KT-436-964

FOR THE LOVE OF A SOLDIER

Also by June Tate

Riches of the Heart
No One Promised Me Tomorrow

FOR THE LOVE OF A SOLDIER

June Tate

HEADLINE

Copyright © 1999 June Tate

The right of June Tate to be identified as the Author of
the Work has been asserted by her in accordance with
the Copyright, Designs and Patents Act 1988.

First published in 1999
by HEADLINE BOOK PUBLISHING

10 9 8 7 6 5 4 3 2 1

All rights reserved. No part of this publication may be
reproduced, stored in a retrieval system, or transmitted,
in any form or by any means without the prior written
permission of the publisher, nor be otherwise circulated
in any form of binding or cover other than that in which
it is published and without a similar condition being
imposed on the subsequent purchaser.

All characters in this publication are fictitious and any
resemblance to real persons, living or dead, is purely coincidental.

British Library Cataloguing in Publication Data

June Tate
For the love of a soldier
I. Title
823.9'14[F]

ISBN 0 7472 7361 8

Typeset by Avon Dataset Ltd, Bidford-on-Avon, Warks

Printed and bound in Great Britain by
Clays Ltd, St Ives plc

HEADLINE BOOK PUBLISHING
A division of the Hodder Headline Group
338 Euston Road
London NW1 3BH

www.headline.co.uk
www.hodderheadline.com

687467

MORAY COUNCIL
Department of Technical
& Leisure Services

With love to my younger daughter, Maxine, who several years ago urged me to join an evening class for Creative Writing, instead of talking about it, and was therefore responsible for starting me on this wondrous journey. How can I ever repay her?

With thanks to my older daughter, Beverley, who brings so much laughter into my life, and to Alan, my husband, my friend . . . my love.

Chapter One

Southampton, 1944

Jack Evans glared balefully across the breakfast table at his daughter. 'I suppose you and your mate are off to the dance at the Guildhall again tonight?'

'Now don't start, Dad,' Maggie protested, sipping her tea.

'Start, I haven't even begun! You know what I think about you and that Ivy, swanning around the town with the Yanks. They're here today and gone tomorrow. These men are only after one thing. People will say you're no better than a tart!'

Maggie's cheeks flushed with anger. 'Thanks a lot. You speak to me as if I'm some loose woman off the streets instead of your daughter. Have I ever brought any disgrace to this house? To you or Mum?'

His tone softened a fraction. 'No you haven't, but I don't want you getting a bad reputation, that's all.'

'For God's sake! We only go to dance.'

His mouth tightened. 'That's what they all say. But I've seen the women pushing prams with their Yankee bastards in them. No doubt before too long we'll see prams full of babies as black as the ace of spades. I don't want that for you. They've got no shame these women, and most of them have husbands in the forces, fighting for their country. I think it's disgusting. Your friend Ivy, for one, should be ashamed of herself,' he continued. 'Her man is with Monty's army. He'd bloody kill her if he knew she was fraternizing with them soldiers.'

Maggie's temper rose in defence of her friend. 'What Ivy does is her business and none of yours!'

He banged the table with his fist. 'It is my business when you're mixing with the likes of her. People will think you're cheap, like she is.'

Rising to her feet, her face white with rage, her green eyes flashing, Maggie snapped at him. 'How dare you speak to me like that! I'm a good girl, and you sitting there all sanctimonious with your preaching, just shows what a hypocrite you are.'

He was furious. 'What do you mean?'

'You think Mum and I don't know what goes on here? You think we don't know that your front room, the one you keep under lock and key, isn't filled with black market gear? Most of it American! But that's a different story, I suppose.' She walked away. 'You make me sick!' she cried as she opened the kitchen door.

Jack was puce. 'What I do is none of your business.'

'And what *I* do is none of yours!'

'Whilst you're living under my roof it is,' he called after her retreating figure.

Maggie slammed shut the front door of the Bricklayer's Arms in College Street and strode off, seething with indignation. She was sick and tired of her father's constant tirades about the American soldiers. It made a change to have fellows in the town that were a bit different, who had a bit of life in them.

Southampton had suffered greatly from the Blitz in 1940. Buildings had been cleared, one-storey shops had been erected, but all around there were still signs of the devastation caused by the constant bombing. Three years later, the arrival of the American Army, billeted around the town in camps, had somehow lifted the spirits of the town. The natural exuberance of these men was welcomed by many, but as they were better dressed than their British counterparts and much better paid, it also caused a great deal of conflict. But the biggest scandal of all was the arrival of a company of two hundred black American soldiers. For many of the townsfolk it was the first time they'd encountered men with black skins and they were horrified when they blatantly walked around the streets of Southampton with white girls on their arms.

Arriving at the entrance of the munitions factory where she worked, Maggie took a scarf out of the pocket of her dungarees and tied it around her auburn hair, turban fashion. As she clocked on she was greeted by Bill the foreman.

'Going out tonight are we?' he asked with a grin. Maggie's love of dancing was well known among her workmates.

'Why, William? Are you asking me for a date?'

'What would my Nellie have to say about that?'

She patted his face. 'What would she say if I told her how you flirted with all the girls?'

'You cheeky tyke! I ought to tan your bottom.'

'Promises, promises,' she teased.

'Now you behave, Maggie Evans. Here. You know what they say about utility knickers, don't you?'

'No, what?'

'One Yank and they're off!' He walked away laughing loudly at his own joke.

Maggie made her way to her machine, shaking her head in mock despair.

In the canteen at midday, listening to *Workers' Playtime*, she was joined by her great friend, Ivy.

'What's up, love?' Ivy asked. 'You're looking a bit down in the mouth.'

'I had another run-in with my father this morning. For God's sake, I'm twenty-one. Old enough to take care of myself.'

'Don't be too harsh with him,' reasoned Ivy. 'If I had a daughter our age, I'd be worried about her virginity too. These Yanks are like bloody octopuses, hands everywhere. All jeeps and genitals they are. It's something they put in their coffee if you ask me.'

Maggie chuckled. 'Well that's something *you* don't have to worry about, losing your virginity. You being a married woman.'

'I don't feel married. Me and Len were only together six months when he was sent overseas. He's been away almost a year now.'

'Have you heard from him lately?'

'I had a letter this morning. He'd been in some place called Tripoli.'

Thinking of her father's remarks, Maggie said, 'Would he mind you going dancing, having a good time?'

'What! He'd go mad. A jealous bugger, my Len. Not that I give a toss. Look, a passionate little sod he is. He used to get the hump when I had the curse. He'll be off having it away with some woman, somewhere. He'd need his oats, wouldn't be able to help himself, of that I'm sure!'

'That's a dreadful thing to say.'

Ivy looked calmly at her friend. 'Look, Maggie, I know my old man, he'll be having a good time all right. It won't mean anything, and let's face it, there's a war on, he could be killed and I'd have missed all this fun for nothing.'

Maggie was shocked. 'You don't even sound upset by the idea.'

Ivy's eyes clouded. 'To be honest, I can't remember what he looks like unless I look at his picture, and then it's like a stranger staring back at me.' She smiled suddenly. 'When he comes home, it'll be all right. We'll start all over again, it'll be like a honeymoon. I doubt I'll be able to walk by the time he's finished with me!'

Maggie smothered a grin. Ivy was quite outrageous, and although she didn't agree with her cavalier attitude to marriage, their friendship was strong. She worried, though, that when her husband came home, he might learn of Ivy's adventures and she was fearful of the consequences.

She supposed her own parents were happy in their way. She adored Moira, her mother, but her father was a difficult man to love. He had been born with one leg shorter than the other and she knew that at times this made him feel less than a man. Yet he was able to clear a bar of awkward customers when there was any trouble, and fights did break out now and again in his pub in the docklands of Southampton. For a cripple, he was able to move surprisingly quickly. He was wiry in build and very strong.

3

It was because of the love she felt for her mother that she had elected to stay in Southampton and work in a factory, as opposed to joining one of the women's forces and getting away, tasting a bit of freedom. Her father gave her mother a hard time on occasion with his sharp tongue, although Moira, a spirited woman of Irish stock, only took so much, then she let rip.

Behind her husband's back, Moira encouraged Maggie to enjoy herself.

'You have a good time, darlin',' she would tell her. 'You're only young once and sometimes life can turn out to be disappointing. None of us knows what's before us.'

It made Maggie wonder just how happy her mother was with her chosen mate. Yet she never said a word against her husband and when she felt he was right, she stood by him against her daughter; but this didn't happen often.

Jack Evans limped to the side door of the pub in answer to the urgent knocking. On the doorstep stood Sonny Taylor, a local spiv, wearing his wide-shouldered camelhair coat, with the usual silk tie. His blond hair was sleeked back with Brylcreem.

He handed a heavy box to Jack then picked up another, pushing his way inside. 'Close the bloody door then,' he ordered sharply. 'Don't want any of your neighbours poking their noses in, do we?'

Unlocking the door of the front room, Jack ushered the man inside. 'What you got this time?' he asked, his eyes bright with greed and anticipation.

Sonny grinned at him. 'Nice little haul,' he said. 'Cartons of Camel and Lucky Strike cigarettes, nylon stockings, large tins of pineapple chunks and a dozen bottles of bourbon. Know anyone who needs petrol? I've got a contact that's very well placed.'

'I can get rid of anything you can find,' said Jack. 'Put that down there and come into the bar. We'll have a drink and I'll pay you.'

They sat on the wooden bench against one of the walls in the horseshoe-shaped bar. Jack poured them each a scotch from a bottle hidden beneath the counter. 'I keep it here because if the bloody Yanks see it on the shelf they want to buy the whole bleedin' bottle!'

They had the place to themselves as it was too early for opening. Sonny Taylor was well pleased. He'd make a nice little pile from this haul. It didn't bother him that Jack would make more. He was the one storing the stuff, taking the risk. The police could come to Sonny's gaff at any time, they wouldn't find a thing, he'd always made sure of that, but Jack Evans stood to lose a great deal if ever his haul was discovered.

'Got a buyer for that lot?' asked Sonny.

Jack tapped his nose, knowingly. 'Now then, I don't ask where you got the gear and you don't ask where I sells it. OK?'

'Fair enough.' He downed the last of his scotch. 'I'll be on my way. I'll probably see you next week.'

The landlord let him out of the pub and, opening the door to his room, went inside, locking it carefully behind him. The room was stacked with cardboard boxes. He looked around with glee. This should earn him a small fortune.

He took a cigarette from a packet of Gold Flake and lit it. This was better than earning a pittance being in the armed forces any day! He had a nice little business going with the pub as well. Sometimes beer was short, but he knew a few of the draymen from the brewers and he helped them out with stuff now and again. The odd barrel of beer came his way often enough to keep things ticking over nicely.

Being in the heart of the docklands, his pub was busy. Not only with the locals, those who lived in the two-up-two-down council houses that lined the shabby street, but many merchant seamen knew they could always get a beer at the Bricklayer's, and he had a steady stream of regular American soldiers too. They paid over the odds for a shot of the bourbon that he carefully rationed out. He couldn't abide the brash buggers, but Moira found them attractive: their unusual accents, their flattering ways with the ladies. It used to sicken him hearing them paying compliments to his wife, but it made her happy.

He puffed on his cigarette and frowned. Deep down he knew she was disappointed with her lot. She had been a sparky Irish colleen when first they met, full of life, but the years had dimmed her happiness. It was only when she was serving in the bar, flirting with the punters, she really came to life and was like the young girl he'd wed.

Maggie had inherited her spirit and that worried him. She loved to dance, to have a good time. That in itself was no bad thing, but now it was wartime. He'd watched the thousands of troops marching through the dock gates in preparation for D-Day, earlier this month. Behind all the cheerful faces he'd seen the look of fear in their eyes. Servicemen, of any nationality, didn't know what was before them and that led to a kind of madness. Live for today and to hell with tomorrow. That was fine for them, but not for his daughter. Despite their continuous haranguing matches, he loved her and worried about her.

Later that evening, Maggie and Ivy queued to get into the Guildhall. They paid their three-shilling entrance fee and rushed to the cloakroom to hang up their coats and gas masks. They preferred the Guildhall to any other dance hall as the floor was sprung and the ballroom large, although by the end of the evening they knew that the floor would be full with heaving bodies, jitterbugging away to the music of Bert Osborne and his band.

The girls stood near the edge of the dance floor. They never sat in the row of plush seats and waited to be asked to dance. As Ivy said, 'Some shortarse may ask you, then when you stand up you tower over them. It's just too embarrassing!'

There were representatives from all the armed forces in the hall, but before very long they saw two American soldiers making their way towards them.

'Don't like the look of yours,' Ivy joked, but in fact both the young men were good looking.

One of them headed straight for Maggie. He was tall, with an olive complexion, a shock of dark hair, neatly cut, and large blue almond-shaped eyes. He smiled as he swaggered confidently to her side.

'Hi, Red,' he said. 'I saw you as soon as you arrived. Did anyone tell you you look just like Rita Hayworth?'

Maggie burst out laughing. These Yanks, they were all full of bull.

'And I suppose you could get me into films as soon as the war is over!' she retorted.

He looked knowingly at her. 'Nah! You're too smart for that old line. I'm Staff Sergeant Steve Rossi, and this is my buddy, Bob Hanson.'

'Maggie Evans,' she responded, and turning to Ivy she introduced her.

'Like to dance?' asked Steve as the band started to play Glenn Miller's 'American Patrol'.

She held out her hand. 'That's what I came for.' They moved towards the dance floor.

Steve was very adept on his feet. He had a natural rhythm and they matched each other's steps without any trouble. The petticoat under her skirt swirled, showing her long slender legs off as he twisted her about. They were both breathless at the end of the number but as the poignant strains of 'Moonlight in Vermont' started, he drew her into his arms, holding her firmly, looking into her eyes.

'This is much better,' he said softly into her ear as he put his cheek next to hers.

Maggie could feel his strong arms about her, the broad shoulders, the taut muscles, the pungent smell of his cologne. Maleness exuded from him as strongly as his personality. This was a real man, she felt. Someone who knew his way around.

He talked softly to her. 'You move real well, Maggie,' he said. 'You're a natural dancer and what's more you really enjoy it, don't you?'

Her eyes shone as she said, 'I do. I just love to dance . . . I've not seen you here before,' she added.

'I've been here a couple of times,' he answered. 'But I'm sure glad I came tonight.' He drew her closer.

When at last the music stopped, he led her to the bar and bought her a gin and tonic. They sat at a small table. He moved his chair next to hers and put his arm along the back of her seat.

'How long have you been in Southampton?' she asked.

'I came last year,' he told her, 'with the 14th Major Port Transportation Corps.'

'And what exactly does a staff sergeant do?'

'I'll have you know, young lady, I'm a mighty important guy. Our role is to coordinate the shipment of our troops, military equipment, and stores throughout the port. I run the stores. I'm in charge of all the victuals. The food – eggs, bacon, meat, fruit, vegetables – cigarettes and booze. Without me, the army couldn't function!'

Maggie found herself liking this man. He was full of himself all right, but he had great charm and charisma.

He put his arm around her shoulder, leaned forward and added, 'I'm also in charge of ladies' perfume, nylon stockings, candy and gum. Whatever you want I can get it.' He stared at her with his deep blue eyes that twinkled and with a slow smile asked, 'Do you want it, Maggie?'

'Are you trying to bribe me, by any chance?' she asked.

'Damn right I am. You stick with me kid, you won't want for anything.'

The band struck up another slow number and again they danced. Steve didn't speak and they both took pleasure in matching their steps, gliding around the floor to the slow foxtrot, her favourite dance. Maggie thoroughly enjoyed it. Too often she'd be asked to dance by someone who spent most of the time stepping on her toes, or being marched around the ballroom by a man who didn't know how to turn, so it added to her enjoyment immensely to be in the arms of such an expert.

When the music stopped, Steve didn't release her at once, but just gazed into her eyes, his brashness gone. Not a word did he utter and for a moment Maggie was thrown. It was as if she was with another person. The confidence was still in his posture but suddenly she felt the power of the man and wondered just what was beneath the façade.

The moment passed as quickly as it came and Steve returned her to her seat. She watched him swagger to the bar, his broad shoulders straight, his uniform pristine and his forage cap tucked neatly in one epaulette. Whilst he was waiting to be served, another soldier came up to him and Maggie watched the encounter with interest. There was a quiet but heated exchange, and Steve kept poking the other man in the chest with his index finger, the expression on his face grim and menacing, until the soldier produced some money and handed it over. Steve took a wad of notes from his own pocket, and added the other man's contribution to it.

When he returned to the table he was as jovial as before. Maggie was curious and wondered what the confrontation had been about. 'That man at the bar, was he a friend of yours?'

7

'No, he owed me some money and he didn't want to settle his dues.' He smiled at her. 'But now it's all been sorted.'

'Oh, I see. Tell me, what did you do for a living before you joined the army? Did you work in a shop or in an office?'

'Jeez, no!' he laughed. 'A nine-to-five job would drive me crazy. I dealt in merchandise. If people wanted something, I found it for them. Wheeling and dealing, we call it. Now I do it for the army and get paid for it.'

'Where are you from?' she asked, her curiosity growing.

'New York City. Or a small part of it called Little Italy.' At her puzzled expression he explained. 'Within the city there are various sectors that are inhabited by certain nationalities. In German Town, the residents are of German extraction, Chinatown, the Chinese, Harlem, the coloureds. I'm from Italian stock. Third generation. My grandfather was an immigrant who came over from the old country.'

'Tell me about New York,' urged Maggie. 'I've seen it in the films of course, it looks an exciting place.'

'It's wonderful, you'd love it. The tall skyscrapers, the stores. You wouldn't need any clothing coupons there. You'd have a great time in Macy's store; it's the largest one in the world, you know. Then there's Broadway with all its theatres and bright lights. Times Square. The place buzzes, it's fascinating. But what about you?'

'There's not much to tell. I was born here, went to school of course, then I worked in an office for a while. Now I work in a munitions factory, doing my bit for the war effort. All very dull.'

'And your parents?'

'Dad and Mum run a pub.'

'Really? Where?'

'In the docklands. The Bricklayer's Arms in College Street.'

'I'll have to find it and come and have a drink. Taste some of your warm beer.' His tone was teasing. 'You limeys always drink warm beer and your coffee stinks!'

She burst out laughing. 'I've heard it all before. Some of the Yanks use our place and they always say the same. What about your family?' she asked.

There was a sudden change in his expression and his jaw tightened for a moment, then he smiled. 'My old man's Italian, Momma too. I have several brothers and sisters but I don't see much of them. We live different lives.'

'Does your mother write to you? I know that letters from home are important.'

The smile faded. 'No. Momma's not into writing much. I send her a card now and then. How about we get some air, Maggie? It's very hot in here.'

It was obvious that he didn't want to continue the conversation and Maggie wondered why. But it was very warm in the ballroom and she'd welcome some air.

Carefully pulling back the blackout drapes, they made their way outside. There was a chill in the June night and Steve put his arm around her. 'We should have brought your coat,' he said. But she was warm within the fold of his arm.

They leaned against a wall and he pulled her to him. His mouth covered hers and he kissed her without hesitation; at first gently, moving his lips over hers, then more deeply and she felt the tip of his tongue softly probing the warm cavern of her mouth. It was enjoyable and she returned his kisses. His arms enclosed her and his hands expertly undid the back of her bra through her dress, releasing her firm full breasts, but she stopped him as he moved to caress them.

'That's far enough, sergeant,' she said firmly.

'Oh gee, honey. Don't stop me now,' he entreated.

But she could feel his erection against her body and knew this could only continue one way, unless she put a stop to it. 'No, Steve. I'm not a pushover. I didn't come here for sex. I came to dance.'

He reluctantly released her. 'You don't mean that.'

'I certainly do. Besides, we've only just met.'

He stroked her cheek gently. 'What happens if we get to know each other better? Does that change anything?'

'I don't know.'

'Will you let me see you again, Maggie?'

'Maybe, but only if you keep your hands to yourself!'

In the darkness, she heard him chuckle. 'That I can't promise.' But as he drew her closer once more, he just held her, gently caressing the back of her neck as his mouth moved sensuously over hers.

Feeling the hunger in his kisses, she knew this was different. He was not a man to dismiss lightly – and he attracted her like no other man had done before. There was a drive about him, a certain magnetism, a hint of danger . . . and she knew she was hooked. She badly wanted to know him better.

When they returned to the dance a few moments later, they were joined by Bob and Ivy. 'I've been looking for you,' accused her friend.

'We stepped outside for a breath of air,' explained Steve. 'Come on,' he said to his buddy. 'Let's get the girls a drink.'

As the two men left, Ivy said, 'A breath of air, eh! That's one way of putting it, I suppose.'

'It was stifling in here,' Maggie protested.

'Of course it was, love,' Ivy grinned. 'You seeing this bloke again?'

'Yes, probably.'

'He'll make sure you do. I saw the way he was looking at you. I'm going out with Bob some time next week. It's all arranged.'

Maggie frowned. 'Do you think you should?'

'Now don't start getting all righteous on me,' snapped her friend.

Putting a hand over Ivy's, Maggie said, 'I know it must be hard for you with Len away for so long, but do be careful. If you start to see Bob on a regular basis and Len finds out . . . what then?'

'How will he know? Unless you tell him.'

'Of course I won't! How could you think of such a thing?' Maggie was outraged.

'All right. Keep your hair on.' Ivy gave a sly smile. 'I know you wouldn't.' She leaned forward and confided, 'this Bob is so nice, not like my Len. He's been telling me all about his home town in Idaho. Some place called Zanesville.' There was a dreamy look in her eye as she gazed into space. 'They live a different kind of life there.' She sighed deeply. 'It sounds wonderful.' She looked at Maggie. 'He isn't married, you know.'

With an anxious expression, Maggie snapped, 'But you are. Or had you forgotten!'

The two men returned and so stopped any further confrontation between the two girls.

When the dance was over, the four of them met up outside after the girls had collected their coats. Steve put his arm around Maggie. 'I've a pass for next Saturday, how about we take in a movie?'

'Yes, I'd like that,' she agreed.

'Fine. I'll meet you outside the Odeon cinema at six thirty. After, we'll go for a meal somewhere.' He drew her to him and gave her a long lingering kiss. He cupped her face in his hands and stared into her eyes. 'We're going to have such a good time together in the future, Maggie.'

'We are?'

He kissed the tip of her nose. 'I promise,' he said. As the two girls walked home through the darkened streets, clutching their torches to show the way, their gas masks over their shoulders, Maggie knew that her father's fears for her were well founded, for if she continued to see Steve Rossi, she wouldn't be a virgin for much longer. He was a man with a man's desires, no boy to be kept at arm's length. Somehow it didn't worry her a bit. In fact she even found the idea exciting. Thank goodness her father couldn't read her thoughts. He'd kill her.

Chapter Two

Corporal Joshua Lewis of the 552nd Port Company sat beside the driver, looking through the windscreen of the American Army truck with its easily distinguishable white star painted on the side, as it headed out of the army camp towards Fair Oak. As the truck left the environs of the town, he looked around the now verdant countryside, the cows chewing the cud in one field, sheep in another, and thought of home.

If he had been driving through his own state of Mississippi, the scene would have been very different. Those fields would be full of growing cotton, picked by negroes like himself, overseen by white men. He smiled wryly. Nothing had changed. All the officers in his company were white. They still reigned supreme.

There was a smile of affection on his face as he thought of his father, the pastor of the local Baptist church, a leading light in his community, fighting for the rights of his people against insurmountable odds. Joshua closed his eyes and let his mind fill with the sound of the choir that used to sing there every Sunday. The spirituals came from the very soul of every man, woman and child in the congregation; dirt-poor people, but with love and God in their hearts. He started to hum the melody of a spiritual to himself.

'Here we are, corp.' The voice of the driver broke through his reverie and he opened his eyes as the truck turned into an unmade road, leading to Willows Farm.

The vehicle was brought to a halt and they both alighted and walked around the back, ready to unload the scraps from the camp kitchen – the potato peelings, bits of cabbage and other discarded vegetables.

Arnold Biggs came striding over in his wellington boots with his old trousers tucked inside, and torn sweater stretching over his broad frame. He peered inside one of the three bins of waste and cursed.

'I told you before it ain't no good putting coffee grains amongst this lot, it upsets my pigs!'

Joshua apologized. 'Sorry, sir. I gave strict instructions that they were to be dispersed separately.' He looked inside the other two bins. 'These are all right though. I'll take the other one back with me.'

Farmer Biggs, thus mollified, mumbled beneath his breath for a moment and then conceded. 'Fine. Only I can't use it. Upsets them something chronic.'

Joshua put his hand in the pocket of his tunic and handed the farmer a packet of pipe tobacco. 'I got this from the PX stores for you, sir.'

Biggs's face broke into a wide grin. 'Thanks, son. Appreciate it. You going to the dance on Saturday at the village hall? I heard your company was invited.'

'I'm not much into dancing,' Joshua confessed.

The farmer looked surprised. 'Thought you darkies were born with a natural rhythm. You know, being used to dancing to the beat of the jungle drums!'

Joshua felt his companion beside him stiffen with indignation, but he just smiled at Arnold. 'We came out of the jungle a while back, sir. And Uncle Sam prefers to see us march as we go into battle. He don't care much for fancy dancin'.'

There was an uncomfortable flush on the farmer's face as he said, 'Right then. See you tomorrow.' He turned on his heel and walked away.

The two soldiers climbed into the truck and headed back to camp, the driver shaking his head. 'The only jungle I've ever seen, man, is the one in *Tarzan* movies!'

'Don't blame the old guy,' Joshua reasoned. 'It's the first time most of these folk have ever seen a black man.'

His colleague laughed. 'Next time I'll bring some jungle drums!'

A day later, Steve Rossi leaned against the bonnet of his jeep in the New Docks as he checked the list of stores due to be unloaded from the ship that had anchored half an hour earlier from the United States. Waiting near him were several of the company of black soldiers who were to help with the task. He looked over at the laughing group with an expression of extreme distaste.

'Uppity niggers!' he muttered. 'Take them out of the cotton fields, the plantations, put them in a uniform and they think they're somebody.' Although he was a Yankee, and not from the south, he'd an inbred dislike of them. He remembered how although you could walk through Harlem, in New York City, during the day with relative safety, no white person would venture through the district at night without fear of mortal danger.

If he were honest, it was much the same in German town, the Hispanic area and other ghettos. The rivalry between the different ethnic groups was fierce and most times fraught with danger, but he'd learned how to take care of himself. It usually started with exchanged insults. As soon as anyone called him a dirty wop, he'd feel duty bound to defend his culture and himself, for to turn away from such a jibe marked you a coward. It had caused him to fall foul of the law on more than one occasion and his proud Italian father had been angry and ashamed of him until eventually it had caused a family rift when once again his father had had to stand bail for him.

'You think I work all hours to keep you outta trouble?' the old boy asked. 'You take the bread from the mouths of your family, you break your momma's heart. Why don't you get a proper job like your brothers?' He didn't wait for an answer but continued, 'No, you think you're too smart to do an honest day's work. This is the last time, you hear? From now on, you get in trouble, I let you rot! You go and live your own life, you leave my house tomorrow. I don't help you no more. You bring too much trouble to us, to our name.'

Steve had moved out of the family home, despite the tears and entreaties from his mother who gesticulated wildly at her husband as she begged him to change his mind.

'He is our son, our own flesh and blood. Families stick together, that's what you've always taught our children.'

But Mr Rossi remained firm. 'He don't stick with no one, Momma, only himself is he interested in. He don't bring the family down no more. Now he learns how to be a man.'

Steve had left and lived by his wits, wheeling and dealing until he decided that joining the army would be his safety net.

These painful memories were brought to an end when at last he got the signal from on board to start unloading, and as the cranes lifted the goods in a large net from the hold and swung them over the side of the ship, he yelled to the negroes to 'Step lively! Move your black arses and get to work.'

They handled the forklift trucks with speed and dexterity. When this equipment had first arrived from the States, it caused great interest among the English dockers who'd never seen the like before. It took a long time to load all the goods onto the waiting trucks. As one was filled it took off to the main camp to be stored. There was one final load and Steve was getting impatient.

'Come on, Rastus. You ain't picking cotton now. Move it!'

Joshua Lewis looked at him coldly. 'Corporal Lewis is my name,' he said quietly but in a firm voice.

Rossi looked at him in astonishment. 'I don't give a fuck what your name is! To me you're just another black bastard in a uniform.'

Joshua looked at him with contempt. 'And you are just a bit of white trash. There were plenty of them in the cotton fields too. Your uniform doesn't make a man of you. You're still white trash.'

The disgust in the tone of the negro enraged Rossi, but before he could reply, one of the military police walked over, wearing his smart white tin hat with MP emblazoned on it, an armband declaring the same and a baton tucked in his belt. 'You nearly through here, soldier?'

'Yes,' said Steve. He glared at Joshua. 'Get your men onto the truck and get the stuff back to the stores.' He climbed into the jeep and drove off at speed, his wheels squealing as he made a rapid U-turn.

The negro grinned broadly as he climbed into his vehicle.

'Having trouble with the staff sergeant?' asked the driver, who'd heard the exchange.

Shaking his head, Joshua said, 'No. He's just a white boy with a big mouth.'

When he arrived back at headquarters, Steve commandeered the various crates and boxes into different sections, with a separate section of his own. He smiled as the last box containing bottles of bourbon was placed there.

Joshua watched him from a distance, knowing exactly what was going on. He'd caught on to the devious ways of Rossi a long time ago. How long did this man think he was going to get away with his little scam? He shrugged. He supposed it could be for the duration of the time that they were here. Who was going to check? Rossi was in charge and, he had to admit, the man was efficient at his job, even if he was a pain in the butt. He turned away. It was no concern of his anyway. Joshua, having finished his duty, climbed into a jeep with three of his men and returned to camp.

His own negro company were in segregated units and, in many cases, separate work details, billets and recreational facilities. They had their own Red Cross Club too, but when they went into Southampton, to the various pubs, it wasn't possible to keep the different companies apart. This often led to fights.

For the most part the townsfolk found the negroes quieter, and more polite than the other brash soldiers, but they still found their colour strange and treated them as a curiosity.

Joshua made his way to the mess hall, queued up with his tin plate and mug, collected his food, a mug of strong coffee, sat at the end of a long table and took out a book to read as he ate his food. His father had instilled in him his love of reading as a young boy, recognizing his son's studious nature, and had introduced him to great writers as well as the Good Book. Over the years, through such a medium, Joshua had educated himself.

Alone in his office, Steve made a long distance call to London and in hushed tones said, 'The next shipment is in. It'll take me a few days to get it to the place we agreed. I'll call you again. Make sure you've enough money with you and don't mess me around. I can easily find another buyer. Remember that!' He put the receiver down, took a cigar from a box in the drawer, bit off the end, spat it onto the floor, moistened the length of cigar with his mouth, then lit it. He blew the smoke out slowly, making a large smoke ring in the air.

He watched it float across the room before it disintegrated, and thought of the redhead he had a date with that weekend. Feisty little thing, she was. A great body, beautiful full breasts and slender legs. They'd have a good time, he'd see to that. A slow smile spread across his face. He bet she'd be a great lay. He'd take her some nylon stockings, a box of candy, some perfume. That ought to do the trick. Although he'd been frustrated when she'd stopped him fondling her at the dance, he'd admired her for it. Too many women were only too pleased to open their legs just for a drink and a night at the movies. Well, that was fine with him. There was no need for any Yank to go without a woman in Southampton. Apart from the local girls wanting a good time, the town was full of prostitutes. Not that he ever paid for sex. He didn't want a dose of the clap, but with so many women being grateful to his comrades, you could never be too careful. That's why he always kept a supply of condoms. He wasn't going to get caught. Not him.

He stretched, yawned, and decided to grab a bite to eat, then have an early night and save all his energy for Miss Maggie Evans.

It was Friday night and the locals had been paid, so the Bricklayer's Arms was busy. The air was filled with lusty voices singing 'Roll out the Barrel', accompanied by the pianist hired at weekends to play in one corner of the bar.

In another, four men were playing darts. Nobby Clarke took his place on the oche and raised his arm, ready to throw his first arrow, grinning at the barracking from his opponents.

'Go on then, Nobby,' encouraged his partner. 'We just need double top and we've won. Then these two buggers have to buy the beer.'

'Don't be daft,' said his opponent, 'he couldn't hit the side of a house with a bloody great gun, not even one of them Big Berthas!'

Nobby kissed the point of his dart and said, 'Come on, darling. Win for Daddy.' He threw it and grinned broadly as it found its target. Turning he said, 'Mine's a pint of bitter.'

At that moment the bar door flew open and a woman stormed in carrying a plate with sausages and mashed potatoes on it. She marched up to Nobby and yelled at him, 'You told me you'd be home early. Well *here's* your bloody supper.' She tipped it over his head and walked out.

There was a roar of laughter from all the customers as they watched him wipe the potatoes and gravy from his head, his face and his working clothes. He looked at Maggie, who always worked behind the bar on a Friday, and said, 'This gentleman owes me a pint of bitter. Be a good girl and get it for me.'

She put it on the counter in front of him, struggling hard not to laugh. Nobby drank it down in one go, then with an expression of thunder on his face, he walked out of the pub.

'Oh dear,' said Moira quietly to her daughter, 'Grace's in for another black eye, I fear. But she did ask for trouble making her man look a fool like that, especially knowing his temper.' She walked towards the door. 'I'd best go and clear up the mess before someone slips on it.'

As she returned with a mop and bucket, one of the American soldiers in the bar stepped forward and in a deep Southern accent said, 'Let me do that for you, ma'am. A good-looking lady like you shouldn't be doing stuff like that.'

She beamed at him. 'My, but you've a silver tongue in your head. But here you are.' She handed him the mop, aware that Jack was listening and watching with a sour expression.

When the soldier had finished he looked at Moira and asked, 'Shall I take this outside in the back yard for you, ma'am?'

Jack stepped forward and snapped, 'No. Give it here, I'll do it.'

Maggie moved over to her mother's side as her father left the bar. 'Go on like that and you'll end up with a black eye too.

Moira glared at her. 'The day your father raises his hand to me will be the last one he remembers and he knows it!' Picking up a glass cloth she turned away and started to wash glasses in the small sink beneath the counter.

Maggie chuckled to herself, knowing that her mother spoke the truth. Her parents often exchanged angry words, but that was all. Her father, for all his difficult ways, loved his wife, and even if he was able to throw a punch in the bar if it was absolutely necessary to calm a fight, and she had seen him do it on occasion, he would never raise a hand to Moira.

Later in the evening two of the local prostitutes arrived with two black soldiers. One came to the counter and asked Maggie politely for two pints of beer and two gin and tonics. There was a sudden feeling of hostility amongst the small group of white Americans, led by the Southerner who'd mopped up. He walked over to the lad who was waiting for the drinks.

'You're in the wrong place, ain't you, *boy*?'

The negro looked at him and answered softly, 'No, I don't think so.'

Jack stepped forward at once. 'All right, Yank,' he said, addressing the white man. 'We don't want any trouble here.'

The soldier looked at him. 'You let these no count niggers drink with decent folk?'

Quietly Jack said, 'Look, son, one war's enough, don't you think?'

One of the locals, already in his cups, joined in. 'His money's as good as yours, mate. On the field of battle he bleeds the same as you do and it's the same colour. Funny that, ain't it?'

The Southerner was getting annoyed. 'Well, you limeys would know about bleeding, wouldn't you? Especially after that fiasco at Dunkirk!'

The mood of the bar turned ugly. Someone else called out, 'Bloody cheek you've got, you only came into the war because you was caught with your trousers down at Pearl Harbor!'

Suddenly the soldier was faced with a room filled with irate Englishmen. Jack leaned over the counter and said grimly, 'I think you and your mates had better leave, don't you?'

One of his companions pulled the soldier's sleeve. 'Come on, Hank. It's time we were going.'

'I wouldn't stay in this flea pit if you paid me,' he snapped. 'You prefer niggers, you have them!' He turned on his heel and left, followed by his two buddies.

Jack turned to another GI drinking alone. 'Do you feel the same way as your friends?'

He grinned. 'Not me, Pops. I got my own troubles.'

'Whew,' said Maggie to her father. 'I thought we were in for a free-for-all for a minute.'

Jack shook his head in disgust. 'Why the bloody hell they have to fight amongst themselves beats me. Why don't they take all their frustration out on the bleedin' Germans!' He lit a cigarette and turned away to serve someone.

Maggie walked over to the lone GI and asked, 'Have you been over here long?'

'No, I arrived last week, soon to be shipped out I guess. His brow furrowed. 'It wasn't until we landed in England most of us realized just how bad things had been for you. You folk must have had a pretty rough time.'

It had been bad of course, and frightening. The docks had been a prime target in the Blitz and there was many a night when Maggie, huddled in their leaking Anderson shelter with her family, wondered if they would all live to see the next day.

'You soon forget,' she said.

The evening passed quickly. One of the negroes had a word with the pianist, slipped him a couple of pounds, and took to the ivories, playing boogie woogie and jazz. Everyone's feet were tapping to the beat. Jack stopped a few as they started to jive.

'Enough of that, you lot! I only have a licence for music, not for dancing. You want to dance, go to the bloody Guildhall.'

Eventually it was time to close the bar. Last orders had already been called and Jack started with the same spiel as he did every night.

He clanged a small bell hanging behind the bar. 'Time, ladies and gentlemen, please! If you haven't got a home to go to we've got an air raid shelter. Now come along, I don't want to lose my licence. Drink up and bugger off home.'

They closed the bar, swept the floor, emptied the ashtrays and washed the dirty glasses, then went into the back room for a cup of cocoa before bed. Moira and her mother sat together chatting about the night's events.

'Those Southern boys really hate the darkies, don't they, Mum? I can't understand it. The ones that have come in here have always been polite and no trouble.'

A line creased her mother's brow. 'I don't understand either, darlin', but I have to say it doesn't look right them being with white women. Even prostitutes. They should stick to their own kind.'

'That would be a bit difficult,' Maggie retorted. 'How many black women have you seen around?'

'You know what I mean. If a white woman fell in love with one of them, think of the trouble it would cause in the future. The blacks in their home town wouldn't like it.'

Maggie rose from her seat, kissed Moira goodnight and went to her room. The two bedrooms were over the front entrance of the pub. Maggie turned off the light, opened the blackout curtains, pulled down the top window, leaned out and look around the darkened street. Raised voices could be heard from the Clarke residence. Oh dear, she thought, they're really at it tonight. The arguments of Grace and Nobby were legendary in the street, but the couple had been married for many years, nevertheless.

She heard the sound of a car's engine and watched as a vehicle drove slowly up the street, stopping outside the pub, its lights faint between the narrow slits of the covered headlamps. Two men got out. She saw the tips of their lighted cigarettes and was surprised when she heard one knock softly on the side door of her place. She recognized her father's voice and leaned forward, peering into the darkness.

There was a lot of to-ing and fro-ing and she guessed that whatever goods he had stashed away in the front room were being moved. Shortly after, the side door closed, and the car was driven away. She heard the sound of the bolt being put across. Then she heard her father's footsteps as he came up the stairs to bed.

She frowned. He was playing a dangerous game. What would happen if the police caught him in his illegal activities? What would happen to her mother? She was angry with him, putting everything at risk: his future, her mother's. But she knew whatever she said to him, he'd go his own way.

She undressed and climbed into bed. Tomorrow she had her first date with Steve Rossi. She snuggled under the blankets and pictured the sexy Italian in her mind. He would be hard to handle, of that she was sure, and with a frisson of excitement she wondered if she had bitten off more than she could chew. She wasn't going to give her virginity away easily, but she wondered just how long she could make him wait. It was a dilemma, but one she felt she was going to enjoy. She would know tomorrow how much of a problem she had. One thing was for sure, she wasn't going to end up with an illegitimate child. She had plans for after the war. She wanted to get away from the docklands of Southampton. Work in London perhaps, see a bit of life. Many of her school chums had married far too young; this was not for her. She wanted much more, and maybe her first step into real womanhood would be with Steve Rossi.

She turned over, closed her eyes, and was soon asleep, but she was beset with confused dreams: her mother sitting outside the Bricklayer's Arms surrounded by her furniture, and herself pushing a pram with twin babies – one white and one black.

Chapter Three

Sitting in front of the dressing table, Maggie swept her hair up at the back, securing it with kirby grips and combs. She twisted the ends into curls on the top of her head, and paused to look at her reflection, turning her head first one way, then the other. It certainly made her look older and more sophisticated. She'd seen Betty Grable wear her hair this way in one of her films and liked it, and as Steve Rossi had appeared so much more a man of the world than other young men she'd encountered, she wanted to impress him. She dabbed Coty's L'Aimant perfume behind her ears then rose from her seat, grabbed her coat and walked downstairs.

Her mother was alone in the bar. She looked at the new hairstyle. 'Very chic,' she said with a knowing smile. 'Going out on a date?'

'Just to the pictures, and maybe after for a meal,' said Maggie. 'I won't be late.' She kissed her mother's cheek.

'Have a good time,' said Moira. 'But take care,' she added.

'I'll be fine, don't you worry about me,' Maggie assured her.

Walking down to Bernard Street she waited for a tram to take her to Above Bar. She was looking forward to the film. She liked Gary Cooper and this time he was teamed with George Raft. *Souls at Sea* sounded exciting, and the second feature with Joel McCrea looked good too.

Alighting from the tram, she thought how nice it would be when the war was over and the vehicles could once again be painted in their vibrant red, instead of the awful gunship grey of wartime. She peered along the road and saw Steve Rossi leaning casually against the wall of the cinema, smoking a cigarette. Her stomach tightened with anticipation and nerves.

'Hi, honey!' he greeted her as she walked up to him. He looked appreciatively at her hair. 'My! Very Miss Hollywood,' he said as he took her arm and led her into the cinema. He handed her a box of American candy. 'Here, I hope you like it.'

Her eyes lit up with delight. 'Thank you. What a treat.'

'There's plenty more where that came from.'

Upstairs in the circle, the usherette showed them to their seats. Maggie was glad that Steve hadn't asked for seats in the back row. Many a time she'd had to struggle with the groping hands of some young man, when all she'd wanted was to look at the screen. As the lights went down and the programme began, Steve put his arm around her, but that was all he did, and she was greatly relieved.

After the main feature, the newsreel came on, and Steve watched closely as it showed American troops in the Pacific, storming ashore on the Japanese-held island of Saipan. Then there was footage of the storm, the worst for forty years, that destroyed the Mulberry Harbours off Omaha Beach. She heard Steve curse under his breath as he lit a cigarette and she realized that one day he and his company may well be over there too and she was aware, more than ever, that life was full of uncertainty.

When the programme finished, everyone stood as the national anthem was played, then, taking her arm, Steve escorted her down the stairs. Outside he said, 'Come on. Tonight you'll eat some really good Italian food.'

He took her to a small restaurant in a back street and was greeted warmly by the owner. She was faintly amused as the men chattered away in a foreign tongue and kissed each other on both cheeks. She smothered a smile as she pictured her father's reactions if that was to happen to him!

'Was that Italian you were speaking?' she asked.

'Si, signorina. My family only speak Italian at home, so I grew up to be bilingual.'

She was impressed. 'I never knew this place existed,' she said. 'Is that man a friend of yours?'

Steve laughed. 'No. But I was told about this place.' He shrugged. 'We Italians stick together. The owner cooks Italian food if you ask for it. If you lived abroad and you found an English restaurant, you'd be the same. You'd be asking for roast beef and yorkshire pudding.'

'You're probably right, but we would shake hands formally. The men would think it sissy to kiss one another!'

'That's because you're born in this cold and wet climate. We have hot Latin blood in us. We are a passionate race, as you'll soon find out,' he said with a cheeky grin.

The owner brought a bottle of wine to the table and poured it into the glasses. 'This is Chianti,' Steve said. 'The life blood of an Italian.'

She took a sip and liked it. Although she worked in a pub, there was not a bottle of wine in the cellar and this was a new experience. As was the spaghetti Bolognese. The homemade pasta was delicious, but Steve had to show her how to twist it round her fork.

'*You* have to be in charge, Maggie,' he laughed. 'Not the pasta!'

In the background soft music of Italy was playing. Pictures on the walls were of Rome, the Bay of Naples, palm trees, sunlit beaches and vineyards.

'Have you ever been to Italy, Steve?'

He shook his head. 'Not yet. But it's inbred in me. One day I'll go and visit the old country.' He looked at her with his almond-shaped eyes, leaned across the table, took her hand and said, 'Maybe I'll take you there.'

Maggie was no fool, she knew that such remarks had no real significance in wartime, but it was a pleasant thought. 'I'd like to travel,' she said. 'When the war is over there's a lot I want to do.'

Steve looked at her, his eyes full of mischief. 'Live for today, Maggie. Life is here, now. Take it in both hands and enjoy it!' He held her with his gaze. 'Don't be scared of taking a chance. This isn't a dress rehearsal, you know. You only get one bite of the cherry!'

She laughed. 'You don't understand the British. We are a nation full of reserve.'

'I've learned that already.' He poured her another glass of wine, then he stared intently at her. 'It's time you learned to let your hair down. I have an all-night pass,' he said softly. 'Come and spend it with me. I've booked a room at the Dolphin Hotel. The Star Hotel is full of the US Navy.' He smoothed her cheek. 'Let's really get to know one another.'

She was taken aback by his brashness. She didn't know whether to be flattered or insulted. 'You've got a bloody cheek!'

He wasn't fazed. 'No I haven't. You're a desirable woman. I want to hold you in my arms, make passionate love to you. What's wrong with that?'

'For one thing we've only just met, and you've taken for granted that I leap into bed with anyone. That's what's wrong!'

'Not at all,' he protested. 'I didn't think that for a moment. But don't you see, war doesn't give you the time for niceties. I could be shipped out tomorrow, next week, any day. Let's not waste a moment of the time we have together.'

'All the more reason to be sensible,' she retorted. 'I sleep with you, and then you're gone. I'll be just another conquest to add to your list. No thanks!'

He caught hold of both her hands. The feel of his flesh against hers as he stroked the back of one hand with his thumb, sent her pulses racing. 'Oh, Maggie honey, don't you see? If I wanted just another conquest as you call it, all I have to do is walk down the street. I want much more. I want you. I want you to be my girl.'

'Why me?'

'Because you're beautiful, intelligent. You're not like the others, good-time girls. That makes you very special.'

She was flattered of course; nevertheless, she wasn't going to give in for a lot of sweet talk. 'Then if I'm that special, you'll wait.'

He shook his head. 'What are you afraid of?'

'I'm not afraid,' she declared. 'But I'm not easy either. If that's all you bought me dinner for, I might as well leave now!'

'Hey! Calm down. There's no need to get mad with me. OK, I'll wait . . . but only if that means you'll be my girl and that eventually, you'll let me love you as I want to. I'll take care of you, Maggie. I won't make you pregnant, I promise.'

Her senses were reeling. Yes, she'd had to cope with young men who took her out and tried to get fresh with her, but no one had ever put into words what exactly they wanted, until now. And to talk about pregnancy. This was all too real and she knew that Steve meant every word. He would expect to sleep with her and soon. How brave was she? It had been drummed into her by her mother that men expected to marry a virgin, that they wouldn't want secondhand goods.

'What do you mean by being your girl?' she asked.

He burst out laughing. 'I would have thought that was very clear. You don't go out with other men.'

'And what about the times when you'd be on duty? I'm not sitting at home, if that's what you think. I like to go dancing and I'm not giving that up for anyone.'

He didn't look particularly happy about this, but after a moment's consideration he said, 'OK. But you don't let anyone take you home. I don't want some other guy smooching with my girl.'

It was her turn to be amused. 'You make a lot of rules, don't you?'

He gave her a cheeky grin. 'It's best if we both know what's expected of each other.' He kissed the palm of her hand. 'You won't regret it, Maggie. We'll have such fun together. I'll spoil you. Italians know how to appreciate a woman.' He took a small package from inside his tunic and handed it to her. 'This is for you, honey.'

She opened the package with barely concealed excitement. Inside was a small bottle of Chanel No 5 perfume and two pairs of nylon stockings. This was indeed manna from heaven. She opened the bottle of perfume and smelt it. She'd heard of Chanel of course, but the scent was so different from her own, or Californian Poppy or Evening in Paris, which was the favourite of the moment.

'Thank you,' she said shyly. 'That's very kind of you.'

He grinned broadly at her. 'Nothing's too good for my girl. You'll learn in time, what it's like to go out with a real man.'

As she looked at him, the firm cut of his jaw, the strong arms, broad frame, she wondered just what it would be like to be in bed with him. Being touched by him. She knew about sex, but as yet hadn't experienced it first hand. It was a daunting thought, now she was really faced with it, and there was no doubt that Steve Rossi was everything he said. A real man. Inside her there were flutterings of fear. What if her father found out? Although she was twenty-one and had railed at him for treating her like a child, she still wanted his approval. And now she was playing with fire.

Steve called a taxi and took her home. He looked at the frontage of the

Bricklayer's Arms and said, 'I'll call in one night soon and have a drink. Meet your folks.'

Maggie wasn't sure that was a good idea. 'Let's leave that for a while,' she suggested. 'Let me get to know you better first.'

He pulled her to him and kissed her. 'I'm all for that,' he whispered into her ear. 'Don't make me wait too long. I'm Italian. I've got a lot of hormones in my body!'

She chuckled. 'You'd better start drinking tea. That'll calm you down!'

'To hell with that! I'll call you soon.' His mouth covered hers again and she felt the passion in his kiss. 'Remember, Maggie. You're my girl now.'

She got out of the taxi, relieved that the pub was in darkness. Her parents would be in bed and she would be spared any inquisition from her father. She was much later than she had intended, but obviously her mother had persuaded him that she was fine. She'd given Steve her telephone number. The public telephone, used by the customers as well as themselves, was situated in the small hallway where at least there would be a modicum of privacy. She didn't want either of her parents to know about Steve Rossi. Not yet.

It was Sunday. In the small council house in Marsh Lane, Ivy put a spoonful of Camp coffee into two mugs, added milk and a meagre portion of sugar, apologizing to Maggie as she did so.

'I had Bob round here and he's got such a sweet tooth, my weekly ration's all but gone.' She grinned broadly. 'But it was worth it!' Maggie shook her head in despair. 'You're looking for trouble,' she warned her friend.

But Ivy was not to be daunted. She sat at the table and told Maggie all about the new man in her life. 'His family have a general store with one of those soda fountains in it. You know, you've seen it in the films, where the kids sit around with all those fancy ice-cream drinks. It was in one of these places that Lana Turner was discovered!' She sat back in the chair with a satisfied smile.

'So now you're telling me you're going to America after the war to be discovered.' Maggie thought it was hilarious, but her smile faded as her friend became serious.

'Well, I did think I could. Not to be discovered, that's being silly, but it's not an impossibility, you know. American soldiers do get married.'

Maggie's eyes widened with alarm. 'But you're already married!' Seeing the flush of guilt on Ivy's face she said, 'You haven't told him, have you?'

Ivy wriggled with discomfort, then she looked at Maggie and pleaded, 'Please don't tell him. I don't want to spoil it all. He's so different to Len. He treats me so nice. And in bed,' she flushed, 'he is wonderful. I didn't know sex could be like that. He makes sure that I enjoy it as much as he does.'

'Oh, Ivy!' Maggie didn't know what to say. 'But surely you must love Len, or else why did you marry him?'

'I married him to have sex! Yes I liked him, of course I did, but I didn't want to get up the spout and I kept saying no when he tried it on . . . So we got married.'

'But it'll take years to get a divorce!' exclaimed Maggie. 'This whole idea is crazy. Anyway, aren't you jumping the gun a bit? How do you know that Bob is thinking about the future? You know what these servicemen are like, full of promises. For all you know he may have a wife back home!'

'No,' protested Ivy. 'Bob's not like that! He showed me pictures of his family, the store. Oh Maggie, it's huge. When he goes home after the war, he's going to manage it for his father.'

'That's hardly a proposal!' Maggie snapped.

'Bob's told me that above the store is an apartment, a flat, and that's where he'll live.' Her eyes pleaded for understanding. 'I know he likes me, Mags. I'm sure if we keep seeing each other he'll eventually ask me to marry him.'

'Oh my God!' Maggie covered her face with her hands. This was far worse than she had imagined. She stared hard at Ivy. 'You have to stop this now, you know you do.'

'Why the bloody hell should I? I have a chance to get away from all this.' She gesticulated around the small room. 'I can have a new life, a better life, in a different country, away from this whole shabby area.' She caught hold of Maggie's hand. 'Len doesn't earn much money as a carpenter and he hasn't any ambition. We'll go through life scrimping and scraping. He'll spend his nights in the pub and where does that leave me? In America, it all sounds so wonderful, so different.' She sat up straight. 'And I want to be part of it.'

'Living above a general store in a small town doesn't sound very wonderful to me. For God's sake, Ivy! You're living in a dream world.' She looked at her friend's left hand. 'Where's your wedding ring?'

'In the drawer,' said Ivy with an unabashed stare. 'I want a new start and I'm going to get it!'

'So what are you going to do?'

Ivy's eyes clouded. 'I don't know, to tell you the truth, but I'll think of something.' She looked hopefully across at Maggie. 'You might want to go to America after the war, with Steve. We could go together.'

But somehow Maggie wasn't at all sure about this. Steve fascinated her, but the future was very uncertain for everyone with a war still raging. She changed the subject. 'Come on, let's go to Bedford Place. I need to take some stockings to be mended. Let's look around the shops, try on a few dresses, forget about men for a while. I think you're mad, but I won't let on about you being married.' It was against her better judgement but hopefully Ivy would come to her senses, once the novelty of her new relationship wore off. God, she hoped so, because she saw nothing but trouble ahead if she didn't.

Staff Sergeant Rossi drove his jeep through the dark of The Avenue, slowed down at a military checkpoint, showed his papers to the sentry and was sent on his way. He smiled to himself. It was all too easy for him to get the necessary documentation. He had a ready supply in his office to cover all his needs: an official stamp which he used for his legitimate dealings and his own personal ones.

Southampton Common was now a military camp, with camouflage nets strewn across the trees to avoid detection from enemy aircraft. Civilians were not allowed access here any more. He drove on to the small village of Otterbourne and turned off by the green, doused his lights and parked. He took a pack of Lucky Strike from his pocket and lit a cigarette, then waited.

He had great plans for after the war. He was making big money, thanks to the shortages, and he had a ready market for all he could lay his hands on. When he returned to New York City, he'd really be somebody. He'd set himself up in business dealing with commodities and he'd show his father just what a man of importance he'd become.

He sensed the arrival of the Rover Saloon before he saw it. Over the years he'd acquired an uncanny sixth sense, and in the ghettos of New York it had saved his skin on more than one occasion. He got out of the jeep.

Two men approached and shook him by the hand. They spoke with the unmistakable accents of the East End of London. 'Got the gear then?' asked one.

Steve led them to the back of the jeep and looked around. All the houses were in darkness, not a light showed with the blackout regulations, and apart from the distant sound of a dog barking, nothing stirred. He unstrapped the bands of leather on the canvas covering and threw them back. Then together they went through a list with the aid of a torch held inside the vehicle to avoid detection. There were boxes stacked with goods and three large jerry cans filled with petrol.

'Did you get the other?' one man asked in a gruff voice.

'Yeah,' said Steve, and from inside his jacket he produced something wrapped in a piece of cloth. He removed the cloth to reveal a military pistol. 'A Colt 45 with three clips,' he said. 'That's all I could get this time, but it'll cost you.'

' 'Ow much?'

There was a great deal of grumbling when they were told.

Steve didn't hesitate, but wrapped the pistol and made to put it away. 'That's all right, gents,' he said. 'You either pay or you don't. I can sell it elsewhere.'

The two men eventually agreed his price and he smirked to himself as they counted out a wad of notes into his hand. 'You won't mind if I don't give you a receipt,' he laughed.

But they weren't amused. They hurriedly removed the goods from the jeep with his help, and drove away.

Steve unwrapped a piece of chewing gum, threw the wrapper on the ground, put the gum in his mouth, got into the jeep and drove away singing lustily, 'This is the Army, Mr Jones.' Yes, and the army was going to pay through the nose and build his future for him.

Chapter Four

Sonny Taylor was getting ready to go for a morning pint at his local boozer when there was a knock at the door. Wiping his hands on a towel, he opened it. On the doorstep stood two local detectives.

'Morning, Sonny,' said the first. 'We were just passing and thought we'd call.'

'Oh yeah,' said the spiv. 'Well, gents, I'm just on my way out. Sorry.'

They pushed past him. 'You won't mind if I use your lav, will you?' said the second man and walked through the scullery to the outside privy.

His companion grinned. 'Sid can't hold his water these days.' He sat down on the sofa and looked around the room. 'Well, I'll say this for you, Sonny. You're a tidy man.'

Taylor wasn't fooled for a moment. The tecs were just sniffing round. They were probably making another concerted effort to curb the black marketeering. It happened fairly regularly, which was why he never kept any goods in his home.

He picked up his jacket and put it on. 'I'm not a bleedin' public toilet! There's one just down the road, why doesn't he use that?'

The detective got up and started to look round, picking up a book here, turning papers over there. He went to pick up a bill lying on the sideboard but Sonny put his hand over it. 'You got a search warrant?' he asked.

The detective grinned back at him. 'Bit touchy, aren't you? Why would I need a warrant? This is just a friendly call.'

'My arse!' exclaimed Sonny and as Sid returned, he opened the front door. 'Time to go, gents.'

The two men left, grinning all over their faces. 'Keep your nose clean, won't you,' they said as they walked away.

Sonny made his way to his local and ordered a pint of beer, then sat and waited. This seedy pub in the dock area was like his office. It was here that all the people with something dodgy to sell knew they could find him. His gaze swept the bar, but there was just the usual punters there. He knew every plain-clothed policeman and he was very careful, always making sure the coast was clear before he did any business.

A shabbily dressed man sauntered over clutching a half-pint glass of beer and sat next to him. 'Want to buy some clothing coupons?' he asked.

'How many?'

'I've got six books,' he muttered.

Sonny looked at the man's poor attire. He himself took great personal pride in his appearance. He knew an excellent tailor who was only too pleased to accommodate him, charging extra for the lack of his customer's coupons, of course. With an expression of distaste, he said to the man, 'I'm surprised you don't use some yourself!'

'No need to get personal!' was the angry retort. 'Do you want them or don't you?'

'Keep your hair on,' said the spiv. 'Yes I'll take them. Usual rates.' He put his hand inside his jacket pocket, took out several notes and handed them over. 'You get any more, you know where to find me.'

Taylor drank up, left the pub and made for a telephone box. He put his pennies in the slot and dialled, then he pressed button A and spoke quickly. 'Jack! A couple of the Old Bill called on me an hour ago. Watch your step.' He replaced the receiver and pressed button B. But nothing came out. It was a habit of his and very often coins came tumbling down the chute. It was like a bonus for using the public facilities.

Jack Evans replaced the receiver with a sigh of relief. Thank God he'd cleared all the stuff from the front room, because he knew he'd get a visit fairly soon. The local uniformed police called during opening time as it was, making sure there was no trouble. This was part of their regular duties and never bothered him. They would stand in the hallway near the hatch where he served those with a jug who wanted a pint to take out. The police always had a glass of beer on the house. He never ever offered them anything else, believing that a copper was never off duty.

Sure enough the same two detectives called on him later in the day, asking questions. Had he been offered any dodgy gear? Jack denied it vehemently. 'Not in my place, gents,' he told them. 'I've got a business to take care of and the missus would half kill me! Mind you, some of the GIs that use the place sometimes give her a tin of fruit or some chocolate. She particularly likes Hershey bars. But that's all.'

When the men had left, Jack smirked as he wiped a few glasses and put them on the shelf. If only they knew! He had a separate bank account for the money made from his dodgy dealings. It was a fair amount already. His retirement would be comfortable, he'd see to that. He fancied a small bungalow beside the sea somewhere. Bournemouth perhaps, or the Isle of Wight. He'd be able to make it up to Moira for the disappointments in her life. She could be the queen bee in her own home. He gave a smile of satisfaction at the thought. He was forty-five now; with a bit of luck he ought to be able to retire when he was still a young man. It would depend how long the war lasted of course. As far as he was concerned, the longer the better.

He had no compunction about such thoughts. Being born a cripple had given him a twisted opinion of right and wrong. He would have given anything to be normal and younger, a man who was physically perfect. If the truth were known, and he'd never confessed this to anyone, he'd have been thrilled to be able to enlist in one of the armed forces, do his bit for his country. But he was too old now anyway and, feeling less than a man at times, he'd decided to make as much money as he could from the situation. He felt it compensated him for the freak of nature that had been his lot. He was still amazed that Moira had consented to be his wife so many years ago. But of course then he was a relatively happy young man. It was only as the years progressed, when he felt he'd lost out on so much, that he became embittered.

At work, Maggie removed her turban, shook out her hair, which had become plastered to her head, clocked off and walked out of the factory, where to her surprise she saw Steve Rossi standing beside his jeep.

'What on earth are you doing here?' she asked. 'And how did you know where I worked?'

He grinned at her. 'So many questions,' he chided. 'Aren't you pleased to see me?'

Several of her workmates walked by, making ribald remarks. Her cheeks flushed with embarrassment. 'Don't take any notice of them,' she said.

He offered her a cigarette. 'Ivy told Bob where you worked and what shift you were on.'

'Oh, I see. Ivy's not on until later,' she said.

'I know,' said Steve. 'It was you I came to see, you silly goose, not her. Look, I've got a couple of hours off this afternoon, why don't we do something?'

'Like what?'

He held her hand. 'It's a lovely day, why don't we take a walk through the park? I want to get to know you better, and what's more important I want you to get to know me, to trust me.' He stared into her eyes, his gaze intense. 'When you learn to trust me, then you'll let me make love to you.'

She quickly looked about her to see if anyone had heard his remark, but most of the people on her shift had gone. 'You don't mince your words, do you!'

He laughed at her consternation. 'Oh you British with your quaint ways.' He stroked her cheek gently. 'Your shyness is very cute. Well, what do you say?'

As soon as he touched her, her heart began to race. This man was outrageous, but that only made him the more exciting. 'I'll have to go home and change,' she said.

'That's fine. I have to go back to camp anyway. Where shall I meet you, or would you like me to pick you up at home?'

31

Maggie shook her head. 'Meet me at the Bargate, near the American Red Cross Club, at two o'clock. Is that all right?'

'That's fine with me, honey.' He kissed her swiftly, climbed into the jeep and drove away.

Bill the foreman walked over to her, having observed the scene. 'You watch that young bugger,' he warned. 'He'll have your drawers off before you can say knife!'

'Don't be disgusting!' she retorted.

He looked at her with raised eyebrows. 'I know men, my dear, and I know that look in his eye. You be careful is all I'm saying. Now get off home and don't be late in the morning.'

The mid-July day was warm as Maggie walked to her rendezvous. Despite the constant reminders of war, the comings and goings of troops through the docks, companies moving out, the wounded being shipped in, today in the full sun and almost clear skies there was no feeling of doom and gloom. People went their own way. Life carried on. Maggie thanked her lucky stars that she wasn't living in London. The city had been suffering from attacks from the flying bombs and a massive evacuation plan had been under way. But here, all seemed well.

Steve arrived at the same time as she did. He jumped from the jeep that delivered him, saluted the driver and walked over to her.

He put his arms around her and kissed her heartily. 'Hi, honey! My, but you look good enough to eat.'

Though pleased at his flattery, she was finding it hard to handle his natural exuberance. Americans were so uninhibited and it took some getting used to. He tucked his arm through hers and they walked past Hanover Buildings to the park.

All the railings had been taken away for the war effort, of course, and in several places deep trenches had been dug, but the flowerbeds were a blaze of glory and it was pleasant just strolling along. They sat on a bench and watched a bunch of American negroes throwing a ball, catching it in their large baseball mitts.

'They're practising for a match next week. Have you ever seen baseball played?' he asked.

She shook her head.

'Then we'll go. It's next Sunday afternoon. I'll tell you the rules as we watch. It's one thing the niggers are good at,' he conceded.

'You don't like the darkies, do you?' Maggie said. 'Why not?'

He lit a cigarette and tried to explain. 'It's something you limeys will never understand. For years the niggers were slaves on the cotton plantations in the South, then Lincoln did away with slavery, declaring everyone equal.' His mouth tightened in an angry line. 'These people will never be equal. They're ignorant, lazy and good for nothing. Put them in a uniform and they get full of themselves. It isn't right.'

Maggie was horrified at his attitude. 'If they're good enough to join the army, fight for their country, die on a battlefield, they are surely due some respect!'

He gave a snort of derision. 'Respect? You've got to be kidding!'

His dismissive attitude began to annoy her. 'No I'm not! What gives you the right to be so superior?'

He looked at her in amazement. 'Because I am.' He saw the anger shining in her eyes and put his arm around her. 'Maggie, honey, don't let's fight. This whole thing is strictly an American thing. You Brits have your problems too, you know.'

But she was still up in arms. 'Really!'

There was a smile of amusement on his face. 'Yes. I mean it. What about the troubles in Ireland between the Catholics and the Protestants? We all have our sore spots, you know.'

With her natural good humour she could see the sense of his argument, and laughed. 'I suppose you're right.'

'Come on,' he said. 'I'll take you out to tea.'

In a small tea shop they sat down and when the waitress brought the tray over, Maggie couldn't help teasing him. 'I imagined you would have ordered coffee.'

He grinned. 'I'm no fool. No one over here knows how to make it. Besides, I'm trying to integrate my ways to yours. If I understand you better, then it'll bring us even closer.'

She burst out laughing. 'I don't believe that for one minute.'

He shrugged. 'Christ, Maggie, I've got to find some way to creep beneath that reserve of yours or I'm going to go crazy.'

She looked sceptically at him. 'I bet you say that to all the girls.'

'No I don't!' He caught hold of her wrist. 'Let's get one thing straight. I don't go round picking up any woman. OK, I'm no saint, but I am particular. From the first moment I saw you, I wanted you, real bad. I'm not some stupid kid in a uniform away from home for the first time. I'm a man. I know what I want . . . and I'll wait.'

She found his steady gaze and the intensity of his words disconcerting and for once was lost for a reply.

'If you want me to go and not bother you any more,' he continued, 'all you have to do is tell me. I just hoped you wanted the same as I did. The decision is yours.'

As she studied his face, the large blue eyes staring into hers, the full passionate mouth, the long sensitive fingers, she knew she didn't want him to leave. But she knew the consequences of telling him so. He'd made that very clear.

'No,' she said softly. 'I don't want you to go.'

He smiled at her. 'You had me worried for a minute there,' he said. He held her hand to his mouth and kissed the palm. 'You won't regret it, honey. I promise you.'

Maggie saw one or two people watching them, but she didn't care. She had taken her first step into the unknown. And it was both exciting and frightening.

During the following three weeks, Steve met her whenever he was able to. He took her to the baseball match and explained the intricacies of the game. She was amused at the enthusiasm showed by the mainly American onlookers. There were a few locals watching, with bemused expressions. 'Just like a glorified game of rounders!' one was heard to remark.

They went dancing, which Maggie really enjoyed, visited the various cinemas, met for a drink, and during this time she grew to know him better. He was excellent company. She liked his sharp sense of humour and admired his air of confidence. He made her feel special, and if they met any of his buddies he introduced her as his girl. His embraces became slowly more intimate, but Maggie tried to keep his willing hands in check. He would complain as he kissed her.

'Christ, Maggie, you're driving me wild. I'm trying hard not to go too far, but the feel of you in my arms, your soft breasts pressed against me, what do you expect from a full-blooded man?'

One evening after a meal at their now favourite Italian restaurant, Steve poured her a glass of wine and said, 'Next weekend I have a forty-eight-hour pass. I have to go to London on business, but that won't take long. Come with me, Maggie.'

'Isn't it dangerous there now with the doodlebugs?' she asked.

'It's not so bad now as it was,' he said. 'They've strengthened the coastal fortifications and are shooting them down as they come over the Channel. You'll be quite safe with me, I'll take care of you.'

It wasn't really the bombs that were worrying her. She knew if she said yes, then she'd be expected to sleep with him. 'When are you thinking of going?' she asked.

'We can catch a train on Friday evening and come back late on Sunday night.' He looked longingly at her. 'Please say yes. London is an exciting city, we can have such a good time.' At her hesitation, he continued to plead his case. 'You're a great girl, Maggie honey. We've really enjoyed being together these past weeks, please come with me. I know you don't give yourself to a man easily, but I desperately want to hold you, love you. I'm not such a bad guy, am I?'

She studied his strong masculine features. He was a very good-looking man and there was this strong chemistry between them that she could no longer deny. Taking a deep breath, she agreed. 'All right.'

As they walked back through the park she wondered just what excuse she could give to her parents. Her father would go mad if he thought she was going to London, let alone with a Yank.

It was in Ivy's house, the following evening, that Maggie voiced her concerns.

'Tell him you're staying with me,' said her friend. 'After all it's not the first time you've done so.'

'But this will be two nights. What excuse can I give?'

'Why do you need an excuse!' exclaimed Ivy. 'Blimey! You're always saying you're old enough to take care of yourself, but listen to you, you sound like a child.'

'You don't know my father!'

'Oh yes I do. Just say you're keeping me company because I'm a bit down. Monty's army has been having a tough time in Italy. Tell him I'm worried about Len.'

Maggie looked immediately concerned. 'Oh Ivy, I'm sorry. I didn't realize.'

'It's all right. I'm sure he's fine. I'm bound to worry of course.' She looked at Maggie. 'Yes, I know I'm having a good time, but naturally when you read the papers about the fighting, you wonder.'

Maggie put her arm around Ivy's shoulders. 'Of course you do, it's only natural.' Secretly she was delighted to see the concern being shown by her friend. Perhaps the novelty of Bob and his general store was dying a natural death.

'I'm sure you'll hear from Len very soon,' she said, trying to reassure her.

Ivy frowned. 'It takes a time for the mail to get through, but then I sometimes get two letters together.'

'Do you write to him?'

'Of course I do.' She gave a wicked grin. 'I don't tell him what I've been up to of course, but I know that letters are important. I'm not that bad a wife.'

'No of course you aren't. Come on, let's go to the pictures and forget about it all.'

The film, *Hollywood Canteen*, cheered them, but the newsreel showed French women having their heads shaved for collaborating with the enemy. The humiliation was hard to watch.

'Poor bitches,' muttered Ivy. 'Probably some of them were only doing it to survive or get food for their kids. No one knows what they'd do in that situation. War changes everybody one way or another.'

But they put such thoughts behind them as in the interval the theatre organ rose from the depths in all its glory and the organist played a selection of the popular songs of the day.

At the end of the second feature Ivy and Maggie walked home with the aid of their torches, Maggie planning mentally what she was going to say to her father before the next weekend.

The following evening after closing time, as she helped her father to clear away the dirty glasses, Maggie took a deep breath and said, 'I'm going to stay with Ivy over the weekend, Dad, so I won't be able to help in the bar on Friday night.'

He looked at her and scowled. 'But you know how busy we get. I need you here.'

She felt a moment of panic. She'd told Steve she was going and nothing was going to stop her. 'Ivy is in a bit of a state, you see. She hasn't heard from Len and she's worried.'

'Not enough to stop her having a good time!' he replied scornfully.

Maggie leapt to Ivy's defence. 'What is she expected to do? Her husband's been away from home for ages. She can't just sit around at night and worry. It would drive her crazy.'

'Lots of other women do it!'

'Look, Dad. Ivy works hard at the factory. She's doing her bit for the war effort.'

'In more ways than one!'

'Well I'm sorry, but I'm going to stay with her. She's my friend and she needs me.' She walked out of the bar and went upstairs to her room.

As she sat on her bed she saw that her hands were trembling. She didn't like lying, but she really was determined to go to London . . . and now she would.

In the privacy of his room, Steve Rossi lay on his bed in his singlet and underpants, a glass of bourbon beside him and a smile of satisfaction on his face. Maggie had given in to his demands much sooner than he expected.

Wherever he was based for any length of time, he liked to choose one woman to go out with. It suited him better. It saved all the trouble of picking up a girl when he felt like company or sex. With one woman, she was usually content to wait for his call. All he had to do was pick up the phone. Although Maggie Evans was different. She made that clear. She wasn't content to wait at home, she insisted on still going dancing. Well, that was all right by him. He'd told her that she wasn't to leave with a man and she'd agreed. Again his Italian charm had worked.

He was looking forward to going to London. He'd got to know the city well since he'd arrived in England. He'd made many contacts there through nefarious ways and he was on to a big deal. It should make him a lot of money.

He'd show Maggie a good time too. After all, she was his girl now and he did like to spoil his women, as he had told her. He didn't think she would make ridiculous demands on him either. She was much too independent for that, and he was thankful. Some women got so possessive. He'd even promised one or two that after the war they'd go to New York and become his wife. But he only did that if it was really necessary. Usually he just dumped them. But Maggie really did fascinate him. She was different. He wondered how different she would be between the sheets. It would be very interesting and enjoyable finding out and he could hardly wait.

Chapter Five

The following Friday evening, Maggie made her way to the station entrance clutching a small case and her gas mask. Her heart was pounding with excitement and tension. She questioned her decision to go with Steve, every step of the way.

She was filled with trepidation at the thought of a man seeing her naked, touching her, making love to her. What would it be like? Would she enjoy it? Would she be disappointed? Would she disappoint him? So many thoughts filled her mind, but she kept walking towards the entrance, her head held high.

Steve was already there, waiting. His face lit up with a broad smile as he hurried towards her and greeted her with a kiss.

'I was afraid you'd change your mind,' he said as he took her case.

Maggie's cheeks flushed; she'd been so overcome with guilt earlier in the day, she almost didn't go, but the urge to prove to herself that she was a woman and not a child had spurred her on. 'Of course not,' she said. 'Why would I?'

'Never mind, you're here and our train is due in shortly.'

When the train arrived, he ushered her into a crowded carriage and placed their cases on the luggage rack before sitting beside her. As he put his arm around her, Maggie was aware of the hostile glances from their fellow travellers at his open show of affection. The British reserve had been severely shaken at the arrival of the GIs. Their natural exuberance had caused a lot of people to be embarrassed, which had aggravated their feelings of hostility towards the men from overseas.

Maggie was incensed by their judgemental attitude which they made no attempt to hide. She deliberately smiled warmly at her companion and said in a steady voice, 'I'm really looking forward to this weekend.'

He pulled her closer and kissed her cheek. 'So am I, honey. I can hardly wait until I can get you alone.'

Maggie could almost hear the tutting of disapproval from two elderly women sitting opposite. It made her smile mischievously. When did they last share a bed with a man, she wondered. She grinned across at them and was amused when they looked quickly away.

The train eventually arrived at Waterloo Station and as they started to walk, Maggie was shocked at how battered, dirty, worn and scarred was the city of London, which was swarming with people dressed in so many different uniforms.

She looked around her in amazement. This was a different London to the one she remembered visiting with her mother, before the Blitz. Strange languages assailed her ears: French, Polish, an American twang; the occasional British voice, a Cockney taxi driver asking, 'Where to, guv?' London had become a Mecca for all the nationalities who were now part of the war.

ARP wardens mingled with the crowds, their gas masks slung over their shoulders. Barrage balloons floated above. Mountains of sandbags barricaded important buildings as they did in Southampton, but here it was more noticeable somehow, with so many buildings so close together. Yet despite all the trappings of war, there was such an air of excitement about the place. It was like getting a sudden shot of adrenalin.

Steve put his arm around her shoulders. 'Happy, honey?'

She beamed at him. 'This is super. The place is so full of life, especially after Southampton. Where on earth has everybody come from?'

'London's the place to be,' he told her. 'All servicemen and women come here when they can. This is where it's all happening.'

They stopped outside a small but comfortable hotel. 'Here we are,' said Steve. 'A buddy of mine recommended it. He said the rooms were comfortable and it wasn't too noisy.' With a cheeky grin he added, 'And the beds are comfortable.'

Maggie felt her cheeks colour.

They entered the hotel and made their way to the reception desk where Steve signed the register and was given a key. As they made their way to the lift he said, 'How does it feel to be Mrs Steve Rossi for the weekend?'

She laughed and held out her left hand. 'Without a wedding ring? I don't suppose we fooled anyone. Do you?'

'Hell no, but who cares anyway! There's a war on and anything goes.'

The bedroom was comfortable and adequately furnished. Ugly blackout curtains covered the chintz drapes at the windows. A matching chintz cover was on the double bed. Maggie felt a nervous fluttering in her stomach as she looked at Steve.

Putting down their cases he said softly, 'Come here.'

She went willingly to his arms, her lips open to receive his kiss.

As he held her he said, 'I can't tell you how often since we first met I've longed for this moment. I promise you'll enjoy it too.'

He slowly undressed her, smoothing her soft skin with his long fingers. Kissing her eyes, her neck, her mouth. Murmuring words of seduction, promising her delight after delight, sending her senses reeling.

She couldn't believe this was happening to her. Here she was, standing naked in a hotel bedroom, with an American who was undressing in front of her as she watched. As he slipped out of his uniform, she ran her hands across his broad chest, covering him with kisses. She felt the strength of his muscular arms as he lifted her naked body and carried her over to the bed. To Maggie it seemed surreal, like a scene in a romantic novel where the hero rides up on a white horse, but this time he'd arrived by train.

She felt Steve running his fingers through her hair, cradling her head, his mouth exploring the contours of her face. She could feel the warmth of his skin next to hers, his bare body against hers. Her own body was behaving strangely.

'Jeez, Maggie. You're so beautiful.' His warm breath against her skin made her quiver with anticipation. He pushed back her auburn tresses and kissed her slim neck.

She felt the rising tide of desire sweeping through her at his every touch and tenderly ran a finger across his full sensuous mouth. All her feelings of guilt, of nerves, were swept aside, dispelled by the sensations of her body.

Never in her wildest dreams had she thought that sex could be like this: this feeling of abandonment, the thrill of feeling Steve covering her body with his kisses, until she thought she'd lose all sense of reason. She felt his arousal as he lay on top of her and she was slowly filled with an intensity deep inside her she'd never experienced before.

As his hand slipped between her thighs, she felt a throb of desire engulf her. It was almost more than she could bear. It didn't lessen for a moment as he slipped on a condom.

Her lover took possession of her slowly; even so, she felt a sharp pain, but it was one of pleasure and she cried out until her passion was unleashed.

They lay together after, exhausted, in each other's arms.

Steve stroked her cheek and looked tenderly into her eyes. 'You didn't tell me this was your first time,' he said softly.

Unable to speak, she just shook her head.

'You know what they say, don't you?'

Her eyes opened wide. 'No. What?'

'When a man takes a woman's virginity, she belongs to him for ever.'

She traced a finger down his nose. 'I don't belong to anyone but myself.'

He chuckled. 'You're a strange woman, Maggie. But wonderful. We're going to have a great time together, you and I. You have a warm passionate nature and I love that.'

'You're not so bad yourself, sergeant.'

'Staff sergeant, if you please!'

She laughed. 'I'm sorry. This certainly isn't the moment to demote you! You should be wearing at least one gold star after that performance.'

He nuzzled her neck. 'Before this weekend is over, honey, I aim to be a five-star general.'

She lay in his arms and thanked her lucky stars she'd given away her innocence to a man who was as experienced as Steve. With him she'd felt cosseted, desired . . . A woman.

Steve stretched and said, 'I don't know about you, but I feel like a drink.' He slipped off the bed and disappeared into the bathroom for a while. On his return he took a bottle of bourbon from his case and poured drinks into the glasses on the side table. 'No ice, I'm afraid.'

Maggie pulled a face as she sipped the sweet spirit.

'Don't you like it?' he asked.

She shook her head and, caressing his bare chest, whispered, 'I'd rather have you.'

Putting down his glass, he leaned forward and kissed her gently. 'You're insatiable. But now we've got to get dressed. I've an appointment to keep, then we'll go for a meal, have a few drinks . . . and then we can start all over again. OK?'

Reluctantly she agreed.

It was just after nine o'clock at night when they emerged from their hotel. Maggie was amazed as Steve led her around the streets with the certainty of a tour guide.

'You've obviously been here before,' she remarked, as they stopped in front of a door marked with a sign that read The Ace of Clubs.

'After arriving in Scotland on the *Queen Mary*, I spent my first leave here,' he explained. 'I get up as often as I can so I know it pretty well. It's a fascinating city. So many old buildings. In New York the oldest is probably only a hundred years old.' He banged on the door of the club.

To Maggie's surprise, someone slid open a hidden panel, spoke a few words to Steve, then opened the door.

They walked down some steps to a basement bar with small booths around the wall and tables in the centre. The only illumination was from small table lamps. A pianist played softly. Despite the cosy glow from the lamps, the place was decidedly sleazy. The air was filled with the odour of stale beer, cigarette smoke and cheap perfume.

Maggie shivered with apprehension as she sat at the table in a small booth. She looked around furtively as Steve went to the bar. She sensed an air of menace in the place and wanted to leave – now.

There were a few American soldiers sitting at the bar with girls who were obviously prostitutes, a small group of civilians in city suits, three matelots in their bell-bottomed trousers and wide sailor collars, and a couple of English soldiers from the Royal Engineers. But there were two other characters who, although well dressed, looked as if they'd stepped right out of an American gangster movie. To her surprise, Steve went over and sat with them.

A waiter set two glasses on the table in front of her. 'The gentleman said he would only be a moment, miss.'

She thanked him and waited, nervously fingering her glass. The conversation between Steve and the two men was earnest. There was no idle banter being exchanged here. The usual bonhomie that seemed to be Steve's style was now replaced by a tough exterior. He was talking fast and forcibly. Then he produced a small bag that he'd taken from his case in the hotel, and handed it to one of the men. His companion offered a large envelope to Steve, who nodded and pocketed it.

Maggie began to feel uncomfortable as the two soldiers stared across the room at her. They grinned and, to her horror, came over to the booth.

'Hello love,' said one.

'Fancy that bloody Yank bringing a nice girl like you to a place like this. He should be ashamed of himself,' said the other. 'Come along with us, girl, we'll give you a good time, won't we?' he said turning to his mate.

The other man leered at Maggie. 'Yes we will. We'll show you what real men are like.'

Maggie's eyes flashed angrily. 'On your bike!'

The first soldier got annoyed. He leaned over the table until his face was only inches away from hers, breathing fumes of stale beer over her. 'You're just like all the rest – lift your skirts for a pair of nylons!'

Scared by the angry curl of his lips, she clutched her glass tightly.

Suddenly Steve was behind the soldier. He pulled him away and sent him flying across the bar. 'You leave my girl alone, buddy!'

The other soldier stepped towards Steve with a raised fist. 'He's not your buddy, mate!' He swung a punch at Steve, who ducked expertly and slammed his own fist into the other man's face. The man staggered backwards, blood pouring from his nose.

Maggie looked on in horror. She watched, her senses alert, as the bar became silent. The sailors were all for stepping in to defend their countrymen, but the American soldiers at the bar warned them to stay out of it. The mood of the place was ugly and dangerous. The two men Steve had been doing business with watched the scene with interest and didn't move.

The two soldiers made for the GI, a united force of strength. Maggie felt the blood drain from her face as Steve produced a knife from his boot and held it out, blade first. 'I don't advise it, you guys,' he said, as he crouched, ready for their onslaught. 'But if you must, which one of you is going to be first?'

The other Americans moved forward, menacing the soldiers who looked around and saw they were outnumbered.

'All right, Yank! You win this time, but if we see you again, we'll bloody have you!' They turned and walked towards the exit.

Heart pounding, Maggie was stunned as Steve put away the knife, sat beside her and in a perfectly normal voice said, 'I'm sorry about that, honey. Drink up and we'll be off.'

She rounded on him. 'Is that all you have to say?'

He looked at her with surprise. 'I'm sorry, I didn't realize you were so upset. Barman, bring the young lady a brandy!'

'Of course I'm upset!' She glared at him and felt her cheeks flush with rage. 'This may be a daily occurrence in your life, it certainly isn't in mine.'

Putting an arm around her he said, 'Of course this isn't a normal occurrence, don't be so silly. But there is a lot of resentment towards us from the Brits. We get paid more than them, we're better dressed and we take all the women. They hate us.'

'But you had a knife!'

'Oh I see, that's what worried you.' He caught hold of her hand. 'I was brought up in New York City. Believe me it's tough for a kid. If you don't learn to take care of yourself at a very early age, you never get to grow up. I learnt to survive, and no two limey soldiers would ever get the better of me.'

She saw the anger in his eyes. 'Would you have used it?' she asked.

He stared at her intently. 'We'll never know, will we? Now let's drink up and get the hell out of this place.'

As they left the club, Maggie asked, 'Who were your friends? The two men at the table you spoke to?'

'Just a couple of guys I met one day. We help each other out from time to time.'

'They looked as if they'd cut your throat as soon as look at you.'

'You're right. They probably would,' was the sharp reply.

No more was said about the incident as they wined and dined before returning to the hotel, and Maggie decided, as Steve kissed and caressed her, to dismiss the whole incident from her mind. Nothing was going to spoil this weekend for her.

The two days passed in a whirl of activity. On Saturday they shopped at the PX store in Great Audley Street, where Steve purchased his ration of chocolate, razorblades and cigarettes. He also bought toothpaste and shaving cream. 'You can take this all home to your folks,' he said. 'I've got more than I need back at the base.'

They dined in a fashionable restaurant, then Steve took her to an American servicemen's club, called Rainbow Corner.

Maggie was enthralled at the place. It was like being in America. Juke boxes pumped out such favourites as 'Don't Sit Under the Apple Tree' and 'Deep in the Heart of Texas' by the Andrews Sisters. On one wall was a big map of the United States. Steve led her over to it and pointed out New York. 'Maybe one day you'll see it for yourself,' he said.

'What are all the little flags stuck in it for?' she asked.

'When you come in here, you put one in your home town. See? There's obviously lots of guys from my area.'

He took her downstairs to the basement where she ate American doughnuts and drank a glass of Coke. He apologized. 'Sorry, they don't serve anything stronger here.'

But she didn't mind a bit, she was fascinated with the place and was amazed at how well organized everything was. A barber was installed, there was even a lady willing to do mending or sew on stripes.

During their last night, Maggie lay in Steve's arms after they had made love. 'What are we going to do when we get back to Southampton?' he said. 'I'm going to go crazy if I can't make love to you.'

She moved even closer to him. 'I don't know,' she said. She sighed. She didn't want to go back to just holding hands. Not now. She had walked around during the day hugging the secret of their intimacy to her. She found herself smiling constantly. She was glowing in her newly awakened womanhood. She kept putting her hand out to touch her lover. It was such a strange feeling, this closeness.

'I'll think of something,' he murmured. He yawned and apologized in a weary voice. 'You've worn me out, young lady,' he teased.

She watched his eyes close, then he was asleep. But she was wide awake. Despite the thrill of this new and wonderful experience, she couldn't dismiss from her mind the fracas at the club. She'd had a glimpse of a brutal side to the cocky American and it disturbed her. When he made love to her, he was gentle and thoughtful of her needs as well as his own. Yet as he made love to her, she couldn't help remembering the grim expression on his face as he threatened the two soldiers with his knife. Would he have used it had he been pressed? She had no doubt that he would have done.

She tried to analyse her feelings for him. It wasn't love, she knew that. Was it infatuation? No, that was for teenagers. He was fun to be around, and as a lover he was wonderful. He gave her a good time. She felt a tremor of guilt. Was that all she was, a good-time girl? She dismissed the idea at once. She went out with Steve because she liked him, was fascinated by him, not for what he could give her. This was wartime after all, and who knew what was ahead of them. She would grab each moment as it came.

Outside Southampton railway station, Maggie dissuaded Steve from taking her home. Before putting her in a taxi, he drew her into his arms. 'Jeez, honey, I don't want to let you go.'

'I know,' she said as she kissed him.

'I'll be in touch, real soon,' he said as he helped her into the waiting vehicle.

Maggie gave the driver Ivy's address.

When she arrived at her destination and knocked on the door after paying off the taxi, Ivy ushered her into the living room.

As she sat beside Maggie she asked, 'Well. How was your dirty weekend?'

Maggie glared at her. 'It wasn't like that!'

'Oh, sorry!' quipped Ivy with a mischievous grin. 'Don't tell me you spent a weekend with that horny bastard and there was no sex, because I won't believe it.'

Maggie couldn't help laughing. 'I had a great time.'

Stirring her tea, her friend asked, 'What was he like in bed?'

'You don't honestly expect me to give you every detail!'

With a laugh Ivy said, 'Why not? I want a blow-by-blow description.'

'Well you're not going to get one!' declared Maggie.

With a sly nudge Ivy asked, 'Was he hot stuff? Did he wear you out?'

'Ivy! Will you behave.' Despite her indignation, Maggie couldn't keep a broad smile from spreading across her features.

'You don't have to say a word. You look just like the cat who ate the cream. You're absolutely glowing. It's not every day a woman loses her virginity, you know. You'd better wipe that satisfied grin off your face when you get home,' warned Ivy, 'or your dad will catch on straight away. Then the shit *will* fly. Men like their daughters to remain pure and untouched, surrounded by their children.'

Maggie looked thoughtful. 'Strange, isn't it. Sex is wonderful, but I can't picture my mum and dad doing it at all.'

'I know what you mean,' said Ivy.

'Steve's going to call me as soon as he has some free time,' said Maggie. 'I hope it's soon.'

'You won't hear this week, love ... of course, Steve wouldn't know until he got back! They leave early tomorrow morning on manoeuvres. Bob told me last night.' At the look of despondency on Maggie's face she said, 'Don't worry, they're only away for five days. Look, there's a dance on in Fair Oak tomorrow night for the company of darkies. Let's go.'

'How will we get there?'

'A couple of trucks are picking up the girls at the Guildhall at seven o'clock, bringing us back at eleven.' At Maggie's hesitation she added, 'These blokes are meant to be great dancers. Come on, come with me. It'll cheer us up whilst the boys are away.'

'All right. Call for me and we'll go to the Guildhall together.'

'I'll meet you outside the pub,' said Ivy. 'If I come in your dad will have a go at me about having a good time with Len away fighting, you know how he goes on, and he might start asking awkward questions about the weekend.'

With a worried frown Maggie agreed. 'Yes, we don't want that. I'll say we stayed in and listened to the wireless because you didn't feel like doing anything else.'

It was only a short walk from Ivy's place to the pub, and Maggie made her way home. She slipped in by the side door. She couldn't face her father after the lies she'd told. She couldn't possibly behave as if nothing had happened and she was sure he'd see the guilt written in her eyes. She needed time to pull herself together.

She made her way upstairs and started to unpack. As she took out the goods from the PX store, she wondered just how she was going to explain them away. Shaking her head she thought, you start with one lie and that just leads to another. She would put the stuff in a drawer for another time, then she'd think of something.

There was a tap on the door. She hastily covered the goods with a dress as her mother walked in.

'Hello, love. How's Ivy? I expect she was glad of your company.'

'Oh yes, she was,' Maggie said hurriedly.

'What did you do?'

'Nothing much. Sat and talked, listened to the wireless. Just had a quiet time, really.'

'I'm just going down to help your father close the bar and clear up. I'll see you in the morning.'

Maggie walked over to her, held her close and kissed her cheek. 'Goodnight, Mum. I love you lots. God bless.'

She breathed a sigh of relief as she was left alone. She was so worried about being caught out! She'd have to be very careful what she said. It would be all too easy to give the game away. She hated lying to her mother, but how could she tell her she'd been to London to lose her virginity!

As she undressed and washed, she wondered what Steve was doing. He'd said he'd ring her as soon as he was free. She couldn't wait to see him again, to be held in his arms. But where could they go to be together, alone, in Southampton? Living at home made things very difficult. And now that she'd given herself to him, Steve wouldn't be content with just going to the pictures and out for a meal. He had booked a room at the Dolphin Hotel at one time in the hope that she would stay the night, but if he did that again and she went with him, how long would it be before their relationship was discovered? Oh she was playing with fire all right, but she didn't regret her weekend for one moment. She enjoyed being a woman!

Climbing into bed, she hugged her pillow to her, pretending it was the attractive Italian she was cuddling, and fell asleep.

Chapter Six

Jack Evans was much too occupied at the pub to worry about his daughter and her friend. Late the previous night, when his wife and Maggie were in bed, he'd taken in a load of black market goods. His small room was stocked to the ceiling and he was worried about how long he'd have to keep them. His usual punters were away for two weeks and the police were becoming especially vigilant. For once he was feeling nervous about the chances he was taking. Apart from the tinned goods and cigarettes, the nylons and petrol coupons, he had six large jerry cans filled with petrol from Sonny Taylor. If there was a raid or a fire, the pub would go up in a cloud of smoke. Consequently he was very edgy and bad tempered.

Moira had had enough of his waspish tongue, and as Maggie arrived home, she could hear raised voices coming from the kitchen.

'Don't you use that tone of voice to me, Jack Evans!' she heard her mother say. She knew she was angry because when Moira was excited or in a temper, her Irish brogue broadened.

'I've put up with you snapping my head off all day, so I have, and I'll not put up with it any longer.'

Maggie walked into the room. 'What's going on?' she asked.

'You're father's got a cob on. Something's on his mind and I'm bearing the brunt of it.'

Maggie looked angrily at her father. 'What's up, Dad? Got another load of goods in, have you?'

He glared at her. 'What on earth are you talking about?'

'It's always the same. You take a load of stolen goods and then you're so twitchy about it you take it out on Mum.'

'Don't be ridiculous.'

'I'm not the one being ridiculous.' She sat opposite him. 'Don't you care what happens to us, to Mum and me?'

He looked startled. 'Whatever do you mean?'

She tried to reason with him. 'If the police catch you, you'll lose your licence after all these years. What'll happen to Mum then?'

His face was flushed with anger and guilt. 'I'm only doing it for your mother.'

Maggie's anger exploded. 'Don't give me that old crap. Men always lay the blame at someone else's door. You're doing it for yourself, to make money. It's greed, that's all.'

He tried to justify himself. 'I'm saving for our retirement. Then we can have a nice bungalow somewhere.'

'And what good will that be if you're in prison?'

Moira was looking anxious. 'She's right, Jack. I don't know exactly what you've got in the front room, but every time you get stuff in, you're like a bear with a sore head until you shift it. It's too dangerous. I don't want a bungalow anywhere! Stop taking these chances. Please.'

'Now don't you start.' He rose to his feet. 'I know exactly what I'm about.' He glared at his daughter. 'Do you take me for a complete fool?'

'Frankly, yes. Whilst you continue to defy the law this way, you are being a complete idiot.'

'You'll speak to me with a little more respect, my girl. Instead of having a go at me, you'd be better sorting your own way of life out instead of running after the Yanks the way you do!'

Maggie's eyes flashed with anger. 'That's right! Change the subject. At least what I do is legal and above board.'

He stormed out of the room.

Moira sat down and buried her face in her hands.

Maggie went over to her and put a comforting arm about her. 'Don't worry, Mum,' she urged.

'But I do,' said Moira. 'And you're right, if we lose the pub, how could I live?'

Maggie hugged her mother. 'Whilst I'm alive, you'll never have to worry,' she said.

'Ah but you're a fine girl,' said Moira, 'but you have your own life to lead. You shouldn't be concerning yourself with mine.'

'But of course I'm concerned! I love you and I hate to see you unhappy. Look, Mum, if the worst ever happens, you and I will always be together. I'll always take care of you.'

Moira gazed at her with tear-filled eyes. 'You're a darlin' child. What would my life be without you around to cheer my day.'

In the bar later that evening, seeing her mother's drawn features, Maggie insisted she relieve her behind the counter. 'Go and have a nice hot bath. Listen to the wireless. Try and relax. I'll work in the bar.'

Moira gratefully complied.

Maggie went over to her father who was changing a barrel of beer. 'You're worrying Mum to death, you know. Why don't you give it all up. She'll be happier and so will I.'

'And what about *my* happiness?' he snapped. 'This is the one time in my life I can make a load of money. You think I'll throw away such an opportunity? Never. I'd be a fool.'

Seeing the determined set of his mouth, Maggie gave up. Nothing she could say would dissuade him. She was wasting her time.

The following evening, Maggie and Ivy climbed into one of the American trucks that had been sent by the base and were driven to Fair Oak village hall. They beamed with delight as they were given corsages to wear on their arrival.

'These Yanks certainly know how to put things over,' enthused Ivy. 'Look at the stage.'

The humble village hall was bedecked with flags. On the stage was a large Union Jack draped on one side and a Stars and Stripes on the other. In front of them sat an American service band. The army captain in charge of the soldiers came over and thanked them for coming.

The two girls danced until they were worn out.

'Blimey!' exclaimed Ivy as she collapsed into a seat. 'These darkies certainly know how to move, don't they?'

Halfway through the evening the band took a break and the officer announced that a corporal from the company would play the piano for their entertainment.

A tall soldier took a seat and started to run his hands over the keys, playing boogie woogie and jazz. Maggie was fascinated and walked nearer the stage to listen, her foot tapping to the music as she stood. Some people danced but the majority gathered round, clapping their hands, bodies swaying with the music. Once or twice the soldier looked around at his audience and caught Maggie's gaze. He smiled at her and played on.

When the band eventually returned, the applause from the dancers was filled with enthusiastic appreciation.

To her great surprise the man walked over to her. 'Hi there! You were really swinging to the music.'

She smiled at him. 'Where did you ever learn to play like that?' she asked.

'No one taught me, ma'am. I picked it up myself using the piano in my daddy's church.'

'They play music like that in church?'

He chuckled. 'Well as a matter of fact, no they don't, only gospel music. I played that every Sunday, but I'd sneak in and play jazz whenever I could. But if he caught me at it, he used to be mighty angry.'

'I suppose it isn't quite the thing for such a place.'

He shrugged. 'Who can say for certain? If jazz was around in the Lord's day, I'm sure he'd have liked it.'

His reasoning amused Maggie. 'We'll never know, will we?'

'I guess not. Say, can I get you a drink, only I'm really thirsty.'

'Do you have American Coke?'

He grinned broadly. 'Well that's a surprise.'

'I tasted it for the first time recently,' she told him, 'and I liked it.'

He went to the bar, returning with two glasses. 'Here you are. Let's sit at a table, shall we?' When they had settled he asked, 'What's your name?'

'Maggie, short for Margaret . . . and yours?'

'Joshua. Joshua Lewis.' He held out his large hand, and Maggie took it in hers.

'That's a name from the bible, isn't it?' she asked.

He smiled softly. 'Sure is. My daddy is a preacher. All the family have biblical names. I've a brother Abraham, another called Matthew and two sisters, Ruth and Jemima.'

'I don't remember a Jemima in the bible!'

'It was the name of one of Job's daughters in the Old Testament. She hates it,' he added, 'and insists on calling herself Delilah. She says if she must have a name from the Good Book, then she'll be somebody interesting!'

Maggie was highly amused. 'She sounds quite a character.'

'She gives my poor momma many a sleepless night, but she's a good girl at heart, just spirited.' He looked at Maggie. 'Not unlike you, I imagine.'

'Now why would you think that?' she asked, intrigued by his remark.

The corners of his mouth twitched as he tried to suppress a smile. 'It's the way you hold your head, I guess. The way you walk. Almost in defiance. Who do you defy, Maggie?'

She smiled ruefully. 'Mostly my father.'

His laugh was so melodic, she felt she could sit and listen to it for hours. There was something about Joshua Lewis that was unusual, but she couldn't put her finger on it.

'So what do you do to amuse yourself when you're not working?' she asked.

'I play jazz,' he said with a broad grin. 'Music is my life. What kind of music do you like, Maggie?'

'I like Glenn Miller,' she said, 'but Frank Sinatra is my favourite.'

'What about Billie Holliday and Ella Fitzgerald? Do you like them?'

'I don't know much about them,' she admitted.

'Have you ever heard of Count Basie and Duke Ellington? Louis Armstrong?'

'Well I have heard of them, but that's all.'

'Oh my, Maggie. Your musical education has been sadly neglected,' he teased. 'If you haven't heard the golden tones tinged with sadness of Louis Armstrong's trumpet playing, you've missed a real treat. An experience.'

The band struck up a slow number and he asked, 'Would you like to dance?'

'Yes, thank you.' She got up and, walking to the dance floor, turned and felt his arms about her. He was quite a bit taller than her and of slender build but his shoulders were broad and he had a presence about him that was indefinable.

His movements were fluid as they traversed the floor and she felt as light as a feather in his arms. Looking up into his dark brown eyes she said, 'For a pianist, you dance very well.'

'Why thank you,' was all he said.

As the music continued, Maggie couldn't help comparing this stranger with Steve. Whereas Steve would have been talking rapidly, joking with her, teasing her, flirting with her, trying to seduce her, Joshua was quiet. Yet it wasn't an uncomfortable or awkward silence, it was restful, enjoyable, relaxing.

At the end of the dance they returned to their seats. 'Do you like being in England?' she asked.

He beamed at her. 'It's beautiful around here. Not that I've seen much more than Southampton and the docks, and a little of the New Forest, but I've read books about it. The history is mighty interesting.'

'What are you doing here?'

'Our company is here to help unload the goods from the ships that dock, bringing food and equipment for the US Army stationed in your country.'

The band started to play a fast number and Joshua looked at Maggie and said, 'Would you like to jive?'

When she said she would, he led her onto the floor. The pace was fast and furious and Joshua held her firmly as he spun her around and his eyes sparkled as she followed his steps until the end of the number.

'You're quite a mover, Maggie,' he said with a grin.

'You don't exactly stand still,' she said, breathless from the dance.

They stayed on the floor as the last waltz began. He held her close and said, 'I've really enjoyed talking to you, Maggie.'

'I've enjoyed it too,' she replied.

And she had. She wished they'd met earlier in the evening because she was intrigued by this man. But as the number finished, he said, 'You take care now, and don't upset your father too much.'

She saw the mischievous glint in his eye and grinned at him. 'I'm afraid I can't promise that. My dad and me were born to fight with each other.'

He touched her arm gently. 'That's a great pity,' he said.

At that moment Ivy appeared holding their coats. 'Come on, Maggie. The truck's ready to take us home.'

'Goodnight, Joshua,' said Maggie. 'Take care.'

'And you too,' he said as he walked them to the door.

When they were settled in the back of the truck Ivy asked, 'Who was your friend?'

'A man called Joshua, the son of a preacher,' she explained.

'Blimey! Did he give you a lecture on the sins of the flesh?' joked Ivy.

'No, not at all. He talked to me about music. He likes jazz, that was different from the usual line of bull.'

'Don't be bloody daft,' said her friend, 'all men are the same if you ask me.'

'Well I'm not asking you!' snapped Maggie, annoyed at the generality.

'Sorry I opened my big mouth!' retorted Ivy.

Maggie apologized. 'No, I'm sorry, but he really was nice.'

'Did he ask to see you again?'

Shaking her head Maggie said, 'No, of course he didn't.' And she knew that she wished he had.

'Just as well,' said Ivy. 'Steve would blow a gasket. Never mind, love, only another few days and the boys will be back at camp. Ooh! I can hardly wait! I used my precious coupons on some new underwear.' She nudged Maggie. 'Not that Bob needs any encouragement.'

But Maggie didn't want to talk, all she wanted to do was be quiet. Silent, as she'd been when she was dancing with Joshua Lewis.

Chapter Seven

When Steve returned from his manoeuvres, he rang the Bricklayer's Arms to arrange a date with Maggie, who fortunately answered the telephone. She was pleased to hear his cheerful voice and realized how she'd missed him.

They met that evening and went to the Red Lion for a drink.

When he returned from the bar with their order, they sat close together and Steve put his arm around her and kissed her cheek.

'Let me look at you,' he said. 'That was the longest week of my life. I couldn't wait to get back.'

'I've missed you too.'

He stroked her face. 'We had such a good time in London, didn't we?'

'Yes,' she agreed. 'Except for that bit of trouble in the club.'

He frowned as he said, 'You're not still worrying about that, surely?'

She stared steadily at him. 'All I could think about was what would have happened if those tommies hadn't left.'

'When we were in London, I was taking care of you, protecting you.' He smiled confidently. 'At the sign of a knife most guys back off.'

'And what happens if they don't?'

'Believe me, they always do.'

'Have you ever had to use it?' she persisted.

'Look, Maggie, when I was growing up I was in the middle of gang wars every day of my young life . . . and yes, sometimes I had to use it or go under.'

She was horrified.

At the look on her face, Steve defended himself. 'It's all very well for you, honey, living here in cosy old-fashioned England. I've seen pictures of kids with their skipping ropes, boys with catapults. Believe me it's all very tame in comparison.'

'I don't believe it!' she protested. 'Kids are kids, the world over.'

'It all depends on their environment, honey. All right, let me put this to you. If you were a teenager and five young men from another gang came at you, what would you do?'

She hesitated.

'I'll tell you what you'd do. You'd use whatever was at hand. A metal bar, a chunk of wood . . . a knife.'

There was a sick feeling in the pit of her stomach. 'Did you ever kill anyone?' she asked.

'No of course not! I may have nicked someone, cut their jacket. It was them or me. Don't you understand?'

It didn't sound so unreasonable, as she thought about it. Just because things didn't happen like that in her own country, should she condemn him for it? And looking into the smiling eyes of the good-looking Italian, she didn't think she should. 'I'm sorry,' she said.

He squeezed her hand. 'That's my girl.' He kissed her cheek and said softly, 'I've got to be back at camp by midnight, but on Saturday night I've got an all-night pass.' He pushed a stray strand of her hair away and caressed her ear. 'Shall I book us a room in a hotel?'

At his touch she knew she couldn't refuse him. 'Yes,' she said. 'I want to be with you, too.'

As Maggie was getting in deeper with her relationship with Steve Rossi, her friend Ivy was plotting and scheming while she listened to the whispered words of love from Bob Hanson as they lay together in bed.

'Tell me again about your home,' she pleaded.

Bob chuckled. 'You're just like a child, wanting the same story every night.'

She snuggled even closer. 'It just sounds so wonderful. So different from this dead and alive country.'

'What a terrible thing to say,' he chided. 'You should be proud of your heritage!'

With a sigh she said, 'I am really, I just want to see other things, other places.'

He looked at her with affection and caressed her. 'You are a real cute woman, you know that? My folks would love you, I'm sure.'

Ivy held her breath.

Bob rolled over and taking her into his arms said softly, 'Would you like to meet them?'

She looked at him wide-eyed. 'How on earth could I possibly do that?'

'You could if we were married.'

She let out a squeal of joy. 'Are you proposing to me?'

His laughter filled the small room. 'Of course I am. Will you marry me, Ivy?'

She flung her arms about him. 'Oh, yes please.' She pushed him on his back and sat her naked form astride him. 'Mrs Ivy Hanson,' she said with a broad grin. 'I love you, you crazy Yank!' She smothered him with kisses as she moved sensually over him. Feeling his erection beneath her she said, 'I'll show you just how good a wife I'll be. You'll never want to go to work.'

'If I don't, how will I be able to buy food, keep you?' he asked with a chuckle.

But as Ivy nibbled his ear he said, 'Who the hell wants to eat anyway!'

* * *

Two days later, Ivy sidled up to Maggie at the factory and held out her left hand, waving it under her friend's nose. 'What do you think?' she asked.

Maggie was appalled as she looked down at the engagement ring. 'I think you've lost your marbles. That's what I think!'

But Ivy was not to be deterred. 'You can say what you like, but I'm going to live in America!' She turned on her heel and stormed off.

Maggie went to the ladies room and lit a cigarette. Now what could she do? Ivy was crazy thinking she could get away with this. Was she going to commit bigamy? She couldn't get a divorce just like that, it would take ages. And anyway, Bob didn't even know she was married! And what about Len? What would he have to say about all this? She would have to try and knock some sense into her somehow.

But it was to no avail.

When the shift was over, she waited for her friend. She tucked her arm through Ivy's and said, 'For God's sake, be realistic. You can't possibly marry Bob Hanson.'

'He's going to find out all the necessary details,' Ivy declared. 'Then I'll know exactly what I'm up against.' She glared at Maggie. 'I'm going to America somehow and nobody is going to stop me. If you want to walk away from our friendship, that's fine with me!'

'Oh Ivy!' The two walked side by side in silence. Maggie had no intention of leaving her friend, because she felt that soon enough Ivy was going to need her. This stupid idea of hers would only lead to trouble and she couldn't leave her to face it alone.

When she returned home she was met with her own kind of trouble. Her father was waiting in the kitchen for her. 'You were seen in the Red Lion with a Yank the other night, despite what I said,' he accused.

She wearily took the turban off her head and shook loose her hair. She looked straight at her father. 'That's right. His name is Steve and I've been seeing him for some time.'

His thin cheeks puffed up with anger. 'How dare you defy me this way!'

She sat down at the table and faced her father. 'Look, Dad. You made it perfectly clear you intend to go your own way with your black market dealings without any regard to Mum and me, so I don't feel you have any right to dictate to me how to run my life.'

She thought he was going to have a fit. 'Whilst you live under my roof I certainly have the right to tell you what to do,' he yelled.

Maggie felt her anger beginning to rise. 'I pay for my keep. You don't give me anything for nothing.'

He leaned on the table and put his face near to hers. 'Whether you pay or not, you do as I say – or you get out!'

Suddenly she'd had enough. 'If that's the way you feel, I'll leave as soon as I find somewhere else to live,' she said. 'By the end of the week if at all possible. That suit you?' She got up, walked out of the room and went upstairs.

A short while later there was an urgent knocking on her door and a distraught Moira came in. 'What's this your father tells me? You're leaving home?'

Maggie put her arms around her and held her close. 'That's right. I won't have him dictate to me any longer.' She felt her mother tremble as she began to cry. 'It's the only way, Mum. I must be free to live my life. I'll still come and see you.'

Moira looked up, her face wet with tears. 'What if he won't let you?'

'Huh! I'd like to see him try and stop me!' she exclaimed. 'I'll tell him I'll shop him to the police if he doesn't.'

Her mother looked horrified. 'You wouldn't do that, would you?'

Maggie grinned. 'Of course not, but the miserable devil doesn't know that, does he? Now I've got to get changed, I want to see about a flat somewhere.' She tried to smile. 'Imagine . . . if I have my own place you can come and stay when the old bugger gets on your nerves.'

Moira took out a handkerchief from her sleeve and wiped her eyes, smiling bravely. 'That would be nice.' Then with an anxious look she said, 'You will take care of yourself, won't you?'

'Of course I will,' Maggie said gently. 'I'm not moving miles away after all, and I promise I'll see you very often.' The two women clung together.

As she held her mother she thought, Well, I've taken that first step. I'm free. Now I'm in charge of my own destiny. And she wondered just what was before her.

A while later, downstairs, Moira was thinking about her daughter with a sinking heart. So young, so vulnerable. So innocent . . . or was she still? She prayed to God she was. What could she say to her to warn her of the pitfalls of life? She loved Maggie so much and she didn't want to see her get hurt. From the moment the nurse had placed her daughter in her arms she'd adored her. Through the difficult years with Jack, here in the pub, Maggie had been her salvation. Without her, what would she have done? She was filled with despair at the thought of her leaving, but she knew that it was time to let go. It didn't ease the pain she felt deep within her heart.

It was with feelings of both excitement and trepidation that Maggie made her way to an estate agent later that day. She was sad to leave her mother behind, but she felt that things would only get worse between herself and her father if she stayed. This way she could continue to meet Steve and live her own life without any fuss. She would certainly keep a close eye on her mother's welfare, though.

She stopped in front of an agent's window and looked at the flats advertised to let. She frowned as she saw the asking price of some of them. She'd deliberately gone to an up-market agent in the High Street, thinking to get away from the docklands, but she realized that to survive, she would have to lower her sights.

She made her way to an office near Holy Rood, advertising the poorer area of the town, and saw that there was a small selection that suited her pocket. She was about to go inside when a low, deep voice said, 'Hello, Maggie. How are you?'

She turned and looked into the smiling eyes of Joshua Lewis. 'Joshua! What a surprise.'

He beamed at her, his eyes lighting up with pleasure. 'I wasn't sure you'd remember me.'

'The man who played the piano so well . . . how could I forget!'

His melodic laughter flowed. 'What are you doing here?'

He looked a mite perplexed when she said, 'I'm leaving home and am looking for a place to rent.'

His dark eyes twinkled. 'Don't tell me . . . you've fallen foul of your father again.'

She burst out laughing. 'Yes, you could say that. Didn't you ever have any family rows?'

'What, with two brothers and two sisters? We certainly did! All the time.'

'And what did your father do?'

He chuckled. 'He took his slipper to us.'

Maggie started to laugh as she pictured this. 'Did it hurt?'

'Not much. We boys used to put something down the back of our trousers. He didn't do this to the girls, of course, which used to make us mad. But we never left home because of it,' he said with a grin.

'Maybe you didn't, but I've made up my mind.'

'Would you like a cup of tea somewhere?' he asked. 'I have the rest of the afternoon free. We could catch up on the short conversation we had at the dance.'

'I'd like that very much,' she answered, 'but first I'll just pop in here. Come with me if you like.' She opened the door and walked inside.

The middle-aged man behind the desk looked up at his customer with a welcoming smile which disappeared very quickly as he saw her companion.

'Can I help you?' he asked coldly.

Maggie felt the hairs on her neck prickle at the veiled hostility of the man. 'I'm looking for a small, one-bedroom flat,' she said.

'I'm not at all sure that I have anything suitable,' he answered, without making any attempt to assist her.

'Now look here,' she began.

But Joshua stepped forward and with a smile said softly, 'I think you may have jumped to the wrong conclusion, sir. This lovely young lady is just showing me around your town. You folks have all been so kind to us GIs, away from home, and we really appreciate it.'

The man looked slightly abashed and coughed. 'Humph, well I may have something, miss.' He looked through his books and offered her three addresses. 'If you like to take a look at the properties from the outside and if you're interested, come back and see me.'

'Thank you,' she said coldly. 'I'll look at these details and think about it.' She stalked angrily out of the office.

Outside Joshua caught hold of her. 'Hey there! Cool down. My word, you're as fiery as your beautiful red hair.'

She turned to him. 'It just makes me so angry the way other people make judgements about things that don't concern them!'

There was a note of resignation in his voice as he said, 'I've been living with prejudice all my life. You learn to be tolerant.'

She gave him a glance filled with curiosity. 'Why don't we go for that cup of tea and you can tell me all about it.'

The long conversation that followed over several cups of tea was most enlightening and horrifying to Maggie's ears.

'What do you mean, negroes are only allowed to sit in the back of the bus?'

'Because the front is reserved for the white folk,' he said quietly. 'And if all the seats are full, we have to give ours up to them. We even have separate schools. Back home in Mississippi, I wouldn't be allowed to sit in the same place as you to eat.' He chuckled softly. 'Back home if I was caught sitting at the same table as a white woman, as we are now, I could be lynched!'

'You're kidding!'

He shook his head. 'No, Maggie, I can assure you I'm not. That night at the dance was the first time ever that I had held a white woman in my arms. At home if I'd done that I'd be a dead man.' He looked at her expression of horror and said, 'Now perhaps you'll understand why the white GIs hate us so much. Here it's all so different. Here we have so much freedom to mix and it drives them crazy. To them we're just no count niggers, coons. Worse than the dirt beneath their feet. They want to keep us in our place – as they see it!'

But whilst they'd been chatting, Maggie had become aware of angry glances and low mutterings from some of the other patrons of the tea room. She looked around and caught many a hostile look. She straightened her back, defiantly.

It was as if Joshua could read her mind. 'Let it go,' he said firmly, but quietly. 'How about we take a look at these properties that guy gave you?'

She nodded her agreement and waited as he paid the bill, outstaring any who dared to glance their way.

The first two flats were in the Chapel area; Maggie just looked at the addresses and turned them down out of hand. The area had been devastated during the bombing and it was one of the poorest districts. College Street wasn't anything special, but she didn't want to lower her sights that much. The final address was in Bugle Street, and the two of them made their way to the Old Walls.

Joshua was fascinated by the history of the place. 'You can just picture it, can't you,' he said, his eyes shining with excitement. 'The knights of old, the soldiers walking the battlements, protecting the town from marauding forces.'

'You have been reading too many books,' she teased.

He turned to her with a grin and said, 'Well I know all about Robin Hood and King Arthur.'

'But that's all fairy stories.'

'Aw, Maggie don't tell me that! They're some of my favourite characters. Old Henry the Eighth was for real, though. I know that much.'

She knew he was teasing her but she didn't mind a bit.

Before they found the address the estate agent had given them, Maggie took Joshua to look at St Michael's church. As they entered the doorway, he removed his hat. They walked quietly around the church, enjoying the tranquillity of the place. Here, Joshua seemed at home, she thought. She sat in a pew and left him to wander. She watched as he stood in front of the altar, saw him lower his head in silent prayer, and waited patiently until he came and sat beside her.

He looked at her with a soft smile and said, 'Here, in God's house, everyone really is equal.'

They sat in companionable silence until he said, 'Perhaps we'd better find this flat you want to see.'

With some reluctance, she got up and made her way to the door.

The row of flats looked all right and she decided to return to the office and ask the agent to show her around. When she told Joshua her intention he said, 'Fine. I'll leave you now.' At the surprised expression on her face he said, 'It's best, I think, if I'm not around.'

She was immediately defensive. 'It makes no difference to me,' she declared.

'Maybe, but it makes a difference to the guy in the office. It's better this way.'

'I've really enjoyed being with you,' said Maggie.

His face lit up as he smiled. 'It's been my pleasure. I'm glad we ran into each other again.' They stood gazing at one another, reluctant to part.

'Will I see you again? I'd really like to hear more about your family.' As soon as the words were out of her mouth, Maggie wondered why she'd uttered them. She wasn't usually that forward, but she didn't want this unusual man just to walk away.

The pleasure her words gave him showed in his expression. 'I'd be mighty happy to see you again, Maggie.' But suddenly he looked concerned.

'What's the matter?' she asked.

'You saw the effect today, of us being together. It could be the cause of some embarrassment to you, and I wouldn't like that.'

Her green eyes flashed angrily. 'Look, Joshua!' she declared. 'I'm leaving home because I won't be dictated to. When people pay my bills and keep me, then they have the right to have a say in my life. If I won't let my own father do that, I certainly won't let a stranger!'

He burst out laughing. 'Oh, Maggie. All those years ago, all the people of the town would have had to do was have you walking the Old Walls. No one would have dared try to enter the town.'

She too started to laugh. 'I'm not that bad! 'Don't you *ever* get angry?' she asked.

'Only when I really have to,' he said. 'I try to stay out of trouble.'

They made an arrangement to meet again the following week and Maggie bade him goodbye, then made her way back to the estate agent's office.

Chapter Eight

The agent sent his assistant to accompany Maggie to the flat in Bugle Street. As soon as she stepped inside she knew she would take it. The bedroom had a double bed in it, a wardrobe, and in front of the window stood a dressing table. The sitting room was adequate, with a three-piece suite that had seen better days, but with a bit of spit and polish, a couple of cushions and a vase of flowers to brighten it, it would be fine.

The bathroom was small, as was the kitchen, but the cooker was clean and there was a selection of cheap china and a few saucepans. It would be hers. When she locked the door behind her, she would be in her own home. What a thrill!

She walked over to the sitting-room window and look out. To her right was the New Docks and straight ahead, in between other buildings, in the distance, was Southampton Water. But what appealed to her most of all was the quiet. College Street and the pub with its comings and goings was a noisy, busy place, but here, behind the Old Walls, it was a sort of haven.

'The usual tenant is away in the army,' volunteered the agent, 'and the wife has gone to stay with her mother. That's why we're able to offer it,' he explained.

Maggie quickly calculated that she had enough savings in the bank to cover the expense, and at least, unlike with hire purchase, she didn't require a guarantor. Turning to him she said, 'I'll take it. When can I move in?'

He smiled his approval and said, 'If we go back to the office, sign the necessary papers, and you give me a month's rent in advance, you could move in this weekend if you wanted to.'

'That's super,' she said. 'Let's go.'

Having completed the necessary business, Maggie walked out of the office clutching the key to her new abode. She hugged it to her chest and walked home, a smile of satisfaction on her face which faded quickly as she wondered how she was going to break the news. Her mother would be upset, she knew, but she wondered if her father had really believed her when she said she would leave. He wouldn't let her go with a good grace, of that she was certain, and she still had two days before she moved.

Jack Evans was sitting at the kitchen table eating chips and a mushroom omelette made from dried egg when Maggie walked in. He completely ignored her, which under the circumstances suited her fine.

Moira gave her a worried glance and asked, 'Are you ready to eat?'

'Give me time to have a wash, Mum, will you?'

'There's no hurry. I'll just put some chips on,' answered her mother with an uncertain smile.

By the time Maggie returned, Jack had left the room to prepare the bar for opening that evening. When her mother put her meal before her, Maggie said, 'Sit down, Mum. I've something to tell you.'

'You've found a place,' said Moira.

She caught hold of her hand. 'Yes, I have. I move in on Saturday.'

'So soon? Well, darlin', you know I'll miss you, don't you?'

Maggie felt a lump in her throat, but she managed to smile. 'Of course I do, but I intend to come back and work in the bar as usual. So we'll still see lots of each other. And you can come to my place. But you know, don't you, I don't have a choice?'

Moira nodded. 'Tell me about the flat.'

Maggie could barely keep the excitement from her voice as she described it to her.

'And what about this American you told your father you've been seeing?'

The question surprised her. She'd forgotten she'd told her father about Steve. 'He's a staff sergeant. He's really nice,' she said, desperately wanting her mother's approval. 'He's from New York City.'

'I'm glad you've met someone nice,' Moira said. 'But I do hope you'll be careful. War destroys people. Life is so unreal. These men are sent over to the war zones and they don't know if they are going to live or die. Because of this they take every advantage of a good time. They live for today and to hell with tomorrow, and who can blame them. But they leave, and the women stay behind to face everything on their own. Be careful, Maggie. Enjoy yourself, certainly, but for God's sake, don't mess up your life.'

She could see the anxiety in her mother's eyes. 'I promise,' she said. 'You're not telling me anything I don't already know. Steve is nice and I enjoy his company but I know it's only for a short time. He's bound to leave, and who knows when? There's too much I want to do with my life after the war to mess it up whilst the war is on. There's nothing to worry about, I promise.'

Moira took both Maggie's hands in hers and stared at her. 'You know don't you, that if anything should go wrong, and in this life, nothing is certain, you could come to me, no matter what your father says?'

Feeling the tears well in her eyes, Maggie said, 'Who else would I go to?'

'Right,' said Moira, blinking away her own tears. 'I think I'd better put the kettle on.' She got up from the table and asked, 'When are you going to tell your father?'

With a grimace she said, 'I don't know. I'm dreading it.'

'I suggest you start packing when he's busy in the bar and when you're ready to leave, you tell him then. You do it before and he'll be hell to live with.'

Maggie knew her mother was right. She nodded her agreement. 'That's what I'll do then,' she said.

On Friday night, she worked in the bar as usual, trying her best to behave naturally. It was difficult, as Jack only spoke to her when it was necessary. Moira and she tried to make up for the lack of conversation by chattering.

Jack was griping to his customers about all the Yanks in town, digging slyly at his daughter. That started a heated discussion about the war and the necessity of gathering as many troops as possible to fight on their side, no matter what their nationality.

Maggie was grateful to hear her father call time. She cleared the empty glasses and made her escape to the sanctuary of her bedroom, knowing that come tomorrow, she would have to face him.

The following morning, Moira insisted that Maggie eat some breakfast before she left. She handed her ration book over to her. 'Here,' she said. 'You'll be needing this.' She also gave her a small bag with bread, milk, a small amount of tea and a bottle of Camp coffee, a tin of fruit and a small tin of condensed milk. She slipped in a piece of cheese too. As Maggie started to protest she said, 'Don't worry, I managed to get a little extra. I swapped a couple of tins of fruit one of the GIs gave me.'

'You watch yourself,' Maggie warned.

'Now remember,' said Moira, 'you're only allowed one-and-tenpence-worth of meat a week, but chicken, rabbit, sausages and offal are off rationing. Just watch the butter and sugar, it doesn't stretch very far. Buy fish when you can get it, too. You don't need coupons for that.'

Maggie looked at her in admiration. 'I honestly don't know how you managed.'

Her mother looked at her archly. 'The butcher fancies me!'

'Mother!' She handed Moira a slip of paper. 'Here's my address. Are you sure you'll be all right?

'Don't you worry about me,' said Moira. 'You just take care of yourself. I'll ring for a taxi, then you'd better get your cases . . . and then tell your father.'

Maggie's heart was thumping as she walked into the bar where Jack was polishing the beer pumps. 'Dad,' she said. 'I need to talk to you for a moment.'

He looked up and stared coldly at her. 'Well?'

'I'm waiting for a taxi. I'm leaving.'

A frown creased his forehead. 'What do you mean, you're leaving?'

'I've got a small flat and I'm moving in this morning. I think it's for the best.'

He exploded. 'You think it's for the best, do you? The best for who? You break your mother's heart and it's for the best! What about helping in the bar? You're walking out on all your responsibilities!'

Maggie felt the heat of anger burning her cheeks. 'I'm not the one breaking Mum's heart, you are, with your black market dealings. But it's easy for you to put the blame on somebody else. You always do anyway. And I'm not leaving you in the lurch as far as the bar is concerned. I'll come and work as usual.' She moved towards the door.

'You walk out of here, you don't come back. Understand?'

She whirled around and walked back until she was facing him. 'Wrong! I'll come back to work in the bar to ease Mum's load and I'll come to visit her too and you won't stop me. And by God you'd better treat her right or I'll shop you to the Old Bill!'

The blood drained from his face as he looked at her in disbelief. 'You wouldn't dare.'

She glared at him. 'Let's hope we never have to find out.'

At that moment there was a knock on the side door. Moira called, 'Maggie, your taxi's here.'

She walked out of the bar, hugged her mother, picked up her cases and left the Bricklayer's Arms.

Moira watched the taxi drive away then quietly closed the door. She glared at Jack who was standing behind the bar. 'I hope you're satisfied!' She spat the words at him and walked into the kitchen.

Maggie paid the taxi driver, put the key in the lock of her new abode and walked in, placing the cases just inside the door. She went immediately to the kitchen, found a small vase, filled it with water and unwrapped the bunch of flowers she'd purchased on the way. She placed the vase on a small table, stood back and smiled. That's better, she thought, that makes it look more homely. She sat on the settee, pushed herself back into it and spread her arms. It was really quite comfortable. Then she turned and lay on it. Her feet dangled over the end, but she smiled as she thought that she and Steve would be quite comfortable curled up here together.

Oh my God! She sat bolt upright. In all the excitement, she'd forgotten that she was to meet him this evening. He'd booked a room at the Court Royal for them as he had an overnight pass. She looked around. No, she wouldn't bring him here tonight; first she needed to get it just right. The first thing to do was to unpack, then she'd make a cup of tea, do a bit of shopping, have something to eat, then a bath and meet Steve. At least she didn't have to worry about her father's recriminations any more. It gave her a wonderful sense of freedom. Yes, she would enjoy living alone.

Back at the Bricklayer's Arms the atmosphere was tense. Jack was trying to appease his angry wife, without success. Moira stood in front of him, her Irish temper at its height.

'So, now I suppose you're happy, having driven your only daughter away!' she accused.

'Now, Moira, it wasn't like that at all. I didn't want her to leave. That was her decision.'

'You're a selfish man, Jack Evans. You go your own way without regard to anyone. Why I ever married you in the first place I'll never know. I should have listened to my mother.'

Jack knew that Moira's mother had never liked him and that bit deeply. 'She said I'd never amount to anything. Well she was wrong. Haven't we a fine pub, money in the bank, aren't we making a good living?'

'That's all you think about, is making money. You have no heart, no feelings. Well you can take yourself off to Maggie's room and sleep there for I don't want you in my bed!' She stormed out of the kitchen.

Jack knew that he was in deep trouble. Never in all the years they'd been married had they ever spent a night apart. Whatever cross words had passed during the day, they had always been swept away by an arm across his wife's body. Sometimes it had led to sex. They'd often had their best sex after a row. But now . . . God how he hated the Yanks. Without them this situation would never have occurred, he told himself, but in his heart he knew that it would have happened anyway. Maggie was a woman now, not a girl to be ordered about any more. He shrugged. Well what's done is done. Perhaps a taste of life outside the family wouldn't be everything she hoped for. After all, although she paid her mother for her keep, alone, she'd have to cope with electricity bills, rates, food. He gave a slow smile. Moira might keep on about money, but you needed it to live. Yes, Maggie wouldn't find it quite that easy, then maybe she'd come home. This way he managed to smother his feelings of guilt. He could always find a way to do that.

Later that evening, Maggie walked into the bar of the Court Royal Hotel to meet Steve. She saw him standing at the counter talking to the barman.

'Hiya, honey!' He put an arm around her and kissed her cheek. 'What'll you have to drink? The usual gin and tonic?'

'Thank you, that's fine.'

'Right. Sit yourself at a table and I'll bring it over.'

She watched as he ordered. He really was a handsome man, and when he smiled across at her she felt a fluttering of excitement and desire inside at the thought that, later, she would be lying naked in his arms.

He sat beside her. 'What's new?' he asked.

'I've rented a flat,' she said with barely concealed excitement. 'I've left home!'

He whistled quietly. 'Wow! What brought that on?'

Oh dear, she thought. I can't tell him it's because of him, can I? 'My dad and I don't see eye to eye,' she said. 'I want to be free to live my life. After all, I'm not a child any more.'

He slipped his arm around her shoulders and caressed the back of her slender neck. In a low husky voice he said softly, 'No, you're very much a woman. I can vouch for that.' His gaze lowered to the soft swell of her breasts and she felt herself blush. 'So tell me about this place . . . and why the hell are we here instead of there?'

'I only moved in a few hours ago!' she protested. 'I want to have it just right before I show it to you.'

'And that's it?'

She gave a mischievous grin. 'That's it. I want it to be a surprise. I'll cook you dinner the next time you're off duty.'

'Gee, honey, that'll be just great. I'll get a couple of steaks from the cookhouse. Get another key cut, then if I'm free I can come by and leave some things for you. I can supply you with a few stores to help out with the rationing.'

Her enthusiasm waned. She wasn't going to give anyone a key. This was her very own piece of heaven. No one but her had the right to enter it, without invitation. Oh no, that wouldn't do at all. But how could she tell him without seeming ungrateful? She changed the subject. 'Anyway, how are you?' she asked.

'Fine. I can't wait to hold you in my arms,' he said softly. 'It seems ages since we were together in London. By the way, have you eaten?' he asked.

She confessed to having had just a sandwich.

'Right, then,' he said. 'We'll go into the restaurant, have something to eat, then . . .' He kissed her forehead. 'Then I'll take you to bed.'

As they entered the dining room, she thought, Thank heavens I have a place of my own, because much as she wanted to be with Steve, she felt cheapened at staying with him in the hotel. In London it didn't matter, but here in her home town she felt differently. She guessed that the staff would gossip about the Americans and the women they brought here for the night. She didn't think she could face having breakfast in the dining room the following morning. To have dinner was fine, she reasoned, because anyone could walk in off the street for that, but breakfast announced to all and sundry that she'd stayed the night.

She was able to put these feelings of guilt behind her for a while once they were together in their bedroom and Steve took her into his arms. He was as passionate as he'd been in London and Maggie revelled in their lovemaking. He whispered to her in Italian. She didn't know what he was saying but it sounded to her like a language of love.

Neither of them got much sleep that night and she smiled to herself, now knowing what Ivy meant about not being able to walk after her husband came home. But she was happy and content. What did it matter if this was just a passing thing? Steve was her first man and because of this she felt really close to him, even knowing it was a transient liaison.

The following morning, at her reluctance to eat in the dining room, Steve ordered two breakfasts from room service. 'I have to be back at camp by ten thirty,' he said, 'I wish we could spend the day together.'

She too was reluctant to say goodbye. She studied the smiling eyes of her lover, his broad shoulders beneath his open shirt, the dark curls of the hair on his chest peeping out at the top of his olive green vest, the long fingers that had given her so much pleasure. 'Next time you can come to my flat,' she said proudly.

He reached for his jacket and took out a pen and small notebook. 'You'd better give me the address,' he said with a cheeky grin. 'I don't want to lose you now, do I? And don't forget to have a spare key cut for me, because I can't contact you by telephone. I should be free on Tuesday from the late afternoon. What shift are you working next week?'

'The early one,' she told him. She gave him the address but made no mention of the key.

He held her close as they said their goodbyes in their room. 'I'll see you on Tuesday next,' he whispered in her ear as he nuzzled her neck. 'You behave now. You're my girl, remember.' He delved into his jacket pocket and pushed some notes into her hand. 'Here, honey. Buy some things for your new home.'

Maggie looked at the money and then at him. 'I don't want this!'

He was surprised at the hostile note in her voice. 'Jesus! Whatever's the matter? I don't know what you need or I'd get it myself.'

She felt embarrassed. Now she realized that Steve was just being generous, but for a moment it had felt to her that he was paying for the sex they'd had and she felt demeaned. 'It's nothing,' she said hurriedly.

He shook his head. 'Women! As long as I live I'll never understand them!'

She stuffed the notes in her pocket and made for the door. 'I'll see you on Tuesday,' she said.

'Come back here, Maggie,' he said and caught hold of her. 'What did I do that upset you?'

'Nothing,' she said. 'I misunderstood, that's all.' She kissed him on the cheek and left him to pay the bill.

She walked back to her flat feeling deflated. She'd been happy to be with Steve, but as soon as he'd given her the money, the happiness faded. For one moment she'd felt no better than a whore. And he was becoming too possessive, wanting a key to her flat. What right had he to ask such a thing? Next he'd be offering to pay the rent!

She opened the door of her flat, walked in, sat down and lit a cigarette. She might be his girl but that didn't mean she'd give up her freedom just when she'd found it. She was free to invite whoever she wanted here. Just imagine if she had a visitor who didn't know about her relationship with Steve and he walked in. Oh no, she was entirely independent and the sooner he knew it the better. When next they met, she wouldn't mess around, she'd tell him that he couldn't come and go as he pleased and there would be no spare key for anyone!

Whilst she was making a cup of tea she thought how much she would like to invite Joshua to her new home. After all he'd been the one to help her find it. She frowned. Steve had better not find out about him. Knowing the way he felt about negroes she knew he'd be furious. But it was only friendship. She wasn't being unfaithful. She knew, though, that Steve Rossi wouldn't see it that way. Nevertheless, she was determined to meet with the gentle Southerner, as planned.

As Steve made his way back to camp, he was feeling very pleased with himself. The night spent with Maggie had been great and now that she had her own apartment, that would make things even better. For him it would be a Godsend. He badly needed a place to stash his stuff. His London connections were urging him to sell them more of his goods, but he couldn't take too much out of the stores at once without causing suspicion. With a place to put it, however, he could take it out little and often. He was making a great deal of money at the moment and if he played his cards right, by the time the war was over he would have enough money behind him to start a business in a big way.

With a frown he wondered just what had triggered Maggie's sudden anger when he gave her money. How strange, usually his women were only too pleased to accept it, but of course Miss Maggie Evans was quite different from his usual conquests. He shook his head. Women!

Maggie of course was in complete ignorance of Steve's plans to use her place for his illegal dealings and, having decided to put him in the picture about her newfound independence, she pottered about happily, preparing lunch for Ivy. She'd previously arranged this, ringing her friend at the factory, guessing that Steve would have to return to camp early after his overnight pass.

Ivy had been very curious about the move, and Maggie had said she would explain when she saw her. Maggie was also anxious to find out what was happening to her friend's crazy plans to marry Bob Hanson and live in America.

She listened to the Forces request programme, and concentrated intently as they played an Ella Fitzgerald number, remembering that she was an artist that Joshua liked. As the record finished, she could see why. The voice was rich and deep and the music had a beat of its own.

An hour later there was a knock on the door. Ivy had arrived.

She bustled in, full of beans as usual, but as Maggie took her coat she saw that she was still wearing Bob's ring.

She walked around the flat inspecting every room. In the bedroom she sat on the bed and started bouncing on it. 'Well, love, the springs are all right,' she said archly.

'Now behave,' scolded Maggie. 'I'll put the kettle on.'

'Then you can tell me whatever made you move out of the pub,' urged her friend. 'Have another row with your old man, did you?'

She regaled her with the news.

'Your poor mum must be upset, I bet she gives your dad a hard time.'

With a grimace Maggie said, 'Yes, you're probably right.' There was a hint of sadness in her voice as she confessed, 'I really hated to leave her, but I'll still be working in the bar on Fridays and I'll call and see her often, in between.'

Ivy settled on the settee and drank her coffee. 'Some of my neighbours had a go at me for taking Bob home,' she said. 'Bloody cheek! Who are they to tell me how to live my life? I gave them what for I can tell you!'

Maggie grinned to herself. She could just imagine it and she bet the language hadn't been too choice either. 'So what's happening about you and Bob?'

With a sigh her friend said, 'The captain is under orders from his commanding officer to put a hold on marriage applications for the time being. It seems there have been quite a lot of requests and they want the men to take their time and consider what it entails. You know, what with the war, some of the boys may be sent to France to fight very soon. Are you doing the right thing, taking an English girl away from her folks? What about the girl you left behind? All that sort of stuff . . . Bob's furious.'

'If that makes him angry think how he'd react if he discovered you were already married!'

To her surprise Ivy didn't jump down her throat. 'Oh Maggie, I don't know what to do. I've grown to love that crazy Yank. At first it was just lust, and a way of getting out of here, but he's a good man. Kind, thoughtful, he wouldn't harm a fly. He'd make such a wonderful husband and I really want to be his wife. I thought I was happy before, but now I know what real happiness is. I don't want Len any more. He's rough and ready in comparison. You know, all he's interested in is sex, the pub, and his meal on the table when he walks in. My dad was like that and Mum didn't have much of a life. I don't want to be like her, and now I've got the chance of something better.' She looked at Maggie, her eyes reflecting the anguish of her situation. 'If I lose Bob, I've lost everything.'

'Oh Ivy.' Maggie put a comforting arm around her. 'What a mess. I don't know what to say. What if you were honest with Bob and told him the truth?'

Ivy looked horrified at the idea. 'I couldn't do that. What if he walked out on me?' She shook her head. 'Oh no. I can't take that chance. I'll just have to bluff it out. When it comes to filling in the forms, I'll lie!'

Maggie looked at her aghast. 'You'll be committing bigamy! You can go to gaol for that.'

'Who's going to find out? As soon as we're married I'll be shipped to the States.'

'When Len comes home, they'll find out! He's not going to sit quietly after discovering what you've done. If he reports it to the police, then you'll really be in the shit.'

The old Ivy surfaced. 'They'd have to find me first!'

At that point, Maggie gave up. There was nothing she could say to change the situation and make Ivy see sense.

The following day, Steve Rossi took a telephone call in his office. His expression changed on hearing the voice on the other end. 'I told you not to call me here. I'll be in touch when I have something for you. In an emergency you can contact me at —' He took a small notebook from his uniform pocket. 'Flat 2, 14 Bugle Street. But only in an emergency. If I'm not there, leave a message with my girl. And don't call me here again!' He slammed the telephone down. Shmucks! Didn't they realize how dangerous a call to his office was? They could blow the whole deal.

Chapter Nine

Doug Freeman, or the ice man as he was known by the underworld fraternity, due to his predilection for ice picks, slammed down the receiver of his telephone. 'Cocky little bastard! That bloody wop gets right up my nose, telling me where and when to call him. He's getting far too big for his American boots.'

Charlie his trusty helper tried to calm him. 'They're all like that, guv. Don't take no notice. We want what he's got and he bloody well knows it.'

Doug frowned. 'I just don't trust him, he's far too sharp for my liking. The trouble with him is he doesn't know who he's dealing with. Perhaps we should teach him a lesson?' He looked enquiringly at his companion.

Shaking his head Charlie said, 'I don't think we should rock the boat just yet. It would be a pity to lose that connection. Where else could we get such a steady supply of goods? Not to mention the artillery.'

But Doug was not so easily persuaded. 'No one talks to me like that and gets away with it.'

And it was true. Doug Freeman was a hard man. All his life he'd been on the wrong side of the law. He'd spent time in Borstal as a young tearaway, had done a stretch in Wandsworth for grievous bodily harm, and only missed a charge of murder by a hair's breadth, through lack of evidence. He was a person that few ever crossed and if they did, it was usually the last time. Occasionally a body floated along the Thames to be discovered washed up on some muddy bank by the River Patrol.

Doug's hero was George Raft. He would go to the cinema and see all his films. He particularly liked the ones co-starring James Cagney, but he thought Cagney was a tough little bugger, whereas George Raft had an air of sophistication about him that Doug envied. He was also a dapper man, which Doug tried to emulate with his bespoke suits, his black shirts and ties, trilby hat. But where the film star could carry this off, Doug couldn't. He had no class. He was a big chap with ginger hair and a temper to match – with two left feet. He liked to watch the films where his hero would dance the tango with the leading lady, usually a glamorous blonde, but he knew that on a dance floor he was a failure.

He was a big-time villain. The East India docks was on his patch, the Isle of Dogs. Here he ran a string of prostitutes, a protection racket, and was up to his neck in black market racketeering. He was a man to be feared.

He lit a large cigar. 'So he's got a bird, has he?' He stored that piece of information away for future reference. 'Well at least now we have a way of contacting him. I'm not prepared to hang around waiting for his call. He's got half my bloody money up front – he was quick enough to take that, I notice. It's time he showed me a bit of respect! When he delivers his next load, I'll have a word.'

Seeing the menacing smile on his boss's face, Charlie knew that if he wasn't very careful, Steve Rossi would be taught a lesson he wouldn't forget.

Against the might of Doug Freeman, Jack Evans was small potatoes. He didn't consider himself a racketeer, just a bloke trying to take advantage of a situation and make a bit of money for his retirement. But things weren't panning out as he'd hoped.

Sonny Taylor had gone cold on him. Whereas he used to be always popping into the Bricklayer's Arms with a bit of news of another load of stuff, now he was evasive, saying to Jack that things were tightening up. The police were becoming too vigilant. 'Just be patient,' he said. 'When I get some goods, I'll let you know.'

What the landlord didn't know was that Sonny had had a visit from Charlie, advising the spiv that it would be in his best interests to sell any goods he had to Doug Freeman. Unlike Steve, Sonny knew of Doug's reputation and was only too pleased to comply. What the hell! It didn't matter to him who he sold the stuff to, as long as he got the money. The only thing was that now he had to put himself in jeopardy by finding an old lock-up garage to store his ill-gotten gains instead of letting Jack do it, thereby putting himself in danger from the law. He scowled. That sod Freeman didn't pay as much as Jack, but at least, Sonny told himself, he was keeping out of trouble. And if he was clever, eventually he could still put some stuff Jack's way.

Jack had emptied his front room of goods at long last, but now it had been empty for a while and he was frustrated. He stood inside the room with the door open. What was the point of closing it, he thought angrily. There was nothing for anyone to see.

And Moira was still insisting that he stay in Maggie's room. She cooked his meals, did his washing and ironing, but there was little conversation between them as she'd not forgiven him for the departure of her loving daughter. All in all, he was not a happy man.

Maggie, however was in her element. She came home from the factory every day, and with sheer delight put her key into the door of her very own home. It never ceased to give her great pleasure. She'd bought a few things to brighten it with the money Steve had given her, and now as she stood and looked around her she was like a cat with a saucer of cream.

She had been back to the Bricklayer's Arms the night before to do her stint in the bar. Her mother had been delighted to see her, as were the regulars, who had been dismayed to hear of her leaving. She'd taken a bit of stick over that.

'Getting too good for the likes of us, girl?' Nobby had quipped.

'I'm here, aren't I?' she retorted. 'I've got to keep an eye on you,' she said with a broad grin.

'You sound just like the bloody missus,' he grumbled.

She turned to her mother. 'I've got a day off tomorrow, Mum. Why don't you come and see the flat? We can have a cuppa and a long chat.'

Moira's eyes lit up with delight. She was very curious to see where Maggie was living and it would do her good to get out of the pub for a bit. 'I'd love to.'

'Come about eleven,' she said, knowing her father wouldn't be busy and moan at Moira for leaving him alone behind the bar.

The following morning, Maggie was rushing around with a duster, plumping a cushion here and there. She so wanted her mother to approve of her first home.

At long last there was a knock on the door.

Maggie ushered her inside.

Looking around the living room, Moira smiled and said, 'But this is lovely, and so cosy.' She looked at Maggie. 'I'm sure you'll be very happy here . . . and it's so quiet!'

'I know, isn't it great? After College Street it seemed strange at first, but I love it. Come and see the bedroom.'

Moira walked over to the window looking at the water in the distance, wondering if Maggie had shared her bed with a man, praying that she hadn't. But she didn't show any of these anxieties as she turned back.

'I wouldn't mind living here myself,' she said.

The two of them spent a couple of hours chatting before Moira rose from her chair.

'I must get back, love, and prepare a meal for your father. You take care of yourself. If you want anything, you let me know.'

'I can always call you from the telephone box down the road,' Maggie said. She walked Moira to the door, kissed her goodbye and said, 'I'll see you next Friday evening.'

Maggie was really pleased that her mother approved of the flat and this evening Steve was coming round for dinner. She wondered just what his reaction would be.

Just as Maggie stepped out of the bath later that afternoon there was a knock at the door. She answered it, wrapped in a towel, with another around her freshly washed hair.

Steve stepped inside and with a lustful gleam in his eyes said, 'Well, it looks as if I've arrived at just the right moment.' He closed the door behind him and slowly pulled the towel away from her body.

'Steve!' she protested.

'Now don't give me that,' he said as he pulled her to him. His mouth covered hers, his hands explored her naked form. 'Where's the bedroom? You'd better tell me quickly or I'll take you here in the hall.'

'What would the neighbours think?' she asked with a chuckle.

'Who the hell cares.' He lowered her to the ground, and quickly removed his jacket and trousers.

She undid his tie and shirt, removing them swiftly, running her hands over his broad shoulders, his chest, returning his hungry kisses with a fervour. They couldn't get enough of each other. It was like a wonderful spread of delicacies laid before a starving man. Their lovemaking was frantic and exciting, both of them reaching a climax very quickly. They lay puffing and panting, exhausted, on the slightly threadbare carpet. It was only then that Maggie realized that Steve hadn't used any contraception. Oh my God! she thought. I could get pregnant.

He saw the sudden look of anxiety in her eyes.

'What's the matter?' he asked.

She told him.

'Christ!' he exclaimed. 'Gee, honey, I'm sorry. I'm usually so careful. It was the unexpected sight of you half undressed.' He pulled her to him and held her. What a damned fool I am, he thought. Oh well, if the worst came to the worst, I'd pay for an abortion. He helped her up. 'Come on sweetheart,' he urged. 'It'll probably be all right.'

'And if it isn't?'

He held her hand. 'Let's not worry about that until the time comes. When is your next period due?'

'In about a week's time,' she answered.

'Then we don't have long to wait. Come on now, go and get dressed and then you can show me this new place.' He picked up a bag he'd hastily dropped on the carpet. 'I've got two steaks here for us and a bottle of wine.' He kissed the tip of her nose. 'Go along now.' He patted her bottom as she passed him. 'I'll put the kettle on,' he said. 'I've brought you some tea and a few other things as well.'

Whilst she dressed, Maggie tried not to worry, but try as she would she couldn't rid herself of the possible consequences of their reckless passion. That would be the end of her freedom. An unwanted pregnancy was the last thing she needed. Oh how stupid they had been. But she knew she'd been as much at fault as Steve. She slipped into a fresh pair of french knickers, and a floral dress, then made her way to the kitchen.

To her surprise, Steve was already cooking. He'd also brought a lettuce, tomatoes, and a cucumber. He was mixing a salad in a bowl he'd found in the cupboard. There were some slices of a strange-looking meat on a plate.

'What's that?' she asked.

'Italian salami. Try it,' he said with a grin.

She did. The taste was unusual, as was the texture. She wasn't sure if she liked it or not.

He raised an eyebrow. 'What do you think?'

'To be honest, I don't know. It's a bit chewy.'

'Before long I'll have you appreciating everything Italian,' he promised.

She smiled as she watched him. He was completely at home in the kitchen. Around his waist he'd tied a tea towel. 'To keep any grease marks off my uniform,' he explained.

He opened the bottle of wine and when the steaks were cooked they sat at the table.

The meat was delicious, but there was a flavour about it that was alien to Maggie. She asked what it was.

'Garlic. No Italian would cook without it. It does make your breath smell but as we are both eating it, then it won't notice.' He produced some American chewing gum. 'Put this into your mouth tomorrow before you go to work,' he said. 'It'll disguise it.'

Later, they sat in a tight huddle on the settee, drinking the remains of the wine.

'Gee, honey, this is really great,' he said. 'I have to be back by midnight though.'

'Just like Cinderella,' she said.

'Who the hell is Cinderella?'

With a chuckle she told him.

'Yes, very quaint. Very English. But I'm not into glass slippers.' He drew her nearer and kissed her. 'Let's go to bed,' he suggested. 'I promise to be careful.'

They did . . . and he was.

As they sat having a cup of tea together before he departed, he looked around the room. 'This really is a neat place you've got here. Is there much storage place?'

'There's an empty cupboard in the hall,' she said.

'Did you get the key cut for me?' he asked.

She felt her nerves tense. Well, here goes, she thought. 'No,' she replied.

'I guess you've been busy,' he said.

'No it's not that, Steve. I don't want anyone else to have access to my place. It's private. Mine.'

He looked at her with an expression of astonishment. 'What's that supposed to mean?'

She tried to explain. 'This place marks my first step into independence.

Having left home, for the first time I'm free. Free to come and go, have my friends to stay, with no one to answer to. Just imagine if I had a friend here for a cup of tea, or my mother, perhaps, and you walked in with your own key. Think how embarrassing it would be.'

She saw the anger reflected in his eyes. 'Are you saying our relationship is an embarrassment to you?'

'No of course not.' She knew now he wouldn't understand, but she wasn't going to change her mind. 'This place to me is absolutely private. No one is going to have the right just to walk in when they want, but me.' She held her breath. There, now she'd said exactly how she felt.

'I'm damned if I understand!' he exclaimed. 'Aren't you my girl? I know every inch of your body. There isn't a part of it I haven't kissed or tasted. You give me that freedom, but I'm not allowed the freedom of your home. Your bed, yes – but that's it?'

She was a little alarmed at the anger and indignation pouring forth from her lover, but she was angry herself and she was adamant.

'I wouldn't put it quite like that, but yes.'

He was furious. 'I don't understand you. I was delighted that you had your own place. It would give us somewhere private. I was going to suggest that I pay the rent, but I guess that would invade your privacy too.'

That was the last straw. Her temper flared. 'I don't want you to pay my rent, thank you. I'm not a kept woman. This flat is mine. I pay all the bills . . . and you can come when I invite you.'

'When you want a good screw! Is that it?'

'Don't you dare to talk to me like that. You make me sound like some cheap tramp. You of all people know that's not the case.'

This comment stemmed his anger. He knew that she'd been a virgin and he had no reason to believe that she'd been with another man. 'I'm sorry, Maggie, but this doesn't make a lot of sense to me.'

She put her hand out to touch him. 'I don't expect you to understand,' she said, 'but my father tried to rule my life for so long and I must be able to please myself now, or it's all been for nothing.' She looked at him, hoping to make him see reason. 'It wasn't easy for me to leave my mother. My father can be difficult to live with.'

This struck a familiar chord with the American and he studied her face, putting out a hand to caress the worried features. 'OK. If that's how you want it.'

There was such a look of relief on her face that he took her into his arms.

'Hey! You know what? We've just had our first fight. How about that?' He looked at his watch. 'I'd better be going. I don't know when I'll be free. Probably not until the weekend and maybe not even then. There's a lot of movement in the docks during the next few days and I'll be on duty.' He frowned. 'I wish you had a telephone. It would be more convenient. I'll put a note through your door as soon as I know anything. All right?'

She nodded. 'That'll be fine.'

He kissed her goodnight and left.

She collapsed on the settee and lit a cigarette. That had been a bit nasty for a while, and at one time she had thought Steve was going to walk out, he was so angry. It was the second time she'd seen that side of him and she didn't like it. But then, as she admitted to herself, she'd become very heated also. Never mind, at least now he knew where he stood. And tomorrow she had to meet with Joshua. She was sure that he wouldn't have made such demands, but then she couldn't have found two men who were so different.

She went to bed, completely exhausted, praying to God that she wasn't pregnant, telling herself that one week before a period wasn't the most fertile time of a woman's cycle and hoping the book she'd read was correct.

Steve on the other hand was furious. It was essential that he have a key to Maggie's place. He wanted to be able to come and go whenever he slipped goods out of the camp. He'd taken a sneaky look at the cupboard in the hall and found it adequate for his needs. Fortunately, Maggie didn't have a lot of stuff of her own and probably wouldn't require it. He rubbed his chin in contemplation. He'd have to find a way round it somehow.

The following day, Maggie met Joshua outside the bombed remains of Holy Rood church. As she approached she saw him studying what was left of the once beautiful building. She walked up behind him.

'Hello, soldier. Need some company?'

He turned and gave his broad smile as he saw her. 'Maggie. How nice you look. I like the new hairstyle.'

She flushed at the unexpected compliment and marvelled at his observation. She usually wound her auburn tresses up into a Victory roll, but when she'd washed it last time she'd turned the ends under into a smooth pageboy.

'Thank you. Flattery will get you anything,' she quipped.

He chuckled. 'Really? Is there anything special you want to do?'

This in itself was a change. Steve usually told her where they were going, and as she thought about it, all she wanted to do was talk to this man. 'No, not really.'

'It's such a nice day, why don't we go and sit in the park?' he suggested and that was exactly what they did.

Once again Maggie felt calm and comfortable in the company of the Southerner as they walked. She ignored the pointed glares from some of the passers by, but smiled as several children danced around Joshua, chanting, 'Got any gum, chum?'

He just laughed and handed out a couple of packets from his trouser pocket. He didn't take her arm, simply walked alongside her.

They found a quiet spot beneath a tree to shade them from the warm summer sun. 'Is the climate in your home like this?' she asked.

He shook his head. 'Hell no! In the summer it's hot and steamy, perspiration drips off you before you even move. But you get used to it.' He began to tell her about his home; about the Mississippi Delta, an impenetrable wilderness of cypress and gum trees; about the plagues of mosquitoes. 'And of course there are gators.'

She looked puzzled.

'Alligators.' He saw her eyes widen in horror. 'Yes, we have plenty of those. You catch a young one, they cook up real well.'

'You eat them?'

He grinned broadly. 'Sure we do, and catfish, so called because they have whiskers. Then there's the poverty and the music of course. Apart from our spirituals, there's the Delta Blues.'

'What on earth is that?' she asked.

In a low deep voice, he began to sing a song called 'Crossroads Blues', which spoke of a stranded night in the chilling emptiness of the Delta. The poignancy of the words touched her deeply as did the soulful yet melodic tune, but she marvelled at the beautiful voice of the man sitting beside her.

He began to tell her how slaves were brought into America from the African continent to work the plantations. 'They were the property of the plantation owner,' he said. 'They lived in shacks. There they jumped over the broom and had their children.'

'What do you mean, jumped over the broom?'

He laughed, his eyes bright with amusement. 'A man and a woman literally jumped over a broom on the ground and that meant they were married.'

'As easy as that?'

The smile faded. 'Nothing was easy about being a slave, Maggie. Life was hard, the overseers were harsh and the owners left the discipline in their hands.'

'I saw a film about that once. I thought it was so cruel.'

'That was the way it was,' he said. 'Abraham Lincoln of course freed the slaves which certainly didn't please the white bosses. Mind you, some of them did good. They made their way to Oklahoma at the time of the landrush and staked out a claim for themselves.'

'And now?'

'There's still great poverty in the South. The white man is still king . . . But to sit and watch a paddle steamer sail down the Mississippi river is such a pretty sight. You can hear the swish of the water as the paddle turns.

And if you're real lucky, you can hear the music of the jazz band on board.'

There was no note of censure in his voice and she admired his acceptance of the whole situation.

'If there was such poverty where you came from, how did you make a living?' she asked.

Joshua smiled at her. 'I escaped and went to New Orleans.'

'What did you do there?'

'Why, played the piano in a jazz band. New Orleans breathes jazz,' he said, his eyes shining with enthusiasm. 'I was truly among my own there. You know, whenever there is a funeral, a band leads the procession.' He grinned at her look of surprise.

'Playing music?' asked Maggie, incredulous at such a thing.

'Certainly, playing! Why not? I can't think of a better way to start your journey to the pearly gates.'

'Well, it's not like any funeral I've ever seen.'

He laughed at her dismay. 'It sure is the way that I want to go, although my daddy may not agree. In his church it's all gospel singing. Beautiful – but not my style.'

'What are you going to do after the war?' she asked.

'I'm heading for New York. I can always find work there.' He leaned towards her. 'Music is my life, Maggie.'

She'd noticed he was carrying a small book and was curious. 'What are you reading?' she asked.

'It's a book of poems.'

'A jazz musician who reads poetry? You are a constant surprise,' she said.

'I don't know why you find that so odd,' he argued. 'Music is a kind of poetry, isn't it? Art too.'

'I've never thought of it that way.'

'Music, words, pictures, they all tell you something in their own way.' She thought for a moment. 'Yes, I suppose they do.'

He began to recite.

Maggie lay back on the grass and listened. She didn't know when she'd experienced such a sense of peace as she did at this time. For the first time she really listened to the words of Shakespeare's sonnets and wondered why at school they had sounded so different.

A while later, she invited Joshua back to her flat for tea.

He was delighted.

When they arrived, he looked around and admired it. 'Is this better than living with your family?' he asked.

As she poured the boiled water into the teapot, she frowned. 'Well, my father can be a difficult man, and even though I love him, there comes a time when you can't take the arguments any more. I miss my mother a lot. I see her every Friday when I work in the bar. Apart from that, I love my independence.'

They sat side by side on the settee.

'Don't you have a young man, Maggie? A good-looking girl like you would have fellows queuing at the door I would think?'

She didn't feel she had to lie. 'I am going out with an American staff sergeant,' she said. 'He's with the 14th Major Port. Steve Rossi is his name.' She knew that something was wrong as soon as she mentioned Steve's name.

'Have you known him for long?' Joshua asked.

'Not really. Just a few months. Do you know him?'

With a wry smile he said, 'Well, we don't exactly socialize, but yes, I know him.'

'And you don't like him, do you?' she asked.

'Who I like and don't like doesn't matter, Maggie, but I have to tell you that he is trouble.'

'He's very nice,' she argued.

'I'm glad he treats you right,' he said. 'But, Maggie, watch your step, that's all.' He looked at his watch, drank his tea and stood up. 'I really have to go.' He shook her hand. 'Thanks for the company.'

They walked towards the door. 'I would like to ask you out to a movie or something, but your boyfriend wouldn't approve.'

'We can be friends, Joshua, can't we? I'd like to go to the cinema with you.'

'He won't like it.'

'I'm free to choose my own friends,' she said angrily.

He chuckled. 'Keep your cool, girl. If that's fine by you, then it's fine by me. How about Monday evening at six thirty? I'll see you outside the Regal cinema. If we don't like the movie showing there we can go elsewhere.'

'That suits me.' She let him out of the door and closed it.

Now she really was playing with fire. Steve hated negroes with a vengeance. He was also very possessive. Joshua said he was trouble, but he couldn't be right, surely? And in what way was Steve trouble? She hadn't seen anything of it, only that incident in London, but then he was protecting her. When they were together, there was no reason to believe Steve was anything but a charmer. His friends seemed OK – those that she'd met when they were out together. Joshua must be mistaken.

Having convinced herself that Joshua was wrong about Steve, Maggie decided it was too nice a day to stay in. She'd walk along the waterfront and take her mother some flowers. Picking up her handbag, she left the flat.

Chapter Ten

As Maggie turned the corner into College Street, she saw the local children swinging on a rope slung over an exposed beam in the remains of a bombed house. There was a huge knot tied at the bottom of the rope which acted as a seat; they jumped on it and swung across the building, yelling and screaming. She smiled to herself. Nothing's changed.

She stopped at the side entrance to the Bricklayer's Arms and walked in, making her way down the narrow hallway to the kitchen. Through the open door she could see her mother sitting at the table, lost in thought.

'Hello, Mum. How are you?'

Moira leapt from her chair and hugged her daughter. 'What a lovely surprise. Sure and it's wonderful to see you again so soon.'

Maggie handed her the flowers she'd purchased on the way. 'These are for you,' she said.

Moira bustled about filling a vase with water, and arranging the summer blooms. 'So what have you been doing?'

'I met a friend and we walked in the park.'

'Anyone I know?'

'He's a GI I met at a dance.'

'But I thought you were already going out with a GI?'

'I am.' She grew impatient. 'He's just a friend. His father's a preacher and he plays jazz.'

'What, the father?'

'No, Mum. Joshua.'

Moira looked at her. 'Joshua? That's an unusual name.'

'He's from the company of black soldiers.'

Her mother spun round and stared at her. 'You go where angels fear to tread, Maggie. You know how folks look down on girls who go out with the darkies!'

'Negroes, Mother. Negroes! Joshua isn't ashamed of who he is. He's a nice man . . . a negro, not a darkie or a nigger!'

'You have no idea what you're getting into, have you? Don't you care what people think?'

'Frankly, no. I care what you think.'

'You know how I feel about it.'

'I don't want to fall out with you, Mum, so let's leave it, shall we!'

Her mother gave her a hard look. 'You'll go your own way whatever I

83

say. You're stubborn, just like your father!'

Maggie changed the subject. 'How is Dad, when he's not raging at me?'

Moira shrugged. 'The same as ever. He'll never change. Although his front room is empty at the moment and has been for a while.'

Maggie was surprised. 'Has he given all the black market stuff up, then?' she asked hopefully.

'Is it a miracle you're expecting? Of course not, but that Sonny Taylor hasn't been round lately. It's driving your father barmy. He's losing precious money, isn't he? Nothing else is important.'

The bitterness in her mother's voice hurt her and she asked, 'Have you two been rowing?'

Moira shook her head. 'No, not at all.' She lit a cigarette. 'How's the flat?'

It's obvious that things aren't going well, thought Maggie and felt guilty at having left the family home, but she wasn't going to lie to her mother. 'It's just fine,' she said. 'I can't tell you how lovely it is to be independent. Not to have anyone telling me how to run my life. It's such a pity you can't come and live with me. I miss you.'

Moira forced a smile. 'Now that wouldn't do at all,' she said. 'That would spoil the whole point of being a free person.' But oh, how she wished that she was able to do the same. As she looked at her daughter, however, she sensed that she had something else on her mind, yet knew better than to probe. If Maggie had something to tell her, she would do so in her own time.

Maggie would have loved to unburden her worries that she might be pregnant to her mother, but she didn't dare.

An hour later Moira let her out of the side door. Nobby Clarke saw her and called to her. 'Hello, Maggie girl. How are you?'

'I'm fine, Nobby, and you?'

He grinned at her. 'When are you coming home to live, lass? I'm sick of that old bugger's face! We need someone behind the bar who's good-looking and with a bit of life.'

'You should try for the job of barman then,' she said with a broad grin.

Nobby burst out laughing. 'Flatterer! You take care, young lady,' he said.

'I will. Give my love to Grace.'

At the door she hugged her mother. 'You look after yourself. When I know what shift I'm on next week, I'll give you a ring and you come round to the flat again.'

Moira's face lit up. 'I'd love to.'

Maggie told her, 'I'll give you a call in a few days.'

Moira gazed affectionately at her. 'You take good care, you hear?' With a heavy heart she watched her daughter walk down the street, wondering just what it was that the girl had on her mind. I miss you more than you'll ever know, thought Moira. Since Maggie had gone, she'd been really lonely. The girl was the light of her life and her husband was no substitute at all.

When the pub closed that night, Jack walked into the kitchen and said to his wife, 'Now that our Maggie's settled, isn't it time you and I stopped this nonsense and got back to a normal way of life?'

She glared at him. 'You're not the man I married, Jack Evans. Then you were happy, carefree. It didn't matter a toss to me that you were crippled because your spirit was strong and healthy, but now you're an embittered old man. I'll tell you one thing, if I was in a position to leave here like Maggie, you wouldn't see me for dust!' She walked out of the kitchen and seconds later he heard the door of her bedroom slam.

He was shattered by his wife's words. He had expected her to be upset when Maggie had left, but he had been sure now that their daughter saw Moira fairly regularly, she'd be fine, even if he and Maggie had had words. Never ever had he expected to hear her say she'd like to leave him. He went into the bar and poured himself half a pint of bitter. You could never tell with women which way they'd turn. He'd buy her something nice, try to sweeten her up. Perhaps if he didn't get in any more black market stuff she'd come round. He'd think about it, because Moira was his life, if only she realized it.

But when Sonny Taylor came knocking on his door with news of books of clothing coupons, and a promise of more goods in the near future, he forgot all about his good intentions in his eagerness to make some more money.

Later that evening, Maggie had an unexpected caller. When she opened the door, Steve was standing there with a cardboard box, filled with stores. He grinned broadly at her. 'Hi, gorgeous. Santa Claus has called early.' He walked in and deposited the box in the kitchen. 'I can't stop for long,' he said, 'but I thought this would help.'

He unpacked some tea, a bag of sugar, coffee, a couple of tins of ham, a carton of American cigarettes, a tin of sliced peaches and some Hershey bars, chewing gum and American magazines.

Maggie was thrilled with such bounty. She hugged him. 'Thanks, thanks a lot.'

He caught hold of her and kissed her. 'I told you I'd take care of you, didn't I? Look, I have a few things on the jeep, I wonder if I could store them in your cupboard for a couple of days?'

How could she refuse? But as he made several journeys to and fro, she wondered just what was going on here. 'What is all this?' she asked.

'Just a few gifts for some folk who have been good to me, and there is to be a kids' party in a month's time, so I'm collecting a few things. Look, honey, I have to fly. I hope to see you for much longer very soon.' He kissed her briefly and left.

Maggie frowned. She was thrilled with the goods he'd given her but . . . She opened the door of the cupboard and looked inside. There were cartons of cigarettes, nylon stockings, bottles of whisky, gin, bourbon. Tinned goods. She wasn't a fool, this wasn't for any children's party, this was contraband, and she had it in her flat. She was absolutely furious.

She stomped around the sitting room. She had railed at her father for storing such things, putting his livelihood in jeopardy, and now she was in the same position. How dare Steve do this to her! What if the police found out and came round?

She was even more incensed when she got home from the factory the following day to find a note from Steve saying some friends of his would be collecting the stuff.

Two men arrived later in a private car and knocked on her door. A couple of rough diamonds with broad smiles. 'Hello, darlin', got some stuff for us? The Yank told us to pick it up.'

She barely spoke to them as they took the goods, but as they drove away she thought, I suppose the car is filled with black market petrol too! She remembered Joshua's warning. How much did he know of Steve's activities, she wondered. A hell of a lot more than she did, that was for sure. She thought back to the two men in the seedy club in London. How stupid she was not to have put two and two together then!

She made a cup of tea and sat down, trying to think of what to do. What a liberty this man had, not only using her place as a drop but then to send two strangers to collect it. Who did he think he was? She would never be put into this situation again and if Steve didn't like it, he could go to hell! She prayed, fervently, that her period wouldn't be late. That would just about be the last straw. Carrying the child of a black marketeer. How her father would crow.

As Steve made his way to Maggie's flat a couple of days later, he wondered what sort of a greeting he'd receive. Maggie was a bright girl, she would no doubt have realized that something was going on. But he'd been desperate. He'd lost a lot of the money Doug Freeman had given him in a crap game and he knew they'd be getting restless if he didn't come across with the goods. He'd had an opportunity to take a load out of the camp, but with no place to store it he was in trouble and the only way to save his hide was to use Maggie. He knocked on her door. He was sure he'd be able to talk his way out of it.

'Hello, honey,' he said with a broad smile, and stepped inside. He went to take her into his arms, but she pushed him away.

'You bastard!' she said. 'How dare you take advantage of me and send your thugs around here?'

'Aw, come on, Maggie. It was only for a couple of days. I didn't think you'd mind helping me out.'

'You lied to me, Steve Rossi. Kids' party, my arse! Do you think I'm stupid?'

He went to catch hold of her arm. 'Now don't be like that, babe.'

'Don't you babe me!' She threw off his hold and and walked into the kitchen.

He followed, trying to placate her.

She turned on him, her fury reflected in her eyes, as she spoke. 'You bring me a few stores to sweeten me up then you fill my cupboard with stolen goods. Not content with putting me in this dangerous position, you send someone to collect it. You gave out my address to strangers! How dare you?'

'Come and sit down,' he entreated, 'let me try and explain.'

She reluctantly followed him into her sitting room.

'In wartime,' he began, 'everyone is into some kind of scam, or fiddle, as you limeys call it. I'm only doing what everyone else is doing. Making a few bucks on the side.'

'What if you're caught?' she demanded. 'You'd be court-martialled, sent home.'

He gave a confident smile. 'Me, get caught? You've got to be kidding!'

She looked at him and shook her head. 'You didn't even consider that I might have been in trouble if the police had called and discovered your haul. I could go to prison! You're so arrogant. So cocksure of yourself. If you want to take those kinds of risks, fine. But leave me out of your schemes. I don't want anything to do with them.'

'Gee, honey, I'm sorry, but I was really stuck. And why on earth would the police call here?' He put an arm around her shoulders. 'I promise it won't happen again, OK? Come on, don't be mad at me. I only have a few hours, let's not fight.' He stroked the back of her neck.

But Maggie was still seething. She glared at him. 'I don't know you at all,' she said. 'This charming front you put on is all a sham. You used me, and now you come round here all sweetness and light expecting to take me to bed, no doubt!'

He was not deterred by her attitude. With a slow smile he said, 'Of course I was hoping for a few moments of love with my girl, I wouldn't be human if I wasn't, but if you're not in the mood, then that's fine.'

She glared at him. 'You can't use people like this, Steve. It isn't right. It isn't being responsible. You tell me I'm your girl as if I'm supposed to be special and you treat me like this . . . Well, I won't put up with it!'

He gazed into her eyes. 'You know, when you're angry, your eyes go a deeper shade of green and your nostrils flare. It's very sexy. And I can assure you that I am charming.' He caught hold of her hand and kissed her palm. 'Don't be cross, honey. We get so little time together.' He pulled her closer and kissed her gently. 'I really do think a lot of you, you know. That's why you're my girl. I wouldn't do anything to put you in any kind of danger. Honest. I think far too much of you to do such a thing.'

'But you bloody well did!' She was exasperated.

He looked shamefaced and said softly, 'I promise I won't ever do such a thing again. You are my girl and you are special.'

She saw the beguiling look in his eyes and for a moment her anger faded.

Being so well schooled in the art of seduction, Steve knew that he was going to win her round. He kissed her again, at first gently then gradually with more passion. He was relieved and delighted when he felt Maggie beginning to respond, but as he went to slip his hand beneath her skirt, she stopped him.

'That's as far as you go,' she said firmly.

He didn't persist but was content to have overcome her anger. She obviously wouldn't let him use her flat again, he'd have to find somewhere else. Or someone else with some spare room. These guys were prepared to spend a lot of money and he wasn't going to miss the opportunity of making a killing, not for any woman.

After he'd left the flat, Maggie was angry with herself for giving in so easily to Steve's advances. He thought he could twist her around his little finger. It was about time he learned that she was no pushover.

Still wary of Steve and his antics, she began to question Joshua about him when they were sitting in the cinema, during the interval, a few days later.

'Why did you warn me about Steve Rossi?' she asked. 'Why do you think he's trouble to be around?'

Joshua gazed at her with an anxious expression. 'Has he treated you bad?' he asked.

'No, nothing like that,' she said, reluctant at this stage to tell him anything.

'Rossi is a man who makes a fast buck wherever he can,' he started. 'Being in charge of the stores puts him in a mighty useful position. I know that he's selling army goods outside the camp.'

'You do? How?'

'I've been on many a detail to collect stores when they dock. He has them stored away, but he has his own stash put separately. It's so obvious that I'm surprised no one has spotted it yet.'

'Are you certain?'

'Oh, yes. I have a buddy who works as a clerk. He's been keeping an eye on him, but he don't want to be involved. Rossi is clever and my buddy is black. You don't go looking for trouble in this army.' He gave her a sideways glance. 'You make sure you don't get mixed up in his mess, Maggie, because he's involved with dangerous men. Some heavy dudes from London, so I hear.' He paused. 'I know he can pour on the charm, but believe me, he'd sell his mother and his soul for a good price.'

Maggie felt her stomach lurch when she thought of the two men who came to her flat. Were they part of some London mob? She guessed that they were. Well anyway, she'd have nothing more to worry about. Steve would have no reason for them to call again. But she thought how ironic was the situation. She had left home to get away from her father and his bad ways, but here she was going out with someone just like him, if what Joshua said was true. But apart from that one time, Steve had been good to her and she still felt drawn to him, however much he'd annoyed her.

She sat back and enjoyed the film. Somehow she always felt at ease when she was with Joshua.

Joshua walked her home, but refused the invitation to go to Maggie's flat for a cup of coffee. 'No I don't think that's wise, do you?'

'Why ever not?'

He took hold of her hand. 'I really like being with you, Maggie. You're a wonderful girl. But what would happen if Rossi came knocking on the door?'

She didn't answer because she knew that would be a dire thing to happen. Steve would be furious. 'Perhaps you're right,' she said.

He smiled at her, his dark eyes crinkling at the corners. 'But that doesn't stop me from taking you out for a drink, does it?'

She grinned back at him. 'No, I don't see that it does. I'll meet you at the end of the road. When?'

'How about tomorrow, seven thirty. I've arranged to swop my duty with a buddy.'

'Until tomorrow then.'

She went into her flat, but she couldn't put aside Joshua's warnings about Steve. If Steve was in deep with the black market, she was taking a chance being involved with him. Her period was due tomorrow; she'd wait and see what happened then, before she made up her mind what to do about her lover.

Chapter Eleven

Maggie didn't sleep at all well, and when she met up with Ivy in the factory canteen the following day, her friend looked at her and said, 'Blimey! You look a bit rough.' With a sly smile she asked, 'That Steve round last night, was he?'

'No, I went to the pictures with Joshua.'

Ivy looked astonished. 'You mean the coloured bloke you met at Fair Oak?'

Maggie nodded.

'Bloody hell! Does Steve know about this?'

'It's none of his business,' snapped Maggie. 'I'm a free agent.'

Ivy gave her an anxious look. 'I don't know Steve Rossi as well as you do, love, but I can tell you this, if he finds out he won't like it. He's the possessive type.' She sipped her tea. 'You sleeping with this Joshua?'

'No of course not! What do you take me for? We're just friends, that's all.'

'Oh yeah? Listen, Maggie, there's no such thing as friendship between a man and a woman. It may start out that way, but it doesn't end there. They always want more. You either give in or bye bye baby.' She paused. 'Pity really. I've met a few blokes I would have liked purely as friends, that I didn't fancy physically, but their ego and sex drive always got in the way.'

'Well Joshua is different. He hasn't attempted to lay a finger on me.'

'What is he then, some bloody saint?'

'No of course not, just a nice man.'

Ivy didn't press the subject, but knowing Maggie as well as she did, she knew that something was bothering her. 'What's wrong? You've got something on your mind.'

Maggie felt the need to confide her troubles, they were weighing mightily upon her. 'I'm afraid I may be pregnant.'

'Oh, Christ!' Ivy took a cigarette out of her overalls. 'How late are you?'

'My period is due today, but we made love once without using a french letter.'

'You're panicking a bit soon, aren't you? My period is often a couple of days adrift.'

Maggie shook her head. 'Not mine. I could almost set the clock by

91

it and I don't even feel as if I'm due on.'

'Well there's no point in getting in a state about it yet. You start worrying and that in itself might mess things up.'

'Whatever will I do if I am?'

'We'll sort that one out when we have to . . . if we have to. Got any gin at home?' she asked.

Maggie looked puzzled. 'No, why?'

'Buy a half-bottle when you leave here, run a hot bath and sit in it, and drink a hefty slug of gin.'

'What the hell will that do?'

'Damned if I know. It's just an old wives' tale, but it's worth a try.'

That night, Maggie did as her friend suggested. She started running the water and sat in the bath until it was as hot as she could bear, sipping the gin. The taste of the neat spirit turned her stomach and after a time she felt faint. Her head began to swim, and she quickly ran the cold water, soaked a flannel and put it on her forehead, pulling out the bath plug at the same time. She felt desperately ill.

Staggering into the bedroom, wrapped in a towel, she lay on the bed. The ceiling seemed to be in a spin and she knew she was going to be sick. She rushed to the bathroom and threw up.

When the next day Ivy enquired after her health, she glared at her friend. 'All it did for me was make me ill and give me a bloody hangover!'

'Sorry,' said Ivy. 'I was only trying to help. Here, someone once told me about some stuff called slippery elm.'

'Oh for goodness' sake, keep your witch's brews to yourself, will you! You're likely to kill me off with your damned cures.' She walked angrily away.

Afterwards she felt guilty at her outburst; after all, Ivy was only trying to help her. At the end of the shift, she waited for her to clock off.

'Sorry. I shouldn't have bitten your head off like that.'

Ivy caught hold of her arm. 'It's all right. It's only because you're worried.'

A frown creased Maggie's brow. 'How ever would I tell my mother? And as for Dad . . . it doesn't bear thinking about.'

'Well, should the worst come to the worst, you could always have an abortion.'

Maggie looked both appalled and frightened. 'Oh my God! But that's so dangerous.'

With a shrug Ivy said, 'It depends who does it.'

Maggie shot her a suspicious look. 'You seem to know a lot about it.'

'Now don't get clever! I had a mate who had one, that's all.'

'Was it successful?'

'Oh yes, but it was bloody painful.'

Maggie felt her stomach turn at the thought. 'Thanks a lot!'

'Steve Rossi could always marry you, then you'd have no need to worry . . . if you did get caught I mean.'

'No!' The word was out of her mouth before she even thought about it.

The vehement tone surprised Ivy. 'Well it might be better than having a bastard child.'

'Oh, great!'

Ivy looked a bit shamefaced at her lack of diplomacy. 'Sorry, Mags. I always did call a spade a spade and not a bloody shovel.'

'I don't want to be Mrs Steve Rossi, that's all.'

Ivy looked puzzled. 'Whyever not? A good-looking bloke like him, I'd have thought he would be quite a catch.'

But she wouldn't be drawn. 'Have you any more news from Len?' she asked, to change the subject.

Shaking her head Ivy said, 'No, except he's in Italy somewhere. I read in the *Daily Mail* that the Eighth Army were advancing on the Gothic Line, whatever that is. All I can say is that it's a pity the attempt to top old Adolf a couple of months ago wasn't successful. The war might be over if it had worked.'

'And then Len would be on his way home . . . and where would that leave you?'

Ivy gave a cheeky grin. 'Up the bloody creek without a paddle, that's where!

That evening, Maggie washed and changed, then walked down the road to meet Joshua. It was a balmy September evening as they strolled down Bugle Street to the waterfront. Along Western Esplanade, convoys of American trucks were parked, waiting embarkation to the shores of France. Troops sat about chatting to each other, lolling against their vehicles. Waiting, as so many had done before them. Children clambered around in their search for American chewing gum, candy, and bits of the troops' K rations which they gave away. American Red Cross women were handing out hot coffee and doughnuts.

On the other side of the road, soldiers were being marched towards the docks, packs on their backs, rifles slung over their shoulders. They ambled more than they marched, which in the beginning had made many of the local residents compare them most unfavourably to the more precise march of the British tommy. But by now it was an everyday occurrence. Millions of troops had passed through Southampton and no one noticed the difference any more.

It was the same with the German prisoners of war, who arrived, housed behind barbed wire in the transit area outside the gates of the New Docks.

At first they too were the centre of everyone's attention, and it was the pastime of many to go and take a look at the enemy. Now they were part of the norm.

Maggie watched the passing troops and, turning to Joshua, asked, 'Will you be one of them one day?'

'I guess. At the moment we're here to assist with the arrivals of the ships' cargoes, but no one knows for how long.'

'Does it worry you, the thought of going to war?'

'What's the point?' he said philosophically. 'If my number's up, there isn't a great deal I can do about it.' He turned towards her, the corners of his mouth twitching with amusement. 'I'll just get them angel trumpets playing my kind of music.'

'Oh, Joshua!' She paused and with a mischievous grin asked, 'What happens if you go to hell?'

'Maggie! How could you think of such a thing, me a good clean-living boy all my life.'

'But have you been? How am I to know?'

He raised his eyebrows. 'And I'm not going to tell you. You'll just have to take my word for it.'

She found herself wondering about his past. Was there a girl somewhere . . . had there been other women? He was a nice-looking man, with a sense of fun about him. Surely somewhere there had to be someone. Yet she hesitated to ask and find out that there was.

They walked along to the High Street, until they came to the American Red Cross Club used by the negro soldiers. They sat at a table with some of his friends, and as they laughed and teased one another, she was taken by the warmth and camaraderie of the men.

'How about a song, Joshua?' asked one.

He looked at Maggie and refused, saying he was entertaining a lady, but she said she didn't mind, that she'd really like to hear him sing.

He ambled over to the piano and sat down. He sang a couple of popular tunes in a deep melodious voice: 'The Banks of the Wabash', 'Old Man River' and then a rousing rendition of 'Joshua and the Battle of Jericho', where the walls came tumbling down, and others. His comrades sang along with him, and for the first time Maggie heard the haunting music of the negro spirituals. It moved her deeply. Then the mood changed as he began to play his own kind of music and she realized how talented he was.

She told Joshua so, when he came over and sat beside her.

'Next week we're giving a concert at the Guildhall,' he said. 'Will you come? It's on Sunday evening.'

'I'd love to, I'll bring my mother, she'd really enjoy it.' She was thoughtful for a moment and then said, 'I'm surprised you haven't gone into the church like your father.'

Joshua shook his head. 'The church isn't for me, Maggie. Yes, I suppose you could say I'm religious; being a son of a preacher I was bound to be, but I don't have what it takes to dedicate my life to the Lord. Not like my father. But he's an open-minded guy. He knows what music means to me.' He sipped his drink and then asked, 'Tell me, you still seeing the sergeant?'

She felt her cheeks flush. 'Yes. Yes I am.'

He shook his head. 'A pity. You're worth far better than Steve Rossi.'

'It's not serious,' she told him. 'He's only going to be here for a while.'

'Then why bother?'

His straightforward question threw her for a moment and his steady gaze was more than a little disconcerting. 'He's fun to be with, that's all.'

'And dangerous. I guess that adds to the attraction.'

Maggie felt she had to defend herself. 'I don't think of him as dangerous. He's just good company.'

'He has to be more than that, Maggie. Rossi doesn't go in for pure friendship.'

It was as if this man was looking into her soul. She held his gaze and said, 'That's right. He's also my lover.'

'This darned war changes everything,' he said with a note of sadness in his voice.

'What do you mean?'

There was no expression of condemnation on his face as he said, 'Normally a girl like you wouldn't give herself to a man like Rossi. You'd save yourself for the man you plan to marry. But in wartime, things change and that's a pity.'

She looked at him sceptically. 'Are you telling me that you've never made love to a woman?'

He grinned broadly and his eyes were full of mischief. 'What a crazy question. I'm a man after all.'

'You didn't answer me,' she persisted with a smile of amusement, filled now with curiosity.

He shrugged. 'Well there have been a few, here and there. We country boys grow up fast.'

'And is there anyone waiting for you?' She held her breath waiting for an answer.

Shaking his head, he said, 'No, Maggie. No one.'

She thought, how strange. He was a man who was experienced and yet he'd never even tried to kiss her. 'Joshua Lewis, I don't think I've ever met a man quite like you!'

His laughter rang out and one or two people looked over at the table to see what had amused him so.

'I don't know whether to take that as a compliment or not,' he said.

'It certainly was not meant as an insult,' she assured him.

'Thank heavens for that!'

At the end of the evening he walked her home.

'Won't you come in?' she asked.

'If I did, what would you do if Rossi knocked on the door?'

'He won't,' she explained. 'He's on duty.'

He cast a wry glance in her direction. 'When the cat's away . . .'

'It's not like that at all,' she protested. 'I've had such a good time, I thought it would be nice to give you a cup of coffee before you walk back to camp, that's all.'

He thought for a moment, smiled slowly and said, 'That would be real nice.'

Whilst Maggie was entertaining Joshua, Ivy was curled up on the settee in her house with her fiancé, Bob Hanson.

'Once we get the all clear from the CO,' said Bob with a broad smile, 'we'll make a date for the wedding. What about the members of your family?' he asked. 'I've yet to meet any of them.'

'I told you, Mum and Dad have both gone,' said Ivy hastily. 'All the rest are spread about the country. We don't keep in touch.'

'But surely, honey, you want some of them there on your big day?'

She snuggled closer and kissed him. 'All I want is you, you big lug.'

'What about Maggie? At least ask her. I've a lot of my buddies that want to come.'

'Oh, have you?' This was not what she wanted to hear at all. The fewer people that knew about it the better. 'I just want a small ceremony at the registrar's office. Nothing fancy, a nice quiet affair with a couple of witnesses.'

He looked at her in amazement. 'I don't believe I'm hearing this! I thought a bride longed for a big splash. I want to give you a wedding day you'll remember for the rest of your life.'

'But I'll remember a small intimate one as much as a big affair.'

He looked at her tenderly. 'You're a great girl, Ivy, that's why I love you so much. Let me do this one thing for you, it will give me so much pleasure.'

What could she say? 'If you really insist.'

He gathered her into her arms and kissed her passionately. 'We're going to have such a good life together,' he murmured into her ear. He softly caressed her breast. 'And we're going to have lots of kids to look after us in our old age.'

They lay side by side, locked in an embrace, their passion so intense that they didn't hear the key put into the lock of the front door.

'What the bloody hell's going on here?' an angry voice demanded.

Ivy shot up to a sitting position. 'Oh my God, it's Len! He must have got leave!'

Bob got to his feet. 'Who the devil are you?' he asked.

Len glared at him. 'I'm the one who should be asking that. What do you think you're doing with my wife?'

'Your wife?' Bob looked astounded. 'This young lady is my fiancée.'

'Fiancé, my arse! I certainly don't remember having divorced her.'

Bob turned towards Ivy, his face devoid of colour. 'What's this all about? I think you owe me some kind of explanation.'

She got to her feet, her voice trembling. 'I meant to tell you,' she said, 'but I didn't want to lose you. I love you! I want to be your wife, I want to go to America and live with you.'

Hanson was shaken to the core. He looked at Len, who was as stunned as he was. 'Gee, I'm sorry, buddy,' he said. 'I had no idea.' He picked up his jacket and put it on. Turning to Ivy he asked, 'How could you do this to me?'

'Don't go, please don't go,' she pleaded.

He just stared at her in disbelief. 'I have no place here,' he said quietly and walked towards the door.

She ran to him and clutched at his arm. 'I'll get a divorce!' she cried.

But Bob Hanson looked coldly at her. 'How could I ever trust you again?' He opened the front door and left.

Ivy stood with her back against it and faced her husband, tears streaming down her cheeks.

Len's anger began to surface now that he was recovering from the shock she'd given him. 'You bloody slut! There I am, fighting for my country, facing death day after bloody day and you're here having it off with a fucking Yank!' He slapped her across the face. 'I'll teach you a lesson you won't forget in a hurry.' He lunged at her, but Ivy swiftly ran around the table in the middle of the room out of his reach.

'Don't you give me that!' she yelled at him. 'You've been having a bloody good time while you were away and don't you tell me any different. I know you, Len Brooks. You wouldn't go without your oats for very long.'

He glared at her. 'And what if I have? It's different for a man, away at war. It's expected. A bit of pussy here and there don't mean a thing. I was always coming home to you, you're my wife. Something you seem to have forgotten! Were you really going to marry that Yank?'

'Yes, I bloody well was!'

'That would have been committing bigamy,' he said incredulously.

'So what? He was worth it.'

That was it. Len stretched across the table and caught hold of her arm, dragging her round to where he could reach her. He looked down at her engagement ring. 'You couldn't wear my wedding ring, but you could wear his.' He tore it off her finger. Then he hit her.

Back at Bugle Street, Maggie and Joshua were sitting drinking coffee and chatting when there was a frantic knocking on the door. Maggie felt suddenly sick inside, but Joshua, seeing the stricken expression on her face, stood up. 'I'll answer it,' he said, and went to the door.

He was appalled at the sight that met his eyes. 'Maggie! Come quickly,' he called.

She ran down the hallway, just in time to catch Ivy, as she slipped to the floor in a faint. 'Oh my God! Lift her, Joshua, and bring her inside.'

They lay her down on the settee and propped up her head with cushions. Her face was covered in blood. Her eyes were swollen and her mouth. Her clothes had been ripped and her nails broken from trying to fight off her attacker.

Joshua went to the kitchen and returned with a bowl of warm water. 'Get me some cotton wool,' he demanded. Then he proceeded to gently bathe Ivy's face. 'Who on earth would do such a thing to a defenceless woman?' he asked.

Maggie could guess who the culprit was, but she said nothing.

Eventually Ivy came round. She opened her eyes as much as the swelling allowed. 'Maggie?' she whispered.

'I'm here, Ivy. It's only me and Joshua. You're quite safe.'

'It was Len. He came back and found me with Bob.'

'I thought as much.'

'Who's Len?' asked Joshua.

'Her husband.'

'Bob's gone for good,' Ivy wailed. 'I've lost him, I'll never be happy now.' She held out her hand. 'Len even took his ring. What am I going to do?'

'We're going to carry you into my bedroom and you'll rest,' said Maggie. 'I'll call the doctor to take a look at you.'

'No, I don't want a doctor.'

Maggie looked at Joshua and raised her eyebrows in question.

'I think it wise that you get her looked at,' he advised.

'Will you stay with her whilst I go to the telephone?'

He nodded and continued to bathe Ivy's wounds.

On her return, Joshua carried Ivy into the bedroom where he left the two women alone. Maggie carefully undressed her friend, put her in one of her nightdresses and made her comfortable. 'You try and rest,' she said. 'I'll leave the door open, then you can call if you want anything.' She picked up a glass from the bedside table, went to the bathroom to wash it and fill it with fresh water. Back in the room she urged Ivy to take a sip.

It was difficult for her, as her mouth was so swollen. Maggie bit her lip as she watched Ivy's suffering. She settled her, then went back to Joshua.

'How is she?' he asked.

'In a bad way. You were right about the doctor.'

He shook his head, his expression one of sadness. 'This is no way to carry on,' he said.

'It was always going to end like this,' she explained. 'Ivy got engaged to a GI without telling him she was already married. Then her husband came home unexpectedly, and found them.'

'I see,' he said. 'It was very foolish of her, but even so, no woman deserves that.' He looked at Maggie. 'You two are quite a pair, aren't you?'

She smiled wryly. 'We have no one to blame but ourselves.'

The doctor came and examined Ivy. 'She has sustained bruising to her ribs,' he said, 'but they're not broken. The bruising will be worse before it's better, I'm afraid. Just keep bathing with cold water to try and keep the swelling down. Keep her quiet, try to get her to eat something. Soup, porridge, scrambled eggs. Something she doesn't have to chew. If you want me again, give me a call, but it's just a matter of time, really.'

'Thank you,' said Maggie as she showed him to the door.

Joshua walked towards her. 'I have to go, Maggie. Will you be all right?'

'Yes. Honestly, I don't know what I would have done without you.'

He smiled at her. 'I'm glad I was here to help,' he said. He kissed her on the cheek. 'I'll be in touch, OK?'

'OK,' she replied and shut the door behind him, locking it, just in case Len found out where she lived and came looking for his wife. Then she went to see how Ivy was.

Chapter Twelve

Maggie was wondering how she was going to manage to look after Ivy and still go to work. Her friend wasn't well enough to be left alone, she felt, so, quickly slipping to the call box down the street whilst Ivy slept, she rang her mother, explaining her predicament.

'What shift are you on?' asked Moira.

'Eight 'til two.'

'I'll be there at seven thirty tomorrow morning,' she said.

'But what about Dad?'

'He can manage,' said Moira sharply. 'I'll tell him a friend needs me. What he doesn't know won't hurt him.'

'Thanks a lot, Mum. I didn't know who else to ask. See you in the morning.'

She spent the evening bathing Ivy's face with cold flannels, and even managed to get her to eat some scrambled egg.

Ivy didn't say much, but it broke Maggie's heart to see her in such an unhappy state.

The following morning, Moira arrived promptly. She took one look at the sleeping form of Ivy and muttered angrily to herself, 'What a silly girl to put herself in such a position.'

'Yes, I agree,' said Maggie, 'but she thought she'd found happiness at last. She just wanted to better herself with the man she loved.'

'That's as maybe,' retorted her mother, 'but she went the wrong way about it.' She sighed. 'There's many of us would like to change our way of life, but we have the good sense to know when we're beaten!' She looked at Maggie. 'Off you go or you'll be late for work. I'll take care of this wounded soldier. I'll have something for you to eat when you come home.'

Maggie made an excuse to the factory supervisor that Ivy had the flu to explain her absence from work, but later, at her own machine, she couldn't help wondering what her friend would do when she was better. Would she return to Len? Would he have her back? So many problems. But at least she had company for a while, and Ivy could stay with her for as long as it took to make up her mind what her next move was to be. And if her period didn't start soon, she'd have a few decisions to make herself.

And where was Steve? He should be with her, worrying as she was. After all it was as much his fault as hers.

When she returned home, it was to find that her mother had prepared a meal, washed Ivy and brushed her hair, which made her look better. She was sitting up in bed, sipping homemade soup.

'Hello, Mags,' she said through swollen lips. 'What a bloody turn-up for the books. I've really burnt my boats this time.'

'Don't you worry,' Maggie said. 'I'm glad to see you looking a bit brighter. I'm just going to see Mum, and have a bite to eat; then I'll come back and we'll have a chat.'

Moira had made a fish pie, having slipped out to the fishmonger when Ivy woke. She sat with Maggie as they ate. 'You're looking a bit pale,' she remarked.

'I'm just tired, that's all. How's Dad these days?' she asked.

'The same as always, but when he rids himself of his latest haul he'll be happy, no doubt, counting his money.'

'Oh, Mum. I'd hoped that was all behind him.'

'Yes, well, so did I for a time, but Sonny Taylor came round again, didn't he? If he gets caught . . .'

'It's no good worrying,' said Maggie. 'If he does, then we'll face up to it together, but don't get yourself in a state now.'

Moira gave a wry smile. 'And you, Maggie. How about you? Are you happy?'

'Yes, why wouldn't I be?'

'And Joshua? Do you still see him?'

'Yes, Mum. I do.' She looked straight at her mother. 'He's a good friend.'

Moira made no comment.

Maggie placed her hand over her mother's. 'I'm worried about you,' she said softly. 'You seem so very unhappy.'

Moira forced a smile. 'I'm all right, really. Just going through the change, that's all.'

'No, Mum. It's more than that. Perhaps I shouldn't have left home. If I'd stayed, you wouldn't be like this.'

'Now you listen to me, darlin'. You have your own life to lead. You're a woman now, not a child. I made my choice years ago.' With a sad smile she said, 'Your father wasn't always like this. When this damned war is over, perhaps we can get back to the old ways again. War unsettles everyone, not just me.' She nodded in the direction of the bedroom. 'Take Ivy for instance. In normal times that would never have happened to her. Well, I'd better be off. Shall I come again tomorrow?'

'Ivy looks so much better. If I leave her a flask of tea and a snack to see her through the morning, she'll be all right. And Dad might start asking questions if you disappear again. I'll call you in a couple of days though.' She hugged her mother. 'Thanks, Mum. Don't get upset about Dad. It really isn't worth it.'

'No, you're probably right. As long as you're fine, that's all I care about.'

After seeing her mother on her way, Maggie went into the bedroom. 'How are you feeling?' she asked.

'Like shit!' said Ivy. She shook her head slowly. 'It's all gone wrong, Mags. Bob doesn't want me and I don't want Len. What a mess, eh?'

'What are you going to do?'

'Get back on my feet, get back to work, find a flat somewhere and start all over again. I've got a bit of money saved.'

'What about Len?'

'What about him? Yes, all right, what I did was wrong, but he'd been having a bit on the side, he admitted as much.'

'He did?' Maggie was surprised.

'Didn't I tell you he would? Well now he can have as many women as he likes . . . but he can count me out!'

Maggie caught hold of her hand. 'You know you can stay here as long as you like, don't you?'

'Thanks, Mags. You're a real friend.' She wrinkled her nose. 'Do you think I could have a bath?'

'Of course. Can you manage?'

'I think so,' said Ivy getting stiffly out of bed, clutching her bruised ribs. 'You might have to help me,' she said, plaintively.

Maggie ran the water and gently lowered Ivy into it. She washed her back, then left her to see to herself. 'Give me a call when you're ready,' she said, 'and I'll help you out.'

Between them, they managed.

Ivy sat on the settee, snug in Maggie's dressing gown, drinking the ever-welcome tea. 'That Joshua is a really nice chap,' she said. 'Very gentle, very kind. I can see why you like him so much.'

With a smile Maggie said, 'Yes, he's a gentleman in every sense of the word.'

'Still just friends then?'

Maggie gave her a sharp look, but Ivy chipped in quickly. 'You don't need to look at me that way, Maggie. You may not be aware of it, but that bloke thinks the world of you and you know my theory about friendship between a man and a woman.'

'Well this time you're wrong.'

'We'll see,' was all her friend said. 'But where does Steve fit in to all this? I'm worried that he'll find out about Joshua. Then all hell will break loose.'

'Well, so far he hasn't.'

* * *

Steve Rossi had his own problems and the fact that he might have got his girlfriend pregnant was far from his mind. Doug Freeman was getting angry that he hadn't come up with the rest of the goods for which he had paid a lot of money and Steve was in London trying to keep his own head above water, trying to explain to the gang boss that the situation was beyond his control.

They were sitting in a seedy pub alongside the East India Docks and Freeman was glaring at the GI.

'You took my fucking money and I want what I paid for!'

'It's not as simple as that,' argued the American. 'I can't just get the stuff out of the camp when I like. I have to watch my butt. I'm taking one hell of a chance, you must know that.'

Freeman grabbed the front of Steve's uniform jacket and hauled him closer. 'You listen to me, you jumped-up wop. Nobody plays fast and loose with Doug Freeman. You don't seem to realize who you're dealing with, sonny.'

Rossi hadn't been brought up in the back streets and ghettos of New York for nothing. He knew this man was dangerous; he just had to look into his eyes to recognize the cold steely glare of a man who was completely ruthless. He knew he was in real trouble and he was getting desperate.

'There's another big shipment coming in from the States in a couple of days' time,' he said. 'I'll divert the last truck and if you can meet it at a destination that I'll give you, you can switch the cargo from one vehicle to another, but it will have to be something that won't be a cause for curiosity.'

Freeman grinned. 'How about a furniture removal van?'

'Yeah, that should do it,' agreed Steve.

Doug Freeman's smile faded. 'You'd better be on the level, my son, because if you try to be clever, then my boys will be after you and your uniform won't save you, I can promise you that.'

With an expansive smile Steve said, 'Why on earth should I do that? We're in business together.'

'It had better not be monkey business. I want the goods or I want my money back . . . do I make myself clear?'

'Very.' Steve rose from his seat. 'Nice dealing with you guys. I'll be in touch.'

'When?' snapped the Londoner.

'The day after tomorrow.'

Freeman got to his feet too. His big powerful frame towered over the American. 'If I don't hear I'll be down to Southampton myself. Remember that, Yank.'

'There's no need for all these threats, Mr Freeman. It was just a hiccup, that's all.'

'With your throat cut that's one thing you wouldn't suffer from, Sergeant Rossi. Get my drift?'

'Sure thing,' said Steve. 'I must go, I've a train to catch.' He saluted jauntily and left the bar.

Once outside the pub, Steve loosened his tie and undid the top button of his shirt, which felt as if it was choking him. Christ! That was close, he thought. He was in no doubt that Freeman was a man who would carry out his threats. It was no use Freeman asking for his money back, he didn't have it all any more. He'd lost most of it in that crap game. Now he had to work out a plan to get this truck to Freeman. How he was going to do that without being discovered he didn't know, not yet. But he would have to keep his word if he wanted to remain healthy.

He made his way to the station racking his brains trying to formulate a plan.

As he walked through the gates of his camp one of the guards greeted him. 'Hi there, Steve. Haven't seen you around.'

'No,' he answered. 'I had a forty-eight-hour pass. I went up to London for a break.'

'That explains it then,' said the soldier.

'Explains what?'

'I was in Southampton last night. I saw your girl walking along with another GI.'

'You must be mistaken.'

The soldier grinned. 'No sir! You can't mistake that red hair and that figure.' He gave a sly grin. 'I see she fancies dark meat now.'

Steve frowned. 'What the hell are you talking about?'

'She was with one of them niggers.' His grin broadened as he saw the look of fury on Rossi's face.

'Where was this?' Steve demanded.

'Walking down the High Street towards the waterfront. Large as life. Maybe you'd better black your face next time you see her! Perhaps you're a mite too pale for her now.' Steve glared at him and walked through the gates towards his quarters.

It was a further three days until Ivy felt able to go back to work, and then only because she needed to keep the money coming in. She and Maggie had come to an arrangement and decided to work on separate shifts; this way they wouldn't be with each other all the time. It would make the sharing of such a small flat much easier.

When she arrived at the factory, she told Bill she'd fallen down the stairs, being so weak after the flu.

He gave her a jaundiced look and said, 'Of course you did.' He'd had a visitation from Len looking for his wife and had put two and two together.

But when Len had asked if he had any idea where he could find Ivy, he'd said no.

'Your old man's been looking for you,' he warned. 'If he comes again, what shall I tell him?'

Ivy hesitated. If she saw Len outside the factory she'd be fairly safe from his temper, she reasoned. 'I'll see him,' she said. 'But do me a favour, keep an eye on me, will you?'

'You women! You play with fire and wonder why you get burnt!' But seeing the stricken look on Ivy's face his tone softened. 'All right, don't worry, I won't be far away. Now get off back to your machine.'

The following day, Len arrived outside the factory and Ivy was summoned.

She walked outside and faced her husband. 'What do you want?' she asked. 'Come to look at the damage you did, have you?'

He looked at her bruised face. 'You asked for it, girl. Going behind my back like that. What man would put up with it?'

'Do as I say but not as I do! Is that it? You can dip your cock anywhere, but I'm not allowed to have any fun.'

He did have the grace to look a little shamefaced. 'Look, Ivy, I've got to go back to camp today and I want to know what's going to happen.'

She frowned. 'I don't follow you.'

'When are you coming home?'

She looked at him in astonishment. 'You can't be serious! You think I'm going to forget what you did to me and come crawling back?'

'You're still my wife!'

'In name only! When you have your next leave you'll find all my stuff gone. I never want to see you again, Len Brooks.' She turned on her heel and went back inside the building.

Len went to follow her but Bill stepped out of his office. 'Hey! Where do you think you're going? This is government property!'

'I want to talk to my wife.'

'She's said all she wants to, now on your bike!' For one moment he thought the irate soldier was going to argue, but he obviously thought better of it. He scowled at Bill and walked away.

As Maggie was walking home alone from work the following day, Steve Rossi, with a squeal of brakes, drew up in his jeep alongside her. Her smile of welcome died on her lips as he glared at her and said, 'Get in!'

'But you're not allowed to give civilians lifts,' she protested.

'Get in, Maggie, or so help me God I'll come round there and put you in this damned vehicle myself!'

Not wanting to cause a scene and feed the curiosity of the few passers by who had slowed to watch, she did as he asked. They drove in silence to her flat. He jumped down from the driving seat, came around to her, dragged her from the passenger's side and pushed her towards her front door. 'Open it!' he demanded.

'What the hell do you think you're doing?' she asked as she took her key from her bag.

He snatched it from her, opened the door and pushed her inside, slamming the door behind him. 'What sort of game have you been playing behind my back, Maggie?'

She saw the anger blazing in his eyes and was at a loss to know what she'd done to deserve such treatment. 'What on earth are you talking about?'

'Where were you last Tuesday evening?' he asked.

Then she knew. She glared at him, her back straight, her nostrils flared. 'I was out with a friend, someone who certainly would never treat me as you have just done.'

'You were out with a nigger! Go on deny it.' His face was taut with fury.

'I was out with a gentleman.' She stood defiant.

'I told you if you were going to be my girl you were not to go out with anyone else.'

'I'm not *going out* as you put it. Joshua is just a friend. There's nothing more to it than that. It's all quite innocent.'

He stormed into the sitting room. 'How do you think I feel when one of my company tells me he's seen my girl walking along the street with another GI, then tells me it was with one of the coons?'

She flew at him. 'Don't you dare use that expression. It's disgusting. You have no respect for anyone. Not even me.'

'Now you're talking nonsense.'

'Am I?' She stood in front of him, her anger blazing now. 'You force me into your jeep, push me in through the door of my own home. You don't even ask how I am, or whether I'm carrying your child. All you can think about is your bloody pride.'

He was too enraged to consider her feelings. 'Well, are you pregnant or not?'

She was horrified by his coldness. 'My period hasn't started, but don't let that worry you.'

'I don't see the problem. If you are pregnant, I'll pay for an abortion. It's as simple as that.'

She slapped him around the face. 'You callous bastard! That's all it means to you, isn't it?'

He caught hold of her wrist in a vice-like grip. 'These slip-ups happen, it's a fact of life. It's nothing that can't be solved.'

'Like your black market stuff? You've used me all along, Steve Rossi, and I was dumb enough to fall for your line. I don't mean anything to you.

I'm just a convenience. A good lay, isn't that what you Yanks say?'

'That's not how I think of you, you crazy woman. You're my girl, mine. I told you the rules in the beginning.'

'Rules!' she laughed harshly. 'You don't play by any rules but your own. You bend the rules to suit yourself. You tempt fate, my friend, selling off army supplies to London villains. I'm the stupid one for staying with you. Especially now that I realize you don't care for anyone but yourself.'

He grabbed her by the arms. 'I do care about you, Maggie, but I won't have you mixing with trash. And what's more I'm going to put a stop to it.' He let go of her and walked towards the door.

'What are you going to do?' she asked, afraid that his anger could put Joshua in danger.

At the door he paused. 'I'm going to find that black son of a bitch. That's what I'm going to do!' The door slammed behind him and within seconds she heard the jeep being driven away.

Now Maggie was really worried, not for herself but for Joshua. She remembered with horror seeing Steve in London when he was threatened. What on earth could she do? Picking up her handbag, she rushed to the telephone box down the road, and quickly leafed through her notebook until she found the number of Joshua's camp, put her money in the machine and dialled. Her heart pounded as she waited for an answer.

The soldier on duty told her that it wasn't possible to get Joshua to the phone, and could she leave a message? She hesitated. What could she say that would warn him without giving too much away? She racked her brains.

'Tell him that our mutual friend is looking for him,' she said, 'and to be careful.' She put the receiver down and walked back to her flat, beside herself with worry. She reasoned that she'd not given Steve Joshua's surname. Surely amongst the negroes in the camp there had to be more than one with the same Christian name? She was going crazy, wondering if Steve would discover her friend's identity; and if he did, what would he do then? She would never forgive herself if anything happened to that lovely gentle man.

Rossi was getting nowhere with his enquiries at the negro camp. If any of the GIs knew anything they were keeping quiet. He racked his brains. Where would this man have taken Maggie? He enquired in a few pubs near the High Street where they were seen, without success, and eventually made his way to the Red Cross Club, using the excuse that he was only checking to see if they were getting enough stores delivered for their use. Then he casually asked about a red-haired girl who might have been there last night.

The soldier on duty grinned. 'Yeah I remember her. What a sight! That hair. A real looker.'

'Who was she with?' asked Steve.

'Corporal Lewis, a real nice guy. Great jazz musician.'

'Lewis, eh? Thanks. Give me a call if you need anything.' He made his way outside. He remembered Lewis, the preacher's son. He'd been on duty with him several times in the docks. He recalled the man pulling him up when he referred to him as Rastus. Well he'd teach him a lesson he wouldn't forget. Put him in his place. It was time these guys realized they couldn't get away with everything just because they were in this country.

He made his way to the 552nd Port Company camp. At the gate the guard let him pass once again. It was not unusual for Steve to visit the camp to discuss requirements with the quartermaster there, so the guard didn't question his presence. He parked the jeep and asked one of the men where he could find Corporal Lewis.

Chapter Thirteen

In the East End of London, Doug Freeman was gathering some of his boys in preparation for the removal of the army supplies in Southampton. The large furniture van was all ready, parked out of sight in a warehouse in the docks.

'When we hear from the Yank we'll know where the meeting place is,' he said. 'Then it will have to be swift and efficient. We don't want the Old Bill on our tail. There will be some furniture already on the van so you pack the stuff behind it, just in case. You'll carry shooters, but only use them in an emergency. Understand?'

The men nodded.

'Right, as soon as I hear from Rossi, I'll let you know.'

He and Charlie left the warehouse and made their way to their local for a quiet drink. They sat at a table in the corner where they knew no one would disturb them. 'I'm still not happy with that cocky bastard,' said Doug. 'He'd better come across, that's all.'

Charlie frowned and said anxiously, 'You don't think he's going to be a problem do you, guv?'

Doug's eyes narrowed. 'I've got a funny feeling about him, that's all. I hope I'm wrong because if he crosses me, he's in real trouble.'

'I'm sure he wouldn't be that stupid,' said Charlie.

'Let's hope you're right,' growled Freeman. 'If he lets me down I want my money back and then I want his bloody hide! One less soldier among the Yanks won't be missed. There's too many of the bleeders around anyway.'

'At least they pay good money for the toms, guv.'

Doug Freeman grinned. 'Yeah, that's right. Well it's swings and roundabouts, I suppose, but I should really invest in one of them VD clinics. They're the ones doing the most business if you ask me!'

The two men laughed heartily and drank their beer.

Joshua Lewis was in the latrines washing his hands when Steve found him. The staff sergeant slammed the door shut behind him. And locked it.

'What you trying to do, Rastus? Wash the black off your hands?'

Joshua looked up. 'I stand as much chance of doing that as you do of cleansing your black soul,' he said evenly, wiping his hands on a roller towel attached to the wall. He stared at Rossi. 'I've been expecting you, sergeant. What can I do for you? I presume this isn't a social call?'

'The hell it isn't! I heard you were seen out with my girl.'

'And so?'

Steve took a step forward and in a voice full of menace he said, 'I'm here to tell you to keep away from her. Understand?'

Joshua grinned at him. 'Sticks in your craw, doesn't it, man? Maggie is a wonderful young woman, much too good for you. She doesn't look down on us negroes like you do, Rossi. She sees us as real people. But you wouldn't understand that.'

Steve's temper was rising rapidly. He was incensed by the calm attitude of this man. Who the hell did he think he was? 'The trouble with you niggers is that over here the British don't understand. You're jumped up with your own importance, knowing damned well that at home you wouldn't dare speak to a white woman, let alone date her. It's time you were put in your place.'

Joshua's laughter echoed around the small area. 'And you think you're the man to do that, do you?'

Steve bent down quickly and removed a knife from his boot. He gripped it firmly and pointed the blade at the other man. With an evil grin he said, 'Oh yes. I'm going to teach you a lesson you won't forget.'

Ripping the roller towel from the wall and winding it around his arm, Joshua moved away from the basin into the centre of the room and said, 'Come on then, sergeant. What are you waiting for?'

Filled with rage, Steve circled Joshua several times, then lunged at his opponent; Joshua quickly swiped at Steve's hand with his covered arm, knocking it up into the air. But Rossi hadn't been in street fights all his life for nothing. The two men continued to circle each other, stooped, ready to strike.

Joshua smiled at him. 'Maybe you thought, as a son of a preacher, I'd turn the other cheek. Well, think again.'

Again Steve jabbed at him with the pointed blade but the negro was light and fast on his feet, stepping out of danger. Steve came back at him, slicing the fold of the towel. He laughed triumphantly and went for Joshua again, this time nicking his shirt at the shoulder, drawing blood. He jabbed again, but this time the negro took him by surprise and with a fast flick of his foot he caught the hand that was holding the knife and Steve Rossi saw it fly through the air.

'Now,' said Joshua, as he quickly unwound the towel, casting it aside, 'we're on equal terms.'

'You'll never be equal!' snapped Steve and with his hands balled into fists he threw a punch at his opponent catching him on the chin, sending him reeling. Joshua recovered quickly and pushed him in the chest, then as Steve once again flew at him he sent him flying to the floor with a hard punch to the jaw. But as he went to lean over him, Steve pulled his legs up and pushed Joshua in the stomach with his feet. He went backwards, losing his balance.

Rossi leapt to his feet, threw himself on top of Joshua and started to pummel him. They rolled around exchanging blows. Lewis was surprisingly strong. He caught hold of the other man's throat and squeezed until Steve was gasping for breath, then he punched him in the face. Steve collapsed on the floor.

Getting to his feet, Joshua stood over his adversary and said, 'Be grateful I don't finish you off, soldier. And if I hear you've been mistreating Maggie, *I'll* come after *you*. You hear?' He unlocked the door and walked away.

Steve Rossi got slowly to his feet and staggered over to the basin. He looked at his reflection in the mirror. Already he could see his eye was swelling and his lip was split. He was going to look a sight by tomorrow. He bathed his mouth, swilled his face, picking up the towel from the floor to wipe it dry. Inside he was seething.

When he arrived at the gate, the sentry looked at his bruised face in astonishment but made no comment. He lifted the bar and let the driver through, but as he watched the back of the jeep disappearing into the distance he grinned broadly to himself.

'My oh my! Looks like that white boy just got himself a lesson!'

The following day Steve's commanding officer sent for him.

As he stood to attention in front of his CO Rossi felt a flush of embarrassment as the officer stared at him.

'I've heard rumours, Rossi, that you were over at the 552nd Port Company yesterday. Is that right?'

'Yes, sir. I was just checking on their store situation.'

'I suppose you're going to tell me you walked into a door whilst you were there.'

'Yes, sir!'

'Don't give me that crap, soldier! We have enough trouble in the town between the blacks and the white soldiers already. I don't expect this of my sergeants. You're supposed to set the men an example.'

'Yes, sir.'

'Go pack your kitbag. I'm sending you up to Norfolk with Lieutenant Cowalski to go around our camps up there. I want a detailed report on their stocks. It seems some are not getting through. I want to put a stop to this pilfering.'

'But, sir, tomorrow we have a big shipment coming into the docks!'

'That's all right, sergeant. I'll have you covered. There's a jeep waiting to take you both to the station and at the other end someone will meet you. You've got ten minutes.'

'But, sir!' Steve protested.

'Don't argue, Rossi. That's an order!'

'Yes, sir.' Rossi saluted, turned smartly on his heel and left the room. Outside he cursed loudly. What the hell was he going to do now? Doug Freeman was expecting a call from him today to give him the meeting place. Now he wouldn't be here. Jesus! He knew he was in deep trouble.

He quickly packed a few things and carrying his kitbag he headed for his office, thinking to call Freeman, but Cowalski was just walking out of the door.

'Come on, sergeant,' he said firmly. 'We'll miss our train if we don't make a move now.'

Steve followed him, his mouth in a tight line. There was nothing he could do for the moment.

The following day at the factory, Ivy cornered her friend as they were about to swop shifts. 'I've got something to tell you,' she said. 'This morning I went into the paper shop and met one of Steve's mates. He says that Rossi has been in a fight and his face is in a mess, but that was all he knew.'

Maggie then told her what had transpired between her and Steve. 'He was awful,' she said. 'Making me get into his jeep. But I was really worried about Joshua.'

With a grin Ivy said, 'Well if he was the one involved with Steve, he really put up a good fight. And if it was him, I don't know what state he's in of course, but he didn't do bad for the son of a preacher.'

'It's all my fault,' said Maggie. 'I should never have gone out with him, knowing how Steve feels about the negroes. But Joshua is such a sweet man.'

'This guy said that Steve's been sent up to Norfolk,' said Ivy. 'He won't be back for a few days anyway. Got your period yet?' she asked.

'Still late. I'm three days overdue. I'm really worried.'

'Look, love. Three days is nothing. Sometimes it happens. After all, you left home, that was distressing for you. Such things can upset the workings of a woman.'

'God, I hope you're right.'

When she arrived home, Maggie saw Joshua waiting, leaning against the wall of her building. She rushed up to him. 'Are you all right?' she asked anxiously. 'I heard about the fight.'

He smiled, his eyes twinkling. 'One of the good things about being black is that the bruises don't show!'

'Oh, Joshua! I'm so sorry, really I am. Look, come in and I'll make you a cup of tea.'

'OK, Maggie. I think you and I need to talk.'

She fussed about making a pot of tea, casting worried glances in her friend's direction, but he just smiled at her. 'I'm OK, honestly.'

She sat beside him. 'I really feel it's all my fault,' she said. 'I should have known what the outcome would be if Steve found out.' She placed a hand on the negro's arm. 'I'm so sorry.'

He chuckled softly. 'I quite enjoyed teaching him a lesson,' he said. 'It was time somebody did.'

She shook her head, and with a sad note to her voice said, 'I don't really believe that. I think of you as a man of peace, not someone mixed up in a brawl.'

He burst out laughing. 'I don't quite know where you got that idea from, Maggie. I have as much anger in me as the next man. I've had to fight my corner as I grew up. I'm no different to anyone else. I have the same emotions, the same needs.'

'But you control them.'

He stared intently into her eyes and in his rich low voice said softly, 'Maybe, but it ain't always easy.'

There was something in the way he looked at her that threw Maggie for a moment. 'What do you mean?'

'I think it's best we leave it at that. What I want to know is, what are you going to do about Rossi? Are you still going to see him?'

She shook her head. 'No. I've decided that I've had enough. I don't want to be involved with him any longer.' Even if I am carrying his child, she thought. 'After all, as I told you, it's only a passing thing. He's bound to be shipped out at some stage and all I want is a quiet life. I don't want Steve Rossi bullying me, telling me who I can see and who I can't.'

He caught hold of her hand. 'You don't know just how happy that makes me, Maggie. He's no good and I don't want to see you involved with the likes of him.'

'Why should you care?' she asked.

'How could I not?' He frowned. 'He's not going to like it, though.'

'That's too bad!' she said. 'I'm in charge of my own destiny, not Steve Rossi.'

'That's my girl,' he said. He drank the rest of his tea. 'Give me a piece of paper and a pencil. I'll leave you a number where I can be reached when I'm in camp. There's a telephone in my corridor.'

'Why do you want to do that?' she asked.

'Well, you never know,' he said. 'If there's trouble of any kind, you give me a call, you hear?'

'Yes, all right.' If only she'd had this number the other night, she thought, all this trouble could have been avoided.

After he'd written down the number, he rose from his chair and said,

'I've got to get back. I'll come and see you real soon. That's if you want me to. I don't want to complicate your life any more.'

'Of course I want to see you again,' she retorted. 'Why wouldn't I?'

He gazed earnestly at her. 'Going around with a coloured man has its own problems, Maggie. You already know that. I'll understand if you say no. The last thing I want is to bring you any trouble.

She walked with him to the door. 'I'll see you at the concert on Sunday,' she said.

As he walked back to the camp, Joshua could feel his anger growing inside at the thought of Steve Rossi treating Maggie so badly. She was such a wonderful woman. It was a great shame she'd ever met the staff sergeant, who had no principles and no respect for anyone, let alone a woman. It riled him to think of Rossi making love to her, and knew that was because he longed to take her into his arms himself. But there was nothing he could do about it.

When she was alone, Maggie poured another cup of tea and sat ruminating. Joshua wasn't kidding when he said that Steve wouldn't like it when she told him she didn't want to see him any more. He was an arrogant man who wouldn't take rejection lightly. Well, that was tough. She knew now that he was trouble and that he had a violent side. She didn't want to see any more of that. She'd seen plenty in the bar of the Bricklayer's Arms often enough, when some of the punters had turned nasty. She didn't like violence. It frightened her. Bugger all men! she thought. Except for Joshua, he was different.

She got up and walked into the kitchen, and was suddenly aware of that heavy, dragging feeling low down in her stomach and prayed that her period might start. Then her troubles would really be over.

How wrong she was. They were only just beginning.

Chapter Fourteen

Doug Freeman was pacing the floor of his office, his face puce with rage. 'So that bloody Yank hasn't called then?'

Charlie shook his head. 'No, guv. We haven't heard a word.'

'I damn well knew it! I had a feeling about him all along. Right, we'll give him another twenty-four hours and then if we've heard nothing, you and I are off to Southampton for a couple of days. We'll see what that bastard's up to. He's still holding half of my money and I want it – or the goods.'

'Where do you reckon on staying?'

'I know the landlord of the Horse and Groom, in East Street. He'll put us up.'

Charlie grinned to himself. Trust his boss to pick that particular pub. It was notorious, and, being near the docks, was just the place to pick up information. It was full of prostitutes who brought in the foreign troops and a large number of American GIs. All the local villains and spivs used it too. It was a tough place. Many a time he'd seen a fight both inside and out of the pub. The police and military police were constant visitors.

Once there, they'd soon find out where the missing Yank was. He himself disliked Steve Rossi and his bumptious ways. He'd take great delight in roughing him up, teaching him a lesson. It was about time someone took him down a peg or two, and he was just the man for the job. Oh yes, he was going to enjoy himself all right.

Two days later, Doug Freeman and his sidekick were drinking in the Horse and Groom and the place was filling up with people. There were several British tommies, French sailors with their cheeky red pompoms on the tops of their hats, merchant seamen, Canadians and American GIs. At the far end of the bar, in an alcove, were two full-sized, stuffed brown bears, standing on hind legs, towering over six feet tall. Some of the tommies were playing at stabbing them with pretend bayonets.

'Christ!' said one. 'I hope the bleedin' Hun isn't as big as this bugger!'

'Well if he looks as hairy as Bruin here,' said his mate, 'at least we can skin him after we kill him and have a fur coat for the missus.'

Doug and Charlie sat quietly surveying the scene. Charlie suddenly nudged his boss as Sonny Taylor walked in and stood at the bar. Freeman rose from his seat and walked over to him.

'Hello, Sonny. How's business?'

Taylor looked around. His face paled as he looked into the cold eyes of the London villain. He'd been sending him black market stock but had held back on quite a bit which was now sitting in Jack Evans's front room, behind locked doors.

'Mr Freeman,' he said with a forced laugh. 'How the devil are you?' He held out his hand which Doug ignored.

'I'm looking for Staff Sergeant Steve Rossi of the 14th Port. He's a friend of mine. Do you know him, by any chance?'

Sonny shook his head. 'Never heard of him. What makes you think I'd know him?'

'You usually know everyone and everything that's dodgy.' He gripped Sonny's arm in a tight hold, making the spiv wince. 'You hear anything, you let me know. I'll be around for a few days.' Freeman walked away.

'Bugger!' muttered Taylor. The last thing he wanted was this London mobster hanging around his patch. Of course he knew Rossi. He'd dealt with him several times, but not lately. He'd find out where he was hanging out, tell Freeman and get him off his back. He downed his drink and left the bar.

Doug grinned at Charlie. 'That put a fire cracker up his arse. He's bound to know Rossi. If there is anything crooked going on, you can bet your bottom dollar that Sonny Taylor is there at the bottom of it. He'll find out just to get shot of us.' He picked up his glass of beer and chuckled before drinking it down. 'All we have to do is wait.'

Meanwhile, Maggie had arranged with her mother to come around to her flat after the Bricklayer's Arms had closed on Sunday lunchtime. They would have something to eat, then go to the concert at the Guildhall.

Her mother had been delighted with the invitation.

'Mum!' She greeted her with a hug when eventually she arrived at the door. 'Come in,' she urged.

Moira looked around. 'My, but this is looking even nicer,' she said with a smile. 'No wonder you're happy here, so would I be.'

They sat down to some cold tinned ham that Steve had brought, boiled potatoes and a salad.

'So tell me about this concert,' said Moira.

'I'm not too sure,' explained Maggie. 'I know there's a choir, but Joshua didn't tell me too much about it,' she added.

Something in her daughter's voice made Moira look sharply at her.

'Corporal Lewis, the son of a preacher. The man I met at a dance. I told you about him.'

Maggie saw the look of consternation on her mother's face, but was relieved that she didn't question her further.

After finishing their meal, the two women washed up the dirty dishes and made their way to the Civic Centre and the Guildhall. They were sitting very near to the stage and Maggie was thrilled to see Joshua walk towards the piano.

She pointed him out to Moira.

Moira studied the tall soldier. His skin was the colour of ebony, his large, deep brown eyes shone. She noted his proud stature. His uniform was pristine as were those of the other choir members. She watched as he caught sight of Maggie in the audience and saw his broad grin. She felt her insides tighten with apprehension as she turned towards her daughter and saw the look of affection and the warm smile on her face.

But all was forgotten as the concert began. The master of ceremonies told the audience that it was a performance of American music. First of all the choir sang, accompanied only by the piano, a selection of popular songs: 'I Wish I Was in Dixie', the marching song of the Confederate Army, followed by a selection of Irving Berlin tunes. Then Joshua played George Gershwin's 'Rhapsody in Blue'.

Maggie sat spellbound, as did the whole audience, by his expertise and sensitive interpretation of the music. The applause was loud and long as he took a bow. Then a quartet took the stage: a drummer, a man with a trumpet, another with a double bass and the last one with a clarinet. They gave a lively performance of traditional jazz, and Maggie began to understand Joshua's kind of music.

Even the conservative Brits' feet were stomping to the music.

Amidst generous applause, the quartet left the stage and Joshua rose from his piano stool to join the choir who had returned. Moments later, beautiful voices in the closest harmony filled the hall, as they sang several negro spirituals. There was no accompanying music, and indeed it wasn't needed.

The choir's repertoire gave great pleasure; everyone listened intently to the words of the spirituals, sung from the soul of every man. Joshua stepped forward to sing a solo and Maggie's heart filled with pride as she listened to his low rich voice, singing 'Nobody Knows the Trouble I've Seen'. And finally the choir ended with 'Where Were You When They Crucified My Lord?'. It was a most moving experience, which surprised Moira, but not Maggie, who'd heard it before.

She turned to her mother and with shining eyes asked, 'Did you enjoy the concert? Didn't Joshua do well? Wasn't the singing just wonderful?'

'Indeed it was, darlin'. Indeed it was.'

Outside, they had started to walk away when Maggie heard her name called. She looked around and saw her friend coming towards her.

'I'm real glad you came,' he said.

'Joshua, I'd like you to meet my mother.'

Moira felt her hand held in a firm grip.

'Howdy, ma'am. I'm very happy to meet you. I sure hope you enjoyed the concert.'

She found herself smiling at him. 'Yes, thank you, corporal. I did. Very much. Such beautiful music and the words were very touching.'

'The jazz was great,' said Maggie with twinkling eyes.

With a slow smile he said, 'We weren't too sure if you reserved British were ready for that!' Turning to Moira he said, 'I have to get back to camp or I'd invite you ladies to tea somewhere.'

'That's all right,' said Moira hastily. 'I've got to get home.' She walked away leaving Maggie and Joshua together.

'Your mother's a pretty woman,' he said. 'Now I know where you get your good looks from.'

Maggie laughed. 'I'll tell her,' she said. 'She'll be flattered.'

'Have you heard from Rossi?' he asked.

Shaking her head, Maggie said, 'No. He hasn't been near.'

'What time do you finish work tomorrow?' he asked.

'I'm on until two in the afternoon.'

'I may be off for a couple of hours. May I come and see you?'

'Of course you can. Look, I must go, I'm going to walk Mother home.'

'Until tomorrow,' he said with a broad grin and a wave.

As Maggie walked towards Moira, she wondered just what her mother was thinking as she saw the thoughtful expression on her face. She tucked her arm through hers and they set off towards the docks.

'He seems a nice young man,' said Moira carefully.

'Joshua is different somehow, Mum. He's kind, considerate, but more than that; thoughtful, a man of principles. And a brilliant musician, as you saw for yourself.'

'You sound as if you know him well.'

'He's just a friend, that's all.'

'Your father would go mad if he knew.'

'I don't care what Dad thinks, Mum.'

'What about the sergeant you were seeing?' asked Moira.

Maggie could feel the tension mounting inside her. As much as she loved her mother, at this moment she felt like a child, trying to explain away some misdemeanour or other. 'I have been seeing him too, but as a matter of fact that's about to finish. I've decided I don't want to see him any more.'

'Take care, Maggie,' warned Moira. 'These men are all just passing through, knowing they're going off to war. It's an emotional time, be very careful in your dealings with them. Men were never very good at coping with rejection.'

'I know,' said Maggie, secretly wondering just what Steve's reaction would be. He certainly wouldn't like it when she eventually faced him, bringing their relationship to an end. But she'd had enough.

At Holy Rood, they parted and went their different ways.

Giving her mother a hug, Maggie said, 'You take care now.'

Moira held Maggie's face between her hands and stared intently at her. '*You* be careful, darlin'.'

As she walked towards College Street, Moira's heart was heavy. Joshua Lewis was probably everything that Maggie said he was, but she could see something else there. Something that Maggie seemed unaware of . . . for the moment anyway. She prayed that she was wrong. But in her heart she knew she wasn't.

It had taken Sonny Taylor all weekend to discover that Rossi was away in Norfolk on army business and no one seemed to know when he would be returning. On Monday lunchtime he made his way to the Horse and Groom to pass his information on. He was worried that if Doug Freeman hung around for too long, he'd discover that he'd put a lot of stuff Jack Evans's way.

Doug Freeman dismissed Sonny once he'd given him the news, telling him to let him know when the American returned. He glared at Charlie. 'I'm not hanging around for that bastard,' he said. 'I'll get back to the Smoke. You can wait here until he gets back. Have a good sniff about the place, see what's going on.' From his pocket he took out a piece of paper and read it. As the barman called time he said, 'Before I go back I think we'll pay a visit to the girlfriend. See what she knows. Come on!'

When Maggie answered the knock on her door, she was surprised to see two men standing there. As they pushed their way past her, she recognized them from the club in London and felt the chill of fear run through her.

'How dare you force your way into my home!' she demanded. 'What do you want?'

Doug looked her up and down. The girl was a looker all right. Good figure, lovely eyes – and that hair. If he had her working his patch in London she would be worth a lot of money to him. He glared at her.

'I'm looking for your Yankee boyfriend,' he said.

'I don't know where he is,' she said, staring back at him despite her fear. 'He hasn't been around for a couple of days.'

'In that case I know more than you do, girl. He's away in Norfolk, but I want to know the minute he's back. You tell him to give me a call. Understand?'

'If he wants to see you, I'm sure he'll get in touch,' she retorted.

Freeman caught her swiftly by the throat and squeezed. 'Now you listen to me, missy. Don't give me any of your lip or I'll have to teach you a lesson and I promise you, you wouldn't like it, would she Charlie?'

Charlie gave a wicked leer. 'No, love. Take it from me, you wouldn't enjoy it a bit?'

Doug released her and she staggered backwards against the wall. 'I don't know anything about his dealings with you,' she said, hoarsely, holding her sore neck. 'They're nothing to do with me and I don't want to be involved.'

She looked into the steely eyes of the Londoner and froze at the coldness reflected there. She could feel her legs trembling and shifted her position, terrified they would give way beneath her.

'But you are involved, my dear.' He took a step towards her and she stiffened, pushing herself against the wall for support. 'You tell him to pick up the phone the minute he gets back or I'll have to come after him.' He wrote quickly on a scrap of paper. 'You give this to him, then he can't give me any excuse about losing the number.'

They both walked towards the door. There he turned. 'I know you won't forget to pass on my message.' He smiled at her, but his eyes remained cold. He opened the door and the two men left.

Maggie slid down the wall until she was sitting on the floor, she started to shake. She put her hands to her head and began to sob with relief. Never had she been more terrified in her entire life. She tried to swallow what little spittle she had in her mouth, but her throat hurt. She rubbed it gently and was startled when there was another knock on the door.

She shrank back against the wall, terrified that the two men had returned. She remained still, hardly daring to breathe. There was a further knock, then silence. She froze as the letterbox opened.

'Maggie! Are you there?'

She looked at the open space and saw the dark brown eyes of Joshua Lewis peering in.

'Joshua!' With a cry of relief, she staggered to her feet and opened the door.

He took one look at her white face, the bruises deepening on her neck, the fear in her eyes and stepped inside the hallway. 'Maggie! What on earth has happened?'

'Oh Joshua. Thank God you're here.' She collapsed into his arms.

He quickly closed the door and, picking her up, carried her into the sitting room. He put her gently down on the settee, holding her close, comforting her as she wept in his arms. He didn't question her, just held her until her racking sobs had stopped.

He handed her a clean handkerchief and said, 'You'd better tell me what's been going on here.'

As she told him of the visitation of the two villains, she saw the anger in his eyes, but he made no comment until she'd finished.

'My poor Maggie,' he said when she had. 'You must have been terrified. You don't think they're liable to return, do you?'

She shook her head. 'No. They just want me to give Steve a message. If he doesn't get in touch with them, then I don't know what'll happen.' She paused. 'No, that's wrong. I do know what will happen, he said he'd go looking for him. He gave me his number. I was scared,' she admitted. 'This man meant business.'

'And so do I,' he said. 'I'll see that you're not involved in this.'

The harsh tone of his voice surprised her. 'I don't want you getting into trouble, Joshua. This mess is mine, not yours.'

'Wrong, Maggie. This mess is Steve Rossi's alone and I'm going to see that he sorts it out. Trust me.' He grinned. 'After all, I am the son of a preacher!'

Despite her bad experience, she couldn't help smiling. 'But what are you going to do?'

He put a finger on her lips. 'Hush now, no questions. Where's that telephone number? I want to write it down.'

She showed him and watched whilst he copied it into a small notebook. 'Look, I can't stop any longer, I have to get back to camp, but I don't want to leave you alone.'

Maggie shook her head. 'No, I'm all right, honestly,' she assured him. 'Ivy will be home later. I was shaken, but it's not me they want. And besides, this is my home. I'm not going to leave it just because Sergeant Rossi is in trouble! As you said, it's his mess.'

He stared intently at her. 'Are you sure now?'

'Yes, I'm quite sure.' By now she was angry that once again the staff sergeant had involved her and her anger overcame her nerves.

Joshua squeezed her hand. 'I'll see you real soon,' he said. 'But don't you worry none. I'm going to take care of everything. OK?'

Maggie nodded. 'But please don't get into trouble,' she pleaded.

He caught hold of her shoulders and gazed into her eyes. 'Don't you worry about me. I promise to take care.' He held her close for a moment. 'Are you sure you'll be fine? I hate to leave you like this.'

'You go on,' she urged.

And reluctantly he left her.

As Joshua walked down the road, he was seething with anger. God dammit! He wasn't going to let that Rossi get away with causing Maggie so much trouble. He pictured the angry fingermarks on Maggie's neck and knew if he met the sergeant at this moment . . . He took a deep breath and tried to calm down. He knew by now that he was in love with Maggie. In fact if he was honest, he had been for quite a while. He admired her spunky nature, her anger at the way some folk saw him. But what was the use? They were worlds apart. He certainly couldn't let her know how he felt, but he would do his best to protect her.

Once Joshua had left, Maggie firmly locked the door. Not that she was expecting the two men to return, now that they had delivered their message, but she felt more secure. So much for wanting her independence! It had brought her nothing but trouble.

But when she went to the toilet and saw the tell-tale smear of blood on the paper she breathed a sigh of relief. At least one problem was solved.

Chapter Fifteen

Joshua Lewis walked back to the 14th Port headquarters at Hoglands Park. He showed his pass and, strolling past several Nissen huts, made for Steve's office where his friend Ezra worked as a clerk.

Joshua was relieved to find his friend alone.

'Hey!' said Ezra. 'What you doin' here? What's happenin', man?'

'Do you still have copies of those phoney stock invoices Rossi had you make up?'

His friend looked concerned and lowered his voice. 'Yeah. I've hidden them back at camp. I kept them just in case he got caught and tried to put the blame on me. They've got his signature on and he can't squeeze out of that. I ain't anyone's fall guy.'

Joshua grinned broadly. 'Looks like we'll be able to fix him for good. Meet me tonight back in the canteen, then we can make a plan.'

Ezra frowned. 'I sure hope you knows what you're doing. These boys don't take kindly to a nigger putting their white boys behind the eight ball.'

'Trust me,' said Joshua. 'This time we've got Rossi by the short and curlies.'

With a slow smile Ezra said, 'Man I'd give a month's pay to see that. He really gets to me. I hate the bastard.'

Joshua leaned closer. 'It won't cost you a dime, buddy, I promise. See you soon.' He made his way to the gate with a satisfied smile.

Two days later, Steve Rossi returned to Southampton. The first thing he did was call Doug Freeman to apologize for the delay.

'I heard you was in Norfolk,' said the racketeer.

'How the hell did you find that out?'

'Listen, Rossi, when some geezer has my dosh and don't deliver, I make it my business to find out. Now what have you got to say? When do I get my goods?'

'I can't tell you,' said Steve.

He held the receiver away from his ear as Freeman let out a string of expletives. After the tirade had ended, he said, 'Hold your fire! I only just got back in the office ten minutes ago. As soon as I know when the next shipment is, the deal still stands. OK?'

Freeman said, 'This is your last chance, Rossi. I hope you know that?'

'Yes, yes,' Steve assured him. 'I won't let you down. I'll call you tomorrow.'

'If you don't, then my boys will come after you and this time you won't get away.'

'There's no need to talk like that, Mr Freeman. I couldn't help it before, it was army business. I had to follow orders. I'll call you tomorrow, you have my word.'

He replaced the receiver just a second before Ezra, in the outer office, replaced his. He sat back in his chair and chuckled. So . . . the game was still on. He'd tell Joshua what he'd heard, tonight, when he returned to camp. It was only a matter of time now.

Steve summoned his clerk. 'Get me the latest list of shipping arrivals,' he demanded, 'then go and get me a pot of coffee.'

'Yes, sir, sergeant!'

Rossi looked at him sharply.

'I'm on my way.' Ezra went for the list and handed it to his superior then made his way to the canteen. He smirked to himself. You stinkin' son of a bitch, you're going to get yours real soon.

Steve was studying the list. Damn! It would be another ten days before there was another shipment from the States. Freeman wasn't going to like that, but there was nothing he could do about it. He'd look at the manifest and see just what he could deliver to him before he called him tomorrow. That ought to sweeten the pill a little.

But he was really worried. To take stuff out of camp in small doses was fine, he could easily cover the shortages, but he was putting himself in a hell of a position by taking a whole load at once. It was only fear of Freeman that made him take such a chance.

He leaned back in his chair and lit a Lucky Strike from a pack of cigarettes. Later he'd go and see Maggie. He wondered if she'd heard about his run-in with Lewis. If she had she wouldn't be very happy. Well that was tough. She was his girl and it was time she realized that. He hoped she wasn't going to tell him she was carrying his child. He had enough problems as it was!

But Maggie wasn't at home when he called. She was out shopping with Ivy, on their day off. Her friend suggested, to cheer herself up and celebrate the fact that she wasn't pregnant, she should buy herself a dress and dig into her precious coupons.

They first went to C & A Modes in Above Bar, but couldn't find anything they liked, so made their way to Van Allen's. There, Maggie tried on one of several dresses that had a little more style. She turned to her friend. 'These Utility dresses aren't bad, but look at these seams. There's hardly anything there!'

'Of course not, silly. That's why they're Utility!'

Maggie eventually chose a pale green button-through dress with inverted pleats. She stood and posed in front of the mirror. 'What do you think?' she asked.

Ivy stood back. 'Turn round . . . yes, the colour's just right for you, it looks really nice – take it.'

Maggie fished in her handbag for her clothing coupon book and handed it over. 'That's seven coupons down the drain,' she complained.

'Never mind. You'll feel nice when you wear it. A new dress always cheers a woman up.'

As they walked through the town, the two of them chatted away happily. The threat of air raids had now seemingly passed. In certain parts of the town, the blackout had been relaxed. Normal curtains were now allowed, but they had to be pulled at night. Fire watching was abolished except in London and the Home Guard had been partially stood down. Southampton was still full of troops being shipped out as before, and the wounded continued to return, German prisoners still arrived, but somehow the spirit of the town and the people began to lift.

They finished the afternoon with a cup of tea and a trip to the pictures.

It was well into the evening when Maggie arrived back at Bugle Street. She was just sitting down to a meal of Spam and chips alone, as Ivy had gone to meet some friends, when there was a knock on her front door. She froze. Ever since the two men had forced their way into the flat, she was nervous whenever anyone called. The milkman had to knock several times before she would answer, and she would do so only when he proclaimed his identity.

She walked to the door. 'Who is it?' she enquired.

'Hi, honey! It's me, Steve.'

This was an unexpected surprise and one she didn't relish. She unbolted the door and let him in.

'What the hell is going on? It's like Fort Knox here,' he said as he stepped towards her to take her into his arms.

She backed off, away from his reach. 'It's been like that ever since I had a visit from your two London mobsters.'

She saw the shock reflected in his eyes.

'They came here? What did they want?'

'They came here looking for you,' she accused. She glared at him. All the horror of that time was now coming out as anger against the man whom she held responsible for her traumatic experience. 'You could have got me killed, you bastard!'

'Jeez, Maggie. I can't tell you how sorry I am. Come here.'

'Don't you touch me! I don't want any more to do with you, *Sergeant* Rossi. You lied to me all along. You used my place to store your stuff and that's twice your gangsters have come here. As far as I'm concerned you can go to hell!'

'Now Maggie, calm down. This can all be sorted out.'

'He wants you to ring him as soon as you return.'

'I've already done that.'

'You would say that, wouldn't you. I don't believe you.'

'I promise you, honey. It's all straightened out. Honest.'

Her eyes blazed with anger as she faced him. 'I don't give a damn. You and me are finished as of now. I don't want to see you any more. Understand? I want you out of my life.'

He grabbed her arms in a vice-like grip. 'I suppose you'd rather have the company of that nigger!'

She was so incensed that she was beyond reason. 'As a matter of fact, he's more of a man that you'll ever be!' She saw stars as Steve slapped her around the face, sending her reeling.

He stood over her, his face pinched and white with rage. 'You dare to say that to me.'

She was still stunned and sat holding her burning cheek. But she showed no fear, although inside she was shaking. 'Get out!'

He hauled her to her feet. 'You listen to me and listen good. You're my girl and no one else is going to have you. You'd better understand that or no other man will want to look at you ever.'

Maggie was so scared now that she didn't reply. Why oh why had Ivy chosen this particular evening to go out!

He grabbed her arm. 'Now stop this nonsense and make me a cup of coffee and then we'll go to bed.'

'You expect me to make love to you after this? I don't believe it! Well anyway, you can't.'

He looked at her and laughed harshly. 'Why not?'

'Because, you'll be relieved to know, my period has started. And besides, Ivy is sharing the flat with me now.'

'Since when?'

'That's none of your business.'

'Well that shouldn't make a difference. She can make herself scarce when we want to be alone, and now our other problem is solved, we'll be careful it doesn't happen again.'

She looked at him with distaste as she said, 'And that's just about all it ever really meant: a small problem. I'm right, aren't I?'

'Yes, since you asked.'

'You are such a cold-blooded bastard! How could I ever have been fooled by you?'

He leered at her. 'You are such an innocent, honey. You were so easy to convince.'

'Well you can damn well go and find some other poor mut, I don't want you any more!'

He grabbed her again and pulled her close, his jaw taut, eyes bright with anger.

'You still seeing that Lewis?'

'No,' she lied.

'I don't believe you!' He caught hold of her and held her whilst his mouth bruised hers.

She tried to push him away, but his brute strength defeated her.

When at last he let her go, she glared at him. Through gritted teeth she said, 'I hate you. You are despicable.'

He grinned at her. 'You could have enjoyed it if you wanted to. You always did in the past. You couldn't get enough, as I recall.'

She was so enraged that she hit out at him, but he caught hold of her wrist. 'That's what was missing in our lovemaking. A bit of anger. Willing is great for a while, but eventually it becomes boring, like making love in the same position.'

'Have you finished?' she asked coldly.

'Yes, thanks, honey. Looking at his watch he said, 'I'll be off now. But I'll be back another time.'

With great relief, she heard him shut the front door behind him and ran down the hall to bolt the door. She walked slowly back into the kitchen where, with trembling fingers, she automatically put the kettle on. Typically British, she thought bitterly. Whenever there's a crisis, reach for the bloody kettle. But she wanted to reach for Steve Rossi. Then the tears began to fall. If only Joshua were here now to comfort her. She covered her face with her hands and cried, 'Joshua! Where are you? I need you.'

Sitting at the table she pictured his face in her mind. His smile, the way his eyes twinkled when he teased her. The way he'd comforted her the other day. The feel of his arms around her . . . and suddenly she knew it was him she wanted. He was a man worth loving, not a waster like Steve Rossi.

If only she had listened to him in the beginning, none of this would have happened. But how was she to know? And now, she was wiser, but faced with the impossible. Joshua was just a friend and how could he be anything more? Couldn't she just picture the hullabaloo in her family if she told them she was in love with this Southerner.

Why did there have to be wars, she anguished. Without them, people could just get on with their lives and all these complications wouldn't arise. Her father wouldn't be mixed up with the black market, her mother would be happy, she wouldn't have met Steve Rossi . . . or Joshua. She stopped her inner raging. She was glad she knew Joshua Lewis. That she wouldn't have missed for anything.

But life was not that simple, and what the hell was she going to do when Steve called again? She didn't want him to touch her. She couldn't bear the thought of him making love to her, but he'd frightened her tonight. She looked at the bruises beginning to show on her arms where he gripped her so tightly. How was she going to make a clean break? She didn't want to tell Joshua of her fears in case he went after Steve. She couldn't bear to think of him being hurt if he did. God! What a mess!

When Maggie clocked on at the factory the following morning, she encountered Bill, the foreman, who took one look at her and said, 'Good God, girl, what's the matter? You look like hell.'

She didn't answer with her usual witty remarks, but said, 'Nothing. I just didn't sleep very well, that's all,' and walked to her machine, somewhat stiffly.

Knowing her as he did, Bill kept an eye on her during the morning, then later walked over to her, indicating to her to shut down the machine and go to his office. Once inside he told her to sit down.

'Now, are you going to tell me what's been going on?' he demanded.

She looked startled. 'I don't know what you mean.'

'How did you get those bruises, Maggie?' he asked, pointing to her arms.

She cursed inwardly. It had become so warm that, without thinking, she'd pushed up the sleeves of her dungarees.

'Your Yankee boyfriend do that, did he?'

She felt the tears well up in her eyes and didn't answer.

Bill leaned forward. 'Listen girl,' he said. 'If you're in some kind of trouble, you'll feel better getting it off your chest. Anything you say to me remains within these walls. OK?'

It was a relief to tell him what had happened, but she didn't mention the London mob, the black market, or Joshua. Only that she wanted to end their relationship.

Bill was furious. 'He had no right to treat you like that. What are you going to do about it?'

'Nothing.'

'You could have him up for assault. If you went to the police, they would arrest him.'

'My dad would love that!'

'You can't let him get away with it, Maggie.'

'Look, Bill,' she said, 'I don't want any publicity about this. If I make a complaint I'd have to go to court. I don't believe in washing my dirty linen in public. It won't happen again, I'll make sure of that.'

'Does he have a key to your place?'

'No, I wouldn't give him one.'

He looked relieved. 'Will he come back?'

'Oh yes, he'll be back at some time. There's no doubt about it.'

'Can't you move out for a bit?'

Maggie's eyes flashed with anger. 'Why the hell should I? It's my first home.'

'You going there straight away when you finish your shift?'

She nodded.

'I'll walk with you,' he said. 'See you safely inside.'

She was touched by his concern. 'There really is no need. After all, Ivy is staying with me, so I'm not exactly alone, but thanks anyway. You're a marvel.'

'Get out of here!' he said, but the smile on his lips belied the angry tone of his voice.

As it happened, when Maggie walked out of the factory gate, Joshua was waiting.

Bill, who was standing in the office doorway, saw Maggie rush over to the coloured soldier and hug him. 'Bloody hell!' the foreman loudly exclaimed.

Maggie beckoned him over. 'Bill, this is my good friend, Joshua. Joshua this is my boss, Bill, who offered to walk me home.'

'Is something wrong?' he asked anxiously. 'Only I heard that Rossi was back.'

'He came round last night,' she told him. 'It wasn't very pleasant.'

Turning to Bill, Joshua said, 'Are you the cavalry, sir, coming to the rescue?'

'Something like that. But Maggie said she was fine on her own.'

'That's real good of you, sir, but if it's all the same to you, I'll take care of her. That's why I'm here.'

Bill looked at her and raised his eyebrows.

She kissed his cheek. 'I'll be quite safe now, honestly.'

The foreman didn't feel it was his place to interfere any further, but he looked at Joshua. 'You take good care of her, mind, or you'll have me to deal with.'

To his surprise, the GI shook him by the hand. 'You're a good man. Thank you. I'll look after her, you have my word.'

And for some reason, Bill believed him. He watched them walk away together and saw the look of affection pass between them. He shook his head. Young Maggie's troubles were far from over, he was thinking.

Joshua waited until they were inside the flat before asking Maggie what had transpired the previous night and was horrified at what she told him.

'He had no right to treat you that way!' His brown eyes seemed enormous when he was angry.

'I don't want you rushing off and getting into more trouble,' she pleaded. 'It was bad enough the last time.'

'Steve Rossi will be out of your life for good soon enough,' he said.

'What do you mean?' Now she was really worried.

'The less you know the better,' he told her. 'Don't you worry none. Everything will soon be ready and all done legally. But Steve Rossi's days are numbered. Soon he'll be Stateside and out of everyone's hair.'

'You're not going to get into any kind of trouble, are you?'

'No way. And I'll see he doesn't bother you again.'

'Oh Joshua, I'm so worried that you'll do something silly.'

He held her hands. 'I promise that I won't. Come and sit down. You look so pale, you should have someone taking care of you.'

She sat beside him. 'You're such a kind man. You'll make someone a wonderful husband one day.'

He chuckled with delight. 'Sure, I can cook, clean . . . I've had enough experience in the army, that's for sure.' He put a comforting arm around her.

She gazed at him and saw the tenderness in his eyes. 'Have you ever been in love?' she asked.

His gaze didn't flinch. 'Oh yes, just once.'

She felt her heart sink at his words. She realized she loved this man, but until he told her he'd loved another, she hadn't realized the depth of her feeling for him.

'Did you ask her to marry you?'

He shook his head. 'No. I wanted to be with her for the rest of my life, but it wasn't to be.'

This was a devastating thing to be told, but Maggie felt a glimmer of hope. He had said before that he didn't have anyone waiting for him at home, so where was this woman?'

'I wish you could find someone, Maggie. Someone worthy of you, not a man like Rossi.'

This was not what she wanted to hear. She longed for Joshua to want her, not want her to find someone suitable!

She let out a deep sigh. 'Well . . . he was a big mistake. But I won't make the same one twice.'

'Look, you should try and rest. How about I go out and buy some fish and chips for lunch. We can sit here and have a picnic.'

'What, and put grease all over everywhere? You go to the shop and I'll warm some plates.'

'What about Ivy? Will she want some?'

'No, she's working. We're on different shifts.'

As Maggie busied herself she thought, well, at least she could spend some time alone with Joshua, get to know him even better, and she felt that every moment was precious.

Soon after, they were settled at the table and he was telling her more about his family, making her laugh over his childhood memories. It sounded as if his early years were full of happiness, but she knew from other things he'd said on previous occasions that it hadn't been easy. How much she admired his optimistic attitude towards life.

As she listened, she watched the way his mouth turned up at the corners when he was amused, the way his eyes twinkled when he laughed. She longed to stretch out and caress his face, to tell him of her feelings. She was very curious about the person he'd wanted to marry. 'Why didn't it work out with this woman you wanted to spend the rest of your life with?' she asked.

'There were too many complications,' he said. 'I really don't want to talk about it. Let's leave it at that.'

His firm tone convinced her it would be unwise to press the subject and she didn't question him further.

After he left Maggie, Joshua walked purposefully towards Hoglands Park. He had a personal score to settle. He showed his pass to the sentry on guard at the 14th Port headquarters and walked swiftly to Steve's office. Opening the door to the outer office he saw Ezra sitting at his desk, typing. He put a finger to his lips and whispered, 'Is Rossi in there?'

Ezra nodded. 'Ain't nobody there but him.'

'Then I suggest you disappear for twenty minutes. You know nothing about my visit. Understand?'

Ezra hurriedly got to his feet. 'Me, I'm off to the john. I feel an attack of the shits coming on, man. You take care now, you hear?'

Joshua locked the main door, then walking quickly he threw open the door to the other room.

Steve Rossi was standing in front of a filing cabinet and looked up in surprise as Joshua burst in. 'What the—?

Grabbing him by the front of his shirt, Joshua pushed him up against the wall. 'I told you, Rossi, if you ever harmed Maggie I'd come after you.' He brought his knee swiftly up to Rossi's groin.

The Italian doubled over in pain, but Joshua forced him upright and punched him in the stomach. As his adversary slumped to the floor, he said, 'You go near Maggie again and the brothers and I will come looking for you. Understand?'

Steve was writhing on the ground unable to reply.

Joshua hauled on the front of him again until he was looking at him. 'Understand?'

'Yeah, I understand,' the other man gasped.

Joshua looked at him with disgust, then left the building.

Outside he saw Ezra leaning against a tree. 'I suggest you spend a long time in the john, my friend,' he advised. 'I'll see you later.' He walked out of the camp.

Steve Rossi pulled himself up off the floor and sat in his chair behind the desk. His guts ached and he wouldn't want a woman for days. He gingerly touched his private parts. 'Bastard!' he muttered. With this deal coming up with Freeman, this was not the time to make waves . . . But after. After, he'd pay both Maggie and that nigger back. He rang for his clerk – but there was no answer.

Chapter Sixteen

The following day, Maggie, ruminating over past events, began to wonder just what Joshua was up to regarding Steve Rossi. He had seemed so certain that Steve would soon be gone, and he had said he would see that the Italian didn't bother her again in the meantime. She fretted that Joshua would get himself into trouble; yet he wasn't a man to go looking for it, she wouldn't have thought. She hadn't been able to talk to Ivy about her worries, as by the time her friend arrived home the night before, Maggie had been asleep.

At lunchtime in the factory, Bill caught up with her in the canteen.

'You all right?' he asked, sitting beside her.

'Yes thanks. And thank you for your kindness yesterday, I really did appreciate it.'

He dismissed her sentiments. 'Think nothing of it,' he said. 'That darkie . . . a good friend, is he?'

'Yes, Bill. And that's all he is.' She replied tartly.

He gently caught hold of her arm. 'Don't get the wrong idea, girl. It's not my business, but I'd hate to see you jumping from the frying pan into the fire – that's all.' He rose from the bench and left her.

She knew he meant well, but of course she recognized that, as he saw it, he was right. Black and white didn't mix. But in wartime things change. She didn't want to lose Joshua's friendship just because of his colour.

A further week passed and Steve Rossi was getting edgy. In three days' time, the next shipment from the States was due to dock and he knew that his survival hinged on his getting the goods to Doug Freeman. No matter what chance he had to take, he had to deliver. He picked up the telephone and dialled.

Ezra, who had been monitoring all his calls, listened in. He noted down the number Steve gave the operator, then made notes of the time and place for the exchange, slipped the paper into his pocket and carried on with his work.

Later, he and Joshua approached the office of the commanding officer and asked to see him urgently.

Standing to attention, Joshua spoke. 'Sir. What I have to say to you could land me in a deal of trouble, but I only have the good name of the

United States Army in mind. I would like you to remember that.'

The CO frowned, put down his pen and said, 'Carry on, corporal. And this had better be good.'

In the East End of London, Doug Freeman was making his plans. The furniture van was prepared and his band of villains ready to roll. He looked at Charlie. 'I'm coming with you,' he said. 'I still don't trust that creep. I want to be there myself to see that he delivers everything he promised. If he tries to screw me . . .' He drew his finger across his throat.

'He wouldn't dare try anything, guv. After all, he did call, and the haul sounds very good. It should make a pretty penny on the black market. No, I don't think you have a thing to worry about.'

At the dockside in Southampton the cargo was being offloaded, put on forklift trucks, then moved onto lorries. Steve was checking every item, every crate, his stomach churning, knowing he was taking a huge chance, but knowing also that he had no choice.

Joshua Lewis was on duty with some of his company, helping as usual. He kept clear of Rossi, not wanting to interfere and cause any friction; trying to behave naturally. He had no idea what was going to happen. As the CO had told him, 'It's a need-to-know basis. If you don't know, you can't spook Rossi.'

When the commanding officer first learned of the duplicity of his staff sergeant, he was astonished. Then when Ezra showed him the copies of the false invoices he was furious at the scale of the thefts.

'This bastard has cost the US Government thousands of dollars!' he roared.

But when Joshua explained that Rossi was involved with Doug Freeman, a London gangster, things became really serious. Ezra and Joshua were made to give statements, but time was short, with only a few days to formulate a plan of action.

Rossi chewed vigorously on his gum, trying to calm his nerves. Most of the lorries had been loaded and sent to the camp. On one side of the dock stood his stash of contraband, waiting for the final lorryload. He glared across in the direction of Lewis who was supervising his men. Any other time he'd sort him out, but this was not the time or the place. Too much was riding on him. But after he'd got this shipment to Freeman, then he would have time to get even.

The penultimate lorry was on its way and the final one waited to be loaded. When it was finished, Steve dismissed the men and the driver, telling him to take his jeep back to headquarters, that he'd drive the vehicle himself.

The soldier didn't argue, and just handed over the keys.

Steve waited until the coast was clear, climbed into the driving cab and made his way to Hill Lane, a quiet residential area. It had been difficult to decide where was the safest place for the handover. Anything near the docks would have caused some interest. All around the town, troops were parked waiting to board troop ships, heading for France. But in a quiet road off Hill Lane no one would take any notice of a furniture van. The local residents would just think that someone was moving out, or in.

He drove carefully towards Southampton Common, until he came to the cemetery, then turned left into Wilton Road, and eventually left again into Bridlington Avenue. Ahead of him, halfway down the road, he saw the furniture van parked. He slowed the army lorry and brought it to a standstill behind the waiting vehicle. He switched off the engine, opened the door and climbed down.

Steve was surprised when Doug Freeman alighted from the passenger seat of the furniture lorry and walked towards him.

'So you made it this time!'

'I told you I would. Now can we please get this stuff moved as quickly as possible?'

Freeman put his fingers in his mouth and whistled. The back of the vehicle opened and several of his men jumped out. They made their way to Steve's army lorry, and started to offload the gear. Freeman watched very carefully.

'You don't know how lucky you are that you came across this time, son. It looks like you'll live to be an old man after all.'

His nerves taut to breaking point, Steve snapped, 'You got the stuff didn't you? So stop bellyaching!'

Freeman grabbed his jacket. 'You use a little more respect when you talk to me. You may think you're tough, but slick bastards like you are a dime a dozen. You think you're so bloody clever, but you're just an amateur. You'll make a mistake in the end and then you'll be finished, but me, I'll go on for years . . . because I'm a professional.'

Steve shook off his hold. 'I won't have any more stuff for you,' he said. 'From now on I'll have to watch my step very carefully.' He stared at Freeman with an expression of arrogance. 'I'm no amateur,' he said. 'I've been pulling this sort of caper since I was fourteen.'

Doug gave an evil grin. 'Believe me, you'll end up behind bars. I know your type. That cocky attitude only leads to trouble. It makes you over-confident, you take chances and that's dangerous.'

The two men watched the rest of the unloading in hostile silence.

As the last crate was exchanged, the men moved a wardrobe and chest of drawers to the front, covering up the stolen loot. Doug turned to Steve and said, 'I'll be seeing you.'

'No, Freeman, you won't. This is my last business deal with you. Find another source!' He walked to the front of the army lorry and opened the door – then all hell broke loose.

From surrounding gardens uniform police appeared; from others, American military police rushed forward, revolvers at the ready. Police cars screeched to a stop at either end of the road, blocking off any getaway.

Freeman was held by two constables. Others swarmed all over the furniture van, pulling out the men inside. Rossi was held by military police. A constable came out of the back of the furniture van carrying three sawn-off shotguns. 'They came tooled up!' he proclaimed.

As the police put the handcuffs on Doug Freeman, he looked over at Rossi, his face flushed with anger.

'Fucking amateur!' he yelled. 'Didn't I tell you?'

The raid made the headlines in the *Southern Daily Echo* the following day: *Black Market Ring Foiled. London Villain Caught.*

Maggie read it, her fingers trembling as she held the paper. She felt her blood run cold as she read the track record of Doug Freeman. To think that this man had been in her home, threatening her, holding her by the throat. It made her feel sick. Then she saw Steve's name and at last realized just what Joshua had been referring to. What had he to do with all this, she wondered. But with a feeling of relief, she now knew for certain that Steve would not be bothering her again. She showed the paper to Ivy.

'Bloody hell!' she said, when she'd read it. 'And to think I told you to marry him. Well I don't know about you, Mags, but from now on, I'm all for a quiet life!'

Maggie grinned to herself, knowing her friend of old. A quiet life would drive Ivy mad. She had already started to go to dances again, visiting her old haunts, looking for excitement. But Maggie was relieved. Steve's violence had shaken her, and although she'd remained in her flat, albeit securely locked in and with her pal sleeping there, she'd been terrified of his return.

The following day she went to visit her mother, insisting as soon as the pub was closed that they go out and look around the shops, perhaps stop for tea somewhere.

When she saw her father it struck her that he'd aged suddenly. When she worked in the bar on a Friday evening, she scarcely looked at him, but tried to keep herself to herself in the confines of the small space behind the counter.

He barely answered her when she said hello, and she supposed that he blamed her still for his wife's unhappiness. And to some extent she was responsible, she couldn't deny it. If he'd been different, in time he and Moira should have grown even closer. Except of course for his dodgy dealings. She knew that Sonny Taylor was still keeping him supplied, and that didn't help his relationship with Moira. But she wasn't going to fret over him. Today was for her mother.

'Did you read last night's paper?' asked Moira as they walked.

'Yes,' said Maggie.

'Didn't you tell me your boyfriend's name was Steve Rossi, a staff sergeant?'

Maggie pursed her lips and cursed her mother's excellent memory. 'Yes, that's right'

'The same one mentioned in the *Southern Daily Echo*?'

'I'm afraid so.'

'Mm. Just as well that you got out when you did, darlin', otherwise you might have been caught up in that mess. That would have been dreadful.'

Maggie breathed a sigh of relief. Thank God her mother didn't know how close she'd come to being involved.

The afternoon was enjoyable for both women. Their relationship was very special. They shared the same sense of humour, and when Maggie had lived at home they had often giggled together like children over silly things. Jack could never understand them.

As they sat in Tyrell and Greens, having tea, Moira looked happier. 'It always does me good to have you around. I enjoy our Friday nights in the bar, and the odd coffee we have together in the town, but today, I don't think I've laughed so much in weeks.' She sighed softly. 'It would be nice if we could go away on a holiday together, just the two of us,' she said wistfully.

'Why can't we?'

'You couldn't get time off from work and I certainly wouldn't leave your father alone to run the pub! Surely the war can't go on for much longer? I know our boys had a bad time at Arnhem, but they seem to be doing better in Italy. How much longer can both sides continue? So many deaths. That lovely Guy Gibson shot down. It's such a waste.'

'All because of that power hungry paperhanger,' said Maggie. 'Well if there is a God, he surely won't let him win.'

Moira looked askance. 'What do you mean, *if* there is a God! Of course there is. You'd better not let Joshua hear you say such a thing.'

'Joshua?'

'Yes. Now there is a man with a belief.'

Maggie hid a smile. 'He's bound to, his father's a preacher, but what makes you so sure? You only exchanged a few words at the concert.'

Moira's expression softened. 'You only had to look at his face as he sang those negro spirituals,' she said. 'The words came from the heart. It's a pity he's —' She stopped.

'That he's black?'

Her mother looked embarrassed. 'Well I can't pretend. He seems a really nice young man, but, Maggie, there's no future for the two of you.'

'I know that! I've told you, it's purely friendship.'

'I'm not sure that's how he sees it.'

'He's never touched me, or even tried to,' Maggie protested.

'I didn't say he had, but the way he looks at you, my dear. I'm surprised you haven't noticed.'

Maggie was quite thrown by her mother's words. 'I'm sure you're mistaken, Mum.'

'I hope so, darlin', I certainly hope so. Well, I'd better make tracks for home. Come on, we'll walk to Holy Rood together . . . that's if you're going home?'

'Yes, I am. I want to have a bath and wash my hair.'

As they parted, Moira kissed her daughter. 'I've had a lovely time,' she said. 'You could always come home one day and let me cook you a meal.'

Maggie hesitated. 'I'm not sure that Dad would approve. He can hardly bear the sight of me, and the idea of sitting at a table sharing a meal with him . . . well!'

'Think about it.'

Maggie said she would and they parted company. As she walked home, she couldn't get her mother's observations about Joshua out of her mind. Ivy had made a similar remark. She doubted that he would feel the same way as she did. He'd never said anything to make her think he did, except that he worried over her when she was going out with Steve.

If only what they said was true. But if it was . . . where would they go from there? She really did like him. She liked his mind too. He stimulated hers with his conversation. They argued over so many different things, especially music. He'd changed her way of thinking. He'd opened her mind to so much and he soothed her soul. She felt, if only things were different, they could be happy together.

As she entered the front door, she could hear the sound of voices. There in the kitchen were Ivy and Joshua, chatting away.

'Hey Mags,' called Ivy, 'come and see who's here, and he's brought some food with him.'

Joshua looked up. 'Hello, Maggie,' he said softly.

For the first time in his company, she felt embarrassed. 'Hello. I want to talk to you. Just exactly what did you have to do with that raid the other day?'

He gave an impish grin. 'I told you Rossi was on his way, didn't I?' He then proceeded to fill in all the details leading to the arrests. 'The army wasn't too happy having to liaise with the Hampshire police, they like to handle army matters internally, but when they heard about the guy from London, they had no choice.'

'Where's Steve now?'

'In the pokey where he belongs! He'll go before a military court, be sentenced, then do time in a military prison. And after, he'll be shipped home in disgrace.'

'How are the mighty fallen!' quipped Ivy.

'What a fool,' said Maggie. 'He was such a bright man.'

'And a violent one – or had you forgotten?' asked Joshua, sharply.

'I'll never forget anything about Steve Rossi,' she said angrily. 'How could I have been such a fool! I should have known better.'

'Don't be so hard on yourself. Rossi could be charming, and convincing. But at least now he won't be bothering you again.'

She looked at him, a frown furrowing her brow. 'You took such a chance going to see your commanding officer.'

He smiled. 'I had the proof; besides, I had to do something. I was worried about you. Rossi wouldn't have left you alone, especially when he learned of our friendship. That really stuck in his craw. I was concerned for your safety, Maggie.'

'But you put your career on the line for me.'

'That's not how I saw it,' he said softly.

'But won't there be trouble for you from his friends?'

'Rossi didn't have any friends! There's no one going to come after me just because he got caught with his hand in the cookie jar. And at least we were able to keep your name out of it.'

She looked horrified. 'What do you mean?'

'Had the police known you had a visit from Freeman, then you'd be called to give evidence.'

'Oh my God! That would be awful.'

'As it was, they caught the two of them red-handed and that was good enough to charge them.' Seeing the expression on her face he said, 'Now you need to forget all this and put it behind you. Get on with your life. Just be a little less trusting, next time.'

'Next time! There won't be a next time.'

Joshua burst out laughing. 'Don't be silly. A girl with your looks will always have men after her. Just take care, is all.'

'I got myself into this mess. I was in too much of a hurry to be a woman. I let my curiosity get the better of me. Well, now I know about sex.' Her eyes flashed with anger and indignation. 'And I don't need any man!' She saw the hurt look on his face. 'I don't mean a friend like you, Joshua. I mean a committed relationship. Look at my mother's marriage; she's not a happy woman. And Ivy's separated.'

'For goodness' sake, Maggie, don't let your experience with Rossi make you bitter. That's a wasted emotion. As for marriage, with the right partner, it's wonderful. My parents have no regrets, that's for sure. When

141

you fall in love, you'll think differently, I promise.' He caught hold of her hand. 'How about we celebrate? Let's go dancing. There's a dance on tonight at the Guildhall,' he said, changing the subject. 'What do you say? Let's put all this mess behind us and have a good time.'

'Go on, Maggie,' urged Ivy. 'It'll do you good.'

And she agreed.

The Guildhall was quieter than usual, which pleased Maggie because there was more room to dance. As Joshua led her onto the floor when the strains of the waltz came over the microphone, she felt as if she'd come home. Within his arms, she relaxed and moved in unison with him to the music. His face was against hers. The warmth from his skin, the feel of his arms around her, made her wish the music would go on for ever. She felt safe, cosseted . . . loved? She looked up at him and as he gazed back at her, she recognized the expression in his dark eyes.

But she was confused. She'd always known she didn't love Steve, had failed to realize how deeply she cared for Joshua. Now she thought she saw something special in the way he looked at her, but she'd been wrong so many times . . . and what about the other woman? The one Joshua had loved so much?

The music stopped, but he just held her close until the next number started. He didn't speak, just clasped her to him.

When the dance was finished, he led her away from the floor and, seating her at a table, asked, 'What would you like to drink?' As he walked to the bar she watched him. He didn't swagger as Steve used to do, his walk was one of elegance, stature, pride. And she realized here was a man who was happy with who he was. She envied him his composure, his certainty.

He smiled at her as he put the drinks on the table and sat beside her.

Thinking of the expression she'd seen in his eyes, she asked, 'Why did you bring me here with you tonight? What was the real reason?'

'I just wanted to hold you in my arms,' he said, simply and honestly.

Her breath caught in her throat. Could it really be that he thought as much of her as she did of him?

'But apart from the time you found me after those men from London had called at the flat, and you comforted me, you've never given any hint . . .' She was lost for words. 'What are you saying?' she asked. 'I've made so many mistakes in the past . . .'

Putting his arm around her shoulders, he said, 'I'm in love with you, Maggie.'

'You are?'

His eyes twinkled as he said, 'You find that so very strange?'

'But what about the other woman, the one you wanted to spend the rest of your life with?' She had to know.

He gently stroked her cheek. 'Her name is Maggie Evans.'

'But why have you never said anything? How was I to know?'

'Steve Rossi was always in the way.'

She caught hold of his hand. 'Oh Joshua.' She brushed the back of it with her lips. 'You've never even kissed me.'

'You have no idea the many times I've wanted to.'

She looked around. They were surrounded by people. 'I want you to kiss me too. Let's get out of here.'

They left the Guildhall and made their way to the park.

Once alone, Joshua took her into his arms.

She relaxed as his mouth covered hers, let herself respond to the gentle urgency of his tender kisses; felt his strong arms about her, the caresses of his hands on her back. It was a long time before he released her.

In the low light reflected from the moon, he looked into her eyes and whispered, 'I love you, Maggie.'

'And I love you,' she responded. She smoothed his cheek and gazed longingly at him. 'What fools we've been . . . or at least I have.'

He put his finger over her lips. 'Hush now. Better late than never, as they say.'

'But we've wasted so much time and you could be shipped out.'

He held her close and buried her head in his chest, stroking her hair. 'That doesn't seem likely just yet. They need us to work in the docks.' He tipped her chin upwards. 'We'll spend every moment we can together and make up for lost time. What do you say?'

'I'd like that. Let's go home. At least there we can be in comfort.' She gave a cheeky grin. 'And you can tell me exactly when you discovered that you loved me.'

He burst out laughing. 'Oh the vanity of women.'

'Not at all.' She reached up and kissed him. 'I just can't believe that you feel this way and I want to know everything. How, where, when and why!' There was a momentary anxious look in her eyes. 'I can't quite make sense of it, you see.'

He pulled her to him. 'Believe it!' He lowered his lips to hers once again, his kisses ardent and demanding. When he released her he asked, 'Does that help to convince you?'

'Oh, yes,' she said in a soft voice. 'But I may need some further convincing.'

She heard him chuckle softly. 'It'll be my pleasure.'

They walked back to Bugle Street, hand in hand.

When they arrived at the flat, Maggie put the key in the door and opened it. Ivy came rushing forward. 'Thank God you're home,' she gasped. 'Your father has been arrested!'

Chapter Seventeen

The success of the raid and the capture of Doug Freeman had fired the enthusiasm of the Chief Constable who had gathered together all his senior officers.

'The other day was a good result,' he said with a satisfied smile. 'Now we must continue with our fight against these criminals. Strike while the iron's hot! I want more men on the beat. Question your narks, find out who's doing business with who. I want an end to this racketeering.'

When it was known that Sonny Taylor had been talking to Doug Freeman in the Horse and Groom earlier that month, a tight watch had been put on the spiv. Taylor had been panicked by Freeman's arrest and had hastened to his hideaway, in a bid to get rid of his goods. The police had followed him to his lock-up garage and arrested him.

When, in the interview room, he'd been charged, he sang like the proverbial canary. He named all his customers in the hopes that he'd get a lighter sentence for helping the police with their enquiries.

Later that evening, two detectives made their way to the Bricklayer's Arms, with a search warrant.

Jack Evans was cleaning out the beer pumps when he heard an urgent knocking on the side door. He cursed to himself. 'Can't the buggers wait,' he muttered. 'It's only ten minutes to opening time!' He was shocked when he opened the door to see two plain-clothed officers of the law standing there.

They pushed past him into the narrow hallway, one of them waving the warrant under his nose. The older one looked at him grimly. 'We hear you've been a naughty boy, Jack,' he said.

The landlord's face turned pale. 'What the bleedin' hell you talking about?'

'We've just arrested Sonny Taylor,' said the other. 'I believe you're one of his customers.' He turned to the door of the front room and tried the handle. It was locked. 'Open up, Jack,' he commanded, ' and don't give us any trouble, there's a good chap.'

At that moment Moira appeared from the direction of the kitchen. 'What's going on?' She stopped in her tracks as she saw the two men and the look on her husband's face.

'Unlock the door, Jack. Don't mess me about,' said the detective.

Putting his hand in his pocket, Jack Evans reluctantly put the key in the lock and turned it. The officer was the first to enter the room. Looking around he said, 'Well, well. Nice little haul you've got here. The Chief Constable will be pleased.'

Moira had followed them. She stood horrified at the sight of the cases of liquor, tinned Spam, fruit, nylon stockings, cartons of cigarettes, medical supplies and American army bed rolls. 'Jesus Mary and Joseph,' she said, crossing herself. She looked at Jack in disbelief. 'You bloody fool!'

The senior detective said to her, 'We'll be taking your husband in for questioning. There'll be a police car along soon to take this stuff away. It'll be used in evidence.'

'What'll happen to my husband?' she asked.

He gave her a sardonic smile. 'I'm sure you must know the answer to that, love. Just take a look around you. You'll be wanted for questioning later too, Mrs Evans.'

She looked at him with a horrified expression, but didn't say a word.

Jack turned to his wife, a haunted look on his face. 'I'm sorry, Moira,' he said in all but a whisper.

She glared at him. 'I hope you're satisfied!' She watched as they took him away in handcuffs.

By now, several of the locals had gathered. Grace Clarke came over to her and said, 'I'm sorry your man's in trouble. What are you going to do?'

Her mouth in a tight line, Moira said, 'I'm going to open the bar while I still have a business to run.'

'Where's Maggie?' asked Grace.

'She's at home and I don't want her bothered. She's got her own life to run.'

'But she'd want to know,' insisted Grace. 'She'd be furious if you didn't tell her, you know she would. You need her here now. You can't face this alone.'

Moira hesitated. 'Perhaps you're right. Would you pop round to her flat and put a note in the door for me?'

'Of course I will, and when I come back, I'll help you serve in the bar. You can't run the pub on your own. You want any barrels changing, my Nobby can do it.'

'Thanks, Grace, you're a good friend.'

It was almost closing time when Maggie hurried into the Bricklayer's Arms with Joshua. She went behind the bar and hugged her mother. 'I've only just heard, I came as soon as I could. Are you all right?' she asked anxiously.

'To be honest, darlin', I'm damned if I know. I've been serving all night like a zombie. Thank God for Grace and Nobby. They've both been helping.'

Maggie turned to the couple and thanked them. Nobby drew her aside.

'Listen, Maggie,' he said. 'The brewers will probably take your old man's licence away. You need to go and see them if you want to keep this place on.'

She smiled at him. 'I've already decided to do so, in the morning. I'm going to ask them to transfer the licence to my mother or me. Do you think they will?'

'I don't know about your mother, they may think she knew all about what was going on. But you, that's different. These days, with so many men away at war, it has been known for a woman to hold a licence. After all, you've worked in the bar for long enough, you grew up in this place, you know the ropes. Just let them see you mean business, that you have the Bricklayer's and the brewers' best interests at heart. They can only say yes or no.'

'Thanks, Nobby. I'll talk it over later with my mother, and thank you both for helping her. I won't forget that.'

'Your father's an idiot,' he said. 'He's got a good business here.'

'I know,' she agreed. 'We both tried to talk to him, but you know Dad.'

'That I do. Stubborn as a mule. You all right now? Anything I can do?'

'No thanks. I'll see you tomorrow.' She looked at her watch and turning she rang the brass bell. 'Time, ladies and gentlemen – please!' she called, looking at Moira. 'Don't you worry, Mum,' she said, 'we'll manage.'

When the customers had left, Maggie locked the door. 'You go and make a pot of tea, Mum. Me and Joshua will clear up.'

Moira looked at him. 'I'm so sorry,' she said, 'I haven't said hello. You must think me very rude.'

'Not at all, ma'am. You've got a lot on your mind, but I sure would enjoy a cup of tea.'

She smiled at him and left the bar.

He walked over to the tables and started clearing the dirty glasses. 'Your poor mother looks exhausted,' he said. 'I'm really sorry about your dad.'

'I should never have left home!' declared Maggie angrily. 'It was the biggest mistake of my life.'

'Ask yourself honestly, would it have made any difference to this outcome? Could you have stopped your father in his dealings?'

She looked thoughtful. 'No . . . I tried often enough.'

'Then stop blaming yourself. But now you do have a problem, so what's the next move?'

'I'll go and see the brewers tomorrow, I'll ring them in the morning and make an appointment. I need to talk to Mum about the licence.' She looked around the dingy bar. 'This place could do with a facelift,' she said. 'If we could get the licence, I'd like to paint the bar a brighter colour.

The walls are covered in nicotine and beer stains.'

'That would be a good move.'

'But hardly possible. I could never close the bar for two days, could I?'

Joshua studied the area. 'You could close it for a morning, that would be long enough.'

'What are you talking about?'

'If you got the licence, I could get some of my friends to come in overnight and paint it. I could arrange for all-night passes, maybe even get the paint. The final touches could be finished in the morning. How does that sound to you?'

She walked over to him and put her arms around him. 'Joshua Lewis. Why is it that you always seem to be around when I'm in trouble?'

He smiled down at her. 'Maybe I'm your guardian angel?'

'After the way you kissed me tonight, I don't see you as angelic.'

He kissed the tip of her nose. 'Me neither. Come on, let's get this place cleaned up.'

A little later, Moira called from the kitchen. 'The tea's made!'

They walked hand in hand out of the bar.

Joshua didn't linger for very long. He had to return to his base, for one thing, and he knew the two women needed to talk, but he was worried for Maggie's sake.

At the front door he took her into his arms. 'You know, honey, I'm around if you need me, don't you?'

She smiled up at him. 'You don't know just how much of a comfort that is at this time.'

He tilted her chin and looked deep into her eyes. 'I love you, Maggie, and don't you forget it.' He kissed her longingly, then opened the door and left.

Maggie returned to the kitchen. 'I'll stay with you tonight, Mum. I don't expect you feel like being alone.'

'Ah, you're a good girl, darlin', so you are. I could do with the company that's a fact.'

'We need to see the brewery, Mum. Ask about having the licence in one of our names. What do you think?'

A frown creased her mother's brow. 'The detective said that they want to question me. If I'm under suspicion, the brewers wouldn't consider giving me the licence. But you wouldn't know anything about your father's dealings.'

'But I did. We both did.'

'But they don't know that! No, you be the innocent party here.' She thought for a moment. 'No. It's you that must take it . . . if they agree.' She shook her head, her expression one of great sadness. 'You should have seen your father when they took him away. He looked a broken man.'

Maggie's lips pursed in a straight line. 'And so he should! Didn't we warn him often enough?'

'We did that, but we all have our weaknesses, you know. I'll go along tomorrow and see him.'

'What, and listen to his excuses? He'll tell you he did it for you. Stuff and nonsense! He did it for himself. Well, you may be able to forgive him, but I don't think I ever will. Come on, Mum. Let's get to bed, we've a lot to see to tomorrow.'

The following morning, Maggie rang the head office of the brewers and arranged to see them later that afternoon. She rang the factory also and spoke to the foreman, explaining her situation, and was given the week off to sort out her problems.

Later that afternoon, she sat in the reception area of the brewery, waiting to see the managing director, trying to run over in her mind just what to say. She'd slipped back to her flat and changed into a grey costume and a clean, crisp, white blouse, hoping she looked businesslike. Taking a deep breath, she followed the receptionist who had come for her.

Albert Watkins, a middle-aged man with a bald head and bluff exterior, looked at Maggie as she walked into his office. 'Please sit down, Miss Evans,' he said. 'Now, what can I do for you?'

'My father is the tenant of the Bricklayer's Arms in College Street. You may not yet be aware of the fact but he was arrested by the police last night,' she began.

The man looked surprised. 'No indeed, I know nothing about this,' he said, his brow furrowing.

'Unfortunately it's true. He was involved in the black market, I'm sorry to have to tell you.'

'I'm sorry too, Miss Evans. Your father has been a tenant for a number of years at the Bricklayer's Arms.'

'Eleven,' said Maggie. She sat upright in the chair and looked Mr Watkins straight in the eye. 'I know this will reflect badly on the brewery and I apologize for that, but I'm here to ask you to transfer the licence to me. I can promise you that if you were to do so, the brewery would be assured of my loyalty. The business is a good one and, in my hands, it will do even better. After all, I was brought up in the public house. I know how to run the bar, how to please the customers. I know I could succeed.'

He looked at her with an expression of curiosity. 'Why would you want to take such a thing on, at your age?' he asked. 'After all, I would have thought a young woman such as yourself would have other things to occupy her.'

'I want to secure my future and safeguard my mother's,' she said.

149

'Ah, I see. Well it's very commendable of you to be so concerned about your mother, in the circumstances.'

'She's a good, hardworking woman,' said Maggie evenly. 'She's an asset to the Bricklayer's Arms. The regulars all know her, and the other customers are charmed by her.' She smiled at him. 'She's Irish, you know. They have a way with them.'

He smiled back at her. 'You have quite a way with you too. But tell me, aren't you already employed?'

'Yes, I'm doing my bit for the war effort. I work in a munitions factory in Southampton.'

'Then how can you do that and run a business?'

'It's not a problem, Mr Watkins. I can always work an early shift. We can employ a barmaid to help in the morning if it's necessary. I of course will be there myself for the evenings when we're busiest. I know how to change a barrel, clean the pumps, clean the cellar. I've learnt a lot in eleven years,' she said with a note of defiance in her voice.

Mr Watkins's eyes twinkled. 'I'm sure you have. I will have to put this to my board, you understand?'

'Yes of course.'

'I'll let you know in about a week's time. But thank you for coming to see me so promptly. It couldn't have been easy for you.'

His kindness and understanding was almost her undoing. She fought back the emotions that threatened to overwhelm her and rose from her seat, held out her hand and said, 'Thank you for your time. I hope you can convince your board that I will do a good job for them.'

'I'll let you know,' he said. 'Good day, Miss Evans.'

Maggie made her way to her flat, knowing that Ivy was on a late shift. Fortunately her friend was there. 'Ivy, I need to ask you a favour.'

'First tell me what happened to your father.'

'They are holding him until this morning when he goes before the magistrate to be charged. I doubt they'll let him out on bail.'

'Oh, Maggie, I'm so sorry. What can I do to help?'

'This morning I went to the brewers' hoping they'll give me the licence. Meantime I'm staying with Mum. If I get it, I won't need the flat.'

'And if you don't, then I suppose you and your mother will need this place?'

'I'm afraid so. I'm really sorry to mess you about, but I wondered if you would stay on until we get it sorted?'

Ivy put an arm around her. 'Of course. And if it all turns out well, I'll take the flat over.'

'That would be great. At least one problem would be solved, either way.'

Ivy walked into the kitchen. 'I'll make us a cup of tea whilst you pack a few things. I'm sure everything will be fine. After all, so many blokes are away at the war, and you do know the business.'

She walked back into the room. 'Imagine you, a pub landlady!'

Maggie smiled. 'Don't count your chickens.' The smile faded. 'God, I hope it works out that way, for Mum's sake.'

Whilst Maggie was sorting things out with Ivy, Moira went to the local police station to see her husband.

She was shown into an interview room, given a cup of tea and told to wait. Five minutes later, Jack was shown into the room.

He sat opposite her and, taking her hands in his, he said, 'I'm sorry I've got you into this mess. But I told them you knew nothing about it, only that I kept some stuff in the room. You must say the same.'

She shook her head slowly. 'Was it worth it, Jack?'

'It seemed like it at the time,' he said.

'So what's happened?'

'They charged me this morning and I'm on remand. They're taking me to Winchester prison later today. But I'm worried about you and the pub.'

'It's a bit bloody late for that, isn't it?' she snapped.

He lowered his head. 'Yes. I'm sorry.'

'Our Maggie went to see the brewers today. She asked if they would let her take over the licence.'

'Did she!'

'What else did you expect? Someone has to do something. Thank God for her, I say, and you might think a bit more kindly of her too! I have to get back. I'll ask when I can come and visit you in Winchester.'

Later in the afternoon, Maggie arrived at the Bricklayer's Arms in a taxi, with a couple of suitcases.

'What's all this?' asked Moira.

'I'm moving back in,' she said.

'But your flat . . .'

'Ivy's going to take it over.'

Moira's eyes lit up. 'That's splendid. But what happens if we lose the pub, where will we live?'

'We move back to the flat. Ivy and I have it all arranged.'

Putting her arms around Maggie, Moira said, 'Whatever would I do without you?'

She held her mother at arm's length. 'Remember when I was small, that teacher kept picking on me at school, making my life hell?'

Moira smiled at the memory. 'Yes.'

'What did you do?'

'I went and sorted her out. I complained to the headmistress.'

'There you go, now it's my turn to take care of you. Any news of Dad?'

'I went to see him while you were at the brewers. He's been charged and now has to wait for his case to come up in court.'

'Well, that ought to give him some time to think about his mistakes!'

'Oh, Maggie. Don't be so hard on him. He's in a sorry state.'

'Hard! He put your livelihood in jeopardy. What did he care?'

'We all make mistakes, Maggie. You'll make a few in your lifetime. Some can be forgiven, a few never can. But only you know which they are.'

Maggie was filled with guilt. How right her mother was. Hadn't she just made a disastrous mistake with Steve Rossi? Turning to Moira she said, 'You're right. Who am I to judge?'

Her mother looked at her and said, 'I do believe you've grown up whilst you've been away. Before, you would have never been so philosophical, just angry. We'll just have to keep our fingers crossed and hope that the brewers see you as a good tenant. It's all in the lap of the gods, darlin'. Come on, let's get something to eat before we get the bar ready for opening.'

It was a busy night. All the regulars dropped in at some time or other, to tell the two women how sorry they were to see them in this position and hoped that all would work out for them.

Joshua arrived with several of his friends, introducing them to Maggie and her mother. They were a jolly crowd, mixing well with the locals, taking their goodnatured ribbing about their country and their colour. Joshua played the piano and all the customers sang together. The pub almost had an air of celebration about it, which was strange in a way, Maggie thought, with her father languishing in a prison cell.

When the bar closed, Joshua stayed behind to help with the clearing up, making sure the outside gents toilet was locked, and the cellar, sweeping the floor and emptying the ashtrays.

'You'd make a good landlord yourself,' remarked Moira.

He looked at her in surprise. 'Gee, do you think so?'

'What are you going to do when you leave the army?' she asked.

'Me, Mrs Evans? I'm a jazz musician. I'll just go where the music is.'

'Well that sounds hopeful. Music is important, everyone can always do with a cheery tune.'

'He plays jazz, Mum. A cheery tune isn't quite how I'd describe it!' grinned Maggie.

'I can do those too,' he quipped. 'I did tonight, didn't I?'

'Yes, I suppose you did.'

Moira said goodnight and left the two of them together.

'I like your friends,' said Maggie, now held in Joshua's warm embrace.

'I'm glad,' he said, 'because they are the ones who'll be coming to paint up this place when you hear from the brewery.'

'You're jumping the gun a bit, aren't you?' she said.

'No, Maggie. I'm sure when you went to their offices, the man there was impressed by you. How could he not be?'

She kissed him. 'You have such a way with words,' she said.

'That's because I read so much,' he laughed. He gazed at her and said, 'It's so good to feel you so close to me. I don't want to let you go.' He kissed her forehead, her eyes, her neck and her mouth.

She returned his kisses eagerly, responding to the growing passion between them.

He reluctantly released her. 'I must get back, much as I'd like to stay. I'm on duty tomorrow, but I'll call you. Give me the telephone number.'

She wrote it on a piece of paper and put it in the top pocket of his uniform. At the door he took her into his arms and kissed her again.

'If I don't go now I'll be AWOL,' he said as he opened the door. He caught hold of her hands and said, 'Remember that I love you. I'll see you real soon.' Then he walked away into the dark.

As they sat together in the kitchen having a cup of Ovaltine, Moira said to Maggie, 'That Joshua's a nice fellow. He thinks a lot of you, doesn't he?'

'Yes, Mum, he does and I feel the same way about him.' She saw the worried expression on Moira's face. 'I know it may seem wrong to you and other people, but we love one another.' She tried to explain. 'Joshua is a very special person. I don't suppose I'll ever meet another man like him. His colour is unimportant to me. It's what's inside that counts.'

'But it's what's outside that people see, darlin', and they can be so cruel.'

'I've already learned that, Mother! It makes no difference.'

'You have the same stubbornness as your father. Just think about it will you, please? It's not that I don't like the lad, it's you I'm concerned about. There is no happy ending here. Surely you can see that?'

'I'm content to take what is given to me, for as long as it lasts,' said Maggie. She put her hand over her mother's. 'I know it will end in tears. Joshua will eventually be posted and we probably will never meet again, but don't you see, until that happens, we want to be together.'

'Well, Maggie, you're old enough to make up your own mind about such things, and I'll always be here to pick up the pieces. That's what mothers are for.'

Maggie leaned forward and kissed her cheek. 'I really love you,' she said.

In the military prison in Southampton, Steve Rossi paced up and down his cell. He hated being cooped up like this. All the years of his youth in New York, taking his chances with the law, he'd only ever spent one night behind bars, until his father bailed him out the following morning. It was driving him crazy.

He was angry at being caught, furious with Doug Freeman for pushing him into making a mistake, but worse, eating away at him, was the relationship between Maggie and Joshua Lewis. Although Maggie had sworn that the two of them had never been lovers, he didn't believe her. The thought of those black hands touching her body, *his* girl's body, gnawed at him every hour of the day. He wanted to get his revenge on both of them. If only he could get out of this stockade. There must be a way, a moment when the guards were careless. So far there had been no chance, but he'd remain alert. His moment would come and he'd be ready.

Chapter Eighteen

The following week seemed endless, waiting to hear from the brewers. Maggie and Moira spent every spare moment, when the pub was closed, cleaning: washing walls; scrubbing floors, windows and window frames; trying to get the grime out of the benches and tables in preparation for the redecorating, in case she was successful in her bid to take over the licence.

Ivy, too, had come along to help when she wasn't working, and had been roped in from time to time to serve behind the bar, much to the locals' amusement. Ivy with her cheek and ready wit had livened up the atmosphere considerably. It had also been therapeutic for her, helping her to get over her broken marriage and the loss of Bob Hanson.

She'd written to Len weeks ago to verify the end of their relationship and in return had received a letter from him full of vitriolic rhetoric. She'd torn it up, burnt it in the fire and forgotten about him, saying to Maggie, 'He's in the past. Now I have to make a new future for myself.'

Maggie had admired the determination and resilience shown by her friend and wondered just how she herself was going to cope when the day came for Joshua's departure, when he would leave Southampton . . . and her.

He was now a regular in the pub, coming around when he wasn't on duty, helping out whenever he could, even washing the glasses when required. The locals were getting used to him, most of them accepting him into their midst.

Moira, too, could at last see the hidden depths to this man, through her various conversations with him, and could well understand why Maggie felt the way she did; yet still, deep inside, she worried about the consequences of their friendship.

Finally the letter from the brewers arrived and Maggie picked it up and took it into the kitchen, her fingers trembling as she held the unopened envelope.

'It's here,' she said to Moira who was clearing away the breakfast dishes.

'Oh my God!' Moira's eyes grew wide. 'Well, are you going to read it or are you waiting for me to have a heart attack with worry!'

Sitting down at the table, Maggie tore open the envelope, removed the letter and read it. She looked up at her mother without saying a word.

'I knew it!' exclaimed Moira. 'We're out on the street. We'll have to move, I'll have to find a job.''

Maggie grinned broadly. 'You can go if you really want to, but me, I'm staying – if only to see my name over the door!' She held out the letter to her mother.

Moira snatched it out of her fingers and quickly read it . . . then threw the paper into the air with a whoop of joy and, pulling Maggie out of her seat, danced around the room with her. They both eventually collapsed into chairs, breathless and excited.

'My darlin' child,' she said. 'You're a marvel. Dear Lord, what a relief, I was dreading having to move. If that had happened I honestly don't think I could ever have forgiven your father!'

With an expression of amusement Maggie remarked, 'I wonder what he'll have to say about it?'

There was a momentary flash of anger in Moira's eyes as she said, 'He's in no position to say anything. And I'll be honest, it will give me a certain amount of satisfaction to tell him of your success.' She looked at her daughter and asked, 'Will you have him back after he's served his time?'

Maggie hesitated. 'I've not given the matter any thought. In any case he hasn't been tried yet, so we don't know what's going to happen to him.'

'Of course we do! He'll do time! What we don't know is how long.'

'Let's wait and see, shall we,' said Maggie. 'He may not be able to accept that now I'm the landlady. You know how stubborn he is. It's a situation maybe he couldn't cope with. Anyway we have much more important things to think about at this moment. I'll call Joshua at the camp. Now we can get on with brightening up the place.'

Joshua, true to his word, arranged for a working party of three of his buddies to come along a couple of nights later, loaded down with paint, brushes and ladders. As soon as closing time was called, they set about their task with a vengeance.

With pots of cream-coloured paint, supplied by Joshua, the men began. There was much hilarity exchanged between them as they worked. As one of them said to Maggie, 'This is much better than doing army chores with a bad-tempered sergeant watching over you.'

The two women made numerous pots of tea and sandwiches to keep them going, but at one o'clock in the morning, Joshua walked over to them both. Putting an arm around Maggie's shoulders he said, 'You and your mother should go to bed. You have to go to work and Moira has to get the bar ready for opening tonight.' He tilted her chin and kissed her slowly. 'I'll see that everything's all right. And . . . I'll be here when you wake up.'

She put her arms around his neck and looked up at him, the love she felt for him shining out for everyone to see. 'Don't work too hard,' she said and kissed him goodnight.

The following morning, Maggie was awakened by the smell of bacon wafting up the stairs. Feeling ravenous, she quickly washed and dressed, putting on her dungarees ready for the factory, and ran down to the kitchen. There, Joshua and her mother were cooking eggs and bacon and making toast. The boys who'd been working in the bar were sitting around the table, stuffing themselves.

'Hi, Maggie, come on in and get something to eat.'

She looked at her mother, who grinned at her. 'Not only do we have a workforce, but they brought their own food with them. Sit down, darlin', or you'll be late for work.'

One of the boys poured her a cup of tea, saying with a wide grin, 'I'm getting real worried, Maggie, honey. I'm actually beginning to like this stuff!'

She laughed at the look of mock horror on his face. 'I can't begin to thank you all enough,' she said.

'Any time, Maggie. Anyway we're not quite finished, there's just a few little touches, that's all. By lunchtime, we'll be gone.'

'I can't wait to see it.'

She made to get up from the table, but Joshua was behind her and put his hand on her shoulder, saying, 'Now you just finish your breakfast or there'll be no time before you go to work.' He kissed the top of her head and sat beside her.

She looked at him and said, 'You look tired.' She looked around at the others. 'You all look as fresh as daisies!'

Joshua laughed. 'It's because I had to keep this lot working.'

'Yeah,' said another. 'He wouldn't let us rest for a moment. A hard man, this Corporal Lewis is. God knows what he'll be like as a sergeant!'

She looked at Joshua with an expression of surprise. 'A sergeant?'

He looked a mite embarrassed. 'I've been promoted.'

'That's just great,' she said, thrilled for him.

'The army's rewarding him for getting that Rossi put away,' said one of the men.

'Maggie's not interested in hearing about that,' he said quickly. Seeing she'd finished her breakfast he said, 'Come with me and take a look at the bar.'

She followed him. As she stepped into the room from the hallway she gasped in surprise. It didn't look the same place at all. Everything was pristine and clean. The walls were light and bright, the window frames had been painted and the ceiling was now white, all traces of nicotine removed. It made the area seem much bigger. They had even put a fresh coat of varnish on the bar.

She turned to him. 'Oh, Joshua, thank you so much.' She flung her arms around him and rained kisses on him.

He held her at bay after a moment. 'Hey, you're not playing fair,' he said. 'You smother me with kisses and then you take off for work.'

She ran a finger over his mouth. 'Well, it wouldn't make much difference would it?' she said archly. 'You are always in such control of your feelings.'

He gazed down into her eyes. 'You think that's easy for me?' he quietly asked.

'I don't really know. You tell me.'

He held her close and caressed her cheek. 'I want you more than anything in this world,' he said. 'I long to take you into my arms and make love to you. The thought of it keeps me awake at night.'

'Don't you realize that I feel the same?'

His searching gaze looked deep into her eyes as if he needed confirmation. 'Honestly? Do you really want me too?'

She caught hold of his hand and placed it on her breast. 'So badly, that I ache to be in your arms.' As he went to protest she shushed him.

'We'll just have to wait for the right time. I must fly or I'll be late for work.' She walked back to the kitchen and said, 'I don't know how to thank you, boys, you've done a grand job. The next time you come in, the first drink is on the house.'

They all cheered. And Moira smiled.

'I'll see you later, Mum,' said Maggie as she kissed her on the cheek and left for work.

When she returned later that day, it was to see the front of the Bricklayer's Arms covered in bunting and a large notice which read, *Under New Management*. She chuckled with glee, and entered the side door.

Moira greeted her as she walked into the kitchen. 'Did you like the flags?'

Maggie hugged her mother. 'It all looks so good. I hope we have a good night.'

'To be sure,' said Moira, 'there'll be no spare room. Word has got about that you now have the licence and everyone's coming.' She looked at Maggie. 'That Joshua has been wonderful. I can see why you think so much of him.'

'I'm glad you understand. It means a great deal to me.'

That night, the bar of the Bricklayer's Arms was packed to capacity. Ivy, who had come to join in the celebrations, was roped in to help behind the bar, and the place buzzed. The pianist had been hired and the pub rang with the sound of voices. 'Roll me over in the clover, roll me over lay me down and do it again', sang the locals, much to Maggie's amusement.

Joshua arrived at nine o'clock and was greeted warmly by the customers, who knew that he and his men had done all the hard work and, being concerned for the welfare of Maggie and her mother, were grateful to the GI for his help. They all wanted to ply him with drinks. He accepted one or two, buying drinks back for the locals, which went down well with the men.

They tried to teach him how to play darts, and there was much joshing and teasing until he got his eye in and started hitting the right spot on the dart board.

Nobby Clarke, who was his partner, was highly delighted. 'You'd better join the darts team, lad. With a bit of practice you'd be quite useful.'

At last, closing time arrived and Maggie rang the bell. She and Ivy, Moira and Joshua cleared up the mess. Ivy called a taxi and went home, and Moira made some Ovaltine and wished Maggie and Joshua goodnight, going upstairs to her room and leaving them alone in the kitchen.

'I was real proud of you tonight,' he said, pulling Maggie onto his knee. You'll make a good landlady.'

'I'm glad for Mum's sake,' she said. 'At least I've secured a future for her.' She gazed at Joshua, her expression one of uncertainty. 'But I'm wondering about mine.'

'What do you mean?'

'When you eventually leave.' Tears welled in her eyes. 'I can't bear the thought of you going away.'

'Neither can I, darling. I don't want to leave you, ever.'

'Oh, Joshua. What are we going to do?'

'We could always get married.'

His proposal took her by surprise. 'Do you really mean that?'

'Of course I do. I'm in love with you, Maggie. If I get shipped out I don't want to have to say goodbye and never see you again . . . but it wouldn't be easy. You know how people react to mixed marriages. There would be great opposition. I don't know how your mother would feel about it, or your father.'

Maggie closed her eyes in despair. 'My father would go mad! Mother, maybe not, I don't know. But what about your own family?'

'My father's a pretty broadminded guy, but this might throw him. Remember where I come from.' He stroked her hair. 'Why are we worrying about other people? It's how we feel that's important. We love each other, but you have to really think about the consequences. It won't be a piece of cake.'

159

She leaned forward and kissed him. 'I don't care! I love you, Joshua. I don't want to lose you.'

He cupped her face in his hands and kissed her passionately. 'You'll never do that, I promise, but I think we need to tread carefully.'

'What do you mean?'

'Let's keep this to ourselves for a while, get people used to seeing us together. Then, when the time is right, I'll go to the captain and get the necessary details and documentation.'

He frowned and Maggie asked, 'What is it?'

He let out a sigh. 'Getting permission ordinarily isn't that simple, but with us, it's going to be more difficult.' Then he smiled at her. 'As long as we love each other enough, then we'll face such things when the time comes.'

'What will we do when the war is over? Where will we live?'

'Hey, slow down. Let's wait. No one knows how long the war is going to last. When it's over, then we'll make plans. OK?'

She entwined her arms around his neck. 'Whatever you say, sergeant.'

As she climbed into bed that night, Maggie was filled with happiness. Yes, Joshua might be shipped out eventually, but at least she knew that in the end they'd be together. She desperately wanted to share her joy with her mother, but realized the wisdom of the man she loved. In time, the sight of them together would become accepted, and hopefully that would make things easier . . . except for her father. That would be a huge problem to face.

Moira walked towards the prison gates, her pass clutched tightly in her hand, her heart racing. This was her first visit to Winchester Prison. She felt her stomach tighten as the prison gates clanged shut behind her. Handing over her pass, she was sent to the waiting room.

The room was full. The atmosphere was charged as she sat among women alone, others with children. There were one or two older men, maybe waiting to see a son, she guessed.

At two o'clock they were ushered across the cobblestone courtyard into a large room with tables and chairs. At one end were cubicles, and she wondered what they were for.

The woman sitting beside her saw her expression of curiosity and said, 'That's for the lifers.'

Moira nodded, then sat twiddling her gloves with a feeling of shame, not wanting to look at anyone.

There was a sound of footsteps as the assortment of men entered the room from within the prison. She looked up and saw Jack limping towards her. He looked pale and tense.

'You came then!'

'What's that supposed to mean?' she snapped, angered by his attitude. 'I wrote and told you that I would.'

'I'd have thought you'd have better things to do.' He glared at her, his lips drawn in a tight, bad-tempered line. 'Well, did she get the licence?'

Incensed by him, Moira said, 'Yes of course she did. The brewers could see that she was trustworthy and competent. They're not fools!'

'Not like me, is that what you mean?'

'You've changed you bloody tune, haven't you? Last time I saw you, you were full of apologies for all the trouble you caused.'

'Well I hadn't been banged up in this hellhole then.'

Moira sat bolt upright, her back stiff with anger. 'Now you listen to me, Jack Evans. You're here because you did wrong. No one asked you to get mixed up with Sonny Taylor, and if you'd listened to me and our Maggie, you wouldn't be here now. You'd still have a pub to run!'

'Oh yes, it was all my fault.'

Moira looked at him in amazement. 'If it wasn't down to you, I'd like to know just who you blame . . . And don't you dare say you did it for me, because as God is my judge, I wanted none of it.'

There was a sudden flush of guilt on his face. 'I know, I know,' he said, calming down as he took out a cigarette and lit it. 'When did Maggie officially take over?'

'Yesterday – and you wouldn't believe how busy we were.' Moira couldn't stem her enthusiasm. 'Some of Maggie's friends from the 552nd Port Company came and painted the bar. It looks lovely,' she said with a broad, beaming smile.

'That's the niggers' company! What the hell were they doing painting my pub?'

Moira cursed her runaway tongue. But she wasn't going to lie to him. He was going to have to know about Maggie and Joshua sooner or later. 'They were all charming young men. They worked hard, all through the night, to get it done. And it isn't *your* pub any longer!'

He let the jibe pass. 'But I don't understand. How did they come to be there?'

Taking a deep breath, Moira said, 'Maggie is friendly with one of the sergeants.'

'She's still going out with the Yank then?'

Moira was beginning to wish she'd left well alone, but now was the opportunity to put things straight. She'd seen the love shared between Maggie and Joshua, and if necessary she'd stand by her daughter against anyone, as long as she was happy.

'This is a different GI,' she said, 'the son of a preacher, a nice lad.'

Jack's eyes narrowed. 'Are you telling me that my daughter is going out with a darkie?'

'Yes.'

'Well, she's no daughter of mine. I'd be ashamed to own her!'

'Strange that, isn't it Jack? I've never heard Maggie say she was ashamed of her father being a gaol bird!' She stood up. 'If you feel like that when you've served your time, I assume you'll be making your own arrangements. You certainly won't want to come and live with us if you feel that way about Maggie. And after all, she is the licensee.' She walked out of the room before he could answer, leaving him sitting there, open-mouthed.

Moira walked to the station, seething with rage. How dare he talk like that about his own daughter – the girl who stepped in and saved the day and her future. As far as Jack was concerned, she could have been out on the street with no place to go, all because of his lust for money. Joshua Lewis was more of a man than her husband could ever be, and as far as she was concerned, Jack Evans could go to hell! Maggie was the one she worried about. And if she was forced to choose between them, it would be no contest.

Chapter Nineteen

The following weeks went by quickly enough. The pub was doing well, the brewers were pleased and Joshua Lewis was now firmly established as the man in Maggie's life.

Working at the Bricklayer's Arms and the factory didn't give Maggie much free time, so Ivy came to serve in the bar some evenings, to help Moira and to allow Maggie a night off to spend with Joshua.

One evening when he called to take her out, Moira was in a state because a close friend of hers had had an accident and she had offered to go and stay the night.

Maggie quickly changed her plans and stepped in. With Ivy's help, she ran the bar until closing time. She'd insisted that Joshua go and spend the evening with his friends instead of hanging around, wasting his free time. So he went, returning to help them just before closing time.

'I'll get us some sandwiches,' Maggie said to him when they were alone at last. 'Come through to the kitchen.'

As she cut the bread, he stood behind her, his hands round her waist, kissing the back of her neck, caressing her bosom.

'Stop it, I'll cut myself,' she protested.

'For goodness' sake, put the darned knife down will you! I haven't seen you for thirty-six hours.'

She did so and turned to face him. 'I'm sorry about —' she began, but she could say no more as he covered her mouth with his own, kissing her ardently, caressing her softly, until she returned his passion with hers.

When at last he released her, she said, 'About tonight, I'm sorry everything was messed up. What time do you have to be back at the base? How long do we have?'

He gazed into her eyes. 'We don't have any rush, honey. I've got an all-night pass.'

'You do?'

'Mm. So we don't have to worry. We even have time for those darned sandwiches, if you really insist.'

'But I thought you'd be hungry,' she said, giving a mischievous grin.

'I'm sure hungry, but it ain't for food.'

She gently put her finger to his lips, and cried out as he pretended to bite on it. 'You know, darling, I've got an all-night pass too. Mum is away.'

'Are you trying to lead me astray, young lady?'

'Yes please,' she said, 'this is the opportunity we've been waiting for. It would be a pity to waste it.' Taking him by the hand she led him upstairs to her bedroom, closing the door behind them.

He took her into his arms. 'I really do love you, Maggie,' he whispered against her hair.

'I know, and I love you too.' She reached up and kissed him eagerly.

'I've waited so long for this moment,' said Joshua. 'Dreamed of holding you close, making love to you.'

She stepped out of his embrace and unbuttoned her dress, letting it slip to the ground. He helped her remove her underwear until she stood naked before him.

He smoothed her soft skin, as he gazed at her.

'You are so beautiful,' he said, as he kissed her shoulders, her neck, her ears, her mouth.

She undid his tie and cast it aside. He took off his shirt, trousers, his olive green singlet, his socks and lastly his underpants. Maggie looked at his fine frame standing before her and thought he should be cast in bronze, he was so perfect a picture of manhood.

They lay on the bed, close together, exchanging embraces, discovering the delights of each other's body, both wanting the night to be memorable.

Joshua was a gentle, thoughtful lover, whispering in his deep voice, telling the woman in his arms how much she meant to him, how much he desired her.

'I'll always take care of you, darling,' he said. 'We'll have a great future together. We'll be real happy, just like my parents, you'll see.'

Maggie caressed his broad shoulders, kissing him with a passion that showed just how much she wanted him. 'I love you more than anything else in the world,' she whispered. 'Nothing is going to keep us apart.'

Joshua insisted on wearing a condom to protect her, saying, 'The last thing we need is for you to become pregnant before we get married. There'll be plenty of time for a family after.'

'Mrs Maggie Lewis,' she said. 'I like the sound of that.'

He caressed and kissed her, teased her, until the longing for him to take her was almost unbearable. But as she felt him inside her at last, she wanted desperately to have his baby, to have something that was part of him, of their love for one another, but she realized the wisdom of his words. One day she would hold his child. And she was content to wait.

At long last they slept, entwined in each other's arms, content in their love for one another.

When her mother returned to the pub the next day, Joshua had already left. Maggie made Moira a cup of tea and asked after her friend.

'Poor soul,' she said. 'She slipped and broke her ankle. Her daughter couldn't get down from Cheltenham until today. She's taking Elsie home with her until it's better, so that's a relief. I'm sorry I mucked up your night out with Joshua.'

Maggie felt the colour rise in her cheeks. 'It was all right, I didn't mind. He went out with some of his mates, but he came back before closing time to help us.' She looked straight at her mother. 'He stayed the night.'

'I see,' said Moira. 'It's that serious then?'

'Yes, Mum. Joshua has asked me to marry him and I've said yes.' At the look of consternation on her mother's face, Maggie said, 'If I can't have him, I don't want anyone.' She waited, tense with nerves. She would marry him, but she really wanted Moira's blessing.

Her mother stretched out her hand and took Maggie's in hers. 'If you feel that strongly about him, then no one has the right to interfere.'

Maggie flung her arms around her. 'Oh thank you, Mum. I don't care about Dad, but I really wanted you to understand. We know there will be problems, but we're prepared for that. For the moment, though, we'll keep the fact that we intend to marry to ourselves. We want people to get used to us being together.'

Moira thought that was a good idea. 'When you can pick the day is the time to make it public,' she suggested. Then she added, after a moment's hesitation, 'If you're going to marry the boy, then I suppose it's all right for him to stay at night, when he can. After all, you're more or less engaged.'

Maggie was taken aback by her mother's liberal view, but then she'd always been somewhat different from most women. Still, knowing how strongly held were her views, about the two different cultures mixing, Maggie admired her change of heart. It just proved to her the strength of a mother's love.

Although Maggie and Joshua were happy in their love for each other, it was not without its down side. Their relationship, now out in the open, caused a great deal of gossip. People took sides. Angry words were exchanged in private . . . and in public. Human nature being what it was, those who wanted Maggie's happiness gave her no trouble, but for others the relationship was distasteful, and these people made their feelings known to all and sundry. One or two spoke out to Maggie herself.

'How can you bring yourself to consort with a black man?' one of the men asked one day when the bar was quiet. 'If you were my daughter I'd take my belt to you!'

Maggie's nostrils flared. 'Well I'm not your daughter and I'll thank you to mind your own business!' she retorted.

Another spoke up: 'It's not right. What's wrong with your own kind?'

'Now you listen to me,' said Maggie. 'I don't tell you how to run your life, don't you dare try and interfere with mine.'

Later that night a group of women sat in the corner of the bar, talking in low voices. 'Well I think it's bloody disgusting!' said one. She grimaced. 'Imagine those black hands touching you. Ugh! It makes me shudder.'

Another, called Edie, grinned slyly. 'You know what they say, don't you? Black men are very well endowed.' The others looked at her with interest. She leaned closer. 'I was told that a nigger's dick is usually huge.'

They turned and looked at Maggie, each thinking her own dirty thoughts. One turned back to the woman. 'Ask her if it's true. Go on. It's your turn to get the drinks in anyway. Ask her. I dare you!'

Edie glared at the faces all turned towards her.

'Or are you all mouth?' taunted her friend.

Picking up the empty glasses, Edie strode over to the bar and asked Maggie for four halves of bitter. When she returned with the full glasses, the woman asked quietly, 'Could you settle an argument for us?'

Maggie, completely unaware, smiled and said, 'If I can.'

Edie leaned over the counter and said, 'It's a bit personal. I don't want the men to hear.'

Maggie put her head close to the woman's.

'Well . . . me and my friends have heard that the dick of a black man is really big. Is it true?'

Maggie's head shot back and she looked at her customer with a shocked expression, then with one of anger. 'Go and wash your mouth out,' she snapped, 'and at the same time, swill your filthy mind.' She glared at Edie, and over her head at the others, then she walked around the counter and crossed to the women who were sitting at the table smirking, waiting for an answer.

'It seems, ladies, and I use the term loosely, that you're interested in my sex life! Well it's none of your business and I'll thank you to keep your dirty little minds to yourselves.'

'Now look here,' said one, 'that's no way to talk to your customers.'

Maggie froze her with a look. 'You keep a civil tongue in your heads if you want to drink in my pub or I'll bar the lot of you!' She stomped back behind the bar.

Nobby Clarke had overheard some of the exchange and said quietly to Maggie, 'That's all they've got to do, love, is gossip about someone. And after all, girl, you must expect it.'

She pressed her lips together stubbornly. 'It's still nobody's business but mine.'

He gave a sardonic grin. 'Come on, Maggie, you know better than that.

In a local pub everyone knows everyone else's business and has an opinion about it. You must expect the flak.'

She walked away to serve another customer. Nobby was right of course, but such smutty talk made her relationship with Joshua sound sordid . . . and it wasn't.

Strangely, most of the men seemed to accept the American more easily than the women. They saw in him a man of pride and intelligence. He was easy to talk to and was, in their minds, a real man. They admired his skill at the piano, his sense of humour, and easily exchanged quips with him. In a male way, he got on well with them and they with him. In private, however, talking to their wives, now aware that the GI sometimes stayed the night, they didn't feel so at ease with the thought of him sharing a bed with Maggie.

Joshua was not unaware of the hostility of a few of the customers. With those, he kept himself to himself. It was Maggie that he was worried about, and the effect the gossip was having on her. But when he approached her on the subject, her stubborn chin stuck out.

'This is my pub! If they don't like it they can drink elsewhere! I'm not hiding our relationship. I'm not ashamed of it . . . are you?'

He took her into his arms. 'Of course not, how could you even think so? I love you. But it breaks me up to see the looks some of them give you, and the way they whisper behind your back. All because of me.'

She gazed up at him and said softly, 'Joshua Lewis, you're worth more than any of them. No one is going to spoil what we have.' She pulled his face down to hers and kissed him passionately.

The winter of 1944 was a severe one, with a chronic shortage of coal. Maggie managed to get a supply of logs from a farmer who had felled some trees on his land. But the threat of war was still hanging over everyone when the Germans continued their raids over London with the new V2 rockets. Everyone in Southampton wondered if they too would be faced by these terrifying weapons. Fortunately they escaped them, apart from two attacks from the V1 flying bombs, popularly known as doodlebugs. Happily there were no fatalities, but everyone's heart was heavy when in late November one of the rockets scored a direct hit on a Woolworth's store in New Cross, killing 160 people.

Maggie was upset when she read the news and asked Joshua, rather scathingly, 'If there is a God, how can he let this happen?'

Seeing the anguish in her expression he put his arm around her and softly said, 'I don't know, honey, I haven't got all the answers. All I can tell you is that without my faith in the Lord, I wouldn't have survived all these years.'

She snuggled into him. 'Oh, Joshua. If only I could be as certain as you.'

'No one can make you believe, Maggie. It's something you feel in your heart. Even non-believers turn to God in times of trouble. Some of the most hardened soldiers start to pray as they go into battle. There must be something there.'

There was much excitement all round as Christmas approached. Joshua was able to help them out with some food, as whenever any troops were invited into a civilian's home, it was army policy to allow them to take goods with them.

Moira had managed to get enough ingredients together to make a cake, and between them all they decorated the bar with old paper chains from the loft and the pub looked very festive.

Joshua's company gave the local children a Christmas party and a bag of sweets each, saved from the soldiers' weekly ration. Gifts of Canadian apples arrived and even a few bananas. One of the white officers acted as Father Christmas, figuring the children would comment if Santa Claus had a black face.

Maggie had been invited along. She joined in all the games and watched with delight as Joshua played with the children, crawling around the floor with two little ones on his back, giving piggy-back rides to the bigger ones. They all loved it. She thought how wonderful it would be when he'd be able to hold their child in his arms.

They all sang nursery rhymes and played Piggy in the Middle and Blind Man's Buff, the children having a high old time with Joshua in the middle of the room, hands outstretched, trying to find a quarry.

In the military court, Steve Rossi stood before the panel of American officers and heard the sentence. He was to to serve two years in an army prison, after which he would be shipped home, in disgrace.

He marched out of the courtroom with an arrogant glance at the men who had passed sentence on him, but inside he was seething, cursing beneath his breath.

During the forthcoming weeks in the prison, he watched every movement of all the departments, looking for a way out. He monitored the incoming army trucks bringing the food and medical supplies. The laundry from the nearby army camp was sent here to be washed by the inmates and at last, one day, he saw a possible way of escape. If he was very smart, he figured he could do it. But he would have to bide his time and pick the right moment. Timing was everything. Already, though, he was in the right place. He'd been given a job in the laundry.

Christmas Day was busy. The bar was open for a couple of hours, but closed for the evening. The pub was packed with locals, drinking and singing whilst the Christmas dinner was cooking. It was traditional to go to the pub in the morning, and no wife with any sense would plan to eat before closing time.

Nobby Clarke and his wife were in good form, Nobby playing darts with his mates, Grace singing at the top of her voice. He came over to the bar to order more beer and smiled at Maggie. 'You're doing a grand job here, girl. I take my hat off to you. Have you seen your father? What does he think about it all?'

Maggie shook her head. 'He doesn't approve of my association with Joshua, so there's no point my seeing him, I'd only have to listen to him going on about it.'

'What a pity,' said Nobby. 'That Joshua is a grand chap, even if he's black. But being a father myself . . .'

Maggie didn't take offence. 'I know. But I love him, you see, and love is colour-blind.'

'Yes, my dear, love is a very powerful emotion. It can be good and it can be destructive. You just take care, that's all.'

Ivy was in good spirits. As she was still living alone, without a steady boyfriend, she had been invited to stay on after closing time and partake of the Christmas dinner. She was invaluable behind the bar with her quick wit and speed at the beer pumps. The regulars liked her.

She beamed across at Maggie. 'This isn't a bad life, you know. When the war's over, I wouldn't mind a job as a barmaid. Plenty of company . . . you meet lots of men.'

'I'd have thought you'd have had enough of them,' teased her friend.

'Don't be daft!' She sipped a gin and tonic someone had bought her. 'You know me, Mags. I always like to have someone interested. In a bar I can flirt without getting too involved . . . unless I want to.'

'And you want to.'

Ivy pulled a face. 'I miss the sex,' she confessed. 'Ever since Bob left, I've been a bloody saint. What I really need is a good seeing to.'

'Ivy! You're incorrigible.'

Her friend sidled up to her. 'Listen you. You're all right. You get plenty of it with Joshua.' As Maggie blushed she continued. 'And I'm happy for you. Sex is healthy – but I'm getting very frustrated!'

Later, at closing time, Maggie saw Ivy enjoying herself under the mistletoe with several willing customers and smiled. She was such a character. But she was happy to see her bouncing back after her ordeal with her husband and her lover.

The Christmas dinner was a happy occasion. Moira had managed to buy a small turkey and Joshua had arrived that morning bearing gifts which were opened after they'd eaten and listened to the King's speech. He'd

169

bought a scarf and some American chocolates for Moira, nylons for Ivy, who was delighted, and for Maggie, a gold locket on a chain.

She slipped it around her neck and smiled at her lover. 'I'll put a picture of you in it,' she told him. She had some snapshots taken during the summer. She could use one of those. She handed him a gift.

He opened it eagerly and was thrilled to find a book about New Orleans and the jazz musicians that played there. There was also a record of Duke Ellington and his music.

His eyes shone with pleasure. 'I'll cherish these,' he said. His eyes twinkled as he held up the record. 'Maybe there's hope for you after all.'

'Maybe not,' she laughed. 'I still like Frank Sinatra. I haven't changed that much.'

He held her close to him. 'Wait until you come to a few clubdates with me when we're married,' he said. 'Then you'll hear real music.'

After the others had exchanged gifts, they sat and drank a cup of coffee before Ivy said, 'I'll wash up. It's the least I can do.'

Moira insisted she helped, leaving Joshua and Maggie alone to sit in the front room. As she explained to Ivy, 'He has to be on duty at five o'clock. It'll give them some time together.'

'It's been one of the nicest Christmases ever,' he said as Maggie snuggled down in his arms, fingering her locket.

'I'm so happy you enjoyed it,' she answered. Turning, she put an arm around his neck and kissed him. But there was a sudden sadness about her expression that he immediately noticed.

'What is it?'

She looked at him and said, 'I was only wondering where you'll be this time next year.'

'Come on, honey,' he said. 'Cheer up. By that time the war will be over, we'll probably be married and settled down somewhere.'

'I do hope so.' She looked at the clock on the mantelpiece. 'You'd better be off,' she said reluctantly, 'or you'll be late back.'

Joshua went to the scullery and thanked the others for their gifts. He walked with Maggie to the front door, where he took her into his arms. 'This war can't last for ever, darling. We'll be together real soon, you'll see.'

She watched him walk down the street and waved as he turned the corner. Looking across at the houses opposite she could see all sorts of family gatherings through the windows and for once she thought of her father. She wondered what he was doing behind prison bars, and was filled with pity for him.

Chapter Twenty

In the laundry of the military prison Steve Rossi wiped the sweat away from his forehead. His singlet was soaked with perspiration too. The steam from the presses that ironed the damp sheets filled the air, making it like a Turkish bath. He hated it here. Fastidious about his appearance, he knew he reeked of sweat. He was allowed to shower at night, but every day was the same.

Gone were his dreams of a big business, of being able to show his father just what a successful man he was. He would be sent home in disgrace . . . a failure. His hot temper had already got him into trouble, adding more months to his sentence, but he had a plan. He had no intention of staying in this hellhole for very much longer.

Every day a big army truck arrived with the dirty laundry from several of the army camps nearby, taking with them on the return journey the clean linen, stacked in large wicker trolleys. He intended that one of the trucks would take him out in the back of it, as soon as the opportunity presented itself.

He smirked to himself as he pressed yet another sheet and folded it. He'd got it all worked out, and when he was free he'd go looking for that bitch and her boyfriend. He was going to settle the score there all right. Maggie Evans was his. Wasn't he the one who took her lovely little cherry? He grinned with satisfaction at the memory. Well, he'd have her again. Christ! He hadn't had a woman since he'd been shut up inside this place and he ached for sex. Masturbation wasn't the same, not the same at all. He closed his eyes as he thought of the feel of her soft flesh, her open legs, and he felt the movement in his loins as he imagined himself thrusting deep inside her.

'Rossi!' one of the soldiers in charge called. 'Get on with your work!'

Steve cursed. The regime in here was harsh. Every morning they were on a parade ground, marching before breakfast, then they dispersed to do whatever job had been assigned. The army had no time for prisoners and worked them until they crawled into their bunks at night, exhausted. That way, they figured there would be less trouble. Well that was fine with him. He was fit and he was tough, but soon they'd have one less to think about.

Jack Evans sat in his cell, alone, after dinner on Christmas Day, wondering

171

what was going on at the Bricklayer's Arms. He remembered previous Christmases. The bar would be packed as usual, plenty of singing, plenty of beer, an entirely different atmosphere than inside this Godforsaken place.

He admitted to himself, as he smoked a cigarette, that his incarceration had been his own fault. He realized how badly he'd let Moira down and how grateful he should be to Maggie. And he was now scared that when at last he was free he'd have nowhere to go.

Moira was still angry with him. She'd come to see him just before Christmas, but she'd been so cold towards him that it was like talking to a stranger. He longed to tell her how sorry he was and make things right, but he realized that things between them would never be the same.

Deep down he was proud of Maggie, the way she'd stepped in and taken over the licence, and cursed his own foolishness – on occasion. And as the days passed he became more and more depressed. Life inside His Majesty's Prison was no life at all. There were some very dangerous people here; people doing life for murder, for grievous bodily harm; and sexual offenders, as well as petty criminals.

He'd learned very quickly to keep his head down and stay out of trouble. Thankfully his age and disability kept him safe from sexual advances, but many of the young men were in real danger. The screws turned a blind eye to so much, to keep the place peaceful. It was like sitting on the edge of a volcano, waiting for it to erupt.

Only the other day a couple of the old queens had a fight over a new inmate, a pretty boy of twenty. He'd never forget the look of terror in the lad's eyes as he stood, pressed against the wall, petrified. It was at such times he realized just how much he'd thrown away.

He tried to come to terms with Maggie and her boyfriend, knowing if he was ever to return to his home, he'd have to accept whatever the situation was, but for him that was very difficult. In his eyes, people should stick to their own kind. Not just their own racial kind, either; Catholics should marry Catholics, Jews should stick with Jews. The basic cultural differences only led to trouble. That was the way he'd been brought up. He blamed the war. Without all these foreigners around, life would not be so complicated. Wives wouldn't be lonely without their menfolk around, wouldn't be tempted into having a fling. Without the war . . . he wouldn't be here sitting in this cold cell, wasting his life.

A few days later, he was surprised to be told he had a visitor, and even more surprised to see Maggie sitting waiting for him. He sat opposite her, embarrassed that she should see him in his prison clothes, wondering what she was thinking.

Maggie had made the decision to see her father after Christmas Day.

Although she couldn't forgive him for letting her mother down, she remembered the good times, when she was a child, when he was a happy man and when she was close to him, and she felt a little guilty that she'd stayed away. She'd talked to Joshua about it and he'd persuaded her that it was the time to forgive and forget.

As he'd said, 'Bitterness only festers inside, it's like something bad that grows and grows until it seeps into your soul. We all need forgiveness for something at some time in our lives.'

And so she was here; but she was really nervous. She knew well his bigoted attitude, and now that she and Joshua planned to marry in the future, she was more than a little concerned about Jack's reaction.

'Hello, Dad,' she said, shocked by his prison pallor. 'How are you?'

'Not so bad,' he said. 'Congratulations on getting the licence. Your mum tells me the pub is doing well.'

'Yes, it is.' How stilted their conversation was, she thought, but it wasn't easy for either of them to act naturally.

'I believe your friend had the place painted up.'

'Yes, and they made a very good job of it.' She saw the tightening of his jaw as he spoke and, knowing him as well as she did, realized he would find this a difficult thing to accept, knowing who the workforce had been.

'My friend Joshua arranged for them to do it, he supplied the paint too, so it didn't cost a penny.' At least that ought to please him!

'So, who is this Joshua chap?'

'He's a sergeant in the US Army.'

There was a bitter twist to his mouth as he said, 'You seem to go in for sergeants, don't you?'

Maggie could feel her anger beginning to rise inside. Her father always seemed to have this effect on her . . . nothing had changed. But she was determined to stand her ground.

'Joshua Lewis is a fine man,' she said determinedly. 'I don't expect you to like him, because of his colour, and that's a shame, because he's intelligent, talented, and he loves me.' She saw the narrowing of Jack's mouth, but ignored it. 'We plan to get married sometime in the future.'

'You what!' he yelled. The people around them turned and stared at the loud remark.

'You heard me, Dad. We're in love. Do you remember what that was like? Did you ever love my mother?'

This completely shook him. 'Of course I did! What sort of a question is that?'

'Then if you did, try and remember just how it felt.' She saw the look of embarrassment on his face and hoped for once she'd be able to get through to him. 'We want to spend the rest of our lives together.'

'But Maggie, the man's black.'

'I know that, Dad. And I know that things won't be easy for us, but we're prepared to face all that – even if it's against my own father's wishes.'

Jack looked at the stubborn expression on his daughter's face and knew whatever he said wouldn't change a thing. 'I can't help the way I feel, Maggie. And if you insist on this, you'll find life far more difficult than you can possibly imagine.'

'I've already had to cope with prejudice, Dad. Joshua has had to cope with it all his life, but he's a lovely man. I don't want anyone else.'

He shook his head. 'I don't know what to say. I just can't bear the idea – not my own daughter.' He took a cigarette out of a packet and lit it.

Maggie changed the subject. 'When does your case come up? Have you heard?'

'In a couple of weeks' time, so I'm told.'

'Is it awful in here?' she asked.

'Pretty grim, but let's face it, it's my own fault.' He looked somewhat shamefaced as he said, 'I'm sorry I let you and your mother down. If I hadn't, your life wouldn't be in the mess it is.'

He cheeks flamed with anger. 'You haven't understood a word I've said, have you! I love this man and, like it or not, I'm going to marry him and you'd better get used to the idea, Dad.'

He didn't answer.

She rose from her chair. 'There really isn't any more to be said, is there?' She waited but there was silence.

She turned and walked away.

On the journey home, Maggie wondered just what would happen when her father had served his time. She couldn't see him without a home, which meant that there would be trouble on his return. Well, she just wouldn't have it. She was the landlady now, she'd chosen Joshua as her man and her father would have to behave – or else!

She tried to talk it over with her mother when she arrived home.

Moira was furious at his attitude. 'I can't forget that, without you, I could be homeless and penniless. I'm glad that he realizes his mistake, and I'm sorry that he's where he is. It terrifies me when I go there, and it must be a thousand times worse for him. But the least he could do is to see your side of things. That is typical of Jack Evans, though.'

Maggie put her arm around her mother. 'Yes, I'm afraid it is. But when eventually he's free, this is his home. I can't turn my own father away, can I?'

'Sure and where else would the silly sod go,' conceded Moira.

But Maggie knew that when that time came, things would not be easy. Apart from her own situation, there were too many recriminations left in the air. Moira still felt bitter and some of the customers, too, felt angry towards Jack. Oh well, thought Maggie. That would give them something else to chew over for a change! She was fed up with being the subject of their gossiping.

In the military prison where Steve Rossi was incarcerated it had been a busy afternoon with extra work for everyone as two companies had been out on manoeuvres and the battle fatigues, covered in mud, had to be washed. This had entailed the use of two army trucks to bring in the laundry. One of the washing machines had broken down and everyone was working under pressure to get it all finished.

During the rush and confusion to load the lorries, Rossi had hidden at the back of one of them, inside a wicker basket where he'd piled clean linen on top of himself. He held his breath hoping he wouldn't be discovered.

Eventually, to his great relief, he heard the engine start and felt the vehicle move away. It paused at the base entrance gates and a sentry peered inside the truck. Steve let out a sigh of relief as he heard the order to proceed.

It was Friday night and pay day. The Bricklayer's Arms had been busy as usual. The locals still milled around outside after closing time, chatting, whilst in the bar Maggie and her mother cleared the glasses and swept the floor.

Outside in an alleyway hid Steve Rossi, cursing to himself about the small groups of men, laughing and talking, wanting them to go home so he could try and find a way to enter the pub unobserved.

Eventually, one by one, they wandered off and Steve emerged from the dark into the empty street. He tried the doors to the pub but they were securely locked, then wandered along to the gate that led to the gents' toilet. The gate was open. He walked up the alleyway and into the toilet. He stood in front of one of the urinals and relieved himself, looking around to see if there was a back way out. Then he heard footsteps and quickly hid himself in a cubicle, closing the door to.

Maggie made her way to the toilets to put out the lights before she locked the gate. She turned up her nose at the smell of stale vomit and looked around to see where it came from. 'Damn,' she muttered. She'd best go and get a bucket of disinfectant and swill it away now, or by the morning it would be hard to shift. She turned away and was about to walk outside when she was grabbed from behind, a hand over her mouth to stop her screaming. She stiffened with terror as she heard the familiar voice.

'Hello, honey. How you doing? I bet you thought you'd seen the last of me.'

Steve spun her round and grinned broadly as he saw the fear reflected in her eyes. 'Not happy to see me? Now that is a disappointment. Well, baby, I'm sure glad to see you. I haven't held a woman in my arms for far too long.' He grabbed hold of a handful of her hair, trapping her head with his grasp and covered her mouth with his, kissing her roughly, his tongue making her choke.

Recovering from her shock, Maggie tried to push him away with all her might, but he still held her tightly.

'What are you doing here?' she asked. 'I thought they had you safely behind bars – where you deserve to be.'

His cruel laugh echoed around the empty room. 'My God you're a spunky broad, I'll say that for you.' Then the expression on his face changed as he glared at her. 'All the time I've been inside, I've thought of you.' He ran his hand over her breast, pulling her close with his other arm. As she struggled he put his hand between her legs. 'I remember this very well,' he said.

Maggie started to pound him with her fists, but he caught them in one hand and gripped them tightly behind her back, pushing her against a urinal. With his other hand he pulled up her skirt. 'Remember how good we used to be together, honey? Well, tonight will be the best ever. You'll be able to tell that black son of a bitch all about it. He won't want you then.'

Maggie went berserk, kicking out and catching Rossi in the shins. He yelled at the pain and let her go. She made for the door, but was dragged back inside and thrown to the floor.

She felt the cold of the tiles as she lay there, momentarily stunned as her head hit a corner of a basin. She felt Steve tearing at her skirt and knickers, then he was astride her. She fought to gather her senses and lashed out at him, her nails to his face, screaming for help. He hit her and she was silenced, but she continued to struggle, determined that this piece of dirt was not going to rape her. Steve Rossi's strength overwhelmed her and she felt helpless as he gripped her flailing arms in one hand and undid his trousers with the other. He took out his swollen member and leered at her. 'Is this as big as that buck nigger's?' he asked.

'Get off me, you crazy bastard,' she yelled. 'I'll kill you before I let you touch me again.'

He laughed loudly. 'And how are you going to do that? Look at you, you can't move.'

And he was right. Maggie felt the helplessness of her situation. He had her body pinned down beneath him, her arms held above her head in one hand. Every time she tried to move he had her trapped between his knees. Quickly she sat up and sank her teeth into his chin, biting as hard as she could.

With a yelp of pain, Rossi let her go and she pushed him off her and got to her feet. She turned to run but he grabbed her around her ankle. She screamed as loudly as she could, but Steve was relentless. He caught her round the knees and pulled her to the ground.

'What the bloody hell's going on?' asked a voice from outside.

Maggie nearly collapsed with relief as Nobby Clarke stood in the doorway.

He quickly took in the situation before him and, swiftly hauling Maggie to her feet, pushed her outside. Then he grabbed hold of Steve Rossi, heaving him up from the floor and landing a punch any boxer would have been proud of, right on the point of the American's chin. Rossi sank to his knees, unconscious.

Maggie threw her arms around Nobby's neck and sobbed with relief. He extricated himself from her grasp and said sharply, 'Listen to me! Go and call the police. Don't hang about. I don't know just how long this bugger will be out for.' He pushed her towards the gate. 'Go! Now!'

Maggie ran for all she was worth and dialled 999.

Later, she, Moira and Nobby sat in the bar drinking a glass of brandy each. 'I keep it for medicinal purposes,' Moira explained.

'How can I ever thank you, Nobby?' Maggie asked in a trembling voice.

'Well, you could always say I wasn't looking well, about once a week, and give me a glass of this stuff,' he said, shrugging off her thanks.

Maggie, still shaken by her ordeal said, 'If you hadn't come along . . .'

'Now you listen to me, girl. Wondering what might have happened is the worst thing you can do. I got there in time, that's the thing to remember.' He turned to Moira. 'It was quite by chance that I stepped outside to let the cat out and saw the gate to the gents' toilet still open. I thought that was unusual, Maggie is always so careful to lock up. I walked over and that's when I heard her screaming.' He looked across at her. 'You've got a fine pair of lungs on you, my dear.'

She gave a wry smile. 'You did look funny, Nobby, when the police arrived. Sitting on Steve Rossi like that.'

'Well, love, I wasn't sure how long it would take for him to come round. I wasn't taking any chances. Best be off home. My Grace will be thinking I've run off with a blonde.'

Maggie let him out of the side door. She hugged him and kissed his cheek. 'Thanks,' she said.

He patted her shoulder. 'At least he's safely locked up. The army will take him out of the local cells tomorrow. They won't like the idea that he escaped, they'll watch him like a hawk in future. Now you go and get a good night's sleep.'

She watched him walk away, thankful that she had such good neighbours. But the experience had shaken her and her hands were trembling as she locked the door. Much as she tried she couldn't help wondering what Steve would have done if Nobby hadn't intervened. Would she still be alive?

That night she had nightmares.

Joshua was furious when he heard all about it the next day. Maggie had never seen him so angry and it surprised her. 'It's all over,' she said, trying to calm him.

'That scum!' he cried. 'How dare he try to touch you! What right has he to behave in such a way?'

She laid a hand on his arm. 'For heaven's sake, calm down. Nobby arrived in time to save me.'

Joshua gathered her into his arms and, holding her tightly, kissed the top of her head and said, 'If anything bad happened to you, I don't know what I'd do. You should have someone here all the time to protect you from this kind of thing. I want to be here to look after you.'

She snuggled against him. 'I know, I know, but you can't be.'

He led her over to the settee and they sat down. Putting his arm around her he said, 'The sooner we get married the better. Tomorrow I'm going to see the officer in charge.'

She looked up at him and said, 'Even if we'd been married you might not have been here.'

'I know that, but I don't want us to wait any longer. Let's not waste any more time. The sooner you're my wife the better.'

That night in bed, they made love, but this time without any means of protection. They both wanted to be close to one another, to be truly as one. 'I'll never let anyone hurt you again,' Joshua promised as they lay in each other's arms. 'You'll always be safe as long as I'm around.'

Maggie was so happy. It didn't matter what the future held; as long as Joshua was beside her, she could stand up to anything. She would be with the man she loved and the rest of the world could go to hell!

Joshua, too, knew the way ahead would be hard. The first thing he would have to do tomorrow was write to his father and try and explain how it was that he intended to spend the rest of his life with a white woman. In the depths of Mississippi, that would be an unthinkable thing, but he had faith in his father's understanding; he only hoped that he could come to terms with such a situation. He knew also that Maggie's father would find it difficult to accept. Already their problems had begun.

Chapter Twenty-One

When Ivy came around to the pub the following afternoon to visit, she was appalled at Maggie's news.

'You're going to *marry* Joshua? But you can't!'

Surprised at her friend's attitude she asked, 'Why not?'

Ivy looked at her accusingly. 'I can't believe you have to ask. I thought you were just having an affair. You can't marry a darkie!'

Maggie felt the blood drain from her face, but then the rage that surged through her flushed her cheeks. Her eyes flashed with anger. 'How dare you sit in judgement on me. You, the woman who got engaged whilst you were still married to another man!'

Ivy looked embarrassed; nevertheless, she returned Maggie's angry gaze. 'That was different.'

'You're damned right it was different! For one thing it was illegal, and for another you lied to both men. Joshua and I are free to make up our own minds, and no one gets hurt.'

'Oh come on, Maggie. Grow up. No one gets hurt, I can't believe you're that stupid.'

'What do you mean?'

'How does your mother feel about her daughter marrying a black man? And as for your father, he'll have a fit! And how about Joshua's parents? How will they feel?'

'I don't know about Dad, although I can imagine. Mum knows, and she's accepted that we love one another. As for his family, Joshua is writing to them.'

'He's from the Deep South remember. Think about it . . . the Ku Klux Klan! It's for real that, not just like in a film. You couldn't live there. They'd kill you both.'

'We haven't made any plans yet. We'll probably stay in England.'

Ivy shook her head sadly. 'And who would employ him?'

'He's a musician. He'll always find work.'

'If he stays here, he'll have a hell of a life if you get married . . . and so will you.'

'We don't care!' said Maggie, defiantly.

'Brave words – but very foolish ones.' Ivy put an arm around her friend's shoulder. 'Listen to me, Maggie. You're like the sister I never had. I understand you love him and he loves you, but this is wartime, all sorts

179

of madness exists. Afterwards, though, when everything returns to normal
. . . think about it. People will stare at you both wherever you go, they'll
gossip, taunt you. Insult you.'

Maggie would not be deterred. 'What you fail to understand, Ivy, is that
none of that matters. I would rather put up with all that prejudice than lose
the man I love. Life without him would be meaningless.'

'And what if you have children? What sort of a life will they have?' Ivy
was relentless.

Maggie closed her eyes to shut out the angry words she'd heard from
others when they'd seen a woman with a coloured child in a pram. She
could hear them now. 'Harlot! Nigger lover!' But she would be a married
woman. Yet she knew that there was a strong element of truth in her
friend's words.

She gave Ivy a piercing stare. 'We'll bring them up to realize how much
they are loved, and teach them about the ignorance of others. They'll know
what a wonderful man their father is, and in time others will know that too
. . . I'll make bloody sure they do!'

Ivy looked at her friend for a moment, then she went and put her arms
around her. 'I'm sure you will. You have more courage than I do, love. But
if you feel that strongly, no one's going to change your mind. And you're
right, it's not my place to have a go at you, after all you stuck by me when
I needed you, and I'll do the same.'

Maggie hugged her. 'There you are, you see. In time others will accept
us as a couple too, and if they don't, it's their loss, not ours.'

'Your father will be the one you have to worry most about,' said Ivy.

'Well he's just been sent down for six months. At the end of that time
he'll be so glad to come home, he'll be more reasonable. By then I'll be
married anyway.'

To add to her problems, Maggie had to go to the police station to give a
statement about Steve Rossi. The local police knew her through her father
being in the pub business. Many of them had stood in the hallway of the
Bricklayer's Arms, drinking beer; had seen her grow up; and they were
aware of her relationship with a coloured soldier. They were less than
understanding.

The sergeant who took her statement was scathing. 'You young girls
look for trouble, mixing with the GIs,' he said shortly. 'They all look the
same in their uniforms, you have no idea what sort of men they are, yet
you lead them on!'

Maggie's cheeks flamed with indignation. 'I didn't lead him on, I had
no idea he was there. I didn't deserve to be nearly raped!'

'But you'd had a relationship with this man before, hadn't you?'

She couldn't deny it.

'I don't know what the world's coming to. Before the war most women were content to save themselves for the man they married. But nowadays, they give themselves to anybody!'

'That's not true, and you have no right to talk to me like this. I came to give a statement about a man who attacked me, not to get a lecture on my morals.'

He pushed a pad and pen over to her and coldly said, 'Write down exactly what happened, from beginning to end.' He rose from his chair. 'I'll be back later.'

Maggie watched him go, filled with anger at his righteous attitude. And he was the type she would have to face up to when she married Joshua. It made her furious that so many could be so bigoted.

She wrote out her statement, finding it very difficult reliving those terrible moments, knowing that others would read it and know of her humiliation. When she'd finished, she signed it in front of the sergeant and left.

On her way home she walked through the rose garden in front of the Civic Centre. The beds were devoid of flowers at this time of year and the fountain wasn't flowing. Come the spring, the parks would be full of colour, but now most of the trees were bare, standing like sentinels over the parkland.

She hated the winter and longed to see the growth of spring. It was like a renewal of life as the daffodils bloomed and the trees were covered with cherry blossom. Now, in the month of January, there was little to cheer her. But as she stopped at the newsagent to buy a paper and saw the shocking pictures of the skeletal figures of the prisoners of Auschwitz, she counted her blessings.

Joshua had at last heard from his father. The pastor had been shaken by his son's plans, and pointed out that there would be no life for them in Mississippi, but he hoped that if they were to marry and stay in England, they would face a better future. He wrote:

My son, knowing you as I do, you must have found a wonderful woman to make you so determined to go down this path. One hopes and prays that as the years pass, all races can live happily together. My prayers will be with you, and my blessings on your union.

Joshua smiled softly. He could almost hear his father's voice as he read the words. He was a man ahead of his time. One day in the future it would be nice for them all to meet up, perhaps with their own children. He would show the letter to Maggie. At least they had most of their family on their side. If only Maggie's father would accept them, it would make them really happy.

He had confided his plans to Ezra, who had looked at him with eyes wide with astonishment. 'You're going to marry Maggie! Have you gone crazy, man? For Christ's sake, remember where you come from. At home we don't have the freedom we have here, as well you know. You think it will be any better in England, once the war is over? Take a look in the mirror, Joshua. You're still as black as the day you were born and that's what these limeys will see. The colour of your skin. Black and white don't mix, man. Maggie too would have a real hard time.'

'You forget, my friend, my world is music. There, there is no colour bar. With music, your talent is what counts. I can get work in London. We'll be just fine, you'll see.'

Joshua sat in a chair in front of his commanding officer's desk.

'Sergeant Lewis, you've applied to marry an English girl.'

'Yes, sir. That's right.'

'As you know, sergeant, the army is especially concerned about the GIs who apply to us to marry. In wartime things are so different. Once the soldiers return home and settle down, we are worried that when things are normal, the men may decide that it's all been a huge mistake. They catch up with the girls they left behind, then we have unhappy war brides left in a foreign country. It's not a situation that we relish. Apart from which, there is still a war raging in Europe. What happens if you are sent there and killed? Would it be fair on your bride? She'd be a widow before she had a chance to be a wife. These things happen, after all.'

'I do realize the difficulties, sir. But my girl and I love one another.'

The officer smiled kindly. 'If I had a dollar for every time some GI told me that, I'd be a rich man.' He became serious. 'I don't need to tell you of the particular difficulty in your case, Lewis.'

'No, sir. Maggie and I have talked long and hard about the future. We know it won't be easy, but we want to be together for the rest of our lives.'

'And nothing I can say will dissuade you?'

'No, sir.'

'Then we'd better make an appointment for her to come and see me.'

Joshua left the office with a wry smile. The appointment wasn't for another three weeks: no doubt giving him time to change his mind.

Later that evening, after the bar was closed, he and Maggie sat talking about the forthcoming interview.

'I don't care what he says,' she said firmly. 'Nothing is going to change my mind.'

He kissed the tip of her nose. 'That's my girl.' He took his father's letter from his pocket and handed it to her.

When she'd read it, tears brimmed in her eyes. 'What a lovely man. If only my father could think like him.'

Joshua held her close. 'We'll meet the obstacle of your father when the time comes,' he said.

Looking at the letter again she said, 'Your father thinks we should stay in England, rather than go to the States.'

'He's probably right, although New York is pretty cosmopolitan.' He put his arm around her. 'In any case, you would probably feel happier being near your mother. London isn't too far away.'

'Will it be easy for you to find work?'

He chuckled. 'Sure will. Even now there's plenty of clubs with small dance floors needing musicians, and when the war is over, the big bands will come back into their own. Listen, honey, a good pianist can always find work. And in time, I'd like to form my own jazz band. Given the right breaks, who knows, I may make a name for myself.'

'Well if the performance of your group at the Guildhall is anything to go by,' she smiled at him, 'I can see your name in lights!'

'I've been trying to think of a name for a small band. How about "The Cool Cats"?'

She looked a little puzzled.

Joshua burst out laughing. 'I'm going to have to teach you American, honey. If you're hep, you're cool. A real cool cat.'

'Like a smart cookie, do you mean?'

'My oh my, you're learning already.'

'Well I know the pavement is the sidewalk, a vest is a waistcoat and a lift is an elevator. And we go to the movies not the pictures!'

He gazed at her in delight. 'I knew you were a bright girl, but maybe you'd better start teaching me the English way of speaking, if we're going to stay here after all.'

She kissed him soundly. 'Never. I don't want to change you in any way, I love you the way you are.'

Maggie related the conversation to her mother the next morning over the breakfast table.

'Well there's no doubt about it,' said Moira, 'Joshua is a talented musician. And I can't tell you how pleased I am that you won't be far away. But what'll happen about the pub?'

'Now don't you worry. I'll definitely keep it on until the war ends. I can come down maybe three days a week, after all it doesn't take long on the train from London. You can look after it the rest of the time. Hopefully, Joshua will be busy. I'll need something to keep me occupied.' She gave her mother a searching look and asked, 'Were you deeply in love with Dad?'

Moira thought for a moment. 'If I'm honest I suppose I wasn't. I was fond of him, I admired him.' At the look of surprise on her daughter's face she said, 'Your father has been a brave man in his day. He met with prejudice himself, you know. He was taunted at school about his limp. Adults weren't much better, at times, but he rose above it. And he was kind.'

'You married him because he was kind!'

Moira laughed. 'Don't be daft . . . he was a good kisser!'

They both dissolved into laughter.

'Oh, Mum. You really are the end.'

Her eyes still full of merriment, Moira said, 'Listen, your father in his youth was a lot of fun. We had a good time together. It's only as the years passed he became bitter.' The expression in her eyes softened. 'We used to be very happy.'

'Maybe you will be again,' said Maggie quietly. 'He made a terrible mistake, but I'm sure he's learned his lesson.'

Moira nodded. 'Yes. Yes, he has. And who knows, being inside may have made him realize what a good home and family he has.'

'I do hope so,' said Maggie, but in truth she didn't think he would change his outlook regarding her marriage to Joshua.

Chapter Twenty-Two

Whilst working at her machine in the factory the following morning, Maggie wondered just how long it would be before she and Joshua could name the day. She was anxious now to get on with the wedding. She didn't want a big one, just a small gathering at the registrar's office and a modest reception for her close friends and Joshua's.

She thought she'd better think about what she would wear. A simple dress, and a hat, she should have enough coupons for that. Ivy and one of Joshua's friends could be the witnesses. At least her mother would be there; but who could she ask to give her away in the absence of her father? There was only one man: Nobby Clarke. She'd have to ask him.

But when Joshua walked into the Bricklayer's Arms that night, Maggie knew something was wrong. His usual smiling countenance was set in grim lines. He asked her to step out from behind the bar and talk to him. She led him to the kitchen, her heart beating wildly.

He sat her down at the table, seating himself opposite, taking both her hands in his.

'What is it?' she asked.

'My company is being shipped out,' he said quietly.

Maggie felt as if her stomach had been gripped by an iron fist. 'Oh no! When?'

'The day after tomorrow.'

She felt the blood drain from her face and a feeling of nausea sweep over her. Joshua rushed to the scullery to fetch her a glass of water.

'Drink this,' he said.

When she'd recovered she asked, 'Where are they sending you?'

'To Germany. We're to join the US Ninth Army.'

Maggie knew that the fighting in Germany was fierce. The British and Canadian troops were fighting around Reichswald; the Germans were in disarray, drafting women into the army to bolster their forces. And now he was to be part of all this. She closed her eyes in despair.

Joshua rose from his seat and came around the table to her, taking her into his arms. 'We always knew it was possible, honey,' he said.

She sobbed against his shoulder. 'I know. I know. But we were so close to getting married. I've been thinking about it all day . . . even what I was going to wear, who would give me away. Oh, darling, war is so cruel.'

He tipped her chin upwards and looked into her tear-filled eyes. 'But

185

for the war, we would never have met, and that's something I wouldn't have missed for the world.'

She clung tightly to him. 'You will write to me, won't you? I need to know you're alive.'

'Honey, I'll write every second I get. But don't worry if the mail takes a long time to get through.' He kissed her eyes, her cheeks, her lips. 'I love you more than you'll ever know.'

'Will I see you before you go?'

He held her tighter. 'No, Maggie. I have to get back to camp now. I shouldn't really be here. All leave has been cancelled.'

She looked at him in horror. 'This is our last time together?'

He nodded. 'I'm afraid so.'

She looked into his large brown eyes and saw the anguish reflected in them. He kissed her again and she could feel the longing in him. 'I'm going to miss you so much,' she said. She caressed his face, wondering if she would ever see him again, feel his strong arms around her. If he was killed in action, she didn't know how she'd survive.

He cupped her face in his hands. 'I *am* coming back, Maggie. We *will* get married. I promise. I love you, honey,' he whispered. 'Always remember that. These past months have been the happiest time of my whole life, and we are going to grow old together.' There was a note of disappointment in his voice as he said, 'I was going to buy you an engagement ring this week; now I won't have time.'

'I don't need a ring. I'm already married to you in my heart, and I'll be here, waiting for the day you return, no matter how long that takes. I love you too, darling, and I'm going to miss you terribly,' she said. 'Please keep safe.'

They clasped each other in one last desperate embrace, then walked to the door together.

He caught hold of her shoulders and gazed into her eyes. In his deep mellow voice he said, 'Let me look at you, Maggie.' He stroked her hair, her face; he took her in his arms and kissed her longingly, held her close for a moment, then he opened the door.

Outside a jeep was waiting. He climbed in and waved to her as the driver drew away. But there was no smile on his face, only an expression of great sadness.

As she watched the vehicle depart, she fingered the locket around her neck, lifted it to her lips and kissed it.

Moira popped her head around the bar door and asked, 'Has Joshua gone?'

Maggie was unable to do anything but nod.

Her mother closed the door behind her and stepped into the narrow hallway. 'Maggie, love. What is it? What's happened?'

'He's being shipped out. He came to say goodbye.'

Moira drew her into her arms and held her. 'Oh, Maggie, darlin', I'm so sorry.'

'Can you manage on your own, Mum? I can't face anyone tonight.'

'Of course I can. Anyway, Nobby's in the bar. If I get a rush on, he'll give me a hand. You go and have a lie down. I'll come up in a while.'

'I just need to be alone, Mum.'

'I understand. Away you go.'

Moira returned to the bar and served her customers automatically, her thoughts full of Maggie. She knew how distressed she would be. All the wedding plans ruined. If nothing else, however, this would be a true test of their love for one another.

Maggie lay on top of her bed, staring wide-eyed into space. Joshua had gone. She'd got so used to seeing him, of his being such an important part of her life. She tried to fill her mind with all the happy times they'd spent together; with the sound of his deep soft voice as he read poetry to her, his twinkling eyes when he teased her, as he so often did. She willed herself to remember the love they shared, his outlook on life, the tolerance he'd shown when people had been vindictive towards him, the plans they had for their future. But the realization that he was going away to a battle zone swept over her and she sobbed. 'God, if you really do exist, keep this wonderful man safe,' she prayed. And smiled to herself through her tears, remembering how Joshua had said that in times of need, people turn to the Lord. Who else could she ask to protect him, except a superior being?

When Moira crept upstairs some time later, Maggie had fallen asleep. Her cheeks were still wet with the tears she'd shed. Her mother covered her with a blanket and slipped quietly out, leaving the door open a little, as she had done when her daughter was a child.

Two months passed and Maggie read every newspaper to try and keep track of her man. The last newspaper article told her his company was just outside Mönchen-Gladbach and Germany was now recruiting boys of sixteen. Surely the war couldn't last for much longer?

She'd had one letter from him soon after he'd landed on foreign soil, telling her that he was safe and that he loved her, but with the censorship he was unable to say more. And she'd heard again, two weeks later. He was well, missing her terribly, and she wasn't to worry, but she'd heard nothing since. The letters were beneath her pillow and she read them every night, clasping them to her in the knowledge that these pieces of paper had been in his hands.

One morning a few days later she visited the doctor who told her she was almost three months' pregnant. By his calculations, her baby would be due around the middle of September. She left the surgery and walked home through the park. She looked at the daffodils, their bright golden trumpets swaying in the breeze, the crocuses peering out of clumps of grass, the sweep of the cherry trees. All around her was new life, and growing inside her was Joshua's child. She couldn't wait to tell her mother.

Moira was sitting in the kitchen after closing time having a sandwich and a cup of tea when Maggie arrived. She kissed her mother on the cheek, fetched a cup and saucer from the scullery, poured a cup of tea, then sat down. She looked across the table at Moira. 'Mum, I've got something to tell you,' she began.

'When is it due?' asked Moira.

Maggie looked at her in astonishment. 'How did you know?'

'I can spot a pregnant woman a mile away,' she said, as she put her arms around her. 'But I'm afraid you're going to be hurt, being unmarried. You know what people are.'

'I don't care. When Joshua comes home, we'll get married. They can say what they like!'

Seeing the determination in Maggie's eyes, Moira admired her spirit. It reminded her of the time when, as a child, Maggie had climbed a tree, terrified at its height but determined to get as near to the top as possible. She'd made it, with a little help from her father. Now she was going to need all the help she could get.

'*We* won't let them say anything,' said Moira with a smile.

'Oh, Mum. I knew you wouldn't let me down.'

But Moira's brow furrowed with concern. 'What about your father, Maggie? You say he's coming back home when they let him out – what about him?'

'I'll tell Dad myself. He has a right to know.'

Moira shook her head. 'Well, that won't be easy. You know how he feels about . . .'

'Negroes! I'm not ashamed of my child's father and neither will his baby be.'

'Would you like me to come to the prison with you?' ventured Moira.

'No thanks, Mum. This is something I have to do for myself.'

The following day Maggie sat in the bare room in Winchester Prison, waiting with the other visitors. The prisoners were allowed in and she saw the smile on her father's face as he walked towards her. He leaned across the table and kissed her cheek. 'Hello, Maggie, love. How are you?'

'Fine, Dad. You're looking better.'

He beamed happily at her. 'Of course I am. I only have another three weeks in here now, with my time off for good behaviour, then I'm a free man again.' He looked fondly at her. 'I can't tell you how much I'm looking forward to walking out of this place. I can already taste the pint of beer I'm going to have when I get back to the Bricklayer's Arms. How's business?'

'Dad, I've got something to tell you and I'm afraid you're not going to like it.'

His smile faded. 'What? You haven't lost the licence have you?'

Despite the seriousness of the situation, Maggie couldn't help smiling. 'No, that's secure. The business is doing well and the brewers are pleased with me.'

'Then what is it?'

'I'm going to have a baby.'

The shock which registered on her father's face shook her. He looked blankly at her as if he couldn't believe what she'd told him. He leaned forward with his elbows on the table and held his head with his hands.

She sat still and silent, wondering what he was going to say.

Eventually he looked at her. 'I was so very much afraid this would happen. Oh, Maggie, how could you?'

If he'd raged at her it would have been easier to cope with, but the sadness in his eyes and the disappointment in his voice hurt her deeply.

'I really love him, Dad. And when he comes home, we'll get married. We'd have done so before if Joshua hadn't been sent abroad.'

'The father is the coloured boy then?'

'Of course! Who else would it be?' she asked shortly.

Jack didn't answer.

'He was shipped to Germany a few weeks ago.'

There was a flash of the old Jack as he said, 'Gone off and left you in trouble has he?'

'No, Dad, it wasn't like that at all. He doesn't know about the child. He loves me. He's going to return to England after the war.'

'And live off you and the pub, no doubt!'

She fought to keep the anger from her voice. 'Not at all. He's going to work in London. He's a very talented pianist.'

'Well there's lots of them around,' he said. 'We never have trouble getting them to play in the bar.'

'He's not that kind of pianist. He's a proper musician, he plays jazz. One day he's going to have his own band. He is a lovely man, Dad. I wish you could have met him. His father is a pastor in Mississippi. He taught Joshua so much. He loves books, he's kind and gentle and he wanted the best for me.' She hesitated then said, 'I have some photos here if you'd like to see them.' She took the snapshots out of her bag and handed them to Jack.

She watched his expression as he looked at them. He couldn't hide the distaste he felt. He looked up and said, 'You may well have loved each other but this still doesn't look right to me. I'm sorry, Maggie, but I have to be honest.'

She shrugged. 'What you think about Joshua doesn't matter. What I want to know is, how will you treat my baby when it's born? He'll be coloured too . . . and your grandchild.'

He looked surprised. 'Of course it will be.' He looked back at the snaps then at Maggie. 'I don't know . . . I honestly don't know.' He saw the disappointment in her expression. 'I can't lie, Maggie, and as you well know, I always speak my mind.'

'That's very true.'

'All I know is how I felt when I saw young girls pushing prams with their Yankee bastards in them. And now my own daughter will be doing the same.' He saw her wince at his words. 'You'd better get used to such remarks, my girl, you'll hear plenty of them in the future.'

'I know it wasn't what you wanted for me, Dad, but there you are. I'm proud to be carrying Joshua's child. And he will come back – and we will be married.'

'What about your mother? How does she feel about all this?'

'She's upset, I won't deny it, but she's behind me.' She appealed to him once more. 'Mum told me that at school, and even after, people used to taunt you about being a cripple.' She saw him blanch. 'I would have thought that you of all people would have understood.'

'But this is quite different, Maggie.'

She gave him a hard look. 'Is it? That's not the way I see it . . .' She realized there was no more to be said on the subject, and to lighten the conversation said, 'I'll see you back at the pub when you get out. I'll have a pint pulled for you.'

'It had better be clear or I'll complain to the landlady.'

'You won't have any need for complaints . . . and I hope I'll be able to say the same about you.'

'What do you mean?'

'You almost lost us the pub. Well, we – Mum and me – are ready to put that in the past. I expect the same consideration from you about my situation. Think about it.'

'Yes, I will.'

She kissed his cheek and left the prison. As she sat on the train she was still angry with her father. But he'd have to toe the line. Her baby came before anyone.

Alone in his cell, Jack Evans sat on his bunk smoking a cigarette, arguing with his conscience. He was too old to change the way he felt. But in his heart he was worried as to how he would feel when he first looked at his grandchild. He prayed that he would be able to accept it. He loved Maggie and was proud of her. She had looked so unhappy today, and he supposed if she truly loved this fellow, she had reason to be so. But he was afraid that when the baby was born, he'd hate it! And that would break her heart.

He stubbed his cigarette out and listened to the sounds of the prison: the clatter of footsteps, the voices raised in anger, the rattle of the keys. He supposed if he really thought about it, here he'd learned to keep his mouth shut to stay out of trouble. Well, he'd just have to do the same when he got home. But would he be able to, feeling as he did?

Chapter Twenty-Three

Sergeant Joshua Lewis sat, holed up in a half-ruined building, with his men. There was a lull in the fighting and they took time out to rest. Sitting with his back against the wall, near an open window, his rifle at the ready, he took a cigarette from a pack in his pocket and lit one. He tipped his steel helmet to the back of his head and wiped the sweat and dust from his brow. It had been a hard day's fighting. His company and others had followed the tanks into this small German town before peeling off into buildings along the way, searching out the enemy troops hiding there.

He took a snapshot of Maggie out of his jacket and gazed at it. How happy she looked. It had been taken in the park in Southampton last summer. God how he missed her. He hoped like hell she'd received his last letter. It was important for him to let her know he was still alive. He put the picture away as he saw the officer in charge making his way towards him.

'Sergeant. You OK?'

'Yes, sir.'

'Did you lose any men today?'

'Two, sir.'

The lieutenant looked weary. 'We have to make a concerted effort to clear these streets.' He looked at his watch. 'In ten minutes, take your men over there.' He pointed to a house opposite. 'In the next street there's a machine gun post, it's playing havoc with the troops. We can't move from our present position. They've got us pinned down. I want you to wipe it out. My boys will give you cover. OK?'

'Yes, sir.'

The man turned away, heading for the exit. 'Good luck, sergeant.'

Joshua gathered his men together and gave them their orders. 'You three go first, make for the doorway. If it's clear, signal me. We'll give you covering fire.'

He counted down the seconds. Five, four, three, two, one – go!

The sound of rifle fire filled the air as the men ran in a zigzag towards the building. A sniper was seen in an upstairs window and shot, his body plummeting down to the road below. After a few minutes, and more sounds of firing within the building, Joshua got the signal to proceed.

In small groups he and his men managed to cross the road safely. The house was now empty of live opposition, but as they went upstairs, climbing over dead bodies, they could see, in the opposite building, the position of the machine gun, placed on a small balcony, manned by two German soldiers. It could cover three directions, holding up any further advance.

He eyed the situation carefully. There was one blind side; if he and his men could manage to enter the house from the back, they had a chance, but they had no way of knowing if there were any more enemy soldiers in the building. He felt it was more than likely.

Stealthily, they crept out of the house, crossed the alleyway and made it to a wall beside the building. They listened but could only hear gunfire in the distance. He knew the rest of the troops were waiting for him to destroy the machine gun position before they moved in. He looked at the others and, taking a grenade from his belt, said, 'Right! Let's do it.'

On the lower floor they eliminated two of the enemy, then another appeared at the top of the stairs. One of the men shot him, then yet another arrived, crouched low. He aimed his rifle and Joshua heard the cry of pain as one of his men was hit, before the German went down in a hail of bullets.

Joshua leapt up the stairs two at a time and, pulling the pin from the grenade, threw it into the front room, ducking down behind a wall to escape the blast. Guns at the ready, his men entered the room, firing their rifles. The machine gun was in pieces, as were the German soldiers. He looked out of the window and waved to the officer in the distance, waiting to advance. The building was secure.

He and his troops went down into the street below and crouched behind any cover they could find, waiting for the rest of the company to move forward.

'Good work!' said the officer as he passed. 'Let's start on the next street . . . and keep your head down.'

One of the men quipped, 'He's a crazy man if he thinks I'm putting my head above the parapet!'

They moved forward again, from house to house, ducking and diving, firing at any of the opposing army who had lingered, moving along the street until it all seemed clear. Then they took a rest.

'Jeez,' said a voice from the rear, 'that was real hairy and I want my momma!'

There was a sound of laughter as the man who'd spoken was huge. 'No momma ever gave birth to you, Samuel. You'd have killed her. I reckon you was regular army issue.'

The call came for them to advance. They moved down to the end of the street. The tank in front turned the corner. As it did so, Joshua heard the whine of a shell, then there was a massive explosion as the tank in front of him was blown up.

He felt a searing pain in his shoulder as he was lifted from the ground by the blast – then everything turned black.

Men scurried forward, keeping low, pulling the injured away from the burning tank. There were moans from the injured. One of the men cursed. 'That son of a bitch has got the sarge!' There was a burst of gunfire and loud calls of 'medic'.

Ezra came running over as Joshua, sheltered by a wall, was attended to by a medical orderly.

'Is he alive?' asked Ezra.

'Yeah, but his shoulder's a mess. He took some shrapnel in it by the look of it, and he's been hit in the head.'

'Is he gonna make it?'

'Difficult to say, buddy. We need to get him to the field hospital pretty quick. I'll just give him a shot of morphine.'

Ezra looked at the men standing around. 'Well, we ain't leaving him behind. Get the frigging meat wagon over here!'

They stood and watched in silence as Joshua was put on a stretcher and into the ambulance.

At the military hospital, behind the lines, Joshua Lewis waited on a stretcher along with the other wounded. He came to for just a moment, and tensed as he felt the pain from his wounds, then he lapsed into unconsciousness.

His stretcher was lifted and he was taken into the surgery. The surgeon looked at his shoulder after the nurse removed the dressing. 'This looks a bit of a mess. We'll know just how bad when we take a look inside. He's also got a piece of shrapnel lodged in his skull. Let's hope it isn't a big piece. Right, let's get on with it.'

Several hours later, Joshua regained consciousness. He could see that his shoulder was heavily bandaged. He put a hand to his aching head and felt the bandages there too. He tried to move, but found it too painful. He looked around, puzzled. Where the hell was he?

A nurse came over to his side and put a thermometer in his mouth. 'Back in the land of the living I see, soldier. How are you feeling?'

'A bit woozy. Where am I?'

'You're in a field hospital. You were caught in an explosion.'

'I was? Where?'

The nurse smiled and said, 'Don't talk, sergeant. You might swallow that.' She held his wrist and took his pulse.

When she'd removed the thermometer, he said, 'I don't remember anything. Nothing at all.'

She patted his arm reassuringly. 'That's all right, nothing to worry about. It's quite normal. No doubt after a good sleep you'll feel better. The doctor will come and see you later today. You try and get some rest now.'

He watched her walk away. She called him sergeant. How strange . . .

It was early evening before he was seen by the surgeon.

'Hello, Sergeant Lewis, and how are you?' He picked up the chart at the end of the bed and studied it.

'A little sore, doc.' He looked anxiously at the man. 'I don't seem to be able to remember anything.'

The doctor frowned. 'Do you remember your name?'

'No, sir. But you called me Sergeant Lewis.'

The doctor sat on the edge of his bed. 'What month is it?'

Joshua shook his head.

'Who is the president of the United States?'

Joshua looked blankly at him. Suddenly fearful, he asked, 'What's happening to me?'

'You were caught in an explosion, it seems. You took a piece of shrapnel in your shoulder. It went in at an angle and tore one of your ligaments pretty bad, but I patched it up real well, if I say so myself. We've cleaned out where the ball goes into the socket of your shoulder, explored the joint, repaired the ligament, but there's been a lot of internal bruising of the muscles, which will take time to heal. Apart from that you caught some more shrapnel in your skull.' Seeing the look of anxiety on the face of his patient, he tried to reassure him. 'You've been a very lucky man. It didn't go deep enough to cause you any real danger . . . but it is probably the reason for your memory loss.'

Joshua's eyes widened. 'Will my memory come back?'

'Most probably, in time. But I can tell you that you are Sergeant Joshua Lewis. That at least is a starting point. We have informed the authorities of your whereabouts. They'll get in touch with your next of kin – then we can fill in the blanks about your background.' He rose from the bed. 'Try not to worry. I know that's difficult, but if you do, you could impede your recovery. I'll see you tomorrow.' He turned to the nurse. 'See that the patient is put on a light diet for twenty-four hours.' He turned to Joshua. 'In a few days we'll have you back in England in a hospital there. Your war is over for a while, son.'

Joshua lay back against his pillows. He had a name, it seemed, but it didn't sound in the least bit familiar. He felt a rising tide of panic inside and tried to control it. He was a man from . . . where? He was obviously in the army. Had been in the fighting, but that was all.

He looked around the ward with its stark iron beds, all filled with men with a variety of injuries. Several, it was obvious to see, were in a worse state than he was. The doctor said he'd been lucky, and compared with one or two men in beds nearby he could see the truth of the remark, but at least they all probably knew who they were.

His head was throbbing. He closed his eyes and tried to sleep, to blot out the fears that were filling his mind. What if he never regained his memory? What then?

In Southampton, Jack Evans made his way along College Street carrying a small suitcase. When he arrived at the side door of the Bricklayer's Arms, he hesitated. The pub was closed at this hour of the afternoon; he knew the side door would be open, as usual, but should he knock? Taking a deep breath, he opened the door, closing it behind him, and walked down the narrow corridor towards the kitchen, calling as he went: 'Moira! Anyone at home?'

Moira looked up from her newspaper as she recognized the voice of her husband. 'I'm here, Jack.' She rose from her chair and went into the scullery to put on the kettle. When she returned she saw him, standing just inside the door, with a look of uncertainty on his face. He looked like a lost child, and she felt pity for him. It couldn't have been easy for him, coming home after what he'd done. She walked over to him and kissed him briefly on the cheek and saw his expression of relief at her greeting.

'Sit down,' she said. 'I've put the kettle on. How are you, Jack?' He looked pale and drawn.

'I'm fine,' he said quietly, still unsure of his ground. 'Where's Maggie?'

'Working. She'll be back at eight o'clock. They asked her to work the later shift. She only works the early one usually, so that she's home to run the bar in the evening, but Tuesday's normally quiet, until later.' She returned to the scullery and came back with a tray of tea.

They sat at the table together. 'How is she?' he asked.

'Fine. She told you about the baby?' Moira asked as she poured the tea. He nodded. 'It came as a bit of a shock, I must admit.'

'He's a nice boy, Jack. He thinks the world of her, and she of him.'

He sipped his tea slowly. 'How could you let her go out with a darkie?' He looked accusingly at her.

'You think you could have stopped her?'

'I'd have had a bloody good try!'

She gave him a scornful look. 'Remember the last time you tried to put your foot down? She left home. If you hadn't interfered she might not have met him!'

He looked appalled. 'Are you trying to say it was my fault?'

She shook her head wearily and sighed. 'No, it wasn't anyone's fault. I'm just worried about the future . . . when the child is born.' She stared hard at him. 'She's going to need our support, Jack, whether Joshua comes back or not. Can you give it to her, feeling the way you do about coloured folk?'

He looked away. 'To be honest, I don't know. I hope so.'

Moira's temper flared immediately. 'Now you listen to me, Jack Evans. After what you put us through, you'll have to do better than hope so! Maggie saved this place . . . and your neck.'

'What do you mean?'

She glared angrily at him. 'You've got a home to come back to, haven't you? You owe her – and don't you forget it!'

He looked shaken at her outburst, and ashamed. 'I know what I did was wrong.'

All the anger and frustration she had been harbouring inside her these past months came to the surface in a rush. 'Wrong! I'll say you did wrong. As far as you were concerned, I could have been out in the street without anywhere to live. Penniless. Did you bloody care? Did you hell!'

'Oh, Moira. Don't you think I know all this? Christ! I've had a long time to think about it. Believe me I've paid for my mistake. I can only tell you how very sorry I am. You didn't deserve to be treated like that.'

'No I bloody well didn't.' Her eyes flashed with anger as she stared at him with a long accusing look. 'You say you're sorry. Right, now is the time to prove it. Maggie needs both of us. You let her down once more and you and I are finished for good. Understand?'

He knew that she meant every word. 'I understand. Don't you think I'm worried about her as well? She's my daughter too.'

'Then be a father to her, that's all I'm saying.' She rose from her seat. 'I'll get you something to eat.'

He lit a cigarette and drew deeply on it. It would be a very long time before Moira forgave him, if she ever did, he thought. And because he really loved her, for all his thoughtless ways, it hurt. Well it was payback time for him, his chance to prove he was sorry for his misdeeds. Would things ever be right between them? Only time would tell, but he'd have to step carefully.

By the time Maggie returned home, Jack had taken his things upstairs and put them away . . . in the spare room. He had hoped that Moira would have taken him back into their bed, but she'd made it very clear where he was to sleep. He had a bath and a shave, changed his clothes, and for the first time in months he felt like a human being. He was sitting in the kitchen by the fire, reading the newspaper, when his daughter walked in.

'Dad. How are you?' She walked over to him and kissed him. At least she looked genuinely pleased to see him.

She was still in her dungarees, with her turban around her hair. 'I'll go and have a bath and then I'll take you into the bar and pour you that pint I promised.'

He looked hesitant. Moira was working in the bar, but he hadn't had the courage to step inside and see the locals.

She recognized his anxiety. 'There's no reason to hide away. Everyone knows you're coming home today. I won't be long and we'll go together.'

It was only then that he realized just how much his little girl had grown up. She was in charge, and to his chagrin, he didn't seem to mind. When at last she appeared in a clean jumper and pair of slacks, she grinned. 'Come along, you might as well get it over with.'

He followed her along the hallway and paused as she opened the door which led to behind the counter. 'Come on,' she said.

He stood in a corner behind the bar and looked around, feeling very conspicuous. Several regulars called over to him, and he greeted them in return. Moira was busy serving and ignored his presence. Maggie took a pint glass down from the shelf, walked to the pumps and with a grin in his direction, pulled him a pint of beer. She walked back to him and handed him the glass.

'There you are, Dad. That'll be the best pint you've ever tasted.'

He put the glass to his lips. 'Cheers!' he said and took a deep swig. The froth clung to his mouth and he licked it away with great relish. He held the glass up to the light and peered at the remains. 'Good and clear,' he remarked.

'What else did you expect?' said Maggie.

Nobby came into the bar at that moment and, walking over to the counter, shook him by the hand. 'Come on round this side, Jack, and I'll fill you in with all the local gossip.'

Nobby Clarke had always been a good mate and Jack felt at ease with him, and Nobby, being the man he was, didn't beat about the bush. 'Was it tough inside?' he asked.

And Jack told him.

He shook his head. 'You were a bloody fool. I credited you with more sense,' he said bluntly.

'I know,' admitted Jack. 'If I could only turn back the clock.'

Nobby looked across the room at the two women behind the bar and said quietly, 'I wonder if Maggie feels the same?'

Jack glanced sideways at him. 'What do you mean?'

With a sympathetic expression, he said, 'I know she's pregnant.'

Jack looked shocked. 'I didn't know it was common knowledge.'

'It isn't, but Moira confided in Grace, she was so worried. Let's face it, Jack, you weren't here – and if you had been I doubt she would have told you.'

A frown creased Jack's forehead. His feelings were well known. 'Well

199

I know now. Not that I'm happy about it, of course.'

'What father would be? But I have to tell you that Joshua's a nice bloke, even if he is black. He's intelligent, well read, he made me feel quite ignorant beside him.'

'Really?'

'Oh, yes. Pity isn't it?'

At closing time, Jack helped them to tidy up the bar. Maggie asked him to go and lock up the gents for her. Ever since her run-in with Steve Rossi, it was a job she could no longer do. She always got one of the locals to do it for her.

When the bar was finished she sat on a stool beside her father, Moira having gone to bed. 'I need your help, Dad,' she said.

Jack was thrilled to hear this as he had wondered what his place would be in this household now.

'I can't lift the barrels any more, it's dangerous for the baby, so will you take over the cellar?'

'Of course, love. I'd be happy to.'

'And if the brewers are agreeable, perhaps you'll help out in the bar too, give Mum and me a break. But I'll have to get permission first.'

He pursed his lips tightly, then said, 'I'm so sorry, Maggie, for all the trouble.'

She patted his knee. 'It's all in the past now, Dad.'

'I don't think your mother thinks so.'

'Just give her time, she'll come round,' she said. 'Come on, it's late, let's call it a day.'

Jack lay on the bed in his solitary state, tired from the emotions and traumas of the past few hours. But he felt at peace with himself. Maggie needed him and that made him feel good, and the fact that Nobby had spoken so highly of this Joshua pleased him too. Nobby was a canny man and a good judge of character. Knowing that the father of Maggie's unborn child was highly thought of helped him accept the situation a little better. But he knew his greatest test was yet to come.

Chapter Twenty-Four

A week later, Joshua was put on a troop ship and sent across the Channel to a hospital at Netley, just outside of Southampton. But of course in his present state of health it might as well have been Timbuctoo. Places meant nothing to him. He had an American accent and was in the US Army. But where was he born? He knew not.

There had been some snapshots in his uniform pocket that he'd studied carefully time and time again. One was of a family gathering with a minister, a lady who was probably his wife, two sons and a cheeky-looking girl holding a younger girl by the hand. He wasn't in the picture though. Was it his family? Perhaps he was behind the camera. Then there was a picture of this beautiful white girl; with laughing eyes and flowing hair. Who was she?

He kept flexing the fingers on his right hand. It bothered him that they were stiff because of the wound in his shoulder. But deep in the recess of his mind, it was more than that. It seemed vitally important to him that he should get back their natural dexterity.

When he questioned the doctor about the stiffness in his fingers, he was told that in time, he should get the full use of them. 'There was a lot of damage done, Sergeant Lewis. The surgeon did a good job when he operated, but the wound and interior bruising take a long time to heal. Soon we'll give you some physiotherapy treatment. That'll help.'

The following few days were a living nightmare for the injured man. The medical staff were kind and efficient, but he felt as if he was occupying a space in a crowded world of strangers, of which he had no part. He was an unknown quantity.

In the bathroom, he looked in the mirror and this stranger stared back at him. It was a terrifying experience. He touched his face, the man in the mirror did the same, so he knew it was him. But who was he? Had he been a nice person, was he a good man? So many questions . . . and if his memory returned, would he be disappointed at what he discovered? He frowned. He could be anyone. A murderer for instance . . . No, he couldn't believe that; yet how was he to know?

He walked back to his bed, still delving mentally. Perhaps he had a wife and children. If so, they must be mad with worry. By now his head was throbbing and he lay on his bed and closed his eyes. Once the authorities contacted his next of kin, he'd know who he was of course, but he wasn't at all sure he was ready for such revelations.

Later in the week, one of the nurses helped him into a wheelchair and pushed him outside into the expansive grounds of the hospital. She settled him under a large cedar tree, wrapped a blanket around his shoulders to keep out the spring breeze and, putting the brake on the chair, said, 'There you are, Joshua. A change of scenery will do you good. Are you warm enough?'

'Yes, ma'am. I'm just fine.'

'I'll come back for you in an hour.'

Looking out over the lawns he gazed at the horizon and asked, 'Where is this place?'

'You're looking out over Southampton Water,' she said. 'We took over this hospital from the British. Before the war, ocean liners would pass by here on their way to the States. The ones you see now are bringing stores and troops back to the port. Not a bad view, eh?'

He smiled. 'I always did like being by the water,' he said.

'Did you now? I wonder why?'

He frowned. 'I don't remember.'

She patted his shoulder. 'You will, you'll see.'

Alone, Joshua sat back in the chair. It certainly was peaceful here. The sun was shining, the birds were singing and the scent of cedar wafted on the air. In the distance, he looked out over the water sparkling from the sun, and for just a moment a picture flashed into his head of a large paddle steamer . . . a river boat. Then it was gone.

He sat very still and closed his eyes in the hope that it would return. There was nothing – but at least there had been something. He reached into the pocket of his pyjamas, took out the two pictures and looked at them again and again, but as before, they meant nothing to him. He looked at the picture of the girl and wished he could remember just who she was. She sure was pretty.

The war was over! On May 6th at 3 p.m. Maggie and her family sat and listened to Winston Churchill make his speech from 10 Downing Street. The official announcement had been a long time coming. In the morning edition of the *Daily Mirror*, Jane, the scantily clad character in the strip cartoon, had disrobed completely, as she'd promised to do, for peace.

Crowds massed in front of Buckingham Palace, chanting, 'We want the King.' He and his family appeared, waving to the crowds. Such was the enthusiasm, they came out onto the balcony eight times in all.

Moira, Jack and Maggie cheered and hugged each other. At last. No more fighting, no more terrible loss of life, and for Maggie, hope at last that she would hear from Joshua. She had no doubts whatever that he would keep his word and get in touch again. She had convinced herself that the reason she hadn't heard was because he must be a prisoner-of-war. She ran to collect the post every day, hoping for a letter. Now she wouldn't have to worry. Soon she would hear.

That evening, she and Ivy rushed off to the Civic Centre forecourt where there were great celebrations. People danced and sang, drank beer and made merry.

The pub was full to overflowing and nearly everyone had far too much to drink. And why not? There was so much to be grateful for.

'Thank God!' said Moira to Grace Clarke.

'Has Maggie had any news?' asked her friend.

Moira shook her head. 'Not lately. We just live in hopes. It's the not knowing that's driving her crazy.'

There were street parties during the following days. Houses were decorated in bunting and the morale of the locals was jubilant.

'At least your child will be born into a free world,' said Moira, as she sat with Maggie outside the pub at one of the trestle tables.

Looking around at the happy faces, Maggie couldn't help being infected with the jubilation. 'It's a wonderful time,' she said. And thought how nice it would be when eventually all the rationing would be lifted and everyone could get back to normality. She just wished that Joshua was here to join in the celebrations.

She had been making regular trips to the doctor and all was well with the baby. She had requested a home confinement and the doctor had said she was strong and healthy and he couldn't find any reason why she shouldn't. She had seen the midwife and made the arrangements. As she had said to her mother, 'I don't want to be in some strange hospital, alone. I want to be at home, with you to hold my hand.'

'I'll be happy to, darlin'. I can't wait to see my grandchild.'

Jack kept out of such discussions. But he was worried about Maggie. She was convinced that Joshua was in some prison camp, but he wondered, cynically, whether the boy had just forgotten about his time in England with her, as so many GIs would do as they prepared to return home to their families.

There had been great celebrations within the confines of Netley Hospital too. They were a little more tempered due to the condition of the patients, of course; nevertheless, they were very much appreciated. An army band visited the hospital to give a concert. Those who were well enough sat in rows of seats, others in wheelchairs, and some had their beds pushed into the hall.

As the music started, Joshua's feet began to tap and he automatically played every note of the music, using his knees as a keyboard, a thing that didn't escape the attention of the senior sister, who watched him for several minutes. She came to sit beside him.

'Great music, Joshua, isn't it?'

'Yes,' he replied. 'This is a Duke Ellington number. One of my favourites.'

She smiled to herself but made no comment. The following day she took him into a recreation room and sat him at a piano. Lifting the lid, she said, 'Try it!' and left him alone.

He looked a little nonplussed and nervous. The keyboard looked very familiar to him. He ran his fingers over the keys and picked out a bass note with his left hand, then a melody with his right. He suddenly felt alive. He closed his eyes and began to play, finding the slight stiffness in his right hand very frustrating when his fingers wouldn't do as he wanted. But for the first time since he'd arrived in hospital, he was a happy man.

Outside the door, the sister listened to the music and went to fetch the doctor.

A while later the door opened and Joshua looked up with a broad smile on his face. 'Hi, doc. What do you know. I can play piano!'

'And you like Duke Ellington. I'm a Tommy Dorsey man myself.'

'Well then you've got great taste. Have you ever heard Harry James, Benny Goodman or Louis Armstrong? And what about Count Basie?' He looked at the doctor in surprise. 'Hell, where did all that come from?'

The man looked at him and said, 'It's the beginning, sergeant, and an excellent sign. Carry on, but don't do too much.'

'Thanks, doc.' As he continued to play he found himself thinking of the girl with the laughing eyes.

The following day Joshua was sitting at the piano, perspiration beading his forehead as he practised. The left hand played the syncopated rhythm just fine, but the fingers on the right hand were still so stiff. He stopped and stretched them. His shoulder ached. But still he kept going until the senior sister came into the room and stopped him.

'Sergeant Lewis! That's enough.'

He sat up and rubbed his shoulder.

'There you go now! What's the point in us working hard to heal your injury if you go and undo it all? You're too impatient.' She sat alongside him on the stool and placed an arm around him.

'Look, sergeant, I know that discovering you can play has been a boon to you, but unless you listen to me, you'll do yourself untold damage. Your muscles aren't ready for all the pressure you're putting on them.'

He sighed. 'I guess I'm not a very patient man. But don't you see, this is the only thing that has made any sense since I came here.' He had a look of desperation. 'Until now, I've been a nobody with nothing. Just a name. At least I have this . . . and that's all I have.'

'I know it's tough for you, Joshua, but at least you have something. And this is just the beginning. Other things will come back to you, given time.' She took a small rubber ball out of her pocket and said, 'Here, take yourself off for a walk around the grounds and keep squeezing this. Don't let me see you in here again before tomorrow! And then only for thirty minutes.'

He grinned broadly. 'They should have sent you to the front line, sister. You'd have put the fear of God up the Hun!'

'Enough of your cheek. Now get out of here!'

Joshua made his way out into the grounds, squeezing the rubber ball in his right hand as he walked.

He sat beneath the tall cedar tree, which was now a favourite spot of his, and started humming to himself. He felt that music was important to him, more than just being able to play a piano, but try as he might, he couldn't understand why. Where did he learn? Did he just play for pleasure? He didn't think so, but he didn't know why. Perhaps he was a professional.

Putting down the rubber ball, he held out his hand and flexed his fingers. There was no doubt that they were much better, but he was extremely worried that they wouldn't ever be dextrous enough to play properly. He supposed that when eventually he was released from here and sent home, he at least could earn a living.

The authorities would have been in touch with his next of kin – whoever that was – but this took time, he knew that. Especially now he'd been moved to a hospital in England, his papers would have to catch up with him. Even if they arrived with his home address, he'd be writing to perhaps a wife or a mother of whom he had no recollection. These problems weighed heavily with him.

Some of the troops that had recovered would soon be repatriated, and eventually the entire American staff would vacate the hospital; Joshua had elected to stay where he was until they did. Somehow he felt safer. Here, no one would come to visit him. He couldn't bear the idea of a stranger coming towards him, arms outstretched in welcome and him not knowing just who they were. And the doctors were in agreement, feeling that such an experience could be too traumatic for him to cope with at the moment.

Early in the month of August, Ivy's husband Len had returned to Southampton from the war overseas and pleaded with her to take him back. But she was very uncertain. As she said to Maggie, 'I know I was in the wrong, but he was having a good time too . . . and I haven't forgotten the beating he gave me. Yet . . . somehow the war has changed him.'

'In what way?' asked Maggie.

Ivy looked thoughtful. 'I don't know, he's more of a man now. More thoughtful, more inclined to think of me and not his mates and the boozer.

Mind you, some of them were killed overseas.'

'What are you going to do?'

'I really don't know.' She looked at Maggie. 'I've got used to pleasing myself, not having to think about putting a meal on the table at a certain time, and all that. But . . .' She looked at her friend. 'I do get lonely, Mags.'

'I know what you mean,' said Maggie.

'Oh, I'm sorry, love. How stupid of me to run off at the mouth like that without thinking.'

'Come on, don't be silly. Life goes on,' Maggie reassured her. She sat up straighter in the chair, holding her back. 'I'll be glad when this is all over,' she said. 'This child is so heavy to cart about.'

'Do you want a boy or a girl?' asked Ivy.

'All I want is a healthy baby.'

Ivy looked at her, a soft expression in her eyes. 'You make me feel broody.'

'You! I didn't think of you wanting children. Well, not yet anyway.'

'To be honest,' confessed her friend, 'I feel it's time to settle down. But somehow I really don't see me spending the rest of my days with Len. Bob showed me that there are better men around . . . I'll just have to wait until I find one.'

Maggie gave her friend a cheeky grin. 'You won't ever be on the shelf, Ivy. Men have always gathered around you like bees round a honey pot.'

'Yes, and we know why! So I like a good time, but there's more to life. I want a home and kids, like everyone else.' She pulled a face. 'Christ! I must be getting old.'

'What, at twenty-four? Hardly.'

'My old gran thinks I'm definitely on the shelf now I don't have Len. She said as much the other day.' She chuckled. 'I told her, I don't mind, as long as someone takes me down now and then and gives me a dust!'

'What did she say to that?'

'She's a quaint old bird. She said, "Quite right girl, but don't wait too long or all the good uns will have gone." Cheeky sod.'

The following days seemed to drag to Maggie. She couldn't get comfortable at night, even with a small pillow beneath her bump as her mother had suggested. The baby seemed to have settled on a nerve, and to help the discomfort she walked around, lifting the weight with one hand.

'I'll be glad when this is all over,' she said to Moira as they sat in the kitchen one afternoon.

'The last few weeks are the worst,' explained her mother. 'I remember it well. But when you hold that child in your arms . . . there is nothing like the thrill of it.'

'I wish Joshua were here,' said Maggie plaintively. 'I miss him so much.'

'Of course you do, darlin'. If he is a prisoner-of-war, it takes ages before everything is sorted and the men go home. You're bound to hear in time.'

Maggie squeezed her mother's hand. 'I know.'

But Moira was beginning to have her doubts. Perhaps Joshua had been killed in action. If he had, then his parents would have been notified, not Maggie. God! She hoped that wasn't the case. She'd seen the telegraph boy on his bike stop and knock on a couple of doors in this street, delivering the dreaded telegram in its orange envelope. The anguish the family suffered was heart-wrenching. But if Joshua had been killed, Maggie might never know, and that would be even worse!

A week later Maggie went into labour. It took them all by surprise as, according to the doctor's calculations, the baby wasn't due for another three weeks.

Both the doctor and the midwife were summoned and the long wait began. Moira stood at the top of the bed, bathing her daughter's forehead, holding her hand when she had a contraction, soothing her as the pains increased.

Downstairs Jack was pacing the kitchen as he'd done when Maggie had been born so many years before. He was surprised to realize he was as much concerned now as he'd been then. The cries of pain coming from the upstairs room went through him like a knife and he wanted to rush upstairs and comfort her, but he knew better than to do so.

'I can see the baby's head,' said the doctor. He looked up at his patient. 'It won't be long now.'

Moira wiped the sweat from Maggie's brow. 'It'll all be over soon,' she said.

'I didn't know it hurt so much,' complained Maggie.

Her mother smiled at her. 'You'll soon forget all about the pain.'

But she couldn't answer, as another contraction gripped her.

'Push, Maggie. Push!' encouraged the doctor.

With all her might she bore down, her voice loud with the effort.

'Once more,' he pleaded.

Her face puce, she did as she was asked. Then she rested, exhausted, perspiration trickling down her face.

The doctor looked at her. 'One more push ought to do it,' he urged.

And at last it was over.

Dr Pierson grinned at her. 'You have a fine son, Maggie. Congratulations!' He wrapped the child in a clean towel and handed it to her.

She took the small bundle from him and stared into the little puckered face of her newborn child. 'Little Joshua Lewis,' she said and looked up at her mother. 'What do you think of your grandchild?'

Moira peered at the baby. 'Ah. He's absolutely beautiful,' she said. 'I can see both you and Joshua in him.'

Downstairs, Jack Evans heard the baby's cry and was relieved. But at the same time he was terrified. Terrified of what he would think when first he saw the child.

When later he was called upstairs, he made his way with great trepidation. He entered the bedroom and, walking over to the bed, leaned forward and kissed Maggie's forehead. 'Are you all right, love?'

'Fine, Dad. Take a look at your grandchild.' She moved back the fold of the towel so he could see.

Taking a deep breath he leaned over the small bundle. The baby had a smooth skin the colour of caramel toffee. His little mouth was moving, and his fingers. Jack looked at him as he put out his own finger and the baby enclosed it in his tiny hand.

He looked at his daughter and smiled broadly. 'He's lovely. I'd forgotten how small a newborn baby is.' He gazed at Maggie and in a soft voice said, 'It takes me back a few years.' He looked down at the child again. Poor little chap, he thought. None of this was his fault, and he's going to have enough problems as he grows without my adding to them. With a proud note in his voice, he said, 'I am your grandfather.'

Moira came over to him and kissed him on the cheek. 'You'll have to move back into our room,' she said quietly. 'We'll need the spare room for a nursery.'

Later, when she was alone with her baby, Maggie looked at the tiny toes, the fingers, the little tongue, and thought what a miracle childbirth was. It seemed impossible that this beautiful living creature had been growing inside her for almost nine months. She kissed the top of the baby's head. 'You are my precious little miracle,' she whispered. 'How proud your father will be of you when he sees you.' But when would that be? she wondered. She gazed once more at their child. 'We'll just have to be patient,' she said. 'I know he'll come back one day. I just *know* he will.' But deep down she was beginning to experience her first doubts.

Chapter Twenty-Five

Whilst Maggie was coming to terms with being a mother, Joshua was extremely frustrated. Now he was having more of these flashbacks, but they were always so fleeting, never tangible. On the wireless one day he heard a spiritual being sung by a choir and suddenly he visualized the minister in the snapshot, standing in front of an altar – then it was gone. He kept looking at his reflection, but still a stranger stared back. It was driving him crazy.

He had nightmares about an explosion. The scene was fragmented: a burning tank, soldiers, the sound of gunfire, the whine of a shell. He woke up always with a start, perspiration dripping off him.

The nursing staff and the doctors were all very supportive, explaining that this was a good sign, even if it was distressing.

'But they don't last long enough for me to grasp!' he exclaimed.

'One day they will,' he was told. And he held on to this thought. He hoped it would be soon, because the authorities were closer now to giving him all the information about his background. As the doctor explained, 'There are so many wounded and dying to trace. Some dead, with only their dog tags for the office to follow up. But you'll hear very soon and then you'll go home to your family.'

But what if he didn't remember before then? He'd be sent to a home, surrounded by strangers, all making a fuss – and he wouldn't know them. The very idea terrified him.

He walked along the corridor, making for the gardens. Through a window he looked out over the lawn. There in the distance was a girl in a floral dress, her auburn hair flowing in the breeze. He stopped. 'Maggie,' he murmured and started to run, down the corridor, out into the grounds. He didn't even feel the grass beneath his feet as he flew towards the figure. 'Maggie!' he called, but she didn't look round.

Breathless, he caught up with the young woman, grabbed her by the shoulders and turned her round to face him.

She let out a cry of fright. He looked at the features of a stranger and apologized profusely. 'Gee, ma'am. I'm real sorry. I thought you were someone I knew.'

'It's all right, soldier,' she said, somewhat nervously, and walked on.

He made his way to the water's edge and sat on the grass. He took the picture from his pocket and looked at the girl with the smiling eyes.

'Maggie,' he said softly. 'How could I ever forget you?'

He sat for a long time, alone, staring at the picture, then at the other one. He closed his eyes, letting his mind roam freely. Images crowded in one after another, until his head throbbed and he felt sick. He tried to look out at the horizon, but his head spun and his vision blurred. He held his head with his hands and rocked back and forth with the pain.

A nurse came rushing over, took one look at his haggard face and called two orderlies who put him into a wheelchair and took him back to his bed.

The doctor came in and took his pulse. 'What happened, Joshua?'

'I started remembering, then this pain in my head.'

'You try and rest now. I'll give you some pain killers.'

'But what if I rest then I can't remember again?' There was a note of panic in his voice now.

'You will, I promise.'

The nurse took his temperature, it was up. 'Just try and keep calm,' she said.

Joshua tossed from side to side in his bed. How could he keep calm? Memories were crowding his brain until he thought it was going to burst. He lay back and closed his eyes after taking the pills with a sip of water, until the throbbing subsided into a dull ache and he recovered his equilibrium . . . He was so tired. His eyes gradually closed and he slept.

Later in the day, the doctor came back to see him. 'How are you feeling?'

'A bit woozy, but my head doesn't hurt so much.'

'I've got some news for you, sergeant. Your papers have come through, now I can put you in the picture about your family, your home.' He sat on the edge of the bed. 'Your father,' the doctor began . . .

'Is a pastor of the church in Mississippi. I have two brothers and two sisters . . . and I have a girl. We're going to be married.' A frown furrowed his brow. 'But the rest is somewhat hazy.'

The doctor smiled. 'Well done, son. When did all this actually happen?'

'A while back . . . All because of a girl with red hair.'

'No wonder you're in a state. But I'm surprised you're taking it so calmly.'

'Believe me, sir, calm is the last thing I feel. I'm just so happy to know who I am. Before, I knew I was Joshua Lewis because you told me so, but it was just a label to me. Any name would have done. But now . . . well, now it's different . . . I need to spend some time alone to collect my thoughts.'

'Who is the president of the United States?' the doctor asked suddenly.

With a grin, Joshua answered, 'Harry Truman.'

There was a look of satisfaction on the doctor's face. 'I'll need to give you a thorough examination later today, but now I suggest you just rest.'

'My family?' asked Joshua.

'They've been advised of your whereabouts, sergeant. Soon you'll be going home and then you'll be discharged from the army.'

Joshua asked, 'Any chance I could be discharged from here, sir?'

'I'd have to make enquiries about that. You may have to go back to the States.'

'There's someone in Southampton I have to see. It's real urgent.'

The doctor got to his feet. 'You aren't going anywhere for a couple of days. How's your head?'

'Throbbing,' he admitted.

'You need to take it easy. This has been very traumatic for you. Give yourself some time to come to terms with what's happened. We'll talk in the morning.'

He felt so unwell that, although he desperately wanted to see Maggie, Joshua knew he wasn't up to it. After all, he didn't want to collapse on her doorstep! But at least now he could lie back on his pillows and plan for the future . . . if she still wanted him.

It worried him that as she hadn't heard from him for so long she might have changed her mind. She was probably thinking all sorts of things. Maybe that he didn't love her. What would he do if she didn't love him any more? These tortuous thoughts plagued him as he lay in his bed.

'Just one thing, doc.'

'What's that?'

'Have you got a mirror somewhere?'

The doctor looked puzzled and gazed around the ward. He went to a locker, took a shaving mirror from the top of it and handed it to his patient.

Joshua looked in it and with a broad grin said, 'Hey. I know this guy!'

The doctor burst out laughing and shook him by the hand. 'Congratulations sergeant. I'm glad it all worked out.'

'Thank you, sir. So am I.' He lay back on his pillows, clutching the mirror, his mind filled with an image of Maggie Evans.

Baby Joshua was now three weeks old and the pride of the family. Jack had become besotted with the child, cuddling him at every available moment. Talking to him, cooing.

Moira looked on and with a wry smile said to Maggie, 'He never spent this much time with you.'

'It doesn't matter. I'm just so happy to see it. Knowing how Dad felt, I was afraid he'd have nothing to do with his grandchild. And as he grows, he'll need a man's authority and guidance.'

With a sharp look at her daughter, Moira said, 'What do you mean?'

'Well, Mum, I've not heard a word from Joshua, and I'm afraid that

211

something has happened to him, because I know if he was alive, he would have moved heaven and earth to get in touch.'

She looked so sad that Moira's heart ached for her. 'You don't know that, darlin'.'

'True, but I have to be prepared, just in case.' She forced a smile. 'At least I have his child.'

'Moira gathered her into her arms and held her. But neither spoke, both too full of emotion for words.

Most of the regulars of the Bricklayer's Arms fussed over the baby, but there were a few who gathered in small groups to gossip about Maggie being unmarried, with a black bastard. They didn't voice their opinions in front of the family, however.

Maggie was nevertheless very aware of the veiled hostility, and completely ignored it, holding her head with pride. This child was hers and Joshua's. He was born out of love, the child of the man she'd wanted to share her life with. She had nothing to be ashamed of. Had Joshua not been shipped out, they would be a happy family, and as young Joshua grew, she would tell him what a fine man his father was, so that he would be proud too.

Already she would hold her baby close to her and tell him of his father's talent, his gentleness, and how much she loved him.

As she gazed at her child, she could see how much he took after his father. She drank in every detail, remembering how Joshua's eyes twinkled, his laugh, how he held her to him and made love to her. She was scared that the memories would fade in time, but she'd had a snapshot enlarged and framed. It stood beside her bed on the table. It was the last thing she looked at every night, before she slept.

Sometimes she dreamed of him. He was always somewhere trying to reach her, but something always seemed to stop him and she'd wake in the morning feeling bereft.

Her friend Ivy was a great comfort to her. She would hold the baby and play with it whilst she tried to cheer Maggie. 'You'll hear eventually. I know you will. That man loved you so much, nothing will keep him away.'

'But what if he's been killed?'

'I've always thought that when two people are really close, like you were, you'd know. You'd get the feeling that something was wrong.' She looked at Maggie. 'Has anything like that happened?'

Maggie shook her head. 'It's just the uncertainty, that's all.'

Ivy smiled at her. 'He'll come back to you . . . and the baby. I know he will.'

Two days later, the doctor told Joshua he could go into Southampton. 'But I want you back tonight, just to check on your health. If you're all right by the end of the week, we'll see about getting you discharged. Then you'll be free to do what you want.'

'Thank you, sir. That sounds mighty good to me.'

He showered and dressed in his uniform, his fingers trembling with nerves as he tried to knot his tie. He caught a bus and headed for the town, looking around at the streets, buildings, for anything that he recognized. He knew his way to the Bricklayer's Arms, and that was the only thing that was really important.

Getting off the bus, he walked through the park, heading for College Street, remembering how he and Maggie had sat among the trees, talking, on many occasions. He smiled to himself as he recalled their conversations – her liking for Frank Sinatra, his teasing her about her taste in music.

At the corner of Maggie's street, he paused and nervously lit a cigarette. His heart was pounding. Would she be pleased to see him? What if she wasn't in? He couldn't bear the suspense any longer. Tossing the cigarette into the gutter, he took a deep breath and walked towards the pub.

Jack Evans heard the knock on the side door as he walked towards the bar. He was very surprised when he opened the door to see a GI standing there.

'Hello, sir. Are you Mr Evans?'

'Yes, that's right.'

The soldier held out his hand. 'How do you do, sir. My name is Joshua Lewis, and I've come to see Maggie.'

'Bloody hell!'

Maggie pushed the back door open with her backside, her arms full, carrying a basket loaded with dry laundry and wooden pegs. She looked at the open doorway and the silhouette of the man standing there. She heard him mention her name. She dropped the basket and, with a cry, staggered against the wall, her face drained of colour. Then she ran past her startled father and hurled herself into the arms of the soldier.

Moira came running from the kitchen, alerted by the noise and saw the two in an embrace. Jack looked at her, astonishment written over his face. She took his hand. 'Come on, love,' she said. 'This is no place for us old ones.'

When at last Maggie was able to speak, she said, 'Oh, Joshua, darling, is it really you?'

He chuckled softly. 'If it isn't I'd like to know who you think you're kissing so passionately.'

She ushered him into the front room, once filled with contraband, now a cosy sitting room. 'Let me look at you,' she said, gazing at him, touching the face of the man she loved so much. 'I was beginning to think I'd never see you again.'

He drew her into his arms and held her to him. Then he looked into her eyes. 'No one is ever going to keep us apart. I love you, Maggie. More than you'll ever know.' He smothered her with kisses. 'You are just as beautiful as I remember.'

She led him to the settee. 'Where have you been? Why didn't you write?'

'I was in an explosion . . . I lost my memory for a time.'

She covered her mouth in horror. 'Oh darling, how dreadful. Are you all right now?'

He caressed her cheek. 'Now I'm with you.'

'Were you in hospital?'

He nodded. 'You wouldn't believe it, but I've been at the one in Netley.'

'For how long?'

'Since just before the end of the war.'

'Oh no!' Maggie looked desolate. 'To think you were so near for so long. That's really cruel.'

'But I'm here now,' he said softly. 'I have to go back this evening, and if I'm all right, they'll discharge me at the end of the week.'

She gazed at him and, with a note of uncertainty in her voice asked, 'And what then?'

He looked puzzled. 'And then I thought we'd arrange to get married as we planned . . . if that's what you still want?'

She kissed him longingly. 'What else would I want, you goose.'

'Oh, Maggie. Coming here today I was real scared.'

'Why?'

'I was worried that you'd have changed your mind.'

She cupped his face in her hands. 'Joshua Lewis, you're the only man I want, and now I know you still want me, that's reason enough.' She gazed into his eyes and smiled softly. 'I do have another reason, and so do you.'

He looked confused. 'My memory is still a bit hazy. Is there something I should remember?'

She took his hand. 'Come with me,' she said. 'There's someone I want you to meet.'

'I've already met your father,' he said hurriedly.

She walked to the back door and opened it.

He followed, now curious, searching his brain, wondering who it could be. Who had he forgotten?

She led him to a large perambulator, its hood down, a canopy keeping the sun off the occupant. She untied the canopy and put it back, revealing the baby, asleep in the pram.

'Joshua, meet your son.'

He looked at her, eyes wide with astonishment, then he gazed down at the baby. He bent closer and studied the child, smoothing his soft cheek.

Then he looked at Maggie again. 'This beautiful creature is ours?'

'Yes, darling, he's almost a month old.'

She saw the tears in Joshua's eyes as he looked at the child. Then at her. 'I had no idea,' he said in a choked voice.

'I didn't know I was pregnant when you were shipped out.'

'Oh, Maggie . . . you had to go through this all on your own.'

'No, Joshua. Mum and Dad were here. They took care of me.'

'Your father! And what does he have to say about all this?'

She chuckled. 'He's besotted with little Joshua.'

'You named him after me?'

'Who else would I name him after?'

He shook his head slowly as he gazed into the pram. There was a look of wonderment on his face. 'He's so perfect,' he said. Then, gently stroking her face, he added, 'And so are you.' He leaned forward and kissed her forehead. 'We're going to have a good life together, darling. When I get clear of the hospital and discharged from the army, I'll go up to London and look for a job.'

Maggie picked up the baby and looked at Joshua with an expression that was full of love. 'I don't mind what you do or where, as long as we're together.' She placed the baby in his arms.

He looked down at his son and said, 'You are such a lucky little fellow. Your mother is beautiful and your father is going to make good.' He kissed the baby and cradled him. When he could tear his gaze from his child, he looked up at Maggie and with a broad grin said, 'You don't know it yet, but you're marrying one hell of a guy! I'm gonna make it big one day, have my own band and who knows, maybe, eventually, my own jazz club. It may take a little time, but your husband is going to be a successful man. I'm gonna take real good care of you both.'

Maggie kissed him tenderly. 'I know,' she said. She had no fears about the future. She knew it wouldn't be easy, that there would be prejudice from some. But she knew that Joshua had the talent to overcome all this and she had his love, which would shelter her and their baby. 'Come on,' she said. 'Let's go inside, he's due a feed.'

The two of them walked into the kitchen. Moira leapt to her feet and hugged the American. 'Oh Joshua, love. I'm so glad you're all right.'

He smiled at her. 'Gee, it's good to see you.'

'And this is my father,' said Maggie. 'Although you did meet briefly.'

Jack got to his feet, looking first at the baby, then at the GI. He shook Joshua by the hand. 'Nice to meet you,' he said shortly.

Joshua looked into the other man's eyes. 'Whatever your reservations about me are, sir, I want you to know that I love Maggie with all my heart and my wish is to take care of her . . . and my son. Ain't nobody gonna stop me.'

Jack was impressed by the young man's candour and recognized the challenge. 'Good, I'm very glad to hear it. Sit down . . . Moira, put the kettle on for a cup of tea.'

Joshua looked across at Maggie and silently mouthed, 'No coffee?'

She chuckled to herself softly as she put a finger to her lips to silence him. Joshua would learn their quaint English ways in time, including how a cup of tea was the answer to all problems. He had taught her so much and now she would be able to teach him. She could see it was going to be an interesting life.

101311

KT-446-472

62049

ST HELE...

WITHDRAWN FROM
ST HELENS COLLEGE LIBRARY

Agent of Challenge and Defiance
The Films of Ken Loach

cinema voices

Series editor: Matthew Stevens, FLICKS BOOKS
Series consultant: Brian McIlroy, University of British Columbia

This series provides critical assessments of film directors whose work is motivated by social, political or historical concerns, or reveals an opposition to conventional filmmaking systems and structures. The following titles are published˙ or in preparation:

˙Auteur/provocateur: the films of Denys Arcand
Edited by André Loiselle and Brian McIlroy

˙Dark alchemy: the films of Jan Švankmajer
Edited by Peter Hames

˙Queen of the 'B's: Ida Lupino behind the camera
Edited by Annette Kuhn

˙By angels driven: the films of Derek Jarman
Edited by Chris Lippard

˙Poet of civic courage: the films of Francesco Rosi
Edited by Carlo Testa

˙A call to action: the films of Ousmane Sembene
Edited by Sheila Petty

˙Agent of challenge and defiance: the films of Ken Loach
Edited by George McKnight

The last modernist: the films of Theo Angelopoulos
Edited by Andrew Horton

Lucid dreams: the films of Krzysztof Kieślowski
Edited by Paul Coates

Agent of Challenge and Defiance

The Films of Ken Loach

Edited by
George McKnight

cinema voices series

FLICKS
BOOKS

A CIP catalogue record for this book is available from the British Library.

ISBN 0-948911-94-8 (Hb)
ISBN 0-948911-99-9 (Pb)

First published in 1997 by

Flicks Books
29 Bradford Road
Trowbridge
Wiltshire BA14 9AN
England
tel   +44 1225 767728
fax +44 1225 760418

© individual contributors, 1997

ST. HELENS
COLLEGE

791.430233

101311

MAY 2001

LIBRARY

An edition of this book is published in North and South America by Greenwood Press in hardback, and by Praeger Publishers in paperback.

All rights reserved. No part of this publication may be reproduced, stored in a retrieval system or transmitted in any form or by any means: electronic, electrostatic, magnetic tape, mechanical, photocopying, recording or otherwise, without prior permission in writing from the publishers.

Printed and bound in Great Britain by Bookcraft (Bath) Ltd.

· To my parents, Jean and George McKnight ·

Contents

Acknowledgements

I must express my deep gratitude to the contributors – John Hill, Deborah Knight, Stuart Laing, Patrick MacFadden and Julian Petley – and to our publisher, Matthew Stevens, for their generosity and support during the preparation of this book. I am particularly indebted to Julian and to Deborah for their assistance at crucial stages, and to Matthew. I would like to thank the National Archives of Canada and Parallax Pictures for their helpful assistance, and the Dean of the Faculty of Arts and the Dean of the Faculty of Graduate Studies and Research, Carleton University, for their support. I would also like to recognise the Bytown Cinema, Ottawa, which, like so many other independent cinemas throughout the world, continues to show Ken Loach's films.

George McKnight
February 1997

Introduction

George McKnight

For over 30 years, Ken Loach's television dramas, television documentary dramas, documentary films and feature films have established him as a voice of defiance in British film and television. His films have implicitly or explicitly been critical of the British social and political system, and this critical stance has often put him at the centre of general debate, whether in academic circles or in the public press. His films have raised questions not only about film form and aesthetic strategies when dealing with political and historical issues, but also concerning public policy and the political will to deal with problems that are a result of the divisions and inequities within British society. Loach's films have been controversial and they have drawn criticism. Yet, they have also won national and international awards, beginning with a British Film Academy Best Supporting Actor award to Colin Welland and a Karlovy Vary Award in 1970 for *Kes* (1969). In addition, his films have won prizes at Cannes – *Black Jack* (1979); *Looks and Smiles* (1981); *Hidden Agenda* (1990); *Riff-Raff* (1991); *Raining Stones* (1993) – Venice (*Fatherland* [1986]) and Berlin (*Ladybird Ladybird* [1994]). In 1991, *Riff-Raff* took Film of the Year at the European Film Awards.

Loach's career has built on what he is inspired at – the creation of emblematic and memorable central characters such as Cathy (*Cathy Come Home* [1966]), Eddie (*The Rank and File* [1971]), Kerrigan (*Hidden Agenda*), Bob (*Raining Stones*), Maggie (*Ladybird Ladybird*), and David and Blanca (*Land and Freedom*, [1995]). These characters and Loach's distinctive film style combine to engage us emotionally in narrative action, and polemically in the specific issues which each film raises. Loach has been unwavering in his concern with working-class individuals and families, and with characters who are disenfranchised or constrained by their social and economic circumstances – consider *Up the Junction* (1965), *Kes* and *Looks and Smiles*. He has drawn our attention to those at the margins of their own social class and indeed even at the margins of society, as we find in *Cathy Come Home*, *Riff-Raff*, *Raining Stones* and *Ladybird Ladybird*. He has also focused on those who oppose the decisions or defy the authority of the organisations, institutions or political parties to which they belong: for example, the striking dockworkers in *The Big Flame* (1969); the rank

1

and file members of the trade union in *The Rank and File*; and the workers during the General Strike in *Days of Hope* (1975). Kerrigan and David are also part of this pattern.

In films across all the genres in which Loach has worked, his central characters come into direct conflict with dominant social institutions or political organisations. Indeed, these institutions and organisations – more so than the characters who represent them – are the real antagonists in his films. It is one thing for individuals to confront individuals, or groups to confront groups: in such situations, the playing field is something like level, and collective discussion might lead to solutions that benefit all parties. It is quite another matter for the marginalised or disenfranchised to confront whole systems of power. The outcome of such confrontations is virtually predetermined: the structures in place will preserve themselves at the cost of those who challenge them.

Consider the broad range of social and political institutions that have come under Loach's scrutiny. He has been consistently critical of state-administered social services, as well as the medical and psychiatric professions, the police, the courts and the administering of the law, the press, the military, and various forms of state security. These institutions are designed to promote and regulate societal well-being, but, as Loach shows, they regularly fail at this task. In films such as *Cathy Come Home*, *Family Life* (1971) and *Ladybird Ladybird*, they fail through a systemic inability to adapt rules and policies to the actual needs of those whom they are supposed to serve and support. Loach's critique suggests the need radically to transform social services that are shown to be unable to deal fairly and humanely with those who must rely on them. But Loach is also preoccupied with another theme that emerges from his study of state services. In films including *The Big Flame*, *The Rank and File*, *Days of Hope*, *A Question of Leadership* (1980), *Questions of Leadership* (1983), *Hidden Agenda* and *Land and Freedom*, he examines the – often covert – actions of political and social institutions, including trade unions, political parties, police forces and the military. He has consistently examined how allegiances rooted in the maintenance of power are frequently at the expense of the very people – employees, members and/or supporters – whom these institutions are designed to protect. So what we see in Loach's films is not just the incompetence or failure of particular social and political institutions. We also see how these institutions betray the very individuals whom they exist to support and to serve.

Most often, Loach tells stories about the actions of ordinary people, frequently working-class individuals and their families, and about groups of people who take collective action. As a rule, Loach's characters do not act out of narrow self-interest, political or otherwise. Nor is it usual for his central characters to act out of wilful anger or to initiate violence. However, in films such as *Riff-Raff* and *Raining Stones*, pent-up frustration and a sense of abject hopelessness can lead to violence or destructiveness. The construction workers in *Riff-Raff* ultimately prefer to burn down the building they have been converting from a former hospital into cheaply made "luxury" flats as a gesture against both their employers and the new Thatcherite economy. After all, in this new economy, the workers themselves are forced to live in squats or in overcrowded buildings, are underpaid, are subject to scandalously unsafe working conditions, and could never hope to be able to afford anything like the type of flats they themselves are making. Their actions offer one of many insights in Loach's films into the ways in which economic and social policies produce social conflict.

But Loach's films, in fact, do not often privilege characters who advocate radical political action or violence – although the figures of authority in his films view those who do take action as just such a threat. With the exception of Kerrigan and Philip Hargreaves, the Labour MP in *Days of Hope*, Loach's central characters seldom occupy positions of authority, let alone any managerial, administrative or professional position in public life from which they could advocate broad social change. Rather, in Loach's films, characters are driven to local action because of quite specific political and economic circumstances, namely, their own. Yet, in what might seem a paradox, given Loach's political commitments, his characters usually do not set out to challenge the structures of power, nor do their actions constitute a wilful challenge to authority. Initially, at least, their actions are driven by something more like idealism, confidence or hope.

In films where dramatic conflict is located in relation to the public sphere, action is developed around events such as strikes, the social upheaval brought about by military conflict or civil war, the struggle for nationhood, or the divisions within organised labour and political parties. Here, Loach's central characters act with the hope of improving working conditions or of changing the relationship between labour and management. They hope to change how decisions are made and how policies are developed. They want to change how land is used or how a state is governed. They act out of a determination to do what they believe is right and what they believe is just. There is often a spontaneity and enthusiasm about these decisions to act, an enthusiasm fuelled by the expectation that what they are doing will make an actual political difference. We need only think of the men who take over the running of the docks in *The Big Flame*, the striking workers who oppose the practices of their union leadership in *The Rank and File*, or David who volunteers to go to fight against Spanish Fascism in *Land and Freedom*. But Loach's films are hardly as optimistic as this sketch might suggest. For, in the socio-political realm, the idealism of his central characters is often coupled with a naïvety about the power of the opposition they face, the lengths to which those who wield power will go to retain their own political advantage, and the final abandonment of principle in the interests of political expediency. Furthermore, even in films which focus on action in the public sphere, we see the consequences of these actions on the personal lives of the individuals involved, as well as on their families or comrades.

In the films with domestic or family settings, Loach's central characters usually act to bring about some change in their daily lives that seems reasonable within the range of possibilities held up as attainable by the social system itself. In Loach's more obviously political films, characters undertake individual or collective actions that challenge those in authority only when they are denied the opportunity to voice legitimate points of view within a democratic system, or to act upon what are often fundamental social beliefs and political values. The moment of challenge often occurs in (usually doomed) situations where central characters confront those who uphold the blind implementation of regulations put in place by higher authorities. We see this poignantly in films such as *Cathy Come Home* and *Ladybird Ladybird*. But, in the more obviously political films, the moment of challenge is not between central characters and those who blindly uphold regulations: in films ranging from *The Rank and File* through *Hidden Agenda* to *Land and Freedom*, the confrontation occurs between central characters and representatives of the political system who know full well that they are acting to preserve their own position.

Loach's films are invariably about how a hierarchy is maintained, whether or not those in positions of authority recognise that the struggle in which they are engaged is a struggle for power. The assertion of power and authority is in the name of moral or legal right, or is assumed to result in individual or social benefit or betterment, or is said to be in the best interests of the community or even the nation. Parents, the board within the hospital that supports the medical establishment, the union officials, administrators, managers, the representatives of the owners, and those representing social services are all part of how the status quo is maintained through the prevailing opinion and the established practices within institutional structures. These are the often-unseen struggles for power where those in subordinate positions – the child, the doctors who offer innovative forms of treatment, the rank and file, the parents whose desire is to hold the family together – will inevitably lose to those who hold authority.

Many of Loach's films have domestic or family settings: for instance, *Up the Junction*, *Cathy Come Home*, *Poor Cow* (1967), *Kes*,

4

After a Lifetime (1971), *Family Life, Looks and Smiles, The Gamekeeper* (1980), *Riff-Raff, Raining Stones* and *Ladybird Ladybird*. These are films about the daily problems faced by people trying to find or keep a job, deal with employers or their representatives, find a place to live, build a relationship or sustain a marriage, keep a family together, raise children or deal with the differences between family members and between generations. These all seem to be apparently unexceptional everyday situations. Yet, Loach's focus is always turned to points where it becomes difficult or even impossible to maintain the minimal conditions to satisfy such apparently everyday expectations as holding down a job, being able to afford a reasonable flat, keeping a relationship together, or buying a new dress for your daughter's first Communion. As we have seen, Loach has been particularly concerned with the consequences of economic and social conditions on central characters and their families. In some of the films made between the mid-1960s and the early 1970s, normative moral and social values – especially concerning questions of sexual morality, the work ethic, and the expectations of the older generation – were voiced within the family to indicate the changes in expectations and attitudes at the time. In his more recent films, however, the threat of violence within or to the family becomes more explicit, although this only develops a theme already established in, for instance, *Family Life*. It is a measure of the hopelessness which characters experience that they act in ways that put their own relationships in jeopardy, or that their actions have consequences that threaten their families. In Loach's films of the 1990s, this threat of violence is tied more directly than before to desperate economic circumstances.

In films ranging across those focused on the family and those focused on labour, we see a consistent attention to the interconnection between questions of gender and identity. Loach does not come to these issues by way of the recently fashionable trends of postmodernism. Rather, in his films, the family has itself always been treated as an enormously powerful social institution. And any consideration of the family, whether the traditional or the post-traditional family, inevitably raises questions about gender roles and about how patriarchal family structures contribute to or encroach on the development of personal identity for all members, adults and children alike. It is not that Loach's films are concerned with "gender issues"; instead, his characters are defined, in large measure, by traditional gender roles. Male central characters dominate his films. By and large, women characters in Loach's films are not involved directly in political action. When they are (Sarah in *Days of Hope*; Emma in *Fatherland*; Ingrid in *Hidden Agenda*; Blanca in *Land and Freedom*), their roles are subordinate to male characters. When we have a central woman character, she is positioned in relation either to her husband (*Poor Cow, Cathy Come Home, Ladybird Ladybird*) or to her parents (*Family Life*). Central women characters are defined by problems and individual aspirations traditionally identified with home and family. They are figures of empathy (Cathy, Maggie), or they speak the values of the traditional family (Cathy) or of normative social and sexual behaviour (Janice's mother). Yet, it is through such characters that these very roles and values are (hopefully) thrown into question. Central women characters dramatise social issues, particularly the consequences of conditions such as a lack of adequate housing (*Cathy Come Home*) or the effects of physical and/or psychological violence on individuals and families (*Ladybird Ladybird*).

The interconnection of gender and identity is also central to the films centred on labour. Loach has shown working-class men with all their faults and blemishes, as well as with a certain vernacular eloquence. In the early films dealing with labour, men are defined by accent and class, by the work they do on the docks or in factories, by locations identified with their work or the terrace houses identified with industrial towns, by talking and meeting as groups of workers, and by acting collectively. The consequences of their actions on their families, particularly when these actions involve industrial disputes that lead to strikes or to taking over the docks, are a significant but secondary feature of films such as *The Big Flame* or *The Rank and File*. There is a clear division between the roles of men and the roles of women in these early films, regardless of whether the films deal with labour or with the domestic sphere. While a division between gender roles remains in Loach's films in the 1990s, the consequences of such differences are now more marked. With the loss of the jobs that traditionally established and maintained their identity as working-class men, Loach's male central characters seem to experience a loss of personal identity. The men in *Riff-Raff* and *Raining Stones* are no longer members of a union. They are unemployed, taking jobs while on the dole, taking whatever work is available, or resorting to petty theft on the job. They know what they are supposed to be doing and know what they want to do as working-class men, but are stuck: jobless, short of the cash they need to provide for their families, they are without clear prospects and without hope. Their stories are no longer the stories of collective action that could transform the workplace and give working-class men a place in management and decision-making (the hope that motivated the workers in *The Big Flame*). Their stories are now the stories of desperate individual actions to retain something of their identity (*Raining Stones*).

Without filmmakers such as Loach, the kinds of stories he has told for the past 30 years, and continues to tell, would likely remain untold. Loach's central figures are not the heroic individuals of

6

mainstream filmmaking who invariably triumph over adverse circumstances and whose actions lead to resolutions that reassure us. (Loach would, of course, consider this type of reassurance false.) One reason why mainstream cinema does not tell the stories Loach tells is because his characters are, typically, so ordinary: these are individuals who are basically indistinguishable from others we see on the street, in housing estates or in pubs. Loach's stories seldom end with the realisation of the hopes and expectations of his central characters. Yet, Loach tells these stories not as personal stories of individual failure, but as stories of social failure.

If there is a central theme that unites Loach's work, it would be the betrayal of hope. More than this, Loach's films consistently turn our attention to the ways in which his characters are betrayed by their own side. This is the great dilemma for Loach as a political filmmaker. In his domestic morality tales (*Cathy Come Home*, *Family Life*, *Ladybird Ladybird*), individuals are betrayed by the very state services upon which they depend in times of hardship. Being betrayed by your own side connects the seemingly more sociologically oriented domestic morality tales to the films that focus on more overtly political matters, as we see in the television dramas on trade unionism (*The Big Flame*, *The Rank and File*, *Days of Hope*), the political thriller, *Hidden Agenda*, and more recently in *Land and Freedom*. In Loach's films, the social or political struggle being waged is invariably twofold. What is immediately obvious is how his central characters become caught up in various types of factionalism. This is usually depicted as an external struggle, a sort of "us-*versus*-them" situation. We find this most obviously in the films that deal with incidents that go on as a matter of public or historical record: for example, where strikers are in dispute with management, where political conflict occurs in Northern Ireland, or where a civil war erupts in Spain. But we see it in the domestic morality tales as well, where social services become the opponents of characters such as Cathy and Reg, or Maggie and Jorge. Moreover, when it comes to the public arena, Loach's films remind us of how broadcast media or the press report events, particularly when dealing with strikes or when government policy is under attack. His films raise questions about the role of the media and the press in formulating issues and shaping both the public perception of events and the construction of an historical record – particularly when authority is challenged by groups of workers or by groups whose political beliefs lead to violence.

There is, however, another struggle running through Loach's films that is more central to his ongoing concern with betrayal. It is played out within organisations, often out of sight of public debate or scrutiny. We see it in the need to maintain power within a particular organisation, such as a union (*The Rank and File*), or within a political organisation or an affiliation of groups seemingly cooperating with one another to achieve a common goal, such as the different groups fighting the Fascists in Spain in *Land and Freedom*. These internal struggles are what preoccupy Loach. It is here that we see the recurring pattern of covert action and betrayal that leads inevitably to the silencing of oppositional voices, to the betrayal of ideal and principle, and to the forms of loss and failure experienced by those whose initiative and commitment initially held out the hope of social or political change.

This paradox of being betrayed by your own side allows Loach to dramatise, from many perspectives, both the idealism necessary to continue the idea of revolution and the practical failure of that idealism when dealing with the political realities of the world. For, in Loach's world, the innocents become the victims of their own idealism. Their idealism and political commitment land them in jail (*The Big Flame*) or cause them to be fired (*The Rank and File*). In extreme cases, these lead to their own deaths or to the deaths of their comrades (*Hidden Agenda*, *Land and Freedom*). The dockers are betrayed in *The Big Flame*; the militia David has joined is betrayed by its own leadership; Janice is betrayed by her parents; Kerrigan is betrayed by his superiors; and the trade unionists in *The Rank and File* and *Days of Hope* are betrayed by their leadership, the TUC. And if Cathy and Maggie are not betrayed by the social services they need, they are failed by the system that authorises these services. It is not the outsiders who get you: it is the insiders. What Loach recognises in and through this thematic of betrayal is the maintenance of political power. At his most overtly political, it is the maintenance of power achieved at the expense of those groups lower in the hierarchy who work cooperatively in socially democratic ways. Power is maintained by covert means because there is a hidden agenda according to which justice, truth, idealism and equity will be sacrificed to satisfy some larger social or political goal.

It is for these reasons that Loach has remained a defiant voice over the years, despite the criticisms and controversies which his work has generated and the actions taken to silence some of his films. To question and challenge the established practices within any social hierarchy invites various forms of condemnation, not to mention the threat of censorship, particularly by television broadcasters. As Julian Petley points out in "Ken Loach and questions of censorship", there have been unsuccessful attempts to censor some of Loach's films, while others have been cut. There have also been demands made by the broadcaster that additional material be included before transmission. Some have not been transmitted by the broadcaster who financed the film, or their transmission has been delayed. His television documentaries have been accused of bias and a lack of impartiality. These accusations seem to arise when Loach has set out to counter an already existing imbalance of opinion in the broadcast media favouring a point of view that supports dominant political attitudes. In addition to the issue of censorship, *Cathy Come Home*, *Days of Hope* and *Ladybird Ladybird*, for example, have led to criticisms in the press that they may mislead the public because they mix fiction with so-called fact, a criticism Petley deals with in "Factual fictions and fictional fallacies: Ken Loach's documentary dramas". Such criticisms are, of course, another form of censorship because they attempt to discredit films and filmmakers such as Loach who employ techniques and practices identified with documentary filmmaking when dealing with contentious issues in a fictional narrative.

In addition to these more public controversies, there have been debates in academic circles surrounding Loach's realist filmmaking practices. The debate that originated in *Screen* during the mid-1970s centring on *Days of Hope* has been reprinted and supplemented in other publications. The debate raised questions concerning aesthetic strategies for political filmmaking at a time in the history of film theory when the so-called "classic realist" text was deemed inadequate as a means of fostering radical political change. In her essay, "Naturalism, narration and critical perspective: Ken Loach and the experimental method", Deborah Knight looks at his films in relation to the traditions of literary and cinematic naturalism, and examines some of the criticisms of Loach which this debate generated. George McKnight concentrates on the narrative structure of a group of films which he identifies as Loach's domestic morality tales, stories that concentrate on the home and family and which feature people who are pushed to the limit of their endurance by circumstances over which they have little or no control. The question of aesthetic strategies is central to any examination of Loach's work, considering the range of forms and film practices found in his work. John Hill takes up this question in "Finding a form: politics and aesthetics in *Fatherland*, *Hidden Agenda* and *Riff-Raff*". Hill concentrates on Loach's return to fiction filmmaking in the changed political climate of the mid-1980s. He examines Loach's experiments with art cinema (*Fatherland*), the political thriller (*Hidden Agenda*), and the methods of documentary drama (*Riff-Raff*) in the search for a film practice appropriate to radical political filmmaking during the Thatcher regime.

The first and final essays of this volume situate Loach's work in the dual context of film and history. In "Ken Loach: histories and contexts", Stuart Laing places Loach in terms of the contemporary history of British film and television production, and in terms of the social, political and economic situation in Britain as it pertains to Loach's career from the 1960s to the present. In addition, he discusses his career in terms of changing broadcast contexts, especially with respect to developing technologies and new patterns of film exhibition and consumption from Loach's early days with the BBC through his recent films produced in conjunction with Channel 4 Television. Patrick MacFadden concludes the volume with an essay on the issue of filmed history. In "Saturn's feast, Loach's Spain: *Land and Freedom* as filmed history", MacFadden reflects on Loach's most atypical political film, emphasising the political backdrop of the film, especially the conflicts between factions within the Communist Party. Furthermore, MacFadden considers the importance, status and political function of fiction films that represent historical events, where the point of the endeavour is to tell stories about the past that have consequences in the present.

The publication of this book anticipates the release of Loach's most recent film, *Carla's Song* (1996). The book offers a long overdue retrospective on Loach's work and a variety of ways in which to consider his future films. It concentrates on how his films have raised or dramatised issues while, at the same time, being always mindful of the social, economic, political and industrial contexts in which the films were produced. As the different essays demonstrate, there is both a singularity to Loach's work across his career, especially in the political analysis towards which his films direct our attention, as well as a diversity in the forms through which he has sought to engage that attention and our political will. The kinds of characters he has created over the years stand as constant reminders of his own attitude of challenge and defiance. Loach's characters remind us that political struggle is and must be ongoing if systems of power are to be made accountable for their actions. And Loach's films remind us that our own engagement cannot remain in the cinema, but must move into the political sphere if any transformation of social systems is to take place.

Ken Loach: histories and contexts

Stuart Laing

> I've spent as much time defending my films as I have making them.[1]

Ken Loach's work is both a reflection of, and a conscious reflection on, the prevailing social and political condition of Britain over the past 30 years. The specifics of this regarding individual works are the subject of other essays in this volume. The purpose of this essay is to provide a more general setting for understanding Loach's work, by noting some of the conditions of production within which he and his various collaborators have worked. These conditions are to be viewed as both constraining (most obviously where cases of censorship are involved) and enabling – in the sense both of particular institutional arrangements and production opportunities within the cultural industries, and of the turn of political and social change which has altered the questions which Loach's films have sought to address. Two related histories are therefore called for: a broad characterisation of the quite marked and unexpected changes in the character of British political and social life between 1964 and the present day, and a more particular attention to the increasingly interrelated television and film industries during the period.

Britain in the 1950s

Loach entered television production in the early 1960s, towards the close of one of the most remarkable periods of social stability and political apathy in British 20th-century history. The 1950s had combined a widespread rise in living standards, visibly evident in the increase in consumer goods (washing-machines, refrigerators, record-players, cars), with full employment and a dominant political philosophy embodied in the words of Harold Macmillan (Conservative Prime Minister, 1957-1963) that "you've never had it so good". For many among the British electorate, this was at last an appropriate and most tangible reward for the efforts and privations of the Second World War and the period of rationing and austerity which followed. The social democratic welfare state (the achievement of the Labour government of the immediate postwar years) was now supplemented

11

by the affluent society of consumer capitalism. Both major political parties shared allegiance to a mixed economy founded on these twin bases, as well as a common aversion to political "extremism" such as had led to the Second World War and was now seen as having come to reside in the Soviet bloc.

The new patterns of consumption in the 1950s were particularly related to the growth of the so-called "home-centred" society, in which the emphasis was on the family, specifically the nuclear family of two parents and two or three children, as the core unit – and the pre-eminent symbol of such a society was the domestic television set. Television was both a key object of domestic consumption (the purchase of the set and the watching of programmes) and a central ideological vehicle for the spreading of the home-centred gospel, through advertising and the messages of its domestic dramas. The decade itself in fact saw a critical change in the relative positions of the two media of television and film (then synonymous with cinema) within which Loach was to make his career. In 1950, cinema was still a major mass cultural form, with two or three cinemas in any medium-sized town; annual attendance stood at 1396 million – an average of 25 visits for every member of the population. By contrast, television sets existed in only 350 000 homes, watching a single channel service available for about five hours a day. However, particularly during the late-1950s, following the introduction of ITV in 1954 and the rapid expansion of new patterns of consumption, the balance shifted. By 1960, cinema audiences were in terminal decline – down to 501 million annually, while 10.5 million homes (approximately two thirds of the population) had television sets, most of which had access to two channels, with a total of up to sixteen hours' viewing available per day. This dramatic growth of television programming requirements together with the income which licence fees (for the BBC) and advertising revenue (for ITV) brought, and the statutory requirement for high levels of home-produced material (rather than merely cheap American imports or recycled feature films), created an unprecedented need for writers, producers, directors and other creative personnel, all necessarily inexperienced, to work in the new medium.

By the close of the decade, evidence of prosperity seemed everywhere – in the shops, on the roads, and in the media. In fact, these manifest signs of material progress masked other signs of Britain's long-term decline as a world power – the loss of Empire; the refusal to be part of the emergent European Common Market; the decline of the industrial base; and the increasingly futile attempts to match the United States and the Soviet Union as an independent nuclear power. In addition, and closer to home, from the mid-1950s questions began to be asked about precisely what kinds of social changes were taking place, and how far existing patterns of social life, particularly in working-class communities, were being affected by the new affluence. One particular theme began to preoccupy a significant number of younger writers and other cultural commentators – a theme summed up by a comment from Barbara Castle, a leading Labour Party politician, during the 1959 General Election:

> Mr Macmillan has boasted that the TV set is the badge of prosperity. In the back streets of Blackburn the TV aerials are there all right; what we lack are thousands of decent houses to put under them.[2]

The implications of this were to suggest that the growth of new patterns of consumption did not necessarily denote any wholesale transformation in more fundamental conditions of life – especially in the traditional areas of the Northern working class. The realist exploration of this interrelation of the old and the new in traditional working-class areas was a major theme of novels, plays, films and television drama in the period between 1957 and 1964. Loach himself has acknowledged this work as a source of some of his own concerns:

> The novels of the late fifties particularly influenced me; writers like Alan Sillitoe, John Braine, Stan Barstow, and David Storey. They had provincial settings in common with my background, and I became interested in reflecting that non-metropolitan life.[3]

BBC drama

Like many other national institutions, the BBC had also undergone rapid transformation during the 1950s. In 1950, the Corporation was almost exclusively concerned with radio transmission, and, with no serious competition, presented a secure and sedate public service image to the nation and the Empire. Towards the end of the decade, this situation had altered radically; the major business was now television, and the emergence of a strong competitor – the advertising-financed, although still strongly regulated, independent television companies – had caused considerable debate about how the BBC's public service mission could be maintained without a loss of audience. As ITV began to gain a majority of the audience, the BBC began a significant shake-up of senior management, led by the appointment of Hugh Greene as Director-General in 1960, with the intention of regaining its dominant position. The BBC also profited from the outcome of the 1962 Pilkington Report on television, which criticised the standards of ITV and laid the basis for the award to BBC of the third television channel (BBC 2, which opened in 1964), which resecured the BBC's position as the senior partner in the new duopoly which was to dominate British television until the beginning of the 1990s.

Typical of the changes within the BBC during the early 1960s was that which took place in relation to television drama. At the end of the 1950s, the dominant notion of television drama was still to regard it as a variant of the live theatre. Thus, the replacement of the traditionalist Head of BBC Drama, Michael Barry, who resigned in 1961, by the Canadian Sydney Newman, who had previously headed ITV's very successful *Armchair Theatre*, was in many ways only a parallel of the changes which had already taken place in the British theatre with *Look Back in Anger* in 1956. In particular, an expanding BBC Drama Department in the early 1960s looked to the theatre, rather than, for example, to an uncertain film industry for its personnel – and, for preference, to the brightest and best-educated for its young trainees. Like many other Oxbridge graduates with experience of student theatre, Loach (who had been President of the Oxford University Dramatic Society), became a BBC trainee in 1963 – as a more lucrative alternative to continuing in live theatre.

The tradition of theatre which these graduates brought with them was necessarily that of single plays performed within a proscenium arch, and much television drama of the 1950s and early 1960s simply reproduced this in the television studio. However, there were three alternative modes of television which, especially after the departure of Barry, began to be seen as available for combining with "armchair theatre" drama to create new and hybridised forms. Firstly, while the accepted wisdom within British television was, in general, that there was a clear division between the television and cinema genres, it was accepted that in the field of documentary (social or wildlife) there was little effective distinction. The conventions and production methods of the cinema were fully accepted for much television documentary – the key point being that such documentaries were shot and edited on film. Secondly, there was a rather different kind of television documentary, the scripted and studio-based "story documentary" (typically dealing with the work of a professional occupation concerned with social problems) which was clearly distinguishable from television drama by the lack of any requirement of a crafted narrative, and by the style of acting. Thirdly, there was the drama series or serial – again, a form seen as of intrinsically low quality by the advocates of single-play drama. During the early 1960s, owing both to the need to compete effectively with ITV, and to the growth of new technical possibilities through the use of videotape, electronic editing and the increasing use of 16mm film, the interaction of all these different genres allowed a gradual move away from the fixed notion that serious television drama had to consist of live continuous studio performance in a manner akin to the theatre.

Loach entered BBC Television during this time of transition, in which many creative opportunities existed, and a considerable diversity of formal models were available or were being created to try and reflect new forms of social experience. His first significant opportunity was the direction early in 1964 of three episodes of the influential *Z Cars* series, which (from its inception in January 1962) mixed drama, documentary and social commentary, and was located firmly in the context of the Northern working-class thematics of the period. However, *Z Cars* had already become something of a formulaic piece, from which its creators, John McGrath (a contemporary of Loach at Oxford) and Troy Kennedy Martin, had moved on in an effort to develop more original television forms. In particular, they developed a critique of the importation of theatrical naturalism into television drama, and recruited Loach as a director for three episodes of their six-part series, *Diary of a Young Man*, in late-1964. While the theme of this series (two young Northern men seeking their fortune in London) was recognisably of the period, the style was explicitly non-naturalistic and self-regarding, using stills, voice-overs, fantasy sequences and time-shifts freely to disrupt the straightforward narrative. In an article, "Nats go home", in the progressive theatre magazine, *Encore*, Kennedy Martin argued for the need to go beyond naturalism in creating a new television drama, and illustrated his argument by quoting scenes from *Diary of a Young Man*; his argument was sophisticated, stressing the need, for example, to "free the camera from photographing dialogue" and "to free the structure from natural time".[4] This conscious construction of a new television aesthetic was one stream of influence on young directors within the BBC at the time; a slightly different and more forthright approach was to be found in a response from Tony Garnett to Kennedy Martin's article, in which he suggested that "most, if not all, of the traditional differences between film [i.e. cinema] and television drama production are not essential differences, but accidental, historical or imaginary".[5] It was with a mixing of styles underpinned by these two views that Loach's reputation was first made through work in the BBC *Wednesday Play* series, and through feature films during the rest of the decade.

During 1965, Loach directed six plays, including Nell Dunn's *Up the Junction*, in *The Wednesday Play* series. One of the aims of the series was to "find dramas which reflected contemporary situations"[6] in a Britain which, by the time of the opening of the series in October 1964 (the same month as the General Election which removed the Conservative Party from power after thirteen years in government), was already markedly different from that of the 1950s. The last years of the Conservative government were marked by signs of decadence (sexual scandal), a failing economic strategy, and a further decline in international prestige (failure to gain entry to the EEC in 1963; loss of the independent nuclear deterrent; the final stages of loss of Empire), while at home the growth of a commercially-fuelled new youth culture (led by the recorded music and clothes industries) symbolised directions in the national culture with which the ageing patricians of the Conservative Party seemed completely out of touch. The Labour Party, under the leadership of the younger Northerner, Harold Wilson, promised a modernising approach, drawing on science and technology, to transform the country. Through the rest of the decade, the attempts to realise this through some form of central economic planning and control proved repeatedly disastrous, in particular alienating many Left activists within and without the trade unions, and fuelling the growth of alternative Left political groupings. The Prices and Incomes Board, the National Plan of 1965, the devaluation of the pound in 1967, and the 1969 White Paper, "In Place of Strife", were all unable to prevent (and perhaps partly caused) growing inflation, unemployment and industrial discontent. The number of strikes doubled between 1965 and 1970, with the number of working days lost in strikes increasing from under 3 million in 1965 to almost 11 million in 1970. However, just as the sphere of production moved towards crisis, so the spheres of consumption and personal freedom continued to expand and liberalise. Under Labour, public spending on the arts and education markedly increased, and key reforming Acts in the fields of divorce, abortion, homosexuality and theatre censorship helped to create a more "permissive" climate for the exchange of ideas and the development of new lifestyles. Both the industrial conflict and the liberalisation of culture created a climate in which political and cultural thought began to go beyond the stasis induced by the Cold War. The essentially Socialist humanist ideas of the late-1950s New Left became transformed both into more organised political groupings, and into a major rebirth of interest in the writings of Marx (a figure not taken seriously in British intellectual life since the 1930s), including questions of how Marxist ideas could be reflected in the form and content of artistic works.

Events in the years 1968 to 1970 brought this to a head. The student and worker protests in Paris in May 1968; the mass demonstrations in London against American involvement in Vietnam; the growth of racial tension fuelled by the speeches of Enoch Powell; the Soviet invasion of Czechoslovakia; the beginnings of the "Troubles" in Ulster; the first stirrings of an activist women's movement – all created a climate in which the boundaries between the cultural and the political became increasingly blurred. Trevor Griffiths' theatre play, *The Party* (1973), set in May 1968 in the home of a television producer (based loosely on Tony Garnett),[7] and in which rival Marxist analyses of the political situation and how to transform it are set against each other in debate, provides one account of the climate of ideas in which Loach was working at the time.

Developments in Loach's work between 1965 and 1972 reflected this gradual sharpening of conflict, and the emergence of both new and old political forms from the social and cultural changes of the early and mid-1960s: "It was a very political time. The Wilson government was in power and our illusions in that were quickly shaken".[8] Loach's reputation was first made by three of the ten *Wednesday Plays* which he directed – *Up the Junction*, *Cathy Come Home* (1966) and *In Two Minds* (1967), all involving collaboration with Tony Garnett. The common feature was the depiction of social problems through a mixture of film and story documentary styles, with an underlying orientation which implicitly said to its audience: "look how these people are not sharing in the comfortable, satisfied, affluent society of contemporary mythology". In discussing his work of this period, Garnett later observed:

> In a sense, I suppose, from a Marxist point of view, we were trying to create something from the point of view of a materialist philosophy, where the whole tradition of TV drama previously had been based on an idealist philosophy, whether they knew it or not. It had all existed in their heads, or at least in the TV studio. And if somebody pointed out that what they were doing was not remotely like the real world or anybody's real experience, they would say, 'We're doing art.' We were very firmly not doing art, right? We were just trying to make sense of the world.[9]

These plays depicted individuals caught in a web of circumstance which they could not fully understand, and from which they could not engineer solutions or any form of escape; political analysis or solutions were absent or only implicit.

This is largely true also of Loach's two feature films of the period – *Poor Cow* (1967) and *Kes* (1969). At first sight, it may seem surprising, at a time when the film and cinema industries were undergoing rapid contraction, that an up-and-coming television director should seek, or be given, an opportunity to make feature films. However, as the cinema audience shrunk, so it became clear that the core audience remaining was that of young adults ready for a less bland diet than the traditional family audience. At the same time, there was a growth of interest from America (which provided significant amounts of finance for British film production in the 1960s) in British settings; equally, despite the developments in television away from "armchair theatre", there was still a considerable difference in what could be attempted in the two media – in terms of budget, visual effect (all British television was in black and white until 1969, and it was not until 1977 that the majority of viewers had colour sets) and the kinds of events and language it was acceptable to present.

Of the two films, *Poor Cow* was very much of *The Wednesday Play* mould (based on a book by Nell Dunn, who had also written *Up the Junction*), while *Kes* looked forward to Loach's later pattern of work. *Kes* is based on a novel by Barry Hines, and marked the beginning of a series of collaborative works with individual writers; its style leaves behind many of the more self-regarding aspects of *The Wednesday Play* mix of drama and documentary, and its setting, a Yorkshire mining village in which the realities of hard physical labour at the heart of the industrial process are seen to govern the lives and opportunities of the inhabitants, suggests a more direct engagement with the everyday lives of specific communities, rather than a focus on problems and casualties.

Loach's other work of 1969, *The Big Flame*, scripted by Jim Allen, shares some of these features, with its central focus on issues surrounding industrial labour, but also reflects and, in a sense, predicts the nature of the link between industrial and political conflict which was already developing, and which became much more explicit in the early 1970s. With *The Big Flame* and *The Rank and File* (1971), also written by Allen, Loach's work took on a much more explicitly political shape which was both reflective of the evolving political climate and indicative of his move away from working within the parameters of the BBC *Wednesday Play* format towards close collaboration with individual writers.

Loach in the 1970s

In June 1970, the Conservative Party, under Edward Heath, were returned to power, and the incipient social and cultural conflicts of the late-1960s began to assume more widespread and explicit forms. The Industrial Relations Act of 1971 fuelled sharp opposition from a number of trade unions, while the government's stated policy of not helping "lame duck" industries to survive began to falter in the face of the likely collapse of such flagship British names as Rolls Royce. Inflation and unemployment began to rise (although the unemployment figures of less than one million would have counted as full employment by the standards of the 1980s and 1990s), and an apparent U-turn in policy was signalled by the agreement to high public sector pay settlements, notably following the miners' strike of 1972. The Ulster conflict was becoming institutionalized, with the gradual collapse of the more moderate political culture of the full-employment Ulster of the 1950s and early 1960s, and the growth of more extreme Loyalist as well as Nationalist political and paramilitary groups. Bombings began to spread to England from 1972, while 1971 had seen the brief bombing campaign of the "Angry Brigade", an anarchist-inspired group. In more specifically cultural politics, too, patterns of consensus broke down, with the Festival of Light, the Education Black Papers and the censorship of the "underground" press seeking to counter the continuing influence of the "permissive" climate of the late-1960s. Finally, the Arab-Israeli War of 1973, with the associated oil embargo, produced conditions in which the miners could again exert pressure on the government, causing a three-day working week and, finally, the General Election of February 1974 – the first example of an industrial dispute leading to a change of government in contemporary British history.

Through the rest of the decade, a Labour government with the barest of parliamentary majorities struggled to control a volatile social and economic situation. 1975 saw inflation and pay settlements approaching 30%, and also the highly symbolic passing of the one million unemployed figure. For more than a generation, it had been taken as axiomatic that a war had been fought and a peace constructed so that the bad old days of the 1930s of depression and unemployment would not return; that form of certainty had now been swept away, and the late-1970s saw the gradual erosion of the parliamentary majority and the confidence of the Labour government in the face of public expenditure cuts, rising nationalisms in Wales and Scotland, and the final Winter of Discontent of 1978-79, with the poorest public sector workers refusing to accept the restrictions of the government pay policy.

As already noted, *The Big Flame* and *The Rank and File* had marked a turn away from a primary concern with exemplary social victims towards a dramatisation of forms of collective industrial and political action; Loach's London Weekend Television play, *After a Lifetime*, made in 1971, reflected on similar issues in meditating on the life of a veteran of the General Strike. The concerns of all these plays were then fused in Loach's major work of the 1970s, *Days of Hope* (1975), which, although his first fully historical piece, was very clearly created out of the contemporary situation (unimaginable a decade earlier) of the early 1970s, in which the parallels were easily drawn between the political and industrial struggles of the early 1920s and those of the early 1970s. Loach was quoted in *Radio Times* in 1975 as saying:

> We want anybody who feels themselves to be suffering from crises today, people who are caught by price rises, inflation and wage restraint, to watch the films and realise that all this

happened before. And we hope they will learn some lessons from the opportunities that were lost in 1926 and the defeats inflicted on the working class that time.[10]

As this comment implies, *Days of Hope* constituted an attempt at a macro-political analysis, linking the personal, the industrial and the national political in a way unparalleled by any of Loach's previous or subsequent fictional work. The political and cultural conflicts of 1968-73 had, in fact, produced a climate in which it seemed plausible to consider seriously the possibility of some major political change borne out of a combination of an industrial conflict and political will and vision. In retrospect, however, it seems indicative of the beginnings of the development of an unfavourable climate for Loach's style of work that, even on the Left, the main issues debated about the films concerned questions of form and of its mode of historical interpretation, rather than those of the directly political questions it raised. Loach's other major television work of the 1970s, the two-part drama, *The Price of Coal* (1977), also drew heavily on the significance of the industrial struggles of the early 1970s which re-established the miners as the symbolic heart of the working-class movement, with its emphasis on the contrast between different images of England in the year of the Queen's Silver Jubilee. In retrospect, both the title and theme seem prophetic of the increasingly sharp political divides and, for Loach, political defeats of the following decade.

Thatcherism

The election of Margaret Thatcher as Prime Minister in May 1979 marks a major turning-point in postwar British history. It was the final confirmation that the postwar settlement of welfare capitalism (based on full employment) was over; initially, taxes rose and public sector industrial support was reduced. Unemployment rose from 1.25 million in 1978 to 2.67 million in 1982. Politically, the sharp rightward turn of the Conservative Party was matched by a leftward turn by Labour, electing Michael Foot, a veteran intellectual and supporter of unilateral nuclear disarmament, as their leader in 1980. Into the vacated centre-ground came the new Social Democratic Party (SDP), created predominantly out of disillusioned right-wing Labour defectors, which, by 1981 (together with its allies, the Liberal Party) was leading national opinion polls and had created damage to the national standing of the Labour Party, which was to determine the shape of politics for the rest of the decade. It was only the occurrence of the Falklands War in 1982 which enabled the Conservative Party to recover sufficient ground to complete a resounding electoral victory in 1983 against a divided opposition. (In fact, the Conservative proportion of the overall

poll was less than in 1979, while their parliamen
over 100.)

The period between 1983 and 1987 marked (
of Thatcherism, during which time its major pol
implemented. The sale of council houses was no
"privatisation" of major publicly-owned organisatic
Aerospace (1981), Britoil (1982), British Telecom (
(1986), and British Airways and British Petrolei
victories over organised opposition were achieved ...at or
the miners' strike (1984-85), of the Wapping dispute involving Rupert
Murdoch's News International (1986-87), and the abolition of the
Labour-controlled Greater London Council (1985). The underlying
social changes reflected in these events can be noted in the changing
social composition of Britain. Between 1979 and 1987, the numbers of
shareowners increased from 3 million to 8 million, home-owners
increased from 52% to 66% of all householders, and taxation was
adjusted to reduce the "tax burden" on high-earners; meanwhile, trade
union membership among those in work fell from 30% to 22%, while,
by 1986, the total unemployed had climbed to 3.2 million, and it came
to be commonplace to note the appearance of increasing numbers of
beggars and the homeless on the streets of all large cities. During this
period, political opposition to Thatcherism remained divided. The
Labour Party, under the new leadership of Neil Kinnock, began its
long haul back to political respectability, focusing a good deal of its
attention on the need to deal with the Militant Tendency within its
own ranks, although also being considerably influenced by the strong
re-emergence of the Campaign for Nuclear Disarmament (CND). The
subsequent result of the 1987 Election, while only slightly reducing the
Conservative majority, confirmed that the SDP/Liberal Alliance had
failed to "break the mould" of British politics, and it disintegrated soon
afterwards.

The final years of Thatcher's premiership from 1987 to 1990 saw
the gradual unravelling of this climate of confidence in the "enterprise
culture". The "Big Bang" deregulation of the London stock market in
1986 was followed by a dramatic collapse of share prices in October
1987, which began the undermining of belief in the beneficial effects
of the rise of the "yuppie". The credit boom, which had fuelled a fast
rise in house prices (upon which much of the sense of rising
prosperity in the mid-1980s was based), stoked inflation and then
began to backfire as house prices began to stall from 1989 onwards.
The attempted reform of local government taxation introduced in
Scotland in 1989 and in England in 1990 led to massive public
resistance, exemplified most dramatically in the "poll tax" riots in
London and elsewhere in early 1990. Divisions within the Conservative
Party over economic integration into Europe led to senior government

ch in the 1980s

Reflecting on why the early 1990s seem to have been a much more successful period for his work than the 1980s, Loach has noted: "Two things – the effect of the Thatcherite consciousness has eased a bit... also I don't think I came up with very good ideas in the early Eighties".[11] In general, it is not, of course, surprising that the onset of Thatcherism should have produced a generally unfriendly climate for such an explicitly political filmmaker as Loach; however, as Loach suggests, there were also more individual reasons for the difficulties he experienced in the 1980s in sustaining his public visibility and reputation.

Loach's successes in the 1960s and 1970s (whether in television or in the cinema) were almost exclusively achieved through the use of a format which intermingled a fundamental claim as fiction (feature film or television play) with a documentary style and a specific social or historical point of reference. However, towards the end of the 1970s, having concluded his relationship with the BBC, Loach turned for the first time to pure documentary – notably with the Associated Television programme, *A Question of Leadership* (1980), dealing with the conduct of an industrial dispute in the steel industry. One of the issues which then arises, as Loach has remarked in a recent interview, is that, while a television filmmaker is given "a wide tolerance in fiction...in documentaries the constraints are much more narrow".[12] In particular, the issue of a requirement for "balance" is brought to the forefront – a particularly problematic concept in the early 1980s, when the very existence of a consensual middle-ground in British politics was being called into question. It was this which caused the difficulties with Loach's subsequent four-part series of documentaries on trade union leadership, *Questions of Leadership*, made for Central Television, to be shown on Channel 4 in autumn 1983 (a moment of deep crisis for the Labour Party in the wake of the shattering defeat in the June 1983 General Election). The programmes were regarded by the Independent Broadcasting Authority (IBA) as lacking "due impartiality" by giving insufficient attention to the views of the trade union leaders, as opposed to the rank and file members with whom Loach was chiefly concerned; the programmes were never shown. Similar objections were made to Loach's celebratory film about the mining communities and their industrial dispute, *Which Side Are You On?* (1984), made for the LWT arts magazine programme, *The South Bank Show* – although, in this case, transmission did take place two months late, in January 1985, on Channel 4 (where the partisan character of the film was seen as more in keeping with the channel's obligation to transmit a genuine plurality of perspectives and views).

In one sense, Loach's move into (explicitly political) documentaries was a logical extension of the aims of his earlier work, especially in a period of sharpened political attack on the living standards and political culture of the working class. Equally, it reflected the difficulty of finding practical support for the further development of the documentary-drama approach which had characterised Loach's previous work. For, while the political climate was less favourable, it was also the case that, aesthetically, Loach's work was being increasingly called into question; the turn in the 1970s, among film critics and left-wing cultural theorists towards "screen theory", based on the disciplines of linguistics and psychoanalysis, made the fundamentally untheorised work of Loach and his collaborative authors (Barry Hines and Jim Allen) seem naïve and old-fashioned. Loach recalls an attempt in the early 1980s to seek funding for a project from the British Film Institute (BFI):

> It was about...relating nuclear weapons to the problems of unemployment...pointing out that actually they're part of the same economic system...It was all to do with a theatre troupe; a very bold thing for Jim Allen to write...Took it along to the BFI and these...people...sat back in their chairs and talked about 'seventies realism'. They had an image of what Jim Allen's writing was like and superimposed that on the script.[13]

The project was refused funding. In 1987, Allen and Loach suffered another major setback when Allen's play, *Perdition*, to be directed by Loach, was withdrawn from the Royal Court following a major public row about its alleged anti-Semitism.

Even one of Loach's two major completed projects of the decade, *Fatherland* (1986), indicated some of the ways in which the conditions of the early 1980s were inimical to his strengths and inclinations. *Fatherland*, a film jointly funded by German, French and British (Channel 4) television companies, was written by Trevor Griffiths. Griffiths' script and preferred way of working did not sit easily with Loach's low-key naturalism. Despite their close political alliance, their practical aesthetics were in conflict:

> 'Trevor ought to direct. His scripts do,' Loach says. 'If Loach could make a film without a camera he would. He wants the actors to just be themselves so that everything looks as though it has just happened,' says Griffiths.[14]

Such differences contributed to a complex and distinctive film, but not to the sketching of an effective future direction for Loach's work.

Changing contexts of production

At the same time, however, the production context of *Fatherland* did indicate some aspects of the changing cultural conditions which were to underpin Loach's return to major success in the early 1990s. *Fatherland* was the first of Loach's works to be consciously made with both cinema and television screening in mind – a new kind of media hybridity which subsequently proved to sit well with Loach's own preference to work in hybrid forms, and which reflected major and irreversible changes within the organisation of the British media. For, while, in Britain in the 1980s, part of the Thatcherite project seemed to be a forced march back into the past to celebrate "Victorian values" and past imperial glories, it was also the case that, within the cultural industries of film and television, the development of the free market ideologies of Thatcherism coincided with (and, to a degree, enabled) opportunities for expansion in forms of delivery of audiovisual products, leading to consequent changes in the organisation of production. In particular, three kinds of development were taking place, which, by the end of the 1980s, began to open up new cultural spaces for films (using the term now very broadly to include material made for television, cinema and video viewing) to be viewed. Firstly, there was the gradual increase of home video machines – from 0.5 million in 1980 to 13 million in 1990 (61% of all homes), by which time the direct sale of video copies of nearly new films had become a distinctive sector of the market. Secondly, the 1980s saw the final bottoming-out of the drop in cinema audiences, as the shift towards new multiscreen outlets began to be completed; between 1984 and 1991, the total annual attendance nearly doubled, from 54 million to 101 million. Thirdly, there was a significant change in the production contexts of British television – a change whose origins predated Thatcherism, but which fitted certain aspects of the new ideological climate extremely well.

1982 saw the opening of Channel 4 Television, the first new British broadcast channel for eighteen years. The debate about the role of a fourth channel had been in progress since the late-1960s, and became closely linked to the gradual whittling away, during the 1970s, of the cultural authority of the state, and of the concept of public service broadcasting and balance. This was the result, on the one hand, of developments on the Left, following the cultural upheavals of 1968, in both alternative forms of cultural practice, and the argument of media and cultural theorists that "balance" was neither intellectually provable nor practically achievable, and, on the other hand, of the argument from the Right, that the free market should be allowed to introduce proper market disciplines and other forms of cultural "deregulation" into broadcasting.

The emergence of the unique organisation of Channel 4 was the result of a combination of both these pressures, taken together with the continuing force of the argument of the incumbent commercial television companies that their commercial interests and public service obligations should not be unfairly undermined. Among the key features of the new organisation were a less rigid (although somewhat ill-defined) requirement for "balance" within any single programme, and a requirement to act as a publisher of work made by others, particularly new independent companies. In the latter case, a particular ambition, from the beginning of the channel, was to finance "films of feature length for television here [and] for the cinema abroad"[15] through the *Film on Four* series under the leadership of David Rose (whose television credentials went back to his role as the producer of the early *Z Cars*, on which Loach began his career). The significance of the reference to "abroad" was that, until the early 1980s, the controlling interests in British cinema, via the Cinema Exhibitors Association (CEA), operated a system whereby a new film was barred from screening on broadcast television for three years after its release. This acted as a major disincentive for television companies in Britain (unlike, for example, in Germany or Italy) to become involved in sponsoring feature film production. However, Channel 4 first negotiated a deal allowing low-budget films (i.e. those costing under £1.25 million) to be exempted – an arrangement which was extended in 1988 to the figure of £4 million. These agreements, together with the increase of distribution of films for home video viewing, had the effect of progressively removing many of the historic distinctions between production for television and production for cinema. By the late-1980s, Channel 4, often in partnership with new independent companies, the government-backed British Screen consortium or, occasionally, European partners, was involved in initiating or supporting about half of all British feature films produced in any one year. Alternatively, many of the same works could be seen as the major achievements of single-play television drama of the period, since the new production contexts of the 1980s had at last removed most of the "accidental, historical or imaginary" differences between film and television production on which Tony Garnett had remarked a quarter of a century before.

Loach in the 1990s

The political downfall of Margaret Thatcher in late-1990 had been preceded by the final collapse in 1989 of the Warsaw Pact military alliance (symbolised most graphically by the destruction of the Berlin Wall and by the subsequent reunification of Germany). Within Britain, these two events together brought a dramatic end to the political certainties of the 1980s. Unemployment began to rise again, as the housing market continued its free fall and the new Conservative Prime Minister set about replacing the poll tax. Despite the subsequent (relatively narrow) election victory of 1992, the Thatcherite Conservative dominance and confidence of the mid-1980s gave way to a more uncertain and open climate of political possibility, the patterns of which will only become clearer in retrospect.

Loach's work of the early 1990s, from *Hidden Agenda* (1990) through *Riff-Raff* (1991) and *Raining Stones* (1993) to *Ladybird Ladybird* (1994), draws on a situation in which the pressure towards convergence between ideas of film and television production is as strong as at any time since the (rather different) debates and circumstances of the mid-1960s. Loach's practical philosophy of documentary-drama is particularly appropriate for such historical moments. Equally, the twin supports of Channel 4 and independent production companies have provided an institutional framework more supportive of the production of politically committed individual feature films/television plays than has been available at any time since *The Wednesday Play* and *Play for Today* series. Finally, Loach's subject-matter (and that of his partner-writers) is drawn from the social fallout of the destructive side of the Thatcherite project of the 1980s: widespread unemployment (and fear of unemployment); the casualisation of labour; the growth of the black economy; increasing homelessness; and families without security and under stress. While much of this seems a return to the subject-matter of the 1960s, these issues now seem less the experience of a small number of victims than typical experiences through which large sections of the population may have to travel. Above all, Loach is once again in a position to make films which "give a voice to those who are often denied it"[16] – and which resolutely refuse (to the annoyance of film critics and politicians alike) to remain neatly within the domain of aesthetic judgment alone.

Notes

1   Christine Aziz, "Shoulder to shoulder", *The Observer* 22 March 1987: 23.

2   "Still Socialist", *New Statesman* 1492 (17 October 1959): 497.

3   Jonathan Hacker and David Price, *Take Ten: Contemporary British Film Directors* (Oxford: Clarendon Press, 1991): 292.

4   Troy Kennedy Martin, "Nats go home", *Encore* 48 (March-April 1964): 25.

5   "Reaction", *Encore* 49 (May-June 1964): 45.

6   "Face to Face", interview with Ken Loach by Jeremy Isaacs, broadcast on BBC-2, 19 September 1994.

7   Trevor Griffiths, *The Party* (London: Faber and Faber, 1974).

8   "Face to Face".

9   Tony Garnett, "Television in Britain: Description and Dissent", *Theatre Quarterly* 2: 6 (April-June 1972): 19-20.

10   Quoted in Tony Bennett, Susan Boyd-Bowman, Colin Mercer and Janet Woollacott (eds), *Popular Television and Film* (London: British Film Institute, in association with The Open University, 1981): 302.

11   "Face to Face".

12   Ibid.

13   Quoted in John Tulloch, *Television Drama: Agency, audience and myth* (London; New York: Routledge, 1990): 160.

14   Aziz.

15   Jeremy Isaacs, *Storm over 4: A Personal Account* (London: Weidenfeld and Nicolson, 1989): 146.

16   "Face to Face".

Factual fictions and fictional fallacies: Ken Loach's documentary dramas

Julian Petley

One of the longest-running controversies to have raged around British television concerns dramatised documentaries and documentary dramas – two very different kinds of programme format, but both charged with confusing viewers by "illegitimately" mingling fact and fiction, and, implicitly, trying to pass off the latter as the former.[1] Ken Loach, especially in his documentary dramas written by Jim Allen, has attracted such criticism more frequently and more consistently than any other director working in British television. In this essay, I want first to chart the long history of this particular line of attack, and then to suggest the reasons for it, and, in doing so, to try to deflect such criticism.

It has become quite commonplace to regard the 1960s as a golden era of British television, when radicalism and experimentation were not only possible, but also welcomed with open arms. However, although conditions may in some ways have been easier then than now, the work that has come to be regarded as "classic" – that of Loach, Potter, Mercer, Hopkins, Garnett, Allen and Trodd, for exam ple – was always produced to some extent against the grain within the British Broadcasting Corporation (BBC), and, as often as not, to a dismal chorus of complaint from a largely Conservative (and certainly wholly conservative) press. It is all too easily forgotten that the decade which saw the "birth" of Loach and Potter was also marked by clamorous calls for stricter television censorship from Mary Whitehouse's newly-formed National Viewers' and Listeners' Association.[2]

Characteristically, one of the first critics to set the fact/fiction hare running was T C Worsley in *The Financial Times* in his review of *Up the Junction* (1965). Worsley, together with Peter Black of *The Daily Mail*, one of the very few critics to take television seriously at the time, admired much in Loach's work, but not in its documentary drama aspects:

> Audiences may have been a bit confused by the télé-vérité approach (Was this supposed to be reality or fiction?), but they surely couldn't have failed to respond to the liveliness and lyricism which the technique captured, certainly as long as it

stayed with those three girls, brilliantly acted by Carol White, Geraldine Sherman and Vickery Turner. But, note, acted! Here was the centre of confusion (and a pretty gloss it makes on the whole illusion-reality issue). However true to real life their behaviour seemed – and the technique was designed to heighten just that impression, and it certainly convinced me – they were in fact acting out, not life as it was lived in Clapham Junction, but Miss Nell Dunn's personal vision of that life. The truth of the final product to Miss Dunn's vision, and the truth of the final product to life as it is actually lived in Clapham, are two different things, and the truth of Miss Dunn's vision to the life of the Junction yet another thing again.[3]

The biggest storm at that time to hit the BBC over the fact/fiction issue was not, however, a Loach/Garnett film, but Peter Watkins' visualisation of a nuclear attack on Britain, *The War Game*, produced in 1965 (but not transmitted until 1985). This was banned by the BBC on the apparent grounds that it was too horrifying to show, although it now seems clear – or rather as clear as these secretive matters ever become – that the programme was the victim of intense Establishment pressure, exercised mainly via the Chairman of the BBC Board of Governors, Lord Normanbrook.[4] Seen in this light, the press screenings organised by the BBC in February 1966 seem less an attempt to drum up support for the film than a rather cynical ploy to justify its suppression on the grounds of bowing to "public opinion", since the press was, as ever, in an anti-BBC mood, and the Corporation must have realised that the majority of papers would clamour for a ban.[5] Among the many reasons given for supporting the ban was that the film dressed up fiction, and even propaganda, as documentary fact. According to Tom Pocock in the *Evening Standard*:

The film is in the guise of a documentary and the action sequences are broken by the comments of doctors, psychiatrists, churchmen and strategists. While the presentation seems authoritative, the film is straight propaganda for the Campaign for Nuclear Disarmament.[6]

Perhaps the most damaging attack, however, came from Grace Wyndham Goldie in *The Sunday Telegraph*, who claimed that "it's difficult to tell, since everyone is in modern dress, whether the physicians, psychiatrists, and clergymen who talk straight to the audience are really what they purport to be or not".[7] This may not seem very serious in itself, but the author had until recently been Head of Talks and Current Affairs for BBC TV, and had actually worked with Watkins on his previous film, *Culloden* (1964). Worse still, she purported in the same article to reveal that Watkins had given his cast "very little food" and used trip wires on that production, all in the interests of documentary verisimilitude – a charge hotly denied by Watkins, his cast and crew, and very publicly rejected by the BBC.

It is in this context that the reception of Loach and Garnett's next film, *Cathy Come Home* (1966), has to be understood. Today, this remarkably powerful exposé of homelessness and poverty in supposedly affluent 1960s Britain has achieved almost iconic television status, and it is remembered as the film which led to the founding of the homeless charity, Shelter. Because the film is now so famous and highly regarded (certainly, together with *Kes* [1969], it is the film which "made" Loach), there is a tendency to assume that it was hailed as an instant masterpiece at the time of its release, but this is not entirely the case. Certainly there were those who praised it to the skies, but anti-BBC and, more generally, anti-television sentiments were too deeply ingrained in certain sections of British society, and especially in Fleet Street, to let its transmission pass without controversy.[8]

Cathy Come Home, however, was sufficiently popular with some sections of the audience to be repeated only a couple of months after its first transmission. But it is also important to note, especially in the present context, that much of the statistical material which makes the film so distinctive (as I shall discuss later) was omitted from the repeat, because pedantic and nit-picking complaints had shaken whatever confidence the BBC had in its accuracy. Significantly, the most sustained attack on the film came from Wyndham Goldie. Writing in *The Sunday Telegraph* a few days before the second showing, she referred dismissively to the film as "Jeremy Sandford's tear-jerker", and called the decision to repeat it "disturbing". According to her, the film was "an early example of a new and dangerous trend in television drama", and her fears were only sharpened by the *Radio Times* billing it as a "semi-documentary". She continued:

> Such a description surely means we are being offered a production which the B.B.C. accepts as a style, and which deliberately blurs the distinction between fact and fiction. Viewers have a right to know whether what they are being offered is real or invented.[9]

The problem for Wyndham Goldie is that the documentary drama could well call into question the truthfulness of television's factual genres:

> We see on the television screen a succession of images. We expect some of them, news and outside broadcasts, current affairs reports and factual documentaries, to be an accurate

reflection of the real world. If, among them, we get a 'semi-documentary' which intermingles the real with the fictional and which may, in order to establish a greater sense of reality, use film clips from news bulletins or from Panorama or Twenty-four Hours, then a doubt could well be cast upon the validity of what has in fact been real.[10]

Wyndham Goldie was also concerned that *Cathy Come Home* was:

[A] powerful piece of advocacy. But television organisations are not allowed, under the terms of the various charters which have been issued to the B.B.C. and Acts of Parliament which govern Independent Television, to use their privileged position to advocate, in areas of controversy, particular policies and courses of action. Every responsible person in any broadcasting organisation agrees with this rule and every factual programme is planned and scrutinised with it in mind. But if you put advocacy into the semi-dramatic form of a semi-documentary it may in effect be by-passing the fundamental rules under which broadcasting organisations are permitted by society to exercise their privileges. If so, the broadcasting organisations would be vulnerable indeed. So, in its own interest as well as those of the viewer, the B.B.C. must think again about the development of 'semi-documentary' as a television style.[11]

A rather different approach was taken by Philip Purser, also in *The Sunday Telegraph*, who, whilst finding much to admire in the film's style, complained that it "should feel the need to substantiate itself with figures":

[D]rama deals with individuals, not statistics. Its job is to give the particular case universal meaning. Likewise, it is surely an admission of failure if a play has to protest that it is based on fact. The truth that it is supposed to be offering is not the kind to be verified by reference to the Registrar-General's annual report, it's the kind which is concerned with the way people behave and the way their behaviour affects their destiny.[12]

Purser summed up his ambivalent attitude to *Cathy Come Home* by concluding that "I'm sure the play did a great service to social education, but I am certain it did a terrible disservice to television drama". Similarly, in his review of the repeat, whilst refusing to take the by-now familiar line that *Cathy Come Home* and its ilk were somehow sailing under false colours, Purser stated:

My objection to 'Cathy' is that either Jeremy Sandford isn't a playwright or in this instance he ducked the playwright's responsibility. He fell back on statistics and snatches of tape-recorded testimony to shore up his case. Instead of drawing two human beings and letting their characters be part of what happened to them, he synthesised a pair of ideal victims to demonstrate – helplessly – every stage in the dizzy descent from £35-a-week prosperity to despairing dispersal of the family.[13]

A remarkably similar line was taken by Worsley in *The Financial Times*. Again, in the course of a series of articles, he praised much about *Cathy Come Home*, but also entered some serious reservations. In particular, he felt:

Loach the reformer took over from Loach the artist and permitted two solecisms which detracted from it as a work of art. First in the statistics which were read out in the background, and secondly in building up the main characters as a generalised, not a particularised, couple.[14]

Elsewhere he concluded:

Document and fiction cannot mix. What Loach and Garnett achieved at their best in *The Coming Out Party* [1965] and *Up the Junction* was fiction which had the immediacy of real life, the raucousness, the feel, the smell of documented life without being a documentary. It was the realistic convention heightened to the nth degree, and very exciting it was. But the moment they try to blend in actual documentary techniques they lose the very element of truth that was the essence of their particular approach to fiction.[15]

Further controversy was to follow with *In Two Minds* (1967), written by one of British television's major dramatists, David Mercer.[16] *In Two Minds* (which Loach himself remade, very differently, as the 1971 feature, *Family Life*) tells the story of Kate Winter, a young woman from a "respectable" home, who is in fact driven mad by her family environment. It drew heavily on the work of radical psychiatrist, R D Laing, and came in for much of the same kind of Establishment flak that greeted Laing's own pioneering achievements. Thus, for example, in the BBC magazine, *The Listener*, Anthony Burgess condemned it as a "dangerous hybrid" and "not a play at all".[17] But the most negative reaction came from James Thomas in the *Daily Express*:

Inside B.B.C. television, a new battle is blowing up between the men who deal with fact and the men who deal with fiction. Producers are expressing open anxiety at the way the line between drama and documentary is being blurred, leaving the public in doubt about whether they are watching truth or fantasy and exposing them to a new and potentially alarming method of propaganda...It is not before time that the dangers of some of the new forms of so-called drama are coming under discussion at the B.B.C. Too often the drama spots are being used by writers and producers to air opinions so way out that they should not be shown to a massive lay audience without balance. Once a writer with a bee in his bonnet sat down and wrote a documentary which was balanced by an experienced features team to present a fair case. Now he writes a documentary and calls it a play – and under the banner of the drama department he acquires a freedom of expression which could not be tolerated by a current affairs producer...I am strongly against the abuse of dramatic freedom by a writer or producer to hammer home to millions in the guise of a play a biased, one-sided view of any highly controversial subject.[18]

Thomas concluded his polemic with the demand that "[t]he B.B.C. should make it a rule that every play which might be confused with a serious features programme must carry announcements before and after to make it clear to the public that they are watching fiction".

Thomas' suggestion of an internal BBC battle over the fact/fiction question was reinforced by an article in the *New Statesman* by Dennis Potter, then making a name for himself as one of British television's leading writers, and attracting a great deal of flak for daring to stretch the medium's boundaries. In the course of a passionate defence of *In Two Minds*, Potter pointed out, with the voice of direct experience, that:

There are senior executives in the BBC who act upon the assumption that unleashing any major but controversial theory on the mass media is equivalent to allowing mad dogs with bloody fangs to savage innocent old ladies in their own living rooms. There is at the moment the acrid whiff of battle in the Corporation's Drama Department, where scripts – and the elementary rights of their authors – are being strenuously fought over before the plays ever reach the rehearsal rooms.[19]

In 1968, Loach directed a *Wednesday Play* about football supporters, *The Golden Vision*, written by Neville Smith and sometime-newsreader, Gordon Honeycombe. This mixed fact and fiction to a greater degree than ever before, since part of the film consisted of interviews with actual Liverpool players. However, there was less negative criticism of this production than of some of its predecessors for allegedly dressing up fiction as fact, although it is hard to avoid the conclusion that this was because the film did not tackle any obviously "political" subjects. Only Worsley in *The Financial Times* and Michael Billington in *The Times* put up any significant objections, and these on genuinely aesthetic, rather than disguised political, grounds. According to Worsley, the "union of fiction and documentary" is a "bastard form":

> The fictionalised documentary is, I believe, getting the worst of both worlds. It has neither the truth of the best fiction nor the distortions of the best documentary. For it is my firm belief that fiction at its best tells us more about human nature than even the most 'truthful' documentary; and that even the most truthful documentary involves inevitable distortions.[20]

Meanwhile, Billington argued that the problem was that

> [T]he dramatic half of the story was always straining hard to achieve the same authenticity as the documentary half...In other words, the re-creation of reality became an end in itself rather than a means of communicating something.[21]

I now come to one of Loach's most important works for television, *The Big Flame* (1969), and the one over which the growing internal BBC rows about documentary drama came to a head. This was Loach's most directly political film to date – other films had tackled broadly political issues such as poverty and homelessness, but *The Big Flame* dealt head-on with fundamental questions of ownership, class conflict, the role of the state, and political organisation and mobilisation. The story concerns a dock strike in Liverpool, which turns into an experiment in workers' control when the dockers form a port workers' council and attempt to run the docks themselves. Of course, no such experiment could possibly be allowed to succeed and thus set an example for other workers, and so the dockers are defeated (in scenes which eerily prefigure the 1984-85 coal dispute) by the massive weight of the British state – not simply the expected coalition of police, Army, bosses, courts, media and right-wing politicians, but also, crucially, the upper echelons of the trade union movement and the Labour Party. Here appears the key theme which will dominate much of Loach's subsequent work, whether in dramas such as *The Rank and File* (1971) and *Days of Hope* (1975), or the ill-fated documentaries such as *Questions of Leadership* (1983): namely, that Labour politicians and trade union leaders are terrified of mass action by the militant working class, since it threatens the very structures on which their own power and position are based.

To understand the radicalism of *The Big Flame* and its successors, and to understand just why such representations ran into so much trouble, it is imperative to understand the political context in which they were produced. In 1969, a Labour government was in power, and was keen to control wage rises (especially in the public sector) as part of its ill-fated "prices and incomes" policy. This was resisted by many rank and file trade unionists, but posed a problem for the leadership. On the one hand, the leadership did support claims for higher wages and for free collective bargaining, but, on the other, they hardly wanted to endanger the existence of a Labour government and let in the as-always militantly anti-union Conservatives. Furthermore, they were certainly not in favour of rank and file demands for more "workers' power", since this directly undermined their own position in the political hierarchy. Wage disputes, therefore, tended to be fought out purely on the economic level, and on a discrete, one-at-a-time basis, by the union bosses. In particular, any tendency to raise the underlying political issues, or to flex the muscles of organised labour by encouraging inter-union solidarity and mass action, thus mounting a directly political challenge to both bosses and government, was strongly discouraged. There resulted a rash of unofficial strikes and sit-ins, greeted by a ferocious witch-hunt for so-called "reds under the bed" by the media – and not simply by the Conservative press.[22] In this context, *The Big Flame* was bound to cause absolute uproar.

That this was Loach's most directly political film to date, therefore, clearly had a great deal to do with the increasingly abrasive political climate of the times. But the overtly political dimension also marks it out as Loach and Garnett's first collaboration with the writer Jim Allen, with whom they would later make the epic *Days of Hope*. Garnett had already produced Allen's *The Lump* (1967) as a *Wednesday Play*, and this highly critical portrayal of the exploitation of casual labour in the building trade makes for a fascinating comparison with the much later *Riff-Raff* (1991), which Loach directed from a script by Bill Jesse. Allen wrote not only from his own experience, but also from an avowedly Marxist perspective, as Paul Madden has noted:

> The majority of Jim Allen's plays have their roots in a reality directly experienced by the writer, constructed as they are from the working lives of working men, whether miners, navvies or dockers, more often than not politically involved at the raw end of industrial relations in strikes, occupations, and picket lines. They fuse lived experience with Marxist, specifically Trotskyist, beliefs.[23]

British television has always had difficulties dealing with Marxist analyses of anything, and such an analysis of labour relations in late-1960s Britain was never going to have an easy ride. Furthermore, it was particularly unfortunate for *The Big Flame* that it arrived at the end of a relatively liberal era at the BBC, that of the Director-General Sir Hugh Greene, in which radical experiments such as *The Wednesday Play* were able to survive, even if not to flourish unchecked.[24] Significantly, in the light of my earlier remarks about the timidity of the Labour Party, Greene was rather *too* radical for the then Labour Prime Minister, Harold Wilson, who had him replaced with the far more conservative Sir Charles Curran. From now on, documentary dramas and other controversial plays would be that much more difficult to produce and screen. Indeed, even *The Big Flame*'s transmission was postponed twice, due to internal BBC wrangles, and at one point it looked as if it might not reach the screen at all.[25]

Clearly, therefore, after several years of mounting internal tensions over controversial subjects on television, matters were reaching some kind of crisis point within the BBC. In addition, the problems actually crystallised, publicly at least, over the question of fact/fiction and documentary drama. For, in the *Radio Times* of 16 January 1969, there appeared a curious, unsigned article entitled "Keeping Faith with the Viewer", whose decidedly "ex-cathedra" tone clearly signalled that it came from high up within the BBC hierarchy and was meant to be read as some kind of official policy statement – as well as, of course, a warning to the BBC "radicals". Because it is absolutely central to the subject-matter of this essay, it is worth reprinting in full:

> Television is a demanding medium in the way that it compels the viewer to move more quickly in place, mood, and indeed emotion, than could ever be possible in real life; and because it can confuse him by the rapid succession of varying images presented on the screen. At one moment the viewer may be watching a fictional drama, at another a factual wartime scene in Nigeria or Vietnam, at another a sporting event unfolding as it happened, the result of which he can already have read about in his newspaper.
>
> As television techniques develop what are the safeguards for the public? What confidence can the viewer have that what he is watching is what it appears to be? The answer is that the BBC bears the responsibility for ensuring that whatever happens the viewer is not tricked. Bearing in mind that every kind of programme has to appear on the same screen, what he sees must be true to fact or true to art.
>
> Over the years the viewer has learned to distinguish between those programmes which he knows to be fact and those he

knows to be fiction by means of a series of conventions which he has come to respect. The first and in many ways the most important indication of the nature of a programme is given in *Radio Times*. Aside from that, when the set is switched on, the signature tune and a related set of captions indicate whether a news bulletin is about to be shown or a current affairs programme, a documentary, a play, or a light entertainment show.

In a news or current affairs programme the viewer will see a selection of events that have really happened with comments about them by real people. If any world event is shown he knows that this really has taken place and has not been fabricated as were – say – the sequences in Eisenstein's film about the 1917 Revolution in Russia. These are great pieces of film-making, but they were not shots of what actually happened.

Through a different set of conventions the viewer knows that in plays, series or serials what he will see will be true to art: a good story or one episode in a continuing piece of fiction. He knows that this kind of programme will not be a photographic record of real events. It will be art presented as art.

In recent years this simple situation has been complicated by the emergence of many different variations in programme formula and the development of a new tradition of realistic writing. In fictional series great trouble has been taken by writers like Elwyn Jones in 'Softly Softly' to create brilliantly down-to-earth stories, which they have set in a most convincing framework. Elwyn Jones has made a special study of police cases, and he has talked at length to policemen. The result is a credible set of adventures, which can on occasion even startle the audience with their realism, as when one episode which dealt with a major disaster was felt by some viewers to be too close to the recent and real Aberfan tragedy.

Such realism in dramatic writing graphically illustrates how people behave in given situations in a way that a factual programme can never quite achieve. The viewer knows very well that what he is watching is only a story, but a series like 'The Troubleshooters' or 'Champion House' can illuminate, for instance, what it really feels like to be an industrial executive under pressure in a competitive world.

In a creative medium like television, experiments are always taking place, and new programmes are being devised with formulae that are slightly different from anything ever done before. Wednesday Plays like 'Cathy Come Home,' 'Golden Vision' and Mrs. Lawrence Will Look After It' were experimental in the sense that although all three were well-acted dramas, each made a deliberate comment on an important social problem. And it was known that actual real-life material had been used to shape their preparation. This was the essential ingredient that made their impact so outstanding.

Can these new programme techniques be carried too far? Is there any danger that they will lead to confusion in the mind of the viewer, so that he is uncertain whether he is watching a play or a documentary – a criticism which was made of 'Cathy Come Home' by one or two panellists in a recent edition of 'Talkback'? This is in fact one of the problems with which the BBC has to grapple every day as part of its overall task of editorial control. Many factors are involved. Among these are professional judgment and contemporary taste. In order to provide a constant opportunity for development and variety in programme style it is important that both authors and programme makers should be left reasonably free. A work of fiction may borrow some of the techniques of a factual programme. 'Up the Junction' was a programme which did this, and one television critic praised it as 'fiction which had the immediacy of real life, the raucousness, the feel, the smell of documented life, without being a documentary. It was the realistic convention heightened to the nth degree, and very exciting it was.'

As Christopher Ralling wrote in a recent article in *The Listener*:

'Many of the things worth discussing in human life are never going to happen of their own accord in front of a camera. This has led people working in films and television to move further away from the old ground rules...'

But obviously there are limits beyond which experimental techniques ought not to trespass. All the time the BBC is walking a tightrope, but even in its most experimental programmes it seeks to keep faith with the viewers. People like and have a right to know what it is they are looking at. In the history of protest about broadcasting trouble has most frequently been caused when the audience got – not what it did not want – but what it did not expect.[26]

In the *Radio Times* of 13 February 1969, a number of BBC "radicals", including Loach, wrote a letter to the editor. This too is worth reprinting in full:

Readers of the *Radio Times* may be puzzled by the recent article (Jan. 16) 'Keeping Faith with the Viewer.' For many people who work in television it is also very disturbing. Because beneath its bland, sweet reasonableness, which is the house-style of BBC bureaucracy, there is a warning.

The warning is this: if you refuse to take our gentlemanly hints, we shall censor or ban any of your programmes which deal in social and political attitudes not acceptable to us. The odd rebel may be allowed to kick over the traces, occasionally. Provided this is an isolated event, and not part of a general movement, it only helps us to preserve our liberal and independent image. But enough is enough.

The important thing for the viewers to understand is that this is an argument about content, not about form. We are told that 'what he sees must be true to fact or true to art' but there is no acknowledgement of the *fact* that the screen is full of news, public affairs programmes and documentaries, all delivered with the portentous authority of the BBC and riddled with argument and opinion. It is a question of which argument and what opinion. Some are acceptable; some are not.

And the gloves are really coming off in the traditionally safe area of drama. Why? If we go back to our article we are told that it is a question of the techniques used, the conventions established. 'Through a different set of conventions the viewer knows...that this kind of programme (drama) will not be a photographic record of real events. It will be art presented as art.'

Over eighteen months ago a Wednesday Play called *Five Women* was completed. Everyone who has seen it (a very privileged few because the BBC won't allow viewings of material that it bans – despite a written request from twenty-five writers, directors and producers) agrees that its artistic merit is beyond doubt. But it used actresses to tell the stories of women who had been in prison. Used them so convincingly, that despite the end credits to artists, the front titles identifying it as a Wednesday Play by an author and a *Radio Times* billing doing both, the BBC decided that viewers might be misled into thinking it was real! And worse, that the style might be imitated until viewers wouldn't know whether to believe even the News (good point: should viewers *believe* the News?)

The BBC have never given a clear reason for banning this show. After more than twelve months of conversations and correspondence with the BBC, the writer, the director and the producer are still mystified. Was it the form, were the actresses just too convincing (but what else do we ask of art?) or was it the possible uses to which this approach might be put?

What *is* clear is that the objection to mixed forms is only introduced when the content is found offensive by our guardians. Much humdrum television drama contains some example of 'real events' in the use of stock film and sound effects. In fact the BBC regularly exploits so-called fiction as a matter of policy – the Archers constantly peddle hints to farmers from the Ministry of Agriculture and it is, after all, some years since listeners sent wreaths to Grace Archer's funeral. When *Till Death Us Do Part* filmed Alf Garnett and his son-in-law in the middle of a real football crowd no-one in the BBC was worried that this was not keeping faith with the viewer.

A documentary called *Hit, Suddenly, Hit* was also banned last autumn – again with no public explanation. Its form was conventional but its argument was not. It contained people like Marcuse, Erich Fromm, Stokeley Carmichael, Allen Ginsberg and Adrian Mitchell. The BBC found it 'unbalanced.' So it's not just form. It appears that the poor viewer shall only be selectively protected – and the areas selected are sensitive ones where social and political assumptions might be upset. This is spelled out almost innocently in the finger-wagging pay off to 'Keeping Faith with the Viewer.'

'In the history of protest about broadcasting trouble' (ah yes, trouble) 'has most frequently been caused when the audience got – not what it did not want – but what it did not expect.' Are the quietists not aware that the worst thing about most television is that you get exactly what you expect? It is as predictable as the grave. – Tony Garnett, Jim Allen, Roy Battersby, Clive Goodwin, Ken Loach, James MacTaggart, Roger Smith, Kenith Trodd, London, W.8.[27]

Appended to this letter was a reply by Paul Fox, then-Controller of BBC 1:

Tony Garnett represents one reiterated point of view in the argument about 'fact or fiction?' – an argument that has been bubbling ever since Garnett's prize-winning production 'Cathy Come Home.' A different point of view was put recently (December 19, 1968) in 'The Listener' by an equally talented television producer, Christopher Ralling. The debate, no doubt, will continue.

As far as Mr. Garnett's two factual points are concerned:
1. 'Five Women,' produced by Roy Battersby, was rejected as a play and turned down as a documentary because it is neither

one thing nor the other. Subject to some modifications – it is too long at present – we hope to show it on BBC-1 – a fact known to Mr. Garnett and other signatories of his letter.

2. 'Hit, Suddenly, Hit' was overhauled and outdated by the events in Czechoslovakia before the programme was ready. It seemed to us that a documentary dealing with political violence, for showing in the autumn of 1968, could not totally exclude any mention of what happened in Czechoslovakia in August 1968. There were other factors that made the programme, in our editorial view, unbalanced and it was not shown.

Viewers can see Tony Garnett's latest production for BBC Television this Wednesday. Called 'The Big Flame,' it is written by Jim Allen, directed by Kenneth Loach and bears all the distinctions of a Tony Garnett 'Wednesday Play.' It is a remarkable film from the same producer and director team that made 'Cathy Come Home.'[28]

To his credit, T C Worsley took up the defence on behalf of Loach, Garnett, Allen et al, calling the article "a time bomb, or rather...the wrapping in which a time bomb was to be stifled", and accusing it of being "very pussy-footed" and "almost a parody of official timidity". On the question of "form" and "content", he is at one with the "radicals'" letter, arguing that:

The two are not and never can be distinct. A new form is a new way of breaking through: it can be very disturbing just in itself. It is commonly (though not always) associated with the importation of a new or previously inhibited area of thought or feeling into the public domain. Mr. Garnett and his group have produced some of the most exciting and influential television in this area where fact and fiction overlap. And if it sets the bees buzzing, the BBC should be delighted, not afraid. While I think the group's fiction has been marvellous, I have not found their mixed experiments artistically successful...But still I would fight to the death for their right to make these experiments in their own way. And I think that the BBC should have clung to this, the most creative and exciting group working in television, at all costs. To have let them slip through their fingers is a real setback both for the BBC and for television.[29]

This last sentence referred to the fact that Garnett and others had formed their own independent company, Kestrel Films, and had decided to see if they fared any better in the independent television sector. This, coupled with the departure of Sir Hugh Greene, seemed for some to mark the end of an era. *The Daily Mail* referred to *The Big Flame* as "[t]he last of the big controversial dramas from the golden age of *The Wednesday Play*",[30] whilst George Melly in *The Observer* argued that it "provided a useful slide-rule against which future conformism and timidity may be measured".[31]

In the event, these funeral orations for the documentary drama were somewhat premature. In 1971, Loach directed Jim Allen's *The Rank and File* for the *Play for Today* slot, the successor to the old *Wednesday Play*. Although a barely disguised dramatisation of the recent strike at Pilkington's Glass Works in St Helens, the film caused far less outcry than many of its predecessors. Meanwhile, as predicted by many, Kestrel was experiencing difficulties in the independent television sector, and the Loach/Garnett/Smith production, *After a Lifetime* (1971), was held up by problems (mainly over bad language) with both the Independent Television Authority (the forerunner of the Independent Broadcasting Authority [IBA]) and London Weekend Television. Indeed, one of the biggest rows of all was yet to come. This was occasioned by Loach, Garnett and Allen's most elaborate-ever production, the four-part *Days of Hope*, which aimed at nothing less than telling the political history of the British working class from the First World War to the General Strike of 1926. Very much "history from below", it was not a production calculated to please any part of the Establishment, since, like *The Big Flame* and *The Rank and File*, it showed the organised working class being defeated as much by the timidity or treachery of its leaders as by the repressive apparatus of the capitalist state. To understand why *Days of Hope* created such a massive furore, one has to realise just how uncharacteristically insecure the Establishment was feeling in 1975.

I have already noted, apropos *The Big Flame*, that in the 1960s the Labour government of Harold Wilson came into serious conflict with the trade unions over its desire to hold down wages. Not surprisingly, the conflict between government and unions became significantly more bitter when, in 1970, the Conservatives, led by Edward Heath, came to power determined to curb the unions. There followed a whole series of industrial disputes, most notably with the miners in 1972 and in 1973-74. This last led to the fall of the Conservative government, and to a plot by extreme right-wingers within the Conservative Party, aided by rogue elements in the security services and ideologically-motivated journalists, to destabilise the supposedly too "liberal" Heath. This disturbing episode culminated in his being replaced by Mrs Thatcher as Party Leader in February 1975. From this moment onwards, the Conservatives prepared to avenge themselves with great force on the unions, the result of which process Loach was to attempt to document in his ill-fated 1980s documentaries.

Meanwhile, the loose canons in the security services and their friends in the press were able to concentrate on their primary task – the destabilisation of the Labour government by smearing them as "Communist sympathisers" *inter alia*.[32] It is against this background, therefore, that the reception of *Days of Hope* in some quarters has to be understood. Much of the chorus of press complaint focused on the issue of "bias" – indeed, *The Daily Telegraph* actually devoted an entire leader to the subject, concluding with a plea for "ending a situation in which [Left-wingery] is the dominant political philosophy put out by a semi-monopolistic State service".[33] Unfortunately, however, the bias issue *per se* is rather beyond my scope here, although one might pause for a moment to consider whether "unbiased" drama – a "fair" version of *Richard III* or *The Diary of Anne Frank*, for example – would be terribly interesting. More to the point, for my purposes, is yet another leader in *The Times*, which linked the "bias" issue to that of the documentary drama:

> As with many television plays the producers of the series have adopted some of the techniques of the documentary to achieve a greater dramatic effect. A danger of confusion in the mind of the viewer can arise. The very realism of the production can easily persuade an audience unfamiliar with the details of Mr Ramsay MacDonald's first Government to accept a version of history that reinforces the political point the author desires to make. In a documentary political objectivity and historical accuracy are essential qualities; in a play they can have a depressing effect on the creativity of the author or producer. So it is important to retain a clear distinction in the mind of the viewer.[34]

Since the same leader describes *Days of Hope* as "avowedly partisan drama" and "such a partisan series", it clearly follows that there is, in fact, *no* "danger of confusion" between documentary and drama, and that Loach, Garnett and Allen have behaved entirely properly towards their audience!

Significantly, rows over fact and fiction have pursued Loach out of television and into the reception of some of his more recent feature films. This was certainly the case with his first 1990s feature, *Hidden Agenda* (1990). One of the very few British cinema or television films to delve into the highly secretive matter of "dirty tricks" by the security forces in Northern Ireland, and the attendant corruption of political life on the mainland,[35] *Hidden Agenda* was never going have an easy time from certain quarters. When it was shown in Cannes in 1990, it was condemned publicly by Tory MP Ivor Stanbrook as "the official IRA entry" (even through he had never seen it),[36] and a small group of hacks from staunchly Conservative newspapers, which never tire of preaching about patriotism, showed how selectively interpreted is this notion by causing a scene at the premiere of this British film, and then pestering the festival director with demands that it should not be awarded a prize! (Fortunately, the largely foreign audience regarded this absurd and demeaning spectacle as some kind of obscure British joke.) By the time the film opened in Britain the following year (although not widely, many exhibitors having been put off by the "IRA" tag), the usual forces were ready for it. Indeed, *The Times* devoted another leader to it. Entitled "Fictional Faction", it stated that "*Hidden Agenda*, Kenneth Loach's new film, uses the quasi-documentary narrative form sometimes called 'faction' to argue that the British have had (and by implication still have) a shoot-to-kill policy in Northern Ireland, which is deliberately covered up". It then argues that "[f]action is the most disingenuous form of television" since, firstly, it absolves the filmmaker from providing any real evidence for his factual claims and provides a dramatic licence for invention; secondly, "[t]he television viewer, knowing that at least the context is real and the issue a live one, is given no indication which parts of the script are factually and which fictionally based". The piece concludes that "[a]s a vehicle of partisan propaganda, which is how Mr Loach likes to use it, [faction] is justified neither as art nor journalism".[37]

The final film which I want to examine here is *Ladybird Ladybird* (1994). It is a sad but significant reflection on the state of sections of the British press that, whilst *Ladybird Ladybird* was receiving glowing plaudits from foreign papers on the occasion of its various festival screenings, *The Sunday Times* should have chosen to mark its British premiere at the Edinburgh Film Festival with a substantial but extremely snide article by Carol Sarler, in which she claims – not to put too fine a point on it – that Loach has distorted the facts of a true story for commercial and personal ends. The film thus became involved in an even more than usually sterile rehearsal of the fact/fiction debate – sterile because the film's publicity states that *Ladybird Ladybird* is "inspired by real events" and its opening title reads "Based on a true story", both of which, by any reasonable standards, indicate that the film is very far from being an exact documentary reconstruction of real events, and allow Loach and his writer, Rona Munro, a good deal of dramatic leeway in telling a story. Indeed, as Ronan Bennett, himself a victim of a similar spurious row over *In the Name of the Father*, put it:

> Loach doesn't claim *Ladybird Ladybird* is true in all respects. It is a fictionalisation of real events. 'If you can't substantiate every fact, every piece of dialogue, it seems better to follow

the example of a film like *Missing*. To use the old phrase: It isn't whether the film is true, but what is the truth in the film?'.[38]

There is, therefore, nothing in the way in which the film actually presents itself which justifies any journalist prying into the lives of those on whom it is – loosely – based, especially as such snooping threatens to breach the spirit, if not the letter, of the Children Act. It is, anyway, difficult to take seriously an article on *Ladybird Ladybird* from a newspaper which has consistently sniped at Loach, and indeed at any British film which has dared to represent Tory Britain as anything less than heaven on earth,[39] or from a writer with such an obvious axe to grind. Thus, *Cathy Come Home* is criticised by Sarler for following "a well-trodden cinematic path, an easy route to memorable emotion",[40] and we are informed that, in the case of *Ladybird Ladybird*, "Loach appears to have been worryingly selective in some of the areas of research he chose to explore – keeping away, for whatever reason, from facts that might upset the film". Elsewhere, we are left in little doubt that those reasons are commercial ("part truths help to sell films better than whole truths") or have to do with personal vanity: "[Loach] has turned a blind eye to a camera lens and, some would say, has exploited the unhappiness of a family in the process... when all he can possibly win is a nickel-plated statuette or two". Finally, one also instinctively mistrusts any writer who accuses others of "part truths" and then proceeds herself to get certain key facts spectacularly wrong! *The Sunday Times* refused, characteristically, to print Loach's reply to Sarler's allegations, but it did, belatedly (on 18 September), carry an article by Peter Smith, Loach's legal adviser on the film, which points out some of the inaccuracies in Sarler's article.[41] However, the die had now been cast, and certain other critics could not help but wander off down the same cul-de-sac. Thus, for example, Hugo Davenport, the *The Daily Telegraph* reviewer, who, whilst admitting that the film had become "mired in a fruitless controversy", felt compelled to add that Loach and Munro "have to some extent invited this pursuit of red herrings by their own approach to the material...The viewer is left wondering whether Loach and Munro aren't having it both ways – claiming the authority of docudrama at the same time as invoking the dramatic licence of fiction".[42] This is nothing like as bizarre, however, as the line taken by George Perry in *The Sunday Times*, in which he pins the blame for the alleged fact/fiction confusion on the one thing that all commentators agreed constituted the real strength of the film – Crissy Rock's central performance:

The essence of the problem is that although Loach is a fiction director, he has extraordinary power to coax convincing performances from inexperienced actors, and it is hard to accept their pain is simulated. It feels like fly-on-the-wall documentary, rather than something invented.[43]

I want now to tease out certain underlying themes from these various objections to and criticisms of Loach's documentary dramas. In doing so, I hope to draw some of their apparent sting.

Firstly, I want to deal with the argument, put forward by Purser and Worsley against *Cathy Come Home*, and by Worsley against *The Golden Vision*, that documentary drama somehow is not "proper" drama, let alone "art". What needs to be pointed out here is that both critics are operating with a highly prescriptive notion of what television drama, and indeed all drama, should actually be, and then criticising Loach for not adhering to it himself. Such notions basically boil down to a preference for the television equivalent of the "well-made play", and it is no coincidence that Worsley was initially a theatre critic. These biases were hardly unique to Purser and Worsley, however; as Mike Poole has noted: "[t]elevision criticism in Britain has always displayed a strongly in-built 'literary' bias...[and]...a marked dependence on an inappropriately literary model – notably nineteenth-century notions of authorship, pre-McLuhanite assumptions about 'representation' and a general willingness to address individual programmes as if they were discrete art objects".[44] Nor were such preferences confined to television criticism, since Purser and Worsley's strictures bear a quite uncanny resemblance to what British film critics in the 1940s regarded as the essential ingredients of the "quality film". As John Ellis has pointed out in a virtuoso analysis of this particular critical discourse, one of its chief underlying tenets was that

> Cinema's relation to the real is not that of mirroring: it is a more subtle relation of *making contact with the living world* through a process of narrative construction...The power that the drama of actuality has is one of using the concentration of the film form, with its unity, poetry, coherence of purpose and invisibility of technique, in order to go beyond it, to create an experience of the world, its people, its values.[45]

What is needed, therefore, is not a mere copying of reality, but a method of "concentrating the real" to make the narrative "true to life".[46] Thus, "[t]hough documentary – however defined – carries a definite charge of reality, it seems as though it can only reach the spirit of the real if it adopts the procedures of the fictional narrative, together with its stress on the central values of the human".[47] Clearly, therefore, Purser and Worsley's criticisms of Loach and of documentary drama are based on some fairly deep-seated and traditionally British notions of what actually constitutes art and culture, but exploration of these is unfortunately beyond my scope here.

Secondly, I want to examine the assertion that documentary dramas confuse the viewers' sense of fact and fiction. With reference to Loach, this was raised by Wyndham Goldie over *Cathy Come Home*, by James Thomas in the *Daily Express* over *In Two Minds*, by "Keeping Faith with the Viewer" over documentary drama in general, and by *The Times*' leaders over *Days of Hope* and *Hidden Agenda*. There are several ways of approaching this criticism. For instance, one can question its bona fides and the motives of those who voice it, by noting that it tends to be used extremely selectively against works which are perceived to be "left-wing": the fuss over *Days of Hope* and *The Big Flame* was not matched by any such qualms over Leslie Woodhead's *Three Days in Szczecin* (1976), a reconstruction of the famous strike in the Polish shipyard, which clearly took the side of the strikers. As Loach was forced to reply to *The Daily Telegraph*'s campaign against *Days of Hope*: "Criticisms about confusing fact with fiction are reserved by certain papers for political films but ignored when Edward VIII or Churchill's mother are romanticised and glorified".[48] Another way of deflecting the "confusion" argument is to note that those who marshal it are themselves, of course, not in the least confused about what is fact and what is fiction. Leading on from this, one might also note that the very public debates over their subject-matter which Loach's films have engendered provide ample proof that people are by no means "duped", and are fully able to make up their own minds about whether or not they agree with the point of view on offer. Unfortunately, no audience research seems to have been carried out into any of the films discussed here, but it is of some significance that when the Independent Broadcasting Authority (the predecessor of the current Independent Television Commission) undertook audience research into a number of factually-based dramas, they concluded that no one should

> [U]nderestimate the sophistication and common sense of most viewers when dealing with their understanding and interpretation of television...As audience research has shown, even when viewers know that a drama is billed as dealing with events that really happened, they do not invariably accept its evidence without question.[49]

Indeed, it could be argued that it is not television writers, directors and producers who are trying to "dupe" the viewers, but newspaper editors and journalists who are attempting to impose their own, largely unacknowledged and implicit cultural and ideological assumptions on their readers.

A third argument was put forward only by Wyndham Goldie over *Cathy Come Home*, and this claimed that such programmes might well cast doubt upon the validity of "proper" current affairs programmes. Here speaks the voice of the true Reithian mandarin, jealously guarding rigid internal BBC boundaries, and appalled at the prospect of the BBC's famed "impartiality" being in any way called into question, especially by young whippersnappers from the Drama Department. Today, even within the BBC, there is a much greater readiness to accept that "factual" and "fictional" programmes are indeed *both* constructs (albeit ones operating with very different rules and codes), but even at the time there were those who rejected the simple equation of factual programmes with "the truth", and drama with fiction. As seen in the reply to "Keeping Faith with the Viewer", these certainly included Loach and his colleagues. Interestingly, another was Philip Purser who, while discussing *Cathy Come Home* in *The Sunday Telegraph*, attacked the inference that

> [I]f a programme is 'documentary' it must be gospel; one accepts what it says without question, while a play is only a play... This naïve supposition is part of the general prejudice against imaginative fiction which dominates the literary scene... What private line to the truth does the documentarist enjoy?...I would sooner trust a playwright than a documentarist to tell me the truth, especially the truth about people and the way people behave.[50]

Later, over the controversy surrounding *The Big Flame*, Purser took a similarly robust line, stating that:

> It is absurd to require a piece of work to declare itself under some literary Trade Descriptions Act: Guaranteed Documentary, containing 22 per cent. old newsreel, 34 per cent. Robin Day, 43 per cent. studio discussion, 1 per cent. monosodium glutinate. Even more dismaying is the underlying assumption – alas, not confined to television – that fact is necessarily more 'real' than fiction, that it is fact which is going to be the injured party if the two collide. Any serious treatment of the way people behave to each other, and what they want, and what drives them on, must fall back eventually on a degree of interpretation. Whether it's history or biography, 'Panorama' profile or 'Wednesday Play', in the end it's created, and identical standards of honesty and truthfulness and compassion are at stake.[51]

It can also be argued, therefore, that, just as Purser and Worsley's earlier strictures were based on their views not only about television, but also about art and culture in general, so these various concerns about fact and fiction on television are rooted in quite specific, if largely unacknowledged, notions about what constitutes fact and factuality as a whole. Much of the criticism of Loach, and of documentary drama in general, rests on precisely the kind of fetishisation of facts that one would expect to find in so resolutely an empirical culture as that of the British. As E H Carr has stated:

> The empirical theory of knowledge presupposes a complete separation between subject and object. Facts, like sense-impressions, impinge on the observer from outside and are independent of his consciousness. The process of reception is passive: having received the data, he then acts on them. The Oxford Shorter English Dictionary, a useful but tendentious work of the empirical school, clearly marks the separateness of the two processes by defining a fact as 'a datum of experience as distinct from conclusions'. This is what may be called the common-sense view of history. History consists of a corpus of ascertained facts. The facts are available to the historian in documents, inscriptions and so on, like fish on the fishmonger's slab. The historian collects them, takes them home and cooks and serves them in whatever style appeals to him.[52]

But, of course, historiography and, *mutatis mutandis*, any television programme about historical events, are not really like this at all. The historian is necessarily selective and cannot avoid making judgments and interpretations; indeed, Carr quotes the American historian, Carl Becker, that "the facts of history do not exist for any historian till he creates them". Carr concludes:

> The facts are really not at all like fish on the fishmonger's slab. They are like fish swimming about in a vast and sometimes inaccessible ocean; and what the historian catches will depend, partly on chance, but mainly on what part of the ocean he chooses to fish in and what tackle he chooses to use – these two factors being, of course, determined by the kind of fish he wants to catch. By and large, the historian will get the kind of facts he wants. History means interpretation.[53]

The fourth argument here is actually what largely underlies the two previous ones, and concerns the whole question of bias. This is raised explicitly by Wyndham Goldie over *Cathy Come Home*, by James

Thomas in the *Daily Express* over *In Two Minds*, and by *The Times* over *Days of Hope* and *Hidden Agenda*. With Wyndham Goldie, this is another example of concern about possible compromise of a key BBC principle, one which underpins its own self-image as an organisation independent of government and as a source of objective, unbiased information.[54] But, like the old, rigid distinction between "factual" and "fictional" programmes, the notion of television being an entirely "neutral" observer or mirror of reality has increasingly come to be questioned, even by those who do not agree completely with the Glasgow University Media Group. So, *pace* the formidable Wyndham Goldie, it is quite possible to argue, together with the "radicals", that television, albeit implicitly and largely unconsciously, "advocates" all sorts of "policies and courses of action" all the time – it is just that this process remains largely invisible, unacknowledged and taken for granted, since there is often so little difference between the "policies and courses of action" which people encounter on the screen, and those which they encounter elsewhere in their daily lives. It is only when a programme takes on the banal ideological assumptions that underpin daily life, the quotidian "commonsensical" notions such as "there's no need for people to be homeless in Britain" – a sentiment which, shamefully, is given far more credence by the current government than by the one in power in *Cathy Come Home*'s day – that the process of "advocacy" actually becomes visible and, of course, controversial. As Tony Garnett expressed it in the *Radio Times* at the height of the *Days of Hope* brouhaha:

> Our own anger is reserved for the phoney objectivity, the tone of balance and fairness affected by so many programmes. We deal in fiction and tell the truth as we see it. So many self-styled 'factual' programmes are full of unacknowledged bias. I suggest that you are really in danger from them and not from us.[55]

Moreover, of course, like the idea that Loach is confusing the viewers' sense of fact and fiction, the charge of "bias" is always wheeled out extremely selectively against programmes which challenge the status quo. Those who uphold it have, apparently, no viewpoint or axe to grind – they just present things "as they are". As Ronan Bennett argues, what really bothers Loach's critics is not the "facts" as Loach represents them in a particular film: "The real problem is with the man and his work, from *Cathy Come Home* to *The Big Flame*, from *Days of Hope* to *The Price of Coal* (1977). Loach, as the title of his miners' strike film suggests, takes sides and says so. Those who don't like his side tend not to like his films".[56] It is entirely unsurprising that this includes a large section of Britain's overwhelmingly Conservative press

– the only mildly odd thing being that newspapers which are a byword the world over for debased journalistic standards, and which have largely obliterated the traditional distinction between news and editorial columns, should actually have the gall to accuse anyone of bias, let alone of confusing fact and fiction!

Fifthly and finally, I want not to argue against the whole notion of documentary drama, but at least to warn against the dangers of using the label in such a heavily blanketing fashion that it tends to obscure important formal differences between individual works – in the case of Loach, for example, *Cathy Come Home*, *In Two Minds*, *The Big Flame* and *Days of Hope*. This, of course, is precisely what unites the *Screen* Left and the Fleet Street Right – from their very different ideological positions, both construct a convenient ideal type ("classic realist text"; "fictional faction") and then use this as a crude measure by which individual works may be judged and found ideologically wanting and "incorrect". Without getting involved in generalised arguments about realism, naturalism, their differences and their progressive potentials,[57] I would like to suggest that we need to bear in mind John Caughie's concern about the "looseness and ahistorical formalism of the concepts of naturalism which circulate within writing and thinking about television" and the need for "the possibility of a debate within naturalism",[58] together with Raymond Williams' warning that "[t]he problems of immediate form have always to be considered in relation to content and to the nature of the audience. Form, theoretically, is always the fusion of specific methods of presentation, specifically selected experience, and specific relations between producer and audience".[59]

Loach's early works, such as the episodes of *Diary of a Young Man* (1964) which he directed, or *The End of Arthur's Marriage* (1965), are certainly not documentary dramas, and, indeed, there is a sense in which they are quite distinctly anti-naturalist. In *Diary of a Young Man*, in particular, there are echoes of the French New Wave, and especially of Godard. It is not altogether surprising, therefore, to find all sorts of diverse elements cropping up in *Cathy Come Home*, which may indeed be realist, but realist in a way that makes it a very different kind of documentary drama to *Days of Hope*, for example. John Corner has described *Cathy Come Home* as exhibiting a "hybrid aesthetic", one which involves various different kinds of narration and moves the spectator through a number of different subject positions. The film develops both as a "story" and as a "report"; conventional first-person, past-tense narrative is frequently supplemented by anonymous voices, statistics and official-sounding commentary, whilst Cathy's own personal story often seems to stop temporarily "to allow a brief ethnographic trip around its current location".[60] Corner concludes that "one of the characteristics of *Cathy* is not only its 'code

51

mixing' but also the way in which certain depictive elements in it become inflected in different directions, towards different communicative modalities, according to the overall discursive context".[61] This is, therefore, an "interpenetration of modes", a series of forms of address which is actually quite disjointed and disorienting. Paradoxically, it bears a number of similarities to the kinds of highly formalised texts so beloved of *Screen* theorists at a certain moment; by the same token, it is extremely hard to see how a text which takes a good deal of active "deciphering" could be accused (by the "other side") of duping the audience or lulling them into accepting Loach and Sandford's particular viewpoints.

One could make a similar point about the many modalities of realism and of documentary drama by looking at *In Two Minds*, and especially by comparing it with *Family Life*. The latter is indeed a film in a recognisably British realist cinematic tradition, but, in the small screen version of the story, Loach and Mercer borrow the visual language of a certain kind of television interview – not the cool, detached approach of the news and current affairs programme, but the intense, probing, intimate style associated with the ground-breaking (and recently revived) BBC *Face to Face* series. Here "style" is very much to the fore and not at all "invisible", and Loach and Mercer use formal elements brilliantly to communicate the awful contradictory pressures and expectations bearing down on the unfortunate Kate. As Potter stated:

> Loach...banged his cameras in so tight upon eyes and foreheads and mouths that the viewer wanted to brush something out of his own eye – but the tiny insect had by then buzzed out of sight to settle inside the brain, where it stung until it hurt. The mesh of questions from the unseen interviewer...become ever more interlocked, criss-crossed and insistent, pulling us into the centre of the drama as colluding participants rather than cool observers safely patrolling on the outer edges.[62]

As we have seen, *In Two Minds* was criticised as documentary drama, as was *The Big Flame*, for very similar underlying reasons. Yet, the two are strikingly different. As Raymond Williams has pointed out, *The Big Flame* is not only socially extended, contemporary and secular (all crucial defining features of a realist text), but also, more unusually, it is "consciously interpretative in relation to a particular political viewpoint".[63] Thus, it starts out by establishing the level of existing working-class history and consciousness in a specific workplace at a specific time: the Liverpool docks at the time of the Devlin Report. As Williams states, however:

What then happens is perhaps inconsistent with the narrower definitions of realism in that, having taken the action to that point in this recognisable place, a certain dramatic, but also political, hypothesis is established. What would happen if we went beyond the terms of this particular struggle against existing conditions and existing attempts to define or alter them?[64]

Thus, what can be seen here is a fusion and, within this fusion, a certain fracture between

[T]he familiar methods of establishing recognition and the alternative method of a hypothesis within that recognition, a hypothesis which is played out in realistic terms, but within a politically imagined possibility.[65]

In other words, the film is not saying simply "this is how it is", but rather "this is how it could be". So, although *The Big Flame* shows the defeat of the occupation itself, it does not concede the defeat of the motivating idea; here the famous labour song, "The Ballad of Joe Hill", plays a key role, introducing a much wider history and consciousness of the working-class movement as a whole, and adopting "a teaching perspective that the working class must understand and learn from its defeats as well as its victories".[66] Or, as Jack Regan, the play's central figure, puts it: "there'll be no revolution, but you'll have lit a bonfire". Indeed, Regan is very much a crucial part of the film's "hypothetical" element; from the moment he arrives, he introduces "the voice of a different consciousness, and there is a movement in that part of the film from the rather ragged discussion which is done within naturalist terms to the conscious voice-over presentation of an alternative point of view".[67]

So, *The Big Flame* may indeed be a documentary drama of sorts, but it is also quite a demonstrative and even didactic text. To this end, it may not use Brechtian methods, but, like *Cathy Come Home* (albeit in a different kind of way), it does engage in "code mixing". Furthermore, its move away from mere naturalist *description* can also be discerned in a scene in which it actually foregrounds conventions of media representation. The particularly crucial moment here, as Williams has noted, is when, in a battle between the police and strikers, Loach – contrary to established news and current affairs practice – places the camera with the strikers, as opposed to with the police. This pointedly brings home to the spectator both what it feels like to be attacked by the police, and how unusual such a sensation is, given that the placing of the camera on the other side has become such a naturalised television convention. As Williams notes, this scene demonstrates all too clearly how the meaning of an image "is inherently determined by viewpoint in the precise technical sense of the position of the camera".[68] It is, therefore, a scene which realises all Grace Wyndham Goldie's worst nightmares about documentary drama casting doubt on "the validity of what has in fact been real".[69]

In this essay I have tried to show how a number of Loach's works have become caught up in a long-running debate about documentary drama, a debate which increasingly has spilled out of the drama arena into more generalised complaints about "bias" at the BBC. Indeed, as I have suggested elsewhere,[70] the question of documentary drama was, for many Conservative politicians and newspapers, little more than a convenient excuse for an exercise in BBC-bashing. Whether such external attacks had any effect on the development of the documentary drama in the BBC by Loach or its other practitioners is difficult to judge. However, we do know from "Keeping Faith with the Viewer" and from Wyndham Goldie that documentary drama was viewed with concern and suspicion by some within the BBC mandarinate, and it is inconceivable that they would not have used negative press comment to bolster their cause within the organisation itself, on the grounds, of course, that they were simply reflecting "public opinion". It is certainly undeniable that there are precious few television films on our screens today which look like *Days of Hope*, but that does not mean to say that factually-based drama has disappeared. What I would argue has in fact happened in such dramas is that what Caughie called the "dramatic look" has largely eclipsed the "documentary look",[71] and that realism of reference (being *about* the real) has taken preference over realism of signification (*looking like* the real). Here the "documentariness" of the drama no longer resides in the visible presence of certain specific televisual codes normally associated with non-fiction programmes, but rather in the script's documented adherence to documented fact. The reasons for this, which pulls factually-based drama closer to US-style "faction", may well be primarily commercial and fuelled by structural changes within Britain's increasingly deregulated and market-led television system. However, one should not underestimate the steady drip-drip effect of years of negative comment by hostile politicians and newspapers on a mandarinate not known for its enthusiasm for radical ideas. Certainly, if one looks at the sections in the *BBC Producers' Guidelines* devoted to accuracy and impartiality, it is impossible not to be aware of the bruises left by past battles over documentary dramas such as *Days of Hope*. For example, of "Drama Portraying Contemporary Situations", the *Guidelines* state that:

> When drama realistically portrays living people or contemporary situations in a controversial fashion, it has an

obligation to be accurate – to do justice to the main facts. If the drama strives for a fair, impartial and rounded view of events, no problem arises. If it is an accurate but, nonetheless, partisan and partial portrayal of a controversial issue, the commissioning executive should proceed only if convinced that the insight and excellence of the work justify the platform offered; and that it will be judged honest, thoughtful and stimulating.[72]

Similarly, when it comes to "History in Drama":

If a drama of artistic merit is written from an obviously partial standpoint, the producer should consider how to label and publicise it in order to make its nature clear. When a powerful drama of this kind is likely to prove particularly controversial, the BBC may need to consider whether to offer an alternative viewpoint in other types of programmes.[73]

The section concludes with the warning:

Great care must be taken in continuity announcements, trails and promotional material to ensure that the audience is aware of the nature of the drama. Where fact and fiction are mixed the public should be made aware of this. It must be made clear that the drama is only an *interpretation* of a current or historical situation.[74]

There is, of course, nothing in the least wrong with such concerns in themselves. Whether or not it is really necessary to lay down the law in this fashion, whether or not it inhibits what a director such as Loach or a writer such as Jim Allen can now make in the way of television drama, and how (and in whose interests) the *Guidelines* are actually applied in practice, are altogether other matters. In my analysis of the criticisms of Ken Loach's documentary dramas, I have argued that they are either misplaced, groundless, self-interested or ideologically-motivated, and I am bound therefore to conclude that such caution is as regrettable as it is predictable.

Notes

[1]   Andrew Goodwin, Paul Kerr and Ian Macdonald (eds), *Drama-Documentary* (London: British Film Institute, 1983); David Edgar, *The Second Time as Farce: Reflections on the Drama of Mean Times* (London: Lawrence and Wishart, 1988); Paul Kerr, "F for Fake? Friction over Faction", in Andrew Goodwin and Garry Whannel (eds), *Understanding Television*

(London; New York: Routledge, 1990): 74-102; Richard Kilborn, "'Drama over Lockerbie': A new look at television drama-documentaries", *Historical Journal of Film, Radio and Television* 14: 1 (1994): 59-76; Julian Petley, "Fact plus fiction equals friction", *Media, Culture and Society* 18: 1 (1996): 11-25.

2   For a useful series of views of British television drama in the 1960s and 1970s, see Irene Shubik, *Play for Today: The Evolution of Television Drama* (London: Davis-Poynter, 1975); Jayne Pilling and Kingsley Canham (eds), *The Screen on the Tube: Filmed TV Drama* (Norwich: Cinema City, 1983); George W Brandt (ed), *British television drama* (Cambridge: Cambridge University Press, 1981). On the Whitehouse phenomenon, see Michael Tracey and David Morrison, *Whitehouse* (London: Macmillan, 1979).

3   T C Worsley, *Television: The Ephemeral Art* (London: Alan Ross, 1970): 36.

4   Michael Tracey, *A Variety of Lives: A Biography of Sir Hugh Greene* (London; Sydney; Toronto: The Bodley Head, 1983): 252-253.

5   Ample evidence of the sheer amount of negative press coverage is provided in "A Powerful New Anti-War Film from Britain: *The War Game*", *Film Comment* 3: 4 (autumn 1965): 4-13, and also in Joseph A Gomez, *Peter Watkins* (Boston: Twayne Publishers, 1979).

6   Tom Pocock, "MPs see bomb film the BBC banned", *Evening Standard* 8 February 1966: 1.

7   Grace Wyndham Goldie, "Why They Made 'The War Game'", *The Sunday Telegraph* 13 February 1966: 17.

8   Indeed, the BBC undoubtedly had an inkling that *Cathy Come Home* would be used as yet another stick with which to beat it: the writer Jeremy Sandford had had to struggle with the BBC for two and a half years before they would produce the film and, inspite of the huge success of *Cathy Come Home*, they would produce only one more of his scripts, the highly-acclaimed *Edna the Inebriate Woman* (1971), even though they had at least two more on the books. (For an interesting discussion of Sandford, see Martin Banham, "Jeremy Sandford", in Brandt [ed]: 194-216.)

9   Grace Wyndham Goldie, "Stop Mixing TV. Fact and Fiction", *The Sunday Telegraph* 8 January 1967: 14.

10   Ibid.

11   Ibid.

12   Philip Purser, "Black and White Play", *The Sunday Telegraph* 20 November 1966: 13.

13   Philip Purser, "Play or Propaganda?", *The Sunday Telegraph* 15 January 1967: 11.

14   Worsley: 64.

15   Ibid: 157.

[16] Mercer had already made a name for himself with *A Suitable Case for Treatment* (1962), remade as the feature film, *Morgan, A Suitable Case for Treatment* by Karel Reisz in 1966, and *And Did Those Feet?* (1965).

[17] Anthony Burgess, "Television", *The Listener* 77: 1980 (9 March 1967): 335.

[18] James Thomas, "Getting a bit blurred on TV... 'Drama' and 'Real-life'", *Daily Express* 8 March 1967: 8.

[19] Dennis Potter, "Sting in the Brain", *New Statesman* 73: 1878 (10 March 1967): 339.

[20] Worsley: 155.

[21] Michael Billington, "Marrying fact and fiction", *The Times* 27 April 1968.

[22] The Glasgow University Media Group, *Bad News* (London: Routledge & Kegan Paul, 1976); The Glasgow University Media Group, *More Bad News* (London; Boston; Hanley: Routledge & Kegan Paul, 1980); Peter Beharrell and Greg Philo (eds), *Trade Unions and the Media* (London: Macmillan, 1977).

[23] Paul Madden, "Jim Allen", in Brandt (ed): 36.

[24] The best account of the Greene period is Tracey.

[25] At the same time, another Tony Garnett production, *Five Women*, written by Tony Parker and directed by Roy Battersby (both known "radicals" in BBC terms), was being seriously held up by a bad attack of BBC cold feet and censoriousness; this pioneering study of women prisoners was broadcast only in a truncated version as *Some Women* in 1969.

[26] "Keeping Faith with the Viewer", *Radio Times* 16 January 1969: 4.

[27] "Keeping Faith with the Viewer: A letter to the Editor", *Radio Times* 13 February 1969: 2. Emphases in original.

[28] Ibid.

[29] Worsley: 230-231.

[30] John Stevenson, "Is The Big Flame still too hot for the BBC?", *The Daily Mail* 10 February 1969.

[31] George Melly, "Suspension of disbelief", *The Observer* 23 February 1969.

[32] For the full, but still largely ignored, story of this scandalous and disreputable period, see Stephen Dorril and Robin Ramsay, *Smear! Wilson and the Secret State* (London: Fourth Estate, 1991).

[33] "History at the BBC", *The Daily Telegraph* 27 September 1975: 14.

[34] "Does the bias run both ways?", *The Times* 30 September 1975: 13.

[35] Paul Foot, *Who Framed Colin Wallace?* (London: Macmillan, 1989); Fred

Holroyd, *War Without Honour* (London: Medium Publishing, 1989).

[36]   See, for example, Steve Grant, "Troubles shooter", *Time Out* 1063 (2-9 January 1991): 24-26.

[37]   "Fictional Faction", *The Times* 10 January 1991: 13. There is, however, an elementary error here: "faction" is an American term applied to television programmes such as *Roots*, *The Day After* and *Holocaust*, whilst *Hidden Agenda* is a specifically British (although American-financed) cinema film.

[38]   Ronan Bennett, "Still worried about Maggie's children", *The Observer (Review)* 4 September 1994: 2.

[39]   Julian Petley, "The price of portraying a less than perfect Britain", *The Listener* 119: 3046 (21 January 1988): 14.

[40]   See Carol Sarler, "Nothing but the truth", *The Sunday Times (Magazine)* 14 August 1994: 43-44, 46, 49.

[41]   See Peter Smith, "Filming difficulties", *The Sunday Times* 18 September 1994: 4.

[42]   Hugo Davenport, "Unhappy families", *The Daily Telegraph* 30 September 1994: 24.

[43]   George Perry, "First impressions", *The Sunday Times* 21 August 1994: 10.

[44]   Mike Poole, "The Cult of the Generalist: British Television Criticism 1936-83", *Screen* 25: 2 (1984): 53.

[45]   John Ellis, "Art, Culture and Quality: Terms for a Cinema in the Forties and Seventies", *Screen* 19: 3 (1978): 29. Emphasis in original.

[46]   Ibid: 30-31.

[47]   Ibid: 33-34.

[48]   Quoted in Julian Petley, "Docu-drama: truth or fiction?", *Movie* 63 (1981): 1257.

[49]   Barrie Gunter, *Drama Documentaries: The Viewer's Viewpoint* (London: Independent Broadcasting Authority, 1990): 25.

[50]   Purser (1967).

[51]   Philip Purser, "Red cries at night", *The Sunday Telegraph* 23 February 1967: 13.

[52]   E H Carr, *What is History?* (London: Macmillan & Co; New York: St Martin's Press; 1961): 3.

[53]   Ibid: 18.

[54]   See Grace Wyndham Goldie, *Facing the Nation: Television and Politics 1936-1976* (London; Sydney; Toronto: The Bodley Head, 1977).

[55]   Tony Garnett, "Letters", *Radio Times* 4 October 1975: 65.

[56]   Bennett: 2.

[57]   See, in particular, Raymond Williams, "Realism, Naturalism and their Alternatives", *Ciné-Tracts* 1: 3 (autumn 1977-winter 1978): 1-6; Raymond Williams, "A Lecture on Realism", *Screen* 18: 1 (1977): 61-74; Raymond Williams, *Keywords: A Vocabulary of Culture and Society* (London: Fontana/ Croom Helm, 1976); John McGrath, "TV Drama: The Case Against Naturalism", *Sight and Sound* 46: 2 (1977): 100-105; Terry Lovell, *Pictures of Reality: Aesthetics, Politics, Pleasure* (London: British Film Institute, 1980); John Caughie, "Progressive Television and Documentary Drama", *Screen* 21: 3 (1980): 9-35; John Tulloch, *Television Drama: Agency, audience and myth* (London; New York: Routledge, 1990); John Corner, *The Art of record: A critical introduction to documentary* (Manchester; New York: Manchester University Press, 1996).

[58]   Caughie: 22.

[59]   Williams (1977-78): 4.

[60]   Corner: 97.

[61]   Ibid: 100.

[62]   Potter: 339.

[63]   Williams (1977): 68.

[64]   Ibid: 68-69.

[65]   Ibid: 69.

[66]   Ibid.

[67]   Ibid: 70.

[68]   Ibid: 71.

[69]   Goldie (1967): 14.

[70]   Petley (1996).

[71]   Caughie: 26.

[72]   British Broadcasting Corporation, *Producers' Guidelines* (London: BBC, 1993): 25.

[73]   Ibid: 26.

[74]   Ibid. Emphasis in original.

Naturalism, narration and critical perspective: Ken Loach and the experimental method

Deborah Knight

Ken Loach's films[1] are naturalist. This has provoked some predictable responses, many of which are predictable responses to naturalist works in general. His work has been criticised by some mainstream critics as didactic, overwritten, too raw and too political. His work has been objected to by the political left of cinema studies as too mainstream, too much a part of the "dominant ideology", not sufficiently formally "self-conscious", and thus insufficiently political. These are political and aesthetic complaints, dealing with the political content or the political form of Loach's films and television dramas. Other responses are equally predictable. Because audiences often respond strongly to Loach's central characters and their social or economic plights, it is not surprising that the broadcast of *Cathy Come Home* (1966) led to questions being raised in the House of Commons about housing conditions in Britain. One might wonder, watching *Cathy Come Home*, about the seemingly destructive role played by representatives of the state charged with the responsibility of "helping the homeless". Conversely, in the case of Maggie in *Ladybird Ladybird* (1994), one might well wonder whether the state is not right, after all, to take her children into care.

These are responses to Loach as a naturalist. They all speak to naturalism's unnerving directness, which takes us from the discussion of art to the discussion of society, from discussions of characters in a fiction to discussions of people in real life. Loach's films consistently exploit the narrow space between the artistic and the social which is the hallmark of naturalism. In this essay, I want to locate Loach in the tradition of British naturalism, a tradition which goes back to the manifesto of literary naturalism, Emile Zola's "The Experimental Novel". My objective is to rehabilitate naturalism, while proposing that Loach is an exemplary naturalist.

Zola and fictional experiments

In his manifesto, Zola announced what he called the novelist's "great study": it is "just there in the reciprocal effect of society on the individual and the individual on society".[2] Zola's manifesto influenced the earliest British literary naturalists, especially George Moore and

Arnold Bennett. It will not be easy to make his proposal seem at all compelling – especially now, given the objections one can easily anticipate, directed not only to the idea of the experimental, but also (given the language of passions and morals) to heredity and environment, in terms of which Zola presents his view of literature. Even Zola's supporters acknowledge that critics take his views to be "naive...moralistic and propagandistic".[3] Part of my task, therefore, is to extricate Zola's naturalism from such complaints. It will then be seen that Loach's films exhibit the same type of experimentalism found in Zola's novels. Points of connection are clear: as Linda Nochlin remarks, Zola's fictions deal with characters on the margins of society, and, in his novels, he consistently examines "the inexorable depredations of an unjust social system".[4] This description perfectly fits Loach's work. Naturalism's goal from Zola to Loach has been to reflect upon – and not just reflect – the circumstances of socially disempowered individuals and groups.

What sense can we make, some century and a quarter after Zola proposed it, of an experimental method in literature – and, by extension, of an experimental method in cinema? The parallel Zola establishes is between the experimental method in the natural sciences, as announced by Claude Bernard, and a comparable "method" which he proposes for literature. As Zola puts it, "if the experimental method [in the natural sciences] leads to the knowledge of physical life, it should also lead to the knowledge of the passionate and intellectual life".[5] How can narrative fiction, whether literary or cinematic, emulate the experimental method of the natural sciences? How, for that matter, can the general goals and objectives of science be exemplified by literature? If one believes that science deals with objective description, and literature with imaginary invention, it is not initially obvious how a connecting link can be forged between experimental science and experimental fiction.

For Zola, the answer is that one must reconceive the purpose of the novel. Rather than being exclusively a medium for the novelist's creative imagination or fancy, the novel should become a medium in which an experiment is conducted. The novel is an experiment designed and constructed by the novelist after careful observation of her contemporary society. Like the experimental scientist, the naturalist does not set out merely to record or to document some aspect of the observed world; instead, in an attempt to explain what she has observed, the naturalist recreates in controlled conditions – in the novelist's case, in the novel itself – something she has previously observed in an actual environment. When the experimental method is applied to literature, the novelist's objective cannot be merely to describe what she has observed; her objective is to reveal the mechanisms which explain the circumstances that have been observed.

61

The point of the literary "experiment" for Zola – as for British and other naturalists after him – is to show the influence on individuals of heredity and social environment. Naturalist narratives investigate such factors as an individual's social position (class), economic situation (comparative wealth or poverty), region of birth, education (or lack of it), type of employment (or unemployment), ethnicity and gender. Naturalists see these various factors as determining and constraining what it is possible for any individual, group or collective to accomplish. Therefore, naturalism is concerned not with individual characters as imaginary agents of action, nor with individual characters as atomic, self-willed subjects capable of imposing their desires and wills on those around them. Rather, naturalism is, as Zola said it ought to be, about the ways in which society, culture, economic circumstances and so forth impose limits on characters. One may add to this a focus on the institution of the family as a microcosm for the reproduction of social and moral values (thus treating "heredity" as social, rather than as strictly genetic), as well as a focus on the workplace, on the locations and circumstances of waged or unwaged labour. With these in place, the naturalist novelist or filmmaker need only select a set of characters, put in place a familial and/or working environment, and "watch" how particular conditions within that selected socio-cultural situation produce a predictable set of results for the individuals chosen as the central characters of the study.

Zola's experimentalism is tied to the idea that the novel should represent particular social processes so that an audience can come to an understanding of those processes. If the novel represents actual social processes and conditions by means of fiction, the novelist takes on the role of experimental scientist. The novelist frames the experiment and "reports" it. It is not the job of the novelist to comment directly on the experiment. The novelist does not present, in summary form, the *outcome* of the experiment; rather, the novel is the experiment itself, from initial conditions through to conclusion. Like the scientist, the novelist is both an observer and an experimentalist. The naturalist novelist must be keenly concerned with the actual social processes which she will later represent in her novel (i.e. she must be an observer), and must also be a creator of experiments, one who can reproduce what she has observed in experimental conditions.

What is the role given here to the reader or viewer of such an experimental narrative? The reader or viewer's role is also likened to that of the scientist. Both reader/viewer and writer must be able to report how these processes appear, and yet also be able to describe the mechanisms that continue to reproduce circumstances of that sort. So the reader/viewer will also have to observe. But, in order to understand, she will have to be able to show how what she has observed works. It is not the job of the experimental scientist, on Zola's account, to offer the overview or summary: the experimental scientist does not merely state the conclusion of the experiment. Neither does the experimental novelist; if she did, she would be doing the evaluative work that is properly the job of the reader or viewer. The novelist presents a course of events which *are* the experiment; the reader/viewer observes the course of events, and draws her own conclusion. Of course, as should be expected from the analogy to scientific experimentation, the course of events should draw the reader/viewer to a particular conclusion.

Zola defends a strongly moral position relative to the experimental novelist. The concern of the experimentalist is with the moral structure of society. Perhaps in some quarters this is thought to reduce to the shallowly moralistic, but it need not. Zola describes the experimental novelist as an experimental moralist. This means that the sorts of experiments that fiction presents are experiments in the moral or human sciences, rather than in the physical sciences.[6] The perspective of the experimental novelist is a moral perspective, since the experimental novelist is a critic of her society, and wants to diagnose observed problems with a view to changing the actual conditions which the novel reports. The goal of the experimental moralist is to be able to "master certain phenomena of an intellectual and personal order, in order to be able to direct them".[7] The sort of direction that Zola has in mind here is direction towards social betterment.

But only when the reader *also* has "mastered" the conditions reported in the experiment will change occur. The experiment is a catalyst for change. If, as Zola suggests, following Bernard, an unfolding process is already contained in the initial conditions of the experiment (the characters, with their history and heredity, and the circumstances in which they find themselves), obviously the only way to effect a change is to change the initial conditions. No stage of the experiment can tell us how things would go better for characters if, for example, they had just had the luck, sense or prudence to act differently partly through the course of events that we witness. Rather, for novelist and reader – and for filmmaker and viewer – we must come to see how the whole complex course of events is all but guaranteed by the initial conditions themselves. The course of events which make up the naturalist novel or film follow from initial conditions. Yet – and he is quick to emphasise this – this does not make Zola a fatalist. Rather, he is a determinist. Things do not go from bad to worse because of some pre-existing consciousness or intention that causes them to do so regardless; things go as they do because of the whole causal chain that unfolds from a set of initial conditions, given the intervention of the sorts of unanticipated contingent events which confront these characters in their particular situations. To be a fatalist is to believe that one cannot bring about social change; to be a determinist is to believe that changes in initial conditions will lead to changes in subsequent conditions.

So the role of the reader or viewer is a complex one: she is an observer, but, more importantly, she is also a witness. She is a witness in the sense of being an observer, one who watches, but also in the juridical sense of one who can give testimony as a result of what she has observed. The testimonial role of the witness goes beyond even the juridical, however, for, as witness, the reader/viewer is required to draw conclusions about what she has observed. She must come to an independent understanding of the course of events she witnesses. She cannot rely on the experimental novelist to tell her directly what to think, since it is not the job of the experimental novelist to state the conclusions which can be drawn from the experiment, but only to present the experiment itself. And it is the viewer or reader who carries the conclusions from the experiment back into the practical social world, the observation of which was the starting point for the novelist's experiment. In this sense, she too is an experimental moralist, completing the parallelism drawn between science and art. The reader or viewer is the only one who is assumed to possess any ability to effect change at the social, political or cultural level. Change is not what is seen to occur within the naturalist narrative; the need to effect change is the challenge of the experimental method as it is worked out in literature and the other arts. So we might well follow Zola's lead and think of naturalism as a cultural or sociological experiment conducted by means of fiction.

Loach and British naturalism

Narrative naturalism emerges in British literature as a development of 19th-century European Realism – and it is for this general artistic movement that I reserve the capital "R". Contemporary cinematic and literary naturalisms continue to examine many of the key topics, themes and concerns that mark 19th-century Realism. As Nochlin's important study notes, these include: the rejection of beauty as an ideal in artistic representation; the desire to describe and understand contemporary political, economic and social life; the positive valuation of subjects previously ignored by art because they have been judged to be low or ordinary; and a commitment to representing "the changing yet concrete appearances of the contemporary world".[8] This is as true of contemporary naturalism as it was of Realism a century ago.

Zola's influence on George Moore was direct, as was Moore's on Arnold Bennett. Moore's *Esther Waters* and Bennett's novels set in the Five Towns, not to mention *Riceyman Steps*, are some of the key early texts of British naturalistic literature. The tradition of naturalism continues through authors such as George Orwell (*Keep the Aspidistra Flying*), Kingsley Amis (*Lucky Jim*), John Wain (*Hurry on Down*), John Braine (*Room at the Top; Life at the Top*) and Alan Sillitoe (*Saturday Night and Sunday Morning*). In the 1950s and 1960s, literary naturalism crossed over into the cinema, where many of the current concerns and styles of documentary, docudrama, and British New Wave filmmaking combined in the work of filmmakers including Lindsay Anderson (*O Dreamland* [1953]), Karel Reisz (*Saturday Night and Sunday Morning* [1960]), Tony Richardson (*The Entertainer* [1960]; *A Taste of Honey* [1961]) and, of course, Loach.[9] An interesting and more recent development is the emergence of contemporary variations of naturalist narrative in the works of women authors such as Anita Brookner and Margaret Drabble.

Several observations follow from this quick sketch of writers and filmmakers. In Britain, there is a longer and more sustained naturalist tradition in literature than in cinema. Here I am not quibbling about a shorter objective history, that cinema as such was only invented in 1895. Rather, relative to each art form, naturalism has had a much more consistent run in literature than it has in cinema. The mid-1950s to the 1960s is a perhaps the key period of British cinematic naturalism, since some of the best-known films of the period are naturalistic. Postwar social and economic discontent was expressed at a variety of levels through artistic media; naturalism was an obvious choice to express some of that discontent. Not only do we have the emergence of compelling working-class protagonists in the naturalist narratives of this period; we also find protagonists who are clerks, lecturers and business people. In short, we find the sort of range of character that typified Realist fictions in the last part of the 19th century, where lawyers and shopkeepers, society wives and washerwomen were all possible central characters, and where the focus on social status, class position and the relative opportunities provided – or denied – by such factors as family, gender, education and so forth was part of a general criticism of the contemporary social order.

While many naturalist films had their origins as naturalist novels or dramas, others were adapted from the stage (for example, John Osborne's *The Entertainer*; Shelagh Delaney's *A Taste of Honey*). One consequence of this connection between naturalist drama and naturalist cinema is an emphasis on dialogue in some films that is not replicated in quite the same way in the naturalist films of other countries.[10] Of course, the influence of the British theatrical tradition on British filmmaking generally is one that has inflected cinematic naturalism, in some cases producing films with recognisably dramatic structures and exploiting dialogue in all its variety and richness.

Loach's films – for instance, *The Big Flame* (1969) and *The Rank and File* (1971), but also *Ladybird Ladybird* and *Land and Freedom* (1995) – consistently employ a wide variety of types and situations of dialogue: discussions, meetings among co-workers, speeches, interviews, recollections, confrontations (whether between members of different levels of the unions; between individuals and representatives of social services, the police and doctors; between members of one family or between couples) and many more. Very often, his films begin with one character asking questions of another character, where initially we know little or nothing about either the characters or their circumstances, and thus have no obvious cues about how we should respond to either – for instance, a psychiatrist questioning a young female patient about herself and her family (*Family Life* [1971]); a news conference (*Hidden Agenda* [1990]). Loach also uses voice-over tracks of characters speaking to begin films, so that we listen to as-yet anonymous characters, and from what they say we must gather some sense of how to understand the images we see (*The Rank and File*). A more recent variation, in *Ladybird Ladybird*, is Jorge insistently questioning Maggie about her past.

There is a countervailing tendency of equal importance, which emphasises the visual narration of naturalist films. Many British naturalist filmmakers had backgrounds in documentary filmmaking, and their films reflect this – from the uses of location shooting to the types of camerawork, from the selection of actors and actresses to the styles of editing. Even the then-contemporary state of film technology had its role to play in the emergence of the sorts of naturalist films we find in Britain at this time. The state of the technology allowed for location shooting, and location shooting became a hallmark of British naturalist filmmaking in the 1960s, just as it was a hallmark of British documentary in the late-1930s and 1940s.

I think it is impossible to overemphasise the powerful and double role played by location shooting in naturalist films. There is simultaneously a literal, documentary use of location, and a metaphorical use. Location shooting allowed scenes to be shot where the novels or plays from which they were adapted were set – or even where the novelist or dramatist worked or lived. For instance, the opening shot of *Saturday Night and Sunday Morning* shows Albert Finney at the workbench at which Alan Sillitoe had worked in the bicycle factory at Nottingham, while much of *A Taste of Honey* is shot in Manchester and Salford where Shelagh Delaney grew up. But we cannot dissociate the literal from the metaphorical function served by these actual locations, especially when the locations are the decaying industrial towns of the Midlands – the same towns that so influenced the writing of Bennett. These locations draw our attention to decrepit factories and putrid smokestacks looming across the horizon or crowding up against residential areas, and to streets which suggest by virtue of the relentlessly bleak uniformity of terrace housing that the characters we see are trapped in a dead-end existence. In Loach's films, location shooting is a forceful and consistent reminder of the actual conditions of the English working class; the panoramic opening shots of *The Rank and File* are, like the cityscapes of *Saturday Night and Sunday Morning* and *A Taste of Honey*, preternatural reminders of the filth and decay of the towns of the industrial Midlands. It is a theme on which Loach plays many variations, from shots of polluted, sludge-covered rivers to the contrast between premodern and modern housing tenements in films such as *The Rank and File*, *The Big Flame* and *Cathy Come Home*; to the ominous regularity of housing estates in films such as *Family Life*; to later observations of the decay and collapse of the 1960s housing projects by the time of *Riff-Raff* (1991) and *Ladybird Ladybird*.

Protagonists in the tradition of British naturalism are quite unlike protagonists in non-naturalistic genres. They are unheroic or anti-heroic protagonists caught up in what is obviously a difficult struggle to make a better lot for themselves. Because naturalism has an inherently critical perspective, we see why the central protagonists of naturalistic narratives are not "heroic". Heroes are capable of great actions. The protagonists of naturalist narratives are seldom able to break free from the constraints of their socio-cultural environments. The dreams to which they aspire are ones which they cannot realise – or, if they realise them even in part, it is at a much greater cost than they had previously imagined. Often the struggles of central characters are worked out generationally in relation to figures of familial authority, and/or confrontationally in relation to figures of a more general social authority – social workers, police, teachers, bosses and so forth. Loach's films exemplify these tendencies. *Cathy Come Home*, *Kes* (1969), *Family Life* and *After a Lifetime* (1971) all involve generational and family-oriented struggles. Loach looks at confrontational problems within the workplace, or between individuals and those empowered by the state to supervise and govern their lives, in these four films as well, and also in works such as *The Big Flame*, *The Rank and File*, *Riff-Raff*, *Hidden Agenda* and *Ladybird Ladybird*.

Like other British naturalists, Loach consistently locates his films in contemporary settings which are, potentially at least, known to his audiences. The apparent exception of *Land and Freedom* does have a "present-time" location that is the context for the story from the Spanish Civil War. But, while the locations are recognisable, the actors and actresses are mainly not. He prefers actors and actresses who are for the most part little-known or actually unknown. Some of these are social actors seen in "grab shots" of housing projects or streets – a familiar documentary practice. Yet, even the main roles of his films are often played by virtual unknowns: Crissy Rock is a recent example. When we think about the use of actual, rather than studio, locations for much of Loach's filmic work in conjunction with the use of actors and actresses with whom, in the main, film audiences have little if any previous familiarity, we see another means by which cinematic naturalism walks the fine divide between film as an art form and film as a means of examining one's contemporary society. It is this fine line between the artistic and the social that can land naturalist narratives in the critical soup produced by opponents of "classic" realism.

Naturalism: critical, not classic, realism

On the political left of film studies some two decades ago, and particularly in the pages of *Screen*, cinematic naturalism was viewed as a debased version of realism. But naturalism is not a debased or lesser form of realism; rather, it is a form of critical Realism. Naturalism is not just another version of what Colin MacCabe called "classic realism".[11] "Classic realism" remains an entrenched notion in cinema studies, despite the fact that its centrality is, as George M Wilson has remarked, "almost wholly a function of the grand obscurity with which it is normally formulated combined with a wholesale failure to think through even the limited implications of a minimally adequate account of cinematic point of view".[12] The reduction of naturalism to realism, and realism to something like "classic realism", appears even in the work of those who are sceptical about the general anti-realist position adopted by *Screen*. In an essay which hints that realism might deserve to be rescued from the purgatory to which *Screen* had condemned it, and which approvingly quotes Raymond Williams' "A Lecture on Realism", Colin McArthur discusses "realism/naturalism" as if realism and naturalism were just one phenomenon. Yet, this is just what Williams warned against. In fact, he warned against thinking of *realism* as just one phenomenon. Instead, Williams' recommendation, which McArthur quotes, is that the discussion of realism would do well if it were to move away from "what...it has been in some danger of becoming – a description in terms of a negation of realism as single method".[13] As MacCabe describes it, a "classic realist text" refers to any text "in which there is a hierarchy amongst the discourses which compose the text and this hierarchy is defined in terms of an empirical notion of truth".[14] What seems to be meant by "empirical" has to do with the idea that what we see is what is true. In the context of cinema, what we are shown by a "classic realist" film is "the truth" (whatever that is), and this visual register of representation overrides whatever we might discover about characters or the situations in which they find themselves as expressed through dialogue.

Wilson, Christopher Williams and David Bordwell[15] have already observed that MacCabe's notion of "classic realism" relative to 19th-century novels is so inexact that we should instead try to see what of substance comes to be said about cinema – despite the fact that it is central to MacCabe's claim that 19th-century realist fiction shares the same basic form as "classic realist" films.[16] As Wilson notes, when we sort through the overblown and occasionally simply inadequate terminology which MacCabe employs,[17] the outcome of his position concerning the so-called dominant discourse of classic film – the governing discourse of the hierarchy, the one that is "defined in terms of an empirical notion of truth" – is quite straightforward. What MacCabe is talking about is narrative point of view. For MacCabe, a film is classic realist if the role of the visual narration (construed primarily as what the camera shows us, rather than how the film is edited together) is to "[tell] the truth against which we can measure" what the characters say about themselves, each other and their situations.[18] As Wilson untangles this idea, it means that the visual narration of classic realism has these two main features. Firstly, the visual narration gives us "superior" epistemic access to the characters – it tells us more about the characters, and about "the truth" of the characters, than they could tell us about themselves. Secondly, the visual narration "explains 'how things are' in relation to the characters" so that we can make sense of what the characters are saying and doing. On these two grounds alone, it is easy to see why, for instance, *L'Année dernière à Marienbad* (*Last Year at Marienbad* [1961]) is not classic realist – if anything is.[19] However, these two grounds are sufficient to suggest why naturalist fictions are also not classic realist. For, in naturalist narratives such as those of Loach, what characters say is in fact central to how we must understand them and their situations, and only a global understanding that unites visual narration with dialogue, given due attention to the situations in which characters find themselves, begins to allow us to say "how things are" with characters.

Ultimately, MacCabe charges the classic realist text with being formally unable to deal with contradiction. The point here is that, despite whatever one might think of as palpable contradictions at the level of "content" – i.e. in terms of the represented story – the form of the classic realist text tends towards unification, homogenization, coherence, consistency and closure, and thus does not require that the audience sort out the contradictions raised within the story. In Loach's case, I suppose that typical "contradictions" would include the confrontation between the interests of the rank and file union members and the union leadership (*The Rank and File*; *The Big Flame*); between social services and those it "serves" (*Cathy Come Home*; *Ladybird Ladybird*); and between the many different political factions in Northern Ireland (*Hidden Agenda*). On MacCabe's account of "classic realism", the audience does not have reason to deal with contradictions within the story, because "classic realism" as a form resolves those contradictions for us, binding us back into a peculiar complacency and passivity that MacCabe dubs "dominant specularity".[20] The visual narration of the classic realist film, it is claimed, is neither self-conscious nor self-reflexive; it does not attempt to present a fiction while simultaneously breaking in to remind us that what we are watching is a fiction. On MacCabe's account, classic realism just is not Brechtian – or as Christopher Williams puts it, it is not "Toutvabienist anti-illusionism"[21] – and this means that it is not political in the right sort of way. Insofar as "classic realism" is wedded to characters represented as psychologically coherent individuals, a basically Aristotelian narrative structure which moves from some state of equilibrium through disequilibrium to a re-establishing of equilibrium (and, with that, closure), and to a mostly transparent or non-self-referential narrational perspective, then "classic realism" *cannot* be anything but politically conservative. Yet, it is far from obvious that anything like a resolution of confrontations occurs in Loach's films. Nor is it the case that, in general, satisfactory closure is achieved in his films, where the disequilibrium that has motivated plot action is resolved and a new equilibrium achieved. It is much more likely that Loach's films "conclude" with the problem that has been investigated still quite totally unresolved. Thus – in a way that is not inconsistent with naturalist practices in general – Loach's films are open-ended rather than closed.

Yet, for MacCabe, nearly all narratives are examples of "classic realism", however different from one another the particular examples might be. The exceptions are various sorts of anti-narratives: avant-garde narratives, films from the art cinema, experimental films and the like. One might ask what of explanatory or interpretive relevance follows from the claim that one form, "classic realism", is shared by *The Grapes of Wrath* (1940) and *The Sound of Music* (1965), not to mention *L'Assommoir* (one of the landmark naturalist novels) and *Toad of Toad Hall* – and shared across their literary, dramatic and cinematic versions! MacCabe himself provides us with these examples; he seems untroubled by the absurdity of a net so large that it captures all these examples. What is perhaps most important for any defence of naturalism is MacCabe's misplaced notion that visual narration functions so simplistically and so totalizingly across the extraordinary range of examples that get caught in this net.[22]

Despite this, in the 1970s there was a tremendously keen sense in some theoretical quarters that MacCabe's diagnosis of the political and narrational problems exemplified by the "classic realist text" were as omnipresent as they were odious. The general repudiation of "classic realism" wound up condemning many films that were not, in fact, examples of classic realism, and the result has been a failure to see that naturalist films such as those of Loach demand that viewers interact with them in a way that is not adequately captured by the idea that we are all made subservient to some dominant ideology. It strikes me as part of the general problem of the absurd scope of "classic realism" that it cannot begin to explain why Loach's films should provoke such extreme reactions from critics and the public alike. If they were examples of "classic realism" as MacCabe describes it, they could not possibly provoke the responses they do.

Clearly, any suggestion that films such as *Cathy Come Home*, *The Rank and File*, *Raining Stones* (1993) and *Ladybird Ladybird* are "classic realist" is misplaced. In none of these films is it sufficient for spectators to just "look and see". In a bewilderingly opaque remark that seems to function as a summary of his objections to "classic realism", MacCabe says: "The unquestioned nature of the narrative discourse [i.e. of the visual narration of 'classic realist' films] entails that the only problem that reality poses is to go and look and see what *Things* there *are*".[23] Surely no one who wants to understand *The Big Flame* or the socio-political concerns it addresses thinks that all they need do is "go and look and see what *Things* there *are*". Loach's films, like naturalist narratives generally, are not concerned with "*Things*". They are concerned with *processes* – with social processes, with political processes, with the courses of events that come to define individuals' social, political and economic lives, positions and opportunities. You do not just leave the cinema and go and look at a complex social process as if it were there to be read off like a sentence from a page. Nor, as we find with Loach's films, do we go to the cinema just to "look and see". Naturalism is a much more complex representational form than that, which is why we get greater explanatory purchase on Loach's films by considering them as examples of naturalism – as films which are examples of critical Realism, not "classic realism".

Narration and narrative

For anti-realists of a MacCabean persuasion, the allegedly "transparent" point of view of "classic realism" is what establishes "the truth" of the narrative situation. Yet, as I have suggested, the idea that even generic Hollywood films are quite as narrationally facile as the anti-realists supposed cannot be sustained by examination of typical texts. One does not just "look and see" to understand what is going on in films such as, for example, *The Maltese Falcon* (1941) or *Casablanca* (1943). Nor does one just "look and see" to understand *The Searchers* (1956) or *Rebel Without a Cause* (1955).[24] The objection of the anti-realists concerned the "subject positioning" that is supposedly brought about by classical narration. This "positioning" was assumed to be produced by a third-person narrational perspective which cinema spectators had, perforce, to adopt. They had to adopt it because, as it were, there is no way to see a film except through the images as they are presented onscreen. This is less a truth of cinema spectatorship than a truism. But it does not follow that spectators must accept "the truth" of whatever the camera observes and represents to them. This is a gross oversimplification of visual narration, ignoring the various ways that visual narrations convey information, the different audience-text relationships these narrations make possible, and the importance of the audience's pre-understanding of various story structures and generic conventions.

This is what makes the particular sort of third-person narration which characterises naturalist filmmaking so important. When discussing third-person narration, one commonly just assumes that if it is third-person, it must be omniscient. But this is, of course, not so. In naturalist filmmaking, narration is most often "behaviourist" and not omniscient. Behaviourist narration is a third-person, observational, non-interventionist and descriptive narration, which nevertheless is no guarantee that things are as they appear to be, or that there is a narrator who knows everything about the characters and their circumstances. As Gerald Prince defines it, behaviourist narration is dedicated to the "conveyance of the characters' behavior (words and actions but not thought or feelings), their appearance, and the setting against which they come to the fore".[25] It is "objective" in the sense of restricting itself to describing how characters act; it does not try to get "into" the characters' minds, and it cannot communicate "subjective" states of characters. Like naturalism itself, behaviourism has fallen into theoretical disrepute – especially in psychology and philosophical psychology – and it is not my intention here to try to rehabilitate it. But it is important to be clear about the characteristics of behaviourist narration. What behaviourist narration makes plain is that how things appear to be, how they present themselves to us, is not immediately self-evident. How things appear demands that we interpret them. Behaviour is a semiotic system, a system of complex signs, of which observers must make sense. In addition, as with all semiotic systems, any piece of behaviour may be a sign of more than one thing. A behaviourist narration does not mean that we can just say directly and singularly what characters are up to; behaviourist narrations preserve the semiotic complexity of actions and of circumstances. They are "objective" in the sense that they do not suggest that there is some privileged level of subjective intention, to which they bear direct witness, that can fix the meaning of what characters do or say.

Clearly, most visual narrations cannot communicate the "subjective" states of characters – cannot, as it were, get "into" the characters' minds – and thus are, in this sense of the term, "objective". But this does not make a third-person, objectivist, behaviourist narration "omniscient". Quite the contrary, for, as Prince remarks, a behaviourist narrative tells (or shows) the audience *less* than what some of the characters know, think or feel, because what it can tell or show about the character is restricted to what the character does or says. A behaviourist narration can only "report" or "present" what characters say; it cannot say whether the character is, for example, rationalizing, speaking ironically, saying less than she or he knows, or merely speculating. Not only do behaviourist narrations tell us less than characters know or think, they also (and here Prince is clearly thinking about literary narrations) "abstain from direct commentary and interpretation".[26] Most visual narrations abstain from this sort of commentary or interpretation, and for the same reason that they abstain from giving access to what characters think: visual narrations, because they are non-linguistic, *cannot* directly state or express any sort of comment or interpretation. Any sort of comment or interpretation about a character's situation or motivation must be inferred from the narration; such commentary or interpretation is not literally stated or spoken by the visual narration, and cannot be.[27] This is also quite consistent with Zola's experimentalism. The moral perspective of the experimental novelist, according to Zola, was to be communicated not verbally, but through the selection of subject-matter and the style of presentation. Loach similarly uses subject-matter and style to establish a moral perspective for the examination of his characters; what his films do not do, at the level of visual narration, is *tell* us what to think.

So, in the case of cinema, naturalist narratives are, perforce, mostly behaviourist, and Loach's are no exception. But the "objectivity" of naturalist visual narratives is not to be confused with any range of discourse which establishes "the truth" of "how things are" by itself, independently of the audiences' task of understanding those situations and what they mean. Naturalism is on the side of a cultural or social psychology, one which sees individuals as constructed and constrained through their socio-cultural environments. As such, the function of naturalist fiction generally, and certainly the function of Loach's naturalism in particular is to examine that interaction between socio-cultural environment and various characters.

Anti-realists are quick to object on ideological grounds to the putative "objectivity" of realist and naturalist narrations, mistaking behaviourist objectivity for omniscience of narration. Moreover, of course, it is true that both 19th-century Realism and the naturalisms which follow it are marked by the idea (or ideal) of an objective, dispassionate, neutral mode of representation – an ideal often thought to derive from the materialist, observational methods of the 19th-century natural sciences, but one which is also exemplified in, for example, the rise of journalistic reporting and certain practices of historiography. In the case of Realist and naturalist literature, the idea was that the author ought not to tell her readers what to think about the characters and their situations; rather, by presenting them in their own right, by letting them speak for themselves (as it were), the audience would be able to come to an independent judgment about them. In Loach's films, there is a consistent interchange between individuals and groups or collectives. The aims and actions of individuals *and* of groups or collectives are equally presented for questioning reflection by the audience, and the origins and explanation of actions and events are seen to result, not principally from features of individual psychology, but from the complex ways in which individuals are constituted in and through social, economic and political relations.

Character, action, emplotment

Cinematic naturalism is stylistically quite distinct from, for example, Hollywood genre films or art cinema films, although it is just as conventionalized. Because of the influence of documentary and docudrama in these films, the audience might treat Loach's films less as artworks, and more as documentary records of social conditions. This appropriation of the conventions of documentary and docudrama is part of the aesthetics of cinematic naturalism. Naturalism, as practised by Loach, maintains what we might refer to as the "authority" of documentary: the idea that a film camera recording images of a housing project is, whatever else is going on, presenting images shot in that housing project. But such "authenticity" must be thought about in terms of the plot structures and characterisation which naturalist narratives employ, for, without these, the point of the documentary stylistics would be lost. One could just as easily use these same documentary techniques to show the beauties of, for example, the interiors of British castles, or the dramatic effects of light and shadow on a moors landscape; it is a tendency of naturalism to use these techniques to examine, not beauty, but decay, squalor, the ugliness of the urban environment and so forth.

But naturalism is not just an attitude or an aesthetic about what images to present. Narrative naturalism has a recognisable dramatic form. The two most important conventions of naturalism concern characterisation and plot structure. Central characters, as I have mentioned, are marginalised, comparatively powerless figures. They are what McKnight calls "emblematic"[28] figures representative of their class, race, gender, and economic and social positions. Plot structures are inevitably and inexorably deterministic. From the works of Zola to those of Moore and Bennett, and to those of Loach, the inevitable plot pattern is from bad to worse.[29] Even in situations where characters are materially better off by the end of the story than they were at the beginning – which never happens in Loach's films – there is always a moral, emotional and experiential cost that goes with moving up the social ladder. In any event, even in the new situation, characters are still marked by the circumstances and by the class background which they have wanted to leave behind (witness Joe Lampton in *Room at the Top* [1958]). Here I want to recall Zola's insistence that he is a determinist, not a fatalist. The whole point of the literary or cinematic experiment is that it should carry through, inevitably, the consequences that are inbuilt in the initial conditions of the narrative situation. Part of the emotional force of these narratives is the result of just this sort of inexorable narrative structuring. Whatever we might hope for naturalist characters, and whatever they might hope for themselves, the audience realises that the aesthetic conventions of naturalism are such that these hopes will likely go unrealised, or only be realised at a cost to the characters involved.

By the conventions of naturalism, an audience will in all probability be aligned with characters who are, in the Realist sense, "low", who are anything but heroic, and who might very well be difficult to like. It should be obvious that an audience can relate in a variety of ways to characters and their situations. Not all film protagonists are heroic or idealised figures whom we wish to emulate. Alignment can shift between characters, or move from one character to another, as a narrative unfolds. We can be aligned with characters for reasons of emotional response – pity, admiration, sympathy and so forth. In *Cathy Come Home*, we can be aligned with Cathy and Reg whether or not we are members of their class, whether or not we have ever had similar experiences – because we feel sympathetically towards them. In *Family Life*, we can be forcefully aligned with Janice, although she scarcely initiates any plot action – she is not an agent but rather a patient, literally as well as narratologically. In *Ladybird Ladybird*, we can be aligned with Maggie whether or not we are sympathetic to her. Indeed, *Ladybird Ladybird* aligns us with Maggie even if we actively dislike her. In this sort of case, which is by no means a common one, the alignment may be based on a strong negative emotional response, rather than a positive one.[30] "Alignment" can be a misleading term if it is thought to suggest convergence of identification between viewer and character. Often, the alignment between characters and audience members depends upon what makes the characters different from, rather than similar to, us.

Whether we judge naturalist characters to be likeable, and whether we feel sympathetically towards them, the plots of these films direct our attention to the situations in which they find themselves –

situations which are not obviously of their own making. Certainly, there is a set of character traits that we often find: stubbornness, imprudence, rebelliousness, disrespect for conventional figures of social authority, and so forth. Yet, if one were so inclined, one could make comparable observations about figures as various as Hamlet, Anna Karenina and Dracula. If all protagonists were duly prudent and rational, fiction would be significantly impoverished. Nevertheless, because of factors such as general expectations about fictions derived from generic narratives, not to mention a propensity to deal with moral issues raised by fictions as exclusively or primarily in the domain of individual agency and responsibility, viewers or readers might be inclined to conclude that what happens to naturalist protagonists is their own fault.

In naturalist fictions, while characters might act rashly or imprudently, and while they often act with single-minded stubbornness (especially in Loach's films: consider the number of characters who try to persuade Bob in *Raining Stones* that he does not have to *buy* his daughter a Communion dress, especially given that he cannot afford to do so), they nevertheless act in ways that make sense, given the social or cultural contexts in which they are located. This embedding of characters in contexts forces us to recognise the pressures which lead to – or, in some cases, prevent – certain actions or decisions. In *Family Life*, it is obvious that Janice's elder sister should do what she says – namely not leave her parents' home without taking Janice with her. Yet, she does not. This is not through anything so simple as lack of willpower. She is simply unable to get the agreement of either her parents or her sister. That Janice stays is, all things considered, a tragedy. But it is not simply Janice's fault, nor that of her sister.

Naturalist characters are unlike the central characters of "classic realist" films, who are able to initiate and complete actions which result in dramatic change. Naturalist characters cannot act successfully to bring about profound changes – least of all profound changes for the better in their own circumstances, or in the circumstances of those around them. In naturalist narratives, the range of possible actions for any character is profoundly circumscribed. So too is the power of the characters to act. As members of the audience, we observe and possibly also feel the frustrations such characters suffer, the aggravations they must tolerate, and the humiliations to which they are subjected. We watch while things go wrong, despite the best efforts of characters to try to make things go right.

Naturalist films do not select characters such as these because we should like or admire them, identify with them, or want to emulate their actions. Rather, the naturalist perspective asks us to recognise that, given the social and cultural contexts in which these characters act, things could scarcely have been otherwise. Naturalist films do not fix characters' problems or resolve their conflicts. Nor do they reconcile the vague and romantic aspirations of these characters with the hard facts about their own situations which make these aspirations unrealisable. On the contrary, naturalist films offer a perspective from which to understand the social mechanisms that perpetuate just these very sorts of irreconcilable conflicts between what characters desire and what they can achieve. At the level of plot action, we do not find anything like a slow progression towards the successful accomplishment of a goal. Rather than directing our attention towards some future resolution to the current set of problems, these episodic yet repetitive structures underscore the general determinism of naturalistic narratives, and arguably give an added poignancy to the inability of characters to bring about positive changes in their circumstances. In addition, it is also characteristic of naturalist films that they should be open-ended; since there are no "solutions" to the situations in which naturalist characters find themselves, there is no "resolution" at the level of plot action.

Perhaps the inexorable move from bad to worse is the most striking aspect of naturalist narratives. It certainly has an important impact on audiences. While viewing a naturalist film, an audience does not just experience frustration empathetically through a projective engagement with the character – an engagement which might nevertheless allow them to remain optimistic that, in the end, things will turn out right after all. Rather, an audience experiences frustration directly as a consequence of the dramatic structure of naturalist films. Not only are Loach's characters powerless to change their own circumstances, but also the audience watches knowing that there is no way to intervene in the downward spiral. We do not know this inferentially, by watching the characters and drawing reasonable conclusions about how things might be going for them; we know it somatically and emotionally because of the aesthetic choices involved in structuring these stories.

Conclusion

To approach films such as *Cathy Come Home*, *The Big Flame*, *Family Life*, *Ladybird Ladybird* and even the more apparently "generic" films such as *Hidden Agenda* as naturalistic allows us to see what is most consistently striking about Loach as a filmmaker. It allows us to recognise the rawness as well as the intensity of his films, their blackness, the determinism of their story-lines – including the story-line of *Raining Stones*, which owes its "happy" ending to the conventions of the mode of comedy as described by, for example, Northrop Frye, but in which nothing of significance has changed to improve the living conditions or job opportunities of the characters. Thinking about Loach as a naturalist allows us to see the reciprocal effect of characters and their social situations, whether we are talking about the dockworkers of *The Big Flame*, the builders on the construction site in *Riff-Raff*, or the women and children in temporary shelters in *Cathy Come Home* or *Ladybird Ladybird*. Like the other premier British naturalists of the postwar period, Loach's films examine subjects that are beautiful neither to look at, nor to think about. His subjects are frequently "low" or "ordinary" (meant non-pejoratively) – members of the working class and the underclass, the unemployed and the underemployed, people from housing projects, or dependent upon the dole or the social services. In addition, a primary objective of these films is not so much to tell us that there has to be a social revolution to begin to effect the sorts of structural changes needed to redress these actual social conditions. Rather, as we might expect from a naturalist, the point of these narratives is not to present and resolve a problem, but to make plain the nature of the problem and its consequences in terms of characters' lives. In naturalist narratives and in Loach's work, it is not the case that disequilibrium is succeeded by equilibrium. Things do not come right in the end. The point of these narratives is not to pretend that artistic representations fix – or show us how to fix – actual social or political problems. Rather, in the spirit of naturalistic experimentation, their point is to present the complexities of a given situation, knowing full well that a satisfactory resolution may be as impossible in life as in naturalistic art, but that the only place where the attempt to improve matters makes any sense is not in art, but in life.[31]

Notes

[1]   For this essay, when I speak of Loach's films, it is meant as an inclusive shorthand recognising the contributors and collaborators with whom Loach has worked, including Tony Garnett, Jim Allen and Chris Menges, and is also meant to embrace both his work for television and his work for the cinema.

[2]   Emile Zola, "The Experimental Novel", in Maxwell Geismar (ed), *The Naturalist Novel* (Montreal: Harvest House, 1964): 11.

[3]   Maxwell Geismar, "Introduction", in ibid: ix.

[4]   Linda Nochlin, *Realism* (London: Penguin Books, 1971): 49.

[5]   Zola: 1.

[6]   Ibid: 14.

[7]   Ibid.

[8]   Nochlin. This paragraph refers to her chapter 1; the quotation is from 45-46.

[9]   John Hill, *Sex, Class and Realism: British Cinema 1956-1963* (London: British Film Institute, 1986).

[10]   Canadian naturalist filmmaking is a case in point: one simply does not find the kind and quality of dialogue in Canadian films such as *Nobody Waved Goodbye* or even *Le Chat dans le sac* (*The Cat in the Bag*); the influence of British drama and British dramatic screenwriting cuts across some of the 1950s and 1960s naturalist films. On the other hand, the emergence of naturalist literature which preserves regional accent and dialect (as found in the work of, for example, Sillitoe) is carried over into the cinema.

[11]   Colin MacCabe, "Realism and the Cinema: Notes on some Brechtian theses", *Screen* 15: 2 (summer 1974): 7-27.

[12]   George M Wilson, *Narration in Light: Studies in Cinematic Point of View* (Baltimore; London: The Johns Hopkins University Press, 1986): 192.

[13]   Colin McArthur, *Television and History* (London: British Film Institute, 1978): 50. Sections of this book have been excerpted as "Historical Drama" and published in Tony Bennett, Susan Boyd-Bowman, Colin Mercer and Janet Woollacott (eds), *Popular Television and Film* (London: British Film Institute, in association with The Open University, 1981): 288-301.

[14]   MacCabe: 8.

[15]   Wilson; David Bordwell, *Narration in the Fiction Film* (London: Methuen, 1985); Christopher Williams, "After the classic, the classical and ideology: the differences of realism", *Screen* 35: 3 (autumn 1994): 275-292.

[16]   Wilson: 193.

[17]   To note only one such example, the appropriation by MacCabe of the terms "object language" and "metalanguage" strains beyond use the technical senses of those terms as established in philosophy of language. Granted that these terms had become fashionable in structuralist writing, notably in the work of Roland Barthes, it is just mistaken to think that quoted speech is an "object language" and the rest of the narration which "surrounds" those quotes is a "metalanguage". Christopher Williams' criticism of MacCabe's notion of "metalanguage" remains caught in the misapplication of the term (see in particular: 277). This is peculiar, given that, years earlier, Bordwell had already noted that MacCabe's inapt usage derives less from Barthes than from Tarski (18).

[18]   MacCabe: 10.

[19]   From these two main features, three more follow to which Wilson draws our attention. The third is that spectators can discover "how things are" just by looking, or, if just looking is not quite sufficient, by bringing "commonsense forms of inference" to bear on what the film presents to us. The fourth is that classic realism denies its status as discourse. Finally, the

fifth is that the "image track is presented as overall transparent". See Wilson: 193-194.

[20]   MacCabe: 12.

[21]   Williams: 289.

[22]   Not only are naturalist films not examples of "classic realist" texts; many realist films are not either. Worse yet for MacCabe, many generic Hollywood films are not "classic realist". For that matter, MacCabe's key example of *Klute* is not classic realist: it is not the case that all we have to do is look and see how things are, and it is not the case that the film's closure is unambiguous. See also Richard Maltby and Ian Craven, *Hollywood Cinema: An Introduction* (Oxford: Blackwell, 1995): 329-330 (and relevant footnotes); Bordwell: 18-20.

[23]   MacCabe: 12. Emphases in original.

[24]   Wilson discusses both these latter films.

[25]   See Gerald Prince, *A Dictionary of Narratology* (Lincoln: University of Nebraska Press, 1987): 10.

[26]   Ibid.

[27]   Literary naturalism, on the other hand, has the opportunity to use a wider range of narrations, and does not necessarily abstain from direct commentary or interpretation. In *L'Assommoir*, for instance, Zola himself offers commentary and interpretation about his characters and the situations in which they find themselves – and does so, in some instances, as a direct address to the reader, for example: "You might say that her [Gervaise's] first bouts of laziness dated from this moment, in the asphyxiating fumes of these old clothes spreading their poisonous miasma around her". Other naturalist narratives employ a first-person narrator who is also the central protagonist of the story – for example, John Braine's *Room at the Top* and *Life at the Top* – and thus give us access to the narrating character's thoughts and feelings. Some naturalist narratives use third-person narration which tells us what at least some of the characters think, and so are not merely behaviourist, yet nevertheless are focalised on the central characters. This thus leaves us in a situation where we know a great deal about those characters' situations and actions, as well as their reasons for acting, without letting us know what other central characters think (*Saturday Night and Sunday Morning* is one example).

[28]   See George McKnight, "Introduction" in this volume: 1.

[29]   In his 1954 "Introduction" to *Anna of the Five Towns* in the Penguin series, Frank Swinnerton uses just this phrase to describe the plot of *A Mummer's Wife*, a novel by Moore that profoundly influenced Bennett: "It told the painful story of a young woman who ran away with an inferior actor and went from bad to worse until she died" (9).

[30]   In an observation about women protagonists that has obvious relevance to any consideration of Maggie, Marilyn French has written: "If the definition

of a 'good' woman no longer involves chastity, heroines are still required to be sweet, vulnerable, *likeable*. Readers do not expect sweetness or honesty of male protagonists: they do not even have to be likeable: consider the heroes of *Under the Volcano*, *Notes from Underground* and *Look Back in Anger*. Authoritative, angry, rebellious heroines make most readers impatient; they tend to blame the character for not finding a way to be happy." See "Is There a Feminist Aesthetic?", in Hilde Hein and Carolyn Korsmeyer (eds), *Aesthetics in Feminist Perspective* (Bloomington and Indianapolis: Indiana University Press, 1993): 71. Emphasis in original.

[31] I wish to thank George McKnight and Julian Petley for their generous comments on this paper, and the Social Sciences and Humanities Research Council of Canada for their ongoing support of my research. I am also indebted to the late Tom Coulsen, Professor of English Literature at Carleton University, who introduced me to British naturalism.

Ken Loach's domestic morality tales

George McKnight

Ken Loach is a teller of morality tales, albeit unconventional ones. This essay focuses on his domestic morality tales: *Cathy Come Home* (1966), *Family Life* (1971), *Raining Stones* (1993) and *Ladybird Ladybird* (1994). What makes these unconventional as morality tales is the consistent way in which Loach ties the personal and domestic circumstances of his central characters into national issues and questions of public policy such as housing, unemployment, and the role and function of institutions in daily life. As we might expect from a domestic morality tale, these films examine interpersonal and familial relationships and everyday social and community relations. What we might not expect is the way in which Loach contextualises these typically domestic or community scenarios in terms of the impact of social and economic policies and institutional practices on the emotional and psychological life of his central characters. Therefore, while his central characters are sufficiently ordinary individuals, the dramatic conflicts of these films arise at the point where social and economic circumstances make it impossible to realise apparently ordinary desires – such as the desire for a place to live; for understanding and affection from one's parents; for a job; for a Communion dress.

To say that Loach is a teller of morality tales is not to say that these films offer a moral position that is clear and unambiguous. In conventional moral tales, we might expect to see characters facing the consequences of individual moral failure. Or we might expect to see characters whose actions demonstrate some moral ideal, or who struggle successfully against adversity, or who, through prudence or fortitude, manage successfully to resolve a crisis. Loach's morality tales do not operate in this way. They do not offer morally instructive lessons or cautionary advice, nor do the actions of the films' central characters serve as models for the audience. Loach's tales do not provide morally unambiguous resolutions to the problems faced by his characters. Nor do they provide morally unambiguous justifications for the actions of these characters. This is enough to make his films untypical as morality tales. What is even more untypical is that there is often no morally unambiguous condemnation of the actions of his characters. What Loach confronts us with is something of a paradox:

morality tales without any obvious moral that tidily sums up the lesson of the tale and allots praise or blame to the various characters and their actions. The moral lessons of these tales are ones which we must draw ourselves. Loach challenges us to draw these moral lessons – to interpret his morality tales, not in terms of the praise or blame of individuals, but in terms of a critique of social and institutional policies, and their impact on individuals' lives.

What makes Loach's domestic morality tales dramatically compelling is not just the way they raise contentious social and political issues, nor just the way they detail and document the circumstances in which his central characters find themselves, nor the way they dramatise the conflicts which these conditions foster. What makes these films dramatically compelling are the central characters themselves. The emotional impact of these films is rooted as much in the performance of his lead actors or actresses as it is in the narrative structure of the films. But it would miss the mark to say that the audience identifies with, or is aligned with, the central characters in these films. Not all of Loach's central characters are sympathetic; indeed, some are extremely unsympathetic – for instance, Janice's parents in *Family Life*. Nor are his central characters necessarily strong figures, as we see with Janice herself. Moreover, even if we happen to find some of his central characters sympathetic – indeed, even if we empathise with them, as we might do, for instance, in the case of Cathy and Reg in *Cathy Come Home*, or in the case of Bob in *Raining Stones* – alignment and identification with these characters are often at best problematic, and the problems posed are often different from film to film.

By and large, the central characters in Loach's domestic morality tales are not figures with whom we identify in an individual and personal way as figures we admire, or would wish to emulate, or would want to be. Not only would we not want to be in the situations in which many of his characters find themselves, but also we would not want to be like many of his characters. For many members of the audience, the forcefulness of Loach's work is a curious consequence of how different we are from these characters, and how different our circumstances are from theirs. Therefore, "identification" with these characters, either as moral agents or as psychologically unified individuals, cannot by itself explain what makes these films emotionally compelling.

What, therefore, aligns us with Loach's central characters, if it is not necessarily either sympathy or empathy? To answer this, we have to think about the depiction of character in these morality tales. We have to differentiate between character in the sense of represented individuals, and the notion of character itself. In Loach's films, character tends to be Aristotelian, which is to say that it is basically a constant set of qualities that we find emerging over the course of narrative action. In most cases, the values and ideals fundamental to the identity of Loach's central characters are not simply individual, but should be recognised as shared and indeed profoundly *social*. What we identify as the motivations of a character are, quite often, familiar social desires and expectations. Character in this Aristotelian sense personalises these desires or expectations, and individuates social and economic conditions. What are represented as individual or family problems are, in fact, society's problems. Characters such as Cathy or Bob individuate systemic conditions or, as in the case of Janice and Maggie, individuate problems that originate in or are compounded by social or institutional practices. The personal or domestic circumstances of these central figures draw attention to questions of social agency, and, in particular, to the ways in which the state regulates the lives of marginalised individuals and families.

Yet, while I have been emphasising the shared and often normative nature of the social goals and aspirations of Loach's central characters, it is nevertheless true that, within each film, a range of different characters will represent a variety of perspectives on particular situations. Different central and secondary characters will have quite distinct senses of just what is the normatively correct thing to do in particular circumstances, and dramatic action is often developed around confrontations and disagreements between members of the family and those outside the family, particularly those representing the state or social institutions. Indeed, we find just such divergence of perspective within the family itself. Loach's films do not so much align us with characters as offer different positions that could be seen to oppose one another, or that formally shift the point of view from which we consider the action in relation to different forms of address.

In *Cathy Come Home*, the normative figures tend to be associated with the state: whether magistrates or those in charge of the shelters, both administrators and nurses. But we also find a group of ratepayers who want the caravans moved without concern for the circumstances of those living in these conditions, just because the presence of the caravans could negatively affect the value of their own properties, and offends their sense of community. At the same time, the film employs the anonymous, official-sounding voice-over to cite figures documenting the numbers on waiting lists for council houses and the number of houses built in Britain since the war. This voice is not the conventional third-person omniscient voice of reassurance – the kind of voice that is often otherwise employed to reinforce social norms – but a voice that points to the failure of current housing policies and calls for a new policy. Comparably, in *Family Life*, Janice's parents are the normative voices within a patriarchal family structure, while the majority on the hospital board uphold the norms of conventional psychiatric treatment when they refuse to renew Dr Donaldson's appointment. In *Raining Stones*, the priest takes on something of this normative function, although his position is anomalous. On the one hand, he consistently counsels Bob not to buy the Communion dress which Bob plainly cannot afford. Later, however, motivated by his disdain for the exploitative power of moneylenders and loan sharks, he protects Bob after the death of Tansey.

What becomes clear in viewing these domestic morality tales is that even a quite basic alignment between character and audience is not necessarily synonymous with either an uncritical sympathy or a moral approbation for the characters with whom we are aligned. Indeed, the actions of the central characters in Loach's domestic morality tales invariably raise moral questions for the viewer. In addition, the domestic morality tales are developed by dramatising various (often dehumanising) crises that follow immediately from the social and economic circumstances of the central character(s). One consequence of this narrative structure is that a sympathetic or empathetic alignment might emerge not initially because of the characters, but because of our progressively greater awareness of the conditions in which they find themselves, or our growing appreciation of their inability to control the circumstances that often force them to act as they do. Our alignment may not initially be with them, but with their struggles in given circumstances, although we do not always agree with their actions. Therefore, whether or not we sympathise or empathise with Cathy or Reg, or with Janice or Bob or Maggie, we recognise the social or familial goals they strive for, and feel the frustrations they experience in their often unsuccessful attempts to realise them. Moreover, in fact, we may also feel their anger, their sense of outrage, or their helplessness in relation to their given circumstances.

Therefore, whether or not we find ourselves drawn to the central characters of these films, we quickly come to face the consequences for them of their particular situations. What we find in Loach's films generally is certainly present in the domestic morality tales: the juxtaposing of a range of conflicting responses, different ideas about how characters ought to act, and even various ways of describing the nature of the problems and quite different diagnoses of what ought to be done, and by whom, to sort out the immediate problems or crises. We find this strategy used in *The Rank and File* (1971) and *The Big Flame* (1969) in discussions about how the union members should proceed, and again in *Land and Freedom*'s (1995) extended debate about whether or not to collectivize.

Viewers must deal with their engagement with these characters in an ongoing way in the course of the film. Indeed, it is often an open question, at least initially, with which of the characters in any of Loach's films we will come to align ourselves. It is equally a question just what perspective we should adopt with regard to the characters and the problems at hand, since, in the early stages of these films, it is far from obvious just how any given "problem" should be understood, and, in turn, which character or set of characters should be relied upon to establish either the nature of the problem or the appropriate response(s) to it. These things are often far from obvious at the outset because of the range of voices which articulate different perspectives on the given situation, thus producing a range of opinions about where the problem lies, or who the problem is, or what is to be done about it. Sorting through this multiplicity of voices is complicated because what each speaker has to say cannot be divorced from the social or institutional position from which the individual speaks, and this is just as much a factor for those whose primary role is to represent the public domain – for example, the Church or the social services – as it is for those whose primary role is to represent the private domain. Whether we are considering views articulated by a police officer or a psychiatrist, or those articulated by a father or a daughter, what is said must be understood in terms of the comparative authority and power (or lack of same) enjoyed by the speaker.

Equally important, although adding to the general complexity of Loach's film narratives, is the visual level of narration of these films, considered in terms not only of the camera's perspective on characters and action, but also of the complex cutting that Loach often uses, itself an extension of the documentary stylistics which we see most plainly, although not exclusively, in such films as *Cathy Come Home* and *Family Life*. The visual narration often functions contrapuntally to what we hear, meaning that there is always a question of just which register – the spoken or the visual – should be given priority in our attempts to understand what is going on in each film. What seems fair to conclude is that very often neither register should be given priority over the other; we must assess each in terms of the other. Therefore, in the opening sequence of *Family Life*, for example, we must negotiate between the spoken and visual perspectives on action offered by the psychiatrist, Janice, the police and Janice's parents, as we begin to sort through just where the problem lies. Viewers must also take into account moral positions represented by various secondary characters who are unsympathetic or not entirely sympathetic to the central character. Loach occasionally positions viewers so that we share the perspective of just such a secondary character, although we may not share the moral position these characters speak. In *Cathy Come Home*, we are positioned both behind Cathy and behind those deciding her fate at the temporary shelters when she becomes angry and loses her temper. In *Family Life*, we are often aligned visually with Janice's parents. In *Ladybird Ladybird*, we are positioned *behind* the figures from social services when Maggie refuses to answer the door. Factors such as these momentarily establish a critical distance between the viewer and the central character(s), so that we do not simply watch the action, but have a perspective on the action. Just what our individual emotional or moral response(s) may be as a consequence of such shifts in perspective could very well differ. We could be drawn more sympathetically to either Cathy or Janice or Maggie as a consequence of how they are treated, or we might come to share the moral position of those seeking to "help" these figures. In either case, how we respond as viewers of these tales always involves some recognition of the context of a character's actions, and of the social and institutional forces that contribute to such actions.

Whatever our responses, or whatever form our engagement with the central characters takes, Loach's domestic morality tales leave us to resolve questions concerning the relationship between the effects of social and economic circumstances on the actions of these characters and the moral nature of their actions. We are left to consider questions of public policy, and questions concerning the social responsibility of institutions and the actions of both those who administer policies and those representing the different forms of authority with which the central characters must contend. Such questions are developed in the course of these narratives around the identity of the central characters – Cathy, Janice, Bob and Maggie – and the particular structure of their experience.

Accidents of character

Loach's domestic morality tales share a structural pattern that is broadly similar, despite obvious differences in the ostensible concerns of these films and in the apparently different stories they tell. The narrative structures of Loach's films emphasise the fundamental role of contingent, accidental or unintended events in relation to the social and economic conditions which his central characters face, and the consequences such events have on their lives. I term this section "Accidents of character" because the ideals and values that are fundamental to the identity of the central characters are thrown into question in the course of actions that follow on from a conjunction of contingent and coincident events in these narratives. Such events and their consequences are played out in relation to the dreams and aspirations of these characters, their domestic circumstances, and their marital and family life.

The opening scenes that establish the central character(s) of

Loach's domestic morality tales are invariably marked by instability. Any stability is only momentary. *Cathy Come Home* opens with the credits above a shot of Cathy, who has left home and family, alone on the road – an opening that prefigures the film's final shot of Cathy, who is again homeless, separated from family and alone on the road. The opening credits of *Family Life* appear above shots of the façades of houses suggesting the sameness, regularity and uniformity of the housing estate. Early in the initial post-credit sequence, Janice is asked about her family. The question as to whether her mother gets upset because she has had so many jobs becomes a sound bridge to a shot of Janice at work, looking desolate, followed by Janice speaking over discontinuous shots of herself and customers, while she relates how she often did not return from work after lunch and how her mother thinks she is irresponsible. There is an abrupt cut to a crowded Underground platform where Janice sits disconsolate until she is approached and led away by a platform guard, questioned by police, and eventually driven home by the police to her parents who question her about her behaviour. Her father's attitude is aggressive to the point of being abusive. In the opening sequence, Janice is always located in relation to figures identified with authority or institutions – doctors, police, and so on. The question about her mother produces a striking visual discontinuity between shots (characterised by Loach's use of docudramatic spatial and temporal dislocations). This discontinuity might be seen as a trope for the fragmentation of Janice's state of mind. The opening sequence makes it quite clear that we cannot understand Janice's mental and emotional state separately from the social and institutional conditions, particularly those of the family, within which she has been raised.

In *Raining Stones*, the black comedy of the opening scenes where Bob and Tommy steal a sheep, attempt to butcher it, find a butcher who will do the job, and try to sell the mutton in a pub (during which time Bob's van is stolen) only underscores the desperation of men who turn to petty crime – in the face of chronic unemployment – in order to support their families. During the opening scenes of *Ladybird Ladybird*, when Maggie meets Jorge in a pub on karaoke night, he tells her that she "looked sad" while she sang. The opening scenes include a reference to the loss of her "four babies"; a flashback of herself as a child playing in a sunlit park; shots of spousal violence, as her initial idyllic recollection turns abruptly into a scene in which her father beats her mother; and reference to the intervention of social services in Maggie's life. These scenes establish the narrative role of flashbacks which isolate key incidents in her past that will have consequences for her future family, scenes that play a significant role in the structure of the film's early sequences, especially in relation to the idea of contingency.

A unique feature of Loach's domestic morality tales – not to mention several of his other films – is how they are structured initially around a conjunction of accidental or otherwise contingent events and events with which these accidental events are coincident. The kinds of contingent events I am thinking about are those over which characters have little or no control. These would include Reg's injury when the brakes on the van fail in *Cathy Come Home*; Janice being locked out of the house by her mother in *Family Life*; the theft of Bob's van in *Raining Stones*; and the fire at the shelter in *Ladybird Ladybird*. Events become coincident with contingent events through some form of juxtapositioning in the organisation of the narrative. Cathy's pregnancy is coincident with Reg's accident; Janice's pregnancy and abortion become coincident in the narrative with Janice being locked out by her mother following the scene where she visits her boyfriend, Tim, and tells him that her mother "killed my baby"; preparations for Coleen's first Communion are coincident with the theft of Bob's van; and, through the use of flashback sequences in *Ladybird Ladybird*, the beginnings of Maggie's relationship with Jorge is made coincident in the narrative with the fire at the shelter.

In these films, the coincident events are significant personal or domestic events that may or may not have been foreseen. Contingent events represent a setback or a loss for the central character(s), whereas the events that are coincident in the narrative – Cathy's pregnancy; Janice's pregnancy; preparing for Coleen's first Communion; and Maggie's initial meeting with Jorge – would appear to be a cause for celebration. Indeed, this particular conjunction of contingent events and events that become coincident with them makes evident some desire, need, value or goal that is normative and entirely within the conventional aspirations of society: Cathy's initial enquiry about buying a house and establishing a home for her family; Janice's emotional and psychological needs that are not met within her own family; Bob's decision to buy a new dress for Coleen's first Communion; and Maggie's desire to re-establish a home and family. Whatever the desire, need, value or goal, it is fundamental to the identity of that character. The domestic morality tales make it quite clear that the desires that motivate Cathy, Janice, Bob and Maggie are thoroughly and conventionally social.

In *Cathy Come Home*, the relationship between Cathy and Reg is developed initially in relation to cultural ideals and social goals associated with romance, courtship, and the belief in marriage as the basis of family life. In particular, Cathy is characterised by her desire to establish a secure home and to raise a family. Her words and actions demonstrate a belief in the sanctity of the life of the child, and her determination to keep both her marriage and her family together in the face of their ongoing homelessness. There is an almost total absence of personal self-interest in Cathy. Her actions are invariably on behalf of her family, especially the children. She is unselfish and without self-pity; Reg is either working or looking for work, and disappears only after the regulations at the reception centre separate him from the family and further aggravate their circumstances. Even in *Ladybird Ladybird*, where there is considerable moral ambiguity surrounding Maggie's behaviour, her actions are nevertheless motivated by an overriding determination to keep her children with her in the face of spousal violence, the fire at the shelter, and the actions of social services.

If one can speak of a social goal or ideal in *Family Life*, it is the ideal of family as the fundamental social(izing) unit providing emotional and psychological support, guidance and affection in the child's life. Such an ideal might be taken to be fundamental in the formation of the child's social identity. In this context, Janice's actions can be understood in relation to the absence of such support and affection in her family life – regardless of her parents' protestations of concern. Her actions are often an implicit call for help and her desire for affection and physical intimacy a need for acceptance and love – whether it is the affection and approval she seeks from her parents, or the affection she gives to others.

In *Raining Stones*, Bob's determination to buy Coleen a new Communion dress stands as a symbol or sign that fixes part of his identity. His actions are bound into notions of masculinity and the traditional role of the male in working-class family life. Part of that identity is the ritual playing out of his social role as father, part the fulfilling of the conventionalized role of the male as the family provider. This would include the idea of doing things properly, doing things the way they should be done. Insisting on a new Communion dress when he cannot afford it can be tied into ideas such as that the new dress is the sign of his daughter's purity; demonstrating his economic self-sufficiency; reaffirming his own individual self-worth as a male; retaining the traditional male position as decision-maker when larger sums of money are involved; and maintaining social appearances. Having been driven by his determination to do the proper thing on behalf of his daughter, he has rejected the sound advice of everyone: his wife Anne, his priest, and even the assistant from the shop where he orders the new Communion outfit. What he has failed to examine are the motives and values that govern his actions. Driven by motives that are obviously secular and profoundly determined by class, Bob does not recognise that insisting on a new Communion dress in a secular society winds up reducing Communion to being about what you wear, not about the meaning of the ritual (which he has touchingly and ineptly explained to Coleen).

The conjunction of contingent and coincident events, and the actions of the central character(s) immediately following such events, marks a turning-point in Loach's narratives. From this point through to some form of narrative closure, plot action is organised as a series of escalating personal and domestic crises. The central character's will and determination to achieve what are taken to be fundamental social goals – despite circumstances which constrain or limit their actions – invariably result in a series of confrontations. Such confrontations are often within the family, although more often than not in the domestic morality tales they involve either figures identified with institutionalized authority, or figures, such as Tansey in *Raining Stones*, whose visible presence in the everyday life of the community is one of the ongoing consequences of chronic unemployment. These are confrontations that are not simply personal or individual, but invariably refer us to some broader set of social issues.

When Cathy and Reg marry, they initially take a comfortable flat, with the suggestion that they have nowhere to go but up the economic ladder. Yet, following Cathy's pregnancy and Reg's accident and the loss of his job, the narrative, in fact, takes them on a largely unbroken pattern of descent – economically and socially – with each situation worse than the previous one. The narrative moves away from scenes that exemplify the idealisation of romantic love to scenes that dramatise any number of quite unidealised social hardships: the economic problems which the couple face trying to purchase or rent a house; the social attitudes they face when looking for accommodation; homelessness; the regulations governing the reception centres, and the attitudes of those who administer the centres; and, finally, the actions of social services. What Loach depicts is a society that holds out promises which it cannot deliver or sustain for many people. Pop tunes vanish from the soundtrack to be replaced increasingly by ambient sounds and voices, the narrator's voice, children crying, argument and conflict. Despite their best efforts to find a home and keep the family together, Cathy and Reg become increasingly entangled with authority and bureaucracy; their lives become increasingly institutionalized and dehumanised. The film is structured to suggest how a conjunction of social and economic conditions, contingent events in the lives of those with minimal resources, and social policies that further marginalise those in need, can destroy the ideals a culture has constructed around romantic love, marriage and family life.

In *Family Life*, Janice's being coerced into the abortion of her child, and then being locked out of the house by her mother as a form of moral censure for staying out late, result in the withdrawal of Janice into herself, and in her subsequent hospitalization and treatment. Following this conjunction of events in the narrative, the conflict between Janice and her parents and the issue of Janice's treatment are brought together through parallel scenes and situations that suggest how both the family and the institution can act with relative impunity when upholding socially normative or institutionally sanctioned values. Both Janice and Dr Donaldson are subject to the structure within which they exist, whether it is the patriarchal family structure or the administrative structure of the institution. These are examples of how control is exercised over the individual whose actions fail to conform to some authorised model, whether it is a model of personal behaviour or of professional conduct. The meeting of the committee to discuss Dr Donaldson's appointment reveals the conflict within the institution, just as the conflict within the family is revealed during a family dinner during the visit of Janice's sister, Barbara, and her children to the parent's house. The violence of Janice's father finds its parallel in the violence of the shock treatment employed by the hospital. It is violence that reproduces itself in Janice's violence. Finally, Janice's visit to Tim on the night she is locked out has its parallel in her visit to his house after he takes her from the hospital, a visit that ends when the doctor and the authorities return her to the confines of the hospital. In *Family Life*, Janice's parents and the hospital legitimate each other's actions at the cost of Janice's mental health. Her parents find professional authorisation of the values they uphold in the final course of treatment which Janice receives. At the same time, the hospital finds no discernible connection between the various symptoms Janice exhibits and her family environment.

In *Raining Stones*, following the conjunction of the theft of Bob's van and the purchase of a dress for Coleen's first Communion, we see a series of plot incidents that indicate something of the social, economic or personal cost that these unexpectedly twinned incidents cause the family. The loss of potential (although illicit) income, the cost of another van, and the cost of a Communion dress produce a series of crises in their already marginal economic circumstances, particularly when Bob insists that Coleen has a brand new outfit for her first Communion. Here is the film's example of a general social ideal being upheld regardless of personal circumstances. The film becomes organised around an escalation in the desperation of Bob's attempts to earn money and a corresponding escalation in violent actions. The mix of black comedy and the threat of violence in the sheep-stealing; the violence of Tansey's actions towards others that initially take place as part of the background to Bob's actions; or the violence prompted by the desperate acts of others, such as Tommy's daughter who is selling drugs at the rave club – all suggest that chronic economic hardship can only result in yet more extreme conditions. Plot incidents represent how various figures are caught between social needs and social expectations, on the one hand, and the often extreme measures they are prepared to take in order to meet their economic needs and obligations. The petty theft in the opening scenes (stealing sod from the bowling green), Bob's abortive security work at the rave club, and his futile attempt to earn money cleaning drains lead him inevitably to Tansey, the moneylender. Each of Bob's actions emphasises both the failure of these actions to resolve the problems, despite what we understand are his best intentions, and the effects that these actions have on the family. The futility of his actions leads Bob to lie to Anne about their financial situation. His actions also lead to Tansey's threat to the family, to the emotional and psychological cost to Anne and Coleen, who have been terrorised, and, in turn, to Bob's retaliation.

The complex structuring of *Ladybird Ladybird*, with its initial flashback sequences, continually positions the relationship between Maggie and Jorge in the context of broader social and legal issues. As we have seen in Loach's other tales, the emotional and psychological effects of various crises on the personal and domestic life of the central character(s) individuate a variety of concerns. *Ladybird Ladybird* is organised around two interwoven lines of action: one line deals with Maggie's attempt to leave an abusive relationship, her new relationship with Jorge, and their determination to establish a home and family, while the other line is developed around an escalating series of confrontations between Maggie and various figures representing institutionalized authority, including confrontations with figures who support her. We are moved back and forth between personal and public issues, such as spousal violence; the problems which women face when they have little social or economic support; the conditions at shelters for women seeking to escape abusive relationships; the way in which non-institutional support, such as shelters, is marginalised within the hierarchy of social assistance; the exploitation of individuals whose immigration status is in question; and the actions of authorities who represent an ongoing threat that children will be taken into care as a consequence of past failures. Furthermore, like the other domestic morality tales, it is constructed around the determination of its central character to achieve some seemingly perfectly normal social goal.

An odd nostalgia

In the previous part of this essay, I argued that the ideals and values of the characters, their social and economic circumstances, and the conjunction of contingent and coincident events in the narrative are all part of the various crises in these films. In a fundamental way, both the ideals and values of the central characters and their social circumstances are in crisis at the same time. When a contingent event occurs in these films, it is an anomaly, not part of a pattern. However, it will become integral to a causal pattern of events in the narrative. When two such events are coincident in the domestic morality tales, the contingent event becomes causal. The contingent event serves as a catalyst in the subsequent development of the narrative and marks a change in the pattern of everything that follows in the lives of the central characters. Contingent events reconfigure the narrative. The action immediately preceding the conjunction of a contingent event, and an event that is coincident, mark the last point in the narrative where the central character(s) are seen to have some reasonable measure of control over their circumstances, as tenuous as that control may be at times. Thereafter, the central characters act in the face of a permanently altered set of circumstances. Their lives become increasingly subject to the consequences that arise from this configuration of events, and they become increasingly subject to the decisions and actions of others.

The structural use of the contingent in Loach's work, however, is not simply a narrative trope. The contingent should not be seen as a chance event or some misfortune or event outside everyday social practice. In the domestic morality tales, the contingent directs us to details of the characters' everyday circumstances and to their social locatedness. The use of contingency in these narratives suggests that what initially happens to these characters is the result of social and economic factors, rather than simply the consequence of something arbitrary or some personal failure. This has the effect of directing our attention to the immediate consequences of such events on the domestic lives of these characters, because such events result in a series of crises. The working out of such crises in Loach's domestic tales, however, can never be disassociated from how the individual circumstances of these central characters refer us to issues that often raise questions of public policy: to the conditions of labour – such as the faulty brakes that contribute to the van accident, the lack of compensation, and the loss of Reg's job (not to mention policies dealing with housing and the regulations governing shelters); to the forms of treatment prescribed for Janice and to how that psychiatric treatment is authorised; to the kind of crime that desperate economic conditions produce – such as petty theft, drug dealing and moneylending where the working class and underclass exploit one another; or to the condition of facilities for women and children subject to family violence, such as the shelter that has earlier been described as a fire-trap because of poor wiring.

Contingent events throw into focus the way in which central characters accept some normative set of social ideals or values around which they have organised their lives and plans. None of these values is very unique or unusual, as we have seen. These characters, however, are singularly unable to see or recognise how the first step is wrong. They fail to recognise that their values, ideals or aspirations – the very things that are fundamental to their identity – both help to cause and, in fact, aggravate their problems. The characters cling to a set of ideas in order to deal with a crisis, without being able to recognise that these ideas are part of the problem. As a consequence, certain events in their lives are tied to their failure to see the unrealisability of their expectations and goals in the circumstances. We might even say that they cling stubbornly to the very ideas that are generating the problems, as if the ideas that are causing the problems could possibly be a solution to them. A conclusion that might well be drawn is that, in fact, there is no individual solution to their problems.

The problem, in fact, is just how social ideals are constituted within a political structure whose social divisions and economic inequities can only produce frustration and forms of isolation when these characters attempt to realise their dreams and goals. Yet, it is also part of the identity of the central characters in these films to persist regardless of personal or economic circumstances for the very reason that their identity is tied inescapably to these social ideals and values. The actions of these characters are symptomatic of a certain kind of nostalgia – one that suggests a desire for a way things were under a misconstrual of how things were. It is the ideal of how things should be or should have been. In the circumstances, such an ideal is nihilistic.

This use of the contingent in the structure of Loach's narratives also dramatises how those who are marginalised suffer most from such events. It draws our attention to an already difficult set of circumstances, where characters live at the limits of their resources. It draws our attention also to the limited range of choices that social circumstances and economic conditions allow in the lives of these individuals, and to the kinds of actions they are forced to take in response to such conditions. Contingent events are obviously a staple of fictional narratives. What is important in Loach's domestic morality tales is that contingent events and events that become coincident with these contingent events invariably bring the characters' social and economic circumstances to a point where the characters no longer have the means to recover what has been lost.

In Loach's domestic morality tales, there is an increasing sense of desperation in the lives of the characters, and a corresponding sense of estrangement from or within the family. In fact, these tales are in some large part about the anomaly of the domestic. The family is one of a number of basic social structures, organisations or institutions we see in these films. Arguably, the family should be the centre, the supportive structure for the individual. Yet, these tales are about divisions within the family and how the family itself becomes divided.

Reg and Cathy become increasingly estranged from one another because there are no provisions at the reception centres to accommodate husbands. The underlying assumption seems to be that husbands want simply to disappear – and also that males, unencumbered by their families, can rebuild their lives. Yet, we recognise that Reg is driven to this unwanted separation by the institutions which are in place to preserve the family. In *Family Life*, Janice's parents uphold traditional roles within the family structure and speak normative values (particularly Janice's mother, who upholds the values of conventional sexual morality) that are a means of exercising control. It is the family that constructs Janice as someone suffering psychological difficulties; it is the family that destroys her. In *Raining Stones*, Bob increasingly makes decisions and acts on his own without any discussion with his wife, while lying to her or withholding information about their problems. His actions result in the totally unexpected violence which Anne and Coleen face at the hands of Tansey and his thugs. In *Ladybird Ladybird*, Maggie often acts against her own best interests – let alone those of her family – and even against the best interests of Jorge, who patiently and consistently offers her the stability and support her life has lacked.

In Loach's domestic morality tales, the confrontations that are the focus of ongoing narrative action are marked by a progressive escalation of violence. The circumstances faced by individuals and families in these narratives are, in fact, often represented as desperate. Violence often seems the only alternative. The inexorable movement towards violence plays out at two levels: physical and psychological. Central characters otherwise represented as law-abiding either become subject to violence, or are brought near to violence, if not to actual violence. Their violence would be misunderstood, however, if we attributed it wholly or simply to individual psychological causes. In the domestic morality tales, violence is a consequence of the conditions that drive these figures beyond the point of frustration, anger, and a sense of hopelessness to strike out when there is no obvious means of righting their circumstances. Moreover, it is fuelled by the unsympathetic, callous or intransigent figures who act on behalf of the state.

Clearly, the problems which Loach's central characters face are compounded by the different institutional structures and forms of authority to which they turn for support. But institutions often serve as the antagonist in much of Loach's work. In their various ways, institutions or organisations serve a regulatory function in the lives of the very characters they were designed to help. For a time, the central character is dependent upon, or trusts, or accepts, the authority which some institution represents. But it soon becomes evident that the institution has its own vested interests and its own goals, and will finally act in its own best interests or in the name of regulations – at the expense of those it purports to serve. Loach's central characters are increasingly subject to the conditions, will and authority of institutional structures, and end up more isolated and alienated as a result. Their frustration and helplessness cannot be disassociated from a sense of the betrayal of the very values and ideals these institutions should embody – a theme found throughout Loach's films in various forms and in relation to various institutions, organisations and political structures. As a consequence, these tales are invariably about the regulatory power of those in authority.

Loach's central characters cannot see that their most basic ideals and values *are* the source of their problems. In turn, the figures identified with authority cannot see, or fail to recognise, the chain of events that has led to a crisis. As a result, figures of authority often compound the damage which these characters experience. While the various social workers, magistrates or administrators fail to see what has brought these characters to a particular situation, *we* see the chain of events. We recognise how things have played out. We may not condone many of the actions of the films' central characters. This, however, is what makes Loach such a compelling social-issue dramatist.

Morality tales without morals

Loach creates a particular kind of morality tale that speaks to the politics of social and economic inequities within the social structure. It is often assumed that, for Loach, the moral is to be found in the political: that any moral position in the films which set stories of family life in relation to specific social issues is inevitably bound into a radical politics. In Loach's morality tales, the circumstances with which characters must deal call for social and economic solutions that demand political action. These films may lead viewers to conclude that a fundamental change in the economic and social structure of Britain is necessary, that any change can only be achieved through some revolutionary transformation of social relations.

So Loach is a radical moralist. The kinds of morality tales he tells are tales without a conventional moral. In fact, what Loach's films offer is a rereading of the conventional morality tale. The conventional view of a moral tale is that a moral can be drawn at the closure of the narrative, or takes the form of a maxim that stands independent of the story. In the latter case, a conventional moral is not a summary or synopsis, nor an account of the story. It is perhaps closer to the theme, and is a prescription for action. The social issue films which Loach makes do not have this kind of moral closure. Yet, narrative closure in the domestic morality tales does not provide a resolution.

Instead, closure draws attention to an ongoing and apparently unfixable set of conditions. *Cathy Come Home* ends with Cathy and Reg separated, the children forcibly taken into care, and Cathy homeless and alone in circumstances similar to those in which we first saw her. *Family Life* ends with Janice institutionalized, her parents certain that they have acted properly and that things could not have been otherwise. She ends in an institution – the metaphor for the increasing institutionalization of social life. *Raining Stones* closes with a totally ironic "happy" ending, even though everything has just fallen short of disaster. Coleen has had her first Communion in a new dress, as Bob insisted; his stolen van has been recovered; and Tansey is dead without any suspicion falling on Bob. Yet, the conditions that led Bob and Tommy to steal a sheep remain unchanged. *Ladybird Ladybird* ends with Maggie still denied access to two of her children who were taken into care by social services. Here we have a range of closures without any sense of a restoration of order or equilibrium – without recovery of the characters from the pattern of disruption and loss, and without any prospect of a resolution to the problems, even at an individual level.

The tales which Ken Loach tells are about the failure of conventional morality tales. Conventional morality tales do not help anymore. Loach appears to take the position that a conventional morality tale with a moral would simply get the diagnosis wrong. His morality tales critique the kinds of diagnoses and actions of those in positions of authority. Their diagnoses do not provide a solution to the problems his characters face. Loach's morality tales expose the vicious circle of the British social welfare state, where social institutions destroy the apparently "normal" social goals and objectives that individuals believe should be realisable in their own lives. There is no point for the working and marginalised classes to be committed to these goals and values with the expectation that they can be realised in the current social and political circumstances. The values in which Loach's characters believe cannot resolve their everyday problems. These values *are* the problems.

Ken Loach and questions of censorship

Julian Petley

Up until 1980, Ken Loach's television works consisted entirely of fiction films (or rather "plays", as they were then anachronistically known), almost all of which were made for the British Broadcasting Corporation (BBC). However, with the election of the first Thatcher government in 1979, and its immediate onslaught on the organised working class in the form of the trade union movement, Loach felt that it was time to tackle the key political issues of the day head-on in straightforward documentary form:

> [T]here were things we wanted to say head on and not wrapped up in fiction...things that should be said as directly as one can say them...Thatcherism just felt so urgent that I thought that doing a fictional piece for TV, which would take a year to get commissioned and at least another year to make, was just too slow...Documentaries can tackle things head on, and you can make them faster than dramas, too – though, with hindsight, it's just as hard, if not harder, to get them transmitted.[1]

The experience was to be a particularly painful and frustrating one, which illustrated all too clearly the limits of the politically possible on British television, and especially during the Thatcher regime. The repeated instances of censorship which Loach suffered during these years meant that one of Britain's leading radical television programme-makers was virtually silenced at a time when dissident voices such as his most desperately needed to be heard.

There are certain topics which British television has found it extremely difficult to treat without directly or indirectly falling foul either of self-censorship or of state interference. Traditionally, these have been the nuclear issue, Northern Ireland, anything which could be construed as having a bearing on "national security", and labour relations. All of these remain sensitive, except the last; however, this is only because, since 1979, wave after wave of Conservative anti-trade union legislation has destroyed any possibility of effective industrial action by working people, and reduced their rights to a level far below that of their fellow workers in any other Western European country. All this, of course, is in the interests of creating a so-called "flexible" economy, a sort of Taiwan moored off continental Europe, eager to lure employers from the mainland with visions of a low-wage, low-skill, no-rights workforce.

In 1980, however, the trade union issue was the hottest potato around, the Thatcher government having come to power on the explicit promise to curb the allegedly over-mighty power of the unions. During the 1970s, both Labour and Conservative governments had come into conflict with the trade unions; by 1979, the Conservative opposition, greatly aided by an overwhelmingly Conservative and ferociously populist press, had turned the whole issue into one of "Who governs Britain?". After the so-called Winter of Discontent, in which the Conservative press and Party pulled out all the stops to persuade people that Britain had become "ungovernable" thanks to the supposedly omnipotent unions, the Conservatives were elected and proceeded to neuter the unions (whilst, at the same time, vociferously supporting Solidarity in Poland!). Their theme was that a "moderate" rank and file was constantly being "led astray" into industrial action by a "militant" leadership, and that power needed to be "handed back" to the members.

The trade union theme had been central to some of Loach's most notable television films, namely *The Big Flame* (1969), *Days of Hope* (1975) and *The Rank and File* (1971). In all these films, Loach and Allen's point of view had been diametrically opposed to that of the Conservatives, since they had argued that, when it came to the crunch, craven and reformist trade union leaders and their allies in the Labour Party had consistently sold out and betrayed the activist, militant, rank and file membership. It was in these films that Loach really began his project of giving voice to the politically silenced and marginalised:

> I think it's a very important function...to let people speak who are usually disqualified from speaking or who've become nonpersons – activists, or militants, or people who really have any developed political ideas. One after the other in different industries, there have been people who've developed very coherent political analyses, who are really just excluded. They're vilified – called extremists and then sort of put beyond the pale.[2]

Inevitably, such heresy had attracted a good deal of huffing and puffing from Loach's right-wing critics both within the BBC and outside it; the BBC had tried (without success) to censor the quote from Trotsky at the end of *The Rank and File*, and *Days of Hope* in particular had been the object of the usual dreary old saw that its makers were guilty of misleading the viewer by presenting fiction as if it were fact. However, there was no censorship as such. But when Loach decided to explore this theme in straight documentary form, and in the specific context of the Thatcherite onslaught on the rights of working people, and of trade unionists in particular, all hell was to break loose.

Before exploring this episode in some detail, however, it is necessary briefly to establish the provenance of Loach's analysis of the role of the unions in capitalist society. This is all too often represented as some kind of paranoid delusion, but, in fact, it has a long intellectual pedigree in Marxist thinking. In his work, *On Britain*, Lenin frequently criticised British trade unions' limited and unrevolutionary horizons, and, in *The First International and After*, Marx argued that "[t]oo exclusively bent upon the local and immediate struggles with capital...the trade unions have not yet fully understood their power of acting against the system of wage slavery itself".[3] Likewise, Lenin in *"Left-Wing" Communism – An Infantile Disorder* criticised the emergence of a "labour aristocracy" made up of "workers who have become completely bourgeois" who have overseen the emergence of a "trade-union consciousness" concerned only with the non-political amelioration of the worst aspects of the work situation.[4] Such analyses were to become quite commonplace amongst those on the left of the trade union movement in Britain. Here, for example, and chosen almost at random, is Tony Cliff:

> Trade union officialdom is caught in a contradictory position. Their trade unions are organizations for the defence of workers against the employers; but they themselves live completely differently and separately from the workers they represent. Even the most 'left' of the top union officials is trapped by his social environment. Worse still, he has to work through an official machine whose personnel is very much a prisoner of this same environment...One thing that terrifies the trade union bureaucrats more than anything else is the independent action of workers. Nothing is better calculated to cut down their importance, their status, their prestige. And nothing is more likely to strengthen their attachment to the status quo. That attachment is not straightforward. The trade union bureaucrat is not a capitalist, but he's not a worker either. He lives off class struggle, but he can't let it go beyond the point of mediation, or negotiation. His basic rule is to keep the contestants alive and able to fight – gently.[5]

Similarly, Ralph Miliband has argued that union leaders operate under significant "structural constraints", and are essentially brokers between those who want to buy and sell labour power. Trade unions are really "defence organizations" whose prime function is to improve the "relations of production" which govern their members' working lives; as such, they exist "not to promote conflict but to avoid it, or at least to 'routinize' it, to render it more manageable, and to reduce its intensity". Thus, according to Miliband, unions are *"agencies of containment of struggle*, of crucial importance in the management of class conflict and the subdual of activism".[6] That such views of the unions differ so wildly from the stereotypes of overweening power and ferocious anti-capitalist activism routinely offered by the media (and especially the client press) in the long run-up to the Thatcherite experiment says a great deal about the role of the media in the hideous lurch to the Right in the 1980s, as well as about gross inequalities of access to the media, which means that certain representations are virtually ubiquitous whilst others remain largely invisible.[7] The issue here is not whether one agrees with views of the kind expressed by Cliff and others, but simply that, contrary to the impression given by the mainstream media, such views do in fact exist and have their proper place within the spectrum of political debate – but not, as we shall see, within the spectrum of *broadcast* political debate.

Loach's first documentary attempt to examine the impact of Thatcherism on the trade unions was *A Question of Leadership*, which was made in 1980 for the independent television company, Associated Television (ATV), the forerunner of the present Central Television. The programme is basically a discussion among a group of steelworkers and other trade unionists, filmed shortly after the former were defeated in the 1980 steel strike, the first victims of the government's anti-union strategy – which consisted of quite deliberately picking fights with specifically selected trade unions, starting with relatively weak ones before moving on to the stronger, and which was to reach its ugly climax in the coal dispute of 1984-85. The discussion revolves around the Conservatives' industrial strategy, the partisan role played by the police, and, of course, the part played by the union leadership in the débâcle. Its tone is quite overtly political; of the government, a miner from the Kent coalfield (since entirely closed down in the wake of the miners' defeat in 1984-85) says: "They export capital into areas where it's going to make a profit, they create mass unemployment, they destroy the basic industries...It's a consistent plan to break down trade union resistance to the reorganisation of the economy". Of the unions, a South Yorkshire steelworker complains:

> There is no one union in this industry that has done one solitary thing to defend jobs. They will tell you at conferences, in the press, at meetings like this, that they are opposed, but the strength of their opposition is less than a two-day-old baby.

The expressly political nature of the analysis presented by the participants in the programme seems to have set alarm bells ringing at ATV, according to Loach:

> I think there's a nervousness in TV about ordinary people showing articulate political views. They like working class people to be complaining about unemployment or bad housing, they like social distress, but they don't like numbers being added up and conclusions drawn...Conclusions have to be drawn by experts in studios, because 'ordinary folk can't talk politics'.[8]

Elsewhere Loach explained:

> [W]hat tends to alert the powers that be is if you use words like 'Marxist' or 'Capitalist' and 'Working Class'. If you use these terms they start to get very suspicious, whereas if you can express these ideas without using those words then they're not so suspicious. I think it really operates at quite a crude level, so we found ourselves trying to take out the words that would trigger their response, whilst leaving the ideas in.[9]

This was to no avail, however, as ATV were concerned that the programme contravened the Independent Broadcasting Authority's (IBA) guidelines on objectivity and balance – no matter, of course, that the programme could itself be regarded as a sorely needed piece of "balance" offsetting the views of the trade union leadership, which at that time received regular airing on television, not to mention counterbalancing the kind of routine, anti-union broadcasting bias enumerated by the Glasgow University Media Group. As Loach himself said: "We felt it was important to make a film in which trade unionists weren't on the defensive. Television never allows them to argue about issues beyond initial statements of policy".[10] However, the absence of the "other side" seems to have been an insuperable stumbling block for both ATV and the IBA. One is left with the distinct impression that everything would have been alright if only the programme had been fronted by the usual onscreen journalist/interviewer hectoring the assembled trade unionists with the usual clichéd question about "militancy" every time they vainly attempted to present their analyses of the situation in which they (unlike the questioner) had actually been involved. But, of course, precisely what makes the programme so distinctive and Loachian is its quiet, unobtrusive, unhurried tone, and the way in which the camera carefully follows the ebb and flow of the debate. The much-praised scene in *Land and Freedom* (1995) in which land reform is debated is distinctly pre-echoed here in this unassuming film which languished unseen for over a year, was never shown on network television, and was cut in order to enable a "balancing" discussion to be tacked on at the end – a discussion which, Loach has argued, "anaesthetises the rest of the programme" and is "entirely redundant".[11]

Undaunted and still eager to pursue his enquiries into union democracy and effectiveness, Loach, through Central, approached Channel 4's commissioning editor for single documentaries, Paul Madden, with a series of proposals. What eventually emerged were a film on the party conferences: *The Red and the Blue* (1983), and *Questions of Leadership* (1983), four 50-minute films with the subtitle of "Problems of democracy in trade unions: some views from the front line". The story of their banning is labyrinthine, but remarkably revealing of the way in which censorship works in British television.

The first film dealt with the Lawrence Scott and Electromotors closure, the steel strike, British Leyland, the flexible rostering dispute on British Rail, and the National Health Service pay dispute. The second looked at democracy in the electricians' union, the Electrical, Electronic, Telecommunications, and Plumbing Union (EETPU), and includes an interview with its leader, Frank Chapple, which he cuts short by walking out. The third returned to British Leyland and told the story of the sacking of shop steward, Derek Robinson (the famous "Red Robbo" of Conservative press demonology), and the ensuing assault on the shop stewards' movement. The final film was an edited version of a day's discussion at Warwick University, in which the issues raised by the films were debated from a number of different positions. Taken as a whole, the films tend to suggest that large unions such as the engineering union, the Amalgamated Union of Engineering Workers (AUEW), and the EETPU are undemocratic and do not adequately represent the interests of the rank and file, and that the Trades Union Congress (TUC) hierarchy has a vested interest in preventing the formation of inter-union solidarity in industrial disputes. However, both Chapple (until he walked out) and Sir John Boyd (AUEW) were given ample opportunity to answer specific charges, and the final discussion programme includes such authoritative exponents of the "official" Labour and trade union line as John Golding MP, Kate Losinska of the Civil and Public Services Association (CPSA), Dianne Hayter of the Fabian Society, and the AUEW national official, Ken Cure (who was named during the analysis of the Lawrence Scott dispute in the first programme). Union leaders Alex Kitson, Frank Chapple and Sir John Boyd were invited, but declined to participate.

The series' viewpoint can be gauged right from the opening sequence of the first programme, in which, over archive footage of a mass meeting of trade unionists during the 1930s Depression, we hear the strains of "Bow, bow, ye lower middle classes" from Gilbert and Sullivan's *Iolanthe*. Then we dissolve to a succession of earnest young men standing on platforms and exhorting the masses. Gradually, these give way to a series of portraits of older, much more regal figures, dressed in the ermine of the House of Lords – the ennobled former trade union leaders, Joe Gormley, Vic Feather and Richard Marsh. The commentary drily states: "There are some trade union leaders who are so prosperous that they have in their own person achieved the harmony of the classes". After this, however, the programme and its successors settle down to the analysis of the cases mentioned earlier, showing how, in each one, the trade union leadership worked against the interest of its members, and collaborated with the government to circumscribe shop-floor power and subordinate the workforce. The voices heard are those of radical union leaders such as Arthur Scargill of the the National Union of Miners (NUM), activist shop stewards such as Alan Thornett and Derek Robinson (both from British Leyland), convenors in the steel industry such as Ray Davies and Bernard Connolly, and EETPU steward, John Aitken. In the second programme, there are also appearances – in silhouette only – by various EETPU members scared to be identified publicly in case their criticism of the lack of democracy in the union provokes reprisals from the leadership. As already indicated, the "other side" is also heard. However, what makes these programmes so unusual in British broadcasting terms is that it is the activists who set the agenda, and the leadership who have to respond to it – not the other way around, as would normally be the case. What also makes the programmes stand out is the viewpoint which emerges from them, from both the commentary and the testimonies of many of the participants. Thus, for example, the commentary boldly states:

> The industrial tactics of the Conservative government were clearly set out in a report prepared for the Party before the last election. It was written by Nicholas Ridley, a leading Conservative MP, and said that the trade unions were a principal barrier to the reshaping of the economy. They would have to be disciplined. Ridley then set out the industries where confrontation should be avoided: the mines, the power supplies and essential services; and those industries where the trade unions could be taught a lesson without immediate damage to the rest of the community, for example in steel and motor manufacture...The steel strike set the pattern: at a time when inflation was running at over 18%, the steelworkers were offered a wage rise of 2%, a move which was bound to provoke an angry reaction. The steelworkers' anger was such that an all-out national strike was called in December 1979, but

several weaknesses were built into the strike from the outset. It seems that the unity of large groups of workers in action was consciously headed off, not only by management and behind them the government, but by trade union leaders themselves.

It concludes that:

> In steel, at British Leyland, on the railways and in the Health Service, the Conservative government has won victories because the strength of the labour movement has not been mobilised. In a very real sense the leaders of the trade unions have kept this Conservative government in power.

In the final discussion, the British Leyland shop steward, Alan Thornett, delivers an analysis that is generally conspicuous by its absence from British television:

> The working class develops its consciousness to a great extent when it's in struggle, trying to improve its conditions and therefore putting itself against the employers and the government. It's forced, then, to tackle the real problems, and I think that that's one of the reasons why trade union leaders are in general opposed to mass struggle...It's in the course of the fight that you're going to create from the working class the people that can achieve Socialism. But if they're continuously sold out and continuously dispersed and never allowed to unite, and never allowed to get at the main enemy, and never allowed to get at the government, and never allowed to seriously get at the employers, then you can't create the conditions in which to end capitalism and establish Socialism.

As John Pilger bluntly put it: "[n]othing like this perspective of the trade unions had been seen in a sustained form on television".[12] As things turned out, it was to remain unseen.

The finished programmes were passed from Central to Channel 4 in May 1983. By August, it became apparent that the IBA and Channel 4 had cobbled together the following scheme (although each put responsibility for it on the other): because the programmes were deemed so "unbalanced" as to contravene the 1981 Broadcasting Act, Loach was to reduce them to three, each to be followed by a half-hour "balancing" discussion made by someone else, and the whole series was to be concluded by *another* programme not of Loach's making! According to Jeremy Isaacs, the channel's chief executive, the main problem was "a matter of quantity".[13] In other words, the programmes would have a cumulative effect (presumably this was precisely Loach's intention).

Channel 4's senior commissioning editor for news and current affairs, Liz Forgan, approached the independent production company, Blackrod, to make the additional discussion programmes; by this time, however, Frank Chapple was making disgruntled representations to the IBA Chairman, Lord Thomson of Monifieth, and other union leaders showed little inclination to become involved in the "balancing" act.[14] However, Isaacs warned that "censorship by non-appearance is unacceptable".[15] The delay caused, however, meant that the programmes had to be pulled from their original schedule: Saturday evenings at 8.00, starting on 10 September 1983 to coincide with the TUC Conference at which a new leader was to be elected. On 22 September, Channel 4 announced that it had now asked Central itself to make the "balancing" programmes, but, as Loach remarked: "How on earth can they need 'balancing' when they are saying something that hasn't been said before and the other point of view has been put so many times?".[16]

David Glencross, the IBA's recently appointed Director of Television, answered this point in *The Guardian* on 14 October, arguing that "[t]he trouble with this is that it does not take sufficient account of the very specific nature of much of the content", and that the films "make specific charges about specific individuals and trade unions in connection with specific industrial disputes". He continued:

In the IBA's view and in Channel Four's view those directly involved should be offered an opportunity to comment immediately following the films. That is the reason for the postponement...No...right of veto [has] been given to those who may still decline to take part.[17]

This ignores the fact that Chapple and Boyd had had the chance to comment on the "charges" during the actual programmes, and that, although no actual right of veto may have been given, trade union heel-dragging was effectively holding up the programmes' transmission. As Loach complained in *The Guardian* on 31 October, "effective censorship is best achieved not by an outright ban but by delay and inaction, by passing the item from one desk to another, from one Board to another, so that the programme gradually loses its topicality and relevance". He also outlined what he saw as the *unspoken* objection to the films:

Working people are allowed on television so long as they fit the stereotype that producers have of them. Workers can appear pathetic in their ignorance and poverty, apathetic to parliamentary politics, or aggressive on the picket line. But let them make a serious political analysis based on their own experiences and in their own language, then keep them off the air.[18]

If Glencross had suggested that the question was less one of "balance" than one of giving certain individuals the chance to answer specific "charges", then Edmund Dell, Channel 4 Chairman (and, like Lord Thomson, another former Labour Minister who had defected to the Social Democratic Party [SDP]), put the "balance" issue firmly back on the agenda in *The Guardian* on 14 November. He argued that, in the case of Channel 4 programmes, "[w]e will stick to the view that balance within a particular programme is not required",[19] but, nevertheless, "where a producer is heavily committed to a particular point of view, his opponents may not be prepared to have their answers mediated through his editorial judgment...in a case like this...it is necessary in fairness to provide additional balancing material produced by some one else".[20] However, as Loach was to reply:

> I am no more committed to allowing the issues which seem to me to be of fundamental importance to be discussed than any news editor or current affairs producer. Each makes editorial judgments according to his perception of events.[21]

Presumably, at the time, many on the Left were not particularly happy at having *their* answers mediated through the editorial judgments of such broadcasting luminaries as Sir Alastair Burnet, Brian Walden or Sir Robin Day, but the IBA never sprang to their defence so assiduously. This was the gist of Labour MP Bob Clay's House of Commons Motion on 8 November, prompted by the *Questions of Leadership* affair, to the effect that:

> This House...hopes that since the Independent Broadcasting Authority believes that the views of rank and file trade union members must not be broadcast without balance, when in future on any occasion when a Government Minister, any honourable Member, broadcaster, or certain trade union officials express views on independent television critical of rank and file trade union members, ordinary trade union members will be given the opportunity to provide balance.

In December 1983, Central asked Loach to cut down the four programmes to two of 50 minutes each. Central would add one "balancing" discussion, and the whole package was scheduled for transmission in March 1984. Loach did as requested, merely shortening each programme item. But Central did not record their part of the deal until April, thereby causing yet another postponement. Union leaders Frank Chapple, Terry Duffy and Bill Sirs all apparently declined to take part, but those present included miners' leader Arthur Scargill, Social Democrat MP Ian Wrigglesworth, Conservative MP Peter Bottomley, and Bob Clay.

On 17 April, Loach and various Central representatives (including Central's solicitor) met with a leading QC. Loach agreed to make one small cut in one programme, but otherwise it was his impression that the programmes were pronounced a fair risk. However, the programmes still did not appear in the schedules. Isaacs and Charles Denton (Director of Programmes at Central) spoke of "legal difficulties".[22] The coal strike had begun. Loach commented:

> Clearly the union leaders who are criticised in the film are the ones who are at present intent on leaving the miners isolated.[23] They are the ones the Government and the Coal Board are relying on to leave the miners isolated. Anything which criticises them is really too sensitive to broadcast now.[24]

As the programmes still languished unscheduled, the Directors Guild of Great Britain intervened and stated that: "The excuses for this are lame and palpably unreasonable...It amounts to political censorship which is both dangerous and against an accepted principle of democracy".[25] The director Michael Winner, the Guild's censorship officer (and, politically, no admirer of Loach's views) accused the authorities of "deliberate delay and prevarication amounting to de facto censorship".[26] In July, Central announced that they were seeking fresh legal advice and, shortly afterwards, issued the following statement:

> The board of Central Independent Television has been advised that the programmes Questions of Leadership are defamatory and would have no adequate defence at law...[A]fter extensive legal argument has been heard, the board has reluctantly concluded that the clear risk of a successful action for defamation precludes the programmes being offered to Channel Four for transmission.[27]

It is hard to avoid the conclusion that this decision represented political censorship masked by legalistic pretext. As Loach himself pointed out:

> The films were edited under the guidance of an expert lawyer, and we conceded to every request for changes. If there are elements in the two remaining films which are still thought to

be libellous, then there is additional material which could be put in its place, so the argument simply doesn't stand up. The only explanation therefore is that this is not a legal, but a political decision, and therefore of concern to anyone who is concerned with freedom of speech.[28]

Before discussing what the *Questions of Leadership* fiasco tells us about the limits of the politically possible on British television, and the way in which television censorship actually works without there being any "television censor" as such, it is useful briefly to examine the fate of the film which Loach made during the coal dispute: *Which Side Are You On?*. This film was commissioned by Melvyn Bragg for *The South Bank Show* in 1984, the idea being – as befitting an arts programme – to look at the songs, poems and other writings of the striking miners. However, although Loach strongly maintains that he kept strictly to his original brief, London Weekend Television, who produce *The South Bank Show*, refused to transmit the finished programme on the grounds that it took a particular point of view on an industrial dispute, and thus infringed the IBA guidelines on impartiality. As Loach put it at the time: "It is clear that only approved people can make comments about a struggle as decisive as the miners. The way the news is covered is crucial to who wins in this dispute and certainly some people are allowed to comment and others are not".[29] It is hard not to agree with Loach here: during the strike, the Conservative-supporting press became even less like proper newspapers than they usually are, and turned themselves into outright propaganda organs for the government and the National Coal Board.[30] The broadcast media were certainly less *overtly* biassed against the striking miners, but no fair-minded person could have called the totality of their coverage "balanced" or "impartial".[31] Loach's film barely begins to counterbalance the massive, daily weight of hostile media coverage with which the striking miners had to cope; perhaps the real problem with it, from an Establishment point of view, was that it was one of the very few television programmes to show some of the horrific violence inflicted by the police on the striking miners – most preferred to turn a blind eye or to concentrate on violence by the pickets.

In the end, the film was shown, unlike *Questions of Leadership*. Ironically, it ended up on Channel 4 in January 1985. At least the strike was still on, but the price to be paid for transmission was a "balancing" programme in which Jimmy Reid, once a militant shipyard worker but now moved considerably to the Right, bitterly attacked the miners' union and especially its leader, Arthur Scargill, thereby only adding to the already groaning pile of negative media coverage of the striking miners.

110

Since it is obvious from what has been said so far that *Questions of Leadership, A Question of Leadership* and *Which Side Are You On?* ran into difficulties over matters of "balance" and "impartiality", it is obviously crucial to establish just what these terms actually mean within the context of British broadcasting. At the time of the making of these programmes, the IBA was bound by the terms of the 1981 Broadcasting Act, which required it to ensure that "due impartiality" was preserved by programme-makers when dealing with matters of political or industrial controversy, and it had the power to preview programmes to ensure that this requirement was being fulfilled. The BBC's Licence contains a similar stipulation, and so, to all intents and purposes, the IBA's and BBC's positions on this matter are identical. However, this position is nothing like as unproblematic as these institutions are wont to make out. As Philip Schlesinger has pointed out, British broadcasting's claims to impartiality are open to the same objections as "value-free" sociology, namely that they are premised on an "uncritical and generally unarticulated commitment to the established order".[32] As Schlesinger puts it, impartiality "can only have meaning in the context of an existing set of values", and, in the case of British broadcasting, "the relevant complex of values is that of the 'consensus'".[33] Furthermore, adherence to consensual values goes hand-in-hand with a commitment to the established institutions of the constitution and parliamentary democracy. Lord Reith himself described the BBC as "an institution within the constitution"[34] when defending the BBC's partisan behaviour during the 1926 General Strike, and Schlesinger cites a number of more recent sources which make the same point even more explicitly. For example, the former BBC Director-General Sir Charles Curran, who liked to echo one of his senior editors' remarks that "Yes we are biased – biased in favour of parliamentary democracy";[35] similarly, the 1976 BBC document, *The Task of Broadcasting News*, states that "[t]he BBC takes it for granted that the parliamentary democracy evolved in this country is a work of national genius to be upheld and preserved".[36] Meanwhile, Sir Geoffrey Cox, former editor of Independent Television News, once went so far as to suggest that it is the broadcasters' duty "to probe the *bona fides* of those who criticize our present democracy, not to make it better but to supplant it".[37]

Such claims (and there are many more one could cite) amply demonstrate that broadcasting, although not "state-controlled", is certainly one of the established institutions of the state, that notions of "balance" and "impartiality" are framed largely in terms of the balance of forces in Parliament, and that broadcasting is indeed an organisation within the political spectrum, and not the entirely detached, disinterested Olympian presence that its rhetoric tends to suggest. As Schlesinger concludes, in this scheme of things, "impartiality is itself predicated on the existence of the present British political system and its underlying social and economic order".[38] This is not, of course, to suggest that there is never any political controversy, conflict or criticism on television, but merely that it tends very strongly to take place within the party-political consensus and thus a relatively safe and narrow spectrum of views – typically, "moderate" Labour vs. "moderate" Conservative vs. "moderate" Liberal-Democrat. Stuart Hood, a former head of the BBC World Service and Controller of Programmes at BBC Television (and one of the very few radical figures ever to have risen so high within British broadcasting), has used his insider's view to portray the "consensual" mind-set of the typical broadcaster:

> Because of the way in which they are selected they are likely to accept as 'obvious' or 'merely commonsense' the central assumptions of consensual politics in this country – will believe that parliamentary democracy as we know it in Britain has only minor blemishes; will not question the capitalist system; will believe, at best, that a mild form of social democracy is the answer to the general crisis of capitalism; will respect the monarchy and the other institutions of the British; will, although themselves probably agnostics, believe that it is important to purvey on television the values of 'mainstream christianity', which is the theological equivalent of the political consensus. They do not see themselves as reactionary and indeed will uphold liberal views on a variety of topics like race, feminism, education, the welfare state; a graph of how political attitudes are distributed among them would probably be skewed slightly left of centre. They are unlikely, however – given the nature of the security screening (although a few odd cases have slipped through the net) – to include more than a handful of people who accept the marxist analysis of capitalism or the need to replace it by a socialist society. It is however, one of their professional duties to learn the limits of what is politically possible on television. If they are in any doubt they will refer the matter up to their immediate superior, who – if in doubt – will refer it to his superior and so on. It is a process which can end with the problem being discussed and ruled on by the Board of Governors.[39]

In such a situation there is rarely any need for governments to lean on broadcasters since, as Miliband puts it, the latter have "unequivocally dwelt within the spectrum of thought occupied by 'reasonable' men and women on the Conservative and Labour sides".[40] In addition, not subject to direct governmental pressure or political string-pulling, broadcasters continue to believe themselves "free" and "independent". But, quite apart from anything else, this ignores what Richard Hoggart has called "the cultural air we breathe, the whole ideological atmosphere of our society, which tells us that some things can be said and others had best not be said. It is that whole and almost unconscious pressure towards implicitly affirming the status quo, towards confirming 'the ordinary man' in his existing attitudes, towards discouraging refusals to conform", which permeates daily life, including, of course, the media.[41]

Clearly, therefore, notions of "balance" and "impartiality" founded on a consensual model of broadcasting risk narrowing considerably the range of views routinely available on television. To identify democracy and politics entirely with the workings of Westminster carries with it the very real danger that any form of extra-parliamentary political activity will be judged "anti-democratic", even deviant, and treated accordingly. Broadcasting may indeed display a fair degree of impartiality between the major political parties, but "[i]mpartiality and objectivity, in this sense, stop at the point where political consensus itself ends – and the more radical the dissent, the less impartial and objective the media".[42] Furthermore, it can be argued that, as the postwar political consensus began to fray from the late-1960s onwards, the broadcasters' position became increasingly untenable. As Schlesinger stated as early as 1978, before Thatcherism finally burst the consensus asunder:

> There is sharp competition over definitions of social reality, and over the general direction to be followed by British society, and hence it is increasingly difficult to sell the idea that there is some Olympian vantage-point from which the arguments below may be surveyed.[43]

The idea, therefore, that British broadcasting has provided audiences with a "balanced", "impartial" and "politically neutral" view of social reality is true only in an extremely narrow and ultimately highly misleading sense of those terms. As John Pilger, himself the victim time and again of the kind of censorship which flows from these conceptions, has concluded from bitter experience:

> There is no such thing as a genuine consensus view. Britain is not one nation with one perspective on events and with everyone sharing roughly the same power over their lives. 'Consensus view' is often a euphemism for the authorised wisdom of established authority in Britain.[44]

It must be obvious from the above quotation that programmes such as *Questions of Leadership* would always face difficulties in the British broadcasting system. However, their censorship is indicative not simply of certain general tendencies within British broadcasting, but, equally importantly, of some of the particular problems which it faced in the 1980s. It is these that I now wish to explore.

Firstly, it is significant that these films could not be shown *even* on Channel 4. I say "even" because one of the main reasons why so many people agitated for a fourth television channel, and why it was eventually set up in a particular way, was to offset some of the perceived shortcomings of the other three channels, including, quite specifically, the narrow spectrum of views which they presented.[45] As its own founding chief executive, Jeremy Isaacs, has noted, the 1980 Broadcasting Act which brought the channel into existence legally required the IBA "to ensure that the fourth channel service would contain 'a suitable proportion of matter calculated to appeal to tastes and interests not generally catered for by ITV'...The channel was to be required by statute, uniquely among the world's broadcasting institutions, 'to encourage innovation and experiment in the form and content of programmes'. The channel was to have 'overall, a distinctive character of its own'".[46] Indeed, Isaacs' own book contains a number of sideswipes at "consensual" broadcasting. For example:

> There *is* a subtle centrist, conformist bias in much television output, fact and fiction, whose coded messages convey a reassuring view of the world. A complete broadcasting service ought to carry in itself also regular antidotes to complacency.[47]

Again, talking about controversial issues such as Republicanism or the Falklands War:

> Society is not a slab of solid feeling on these or on any other issues; it is composed of different strands of people with differing views and varied tastes. It was a pluralist Britain in which Channel 4 was called on to broadcast. In our appeal to different audiences we needed to cater for that diversity of taste, reflect that plurality of view.[48]

Isaacs also quotes his 1979 MacTaggart Lecture at the Edinburgh International Television Festival, generally regarded as his "calling-card" for the Channel 4 job, in which he argued that

> We want a fourth channel which extends the choice available to viewers: which extends the range of ITV's programmes; which caters for substantial minorities presently neglected; which builds in to its actuality programmes a complete spectrum of political attitude and opinion.[49]

Indeed, one of the "specialized interests" which Isaacs wanted the channel to cater for were the trade unions, who "believed that, pulverized in a popular press which knew no inhibitions, they were entitled to a fairer deal in publicly accountable media".[50]

This seems a bitterly ironic remark in the light of what happened to *Questions of Leadership*. Is Isaacs being disingenuous, or did the fault lie elsewhere – with the IBA, for instance? On the surface at least, the IBA seems to have taken a fairly liberal attitude to the channel's special remit. Thus, in the IBA's blueprint for Channel 4, *The Fourth Channel: The Authority's Proposals*, it states that:

> Our wish is that the Fourth Channel will take particular advantage of this freedom, and that enterprise and experiments will flourish. *It must provide opportunities for talents which have previously not been fully used, for needs to be served which have not yet been fully defined, and for the evolution of ideas which, for whatever reason – personal, structural, institutional – have yet to be revealed.*[51]

On the matter of controls, it merely says that:

> The Home Secretary has made clear that the general statutory provisions for programme content will be the same for both channels. We believe it is possible, however, that the availability of a wider choice of programmes *will allow controlled encouragement to be given to the presentation of a wider range of opinions and assumptions.*[52]

Moreover, at the start of the *Questions of Leadership* saga, the IBA's David Glencross, in *The Guardian* article quoted earlier, argued that:

> Channel Four has quite properly and with the IBA's support, opened its doors to a great deal of strong opinion, sometimes raw and unformed. That is part of the Channel's brief for innovation and distinctiveness. Due impartiality in a series of programmes has been deliberately interpreted in a most liberal fashion.[53]

It is, however, hard to examine the controversies, including *Questions of Leadership*, surrounding the early years of Channel 4 without coming to the conclusion that the IBA behaved in a less liberal fashion than its public pronouncements suggested. This is certainly the impression given by Isaacs' book. For example, he says he felt that the IBA Chairman, Lord Thomson, saw the channel as "the creature of the IBA",[54] admits that he "never looked forward to liaison meetings at

Brompton Road" (the IBA headquarters), reveals that the IBA exhibited in private "almost constant anxiety"[55] about the channel, and, of its Finance Director, Peter Rogers, who sat as an IBA representative on the Channel 4 board, remarks that

> [I]n spite of his previous ignorance of all broadcasting matters, [he] did not hesitate to hold forth on contentious issues at considerable length. He was particularly strong on the interpretation of the Broadcasting Act.[56]

Isaacs concludes that:

> The simple notion that public feeling was unitary suited both the regulator and the purveyor to mass taste. It suited both to suppress matter that risked offence; the former because it made the Act simpler to administer, the latter because it maximized the audience.[57]

Isaacs' view is all too clearly confirmed by the remark of an anonymous IBA spokesman quoted in *Broadcast* on 23 September 1983 apropos the growing furore over *Questions of Leadership*, to the effect that "[t]he Act does represent the general view of life and it is inevitable the majority view will be more reflected than the minority".[58] Just how this sage gauged "the general view of life" was left unclear; however, long observation of the workings of the IBA leads one to the profound suspicion that, if pressed on the point, the spokesperson would have replied: "by what appears in the media", thus neatly demonstrating the perfectly circular process by which "minority" views are routinely excluded. As Loach himself said of the trade union view that proved so contentious in *A Question of Leadership*: "Because the news hadn't covered it, when we showed that opinion, the IBA said it was not representative".[59]

However, not all the blame for the banning of *Questions of Leadership* can be laid at the door of the IBA. Although Isaacs himself did defend (up to a point) *Questions of Leadership* and argued that it should have been shown, it was not exactly helpful to refer to it dismissively as "the basic Trotskyist view of trade unions" at the 1984 Edinburgh International Television Festival.[60] In the last analysis, it is very difficult to read his book without wondering just how strongly and convincingly the Channel argued for the series with the IBA. Even Isaacs is forced to admit that the heavy SDP presence on the Channel 4 Board was "all a bit much",[61] and one must ask just how enamoured these people would have been of Loach's series in particular, and of his politics in general. After all, the SDP was formed by people who split from the Labour Party because they found it too *left*-wing, and here was Loach criticising the Labour hierarchy for being too *right-wing!*

In this respect, it is worth concentrating a little on Edmund Dell, the Chairman of the Channel 4 Board, whom we have already encountered in *The Guardian* accusing Loach of being "heavily committed to a particular point of view".[62] Dell had been a Labour Minister of State at the Board of Trade (1968-69) and Paymaster-General (1974-76). On the Right of Prime Minister James Callaghan's Cabinet, he had supported Denis Healey when, as Chancellor of the Exchequer, and at the bidding of the International Monetary Fund, he had introduced monetarist policies to Britain in 1976. Dell stood down as an MP in 1979, and his name was amongst those published in *The Times* in February 1981 in a full-page advertisement announcing the formation of the SDP. At the time of his appointment to the channel, he was chairman and chief executive of the major banking firm, Guinness Peat, he did not own a television, and had never heard of Jeremy Isaacs, who, as producer of the Thames Television series, *The World at War*, was one of the best-known names in British broadcasting.[63] He was, like Isaacs, a passionate opera fan, and was also on the Board of the English National Opera. In other words, he epitomised the Labour – and former Labour – Establishment that *Questions of Leadership* denounced.

This does not, of course, mean that Dell was incapable of judging these programmes in a disinterested fashion. However, his own pronouncements about them, allied with certain passages in Isaacs' book, give one pause for thought. According to Isaacs, Dell's idea of the person to take charge of the channel's journalism "would have been something between a Harvard professor of economics and the editor of the *Financial Times*".[64] Elsewhere, he reveals that Dell

[H]ad high expectations of the intellectual quality of television journalism, never having seen anything of it before being appointed to Channel 4. He was gravely disappointed – appalled is probably more accurate – by what he found. He had, he said, no overriding political objection to the work he most despised; it was simply that it was not good enough. Put that right, and any associated political problems would vanish.[65]

The suspicion that what Dell really wanted was good old traditional, heavyweight, "thumb-sucking" journalism to which Channel 4 was meant, at least some of the time, to provide an alternative, is only heightened if one examines his objections to Loach's films, stated in *The Guardian* article quoted earlier. In fact, Dell does defend the principle of "unbalanced" programmes, but then adds that "there does

117

need to be more discussion of the role in such programmes of professional television journalism".[66] However, if one of the norms of "professional television journalism" is "balanced reporting", it would be hard to see the point of such discussion. He also argues of "unbalanced" programmes that they can be

> [D]one well or badly. When Keynes was 22, he wrote: 'My heroes must feel and feel passionately – but they must see too, everything and more than everything.' To some of our suppliers, this seems an impossible ideal, to outline the whole of a problem and yet argue a strong point of view; to ask the searching questions and yet demonstrate that they can be answered with conviction. But that seems to me to be the right ideal both for a politician and for a journalist. When therefore I see a programme or a series of programmes in which none of the most obvious questions are raised to test the point of view of the producer, I do feel that that programme falls short of the highest standards by which it should be judged.[67]

It is hard to avoid the conclusion that someone with this particular conception of journalism was not the best person to defend *Questions of Leadership* – nor any kind of "committed" or "alternative" forms of journalism for that matter – before the IBA.

Finally, I want to consider the wider political background against which these events took place. These were, of course, the early years of the Thatcher regime, with its bleak, ideologically driven hostility to public institutions of any kind. The broadcasting institutions came second only to the unions in the Thatcherite demonology, and seemed to personify all that she detested in public institutions. Their very worst sin, however, was to epitomise the liberal, consensual ethos which Thatcher, as a thoroughgoing conviction politician, regarded as an absolute anathema; indeed, she once went so far as to denounce Conservatives who believed in consensus politics as "Quislings" and "traitors".[68] As already noted, there are all sorts of problems associated with consensus politics and with their application to broadcasting – namely that they tend to work to the exclusion of a wide range of political views. Needless to say, this was not Thatcher's objection! What appeared most to infuriate her about broadcasting's attachment to "balance", which tended to deliver a rather middle-of-the-road view of political life, was that the outright adulation which she received from a quite appallingly fawning and sycophantic press was not replicated on television, whose attempts to remain "impartial" were, at moments of particularly heightened tension with the government, denounced as quite literally treasonable and traitorous.

Although the hated BBC was the main target of Thatcherite wrath, and narrowly avoided being broken up and privatised in a characteristic act of vengeful spite, Channel 4 was far from immune from attack, as Isaacs' book makes abundantly and repeatedly clear. Here the main aggressors were the Conservative press (although greatly aided and abetted by the usual dismal gang of rent-a-mouth Conservative MPs), and the targets were precisely those "minority" programmes which the channel had been established partly to provide. Isaacs communicates all too clearly the virtual siege mentality which the press created at Channel 4 in its early days, and it is impossible to believe that this did not discourage the channel from continuing with some of its more radical experiments. More to the point, however, it is inconceivable that this onslaught did not have a considerable impact on an already anxious and fretful IBA.

It is thanks to a combination of all the factors outlined above that one of Britain's most radical filmmakers was either marginalised or completely silenced during one of the most momentous, not to say catastrophic, decades in British political history. It proved quite impossible in the 1970s with the BBC, and in the 1980s with Channel 4, to set up a film on any aspect of the situation in Northern Ireland, either past or present. In the end, all that Loach managed, on a subject about which he cares passionately and has a great deal to say, was *Time To Go*, a short contribution to the BBC *Split Screen* series made by the Community Programmes Unit, which each week gave space to opposing viewpoints on a specific subject; Loach put the case for the withdrawal of British troops from the North. In addition, on the wreckage of young lives caused by the Thatcher government's policies of de-industrialisation and unemployment creation, Loach found himself squeezed into Channel 4's late-night margins with *The View from the Woodpile* (1989), about a group of young people in Darlaston in the West Midlands, which was a contribution to the excellent (if little-seen) *Eleventh Hour* slot. As for the coal dispute – after the *Which Side Are You On?* furore, all he was offered was a "guest editor" slot on an edition on the strike of Channel 4's *Diverse Reports*, entitled *The End of the Battle but not of the War*.

At this present time, with the neutering of the unions and the steady drift of "New" Labour to the Right, these battles already seem to have the aura of History about them. Today, those who are concerned with freedom and pluralism in broadcasting are worried above all about the effects of increased competition and "deregulation" on the sorts of programmes which we see on our television screens. Some people are even beginning to look back nostalgically to an age in which "problematic" programmes could at least be made, even if, in the end, they languished unseen on the shelf, Soviet-style. Meanwhile, out there in the real world, the gap between rich and poor, haves and have-nots, grows at a faster rate than at any time in

Britain this century, and faster than in any other EU country at the present moment. Television programmes do wring their hands over this from time to time (some of those in Channel 4's June 1996 *Broke* season being a case in point), but where are the *political* analyses of what is, at heart, a *political* phenomenon, the result of quite deliberate *political* policies and choices? The answer is: nowhere – with the partial exception, perhaps, of Will Hutton's series, *False Economy*. This brings us right back to our discussion of consensus, since the Conservatives have always refused, and "new" Labour has become increasingly unwilling, to discuss the issue in these terms. Broadcasting, taking its cue from the terms of parliamentary debate, does likewise. As Pilger has so eloquently put it:

> [I]t is a rare programme that captures the impact of poverty and dares to place it in its proper political context. To those of us who are not poor, 'modernised' poverty can be disguised and isolated in enclaves where outsiders seldom go and which are beyond the reach of Reithian notions of impartiality and balance. How can the 'impartial' camera possibly describe the shredding of spirit, the loss of self-esteem, the frustration and rage not articulated by the unemployed and the impoverished employed who are forced to watch their possessions borne away by bailiffs?[69]

The answer is: it cannot. Of course, it can present absolutely heart-rending images of the poor as victims, in seasons such as *Broke* and series such as *Undercover Britain*. Indeed, television's record in this respect is good compared to those odious Conservative newspapers which stoutly deny that poverty even *exists* in that best of all possible worlds bequeathed to her subjects by Mrs Thatcher. Moreover, without television and specifically Channel 4, we would not have had *Riff-Raff* (1991), *Raining Stones* (1993) and *Ladybird Ladybird* (1994). But these are fictional features, and Loach is simply too good a filmmaker to turn them into didactic documentaries *manqués*. We know from the programmes discussed in this essay that Loach is one of the few filmmakers who can transcend televisual notions of "impartiality", but we also know the price which he paid for doing so. However, it is not Ken Loach but British television and, in a wider sense, Britain's reputation as a democratic state that is the poorer for the censorship of his documentaries of the dog days of the Thatcher era.

1   Quoted in Paul Kerr, "The Complete Ken Loach", *Stills* 27 (May-June 1986): 148.

2   Gavin Smith, "Voice in the Dark", *Film Comment* 24: 2 (March-April 1988): 42.

3   Quoted in Ralph Miliband, *Marxism and Politics* (Oxford: Oxford University Press, 1977): 132.

4   Quoted in ibid: 133-134.

5   Tony Cliff, *The Crisis: Social Contract or Socialism* (London: Pluto Press, 1975): 120, 126.

6   Ralph Miliband, *Capitalist Democracy in Britain* (Oxford; New York: Oxford University Press, 1982): 55-56. Emphasis in original.

7   On this matter, see especially the Glasgow University Media Group, *Bad News* (London: Routledge & Kegan Paul, 1976), and Peter Beharrell and Greg Philo (eds), *Trade Unions and the Media* (London: Macmillan, 1977).

8   Stephen Cook, "Film maker accuses ITV of 'nods and winks' censorship", *The Guardian* 12 August 1981; Stewart Lane, "Loach gasps at IBA's 'sharp intakes of breath'", *Broadcast* 1121 (17 August 1981): 5.

9   Julian Petley, "An Interview with Ken Loach", *Framework* 18 (1982): 10.

10 John Wyver, "A Brace Of Loach", *Time Out* 556 (12-18 December 1980): 75.

11 Barthélemy Piéchut, "Muting the voice of Militants", *Free Press* 9 (September/October 1981): 5.

12 John Pilger, *Heroes* (London: Jonathan Cape, 1986): 501.

13 Quoted in Ken Loach, "A question of censorship", *Tribune* 47: 47 (25 November 1983): 7.

14 Incidentally, Lord Thomson was a former Labour Cabinet Minister, but by this time had defected to the Social Democrats.

15 Pilger: 502.

16 Quoted in Alan Rusbridger, "Diary", *The Guardian* 31 August 1983: 15.

17 David Glencross, "Double vision lets you see both sides of the question", *The Guardian* 14 October 1983: 12.

18 Ken Loach, "Broadcasters who uphold the established order through the charade of impartiality", *The Guardian* 31 October 1983: 9.

19 Edmund Dell, "A balanced view of television that leaves room for searching polemic", *The Guardian* 14 November 1983: 21.

[20]   Ibid.

[21]   Ken Loach, "How Channel Four's balancing act falls down", *The Guardian* 22 November 1983: 12.

[22]   Quoted in Michael Winner, "Guild claims Loach docs were held back", *Television Today* 26 July 1984: 15.

[23]   Witness the bitter attack by Chapple's successor, Eric Hammond, also named in *Questions of Leadership*, on Arthur Scargill at the 1984 TUC Conference.

[24]   Winner: 15.

[25]   "Loach films have been buried, claim directors", *Television Today* 26 July 1984: 13.

[26]   "C4 Loach films in 'censorship' row", *Screen International* 456 (28 July-4 August 1984): 25.

[27]   "Central has to abandon the two Loach docs", *Television Today* 2 August 1984: 15.

[28]   "'Defamatory' Loach films will not be broadcast", *Screen International* 4 August 1984: 17, 21.

[29]   RF, "LWT dumps Loach's miner masterpiece", *Broadcast* 7 December 1984: 12.

[30]   See Mark Hollingsworth, *The Press and Political Dissent* (London: Pluto Press, 1986): 242-285.

[31]   See Len Masterman (ed), *Television Mythologies: Stars, Shows & Signs* (London; New York: Comedia/Routledge, 1984): 99-109; Huw Beynon (ed), *Digging Deeper: Issues in the Miners' Strike* (London: Verso, 1985); David Jones, Julian Petley, Mike Power and Lesley Wood, *Media Hits the Pits: The media and the coal dispute* (London: Campaign for Press and Broadcasting Freedom, 1985); and Greg Philo, *Seeing and Believing: The influence of television* (London; New York: Routledge, 1990).

[32]   Philip Schlesinger, *Putting 'reality' together: BBC news* (London: Constable, 1978): 164.

[33]   Ibid.

[34]   Ralph Negrine, *Politics and the Mass Media in Britain* (London; New York: Routledge, 1989): 120.

[35]   Quoted in Schlesinger: 167.

[36]   Quoted in ibid.

[37]   Ibid.

[38]   Ibid: 170.

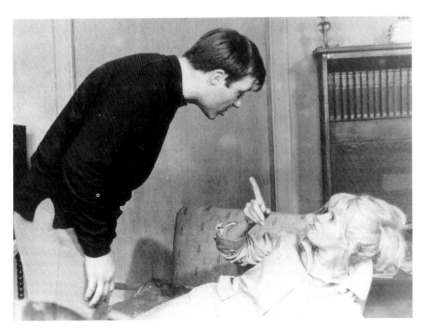

Poor Cow (1967)

After a Lifetime (1971)

Kes (1969)

Family Life (1971)

Days of Hope (1975)

The Gamekeeper (1980)

Looks and Smiles (1981)

Which Side Are You On? (1984)

Fatherland (1986)

Riff-Raff (1991)

Hidden Agenda (1990)

Raining Stones (1993)

Ladybird Ladybird (1994)

Land and Freedom (1995)

[39] Stuart Hood, *On Television*, second edition (London: Pluto Press, 1983): 51-52. Incidentally, the "security screening" mentioned by Hood refers to the fact that potential BBC employees were secretly vetted by MI5 from 1937 to 1985, when a highly embarrassed BBC was forced to abandon the process after it had been exposed by *The Observer*, a revelation which, of course, serves impressively to underline the fact that broadcasting *is* one of the key established institutions of the state. For a detailed analysis of this episode, see Mark Hollingsworth and Richard Norton-Taylor, *Blacklist: The Inside Story of Political Vetting* (London: The Hogarth Press, 1988): 97-121.

[40] Miliband (1982): 81.

[41] Glasgow University Media Group: x.

[42] Ralph Miliband, *The State in Capitalist Society* (London; Melbourne; New York: Quartet Books, 1973): 200.

[43] Schlesinger: 167.

[44] Pilger: 475.

[45] Simon Blanchard and David Morley (eds), *What's this Channel Fo(u)r?: An alternative report* (London: Comedia Publishing Group, 1982); Stephen Lambert, *Channel Four: Television with a Difference?* (London: British Film Institute, 1982).

[46] Jeremy Isaacs, *Storm Over 4: A Personal Account* (London: Weidenfeld and Nicolson, 1989): 22.

[47] Ibid: 85. Emphasis in original.

[48] Ibid: 114.

[49] Ibid: 19.

[50] Ibid: 37.

[51] Quoted in Lambert: 100. Emphasis in original.

[52] Ibid: 101. Emphasis in original.

[53] Glencross.

[54] Isaacs: 74.

[55] Ibid: 76.

[56] Ibid: 74.

[57] Ibid: 114.

[58] RF, "Is Loach new C4 'victim'?", *Broadcast* 23 September 1983: 32.

[59] Nicholas Wapshott, "The acceptable face of radicalism", *The Times* 13 November 1981.

[60] Quoted in "Four into two won't go – for the time being", *The Guardian* 3 September 1984: 11.

[61] Isaacs: 74.

[62] Dell.

[63] Isaacs: 24.

[64] Ibid: 39.

[65] Ibid: 79.

[66] Dell.

[67] Ibid.

[68] Hugo Young, *One of Us: A biography of Margaret Thatcher* (London: Macmillan, 1989): 223.

[69] Pilger: 504.

Finding a form: politics and aesthetics in
Fatherland, Hidden Agenda **and** *Riff-Raff*

John Hill

In 1986, Ken Loach completed *Fatherland*, his first feature film since *Looks and Smiles* in 1981. In the intervening years, Loach had concentrated on documentary work. The reasons for this were partly economic, insofar as Loach was unable to raise the finance for film features, but also political. For Loach, the rise of Thatcherism in Britain "felt so urgent" that he wanted to produce material more quickly and in a more "head on" manner than was possible with feature film production.[1] If the resulting confrontations with broadcasters provide any measure, it is clear that this "head on" approach was achieved. *Questions of Leadership* (1983), a four-part series on trade union democracy, was made by Central Television for Channel 4. However, despite a re-edit, the series was still refused transmission.[2] *Which Side Are You On?* (1984), a documentary about the songs and poetry of the miners' strike, was made for London Weekend Television's *The South Bank Show*. LWT, however, declined to show the programme, which eventually appeared, logo-less, on Channel 4. Despite such setbacks, Loach still considered documentary to be "the appropriate form for the time".[3] In going back to features, therefore, he not only began a new phase of his career, but also returned to the question of how fiction, rather than documentary, could provide the appropriate form for engaging with political concerns.

For Loach, *Looks and Smiles* represents "the end of an era" in his work.[4] This film charts the experiences of three young people as they come to terms with the realities of life around them. It focuses, in particular, on the young school-leaver, Mick (Graham Green), as he engages in a futile search for a job, and reconciles himself to the prospect of life on the dole. For Loach, however, the film was insufficiently hard-hitting. Unemployment surged dramatically in Britain during the early 1980s, and Loach believes he "missed creating the outrage in the audience that should have been there".[5] A reason for this, he suggests, is that the distanced and observational methods which he had evolved with *Kes* (1969) were no longer fresh, with the result that the film came across as "old and lethargic".[6] This is undoubtedly too harsh a judgment upon the film which achieves much of its effectiveness precisely because it is quiet, rather than openly angry. Nevertheless, given Loach's feelings about the film, it

125

was unlikely that his first feature to follow *Looks and Smiles* would simply take up from where it had left off. Thus, while *Fatherland* does display some undoubted continuities with Loach's previous films, it also represents a significant departure for Loach from the aesthetic strategies which he had previously adopted.

This may be explained in part by the circumstances surrounding the film's production, but it also seems to reflect a certain rethinking of the relationship between aesthetic form and political content. Loach's work has characteristically been associated with a tradition of "realism". During the 1970s, in particular, the conventions of realism were subject to considerable criticism for their apparent inability to deliver a "genuinely" radical cinema, and Loach's four-part television drama, *Days of Hope* (1975), became embroiled in the ensuing debate.[7] Above all, what fuelled "the realism debate" was the question of how well different aesthetic strategies serve radical political ends. Insofar as Loach has remained committed to the making of overtly political films, this is a question which continues to be pertinent. However, with *Fatherland*, and his two subsequent films, *Hidden Agenda* (1990) and *Riff-Raff* (1991), Loach has adopted three quite diverse sets of aesthetic conventions. This suggests that, following the hiatus of the early 1980s, Loach's films display a certain hesitation about the aesthetic form most appropriate to the changed political circumstances of the period. As such, they provide an instructive illustration of the possibilities and pitfalls facing radical filmmakers in the late-1980s and early 1990s.

Clearly, the changed conditions of British film and television financing were an important factor in the production of *Fatherland*. Loach is a director who has always moved easily between film and television; and a part of the importance of his early television work, such as *Up the Junction* (1965), derived from the use of cinematic techniques. At the end of the 1970s, Loach was also tempted from the British Broadcasting Corporation (BBC) to Associated Television (ATV) by the prospect of making films for television (such as *Looks and Smiles*) which would also be seen in cinemas. This particular arrangement effectively anticipated the relationship between film and television which became the norm in Britain during the 1980s. Thus, while the television single play continued its decline, the drama series and the television-funded film grew in importance for the broadcasters. As a result, the number of films produced or co-produced by television companies during the 1980s grew from virtually nil to a total of 49% of all UK productions in 1989, a figure which would be even higher if the "offshore" – and nominally British – productions of American companies were excluded.[8] Channel 4, launched in 1982, was particularly important in this regard, and its Drama Department (which was responsible for *Film on Four*), as well as its Department of Independent Film and Video, contributed many of the decade's most distinctive British features. Although financed by advertising, the channel possessed a clear "public service" remit, which was evident in the support which it gave to original drama dealing with contemporary Britain. It was thus Channel 4 which provided 52% of the budget for *Fatherland*, contributed (together with British Satellite Broadcasting) to the financing of *Hidden Agenda*, and fully funded *Riff-Raff*.

Fatherland (together with *Looks and Smiles*, which was partly German-funded) also reflected another trend within the British film industry. Due to the relative lack of finance available in Britain for British filmmaking outside television, European co-production became an increasingly attractive option for British filmmakers during the 1980s. Thus, whereas in 1980, only three out of 31 British features were international co-productions, the corresponding figure for 1991 was 22 out of 46.[9] However, while co-production has had undoubted economic benefits for British filmmakers, it has not always clearly benefited the films themselves. The financial involvement of different countries has exerted pressures on the types of project which have been put together, and many of the films financed in this way have suffered as a result of the incorporation of spurious pan-European elements, or the avoidance of material which has been considered too culturally specific.

Certainly, there are a number of features characteristic of the European co-production to be found in *Fatherland*, which, in addition to Channel 4, was financed through production partners in France and Germany. Thus, unlike so much of Loach's previous work, the film's story lacks a firm grounding in English social life, and offers instead a self-consciously international mix of both characters and settings. Klaus Drittemann (Gerulf Pannach) is an East German *Liedermacher*, or protest singer, denied work in the East, but permitted to move to the West with a one-way visa. In West Berlin, he is involved in a number of dealings with Taube Records, and their American record executive, Lucy (Cristine Rose). He decides, however, to depart for England with a young French woman, Emma (Fabienne Babe), whom he believes to be a journalist in search of his father who had apparently defected to the West over 30 years before.[10] This shifting in localities and mixing of nationalities undoubtedly have consequences for the way in which the film is able to deal with each country and culture, and for the sense of genuine engagement which it can provide. This is partly in evidence in the film's treatment of Berlin (where Loach was hampered by not speaking German), but also, more surprisingly, in its representation of England.

Writing on the aesthetic and cultural implications of European co-production, Vincent Porter has suggested that it is "how a film-maker deals with the sense of place" which is crucial in identifying "the cultural and ideological world...the film inhabits" and whether the filmmaker "is a tourist or a resident".[11] Loach does, of course, live in England, but, in contrast to his previous work, *Fatherland*'s treatment of place appears to lack inwardness, providing curiously unresonant images of the England portrayed. Thus, while the choice of Cambridge may have some validity as a hideout for Drittemann's father, it is also an archetypically "tourist" location which fails to offer the opportunity for socio-political comment which the film otherwise seeks to make.[12] It may, of course, be the case that the film's disengaged viewpoint mirrors the estrangement of Klaus and Emma as they move through a foreign country. Nevertheless, the film fails to make use of this distancing perspective to present fresh perceptions of English society, and, as a result, is dependent upon rather heavy-handed narrative insertions, rather than textured *mise en scène*, to deliver some kind of political perspective. Thus, when the couple listen to their car radio, they coincidentally hear a phone-in host dismissing a question on cruise missiles; and, when the same couple are stopped at a police checkpoint, striking miners on their way to picket lines are observed being prevented from travelling further. The treatment of England as a landscape which reflects the primarily psychological "alienation" of the two central characters may be linked to the characteristics of the film more generally.

According to the film critic Derek Malcolm, *Fatherland* represents "a complete change of style" for Loach, and this results from an attempt "to tell a European story in a European way".[13] Malcolm does not explain what he means by this, but it is evident that he wishes to locate the film within a tradition of European "art" cinema, rather than within that of British social realism. The implications of this point for an understanding of the film can be pursued. For David Bordwell, the European art film is characterised by a distinct set of narrative and stylistic conventions. In contrast to those of "classical" narrativity, the main features of the art film, he argues, are confused or goal-bereft protagonists; looser and more episodic plots which often make use of a central "boundary situation"; expressive effects; and narrational self-consciousness.[14] It is these conventions which *Fatherland* may also be seen to employ. Like other Loach films, the plot is loose and lacks the highly wrought causal dynamics of "classic" Hollywood. It also relies on a certain degree of parallelism which, Bordwell suggests, may take the place of causality (as when Drittemann finds himself being followed in the West as well as in the East). But, unlike other Loach films, the central protagonist, Drittemann (particularly as played by an impassive Pannach), is troubled, introspective and equivocal in a way more typical of the European art film. He also undergoes what Bordwell, after Horst Ruthrof, describes as a "boundary situation",[15] when he discovers that his father was a traitor, working firstly for the Gestapo and then for the Americans. The film is also unusual for Loach in its more overt use of expressive techniques.

For Bordwell, the European art film characteristically combines realist and expressionist techniques. Loach's work is usually distinguished from Hollywood by its use of documentary devices (such as distanced camera placements, unobtrusive lighting, long takes and unexpected camera movements) in the context of film fiction. This "documentary realist" approach is in evidence in *Fatherland*, but it is also combined with more obtrusive, modernist elements which have largely been absent from Loach's work since *Up the Junction*.[16] Thus, there are a number of temporal jumps, the introduction of dream and memory sequences (Drittemann running from his pursuers; Drittemann fantasising about his father), and the adoption of loosely Brechtian techniques, as in the use of titles, songs and music. Indeed, the central character's role as a musician, politically at odds with both East and West, is itself something of a commentary upon the film's own efforts to use art as a means of political intervention.[17]

The reference to Brecht does, of course, suggest that, under the influence of scriptwriter Trevor Griffiths, *Fatherland* may represent a move towards precisely the kind of "anti-realist" cinema which Loach's critics in the 1970s sought to champion, and which Bordwell suggests may be identified as "historical-materialist", rather than "art", film.[18] However, the Brechtian elements in the film are relatively muted and do not significantly interrupt or intrude upon the basic flow of the film. What might be said is that the "historical-materialist" elements are effectively incorporated into, and subordinated to, the more general use of art cinema conventions. This, in turn, has a consequence for the kind of politics which the film is then able to deliver.

Conventions are not, of course, neutral, and both permit and constrain what may be said within them. The conventions of the art film in this respect tend to encourage meanings associated with the themes of "alienation", communication breakdown, uncertainty and emotional discontent, which are themselves conceived in primarily psychological, rather than social, terms. As such, the conventions of the art film are not necessarily congenial to the political filmmaker concerned with social and political considerations. To this extent, the conventions employed by *Fatherland* work against its political objectives, and its apparent concern with the limits of freedom in both the East and the West tends to become subordinate to a more general, more existential sense of malaise. Thus, while Drittemann may contain elements of the "typical" hero characteristic of the historical-materialist film (his name translates as "third man" – in suggestion perhaps of a third politics between Stalinism and capitalism), his predicament is primarily communicated in terms of personal and psychological unease. This becomes more so once the plot moves to England and Klaus is almost exclusively preoccupied with the search for his father. Again, the father's revelations have emblematic value (given his successive involvement with the Communists, Nazis and Americans), but the film's final focus on his son on his own with some session men tends to add to the sense of melancholia and isolation which much of the film has communicated.

Loach himself has acknowledged how "damaging" the ending is.[19] The original intention was to film Drittemann at a peace concert amidst a large crowd, and so communicate his involvement in a larger movement. Undoubtedly, this would have tempered the film's pessimism, but it would not have overridden what had preceded. Drittemann has been isolated throughout the film (reaching no real rapport with Emma, and choosing not to reveal his identity to his father who mistakes him for a Stasi), and he has never successfully understood the powers which are arraigned against him.[20] On arriving in the West, he is accused by Lucy of paranoia, and then again in England when she phones him. But what the film appears to indicate is that this paranoia is warranted. Klaus is followed not only in West Berlin, but also in England, where his phone calls are monitored and he apparently leads his pursuers to his father (who dies in mysterious circumstances). However, the precise nature of his pursuers – or "they", as Drittemann refers to them – is never revealed. What the film suggests is a vague sense of conspiracy and hidden power stretching back to Stalin's Russia, Hitler's Germany and Roosevelt's America. For Loach, the film is concerned with "the unfreedom of the West that arises out of the economic system".[21] However, this is not an analysis which the film actually provides. As a result of its narrative and stylistic conventions (ambiguous, episodic plot; psychologically introspective and troubled hero; fusion of realist and modernist techniques) and the mood of melancholia and paranoia which results, the film is quite vague in its diagnosis of the economic and social ills of the West (a mixture of conspiracy and, as in the belaboured party scene, straightforward "decadence"). Ironically, it is a reliance upon a vague sense of conspiracy which is also evident in the otherwise quite different *Hidden Agenda*.

Hidden Agenda is a political thriller (written by one of Loach's regular collaborators, Jim Allen) which sets out to investigate events both in Northern Ireland (the question of a "shoot-to-kill" policy in the early 1980s) and in Britain (the "dirty tricks" campaigns of the security services during the 1970s). The conflict in Northern Ireland is a topic which most filmmakers have preferred to avoid. Those few films which have tackled this complex subject, such as *Angel* (1982) and *Cal* (1984), have successfully hammered home the destructive consequences of the "Troubles", but have shed little light on the motivations and causes which have sustained the violence.[22] With its more overt political concerns and readiness to ask uncomfortable questions about the role of the security services in both Britain and Northern Ireland, there can be little doubt that *Hidden Agenda* represents a serious attempt to engage with the situation in Northern Ireland. Nevertheless, the way that it does so is not without its problems.

As with *Fatherland*, these problems relate to the formal conventions which the film adopts, and their suitability for the expression of political ideas. During the 1980s, political thrillers, such as *Defence of the Realm* (1985) and the two television series, *Edge of Darkness* (1985) and *A Very British Coup* (1988), proved sufficiently popular for the BBC arts programme, *The Late Show* (11 March 1991) to declare that "the conspiracy drama" had provided the "perfect form" for 1980s writers. However, while there can be no doubt that the work being referred to was both impressive and important, the political thriller format was not necessarily as "perfect" as this comment would have it. For at least one critic, *Hidden Agenda* represents the type of "political thriller...that might have been made by Costa-Gavros [sic]", and, by referring to the debates which initially surrounded his films, it is possible to identify some of the relevant issues.[23]

The background to "the Costa-Gavras debate" was the worldwide social and political upheavals of the 1960s, when it was only to be expected that questions regarding what political role films could perform would come to the forefront.[24] In common with the realism debate with which it was associated, the central issue concerned the possibility of making a radical film employing conventional cinematic forms. Two directors, in particular, seemed to crystallise the choices at hand. On the one hand, the films of Jean-Luc Godard, especially from *La Chinoise* (1967) onwards, demonstrated an insistence on the need for revolutionary messages (or content) to be accompanied by an appropriate revolutionary form, and were characterised by a deliberate abandonment of the traditional Hollywood conventions of linear narrative, individual, psychologically-rounded characters, and a convincing dramatic illusion (or "classic realism"). On the other hand, the films of Costa-Gavras, beginning with his exposé of political assassination, *Z* (1968), exemplified a model of political filmmaking which sought to bend mainstream Hollywood conventions to radical political ends. In doing so, they attempted to "sugar the pill" of radical politics with the "entertainment" provided by the conventions of the thriller. For supporters of political thrillers, their great strength was their ability both to reach and to maintain the interest of an audience who would normally be turned off by politics; for their detractors, the weakness of such films was that their use of popular forms inevitably diluted or compromised their capacity to be genuinely politically radical and to stimulate active political thought. From this point of view, radical political purposes were more likely to be bent to the ends of mainstream Hollywood than vice versa.

What critics of political thrillers highlighted was how the use of the general conventions of narrative and realism characteristic of classical Hollywood, and of the specific conventions characteristic of the crime story or thriller would, by their nature, encourage certain types of political perspectives and discourage others. Hollywood's narrative conventions characteristically encourage explanations of social realities in individual and psychological terms, rather than economic and political ones, while the conventions of realism, with their requirement of a convincing (or "realistic") dramatic illusion, not only highlight observable, surface realities at the expense of possibly more fundamental underlying ones, but also attach a greater significance to interpersonal relations than to social, economic and political structures.[25] Moreover, it is because of these tendencies, implicit in the conventions of Hollywood's narrative realism, that political thrillers so often gravitate towards conspiracy theory or, as Kim Newman drolly observes of US thrillers of the 1970s, the view that society and government are run according to "the same principles as the coven in *Rosemary's Baby*".[26] Conspiratorial actions can be seen and dramatised (as in *Hidden Agenda*, when a senior Tory politician and senior member of MI5 are brought together to admit what they have done) in a way that underlying social and economic forces cannot within the conventions of narrative and realism. As a result, "conspiracy" becomes the preferred form of "explanation" for how power is exercised in society, and how events are to be accounted for. In *Days of Hope*, Loach and Allen presented the failure of the British 1926 General Strike as simply the result of individual treachery on the part of Labour and trade union leaders; in *Hidden Agenda*, no less than two conspiracies are unveiled – both the conspiracy to pervert the course of justice by the security services in Northern Ireland in the early 1980s, and the conspiracy on the part of a small group of businessmen, security personnel and politicians (led by a thinly disguised Airey Neave) to overthrow a Labour government and replace Edward Heath with Margaret Thatcher as leader of the Conservatives in Britain in the 1970s.

To be fair to the makers of the film, they appear – on the basis of the revelations of Colin Wallace (who read the script), Fred Holroyd (who acted as adviser to the film) and the magazine, *Lobster* – to be convinced of the evidence for conspiracy in 1970s Britain.[27] Moreover, there is undoubtedly a case to be answered. Conspiracy, nevertheless, provides a singularly problematic basis for political analysis and explanation, and is certainly of little value in helping us to understand the crisis of social democracy and labourism which occurred during the 1970s, and the subsequent rise to power of the New Right. According to Malcolm, "the film seems almost ludicrously committed to a view of things that could only be sustained by the most paranoid of Marxists".[28] On the contrary, it seems to me that the underlying viewpoint of the film is fundamentally a liberal one, insofar as it places such stress on the capacity of strong individuals to will change and alter events almost outside of history. What is lacking is some sense of the context in which such actions occurred and the constraints imposed upon them. The rise of the New Right was not simply willed or manufactured, but grew out of a complex set of economic, political and ideological circumstances.[29] Conspiracy would, at most, have been a response to these circumstances, just as the likelihood of its success would have depended upon them. In this respect, conspiracy theory has the virtue of neatness, but its cost is the loss of genuine social and political complexity.

The tendency towards personalisation which is encouraged by the conventions of narrative realism is reinforced by the specific properties of the crime thriller, especially when it is structured around the investigation of an individual detective and his quest to reveal, or make visible, the truth behind a crime or enigma. Moreover, as a number of critics have suggested, the detective story formula is also characteristically a conservative one.[30] It depends upon the superior powers (either intellectual or physical) of an individual investigator (who is often a loner) and, in doing so, tends to prefer the values of individualism to those of the community. In addition, the conventional narrative movement towards a solution of the crime will encourage both an identification with the forces of "law and order" (even when the investigator is not actually a member of the police), and a general confidence in the ability of the current social set-up to triumph over injustice and right wrongs (which are then characteristically identified as the responsibility of an isolated or atypical individual, rather than of social institutions or political regimes). It is partly in recognition of these problems that political thrillers have attempted to blunt the affirmative and socially conservative impulses of the crime story by stressing the limitations of the individual detective hero and the difficulties of actually getting to the truth. Thus, the investigator may prove unable to solve the crime due to the complexity and deviousness of the forces confronting him, or he may indeed succeed in solving the mystery but then find himself unable to do anything about it – the most paranoid example of which is undoubtedly *The Parallax View* (1974), in which Warren Beatty's reporter uncovers the inevitable political conspiracy, but is then himself assassinated. *Hidden Agenda* adopts a similar, if less dramatic, strategy. CID Inspector Kerrigan (Brian Cox), loosely modelled on John Stalker, is brought from England to Northern Ireland to investigate the murder of Paul

Sullivan (Brad Dourif), an American lawyer who was working for the League for Civil Liberties.[31] He uncovers evidence of both a shoot-to-kill policy and a conspiracy to overthrow a democratically elected Labour government, but is unable to do anything about it, having been effectively silenced by the military and political forces arraigned against him. Admittedly, Ingrid (Frances McDormand), Paul's widow, is still in possession, at the film's end, of an incriminating tape which Harris (Maurice Roëves), the renegade Special Branch officer, has provided. However, given that the film has already made clear that the tape will lack credibility without Harris (whom we now know to be dead at the hands of the security services), the film's ending remains resolutely pessimistic.

While such an ending avoids glib optimism about the prospect of social reform, the film's negative inflection of the thriller format has its limitations, not only projecting the paranoia characteristic of the political thriller genre, but also engendering a sense of powerlessness about the possibilities for social and political change ("You can't win against these people", Kerrigan informs Ingrid). Ironically, Loach himself has criticised the limited politics of his own *Cathy Come Home* (1966) on precisely these grounds. "It tried to make people concerned about a problem", he observes, "but it gave them no indication of how they might do anything about it".[32] However, if this is the case with *Cathy Come Home*'s treatment of homelessness, it seems even more so of *Hidden Agenda*'s grim brew of conspiracy and paranoia. For, if *Cathy Come Home* failed to offer solutions and simply rested upon the hope that, by exposing social ills, it could do some good, *Hidden Agenda* not only offers no solutions, but also, given its conviction that it is virtually impossible to make the security services democratically accountable, seems even to cast doubt upon the political value of its revelations. From this point of view, one possible explanation for the popularity of the political thriller with film and television producers during the 1980s was the way in which it allowed expression of the sense of political impotence felt by liberals and the Left during this period (the grafted-on attempts at optimism of *Defence of the Realm* and *A Very British Coup* notwithstanding).

This concern about the absence of any perspective for political change is linked to the final criticism which has traditionally been directed at the political thriller. For, whatever the strengths and weaknesses of the actual message which the political thriller succeeds in communicating, it is still one that is, so to speak, "pre-digested". That is to say, opponents of the political thriller have argued that, by virtue of a reliance upon individual characters and stars with whom we identify, and upon the tightly structured patterns of narrative suspense which engage us emotionally rather than intellectually, the political thriller "makes up our minds for us". It may challenge, as

Hidden Agenda does, the prevailing ideologies of society, but it does so by employing the same emotional patterns of involvement as films which offer the contrary view, and hence fails to encourage audiences to engage critically with political ideas. To some extent, this is true of *Hidden Agenda*, which is generally content to present us with an interpretation of events which we can either take or leave, rather than engage us in active political dialogue.[33] It does make some attempt, however, to meet this type of complaint. While, in comparison to Loach's earlier work, the film employs relatively well-known actors, it seeks to encourage identification less with individual characters than with their situation. Thus, the "honest cop" Kerrigan represents more of a "type" than a fully fleshed-out hero. In the same way, by staging the killing of Paul early in the film, the reliance of the narrative on delayed revelations and the mechanics of suspense is kept to a minimum. However, such tactics tend simply to subdue, rather than subvert, the thriller elements, with the result that *Hidden Agenda* ends up falling between two stools, offering neither the narrative energy and visual expressiveness of the best thrillers, nor the "authenticity" and distance from conventional dramatics which are the hallmark of Loach's earlier work.

This problem is also evident in the film's use of visual imagery. The cinematic thriller is, in origins, a North American genre which has evolved an elaborate iconography of dress, objects (such as cars and guns) and settings, often in relation to specific places (New York and Los Angeles, for example). This iconography is not, of course, inanimate, but cues many of the genre's characteristic meanings. Thus, it is not always easy simply to transplant the thriller to a novel environment (as thrillers set amidst the streets and traffic of London have often discovered to their cost). In the case of *Hidden Agenda*, the attempt to find the right iconography for a thriller set in Belfast leads it towards the most typical images of the "Troubles": an Orange band; murals; a cemetery; religious icons; and security forces on the streets. The problem with this is that, while such images clearly conform to the thriller's demands for the dramatic and striking, and also cue an audience (to the "universe" of the "Troubles") in the way that thriller icons conventionally do, they nevertheless do so only by virtue of being the most obvious and, indeed, clichéd of images. Thus, a film which, at the level of manifest content, seeks to challenge dominant perceptions of the "Troubles" actually reinforces them at the level of formal imagery. In this respect, the thriller format has encouraged too easy an acceptance of conventional ways of depicting the city and hence the "Troubles", but at the expense of the freshness of observation which might normally have been expected of Loach's documentary realism.

It may be no coincidence, therefore, that Loach's next film

abandons his experiments with art cinema and the political thriller to return to more familiar territory and techniques. *Riff-Raff* takes as its subject the lives of ordinary people, struggling to survive in the late-Thatcher era. Indeed, in a kind of metaphor for the period, a group of labourers (some themselves homeless) convert a disused hospital into luxury apartments. The plot itself is loose and episodic, often devoting time to apparently incidental business (such as the funeral sequence). In style and approach, the film also strives for the appearance of documentary accuracy. The script was by Bill Jesse, based on his own experiences on building sites. The cast were expected to have worked on a building site, and were encouraged, through improvisations, to bring their own experiences to bear upon their performances. The film was shot on a real building site and in a style designed not to interfere with the action.

This style is not, however, straightforwardly "invisible". As John Caughie suggests, it is the "classic realist" film which "depends to a greater or lesser extent on the illusion of unmediated vision". Documentary drama, on the other hand, "operates a rhetoric of mediated style which is clearly marked, but which has a prior association with truth and neutrality" by virtue of its use of techniques associated with documentary.[34] In this respect, the special feature of documentary realism is its use of "the documentary look". Thus, whereas "classic realism" engages the spectator in a system of "dramatic" looks between characters through the use of such techniques as reverse-field cutting, eyeline matches and point-of-view shots, the documentary look is more observational, and looks at, rather than looks with, those in front of the camera. It is this blend of dramatic and documentary looks which is also a feature of *Riff-Raff*.

However, if *Riff-Raff* does seek to explore contemporary social problems through the use of documentary drama methods, the issue remains as to how successful it is as a political film. The strength of the form, as Caughie suggests, is simply its ability to *show*, and give testimony to, experiences which are not traditionally dignified with cinematic representation. For Loach, this is possibly the main purpose of the film: to present the lives of "people who get by on the margins", and to give recognition to both their plight and their fortitude.[35] However, as has already been noted, the question traditionally raised in relation to this realist mode of presentation is its ability to move beyond observable realities and to provide a more analytic or explanatory perspective. One solution, often resorted to by realism, is that a character is required to state verbally the film's preferred explanation of the situation or issue at hand. The danger of this, however, is that the very conventions of the film, which rely upon the creation of a convincing dramatic illusion or sense of "authenticity", risk being ruptured by virtue of the implausibility of the speeches which characters have to make in order for the film's politics to emerge clearly. In *Riff-Raff*, it is the character of Larry (Ricky Tomlinson) who is allocated this role, making a speech, for example, to his fellow workers about the iniquity of housing policy under Thatcher's government. In this case, the film is probably able to contain the potential strain placed upon its "authenticity". Larry is linked to both union activism and Militant politics, and his speeches are the source of humour to his colleagues ("he only asked for a fucking squat", remonstrates a fellow Liverpudlian in the face of Larry's anti-Thatcherite sermonising). Indeed, what the film successfully demonstrates is that the resistance to change comes not only from ruthless, cost-cutting employers (who eventually sack Larry), but also from the workers themselves, who generally lack the will and the means to fight back. When they do, as in the final arson attack, it is this which strains plausibility, signifying an unprepared-for action which goes against the grain of what has preceded – a sort of grafting-on of defiance which does not emerge "naturally" from the drama.

The film also has some difficulty in welding together the personal and political aspects of its drama. For Loach, the benefit of combining fictional and documentary methods is the ability to move between private and public worlds: "to get the insights into personal relationships and experiences that you can get through fiction, and yet to set them in a firm, concrete context".[36] In *Riff-Raff*, this twin focus is particularly evident in the combination of the scenes at the building site with those concerning the evolving relationship between the young Glaswegian, Stevie (Robert Carlyle), and his would-be singer girlfriend, Susie (Emer McCourt). For Caughie, there is always a risk involved in this mix of documentary and drama, public and private. As he explains, "though documentary drama within its naturalist project wishes to be about the community and the social environment, there is always the risk that the balance will fail, the dramatic narrative will impose its resolutions on the documentary disorder, and the drama will end up being about the privileged, centred individuals".[37] In the case of *Riff-Raff*, however, it is less that the balance swings too much in favour of the private, personal drama (although certainly a rather excessive amount of time is devoted to it, given the limited insights which it provides) than that the personal drama lacks a clear sense of relationship to the communal drama. As one critic complained, the film "builds a central relationship round, but not from, the scattered bricks of a communal experience".[38] Therefore, while there are undoubtedly scenes which do link private emotion with communal solidarity (Susan's singing of "With a Little Help from My Friends" following Larry's reproach to a club audience; the builders' applauding of the couple's embrace), the film does nevertheless tend to keep separate the "political" world of work from the private sphere of relationships and romance. In this respect, the relationship between the couple does not really connect with the "concrete context" of work, and often appears to be set in opposition to it. The effect of this, as Sheila Johnston suggests, is problematic. Thus, while "the romantic relationship" of the young couple is presented as "a nagging, dead-end one", "the male bonding" provided by Stevie's fellow workers is seen as "energising and supportive".[39] In this respect, Loach's return to the conventions of documentary realism may have brought with it a too clear-cut version of class politics. While this has the undoubted virtue of drawing attention to the severe economic divisions which continue to be a characteristic of British society (and which significantly widened during the Thatcher years), it may also be at the expense of an ability to deal adequately with other social divisions, such as those of sex and ethnicity, and the ways that these may be seen to complicate a basic class perspective.

Nevertheless, there can be no doubt that *Riff-Raff* did strike a chord when released, and that it was welcomed by many for its revivification of political filmmaking in Britain.[40] What this suggests is that the significance of such films cannot be viewed in isolation or in purely "textualist" terms. One of the weaknesses of "the realism debate" and of its variants such as the political thriller debate, was that it tended to be conducted in relation to the textual properties of films, independent of the context in which such films were produced and consumed. However, with the waning of 1960s and 1970s radicalism, and a corresponding shift away from both political and artistic vanguardism, it is evident that support for the "revolutionary text" (as exemplified by the work of, for example, Godard) has also declined. At the same time, there has been much greater tolerance (and, given the experiences of the 1980s, even gratitude) amongst the Left for the strategies of the political thriller and documentary drama, despite the often quite limited politics which they can provide. In the case of documentary realism, it might also be the case that it is precisely its straightforwardness and simplicity which has made it attractive in a culture increasingly dominated by the significatory playfulness (and very often emptiness) of postmodern culture. Thus, for Michael Eaton, the "comeback of British realism", signalled by the work of Ken Loach and Mike Leigh in the early 1990s, represents not only "a return to a particular style", but also "a return to value".[41]

In revisiting some of the criticisms of realism and the political thriller, it should be clear that I am doing so from a changed political context, and that I am not therefore advocating any return to the Godardian or "counter-cinema" model of political filmmaking. Indeed, two major shortcomings of the traditional critique of realism was its characteristic reliance on crude binary oppositions (*either* narrative realism *or* the revolutionary avant-garde; *either* Costa-Gavras *or*

Godard) and general tendency to assume that certain aesthetic strategies (primarily Brechtian) would almost necessarily deliver a radical politics. It is evident that the unitary model of political cinema which underpinned such formulations is inadequate, and that changed political circumstances now require more diverse forms of political filmmaking. It is for this reason that the revival of the concept of "third cinema" has also been helpful.[42]

The concept of third cinema was initially employed by the Argentinian filmmakers, Fernando Solanas and Octavio Getino, to identify an emergent political cinema which was distinct from both mainstream Hollywood (first cinema) and European "art" cinema (second cinema). Current usage of the term has continued to emphasise third cinema's original commitment to political explanation and dialogue, but has also recognised that this commitment cannot be fulfilled by any pregiven artistic recipes. As Paul Willemen has stated, third cinema is not only engaged in the creation of "new, politically... (and)...cinematically illuminating types of filmic discourse", but also is aware of "the historical variability of the necessary aesthetic strategies to be adopted".[43] What artistic means are appropriate to third cinema, therefore, will vary according to the social, political and cultural contexts in which it is produced and to which it is addressed. The virtue of third cinema in this respect is that, unlike models of counter-cinema, it does not prescribe one "correct" way of making political cinema which is universally applicable, but recognises the need for aesthetic diversity and a sensitivity to place, and to social and cultural specifics. In doing so, it also insists upon the importance of constantly rethinking and reworking (but not necessarily overthrowing) traditional artistic models (including those of both Hollywood and the avant-garde) if cinema is to continue to be critically lucid and politically relevant. The great strength of Loach's work has been, with some exceptions, its rootedness in a specific social context, and its nuanced relationship to both first and second cinemas. However, Loach's work at the end of the 1980s and start of the 1990s does also suggest that it may have been too dependent upon pregiven aesthetic recipes, and, as a result, failed to re-imagine, in a way which was entirely successful, a political cinema appropriate to the changed circumstances of the period. Loach is a formidable filmmaker whose continuing commitment to using film for political purposes places him in an uniquely important position in British cinema. As such, his work demands both attention and respect. However, precisely because he is such a significant filmmaker, it is important not simply to celebrate his achievements, which are considerable, but also to enter into dialogue with his work and engage with the issues which it raises.

Notes

[1] Quoted in Paul Kerr, "The Complete Ken Loach", *Stills* 27 (May-June 1986): 148.

[2] See Julian Petley, "Union Blues", *Stills* 14 (November 1984): 44-47.

[3] Loach on *The South Bank Show*, LWT, 3 October 1993.

[4] Kerr: 148.

[5] Ibid. In the period 1979-82, unemployment in Britain more than doubled, reaching well over three million. See Stephen Edgell and Vic Duke, *A Measure of Thatcherism: A Sociology of Britain* (London: HarperCollins, 1991).

[6] Kerr: 148.

[7] See, in particular, Colin MacCabe, "Realism and the Cinema: Notes on some Brechtian theses", *Screen* 15: 2 (summer 1974): 7-27; Colin McArthur, "Days of Hope", *Screen* 16: 4 (winter 1975/76): 139-144; and Colin MacCabe, "Days of Hope – A response to Colin McArthur", *Screen* 17: 1 (spring 1976): 98-101. The relationship of Loach's work to "realism" is not straightforward. MacCabe's critique is of the "classic realism" or "illusionism", characteristic of mainstream Hollywood, and, as such, applies to films which are often not regarded as "realistic" (such as *The Wizard of Oz*). MacCabe discusses *Cathy Come Home* as a socially "progressive" form of classic realism which simply challenges dominant discourses at the level of content. John Caughie, however, distinguishes Loach's work from classic realism in terms of its use of naturalist and documentary techniques; see John Caughie, "Progressive Television and Documentary Drama", *Screen* 21: 3 (1980): 9-35. For a recent reassessment of the realism debate, see Christopher Williams, "After the classic, the classical and ideology: the differences of realism", *Screen* 35: 3 (1994): 275-292.

[8] See Richard Lewis, "Review of the UK Film Industry: Report to BSAC", mimeo (London: British Screen Advisory Council, 1990).

[9] *Screen Digest* April 1992: 82.

[10] The casting of Fabienne Babe as Emma, the French Nazi-hunter, provides a clear example of the compromises struck in the interests of co-production. The original character was Dutch, and the casting of Babe adds an element not only of confusion to the plot, but also of unintelligibility, given that the French actress's command of English is so poor. This is particularly unfortunate insofar as Trevor Griffiths' script gives much more weight to the dialogue than would be characteristic of most of Loach's other work. For a discussion of the film's production by Trevor Griffiths, see Simon Banner, "Drittemann, poor man", *The Guardian* 26 March 1987: 13. His original screenplay has also been published; see Trevor Griffiths, *Fatherland* (London; Boston: Faber and Faber, 1987).

[11] Vincent Porter, "European co-productions: aesthetic and cultural implications", *Journal of Area Studies* 12 (autumn 1985): 7.

[12] The film, in this respect, is somewhat at odds with Griffiths' screenplay which seeks to incorporate the traditional images of Cambridge into what he describes as "an essential imagery of a rotten Britain": "King's College Chapel choristers progressing down the street; skins on the town; punks at corners; paired police; NF slogans; dole queues; banks, churches; bad TV in pubs; dossers and dogs picking a decorous way through the Bentleys and Mercedes". See Griffiths: 53.

[13] Derek Malcolm, "Loach's song for Europe", *The Guardian* 4 September 1986: 11.

[14] David Bordwell, *Narration in the Fiction Film* (London: Methuen, 1985): 205-213.

[15] Ibid: 208.

[16] Loach's early television work was influenced by the anti-naturalistic polemics of Troy Kennedy Martin and John McGrath, who scripted the six-part series, *Diary of a Young Man*, three episodes of which Loach directed in 1964. However, as Kerr suggests, Loach's career has largely been characterised by "a gradual shedding" of the "non-naturalist devices" which were a feature of his early work. See Kerr: 145.

[17] According to John Tulloch, Griffiths' intention was to use the "cool" conventions of the European art film, but to invest them with greater social and political "matter". He also indicates how Griffiths' screenplay was intended as a kind of response to Milan Kundera's *The Book of Laughter and Forgetting*. See John Tulloch, *Television Drama: Agency, audience and myth* (London; New York: Routledge, 1990): 152-165.

[18] Bordwell: 234-273. For Bordwell, the most pertinent characteristics of "historical-materialist" film are the refusal of psychologically-defined, individually-centred plots, an emphasis upon typicality and historical reference, and overt and politically-conscious narrational strategies.

[19] Quoted in Gavin Smith, "Voice in the Dark", *Film Comment* 24: 2 (March-April 1988): 42.

[20] Drittemann's relationships with women in the film are significantly different from the relationships described in the screenplay, where Drittemann makes love to his ex-wife before leaving East Berlin, has sex with Lucy, and evolves an uneasy "comradeship" with Emma. According to Tulloch (163), the lovemaking scenes were shot by Loach but then omitted "on the grounds of naturalistic plausibility". For Tulloch, this is symptomatic of a more general tension within the film between the "critical realism", or interpretive approach, of Griffiths and the "naturalism", or observational approach, of Loach.

[21] Quoted in *Stills* December 1985/January 1986: 33.

[22] For a discussion of these films and their relationship to an ongoing tradition of representing the "Troubles", see my analysis, "Images of Violence" in Kevin Rockett, Luke Gibbons and John Hill, *Cinema and Ireland* (London: Routledge, 1988): 147-193. An earlier discussion of *Hidden*

Agenda appeared as "Hidden Agenda: Politics and the Thriller", *Circa* 57 (May-June 1991): 36-41.

23   Derek Malcolm, "The plot thickened", *The Guardian* 17 May 1990: 27.

24   For an influential account of the Costa-Gavras debate, see Guy Hennebelle, "Z Movies or What Hath Costa-Gavras Wrought?", *Cineaste* 6: 2 (1974): 28-31. For a retrospective overview, see John J Michalczyk, *Costa-Gavras: The Political Fiction Film* (London; Toronto: Associated University Presses, 1984): especially chapter 1.

25   For a fuller discussion of these matters, see my "Narrative and Realism", in *Sex, Class and Realism: British Cinema 1956-1963* (London: British Film Institute, 1986): 53-66.

26   *Nightmare Movies: A Critical History of the Horror Film, 1968-88* (London: Bloomsbury, 1988): 79.

27   Colin Wallace (who is loosely the model for Harris in the film) and Fred Holroyd were Army Intelligence officers who subsequently made allegations of "dirty tricks" against the security forces in Northern Ireland. See Paul Foot, *Who Framed Colin Wallace?* (London: Macmillan, 1989). Jim Allen acknowledges his debt to *Lobster* in an interview: Patsy Murphy and Johnny Gogan, "In the Name of the Law", *Film Base News* 19 (September/October 1990): 13-17.

28   Malcolm (1990): 27.

29   For a discussion of these circumstances and an indication of their complexity, see Andrew Gamble, *The Free Economy and the Strong State: The Politics of Thatcherism* (London: Macmillan Education, 1988); Stuart Hall, *The Hard Road to Renewal: Thatcherism and the Crisis of the Left* (London; New York: Verso, 1988); and Bob Jessop, Kevin Bonnett, Simon Bromley and Tom Ling, *Thatcherism: A Tale of Two Nations* (Oxford: Polity Press, 1988).

30   For a trenchant critique of the social conservatism of the crime story, see Ernest Mandel, *Delightful Murder: A social history of the crime story* (London; Sydney: Pluto Press, 1984).

31   John Stalker was the Deputy Chief Constable of the Greater Manchester Police Force who was asked to undertake an enquiry into the deaths, at the hands of the Royal Ulster Constabulary, of six men in Northern Ireland in late-1982. Stalker was removed, in controversial circumstances, from the case before his report was completed. For further details, see John Stalker, *Stalker* (London: Harrap, 1988) and Peter Taylor, *Stalker: The Search for the Truth* (London; Boston: Faber and Faber, 1987).

32   Quoted in Kerr: 146.

33   One of the weaknesses of the political thriller debate was its tendency to assume that realism necessarily implied a "spectator-position", and that audience response, or "ideological effect", could simply be read off the text. In contrast, more recent work in media studies has stressed the creativity

and interpretive licence enjoyed by media audiences. However, while it is evident that texts cannot simply determine audience response, it is still appropriate to suggest that some aesthetic strategies are more likely than others to engender a dialogue with audiences.

[34] Caughie: 27. In identifying Loach with documentary drama, Caughie is, in effect, distinguishing documentary drama from drama documentary. Drama documentary, in this respect, derives its "documentariness" from its content, which is based upon real people and events. Documentary drama, on the other hand, achieves its "documentariness" on the basis of its style and formal techniques. Thus, while Loach's films have only rarely dramatised actual events (as in *Ladybird Ladybird* [1994]), they have characteristically aimed to provide a documentary look (even though the methods used to achieve this may involve careful planning and rehearsal). For discussion of the issues raised by the mixing of drama and documentary, see Andrew Goodwin, Paul Kerr and Ian Macdonald (eds), *Drama-Documentary* (London: British Film Institute, 1983).

[35] Annalena McAfee, "Hard labour for tragic Bill", *Evening Standard* 20 June 1991: 35. In her discussion of realism, Terry Lovell also suggests how the pleasure of a text may be grounded in "pleasures of an essentially public and social kind" such as "pleasures of common experiences...solidarity... and...a sense of identity and community" (*Pictures of Reality: Aesthetics, Politics, Pleasure* [London: British Film Institute, 1980]: 95). It is some of these pleasures which *Riff-Raff* also appears to invite.

[36] Kerr: 146.

[37] Caughie: 29-30.

[38] David Wilson, "Riff-Raff", *Sight and Sound* 1: 1 (May 1991): 61.

[39] Sheila Johnston, "Another brick in the wall", *The Independent* 19 April 1991: 18.

[40] According to Lizzie Francke, "[i]f the British political film might have seemed [to] have lost its way, Loach brings it back home" (*City Limits* 18 April 1991: 24). Gilbert Adair also praised Loach's success in reviving political filmmaking but tended to confirm the argument of this article by describing *Riff-Raff* as "the finest mainstream 'liberal movie'" he had seen in recent years ("If you don't buy the politics, we'll shoot the movie", *The Guardian* 27 February 1992: 22).

[41] Michael Eaton, "Not a Piccadilly actor in sight", *Sight and Sound* 3: 12 (December 1993): 32.

[42] See Jim Pines and Paul Willemen (eds), *Questions of Third Cinema* (London: British Film Institute, 1989).

[43] Paul Willemen, "The Third Cinema Question: Notes and Reflections", in ibid: 4, 7.

Saturn's feast, Loach's Spain: *Land and Freedom* as filmed history

Patrick MacFadden

There was reason to fear that the Revolution would, like Saturn, devour all of its children in turn. (Pierre Vergniaud, *Girondin*)[1]

History, as Fredric Jameson has remarked, "is what hurts".[2] No more poignant example can be found than in Spain. The English war correspondent Noël Monks recalls the aftermath of Guernica, destroyed by Hitler's bombs on 26 April 1937:

> [W]hen the grim story was told to the world, Franco was going to brand these shocked, homeless people as liars. So-called British experts were going to come to Guernica, weeks afterwards, when the smell of burnt human flesh had been replaced by petrol dumped here and there among the ruins by Mola's [Franco's general] men, and deliver pompous judgements: 'Guernica was set on fire wilfully by the Reds.'[3]

Franco's army marched into Barcelona on 26 January 1939. The French and British governments recognised his regime on 27 January. The war was over. No peace terms were granted by the victorious Fascists, with Franco taking time out to denounce "the eternal Jew – whom nobody wants because they are a communist horde which advances".[4]

For scriptwriter Jim Allen, the issue is straightforward. The Communist parties knew "that if a democratic revolution had succeeded in Spain then Stalin's days were numbered. It was the last thing he wanted because then the dictatorship in Russia would not have been tolerated".[5] This broadly coincides with the view held by Isaac Deutscher:

> The working classes, armed for the defence of the Republican Government, might attempt to establish a proletarian dictatorship, Communist or Anarcho-Communist. The landless peasants, in a country as feudal as old Russia, might press for agrarian revolution. But if Spain were to have its 'October', western Europe would be split even more sharply; and the chances of agreement between Russia and the west would be even more slender.[6]

History written in the subjunctive mood is quite properly grounds for intelligent speculation, and perhaps one should not ask for much else. The cautionary note struck by the Spanish writer, José Bergamín, is relevant here: "When I testified to the truth, I put my hand to the flame, and I burnt myself; for the truth was not my hand, it was the flame".[7]

Nevertheless, Loach's *Land and Freedom* (1995) is a passionate re-enactment of the story of people as the objects of history – this time as pawns in a game, the main rule of which is that everyone has his reasons. The fragmented incoherence of the contemporary European Left is on display in the French-financed film by the Yugoslav-born Stanislav Stanojević, *Illustres Inconnus* (1985) – *Notorious Nobodies* in its English-language release, but more aptly translated as "Distinguished Unknowns". Its disillusioned protagonist declares: "Modern states are murderers...Political parties are grave diggers... schools of thought merely encourage idiocy, blindness. In such conditions, the only possibility is individual action". The film bears a commendation from Costa-Gavras.

In this view, history is a hair shirt, Clio an inveterate attender at wakes, the owl of Minerva a permanent screech. It is a view that perhaps can only be challenged by alternative readings *à la longue durée*: "And yet, the Spanish Civil War anticipated and prepared the shape of the forces which were, within a few years of Franco's victory, to destroy fascism. It anticipated the politics of the Second World War, that unique alliance of national fronts ranging from patriotic conservatives to social revolutionaries, for the defeat of the national enemy, and simultaneously for social regeneration".[8]

* * *

"In this film more than any you have to be painstakingly accurate and have all your facts correct and at the same time make a very heavy subject entertaining" (Jim Allen).[9] Apart from his own artistic and political investment, he echoes here what most people seem to feel: that we make more demands on the historical film than on any other. Quite why this is so is a matter of some debate, as is the related question of whether we ought to be doing anything of the sort. Nor is it certain that people always did so in relation to the stories they hear or the stories they tell. It seems unlikely that contemporary audiences would meekly accept the version of *Giovanna D'Arco* offered by Verdi at La Scala in 1845: Joan escapes from the English, dies with her standard bravely in hand, with the voices of angels as her accompaniment. Does this matter, except that the English would be left with no French witch, Shaw no play, and Honegger no stage-oratorio? Part of the answer is supplied by Allen himself:

145

It's got to be relevant today, otherwise it's meaningless, a historical tombstone. The film shows a group of people prepared to offer their lives for some big noble principles. It's a million miles from the cynical outlook on life. It's a great moral issue that is unfolding on that screen.[10]

In other words, we look to history, on the screen or on the page, to make sense out of the present. That goes some way towards explaining the heightened demands that attend filmic history.

It is predictable, therefore, that professional historians are even more likely to be dismayed when filmic history turns out to be something less than they had anticipated. Robert A Rosenstone's scholarly dissertation on the Lincoln Battalion of the International Brigades led him to an involvement with a documentary film on the subject, *The Good Fight* (Noel Buckner/Mary Dore/Sam Sills, 1983). In his account of this experience, he lists many of the ways in which the film differs from the historical record. Common sense would suggest that most of them spring from the ethnomethodology of documentary cinema: the colourful interviewee, the symbolic image, the heightened emotion and immediacy of documentary footage and actuality sound accompanied by an appropriate score, and so on. He sees documentary as suffering under "a double tyranny – which is to say an ideology – of the necessary image and perpetual movement".[11] Although it could be argued that commercial fiction film must also meet these demands – as well as the added bugbear, since it is inevitably headed for the small television screen, of endless close-ups.

But it is when he moves away from the constricting conventions of filmmaking that Rosenstone raises more complex matters. There is what he terms, in relation to this film about the Lincoln Brigade veterans, history as homage – "homage to a certain kind of commitment and to a tradition of activism, one in which the filmmakers clearly situate themselves. This desire to do homage is hardly a neutral factor. It underlies the aesthetic decisions that shape the film and helps to provide its structure, meaning, and message".[12] The overall result is that the format (of talking heads) "privileges memory (and nostalgia) rather than history...never asks questions of its witnesses, never comments upon their opinions, however wrong or inaccurate they may be".[13]

Whether these strictures apply to all such documentaries is open to question. Lanzmann's *Shoah* (1985) comes to mind. But what is not in doubt is that Rosenstone the historian is not prepared to assent to the proposition that *The Good Fight* is good history and that he thinks it should try harder so to be. His summary raises more questions than it settles: "they [the filmmakers] tended to make decisions on the basis not of some notion of written truth but of a filmic truth (or belief, or ideology), one which asserts that anything that cannot be explained in images, or which slows the relentless filmic pace of twenty-four frames a second, will destroy some larger truth by boring or losing the audience".[14] However, what that "larger truth" might be is not vouchsafed to us, and his parenthetical equation of truth with belief or ideology collapses all comment. In fairness to Rosenstone, he retrospectively sees his view at that time as being that of a "Dragnet historian".[15] Why this is a bad thing is left unexplained.

What happened in history is also the concern of Natalie Zemon Davis, the Harvard historian who collaborated with Buñuel's great screenwriter, Jean-Claude Carrière, on the film, *Le Retour de Martin Guerre* (*The Return of Martin Guerre*, 1982). Not surprisingly, she notes that the film, based on a story that had already been turned into a play, two novels and an operetta, did not comport with her historian's view of the 16th-century Basque country:

> At the same time, the film was departing from the historical record, and I found this troubling. The Basque background of the Guerres was sacrificed; rural Protestantism was ignored; and especially the double game of the wife and the judge's inner contradictions were softened. These changes may have helped to give the film the powerful simplicity that had allowed the Martin Guerre story to become a legend in the first place, but they also made it hard to explain what actually happened.[16]

Filmed history or the historical film is "a different way of telling about the past"[17] – as, of course, is balladry, epic or theatre. That we ask particular questions about cinematic accounts of history may be a tribute to the very concreteness and the apparent palpability of the image. We trust the camera because we want to trust ourselves. This insistence upon an unseverable relationship between filmed history and something outside the text is an irritant to some. In the course of a formidably acute interrogation of the famous Rodney King video, Frank P Tomasulo takes time out to warn of "the reemergence of the spectre of positivism that the film studies discipline had been trying to exorcise for years".[18] What is a good pastor to do? Clearly these sprightly demons are proving more resilient than the "discipline" had bargained for.

Could it be that the idea of the historical film is a flag of convenience? In a tautological sense, all stories – filmed or otherwise – are about the past. (What happened, or what might have happened – *Se una notte d'inverno un viaggiatore* (*If on a winter's night a traveller*, 1979) of Calvino sets the tone.) To interrogate historical truth through these films is ultimately unrewarding: a sphinx in wistful pursuit of a riddle, an irredeemably reified category.[19] But this is not to say that the facts of history are incapable of representation in the writing of filmic history:

> If the nature of the particles that make up physical reality is up for grabs in contemporary philosophical and scientific thought, then the concept of a once-lived reality in the past and its relation to historical representations is even more vexed. Yet the mere existence of questions and doubts does not prove the inherent falseness of the narrative form with its incorporation of causal language...We see no reason to conclude that because there is a gap between reality and its narration (its representation) the narration in some fundamental sense is inherently invalid. Just because narratives are human creations does not make them all equally fictitious or mythical.[20]

The authors refer here to the writing of history, but there is no overwhelming reason to suppose that their remarks should not apply equally to filmic history.

The conclusion, therefore, is that, since there is no *a priori* reason to dispute the relationship between historical fact and its representation, there is equally no need to demand that filmed history should be treated as if in need of some analytical version of affirmative action.[21] In any event, the Loach/Allen ventures seem never to have sought landfall on the wilder shores of poststructuralism.

* * *

Jaime Camino's documentary, *The Old Memory*, brings together the iconic Communist, Dolores Ibárurri, with other ageing combatants from the Civil War past: Catalanists, Socialists, anarcho-syndicalists, Trotskyists and Fascists. In the spirit of Welles' last completed work, *F for Fake* (1973), Camino juggles the interlocutor's questions and the interviewees' replies and comments; the addition of strategically placed documentary footage makes for a richly-textured complexity: memory, illusion, reality and political *parti pris* are implicitly contested and contestable, as, indeed, the film contests itself.[22] Displaying much more confidence, *Land and Freedom*[23] positions itself firmly in this troubled field.

David Carne is a young unemployed working-class man in Depression Liverpool. A member of the Communist Party of Great Britain (CPGB), he attends with his girlfriend (later his wife) a recruiting meeting addressed by a Spanish Republican militia man. David enlists, and sometime in 1936 is on a train headed for Barcelona, centre of the Revolution and capital of Catalonia. In the carriage, he meets other volunteers off to join the Partido Obrero de Unificación Marxista (POUM).[24] He proudly mentions his Party affiliations to his new comrades before joining up with them. "I'm not in the Communist Brigade", he later writes home to Kitty, "but it doesn't matter, we're fighting the same enemy".

It has been suggested that the character of David Carne is based on Stafford Cottman, a friend of Orwell in the POUM.[25] However, Cottman was a member of the British Young Communist League (YCL) and not, as such, a Party member. Given David's age and relative political immaturity, it would seem more fitting to have him in the YCL. In any event, it is unlikely that in 1936 a CPGB member would end up, no questions asked, in the POUM.[26] Orwell found his route to the POUM via its affiliate, the British Independent Labour Party (ILP).

David's first military experience is on a parade ground in Barcelona, where the fatuity of the drilling exercises is grimly frustrating. Maite, a young comrade, displaying the trade mark spontaneity of the anarchist, objects vociferously to this style of aimless regimentation and the exercises appear to be abandoned. (Perhaps prematurely: this "lack of training and discipline" on the part of the POUM is cited by a sympathetic historian as "indubitably among the principal reasons for General Franco's swift advance up the Tagus valley towards the Spanish capital".)[27] The figurative meanings set in train by Maite's intervention resonate throughout the film, inflecting and shaping its political theme.[28]

Together with Bernard, a French comrade, the American Gene Lawrence, Maite from the parade ground, Blanca, an anarchist fighting alongside her lover, Coogan, an Irish graduate of a five-year stretch in Manchester's Strangeways Prison ("for fighting the Brits"), David becomes part of a unit under the command of the *poumista* Captain Vidal on the Aragón Front. A Fascist officer is captured. Despite the inadequacies of the elderly Mausers and the realities of trench warfare in winter against a better equipped enemy, the overall impression is of an egalitarian idyll. The throwing together of strangers to wage war; the growth of shared comradeship amid danger; one recruit's anguish over an errant wife back home; the prevalence of lice; the *badinage* hurled between the trenches across no man's land – these are all the standard tropes of cinema at war.

An attack on a Nationalist-held village is followed by the execution of a collaborationist priest and the death of Coogan. (David has a moment of consternation as his anarchist comrades cart off religious statuary to the bonfire.) The following day, the peasants and victorious POUM militia hold a meeting in the expropriated house of Don Julian, a collaborationist landowner, and an open vote is taken on land collectivization. One peasant, Pepe, wants to hold onto his meagre acreage. It is pointed out that there are two million landless peasants: "The Revolution is like a pregnant cow, it has to be helped". The American Gene Lawrence argues that if the comrades want assistance from the capitalist countries, "you must tone down your slogans". The vote is called, and David votes with the collectivizing majority.[29]

The discussion of land ownership, with its echoes of Dovženko's *Zemlja* (*Earth*, 1930), is central to the literal and figurative meaning of *Land and Freedom*. As the titles tell us, this is "a story from the Spanish Revolution" – no doubt one story among many, but a story chosen by Loach and Allen for its appositeness in collapsing other complexities into one representative configuration. The film is about land and who should have it: the *braceros* who have none of it, or the *latifundistas* who have too much of it. Like Pepe, many small peasant proprietors were reluctant converts. As the Anarchist paper *Solidaridad Obrera* noted: "We militiamen must awaken in these persons the spirit that has been numbed by political tyranny. We must direct them along the path of the true life and for that it is not sufficient to make an appearance in the village; we must proceed with the ideological conversion of these simple folk".[30] This drive for revolutionary purity would take many forms: in Andalusia, such vices as the consumption of alcohol and coffee were abolished.[31] But the scene also hints at the uncertain ideological terrain still ahead for the Revolution: the American comrade Lawrence is ambivalent about the project.

What the Revolution in Spain was or was meant to be is sufficiently clear. It aimed for a society transformed, inasmuch as it sought not to replicate or retool the previous social formation, but to replace it with something new, a revolution, as the old tag had it, "not for more bread in Man's mouth but for a different taste of bread in Man's mouth". For Republican and Nationalist alike, the Spanish war was transcendental. "The Spanish national war is a holy war, and the holiest that history has known", wrote the Dominican Ignacio G Menéndez Reigada, writing from Salamanca in 1937.[32] Given such elevated war aims, this would be a pitiless conflict.

"I recognized it immediately as a state of affairs worth fighting for",[33] Orwell famously wrote. In Barcelona, shops and restaurants had been collectivized – even the shoeshine boys, their boxes now painted in anarchist red and black. Such formalities as "Don" and "Señor" had given way to "Comrade". Tipping was forbidden by law, and all private automobiles had been taken over. The well-dressed people had disappeared. "I did not realize that great numbers of well-to-do bourgeois were simply lying low and disguising themselves as proletarians".[34]

Yet, of this changed state of affairs we see little in *Land and Freedom*, except for references to returning to the old order, as the balance of forces tips towards winning the war at the cost of losing the Revolution.[35] For example, we learn from Blanca that women have been removed from the front lines and returned to more domestic duties: "I must know my place as a woman", she notes drily.

The fight to control the direction of events in Spain exploded onto the streets in May 1937. David sees the Revolution destroy itself as the anti-Franco forces battle one another for control of the Barcelona Telephone Exchange.[36] He has come here to be made well, having been wounded up in the mountains. But Barcelona is the city of dreadful night, "the city of the devil".[37] It is the agora where treachery plays, a place of whispering alleys and fractious cabals; the civil guards are back, conducting door-to-door searches. Where does loyalty lie? Blanca finds David's International Brigade uniform – to her, another betrayal. It is the beginning of the end; when David overhears the slanders put about by some young soldiers of the International Brigade, he tears up his Party card and returns to the relatively untainted company of the *poumistas* in the sunlit mountains.[38]

It is his last battle. He and his unit come under heavy fire from the Fascist lines; they are rescued by the arrival of a Popular Army unit, only to find that they are forced to hand over their arms. (Among the officers of the Popular Army are Gene Lawrence and the Fascist previously captured by Captain Vidal.) During the exchange, Blanca is killed, shot in the back, the betrayal complete. "We fought for nothing", David declares. "If we had succeeded here – and we could have done – we would have changed the world".

On one reading, *Land and Freedom* may be taken as the case for the prosecution – in this instance, of Stalinism. (Although, since Stalinism, in the triumphalist discourse of Western capitalism, as in the more discreet flutings of its acolytes, has by now become a synecdoche for all Moscow-friendly Communists back-projected to 1917, it is not an exercise that would demand overwhelming reserves of political courage.) Loach's project has often been to give a voice to those rendered mute, in E P Thompson's phrase, by the "enormous condescension of posterity".[39] This has meant pointing to the forces that result in young lives being wasted – the theme of *Up the Junction* (1965), *Cathy Come Home* (1966) and, in a different register, *Land and Freedom*.

Loach has remained consistent in his admiration for such syndicalist theories as workers' control: "Let's use the docks as a laboratory for the working class to try out the gear and draw the lessons", urges the ex-Communist Trotskyist Jack Regan to Danny Fowler of the dockworkers in *The Big Flame* (1969). Again, in *Days of Hope* (1975): "The trouble with you lot is that you judge everything from the Russian experience. You behave as if every social revolution has to go along the same lines". (During the Merseyside strikes, the "official" Communist Party, hewing to its "pure electoralism" line, took a dim view of the tactics of the Workers' Revolutionary Party and other elements of the "Militant Tendency".)

There is a sequence in *The Rank and File* (1971), in which the striking glassworkers parade under their trade union banner through the wasteland of their company town. They are singing "Solidarity Forever". For a moment, the viewer is sharply reminded how the iconography of mid-20th century Northern England has its roots in the 19th century. All of this – the trade union banners, the brave words, the slag-heaps – in Peter Laslett's phrase, evokes "the world we have lost".[40] (Similarly with E P Thompson's seminal work, *The Making of the English Working Class*, in which one is closer to threnody than nostalgia.) In these early films, there is a brooding sense that the workers, far from taking over the stage of history, are vacating it. And, of course, by the end of the Thatcherite era of sado-monetarism, they are changed utterly.

"A battered landscape, a company town for 142 years", the voice-over narration tells us in *The Rank and File*; every Christmas, a free bag of coal for the employees of the glass factory, "together with a contribution to the television licence". (It is important to keep folks at peace.) There has not been a strike for 100 years, and the company union rarely meets. Then, a minor discrepancy over a pay slip "bursts like a carbuncle that had been left festering". A strike vote is called. Brother Hagan of the union executive, "a clown executive of a clown union", intervenes to no avail. The strike is on. It is declared illegal by the London union bosses. There is therefore no strike pay.

The outcome of this uneven contest is never in doubt. An unofficial strike committee, with rents to pay, children to feed and wives to console, is pitted against the bosses, the union, the Trades Union Congress and the Labour government. (It should be borne in mind that, in cities such as Glasgow and Liverpool, Labour Party bossism has traditionally been quite comparable to, for example, Chicago levels.) Barbara Castle, the Yorkshire-born Labour MP, once something of a firebrand but, in the time frame of the film, Secretary of State for Employment and Productivity in the Labour government of Harold Wilson, is selected by the strikers as the ultimate symbol of sell-out; she also gets her comeuppance in *The Big Flame*.

"The role of the TUC", explains one striker in *The Rank and File*, "is the broker for the government, Labour or Conservative". Again, "Barbara Castle and the phoney Left" are all part of the enemy; the TUC leaders are "Judas goats leading the sheep". It is in this depiction of the constellation of opposing forces that the Loach-Allen dramas diverge sharply from such classic treatments of industrial struggle as Monicelli's *I compagni* (*The Organizer*, 1963), Sayles' *Matewan* (1987) or Widerberg's *Ådalen 31* (*Ådalen '31/The Ådalen Riots*, 1969). The battlefield here is littered not only with the corpses of the defeated, but also with the hopelessly compromised. And the defeats are never just those of another lost strike or missed opportunity: "We could have done anything", says one embittered striker, "we could have stopped the world", words echoed by David Carne surveying the defeat in Spain, "we would have changed the world". A kind of obdurate idealism accompanies defeat.

A similar trajectory is followed in *The Big Flame*. After a strike lasting some six weeks, 10 000 dockworkers take over the docks, and, for a glorious five days, put into practice the theory of workers' control until the troops are sent in. The issue here is the unemployment that will inevitably follow the introduction of containerization to the docks as recommended in the Devlin Report. Four of the leaders – Danny Fowler, Joe Ryan, Peter Conner and Jack Regan – are given sharp three-year jail sentences, ostensibly for "conspiracy to affect a public mischief", but obviously from the presiding magistrate's summation, to encourage the others: "The doctrine of Marxism is not on trial here...But, when placed in the hands of determined working men this doctrine becomes as dangerous as a loaded pistol in the hands of a criminal. It is the use, the practice rather than the theoretical speculation, that we are here concerned with". He wishes to make it clear that, indeed, this revolutionary doctrine is favoured "in some of our better universities", and that to the degree that it sharpens the wits of the students and helps remedy "the distemper" affecting young people, he, the magistrate, is in favour of it.

In a delicious irony, Jack Regan's speech from the dock finds common cause with this "Uriah Heepery". He congratulates the magistrate's notion of Marxism as social therapy for young pseuds, "folksinging church Socialists" who preach Socialism on their visits to Havana, but "keep quiet in their own backyards". (The writerly voice of Jim Allen is unmistakable here, as is the reference to the heated debates in Left circles over the vexed question of praxis.) Regan concludes with a summary of the brief dawn of workers' control: "For five days we ran the docks and shifted more cargo than ever before...I never seen harmony like that before...fellows suddenly sprouted...and that's a picture worth remembering".

To the enemies of the dockers in *The Big Flame* – the unions, the TUC, the Labour government, the shipowners – are added the London-based media, the Moral Rearmament movement (a Christian-based self-styled "alternative" to capitalism and Communism that made inroads among trade union officials, as well as among some leaders of post-colonial countries in the late-1950s and early 1960s) and a Cockney docker who turns out to be "with the Cossacks" and who betrays the leadership to the police. And again, as so often in the

Loach-Allen schema, there are hints that the example set by the dockers may set off labour unrest elsewhere: there is news on the radio of a sit-down strike among car workers, dockers have come out in other British ports, and later that night there will be another meeting to elect replacements for the fallen. "The jails won't be big enough". In the 1980s, Loach returned to his attack on trade union officialdom in a series of documentaries, notably in *A Question of Leadership* (1980). This time, he concentrates on the response of the official labour movement to what he calls the "Thatcherite onslaught", in which he castigates the leadership for what he sees as a deliberate policy of narrowing the potential opposition of workers to attacks on their living standards.

In conclusion, the themes introduced in these earlier films show up again in *Land and Freedom*. There is the question of betrayal on the part of those who are ostensibly the class ally; there is what amounts almost to a Puritan interrogation of revolutionary purity; and finally, there is the promise that, by revolutionary example, by – in Christian terminology – bearing witness, the defeated protagonist will cause others to emulate him in the strife that lies ahead. Perhaps it should be added that apart from these quite explicit themes, Loach's canvas of England and its condition is informed by his palpable contempt for what he sees as the inbuilt hypocrisy of its public face. In this as in much else, he is in a long line of descent.[41]

Land and Freedom is also an implicit commentary on the course of the political idealist or the politically innocent. David Carne's *rite of passage* emblematically replicates the titles of Isaac Deutscher's great biography of Trotsky: *The Prophet Armed*, *The Prophet Unarmed*, *The Prophet Outcast*. Yet, there is nothing of Trotsky's guile in David; his is a pilgrimage closer to Bunyan than to Bakunin (or Bukharin), but with no hope of transcendence, the road to the Holy City of the virtuous blocked. There is in him something of that fatalism identified by Gramsci as "nothing other than the clothing worn by real and active will when in a weak position".[42]

But again, it might be argued that Loach's film resists the despair of this impasse. David Carne's journey begins and ends in contemporary England. Taken by ambulance from his Liverpool council estate after a stroke, he dies on his way to hospital. His granddaughter, Kim, finds his letters home from Spain as she sorts out his effects; her reading of the letters merges into the extended flashback of the film. David's funeral, with which the film ends, has Kim opening the red handkerchief she had found among his things, and spilling the dust inside onto his coffin. It is the red handkerchief Blanca's mother had given him at her daughter's funeral, in which he had placed a handful of Spanish earth from her grave.

Knowledge and memory are thus secured, and the possibility that "our day will come" not negated but postponed. In *After a Lifetime* (1971), at William Scully's wake, his son laments that he never took the time off from the dances and the parties to find out from his Dad, a veteran of the 1926 General Strike, what it was to be a "political", to lead a political life: "Now, y'know, I wanna know, I wanna know...but I want to hear him tell me, but he never will, y'know. This is what hurts". In his own way, David Carne has told Kim. She is now the carrier of Red memory. It is a proleptic moment.

Notes

[1] Quoted in Angela Partington (ed), *The Oxford Dictionary of Quotations*, fourth edition (Oxford: Oxford University Press, 1992): 710.

[2] Fredric Jameson, *The Political Unconscious: Narrative as a Socially Symbolic Act* (London: Methuen: 1983): 102.

[3] Noel Monks, "The Spanish Civil War: Guernica Destroyed by German Planes, 26 April 1937", in John Carey (ed), *The Faber Book of Reportage* (London; Boston: Faber and Faber, 1987): 521.

[4] Quoted in Mary Biggar Peck, *Red Moon Over Spain: Canadian Media Reaction to the Spanish Civil War 1936-1939* (Ottawa: Steel Rail Publishing, 1988): 54.

[5] Production notes, *Land and Freedom*.

[6] Isaac Deutscher, *Stalin: A Political Biography* (London; New York; Toronto: Oxford University Press, 1949): 424.

[7] Translated from the French: "Quand j'ai témoigné de la vérité j'ai mis ma main au feu et je me suis brûlé car ma vérité ce n'était pas ma main, c'était le feu". Quoted in Barthélemy Amengual, "La guerre d'espagne vue par le cinéma", *Positif* 213 (December 1978): 30.

[8] Eric Hobsbawm, *Age of Extremes: The Short Twentieth Century* (London: Michael Joseph, 1994): 161.

[9] Production notes, *Land and Freedom*.

[10] Ibid.

[11] Robert A Rosenstone, *Visions of the Past: The Challenge of Film to Our Idea of History* (Cambridge; London: Harvard University Press 1995): 116.

[12] Ibid: 111.

[13] Ibid: 115.

[14] Ibid: 112.

[15] Ibid: 7.

[16]   Natalie Zemon Davis, *The Return of Martin Guerre* (Cambridge; London: Harvard University Press, 1983): viii. The homage paid here by Davis to another chronicler of the period, Leopold von Ranke, can hardly be missed.

[17]   This is a reworking of a phrase from Rosenstone (63): "a different way of thinking about the past".

[18]   Frank P Tomasulo, "i'll see it when i believe it", in Vivian Sobchack (ed), *The Persistence of History: Cinema, Television and the Modern Event* (New York: Routledge, 1996): 79.

[19]   "Perhaps film is a postliterate equivalent of the preliterate way of dealing with the past, of those forms of history in which scientific, documentary accuracy was not yet a consideration, forms in which any notion of fact was of less importance than the sound of a voice, the rhythm of a line, the magic of words" (Rosenstone: 78). One has a disquieting apprehension that this may be right.

[20]   Joyce Appleby, Lynn Hunt and Margaret Jacob, *Telling the Truth about History* (New York; London: W W Norton & Company, 1994): 235.

[21]   In the case of Oliver Stone, however, remedial action would seem essential; aficionados of the surreal may, in *JFK*, get something out of Jim Garrison as exemplifying the speaking of Truth to Power; but in his most recent outing, Stone ascribes to Nixon the bizarre assassination attempts on President Castro orchestrated by the Kennedy brothers.

[22]   Appropriate testimony to the rightness of Camino's choice of aesthetic strategy was the decision of the judges at the San Sebastián Film Festival to disallow *The Old Memory* in the documentary class. It won the Critics' Prize.

[23]   *Tierra y Libertad* was the main publication of the Federación Anarquista Iberica (FAI), the insurrectionary vanguard of the Anarchist movement.

[24]   The POUM was formed in 1935 by an alliance of Trotskyists and left-Communist dissidents from the non-Moscow-affiliated Communist Bloc Obrer i Camperol (BOC; Workers' and Peasants' Bloc) and the Izquierda Communista, a Trotskyist organisation. Andreu Nin, wartime political secretary of the POUM, had been Trotsky's private secretary in Moscow, and was now his main political contact in Spain. Although maintaining a relatively arm's-length relationship with Trotsky's Fourth International, Nin and the POUM ("always a muddled organization", Trotsky wrote in January 1936) were committed to the theory of "permanent revolution", a stance directly at odds with the strategy of étapisme pursued by the Comintern (Communist International), the Partido Comunista Obrero de España (PCE) and the Partido Socialista Unificado de Cataluña (PSUC), the Catalan Socialist Party. Almost any attempt to decipher the nuanced affiliations of groups in the Spanish conflict is a charged exercise. Paul Preston settles for "quasi-Trotskyist" as a POUM appellation (Paul Preston, *The Spanish Civil War 1936-39* [London: Weidenfeld and Nicolson, 1986]: 4.) For a complete list of groupings, see George Esenwein and Adrian Shubert, *Spain at War: The Spanish Civil War in Context, 1931-1939* (London; New York: Longman Publishing, 1995).

[25] The suggestion is from the UK Anarchist publication, *Freedom* 10 June 1995.

[26] Compare Peggy Dennis's account of Spanish Civil War recruitment in Wisconsin: "Eighty Wisconsites were fighting with the Abraham Lincoln Brigade. Gene [Peggy's husband Eugene, State Secretary of the Wisconsin Communist Party] and I knew them all well, most of them personally. Each had come for an interview bearing recommendations from people we knew in their local area or organization. *Political orientation was done in New York...*" (emphasis added). The US State Department had already made it an offence punishable by jail for any American to break the government's neutrality embargo. (Peggy Dennis, *The Autobiography of an American Communist* [Westport; Berkeley: Lawrence Hill and Co.; Creative Arts Book Co., 1977]: 7.) Note also Kevin Morgan on CPGB recruiting practices: "In due course ostensibly non-Party organisations were established to organise Spanish aid and support for volunteers' dependants. Recruitment, on the other hand, was from first to last strictly under Party control". (Kevin Morgan, *Harry Pollitt* (Manchester; New York: Manchester University Press, 1993): 96.)

[27] Burnett Bolloten, *The Grand Camouflage: The Spanish Civil War and Revolution, 1936-39* (London: Pall Mall Press, 1968): 208-209.

[28] Orwell similarly underwent "drill of the most antiquated, stupid kind" at the Lenin Barracks in Barcelona. (George Orwell, *Homage to Catalonia* [London: Secker & Warburg, 1959]: 8.)

[29] "For they [the Communists] believed that unless the Western democratic societies and governments were convinced that it was in their best interests to stop fascism in Spain, the republicans stood little chance of winning the war" (Esenwein and Shubert: 246). As David Carne points out in the film, the Soviet Union had already signed "a treaty with France" – actually a mutual assistance pact – in May 1935. "The whole of Comintern policy is now subordinated (excusably, considering the world situation) to the defence of the U.S.S.R., which depends upon a system of military alliances" (Orwell: 58). Moreover: "If the war was lost democracy and revolution, Socialism and Anarchism, became meaningless words" (Orwell: 56). As early as November 1935, Georgi Dimitroff, the General Secretary of the Comintern, had written to Husto Amutio, editor of the Valencia left-wing Socialist newspaper, *Adelante Verdad*: "I wish you success, dear comrades, Socialists, Communists and Anarcho-Syndicalist workers, in, boldly, shoulder to shoulder, overcoming all obstacles to the establishment of unity raised by the splinters of the working class, whether conscious agents of the bourgeoisie or misled opponents of the united front...I wish you every success in achieving this militant unity...so that, in the long run, the victory of socialism will be assured in Spain". See Georgi Dimitroff, "Reply to Spanish Socialists", in *The United Front: The Struggle Against Fascism and War* (London: Lawrence & Wishart, 1938): 154.

[30] Quoted in Bolloten: 71-72.

[31] Preston: 128. It is neither easy nor pleasant to consider how this state of affairs might be brought about.

[32] "La guerra nacional española es guerra santa, y la mas que registra la historia". The statement is quoted by Jacques Maritain in his essay, "The Idea of Holy War", in Justin O'Brien (ed), *From the NRF (La Nouvelle Revue Française)* (New York: Farrar, Strauss and Cudahy, 1958): 335-336. Writing in the same year, 1937, Fr. Maritain observes of Menéndez Reigada's declaration: "One may be allowed a doubt whether Providence has no other means...except by the victory of the Spanish nationalists and their allies".

[33] Orwell: 3.

[34] Ibid: 4. The historic antipathy between anarchist and Communist theory, turning on such matters as the role of the state, long predates the Spanish conflict. It added to the special venom that accompanies a civil war. *Land and Freedom* is the latest chapter in this debate. "But the war against the generals remained to be fought, and they [the Anarchists] were incapable of fighting it effectively either in the military or political sense. This was evident to the great majority of foreign observers and volunteers, especially in Catalonia and Aragon...The inefficacy of the anarchist way of fighting the war has recently been doubted by a new school of libertarian historians (including the formidable intellect of Noam Chomsky), reluctant to admit that the communists had the only practical and effective policy for this purpose, and that their rapidly growing influence reflected this fact. Unfortunately it cannot be denied. And the war had to be won, because without this victory the Spanish Revolution, however inspiring and perhaps even workable, would merely turn into yet another episode of heroic defeat, like the Paris Commune. And this is what actually happened." E J Hobsbawm, *Revolutionaries: Contemporary Essays* (London: Weidenfeld & Nicolson, 1973): 77-78.

[35] It may be presumptuous to explain this absence in terms of budget exigencies; Loach may have felt that the heart of the story rested with the militia at the front. However, Jim Allen states that the decision to use the framing device of the flashback sequence was adopted for budgetary reasons. An original budget projection of £5 million was cut to £2.75 million, a low figure for such an undertaking. (Production notes, *Land and Freedom*.)

[36] As with the General Post Office in Dublin during the 1916 Easter Rebellion, the building had a practical, as well as a symbolic, value. "Those who held the Telefónica controlled all telephone communications between Barcelona and the rest of the world". Víctor Alba and Stephen Schwartz, *Spanish Marxism versus Soviet Communism: A History of the P.O.U.M.* (New Brunswick, NJ; Oxford: Transaction Books, 1988): 189.

[37] Preston: 119.

[38] "During all the time I was at the front", Orwell reports, "I never once remember any P.S.U.C. adherent [the Communist-controlled Catalan Socialist Party] showing me hostility because I was P.O.U.M. That kind of thing belonged in Barcelona" (Orwell: 216).

[39] E P Thompson, *The Making of the English Working Class* (Harmondsworth: Penguin Books, 1968): 13.

40   Peter Laslett, *The World We Have Lost* (London: Methuen, 1965).

41   "The truth...is that in these days the grand *'primum mobile'* of England is *cant*; cant political, cant poetical, cant religious, cant moral; but always *cant*, multiplied through all the varieties of life". George Gordon, Lord Byron, in Ian Jack, *English Literature 1815-1832* (Oxford: Clarendon Press, 1963): 436. Emphases in original.

42   Quintin Hoare and Geoffrey Nowell Smith (eds), *Selections from the Prison Notebooks of Antonio Gramsci* (London: Lawrence and Wishart, 1971): 337.

Interview with Ken Loach[1]

John Hill

What were your early influences as a film director?

There were a number of things in our minds when we started doing what we called plays, recorded plays. First of all I did a series with Troy Kennedy Martin and John McGrath called *Diary of a Young Man* [1964]. At this stage I really didn't know one end of a camera from another, but Troy had written a manifesto for a theatre magazine called *Encore*.[2] This was very influenced by Brecht and the French New Wave, and sought to establish a new grammar for fictional television involving the use of stills, cutting to music, not observing natural time and a lot of things like that. The series was very much a testing ground for those ideas. The ideas were carried on when we did things like *Up the Junction* [1965], which was supposed to be on tape but which we managed to shoot on film, so manipulating the system at the BBC [British Broadcasting Corporation]. Also we were following the news so we tried to work in the style of *World in Action* and other current affairs programmes so that people didn't think "we have had the facts now we will have the fiction" but rather "we've had the facts – now here's some more facts with a different point of view".

How strongly did you identify with these Brechtian ideas, given that so much of your subsequent career has been identified with realism and naturalism? Did you consciously reject the modernism of your early work?

Given that we were very young, we'd try anything and this seemed to make a lot of sense then. Some things have stayed: it's just some of the external mannerisms that have become rather tedious. Cutting to stills, for example, is only good for one or two projects. You can't do that film after film. Doing things that are pared down is something that I've always tried to do, although I have failed on a number of occasions. The aim is to find the most economical way of doing something rather than the flashiest, the most dramatic, the most cinematic or the most stunning. Finding the simplest way of doing something came out of that early work.

At this time you were strongly identified with the producer Tony Garnett. Did he play a creative role?

Yes, particularly with the writers and the working over of a script, and in just being very shrewd about the project. Making the space in the BBC to get them done was also no mean feat.

Following the great success of Up the Junction *and* Cathy Come Home *[1966], you moved into feature film making. What was the reason for this move, and what were the consequences for your relationship with an audience?*

I think what determined the relationship with the television audience was that time. If you made a film for television now you would tend not to have the same relationship. *Up the Junction* and *Cathy Come Home* were made very quickly and went out very soon after. We made *Up the Junction* in about six weeks and it went out almost immediately. That night we were also on *Late Night Line-Up* and you would sit there and get questions from the angry Mary Whitehouses of this world complaining about swearing on television and generally talking about it. So there was a sense of immediacy and real exchange going on. When we did those, there were really only two channels, and so if you did well you would get an audience of ten to twelve million people, or even more. There was a feeling that we were in politics. The plays came after the news and we hoped they had a political vitality about them. That was very exciting. You don't get that in the cinema, but I don't think that you get that in television now either or, if you do, to a much lesser degree than before.

Is there a difference making cinema and making television drama? Do you see television and film as distinct mediums or are they basically the same?

It's basically the same medium. I think there is a difference between doing a straight documentary and doing fiction. A straight documentary is like a pamphlet while a fiction should be like a novel in that it should give that feeling that there is a whole submerged iceberg there and you are just seeing the tiny bit that's on the surface. You should feel there's a world there, a whole set of relationships of people that exist outside the film. It should have that richness. Otherwise it's the same. When you go out to shoot, you are confronted with the problem of the light, with how to get the reactions amongst the people that you want and how to get the moments in front of the camera that you want to happen. You have to steer that and you have to steer the people so that they will respond at a certain time when the camera is turning over on a particular lens. That kind of guiding of cast and crew is exactly the same whether it's a film that's going to be shown on television or is going to be shown in the Odeon, Leicester Square (not that I've ever had a film shown in the Odeon, Leicester Square)!

You have described your development in terms of a paring down process. Kes *[1969] is often regarded as a turning-point in this respect. What was different in the making of this film?*

I think it was working with Chris Menges. I got rather dissatisfied with the jerky handheld camera and the go-in-and-grab-it type of filmmaking. Chris had been the operator on *Poor Cow* [1967] and then had worked with a Czech called Miroslav Ondříček on *If....*, and that had influenced Chris quite a lot. So when we came to work on *Kes* we talked about the process a little bit more. What I had done in *Poor Cow* was do a lot of things in one take, and not cut, and that became very sterile and just throws away a whole lot of things you can do. So we began to put a sequence together a bit more thoughtfully. How it was lit was very important. More generally, it was a case of finding a sympathetic way of looking at the subject, the people in it, rather than using an exploitative cinema style which can be rather crude.

Chris Menges was also the cameraman on Looks and Smiles *[1981] which is visually quite striking. Was it a conscious choice to shoot in black and white?*

I think it's a bit arty-farty now. At the time we just wanted something that was very simple and monochrome. I love black and white photos but hate colour photos. Chris and I felt that black and white would give it a strength. Colour can make things pretty and in a way, with black and white, you can be more truthful in that it isn't necessary to remove things from the shot because their colour is distracting. The problem with that film is that we weren't tough enough with the structure. My memory is that it could have been tighter and there were scenes I could have done better. I had a feeling it should have been a little more dynamic.

In the early 1980s, you moved away from feature film to documentary. Why was this?

When Channel 4 started up in 1982, there was the possibility of making smaller-scale films without the big commercial pressures. Instead of doing that I made documentaries because it was the time of the Thatcher onslaught and rising unemployment and I wanted to try and make some tiny intervention into all that. However, the things got banned and I really wasted two or three years.

Looking back, do you think you should have been more sensitive to the censorship problems you were likely to face? Could you have anticipated the problems, or were you genuinely taken aback by the censorship of a series such as Questions of Leadership *[1983]?*

In a way, the series was made as a challenge because the people at Channel 4 said "we can put these out". We said "are you sure?", and they said "yes". So we made them and they couldn't or wouldn't. I think there is a danger if you say "I can only get away with a certain amount therefore I'll censor myself in advance". That's one of the great catch-phrases in current affairs and documentary television. I have always resisted it. You should challenge them and say "if you are going to use censorship, do so in the open" because they hate that. If their system works, they never have to censor anything because everybody modifies what they can do in order to slip through the net. That, in the end, is absolutely corrupting.

You have indicated that one of the attractions of documentary is that it permitted you to make an intervention at a particular moment. Are you still interested in making documentaries or, given your experiences, are you now happiest making film features?

In an ideal world it would be nice to do both really. To be a novelist and a pamphleteer. There's a place for both. I feel when there's a chance of making some more films I should pursue those. It would be good to do the occasional documentary. The area I try to work in, however, is the most contentious. It's not so much documentary where you observe something happening, but documentary which is involved in current affairs and political issues and political people. Then they are very determined to control the medium and that's obviously where there's the most censorship and often very blatant censorship.

Your return to feature filmmaking was effectively a film that dealt with censorship – Fatherland *[1986]. However, it is a film you do not seem to be terribly happy with.*

Fatherland was a big disappointment. I directed in a way that was not appropriate to the script and so it was a lost opportunity. I think the problem is that Trevor Griffiths [the writer] and I have rather different ways of working, and I guess Trevor spotted this quicker than I did. His writing is quite literary and precise and I'm not very good at that. I'm better at capturing things that are happening or appear to be happening, and capturing the vitality of that. The other problem was that half the film was in German, so Trevor's script had to be translated into German, and he and I had no idea whether the translation was any good or not. When the actors were doing it, they were saying this dialogue is impossible to say and I couldn't be any help. I just had to rely on them with the result that the dialogue became quite placid. We also ended with a long scene in which a huge amount is revealed. Structurally, that wasn't a very good idea.

It's a relatively unusual film for you. How conscious a departure from your earlier work was it?

I'd rather lost touch with the sort of things that I used to do. After not having done any sort of cinema work for a bit, you get more desperate to do a film at all costs, and my judgment wasn't very good about it. I was trying too hard to be a European film director instead of finding a good story and telling it.

Your next film was Hidden Agenda *[1990]. How did you become involved with that?*

I got a call one day from David Puttnam after he had gone to Columbia asking would I be interested in making a film about John Stalker. I said "yes" and that I would like to work with Jim Allen. Puttnam commissioned the script but then, when he left Columbia, the script fell. However, the fact that he had expressed interest gave everyone else the confidence to think that it would be worth investing in it, and two years later we finally raised the money. However, we were turned down by everyone in Britain and then when it came out it was promptly dubbed an "IRA film" by this Tory MP.[3]

As you have indicated, the film reunited you with Jim Allen. You seem to work very closely with particular writers. What kind of relationship do you have with them and do you involve yourself in the writing?

I think writers are the most undervalued people in films, and for me it has always been a fundamental of doing any project that I work side-by-side with the writer. Usually the idea comes up between us through conversation and then we will talk roughly about the shape and pattern that the film will have and then Jim (if it's Jim) will write some scenes and send them down. Jim lives in Manchester and doesn't come to London if he can avoid it. He sends some scenes in the post or more lately the fax machine in the grocery shop nearby! Then we talk on the phone or I will go up and see him, and we work on it together. But Jim does the writing.

How much of Hidden Agenda *did you actually shoot in Northern Ireland?*

We wanted to shoot it all in Ireland but the people who insure films said that they wouldn't insure us if we shot in Belfast. We said "OK, if we can't shoot in Belfast, can we rehearse there?" We rehearsed for a week but actually filmed the "rehearsal". In the end, we shot a week at the beginning and a week at the end, so we did nearly half in Belfast.

It is probably the nearest you've done to a genre piece since you directed Z Cars *in 1964. How did you find working with that kind of genre format?*

We realised two thirds of the way through the film that actually it's not the film we should have done. We tried to bring the "shoot-to-kill" and "dirty tricks" stories together and I'm not sure it was entirely a good idea. I think we felt at the end of the project that if we had not started out with that commission then we would have tried to do a different film which would have been much more on the streets. The actual making was fine. However, because the whole point of a police investigation story is that the information has to come out in a very precise order, we were very much tied to the script. I don't regret it at all but I think with hindsight we would decide to do some things differently.

With Riff-Raff *[1991] you appeared to return to more familiar territory.*
Yes, back to basics!

Did you feel, however, that the changed political circumstances of the 1990s might require any change in your cinematic approach?
If you can be fairly accurate about the way people are and what they are up to that's always interesting and relevant. Providing you are true to people you don't have to invent theories or construct an aesthetic for what you do. Just go and be accurate and that will be contemporary by definition.

Do you think the success of the film, and those that followed, might have been due to some sort of reaction to the Thatcher years? Was there a renewed interest in the very issues, such as unemployment and poverty, which had been neglected during the 1980s?
We never tried to see the stories in that light because human nature is such that if you say "do you want to come and see a film about poverty" everybody says "not likely – I'd rather go and see a comedy or something". We have never tried to present stories as though they are going to be grim and about hardship. I think you have to try and tell stories that give people a lift, or at least a kind of genuine emotional experience, and not make them about issues. I think films about issues tend to be rather tedious.

In the case of Riff-Raff *I get the impression that you are happiest dealing with the workers on the building site and that the actual romance works much less well. Do you think there is any tension between the two, or how do you see the two relating to each other?*
Well, we wanted something that felt quite random and haphazard, and we also wanted the main characters to have a private life. So it was another one of Bill's [Jesse's] recollections and seemed to fit. In the end there were two people who each needed each other for a

time – ships that passed in the night. I enjoyed doing those scenes because Emer McCourt was good to work with, and I think if it had been all hairy-arsed builders we might have got a bit fed up with them. It seemed right that there should be a counterpoint.

What about the end of the film when the two workers set fire to the building site? How were you encouraging us to interpret this?

Well, it's a classic case of alienation. They were building homes they had no chance of living in. It was just a place of exploitation and danger where they were ripped off from morning till night. They had taken enough and just said "to hell with it". They are not political people so it's "up yours"! It would have been false to make them suddenly have a formed political response. Nevertheless, we didn't want them to accept the situation passively either.

In contrast to something like The Big Flame *[1969] which is about organised working-class struggle, is there now a greater pessimism on your part about the possibilities for organised political action?*

It's not a pessimism about the possibility of action, but just that people are not so politicised now for reasons we know. We all voted for our own misery in 1979. We just have to be realistic. On the average building site in England, just as in any walk of life, people are not terribly politicised. We've got a right-wing Labour Party to thank for that. I recently got one of those reproduced letters, supposedly from Tony Blair, soliciting not your political involvement, not that you join the Labour Party, not that you should have any thoughts that might contribute to the direction of the Labour Party, but simply that you should send in your Visa card! The social-democratic left just want to become the Clinton Party. Given the Thatcher attack and the coliusion of the Labour Party, it is no wonder that people have become depoliticised.[4]

There has been an emergence of new forms of politics, particularly around feminism and the politics of ethnicity. Might these give rise to some political optimism?

The problem is that, if it is to be progressive, the heart of the struggle has got to be around the class that's got revolutionary potential. Otherwise its just a liberal cause. Unless in the end you have the power to take the system by the throat and throttle it, it's just a cause. So there has to be some potential for taking power in the issue you are organising around or in the end it just becomes a subject for demonstration. It's important, it's a manifestation of the unfairness of the system, but in the end it won't stop the wheels of industry turning or cause the system to stop.

Does that mean that for you issues of racial and sexual inequality are in effect subordinate to the issue of class inequality?

They are not subordinate in the sense that they are unimportant. But if you are wanting to change the way we live together then the key issues are the ones where power is at stake.

Questions of both class and gender are present in Ladybird Ladybird *[1994]. How did you become involved in this project?*

It was one of those cases where somebody – a social worker – wrote a letter and just described some events that had happened to a friend of hers. The events were so extreme that I thought that they at least deserved looking into. So we went to see the woman and her husband and just listened to their story. It was just such an extraordinary story of loss and grief and elemental emotions that you think how can a human person contain these feelings. It was a story particularly worth telling not simply as a "shock horror this is Britain 1994"-type story, but in order to try to explore the difficulties that people may have of escaping their own stereotype, of the damage that violence can do when you experience it, the anger that it might generate and, when it can't express itself, the kind of unacceptable behaviour and spiral of emotions which it can lead to. It was this which drew us to the story. I don't know if the extraordinary bond between husband and wife came over. He was a most gentle and most passive man, but even he broke in the end under the weight of the kind of anger that the woman had. We tried to tease out those emotions and show why they developed in the way that they had. It was this which really drew us to the story. The important thing from our point of view, the real story of the film, was Maggie and Jorge and the fact that they start off with such possibilities. Then all the problems that Maggie has had give her this rage which practically destroys their relationship, but at the end they are just hanging on.

Crissy Rock gives a formidable performance in the main role of Maggie. How was she cast?

It was a question of finding someone who could do justice to that extraordinary range of emotions and somebody who the audience would identify with, somebody enormously strong and yet credible. So we really started with a blank sheet. We didn't want any of the actresses who are known for doing working-class parts on television because there wouldn't be that sense of originality and we felt really strongly that we had to find somebody that you had never seen before but who could still give you a kick in the solar plexus. I auditioned lots of people in London but couldn't find anybody. I then went to Glasgow, Manchester and Liverpool to try the cities where there is a very strong working-class culture and where there's also quite a strong culture of working men's clubs. I have found that people who work there are very talented and also possess a kind of vitality. There's something of the performer in them but they are not actors, so you don't get an actor's technique. Ricky Tomlinson, who's a friend and was in *Raining Stones* [1993], had worked as an agent for club acts in Liverpool and he set up an audition for about 30 people. There were three people there, all of whom would have been very interesting, and Crissy was one of them. Then, through a process of auditions and improvisations and trying things out, we ended up with her. She was extraordinary to work with. We shot for a long day, ten to twelve hours, at this kind of emotional pitch and when we finished at eight o'clock at night she's saying "Where are we off to then, where's the action?". She is a prodigious woman.

How important is it to you to avoid casting well-known actors?

A key thing is the people you have in the film. One of the things you try to do is give a dignity and an importance to ordinary people. If we had got a well-known star or actor to play Maggie, you would have gone to watch that performance and the whole business of class would have been lost or patronised. It just takes away the basic quality that you want to get onscreen. That's the compromise that is required in order to get into the mainstream. You would have to get more into the *Kramer vs Kramer*-type film: Dustin Hoffman vs Meryl Streep, with the child tugged between the two. There would have to be a much bigger "feel good" factor and so it couldn't be as unremitting as we wanted to make it. Then they expect a certain kind of music and a kind of manipulation of the emotions that would change the nature of the film so much that it subverts the point you are trying to make.

One of the complaints about the film has been its blending of drama and documentary? What is your response to such complaints?

It's a laugh really. Every night there are drama documentaries on television, yet they never attract this flak. Our film was based on a true story, the characters are written and played by actors. So it couldn't be more plain what the film is. Nevertheless, we would stand by every fact in it and we would stand by every line in it: not as the line exactly said by that person at such and such a time, but as being as true a representation of their relationship and those events as we could make it. I remember the same argument came up when *Hidden Agenda* came out. *The Times* wrote a leader saying that you cannot blur facts and fiction in this way. In the same week the film *Reversal of Fortune* came out about someone called Claus von Bulow who was supposed to have murdered his wife. It starred Jeremy Irons and there was a character in it called Claus von Bulow and a character in it called his wife played by Glenn Close. What was fact and what was fiction there? Was Jeremy Irons Claus von Bulow? I don't think he was, but nevertheless there was Claus von Bulow onscreen, no argument about that. But that's apparently okay. We had all fictitious characters. It's just that some of the events bore rather a close relationship to some of the tricks that the British had been pulling in Northern Ireland, and that was mixing facts and fiction. So really it is a completely fraudulent argument and, whether the people who do it are aware of it or not, it's a way of trying to undermine the film without tackling it head-on.[5]

To what extent are your filmmaking techniques influenced by documentary methods?

My techniques are, in a way, classic filmmaking techniques. They are very straightforward techniques. I shoot a scene from two or three angles so that you can cut it together. I repeat the action for each set-up. It's based on a script. It's lit when it has to be. None of these are things you could do on a documentary. The problem with a documentary is you film things that happen only once. I couldn't make these films in a documentary way. You would have to go in with a wide-ish angle and stand in the doorway and poke it around. There are obviously little tricks of the trade to try and make it look as though it is happening for the first time, but it's set up like a piece of fiction.

How far do you encourage actors to improvise?

We do improvise, but in a way improvisation is a technique for fiction because obviously you want to make the audience feel they are watching something that's just happening. But that's not documentary.

How prepared are you to improvise camera movements or are these preplanned?

The camera positions are fairly well decided before we start, but sometimes the camera is positioned in such a way that the actors might be free to move within a room and you can cope with this from the one position.

How many takes would you normally make of a particular shot?

It depends: around six or seven. Sometimes more, sometimes less.

Do repeated takes effect the freshness of the performances which you are seeking to achieve.

Not necessarily. It's a question of keeping it fresh, changing it ever so slightly and getting a question to be rephrased or the like. However, it means you have got to do it two or three times on a looser shot and then a certain number of times with the camera in one position and then again with the camera in another position. So you do work it out.

Ladybird Ladybird is in some ways similar to Cathy Come Home. How conscious of this were you?

I suppose there are similarities, but the similarities are very much on the surface in that a woman is separated from her children. *Cathy Come Home* was more like a report on homelessness in which various things which happened to homeless families were condensed into a narrative. This was with the intention of saying to people who were watching on television that this is actually happening in your name, and we really have to stop it and deal with it. The personal aspects of it really just hung on Carol White being who she was and being, I think, quite moving and very strong. But it was a very raw piece and is much more about the social aspect of the situation than *Ladybird Ladybird*, which tried to be a kind of interior film and is nearer, I think, to *Kes* and *Family Life* [1971]. *Ladybird Ladybird* is not meant to be a social document. It's much more about damaged people, why and how they are damaged, and the consequences of trying to establish who you are in the face of other people. It's a story of grief and of grief that turns to anger and rage and destruction. That's really where the heart of the film is and the best way to show solidarity with Maggie seemed to be to share those feelings as far as we could.

Does this emphasis on the highly moving personal drama threaten the more political aspects of the story?

Not really, because it's the emotional damage that's done to the woman that illustrates the politics of it. The alternative is to detach the viewer from her experience. I think, however, if you can share her experience, then that gives you some of her anger and that's the springboard to be political. Otherwise you sit back and you don't feel her suffering and it's her suffering that drives you to say "what is the politics behind this?".

How clearly is it indicated what the spectator's anger is to be directed towards?

There isn't a simple answer. It is the cycle of poverty, deprivation, victimisation and the social context of that. It's very complicated, but clearly there is something wrong, isn't there? Clearly there's something we've got to try and deal with, discuss and sort out.

Is there a danger that the film may simply be seen as an attack on social workers at a time when they are already under sustained assault from the right?

170

You will be aware there is a whole left wing within the social services who say that despite their attempts to do good work they are nevertheless picking up the pieces of a rotten society and that we shouldn't be afraid of criticising them and obviously we were helped by social workers all the way through. I guess my answer is that these things did happen to that woman, and one of the pressures on social workers is simply to pick up the pieces and therefore they are led into these mistakes. I guess we felt in the end that the story was important enough to tell and that we shouldn't be afraid of political incorrectness. But it was something that weighed with us. We were at great pains to make certain that everybody who played a social worker was involved in some research, went with social workers for a day or so and actually argued it from their point of view. We also tried to put enough in the film to indicate why they took their decisions, so that it was never a black and white issue. If it gives rise to a debate about social workers, I think that's fine, but if it's seen as an attack on them obviously that's a misjudgment.

Do you feel that Ladybird Ladybird *is a less political film than* Cathy Come Home?

Oddly enough, I think we felt that one of the problems with *Cathy Come Home* was that it wasn't political enough because it had some dreadful captions at the end that said that they build more houses in West Germany than we build in Britain. Well, that's a daft thing to say, bearing in mind the Yanks have propped up the German economy and that it was a wholly artificial situation. We should have been ashamed of that. It dealt with homelessness but it didn't deal with the building industry, who controls it, who finances it. It didn't deal with the ownership of land, where you get land to build buildings on. It didn't deal with the location of employment. We very quickly tumbled to the fact of all the issues we left out. We showed it around various places like Parliament and they would all come along and stroke their chins and look at it. We went to meet the Housing Minister who was a supposed left-winger called Anthony Greenwood, and he said what a fine piece of work it was and how it helped us understand the problem of homelessness. We came out having had our heads patted and thought this is a guy that should know all this in the first place. It was a very liberal film in that it didn't challenge any of the issues that you have to deal with if you are going to deal with the question of who decides where houses are built, what price they are and all the rest of it. If we had put those issues in then we would really have challenged people, we would have challenged the Wimpeys and the McAlpines, and we would have challenged the whole structure. Of course, we didn't do that, so that's why the film could be patted on the head and helped to form a charity but nothing else.

I have always been struck by how lukewarm you and Tony Garnett have been about the political impact of Cathy Come Home, *probably one of the most controversial plays in the history of television drama. What are the implications of this for your commitment to political filmmaking? Do you think films really make a great difference to the world of politics?*

I don't know. All you can do is to try to ask a few questions, say things that will have a resonance with people, and be part of a broader movement. A film on its own is not worth much. We used to say that one good shop steward was worth twenty good filmmakers, and I think that was really trying to be provocative. There is, nonetheless, an element of truth in that. The problem is that political cinema is usually very right-wing. It is represented by *Patriot Games*, one guy with a gun who will go and solve all your problems. To try and make left-wing political cinema is very difficult, and by and large you can't do very much. What you can do is try and put an alternative view of the way things are, try and set up alternative values, ask questions and hope that the thing reverberates for a time.

One of your criticisms of Cathy Come Home *has been that it offers no perspective for change. How successful do you feel your most recent work has been in suggesting the prospects for change?*

I don't know. I hope that there's a sense of real solidarity with people in particular situations and that, by giving people their dignity and self-respect, the films prepare the way for a political analysis. I would hope that, without making it explicit, a political analysis underpins the films, and that you can only read them according to one political blueprint. You hope that this is implicit. Otherwise you end up with the slogan at the end and that's hopeless.

Do you have a sense then of who your audience is? Who do you make films for?

I don't think we have a very strong sense, not in the way that a marketing person would have a strong sense of a target audience. You simply hope that it's people like yourself who would enjoy going to watch the people, spending time with the people, sharing their experience, enjoying the story and then recognise that it fits into this view of the world.

How do you feel about people's access to these films? Riff-Raff *became European film of the year but hardly got a showing in British cinemas.*

It's a problem of the free market. If it is simply a market place, then obviously the big American films win. The problem is in the distribution and exhibition and, in the end, who owns the cinemas. I went to Norway where a lot of the cinemas are owned by the municipalities. They are programmed to include a good number of European films and that's been there for a long time. The consequence is that Norwegians are interested in European films and *Ladybird Ladybird*, just to take an example, opened in August 1994 and was still running in November. That's Norway. It shows that you can't just throw the odd British film in amongst a sea of American exploitation movies and be surprised when it fails. It's a question of developing and building an audience, and changing people's perceptions of what the cinema has to offer.

Do you show your films in environments other than cinemas?

Yes, quite a bit at different times. We had a showing of *Riff-Raff* for the Construction Safety Campaign and things like that. That can be very rewarding. The difficulty is usually one of cost. You can take it on video now to a room full of people, but getting a cinema for a 35mm print is quite a big deal.

What are the economics of your films? They are made on a relatively low budget even by British standards. Do they recoup their costs?

Riff-Raff, *Raining Stones* and *Ladybird Ladybird* cost between £800 000 and £900 000 each, and were almost entirely paid for by Channel 4. They write off nearly half that against their own television showings and then they recoup the rest from sales quite easily. So, in fact, I think they are all in profit. They are quite viable.

Are you very conscious of keeping costs down in order to maintain economic viability?

Yes. If you don't make films that are economically viable you won't make many films. And if you have a track record of getting money back, then you have more freedom. That small limitation gives you a much greater freedom.

Your Spanish Civil War film, Land and Freedom *[1995] is a somewhat bigger project. What is the background to your involvement in it?*

It's a subject that Jim Allen and I wanted to work on for some years. I guess that most people know the basic story of what happened in Spain: it was the first war against Fascism and a very important event in 20th-century politics. It was a subject that we thought we would like to deal with, and Jim and I started to work on the script six or seven years ago. We eventually raised the money and shot it in May-June 1994. About a third of it is in Spanish. If you make a film in another country then obviously the language is very important, particularly when people volunteered to fight Fascism from different countries. The language is very important for the sense of internationalism and just to tell the truth about what happened. So we ended up shooting about a third of it in Spanish and some of it in Catalan. In a sense that's part of the politics of the film and part of the politics of the event, but it did make it quite tricky when we got to cutting it.

Given your experience with Fatherland, *was it a problem working with actors who were speaking in Spanish and Catalan?*

Not really. I had somebody giving me the translation in my ear. The biggest scene that's in Spanish in the film is set during the first part of the war. I guess you know that the first part of the war was the Spanish revolution when people took over the land, took over the factories and there was workers' control in some of the industries. One of the key scenes we thought it was important to show was this process of people taking power over their own lives. So there's a scene where a village is liberated from the Fascists and the Republicans come in and take it. Then the people in the village have to decide what to do with the land, and some people want to collectivize and some people just want to take the land of the landowner and divide it up because he was a pro-Franco supporter. Some people want to hang on to their own farm because they reckoned they worked harder than anybody else and didn't want to give up their bit of land for a collective. All these arguments were really important. They had to be argued through and, of course, they had to be done in Spanish. There was no short cut.

All your recent films have been set in the present day and have dealt with contemporary social issues. With the notable exception of Days of Hope *[1975] you have done little historical drama. Was it something that you felt happy about doing?*

I've always had a great resistance to doing pieces set in the past because I think it's one of the blights of the British cinema that it worships the past. It's a kind of nostalgia and is now part of the heritage industry. I find that really depressing. But the story of the Spanish revolution is a story that nobody knows and it's such a terrific story that Jim and I have wanted to do it for years.

Although historical drama, Days of Hope *was also very much about the course of labour in the 1960s and 1970s. Do you think the Spanish Civil War has a resonance for the present?*

I think so. One element of the story that we tried to tell is the splits on the Republican side and the struggle for leadership between the anarchists and the Marxists and the Communists under the direction of Stalin. We also wanted to show why the Communists gained control of the struggle and how they led it. The Communists actually gave the land back to the landlords, so, if you know that about the Communist Party in the 1930s, it makes the whole business of the Cold War something of a charade. But we didn't do it in order to say 1995 reveals the real importance of the Spanish Civil War. It's because it's one of those enduring stories of the struggle for the leadership of the working-class movement or the revolutionary movement or whatever you like to call it, and of the great energy and power that was released then and how it was diverted and subverted. That has perhaps been the tragedy of the 20th century, so in a way it has been an enduring theme.

You have been critical of the heritage film and its nostalgia for the Edwardian upper class. Is there a danger that on the left we could have a nostalgia for the days of revolutionary Socialism?

I don't think it's nostalgia: it's heady stuff. What was interesting was that it was very much an alive issue. We tried to find people who would have fought the revolution today if it were to happen, and it wasn't dead history to them at all. It was very much alive, and with the Fascist standard being raised again in parts of Europe it doesn't seem totally nostalgic.

You've been making films for 30 years now. Has your approach changed significantly during this time?

Well, you try and get bolder each time, to be more adventurous and to take more chances. We felt before we started *Ladybird Ladybird* that there was a hell of a risk trying to do justice to the emotions that a woman would feel when a baby is taken from her hours after she has given birth in a hospital ward. We looked at the story and thought we must be mad. All the time you are trying to adapt whatever tricks you have picked up over the years to get that expression, that feeling, that scene, so that people feel "Christ – that's true!". So that's the risk you take all the time. The methods have only changed insofar as you are trying to refine it all the time in order to take bigger and bigger chances. The scene I was talking about in Spain where we have got a scene of some 40 or 50 people, only about a third of whom speak English. The rest talk in Valencian Spanish. Some are Catalans and they insist on talking Catalan because it's a national issue and somehow you've got to make a scene in which you want to show the excitement of people taking control of their lives, taking over the land they have worked for all their lives. You are right on the edge of the cliff really.

Notes

[1] This is a record of two interviews which took place in November 1994. The first was in front of an audience at the Foyle Film Festival in Derry, Northern Ireland; the second was at the offices of Parallax Pictures in London. The two interviews have been condensed and edited into one. My thanks to Ken Loach for his time and enthusiasm, and to Carol Kyle for the transcription.

[2] Troy Kennedy Martin, "Nats go home: first statement of a new drama for television", *Encore* 48 (March-April 1964).

[3] When the film was shown at Cannes the Conservative MP Ivor Stanbrook dubbed it "the official IRA entry", even though he had not actually seen the film. See Jeff Sawtell, "Where truth really *is* stranger than fiction", *Morning Star* 18779/72930 (11 January 1991): 4-5.

[4] Following the death of John Smith, Tony Blair took over the leadership of the Labour Party in July 1994. His campaign to replace Clause 4 of the Party constitution and its commitment to public ownership has been strongly opposed by Loach, who made a 22-minute video for the Defend Clause 4 Group in early 1995. For his response to Labour Party criticisms of the video, see "Tooth and clause", *The Guardian* 24 February 1995: Sec. 2, 4.

[5] *The Times* leader appeared on 10 January 1991, under the title of "Fictional Faction". A letter from Loach subsequently appeared, in which he defended the film and complained that *The Times* writer had not objected to the "interpretation of real events in dramatic form" in *Reversal of Fortune* (Barbet Schroeder, 1990). The writer, he suggested, was simply "opposed to the politics of one and indifferent to the other" ("'Hidden Agenda'", *The Times* 22 January 1991: 11).

Ken Loach: filmography

Compiled by George McKnight

In compiling this filmography, particular emphasis has been given to the broadcasting institutions and production companies for which Loach has worked, to the television series (programmes) for which a work was produced, and to the producers, writers, actors and craftspeople with whom he has worked at various stages during his career or on a continuing basis. The following abbreviations have been used:

KL	Ken Loach	*m*	music
ad	art director	m	minutes
ATV	Associated Television	*p*	producer
BBC	British Broadcasting	*pc*	production company
	Corporation	*pd*	production designer
bw	black and white	*ph*	cinematographer
C4	Channel 4 Television	*s*	story; source
col	colour	*sc*	scriptwriter
ed	editor	*se*	story editor
ep	executive producer	*ser*	television series
LWT	London Weekend	tx:	first television transmission
	Television		

[Unless indicated otherwise, all films are directed by Ken Loach and produced in Great Britain.]

Catherine
1964   30m   bw   tx: 24 January 1964, BBC-1
pc BBC *ser* Teletales *p* James MacTaggart *sc* Roger Smith *ad* Robert Fuest *m* Dennis Wilson
main cast Geoffrey Whitehead (narrator), Kika Markham (Catherine), Peter Hoy (car salesman), Gilbert Wynne (Jack), Tony Garnett (Richard), David Bedard (Dave), Tony Selby (singer), David Hart, Peter Blythe, John Downey (young men).

Z Cars
1964   50m (each episode)   bw
pc BBC *p* David Rose
[The original *Z Cars* series ran from January 1962 until December

1965. Loach directed three episodes in early 1964.]
: "Profit by their Example" (tx: 12 February 1964, BBC-1) *p* David
Rose *sc* John Hopkins *se* Robert Barr *ed* Christopher La Fontaine
: "A Straight Deal" (tx: 11 March 1964, BBC-1) *p* David Rose
sc, se Robert Barr *ed* Christopher La Fontaine
: "The Whole Truth" (tx: 8 April 1964, BBC-1) *p* David Rose
sc, se Robert Barr

Diary of a Young Man
1964 6x45m bw
pc BBC *p* James MacTaggart *sc* John McGrath, Troy Kennedy Martin
se Roger Smith *ph* John McGlashan *ed* Christopher La Fontaine
ad John Cooper, Peter Seddon *m* Stanley Myers
main cast Victor Henry (Joe), Nerys Hughes (Rose), Richard Moore
(Ginger), Roy Godfrey (Mr Silver), Leslie Dwyer (Mr Gold), Will
Stampe (Uncle Arthur), Glynn Edwards (police constable).
[KL directed the first, third and fifth episodes: "Survival" (tx: 8 August
1964, BBC-1), "Marriage" (tx: 22 August 1964, BBC-1) and "Life" (tx: 5
September 1964, BBC-1).]

A Tap on the Shoulder
1965 70m bw tx: 6 January 1965, BBC-1
pc BBC *ser* The Wednesday Play *p* James MacTaggart *sc* James
O'Connor *se* Roger Smith *pd* Eileen Diss *m* Stanley Myers
main cast Lee Montague (Archibald Cooper), Richard Shaw (Ronnie),
Judith Smith (Hazel), Griffith Davies (Terry), George Tovey (Patsy),
Tony Selby (Tim), Edwin Brown (George), Mark Elwes (pub
customer), John Henderson (Clegg), Tom Bowman (Charlie).

Wear a Very Big Hat
1965 75m bw tx: 17 February 1965, BBC-1
pc BBC *ser* The Wednesday Play *p* James MacTaggart *sc* Eric Coltart
se Roger Smith *ph* Stanley Speel *ed* Norman Carr *ad* Peter Kindred
m Stanley Speel
main cast Neville Smith (Johnny Johnson), Sheila Fearn (Ann
Johnson), William Holmes (Snapper Melia), Johnny Clive (Billy
Mofatt), Malcolm Taylor (Stan), Alan Lake (Harry Atkins), Nola York,
Royston Tickner, William Gaunt.

Three Clear Sundays
1965 75m bw tx: 7 April 1965, BBC-1
pc BBC *ser* The Wednesday Play *p* James MacTaggart *sc* James
O'Connor *se* Roger Smith *ph* Tony Imi *ed* Pam Bosworth
main cast Tony Selby (Danny Lee), Rita Webb (Britannia Lee), Dickie
Owen (Big Al), Will Stampe (Porky), John Blithe (Jimmy the Gent),
Finuala O'Shannon (Rosa), Glynn Edwards (prison officer Johnson),

George Sewell (Johnny May), Kim Peacock (prison governor).

Up the Junction
1965 72m bw tx: 3 November 1965, BBC-1
pc BBC *ser* The Wednesday Play *p* James MacTaggart *sc* Nell Dunn
se Tony Garnett *ph* Tony Imi *ed* Roy Watts *pd* Eileen Diss *m* Paul
Jones
main cast Carol White (Sylvie), Geraldine Sherman (Rube), Vickery
Turner (Eileen), Tony Selby (Dave), Michael Standing (Terry), Ray
Barron (Ron), Rita Webb (Mrs Hardy), George Sewell (the tallyman).

The End of Arthur's Marriage
1965 70m bw tx: 17 November 1965, BBC-1
pc BBC *ser* The Wednesday Play *p* James MacTaggart *sc* Christopher
Logue *pd* Robert Macgowan *m* Stanley Myers, Paul Jones
main cast Ken Jones (Arthur), Charles Lamb (Dad), Winifred Dennis
(Mum), Janie Booth (Mavis), Maureen Ampleford (Emmy), Joanna
Dunham (Mrs Thurloe), Edward De Souza (Mr Thurloe), Neville
Smith, Tracy Rogers.

The Coming Out Party
1965 65m bw tx: 22 December 1965, BBC-1
pc BBC *ser* The Wednesday Play *p* James MacTaggart *sc* James
O'Connor *pd* Michael Wield *m* Stanley Myers
main cast Toni Palmer (Rosie), George Sewell (Ricketts), Dennis
Golding (Scrimpy), Jayne Muir (Sister Bridget), Wally Patch
(grandad), Hilda Barry (grandmother), Julie May (Wendy), Rita Webb
(Floss), Carol White, Will Stampe.

Cathy Come Home
1966 75m bw 16mm tx: 16 November 1966, BBC-1
pc BBC *ser* The Wednesday Play *p* Tony Garnett *sc* Jeremy Sandford,
KL *ph* Tony Imi *ed* Roy Watts *pd* Sally Hulke *m* Paul Jones
main cast Carol White (Cathy), Ray Brooks (Reg), Winifred Dennis
(Mrs Ward), Phyllis Hickson (Mrs Alley), Wally Patch (grandad),
Adrienne Frame (Eileen), Emmett Hennessey (Johnny), Alec Coleman
(guest at wedding), Ronald Pember (Mr Jones), Liz McKenzie (Mrs
Jones), Gabrielle Hamilton (welfare officer), Geoffrey Palmer
(property agent), Anne Ayres (Pauline Jones), Frank Veasy (Mr
Hodge), Barry Jackson (rent collector), David Crane (barrister).

In Two Minds
1967 75m bw tx: 1 March 1967, BBC-1
pc BBC *ser* The Wednesday Play *p* Tony Garnett *sc* David Mercer
ph Tony Imi *ed* Roy Watts *pd* John Hurst
main cast Anna Cropper (Kate Winter), Brian Phelan (interviewing

doctor), George A Cooper (Mr Winter), Helen Booth (Mrs Winter), Adrienne Frame (hairdresser), Peter Ellis (Jake), Christine Hargreaves (Mary Winter), George Innes (Paul Morris), Anne Hardcastle (doctor).

Poor Cow
1967 101m col 35mm
pc Vic Films/Fenchurch *p* Joseph Janni *sc* KL, Nell Dunn *novel* Nell Dunn *ph* Brian Probyn *ed* Roy Watts *ad* Bernard Sarron *m* Donovan
main cast Carol White (Joy), Terence Stamp (Dave), John Bindon (Tom), Kate Williams (Beryl), Queenie Watts (Aunt Emm), Geraldine Sherman (Trixie), James Beckett, Bill Murray (Tom's mates), Ellis Dale (solicitor), Gerald Young (judge).

The Golden Vision
1968 75m bw tx: 17 April 1968, BBC-1
pc BBC *ser* The Wednesday Play *p* Tony Garnett *sc* Neville Smith, Gordon Honeycombe *pd* Malcolm Middleton
main cast Ken Jones (Joe Horrigan), Bill Dean (John Coyne), Neville Smith (Vince Coyne), Joey Kaye (Brian Croft), Johnny Gee (Syd Paisley), Flora Manger (Annie Coyne), Angela Small (Celia Horrigan), Patricia Bush (Muriel Coyne).

In Black and White
aka The Save the Children Fund Film
1969 50m col not transmitted
pc Kestrel *p* Tony Garnett *narr* Alan Dobie

The Big Flame
1969 85m bw tx: 19 February 1969, BBC-1
pc BBC *ser* The Wednesday Play *p* Tony Garnett *sc* Jim Allen
ph John McGlashan *ed* Roy Watts *pd* Geoff Patterson
main cast Godfrey Quigley (Jack Regan), Norman Rossington (Danny Fowler), Peter Kerrigan (Peter Conner), Ken Jones (Freddie Grierson), Daniel Stephens (Joe Ryan), Tommy Summers (Alec Murphy), Meredith Edwards (Logan), Michael Forrest (Garfield), John Riley (Bruno), Harold Kinsella (Andy Fowler), Joan Flood (Liz Fowler), Terence Flood (Liz Fowler's son), Ron Davies, (Steve Fowler), Roland MacLeod (Weldon), Gerald Young (judge).

Kes
1969 113m col 35mm
pc Woodfall Films/Kestrel Films *p* Tony Garnett *sc* Barry Hines, KL, Tony Garnett *s* novel by Barry Hines *ph* Chris Menges *ed* Roy Watts *ad* William McCrow *m* John Cameron
main cast David Bradley (Billy Casper), Lynne Perrie (Mrs Casper), Freddie Fletcher (Jud), Colin Welland (Mr Farthing), Brian Glover (Mr

Sugden), Bob Bowes (Mr Gryce), Robert Naylor (Mr MacDowall), Trevor Hesketh (Mr Crossley), Geoffrey Banks (mathematics teacher). *awards* Karlovy Vary Film Festival; Best Supporting Actor (Colin Welland), British Film Academy 1970.

Family Life
aka Wednesday's Child
1971 108m col 35mm
pc Kestrel Films/Anglo Amalgamated-EMI *ep* Bob Blues *p* Tony Garnett *sc* David Mercer *s* television play, "In Two Minds", by David Mercer *ph* Charles Stewart *ed* Roy Watts *ad* William McCrow *m* Marc Wilkinson
main cast Sandy Ratcliff (Janice Baildon), Bill Dean (Mr Baildon), Grace Cave (Mrs Baildon), Malcolm Tierney (Tim), Hilary Martyn (Barbara Baildon), Michael Riddall (Dr Donaldson), Alan McNaughton (Mr Carswell), Johnny Gee (man in garden).

Talk About Work
1971 16m col 16mm
pc Ronald H Riley Associates, for the Central Office of Information and the Central Youth Employment Executive in association with the Department of Employment *p* Michael Barden *ph* Chris Menges

The Rank and File
1971 75m bw 16mm tx: 20 May 1971, BBC-1
pc BBC *ser* Play for Today *p* Graeme McDonald *sc* Jim Allen *ph* Charles Stewart *ed* Roy Watts *pd* Roger Andrews
main cast Peter Kerrigan (Eddie Marsden), Bill Dean (Billy), Tommy Summers (Les Sanders), Neville Smith (Jerry), Joan Flood (Joan), Johnny Gee (Johnny), Mike Hayden (Mike), Bert King (Bert), Jimmy Coleman (Jimmy), Ernie Mack (Bill Hagan), Michael Forrest (Holtby).

After a Lifetime
1971 75m col 16mm tx: 18 July 1971, LWT
pc Kestrel Films for LWT *p* Tony Garnett *sc* Neville Smith *ph* Chris Menges *ed* Ray Helm *pd* Andrew Drummond *m* John Cameron
main cast Edie Brooks (May), Neville Smith (young Billy), Jimmy Coleman (Aloysius), Peter Kerrigan (Uncle John), Bill Dean (Uncle Sid), Johnny Gee (Frank), Sammy Sharples (Uncle Gus), Joey Kaye (Mike), Joan Flood (Cissie), Mike Hayden (Father MacNally).

A Misfortune
1973 38m col 16mm tx: 13 January 1973, BBC-2
pc BBC *ser* Full House *sc* KL *s* Anton Chekhov
main cast Lucy Fleming, Ben Kingsley, Peter Eyre, Xenia Deberner, Vyvan Ekkel, John Langford.

Days of Hope
1975 col 16mm
pc BBC *p* Tony Garnett *sc* Jim Allen *ph* Tony Pierce-Roberts, John
Else *ed* Roger Waugh *pd* Martin Johnson *m* Marc Wilkinson
main cast Paul Copley (Ben Matthews), Pamela Brighton (Sarah
Hargreaves), Nikolas Simmonds (Philip Hargreaves), Christine
Anderson (Jenny Barnett), Peter Kerrigan (Peter), Patrick Barr (Mr
Harrington), Helen Beck (Martha Matthews), Brian Harrison (Alfred
Purcell), Brian Hawksley (prison chaplain), Clifford Kershaw (Tom
Matthews), Bert King (prison warder), Gary Roberts (Joel Barnett),
Peter Russell (soldier on leave), Neil Seiler (Arthur Pugh), Jean
Spence (May Barnett), Russell Waters (Jimmy Thomas).
[Comprises "Days of Hope 1916: Joining Up" (tx: 11 September 1975,
BBC-1; 95m), "Days of Hope 1921" (tx: 18 September 1975, BBC-1;
100m), "Days of Hope 1924" (tx: 25 September 1975, BBC-1; 80m);
"Days of Hope 1926: General Strike" (tx: 2 October 1975, BBC-1;
135m)]

The Price of Coal
1977 col 16mm
pc BBC *ser* Play for Today *p* Tony Garnett *sc* Barry Hines *ph* Brian
Tufano *ed* Roger Waugh *pd* Martin Collins
main cast Bobby Knutt (Sid Storey), Rita May (Kath Storey), Paul
Chappell (Tony Storey), Jayne Waddington (Janet Storey), Haydn
Conway (Mark Storey), Jackie Shinn (Mr Forbes), Duggie Brown
(Geoff Carter), Bert Oxley (Phil Beatson), Ted Beyer (Harry), Hughie
Turner (Bob Richards), Tommy Edwards (Alf Meakin), Anne Firth
(Sheila), Robbie Platts (Mr Atkinson).
[Comprises "Meet the People" (tx: 29 March 1977, BBC-1; 75m) and
"Back to Reality" (tx: 5 April 1977, BBC-1; 85m)]

Black Jack
1979 110m col 35mm/16mm
pc Kestrel Films, in association with the National Film Finance
Corporation *ep* Bobby Blues *p* Tony Garnett *sc* KL *s* novel by Leon
Garfield *ph* Chris Menges *ed* William Shapter *ad* Martin Johnson
m Bob Pegg
main cast Stephen Hirst (Bartholomew "Tolly" Pickering), Louise
Cooper (Belle Carter), Jean Franval (Black Jack), Phil Askham
(Hangman), Pat Wallis (Mrs Gorgandy), John Young (Dr Hunter),
William Moore (Mr Carter), Doreen Mantle (Mrs Carter).
awards Cannes Critics Award

Auditions
1979 60m bw 16mm tx: 23 December 1980, ATV
pc ATV *p* KL *ph* Chris Menges *ed* Jonathan Morris

A Question of Leadership
1980 50m col 16mm tx: 13 August 1981, ATV
pc ATV *p* KL *sc* Barry Hines *ph* Chris Menges, John Davey *ed* Roger
James

The Gamekeeper
1980 84m col 16mm tx: 16 December 1980, ATV
pc ATV *p* Ashley Bruce, June Breakell, Julie Stoner *sc* Barry Hines
s "The Gamekeeper" by Barry Hines *ph* Chris Menges, Charles
Stewart *ed* Roger James *pd* Martin Johnson, Graham Tew
main cast Phil Askham (George Purse), Rita May (Mary), Andrew
Grubb (John), Peter Steele (Ian), Michael Hinchcliffe (Bob), Philip
Firth (Frank), Les Hickin (Jack), Jackie Shinn, Paul Brian.

Looks and Smiles
1981 104m bw 35mm
pc Black Lion Films in association with Kestrel Films, for Central
Television *ep* Jack Gill *p* Irving Teitelbaum *ph* Chris Menges *sc* Barry
Hines *ed* Steve Singleton *ad* Martin Johnson *m* Marc Wilkinson,
Richard and the Taxmen
main cast Graham Green (Mick Walsh), Carolyn Nicholson (Karen
Lodge), Tony Pitts (Alan Wright), Roy Haywood (Phil Adams), Phil
Askham (Mr Walsh), Pam Darrell (Mrs Walsh), Tracey Goodlad
(Julie), Patti Nichols (Mrs Wright), Cilla Mason (Mrs Lodge), Les
Hickin (George), Arthur Davies (Mr Lodge), Deirdre Costello (Jenny).
awards Cannes Prize, Contemporary Cinema

The Red and the Blue
1983 90m col 16mm tx: 1 October 1983, C4
pc Central Television *p* Roger James *ph* Chris Menges *ed* Jonathan
Morris

Questions of Leadership
1983 4 parts, each originally 50m col 16mm
not transmitted
pc Central Television for C4 *ep* Roger James *p* KL *ph* Jimmy Dibling
ed Jonathan Morris

Which Side Are You On?
1984 50m col 16mm
not transmitted by LWT / tx: 9 January 1985, C4
pc LWT (for the South Bank Show) *ep* Melvyn Bragg *p* KL *ph* Chris
Menges, Jimmy Dibling *ed* Jonathan Morris

The End of the Battle but not of the War
1985 27m col video tx: 27 March 1985, C4

pc Diverse Productions, for C4 *ser* Diverse Reports *p* Alex Graham
d Philip Clark *guest editor* KL *research* Roy Ackerman
[KL edited a programme on the coal dispute]

Fatherland
GB/W Germ/France 1986 111m col/bw 35mm
pc Film Four International (London)/Clasart Film (Munich)/MK2
(Paris). A Kestrel II production. With the participation of the French
Ministry of Culture *ep* Irving Teitelbaum *p* Raymond Day *sc* Trevor
Griffiths *ph* Chris Menges *ed* Jonathan Morris *pd* Martin Johnson
m Christian Kunert, Gerulf Pannach
main cast Gerulf Pannach (Klaus Drittemann), Fabienne Babe
(Emma de Baen), Sigfrit Steiner (James Dryden, formerly Jacob
Drittemann), Cristine Rose (Lucy Bernstein), Robert Dietl (East
German lawyer), Heike Schrotter (Marita), Stephan Samuel (Max).
awards UNICEF A. Venice 1986

Time To Go
1989 15m col 16mm tx: 9 May 1989, BBC-2
pc BBC (Community Programmes Unit) *ep* Gavin Dutton *ser* Split
Screen

The View from the Woodpile
1989 52m col 16mm tx: 12 June 1989, C4
pc Central Independent Television, for C4 *ep* Roger James *ser* The
Eleventh Hour *p* KL *ph* Barry Ackroyd, Robin Proby *ed* Paul Jackson,
Mike Burch

Hidden Agenda
1990 108m col 35mm
pc Initial Film and Television Production. In association with
Hemdale *ep* John Daly, Derek Gibson *p* Eric Fellner *sc* Jim Allen
ph Clive Tickner *ed* Jonathan Morris *pd* Martin Johnson *ad* Nigel
Phelps *m* Stewart Copeland
main cast Frances McDormand (Ingrid Jessner), Brian Cox
(Kerrigan), Brad Dourif (Paul Sullivan), Mai Zetterling (Moa), Maurice
Roëves (Harris), Robert Patterson (Ian Logan), Bernard Archard (Sir
Robert Neil), John Benfield (Maxwell), Bernard Bloch (Henri),
George Staines (Tall Man), Michelle Fairley (Teresa Doyle), Patrick
Kavanagh (Alec Nevin), Brian McCann (Molloy), Des McAleer
(Sergeant Kennedy), Ian McElhinney (Jack Cunningham), Jim Norton
(Brodie).
awards Special Jury Prize at Cannes

Riff-Raff
1991 95m col 16mm

pc Parallax Pictures for C4 *p* Sally Hibbin *sc* Bill Jesse *ph* Barry Ackroyd *ed* Jonathan Morris *pd* Martin Johnson *ad* Jonathan Lee *m* Stewart Copeland
main cast Robert Carlyle (Stevie), Emer McCourt (Susan), Jimmy Coleman (Shem), George Moss (Mo), Ricky Tomlinson (Larry), David Finch (Kevin), Richard Belgrave (Kojo), Ade Sapara (Fiaman), Derek Young (Desmonde), Bill Moores (Smurph), Luke Kelly (Ken Jones), Garrie J Lammin (Mick), Willie Ross (Gus Siddon), Dean Perry (Wilf).
awards Film of the Year (Félix), European Film Awards; International Critics Award, Cannes.

The Arthur Legend
1991 40m col 16mm tx: 22 May 1991, C4
pc Clark Productions for C4 *ser* Dispatches *p* Lorraine Heggessey *ph* Barry Ackroyd, Stephen Sanden *ed* Jonathan Morris

Raining Stones
1993 91m col 35mm
pc Parallax Pictures for C4 *p* Sally Hibbin *sc* Jim Allen *ph* Barry Ackroyd *ed* Jonathan Morris *pd* Martin Johnson *ad* Fergus Clegg *m* Stewart Copeland
main cast Bruce Jones (Bob Williams), Julie Brown (Anne Williams), Gemma Phoenix (Coleen Williams), Ricky Tomlinson (Tommy), Tom Hickey (Father Barry), Mike Fallon (Jimmy), Ronnie Ravey (butcher), Lee Brennan (Irishman), Karen Henthorn (young mother), Christine Abbott (May), William Ash (Joe), Geraldine Ward (Tracey).
awards Cannes Jury Prize

Ladybird Ladybird
1994 101m col 35mm
pc Parallax Pictures for C4 *p* Sally Hibbin *sc* Rona Munro *ph* Barry Ackroyd *ed* Jonathan Morris *pd* Martin Johnson *ad* Fergus Clegg *m* George Fenton
main cast Crissy Rock (Maggie), Vladimir Vega (Jorge), Ray Winstone (Simon), Sandie Lavelle (Mairead), Mauricio Venegas (Adrian), Clare Perkins (Jill), Jason Stracey (Sean), Luke Brown (Mickey), Lily Farrell (Serena), Scottie Moore (Maggie's father), Linda Ross (Maggie's mother), Kim Hartley (Maggie, aged 5).
awards International Critics Prize, Berlin Film Festival

A Contemporary Case for Common Ownership
aka Clause IV: The Movie
1995 22m col video
pc Defend Clause Four Campaign

Land and Freedom
GB/Spain/Germany 1995 110m col 35mm
pc Parallax Pictures/Messidor Films/Road Movies Dritte. With the
participation of British Screen/The European Co-Production Fund
(UK)/Television Española/Canal Plus (Spain)/BBC Films/Degeto for
ARD and Filmstiftung Nordrhein-Westfalen. With the support of BIM
Distribuzione/Diaphana/Eurimages Fund of the Council of Europe
ep Sally Hibbin, Gerardo Herrero, Ulrich Felsberg *p* Rebecca O'Brien
sc Jim Allen *se* Roger Smith *ph* Barry Ackroyd *ed* Jonathan Morris
pd Martin Johnson *m* George Fenton
main cast Ian Hart (David Carne), Rosana Pastor (Blanca), Iciar
Bollain (Maite), Tom Gilroy (Gene Lawrence), Marc Martinez (Vidal),
Frederic Pierrot (Bernard), Suzanne Maddock (Kim), Angela Clarke
(Kitty).
awards Film of the Year (Félix), European Film Awards

The Flickering Flame
GB/France 1996 50m col Super 16mm/video tx: 18 December
1996, BBC-2
pc Parallax Pictures/AMIP/BBC/La Sept/ARTE *ser* Modern Times
p Rebecca O'Brien, Xavier Carniaux *ph* Roger Chapman, Barry
Ackroyd *ed* Tony Pound, Anthony Morris *narr* Brian Cox

Carla's Song
GB/Germany/Spain 1996 125m col 35mm
pc Channel 4 Television Corporation and the Glasgow Film Fund. A
Parallax Picture in co-production with Road Movies Dritte
Produktionen and Tornasol Films SA. With the support of the
Institute of Culture, Nicaragua, and ARD/DEGETO Film, Filmstiftung
Nordrhein-Westfalen, Television Española and Alta Films, the
European Script Fund, and the Scottish Film Production Fund *p* Sally
Hibbin *sc* Paul Laverty *ph* Barry Ackroyd *ed* Jonathan Morris
pd Martin Johnson *ad* Llorenç Miquel, Fergus Clegg *m* George
Fenton
main cast Robert Carlyle (George), Oyanka Cabezas (Carla), Scott
Glenn (Bradley), Salvador Espinoza (Rafael), Louise Goodall
(Maureen), Richard Loza (Antonio), Gary Lewis (Sammy), Subash
Singh Pall (Victor), Stewart Preston (McGurk).
awards Venice Film Festival: Gold Medal, President of the Senate;
Best Film in the Competition (Youth Vote).

Ken Loach: selected bibliography

Compiled by Matthew Stevens and George McKnight

Primary bibliography

A: Published screenplays

Sandford, Jeremy. *Cathy Come Home* (London: Marion Boyars, 1976).

B: Statements by Loach

"A question of censorship", *Tribune* 47: 47 (25 November 1983): 7.
"Broadcasters who uphold the established order through the charade of impartiality", *The Guardian* 31 October 1983: 9.
"'Hidden Agenda', *The Times* 22 January 1991: 11 [letter].
"How Channel Four's balancing act falls down", *The Guardian* 22 November 1983: 12 [letter].
"La Mort d'une nation", *Positif* 400 (June 1994): 75 [in French].
"Market takes all", *Index on Censorship* 24: 6 (November-December 1995): 158-159.
"Nat Cohen: his handshake was his bond", *Screen International* 641 (27 February-5 March 1988): 6 [letter from Loach, Tony Garnett and David Puttnam].
"Only One Film", *Time Out* 99 (7-13 January 1972): 33.
"Questions of ownership", *Red Pepper* April 1995: 20.
"Run fast to stay standing", *The Guardian* 31 December 1993: 4-5.
"The establishment always prevails", *New Statesman and Society* 4: 145 (5 April 1991): 20-21 [part of *Banned* supplement, under the heading "Banned by the British"].
"Tooth and clause", *The Guardian* 24 February 1995: Sec. 2, 4.
"True record", *The Daily Telegraph* 24 May 1991: 18 [letter].
"Writers' rights and a kangaroo Court", *The Guardian* 18 February 1987: 28.

C: Interviews with Loach

Alion, Yves. "Entretien avec Ken Loach: L'intègre", *La Revue du Cinéma* 476 (November 1991): 28-29 [in French].
Amiel, Mireille. "Kenneth Loach: 'Solidaires des courants de pensée qui dépassent le cinéma..'", *Cinéma (France)* 171 (December 1972): 74-77 [in French].
Aziz, Christine. "Shoulder to shoulder", *The Observer* 22 March 1987: 23.
Birch, Helen. "Ken Loach: A Very British Director", *Empire* 53 (November 1993): 59.

Blaney, Martin. "Ken Loach", *Filmfaust* 56/57 (January-February 1987): 20-22 [in German].

Bourget, Jean-Loup, Lorenzo Codelli and Hubert Niogret. "Entretien avec Ken Loach: 'Milicien plutôt que soldat'", *Positif* 416 (October 1995): 73-79 [in French].

Bream, Paul. "Spreading Wings at Kestrel", *Films and Filming* 18: 6 (March 1972): 36-40.

Brett, Anwar. "Pleasant surprises", *What's On in London* 17 April 1991: 17.

Brooks, Richard. "The prophet incentive", *The Observer (Review)* 28 May 1995: 6.

Brown, Robert. "Continuing...the State of Things", *Monthly Film Bulletin* 50: 588 (January 1983): 11.

Ciment, Michel. "Entretien avec Ken Loach: 'Le sentiment de l'inéluctable'", *Positif* 404 (October 1994): 8-12 [in French].

Collins, Mike. "Spanish Guns", *Film Ireland* 49 (October/November 1995): 24-25.

Crozier, Siobhan. "Loach does the Cannes Cannes", *City Limits* 10 January 1991.

Cryer, John. "No Ken do", *Tribune* 59: 17 (28 April 1995): 9.

"Discussion with Ken Loach", in Jonathan Hacker and David Price, *Take Ten: Contemporary British Film Directors* (Oxford: Clarendon Press, 1991): 292-303.

Eimer, David. "Ken Loach", *Premiere (UK)* 3: 9 (October 1995): 32.

"*Family Life* in the making", *Jump Cut* 10/11 (summer 1976): 41-45 [originally appeared in *7 Days* 12 January 1972].

Garel, Sylvain. "Ken Loach", *Cinéma (France)* 468 (June 1990): 14-15 [in French].

Gilbey, Ryan. "If anyone can, Ken can", *The Independent* 5 April 1996: 6.

Glomm, Lasse. "Socialist utan politisk etikett", *Chaplin* 116: 5 (1972): 182-184 [in Swedish].

Guerand, Jean-Philippe. "A traverse le miroir", *Première (France)* 122 (May 1987): 184-185 [in French].

Guibert, Hervé. "Des jeunes sans importance", *Le Monde* 14 May 1981 [in French].

Hardwick, Claude and Roger. "Ken Loach: Famille et névrose", *Jeune Cinéma* 66 (November 1972): 29-33 [in French].

Hattenstone, Simon. "Rock steady", *The Guardian* 29 September 1994: 10-11.

Hodges, Adrian. "Reflecting the current climate", *Screen International* 294 (30 May-6 June 1981): 11.

Jivani, Alkarim. "Raff justice", *Time Out* 1087 (19-26 June 1991): 62.

Johnsen, Frank. "Politisk rundbrenner", *Film og Kino* 4 (1995): 16 [in Norwegian].

"Kenneth Loach: Choquer le spectateur pour qu'il médite", *l'Avant-Scène du Cinéma* 133 (February 1973): 12 [in French].

Kerr, Paul. "The Complete Ken Loach", *Stills* 27 (May-June 1986): 144-148.

Lavoignat, Jean-Pierre. "Messieurs les Anglais...", *Studio* 99 (1995): 100-103 [in French].

"L'équipe du film s'explique: Conférence de presse de Ken Loach", *Jeune Cinéma* 202 (June-July 1990): 26-28 [in French].

Libiot, Eric. "Ken Loach: L'Angleterre à vif", *Première (France)* 199 (October 1993): 82-83 [in French].

Macnab, Geoffrey. "Ladybird Ladybird: The director", *Sight and Sound* 4: 11 (November 1994): 13-14.

Mackie, Lindsay. "Uncovering the hidden agenda", *The Scotsman* 19 January 1991: 11.

Nacache, Jacqueline. "Entretien: 'Fatherland' par Ken Loach", *Cinéma (France)* 398 (6-21 May 1987): 16 [in French].

Naughton, Mike. "Conspiracy in close up", *Morning Star* 18779/72930 (11 January 1991): 4-5.

Nave, Bernard. "Entretien avec Ken Loach", *Jeune Cinéma* 127 (June 1980): 27-30 [in French].

——————. "Entretien avec Ken Loach", *Jeune Cinéma* 178 (January-February 1987): 7-11 [in French; includes extracts from dialogue of *Fatherland*].

——————. "Une fiction enracinée dans le réel", *Jeune Cinéma* 137 (September/October 1981): 10-15 [in French].

O'Hara, John. "Ken Loach: Days of Hope", *Cinema Papers* 12 (April 1977): 298-301.

Olsen, Claus Ib. "Samtale med Ken Loach", *Kosmorama* 20: 120 (April 1974): 179-183 [in Danish].

Ostria, Vincent. "Entretien avec Ken Loach", *Cahiers du Cinéma* 484 (October 1994): 37-41 [in French].

Pede, Ronnie. "Looks and Smiles", *Film en Televisie* 294 (November 1981): 20-22 [in Dutch].

Petley, Julian. "An Interview with Ken Loach", *Framework* 18 (1982): 9-12.

——————. "The Spanish connection", *Living Marxism* October 1995: 38-39.

Pilard, Philippe. "Entretien avec Ken Loach: Vingt-cinq ans de cinéma", *Positif* 392 (October 1993): 18-23 [in French; includes "Biofilmographie de Ken Loach" by Hubert Niogret].

——————. "Rencontre avec Ken Loach", *La Revue du Cinéma/Image et Son/Écran* 350 (May 1980): 59-60 [in French].

Porton, Richard. "The Revolution Betrayed: An Interview with Ken Loach", *Cineaste* 22: 1 (April 1996): 30-31.

Quart, Leonard. "A Fidelity to the Real: An Interview with Ken Loach and Tony Garnett", *Cineaste* 10: 4 (autumn 1980): 26-29.

Rinaldi, Giorgio. "L'ultimo arrabbiato – Conversazione con Ken Loach", *Cineforum* 310 (December 1991): 75-76 [in Italian].

Smith, Gavin. "Sympathetic Images", *Film Comment* 30: 2 (March-April 1994): 58-67.

——————. "Voice in the Dark", *Film Comment* 24: 2 (March-April 1988): 38-46.

"Talking to Ken Loach", *Vertigo (UK)* 1: 6 (autumn 1996): 14.

Waddy, Stacy. "Content with content", *The Guardian* 30 June 1969: 6.

Secondary bibliography

A: Monographs devoted to Loach (on individual films or his work in its entirety)

Fedeli, Sveva. *Ken Loach* (Firenze: Mediateca Regionale Toscana, 1992) [in Italian].

Ken Loach (Barcelona: Filmoteca de la Generalitat de Catalunya, 1986) [in
   Spanish].
Monaco, James. *Loach/Hatton* (New York: New York School Department
   of Film, 1974).
Petley, Julian. *Ken Loach: La mirada radical* (Valladolid: Semana
   Internacional de Cine de Valladolid, 1992) [in Spanish].

B: Chapters or sections on Loach or his work in books, and theses

Bennett, Tony, Susan Boyd-Bowman, Colin Mercer and Janet Woollacott
   (eds). *Popular Television and Film* (London: British Film Institute, in
   association with The Open University, 1981): 285-352.
Brandt, George W (ed). *British television drama* (Cambridge: Cambridge
   University Press, 1981) [includes "Jim Allen" (36-55) and "Jeremy
   Sandford" (194-216)].
Corner, John. *The Art of record: A critical introduction to documentary*
   (Manchester; New York: Manchester University Press, 1996): 90-107.
"Essay on Ken Loach", in Jonathan Hacker and David Price, *Take Ten:
   Contemporary British Film Directors* (Oxford: Clarendon Press, 1991):
   273-291 [also includes "Filmography" (304-307) and "Bibliography"
   (308-309)].
Goodwin, Andrew. *British Television Drama 1946-80* (Centre for
   Contemporary Cultural Studies, University of Birmingham, 1981).
—————————. *Teaching TV Drama-Documentary* (London: British
   Film Institute, 1986).
Goodwin, Andrew, Paul Kerr and Ian Macdonald (eds). *Drama-
   Documentary* (London: British Film Institute, 1983).
"Ken Loach", in John Wakeman, *World Film Directors 1945-1985*, volume
   2 (New York: H W Wilson Company, 1988): 593-597.
"Kenneth Loach", in Richard Roud (ed), *Cinema: A Critical Dictionary. The
   Major Film-Makers*, volume 2 (London: Secker & Warburg, 1980): 630-
   631.
Kerr, Paul. "F for Fake? Friction over Faction", in Andrew Goodwin and
   Garry Whannel (eds), *Understanding Television* (London; New York:
   Routledge, 1990): 74-102.
Levin, G Roy. "Tony Garnett and Kenneth Loach", in *Documentary
   Explorations: 15 Interviews with Film-Makers* (New York: Doubleday
   & Company, 1971): 95-110.
Orbanz, Eva. *Journey to a Legend and Back: The British Realistic Film*
   (Berlin: Volker Spiess, 1977) [includes an interview with Tony Garnett
   (63-76) and "The Way Back from the Legend" by Jim Allen (151-159)].
Petley, Julian. "Ken Loach", in Laurie Collier Hillstrom (ed), *International
   Dictionary of Films and Filmmakers*, volume 2, third edition (Detroit;
   New York; Toronto; London: St James' Press, 1997): 615-617.
Pilard, Philippe. *Le Nouveau Cinéma Britannique: 1979-1988* (Paris: 5
   Continents-Hatier, 1989) [in French].
Rosenthal, Alan. *The New Documentary in Action: A Casebook in Film
   Making* (Berkeley, Los Angeles; London: University of California
   Press, 1971): 164-175.
Thomson, David. *A Biographical Dictionary of Film*, revised and enlarged
   edition (London: André Deutsch, 1994): 447-448.
Tulloch, John. *Television Drama: Agency, audience and myth* (London;

New York: Routledge, 1990).

Vincendeau, Ginette (ed). *Encyclopedia of European Cinema* (London: Cassell/British Film Institute, 1995): 264.

Worsley, T C. *Television: The Ephemeral Art* (London: Alan Ross, 1970) [includes "Active and Passive": 154-157; "The Garnett Ring": 230-232; "Life Caught on the Wing": 63-65; "Facts and Figures": 225-228.

C: Special journal or magazine issues devoted to Loach or his work

Chirivi, Massimo. *Ken Loach* (Venice: Circuito Cinema, 1993) [in Italian]. Contents: "Ken matto da legare", by Alberto Crespi (2-4); "Storia di un sopravvissuto", by Paul Kerr (5-12); "Il 'caso' Family Life", by Alain Marty (12-18); "Questioni di censura", by Julian Petley (19-22); "Impegno e coerenza di un cineasta semplice", by Ken Loach (23-28); "Biofilmografia" (29); "Note biografiche" (30-32); "Regie" (32-55); "Bibliografia essenziale" (55-62).

D: General articles on, or relating to, Loach in journals and magazines

Åhlund, Jannike. "den nödvändiga vreden", *Chaplin* 1 (February-March 1992): 46-48 [in Swedish].

Butler, Robert. "Feeling the charge", *Independent on Sunday* 24 July 1994: 14-17.

Cathcart, Brian. "Pariah with no regrets", *Independent on Sunday* 30 May 1993: 25.

De Santi, Gualtiero. "Il vascello Britannia alla deriva", *Cineforum* 217 (September 1982): 23-29 [in Italian].

Eardley, Susan. "Loach lobbies for hard-core subjects", *Broadcast* 5 July 1991: 25.

Fuller, Graham. "True Brit", *Village Voice* 9 February 1993: 56-58.

Garnham, Nicholas. "TV Documentary and Ideology", *Screen* 13: 2 (summer 1972): 109-115.

Glaister, Dan. "Hollywood vision for British cinema", *The Guardian* 3 August 1996: 6.

Hall, William. "Finding the figures to fit the landscape", *Evening News* 8 February 1980.

Hammond, Wally. "Estate of the art", *Time Out* 1207 (6-13 October 1993): 22.

Hattenstone, Simon. "A slice of Loach", *The Guardian* 8 October 1993: 6-7.

HH. "Ken Loach bei ARD", *Film-Echo/Filmwoche* 36 (7 September 1996): 9 [in German].

Hibbin, Nina. "Dokument och fiktion", *Chaplin* 173 (23: 2) (1981): 48-51 [in Swedish].

Jackson, Kevin. "All that glistens could be gold", *The Independent* 17 February 1995: 23.

—————. "The Parallax view of the cinema", *The Independent* 25 February 1994: 24.

"Keeping Faith with the Viewer", *Radio Times* 16 January 1969: 4.

"Keeping Faith with the Viewer: A letter to the Editor", *Radio Times* 13

191

February 1969: 2.

"Ken Loach", *City Limits* 285 (19-26 March 1987): 58.

"Ken Loach", *Film Dope* 36 (February 1987): 4-5.

Lister, David. "House of Horror (a director's cut)", *The Independent* 2 December 1994: 8.

Littlefield, Joan. "Meet British Film Directors", *Film World* 4: 2 (July-September 1968): 78-79.

"Loach ad in the can...", *Broadcast* 14 March 1986: 27.

"Loach resigns from DGGB", *Film and Television Technician* May 1990: 4.

Lyttle, John. "John Lyttle on cinema", *The Independent* 10 October 1994: 9.

McAfee, Annalena. "Hard labour for tragic Bill", *Evening Standard* 20 June 1991: 35.

MacCabe, Colin. "Realism and the Cinema: Notes on some Brechtian theses", *Screen* 15: 2 (summer 1974): 7-27.

Malcolm, Derek. "The answer to sex and violence", *The Guardian* 16 February 1980: 10.

Marszałek, Rafał. "Kenneth Loach, krytyk kultury", *Kino (Poland)* 101 (9: 5) (May 1974): 46-50 [in Polish].

Mather, Ian. "How the law made Ken Loach despair", *The Observer* 8 February 1976.

Nave, Bernard. "Ken Loach aux rencontres de Saint-Etienne", *Jeune Cinéma* 134 (April/May 1981): 21-26 [in French].

——————. "Portrait d'un cinéaste modeste: Ken Loach", *Jeune Cinéma* 183 (October-November 1987): 19-25 [in French].

Norman, Barry. "Barry Norman on...", *Radio Times* 269: 3519 (1-7 June 1991): 26.

——————. "Ken Loach: a perspective for working people", *The Times* 15 January 1972.

Oakes, Philip. "Loach's line", *The Sunday Times* 9 January 1972.

Pearce, Garth. "I've been blacked, says top film maker", *The Daily Express* 3 September 1986: 13.

Petley, Julian. "Docu-drama: truth or fiction?", *Movie* 63 (1981): 1255-1257.

——————. "Fact plus fiction equals friction", *Media, Culture and Society* 18: 1 (1996): 11-25.

——————. "Ken Loach – Politics, Protest & the Past", *Monthly Film Bulletin* 54: 638 (March 1987): 96.

——————. "The price of portraying a less than perfect Britain", *The Listener* 119: 3046 (21 January 1988): 14.

——————. "Why Cathy will never come home again", *New Statesman and Society* 6: 246 (2 April 1993): 23-25.

Pile, Stephen. "Fall and rise of a radical film-maker", *The Daily Telegraph* 27 March 1993: xvii.

Porter, Beth. "Working Class Gets its Due in Ken Loach's *Riff-Raff*", *Film Journal* 96 (March 1993): 28-30.

Roberts, Glenys. "Loach's commitment to real people", *The Times* 21 February 1980.

Robinson, David. "Case histories of the next renascence", *Sight and Sound* 38: 1 (winter 1968/69): 39-40.

Rubin, Mike. "Getting Good Marx", *Village Voice* 13 December 1994: 70, 72.

Saada, Nicolas. "Ken Loach, années 90", *Cahiers du Cinéma* 449

(November 1991): 65 [in French].

Sandford, Jeremy. "Edna and Cathy: Just Huge Commercials", *Theatre Quarterly* 3: 10 (April-June 1973): 79-85.

Sawtell, Jeff. "Socialist season with Loach in London", *Morning Star* 19040/73189 (15 November 1991): 8.

SH. "Weekend Birthdays", *The Guardian* 17 June 1995: 30.

Swallow, Norman. "Television: the Integrity of Fact and Fiction", *Sight and Sound* 43: 3 (summer 1976): 183-185.

Taylor, James. "Directors find nothing but hot air at the house", *Rushes* January/February 1995: 10-12.

"The Ken Loach approach – and how to film it", *In Camera* spring 1990: 5.

"Tony Garnett", *Afterimage* 1: 1 (April 1970): n.p.

Wapshott, Nicholas. "The acceptable face of radicalism", *The Times* 13 November 1981.

Williams, Raymond. "Realism, Naturalism and their Alternatives", *Ciné-Tracts* 1: 3 (autumn 1977-winter 1978): 1-6.

Wivel, Peter. "Ny Loach-film etter ni år – Black Jack", *Film og Kino* 1 (1981): 23, 29 [in Norwegian].

E: Selected film reviews, and articles about specific films

Diary of a Young Man

Black, Peter. "Peter Black", *The Daily Mail* 10 August 1964.

Furlong, Monica. "War in the BBC for men's minds", *The Daily Mail* 12 August 1964.

Jailler, Mrs. "Vicar attacks B.B.C. television serial", *The Times* 8 September 1964.

Lockwood, Lyn. "2 unendearing Northerners in London", *The Daily Telegraph* 10 August 1964.

"Vicar raps the BBC's 'filthy young man'", *Daily Herald* 8 September 1964.

A Tap on the Shoulder

Jailler, Mrs. "The precision of high crime", *The Times* 7 January 1965.

Lane, Stewart. "Jane tried too hard" *Daily Worker* 10347 (9 January 1965): 2.

Marsland Gander, L. "Bad timing", *The Daily Telegraph* 11 January 1965.

——————. "Warped play about nasty people", *The Daily Telegraph* 7 January 1965.

Mitchell, Adrian. "Villains! But good for a laugh", *The Sun* 7 January 1965.

Purser, Philip. "Sex for All – But Dreary", *The Sunday Telegraph* 10 January 1965: 13.

Richardson, Maurice. "Waiting for the late-night laughter", *The Observer* 10 January 1965: 24.

Wear a Very Big Hat

Lockwood, Lyn. "Good human situation in BBC play", *The Daily Telegraph* 18 February 1965.

Mitchell, Adrian. "A good play..right to the last clinch", *The Sun* 18

February 1965.

"Mod's Honour at Stake", *The Times* 18 February 1965: 16.

Three Clear Sundays

Holmstrom, John. "Black Roses", *New Statesman* 69: 1780 (23 April 1965):
660.

Larner, Gerald. "Three Clear Sundays on BBC-1", *The Guardian* 8 April
1965.

Richardson, Maurice. "Fighting for the throne", *The Observer* 11 April
1965: 29.

Up the Junction

"BBC cuts 'raw and witty' play", *The Daily Telegraph* 3 November 1965:
17.

Black, Peter. "This must be just about THE LIMIT", *The Daily Mail* 6
November 1965: 4.

Dean, Brian. "Doctors lash BBC play", *The Daily Mail* 6 November 1965:
9.

——————. "Kitchen sink plays get the BBC boot", *The Daily Mail* 4
January 1966.

——————. "TV play brings biggest protest yet", *The Daily Mail* 5
November 1965: 11.

Douglass, Stuart. "Struggling to break through the cottonwool curtain",
Morning Star 10604 (6 November 1965): 2.

Garnett, Tony. "Up the Junction by Nell Dunn", *Radio Times* 169: 2190
(28 October-5 November 1965): 45.

Green, James. "TV Drama Chief Defends That Play", *Evening News* 5
November 1965.

Howard, Barrington. "'Up the Junction' Critics All Saw it Through", *The
Daily Telegraph* 12 November 1965: 16 [letter].

Jones, D A N. "Careless Love", *New Statesman* 70: 1809 (12 November
1965): 760.

"'Junction' critics", *Daily Worker* 12 November 1965 [2 letters].

Lane, Stewart. "He doesn't want to be a TV censor, but...", *Morning Star*
39/10784 (8 June 1966): 2.

Lockwood, Lyn. "'Raw & witty' documentary scrapes barrel", *The Daily
Telegraph* 4 November 1965.

Phillips, Philip. "'Working girl' play upsets viewers", *The Sun* 5 November
1965.

"Play for yesterday", *Time Out* 1195 (14-21 July 1993): 145.

Ratcliffe, Michael. "Up the Junction", *The Times* 15 August 1977.

Read, Piers Paul. "The BBC, social engineering and the guilt of the middle
classes", *The Daily Mail* 13 July 1993.

Richardson, Maurice. "Bird life in Battersea", *The Observer* 7 November
1965: 25.

Thomas, James. "One classic that has stood the test of time", *The Daily
Express* 15 August 1977.

"'Up the Junction': A Case for Television Censorship?", *The Daily
Telegraph* 8 November 1965: 12 [3 letters].

Walter, Natasha. "The incredible shrinking men", *Independent on Sunday*

194

18 July 1993: 21.

Wiggin, Maurice. "Little Nell's Curiosity Shop", *The Sunday Times* 7 November 1965.

Worsley, T C. "Experimental Slot", *The Financial Times* 10 November 1965: 26.

The End of Arthur's Marriage

Black, Peter. "Peter Black", *The Daily Mail* 18 November 1965: 3.

Larner, Gerald. "The End of Arthur's Marriage", *The Guardian* 18 November 1965.

Lockwood, Lyn. "Experiment in whimsy falls flat", *The Daily Telegraph* 18 November 1965.

Purser, Philip. "Out of the Rut", *The Sunday Telegraph* 21 November 1965: 13.

Richardson, Maurice. "Remaking a classic", *The Observer* 21 November 1965: 24.

The Coming Out Party

Lockwood, Lyn. "Scimpy in search of a parent", *The Daily Telegraph* 23 December 1965.

Cathy Come Home

"A searing indictment of housing conditions", *The Times* 17 November 1966.

Banks-Smith, Nancy. "Cathy, and why the pen is so ineffectual", *The Sun* 14 November 1968.

Black, Peter. "Peter Black", *The Daily Mail* 17 November 1966: 3.

"Cathy. Twenty years on, she could still be looking for a home", *Today* 25 November 1986: 7.

Connard, Avril. "Carol. When we filmed it, sometimes I really did get hysterical", *Today* 25 November 1986: 7.

Davidson, Max. "Cathy's plight is still shocking", *The Daily Telegraph* 1 April 1993: 19.

Fay, Gerard. "Cathy Come Home on BBC-1", *The Guardian* 17 November 1966: 9.

Fuller, Roy. "Two pairs", *New Statesman* 72: 1864 (2 December 1966): 852.

Gross, John. "Homeless marriage", *The Observer* 20 November 1966: 25.

Hebert, Hugh. "Cathy Come Home, Dispatches, Bookmark", *The Guardian* 1 April 1993: 7.

Holland, Mary, "Keeping Edna at a distance", *The Observer* 24 October 1971: 34.

"Homeless Cathy returns to screen", *The Times* 17 March 1993: 5.

Lane, Stewart. "Now they've seen 'Cathy'", *Morning Star* 226/10971 (14 January 1967): 2.

——————. "Search for homes play on TV", *Morning Star* 178/10923 (17 November 1966): 5.

——————. "This boring ritual of Miss World", *Morning Star* 180/10925 (19 November 1966): 2.

M.B. "Importance of Cathy", *The Times* 14 November 1968.

Melly, George. "Shocking treatment", *The Observer* 17 November 1968.

Pile, Stephen. "Fall and rise of a radical film-maker", *The Daily Telegraph* 27 March 1993: xvii.

Purser, Philip. "A tangled skene", *The Sunday Telegraph* 17 November 1968: 15.

——————. "Black and White Play", *The Sunday Telegraph* 20 November 1966: 13.

——————. "How Cathy changed the face of TV drama", *The Daily Telegraph* 27 March 1993: 6.

——————. "Play or Propaganda?", *The Sunday Telegraph* 15 January 1967: 11.

Reynolds, Stanley. "Television", *The Guardian* 14 November 1968: 7.

Sandford, Jeremy. "Aims of 'Edna' and 'Cathy'", *The Observer* 31 October 1971: 13 [letter].

——————. "'Cathy Come Home' returns along with lingering myths'", *The Independent* 26 March 1993: 21 [letter].

Selway, Jennifer. "Sixtysomethings", *The Observer* 11 July 1973: 70.

Serceau, Daniel. "'La télévision des autres': Cathy Comes Home de Ken Loach", *Téléciné* 178 (March 1973): 39-41 [in French].

Wiggin, Maurice. "The grace to feel a pang of pity", *The Sunday Times* 20 November 1966.

Wyndham Goldie, Grace. "Stop Mixing TV. Fact and Fiction", *The Sunday Telegraph* 8 January 1967: 14.

In Two Minds

Black, Peter. "We can learn from Kate's destruction", *The Daily Mail* 2 March 1967: 3.

Burgess, Anthony. "Television", *The Listener* 77: 1980 (9 March 1967): 335.

Clayton, Sylvia. "Schizophrenia vivid study for play", *The Daily Telegraph* 2 March 1967: 19.

Cooper, R W. "Girl on brink of insanity", *The Times* 2 March 1967.

Lane, Stewart. "Should uncomfortable facts be labelled fiction?", *Morning Star* 274/11019 (11 March 1967): 2.

——————. "Yorkshire – the juiciest plum", *Morning Star* 268/11013 (4 March 1967): 2.

Marsland Gander, L. "Putting Politicians in the Pillory", *The Daily Telegraph* 27 March 1967: 9.

Potter, Dennis. "Sting in the Brain", *New Statesman* 73: 1878 (10 March 1967): 338-339.

Purser, Philip. "Nobody Cares But Us", *The Sunday Telegraph* 5 March 1967: 11.

Thomas, James. "Getting a bit blurred on TV... 'Drama' and 'Real-life'", *Daily Express* 8 March 1967: 8.

"Update on schizophrenia", *Radio Times* 258: 3376 (13-19 August 1988): 80 [3 letters].

Poor Cow

Armstrong, Michael. "Poor Cow", *Films and Filming* April 1968: 26-27.

Barker, Felix. "Hope v misery south of the river", *Evening News* 7 December 1967.

Bolzoni, Francesco. "Poor Cow", *Bianco e nero* 29: 11-12 (November-December 1968): 274-276 [in Italian].

Christie, Ian. "A gem dished up on a grimy platter", *The Daily Express* 6 December 1967.

"Cinema: New Movies", *Time* 9 February 1968: 93.

Coleman, John. "Home Grown", *New Statesman* 74: 1917 (8 December 1967): 823.

Davies, Brenda. "Poor Cow", *Sight and Sound* 37: 1 (winter 1967-68): 43.

"Film shots banned by council", *The Daily Telegraph* 8 April 1967.

Garsault, Alain. "Des tasses de thé sans madeleine...", *Positif* 151 (June 1973): 74-77 [in French].

Gibbs, Patrick. "Tarting Up the Junction", *The Daily Telegraph* 8 December 1967.

Hibbin, Nina. "'Cathy' goes out to primitive picnic", *Morning Star* 504/11249 (6 December 1967): 5.

Hinxman, Margaret. "In at the birth", *The Sunday Telegraph* 10 December 1967: 12.

Hirschhorn, Clive. "The seamy tale of a girl seeking happiness", *The Sunday Express* 10 December 1967.

Houston, Penelope. "Up the creek", *Spectator* 219: 727 (15 December 1967): 756.

J.A.D. "Poor Cow", *Monthly Film Bulletin* 35: 409 (February 1968): 23.

Jarvie, Ian. "Media and Manners", *Film Quarterly* 22: 3 (spring 1969): 11-17.

Lefèvre, Raymond. "Pas de larmes pour Joy (Poor Cow)", *Cinéma (France)* 177 (June 1973): 128-130 [in French].

Mortimer, Penelope. "Wanted – an audience", *The Observer* 10 December 1967.

M.T. "Pas de larmes pour Joy", *Écran* 15 (May 1973): 67-68 [in French].

N.H. "'Poor Cow' story with a heart", *Morning Star* 507/11252 (9 December 1967): 3.

Otta. "Poor Cow", *Variety* 13 December 1967: 6.

Pacey, Ann. "Sentenced to life..outside prison", *The Sun* 6 December 1967.

"Pas de larmes pour Joy", *Le Film Français* 1478 (16 March 1973): 14 [in French].

Pim. "Poor Cow", *Kosmorama* 86 (August 1968): 237 [in Danish].

Porter, Vincent. "Le cinéma anglais en 1968", *Positif* 99 (November 1968): 33-34 [in French].

Powell, Dilys. "The beasts of the field", *The Sunday Times* 10 December 1967.

Rhode, Eric. "Poor Cow", *The Listener* 78: 2020 (14 December 1967): 769-771.

Richards, Jeffrey. "Back to the swinging Sixties", *The Daily Telegraph* 3 March 1989: 16.

Robinson, David, "The Dunn Cow", *The Financial Times* 8 December 1967: 28.

Roud, Richard. "New films", *The Guardian* 8 December 1967: 9.

Serceau, Daniel. "Pas de larmes pour Joy", *Téléciné* 179 (June 1973): 33-34 [in French].

Simon, John. *Movies into Film: Film Criticism 1967-1970* (New York: The Dial Press, 1971): 290-291.

Sulik, Boleslaw. "Encounter in a subway", *Tribune* 31: 51 (22 December 1967): 11.

Taylor, John Russell. "A picturesque view of a messy life", *The Times* 7 December 1967.

Walker, Alexander. "Kids, a room and a man – a blonde's life in Battersea", *Evening Standard* 7 December 1967.

Wilson, Cecil. "The Cathy team adds tenderness to the hard life", *The Daily Mail* 6 December 1967.

The Golden Vision

Banks-Smith, Nancy. "Fiction? Why, it looked truer than fact", *The Sun* 18 April 1968.

Black, Peter. "Peter Black", *The Daily Mail* 18 April 1968.

Billington, Michael. "Marrying fact and fiction", *The Times* 27 April 1968.

——————————. "When football takes over your life", *The Times* 18 April 1968.

Clayton, Sylvia. "Impact of soccer essay blurred", *The Daily Telegraph* 18 April 1968.

Lawrence, Ann. "'Big Fish' and the workers", *Morning Star* 618/11363 (17 April 1968): 2.

Melly, George. "It's not all rubbish", *The Observer* 21 April 1968: 30.

Purser, Philip. "Whose play is it?", *The Sunday Telegraph* 21 April 1968: 15.

Reynolds, Stanley. "Television", *The Guardian* 18 April 1968: 8.

Worsley, T C. "A false trail", *The Financial Times* 24 April 1968: 30.

The Big Flame

Banks-Smith, Nancy. "For fiction, it seemed very like fact", *The Sun* 20 February 1969.

Clayton, Sylvia. "Marxist play presented as sermon", *The Daily Telegraph* 20 February 1969.

Holmstrom, John. "Dockers Arise", *New Statesman* 77: 1981 (28 February 1969): 304-305.

Lane, Stewart. "Docks take-over", *Morning Star* 878/11623 (20 February 1969): 2.

——————————. "Some solid achievements in art of the half-hour play", *Morning Star* 874/11619 (15 February 1969): 2.

Malone, Mary. "Dockland puppets with no room to move", *The Daily Mirror* 20 February 1969.

Melly, George. "Suspension of disbelief", *The Observer* 23 February 1969.

Norman, Barry. "TV", *The Daily Mail* 20 February 1969.

Purser, Philip. "Red cries at night", *The Sunday Telegraph* 23 February 1969: 13.

Raynor, Henry. "Optimists almost right", *The Times* 20 February 1969.

Reed, Christopher. "Cathy meets 'The Lump'", *The Sun* 19 February 1969.

Reynolds, Stanley. "The Big Flame", *The Guardian* 20 February 1969: 8.

Stevenson, John. "Is The Big Flame still too hot for the BBC?", *The Daily Mail* 10 February 1969.

Thomas, James. "Fanning a flame of big trouble", *The Daily Express* 20 February 1969.

Wiggin, Maurice. "Merry-go-round", *The Sunday Times* 23 February 1969: 56.

Williams, Raymond. "A Lecture on Realism", *Screen* 18: 1 (1977): 61-74.

Kes

"Adverse effect of Kestrel film suggested", *The Times* 26 October 1970.

Barker, Felix. "This gem doesn't get a West End setting", *Evening News* 19 March 1970.

Barker, Paul. "Boy in a cage", *New Society* 20 November 1969.

Bartlett, Louise. "Kes", *Films in Review* 21: 8 (October 1970): 507.

Berman, Charles. "Launching 'Kes' in the North", *The Guardian* 30 December 1969: 8 [letter].

Burn, Gordon. "Where the Kes boys ended up", *The Sunday Times* 14 January 1973.

Capdenac, Michael. "L'adolescence à vol d'oiseau", *Lettres Françaises* 17 June 1970 [in French].

Caslin, Fergus. "Gritty", *The Sun* 19 March 1970.

Christie, Ian. "Hero's day", *The Daily Express* 19 March 1970.

Cocks, Jay. "Kes", *Time* 21 September 1970: 68.

Cohen, Larry. "Britain's 'Kes' Shown at New York Film Festival", *The Hollywood Reporter* 212: 47 (17 September 1970): 8.

Coleman, John. "Flown South", *New Statesman* 79: 2046 (29 May 1970): 781-782.

——————. "Flying High", *New Statesman* 79: 2037 (27 March 1970): 454.

Davies, Brenda. "Kes", *Monthly Film Bulletin* 37: 435 (April 1970): 74-75.

Dewhurst, Keith. "Drawing the curtains on Barnsley", *The Guardian* 20 November 1969: 13.

"Double billing", *The Guardian* 13 June 1970.

Gibbs, Patrick. "Story of a real boy", *The Daily Telegraph* 20 March 1970.

——————. "Worth an award", *The Daily Telegraph* 29 May 1970.

Gow, Gordon. "Kes", *Films and Filming* 16: 8 (May 1970): 53-54.

Harmsworth, Madeleine. "Miner's son steals a hit", *The Sunday Mirror* 22 March 1970.

Hibbin, Nina. "A boy, his kestrel and his hard life", *Morning Star* 1036/11781 (26 August 1969): 4.

——————. "Back to the early hey-day style for 'Hitch' and his fans", *Morning Star* 1100/11845 (8 November 1969): 3.

——————. "Cautionary tale for courting couples", *Morning Star* 1247/11992 (2 May 1970): 2.

——————. "Jewel of a film that might surprise cinema managers", *Morning Star* 1212/11957 (21 March 1970): 2.

——————. "Rather folksy, but it wins you in the end", *Morning Star* 1277/12022 (6 June 1970): 3.

——————. "Rosamund and her baby – pardon my irritation", *Morning Star* 1076/11821 (11 October 1969): 3.

Hinxman, Margaret. "When Billy takes wing", *The Sunday Telegraph* 22 March 1970: 16.

Hirschhorn, Clive. "If you've forgotten the joys of youth...", *The Sunday*

Express 22 March 1970.

Houston, Penelope. "True grit", *Spectator* 224: 7396 (28 March 1970): 421-422.

Hutchinson, Tom. "After the apes", *The Sunday Telegraph* 31 May 1970: 14.

Ibberson, Jack. "Kes", *Sight and Sound* 38: 4 (autumn 1969): 214.

"'Kes' decision", *Evening Standard* 9 July 1969.

"'Kes' makes it at last", *The Guardian* 27 April 1970.

McNay, Michael. "Bird in the hand", *The Guardian* 28 May 1970: 10.

Malcolm, Derek. "Carry on, 'Kes'", *The Guardian* 19 March 1970: 10.

M.C. "Kes", *Positif* 119 (September 1970): 14-15 [in French].

Millar, Gavin. "The Caging of 'Kes'", *The Listener* 83: 2133 (12 February 1970): 201-202.

Mitchell, Alexander. "Top film hits snags", *The Sunday Times* 16 November 1969.

Mortimer, Penelope. "Banished to Yorkshire", *The Observer* 22 March 1970.

——————————. "Billy and his kestrel", *The Observer* 31 May 1970.

Nave, Bernard. "Kes", *Jeune Cinéma* 193 (February-March 1989): 46-47 [in French].

"No. England Gab Limits 'Kes' But D.C. Trial Good", *Variety* 28 April 1971.

Norman, Barry. "Just one boy and his bird", *The Daily Mail* 19 February 1970.

Olsen, Claus Ib. "Kes", *Kosmorama* 28: 107 (February 1972): 138-139 [in Danish].

P.A.B. "Kes", *Le Film Français* 1349 (10 July 1970): 14 [in French].

Powell, Dilys. "Bird of freedom", *The Sunday Times* 31 May 1970.

Rich. "Kes", *Variety* 8 April 1970: 22.

Richards, Dick. "Champion...", *The Daily Mirror* 20 March 1970.

Richards, Jeffrey. "Too cute to be true", *The Daily Telegraph* 10 October 1987: 4.

Robinson, David. "Bad lots", *The Financial Times* 20 March 1970: 3.

——————————. "Kes at last", *The Financial Times* 29 May 1970: 3.

Stephenson, William. "*Kes* and the Press", *Cinema Journal* 12: 2 (spring 1973): 48-55.

Taylor, John Russell. "Boy and kestrel", *The Times* 20 March 1970: 10.

——————————. "Hawks and apes", *The Times* 29 May 1970.

——————————. "The Kes Dossier", *Sight and Sound* 39: 3 (summer 1970): 130-131.

Taylor, Peter. "'Kes' trailer", *The Guardian* 5 November 1970: 12 [letter].

Walker, Alexander. "A boy and a bird, adding up to something great!", *Evening Standard* 28 May 1970.

"Why 5 boys volunteered to be caned", *The Daily Mirror* 12 August 1968.

Wilde, Jon. "Rare bird", *The Sunday Express* 7 May 1994: 15-17.

Wilson, Cecil. "Two London homes for Kes", *The Daily Mail* 5 June 1970: 10.

Family Life

Axelsson, Sun. "Familjeliv", *Chaplin* 122 (15: 3) (1973): 100-101 [in Swedish].

Barker, Felix. "A face to tear at your heart", *Evening News* 13 January 1972.

Behrendt, Flemming. "Den onde cirkel", *Kosmorama* 120 (April 1974): 176-178 [in Danish].

Bernardini, Aldo. "Family Life", *Rivista del Cinematografo* 5 (May 1974): 38-41 [in Italian].

Buckley, Peter. "Family Life", *Films and Filming* 18: 5 (February 1972): 52-54.

Caslin, Fergus. "The family life drives a girl out of her mind", *The Sun* 13 January 1972.

Cattini, Alberto. "Loach: family death", *Cinema e Cinema* 1: 1 (October/December 1974): 98-101 [in Italian].

Christie, Ian. "When parents are the problem", *The Daily Express* 14 January 1972.

Coleman, John. "Kubrick's Ninth", *New Statesman* 83: 2130 (14 January 1972): 55-56.

Combs, Richard. "Summer Sonata", *The Listener* 119: 3065 (2 June 1988): 42.

Connolly, Ray. "The Ray Connolly Interview", *Evening Standard* 27 November 1971.

C.P.R. "Wednesday's Child", *Films in Review* 23: 9 (November 1972): 568.

Curtiss, Thomas Quinn. "The French Censors Release 'Family Life'", *New York Herald Tribune* 10 November 1972.

Daney, Serge and Jean-Pierre Oudart. "Sur *Family Life* (de Kenneth Loach)", *Cahiers du Cinéma* 244 (February-March 1973): 44-48 [in French].

Dawson, Jan. "Family Life", *Monthly Film Bulletin* 39: 457 (February 1972): 31.

D.C. "Family Life", *Films Illustrated* 1: 7 (January 1972): 26.

Dell'Acqua, Gian Piero. "'La crisi dell'istituto familiare': 'Family Life' di Kenneth Loach", *Cinema Sessanta* 14: 95 (January/February 1974): 61-62 [in Italian].

Evans, Peter. "Ken Loach films 'Family Life'", *The Hollywood Reporter* 219: 20 (29 December 1971): 3, 4.

"Family Life", *l'Avant-Scène du Cinéma* 133 (February 1973): 50-52 [in French].

"Family Life: Découpage et dialogues in extenso", *l'Avant-Scène du Cinéma* 133 (February 1973): 13-49 [in French; script].

Freeman, Hugh. "Sweet madness", *New Society* 3 February 1972 [letter].

Gaulier, Patrick. "Family Life (la vie de famille)", *La Revue du Cinéma/Image et Son* 267 (January 1973): 119-121 [in French].

Gibbs, Patrick. "Boundaries of happiness", *The Daily Telegraph* 14 January 1972.

Giddins, Gary. "'Wednesday's Child'", *The Hollywood Reporter* 223: 17 (5 October 1972): 13.

Gould, Donald. "Girl with an Identity Crisis", *New Statesman* 82: 2126 (17 December 1971): 848-849.

Hinxman, Margaret. "Grim and glorious", *The Sunday Telegraph* 16 January 1972: 18.

Illman, John. "Jan: Trapped between two schools of psychiatry", *General Practitioner* 14 January 1972.

J.D. "Family Life", *Jeune Cinéma* 64 (July-August 1972): 38 [in French].

Jordan, Isabelle. "Y a-t-il un cas 'Family Life'?", *Positif* 147 (February 1973): 62-65 [in French].

Le Gauley, Guy. "La perte du sens", *l'Avant-Scène du Cinéma* 1331 (February 1973): 10-11 [in French].

Le Grivès, Eliane. "Une descente aux enfers"; *l'Avant-Scène du Cinéma* 133 (February 1973): 9-10 [in French].

Malcolm, Derek. "Who is for sanity?", *The Guardian* 12 January 1972: 8.

Marsolais, Gilles. "Family Life", *Cinéma Québec* 2: 2 (October 1972): 42 [in French].

M.C. "Family Life", *Positif* 140 (July-August 1972): 36 [in French].

Melly, George. "Kubrick's crystal ball", *The Observer (Review)* 16 January 1972: 31.

Mercer, David. "No credit for writers", *Radio Times* 221: 2867 (21-27 October 1978): 91 [letter].

Millar, Gavin. "Treatment and Ill-Treatment", *The Listener* 87: 2234 (20 January 1972): 93-95.

Miller, Michael and Geoffrey Matthews. "Why Family Life is dangerous", *Evening News* 11 January 1972.

"Mindboggling", *The Observer* 5 November 1972.

Mosk. "Family Life", *Variety* 8 December 1971: 20.

Passek, Jean-Loup. "Family Life", *Cinéma (France)* 170 (November 1972): 119-121 [in French].

Porro, Maurizio. "Kenneth Loach: Family Life", *Cineforum* 131 (April 1974): 255-267 [in Italian].

Powell, Dilys. "Roots of terror, paths of survival", *The Sunday Times* 16 January 1972: 27.

r.al. "Family Life", *Cinema nuovo* 23: 227 (January-February 1974): 53-54 [in Italian].

Shorter, Eric. "Loach study disturbs and impresses", *The Daily Telegraph* 22 November 1971: 11.

Silverstein, Norman. "Two R.D. Laing Movies: *Wednesday's Child* and *Asylum*", *Film Quarterly* 26: 4 (summer 1973): 2-9.

"Table ronde: Family Life", *La Revue du Cinéma/Image et Son* 267 (January 1973): 51-64 [in French].

Taylor, John Russell. "A death in the family", *The Times* 14 January 1972.

Tessier, Max. "Family life", *Écran* 10 (December 1972): 63-65 [in French].

Thirkell, Arthur. "After Cathy – Janice", *The Daily Mirror* 13 January 1972.

Tweedie, Jill. "Flowered power", *The Guardian* 20 December 1971: 9.

Walker, Alexander. "Unhappy families", *Evening Standard* 13 January 1972.

Wilson, Cecil. "Cecil Wilson Films", *The Daily Mail* 13 January 1972.

Wilson, David. "Family Life", *Sight and Sound* 41: 1 (winter 1971/72): 50-51.

Wood, Michael. "Sweet madness", *New Society* 13 January 1972: 73-74.

Zambetti, Sandro. "Ecco qual e' il tipo di famiglia che vogliono 'salvare'", *Cineforum* 131 (April 1974): 242-248 [in Italian].

The Rank and File

Banks-Smith, Nancy. "Television", *The Guardian* 21 May 1971: 10.

Dawson, Len. "Price of paternalism", *Morning Star* 1570/12315 (21 May 1971): 5.

Olsen, Claus Ib. "Ken Loach og det politiske magtspil", *Kosmorama* 19: 114 (May 1973): 207-208 [in Danish].

Woodforde, John. "Hiss the villain", *The Sunday Telegraph* 23 May 1971: 15.

After a Lifetime

Banks-Smith, Nancy. "Television: After a Lifetime", *The Guardian* 19 March 1971: 12.

Black, Peter. "Sadly, Billy's story was just too easy", *The Daily Mail* 19 July 1971: 15.

Lucie-Smith, Edward. "Two Englands", *New Statesman* 82: 2105 (23 July 1971): 122-123.

Myers, Nell. "Stick a little label", *Morning Star* 1623/12368 (22 July 1971): 2.

Days of Hope

Amis, Martin. "Bias Will Be Bias", *New Statesman* 90: 2322 (19 September 1975): 348.

"BBC distortion of history", *The Daily Telegraph* 1 October 1975 [4 letters].

Behrendt, Flemming. "Nye tider", *Kosmorama* 22: 130 (summer 1976): 171-172 [in Danish].

Boulton, David. "'Days of Hope'", *The Times* 13 October 1975 [letter].

Buckley, Leonard. "All my eye and Tony Garnett", *The Times* 12 September 1975: 10.

Buckman, Peter. "Good lines and grimaces", *The Listener* 93: 2426 (2 October 1975): 446-447.

——————————. "Urgent messages", *The Listener* 93: 2427 (9 October 1975): 478-479.

Caughie, John. "Progressive Television and Documentary Drama", *Screen* 21: 3 (1980): 9-35.

Clayton, Sylvia. "Good outlaw and articulate villain", *The Daily Telegraph* 19 September 1975: 11.

Cunningham, Valentine. "Ex Cathedra", *New Statesman* 90: 2324 (3 October 1975): 420.

Davies, Bernard. "One man's television", *Broadcast* 831 (6 October 1975): 12-13.

——————————. "One man's television", *Broadcast* 832 (13 October 1975): 14-15.

"'Days of Hope'", *The Listener* 93: 2429 (23 October 1975): 539-540 [2 letters].

"Days of Hope – drama should be clearly labelled", *Television Today* 30 October 1975: 13.

"Did Garnett tell it as it was?", *Radio Times* 209: 2711 (25-31 October 1975): 65 [letters].

"Does the bias run both ways?", *The Times* 30 September 1975: 13.

Dunkley, Chris. "Days of Hope", *The Financial Times* 15 September 1975.

Fay, Stephen. "Did TV play slant history?", *The Sunday Times* 28 September 1975.

Gould, Tony. "Days of some hope", *New Society* 2 October 1975: 25-26.

"History at the BBC", *The Daily Telegraph* 27 September 1975: 14.

"History guise charge against TV 'Days'", *Screen International* 9 (1 November 1975): 14.

Jones, D A N. "Citrine on 'Days of Hope'", *The Listener* 93: 2427 (9 October 1975): 458-460.

———————. "Days of Hope: how did it feel?", *Radio Times* 208: 2707 (27 September-3 October 1975): 69-70.

Lane, Stewart. "Politics of 'Days of Hope'", *Morning Star* 2918/13663 (4 October 1975): 2.

———————. "Rugby togetherness under siege", *Morning Star* 2912/13657 (27 September 1975): 2.

———————. "What lessons in 'Days of Hope'?", *Morning Star* 2906/13651 (20 September 1975): 2.

Last, Richard. "BBC defends 'Days of Hope' as brilliant film", *The Daily Telegraph* 27 September 1975: 6.

———————. "'Days of Hope' serial goes Communist", *The Daily Telegraph* 26 September 1975: 12.

———————. "Play captures tension of mine disaster", *The Daily Telegraph* 3 October 1975: 11.

Lennon, Peter. "History into art", *The Sunday Times* 28 September 1975.

———————. "Point of information", *The Sunday Times (Weekly Review)* 5 October 1975: 37.

———————. "State of the nation", *The Sunday Times (Review)* 21 September 1975: 37.

London Documentary Drama Group. "A response to John Caughie", *Screen* 22: 1 (1981): 101-105.

Lyndon, Neil. "Years of promise", *Radio Times* 208: 2704 (6-12 September 1975): 66-69.

McArthur, Colin. "Days of Hope", *Screen* 16: 4 (winter 1975/76): 139-144.

———————. "The Historical Role and Testimony of the Individual", in *Television and History* (London: British Film Institute, 1978): 16-20.

MacCabe, Colin. "Days of Hope – A response to Colin McArthur", *Screen* 17: 1 (spring 1976): 98-101.

———————. "Memory, Phantasy, Identity: Days of Hope and the Politics of the Past", *Edinburgh '77 Magazine* 2: 13-17.

Mills, Bart. "'Days of Hope' – going to extremes", *The Listener* 93: 2423 (11 September 1975): 337-338.

Murray, James. "The classiest propaganda", *The Daily Express* 26 September 1975.

Myers, Nell. "Looking back at a crucial decade", *Morning Star* 2900/13645 (13 September 1975): 2.

Nash, Mark and Steve Neale. "Reports from the Edinburgh Festival: Film: 'History/Production/Memory'", *Screen* 18: 4 (winter 1977-78): 77-91.

O'Hara, John. "Days of Hope", *Cinema Papers* 12 (April 1977): 344-345.

Potter, Dennis. "Counterweight", *New Statesman* 90: 2325 (10 October 1975): 451-452.

———————. "Living under the great sickle of equality", *The Sunday Times* 30 April 1978: 37.

Pryce-Jones, David. "Chronicles of England", *The Listener* 93: 2424 (18 September 1975): 376-377.

———————. "The blinkers of protest", *The Listener* 93: 2425 (25 September 1975): 418-419.

Purser, Philip. "Bend of hope", *The Sunday Telegraph* 5 October 1975: 15.

——————. "Past with us", *The Sunday Telegraph* 14 September 1975: 13.

——————. "Seeing red", *The Sunday Telegraph* 28 September 1975: 13.

Rae, John. "'Days of Hope'", *The Times* 17 September 1975 [letter].

Russell, Dora. "'Days of Hope'", *The Listener* 93: 2426 (2 October 1975): 444 [letter].

Stevens, Tony. "Reading the Realist Film", *Screen Education* 26 (spring 1978): 13-34.

Tribe, Keith. "History and the Production of Memories", *Screen* 18: 4 (winter 1977-78): 9-22.

Usher, Shaun. "Perhaps this was just one disaster too many...", *The Daily Mail* 3 October 1975.

——————. "The most powerful TV plays of the year...or just a political broadcast for the far left?", *The Daily Mail* 23 September 1975: 7.

——————. "This sad but faithful look at the forgotten days of hope", *The Daily Mail* 26 September 1975: 23.

——————. "This spell-binder is so easy to forgive", *The Daily Mail* 19 September 1975: 21.

Ward, Alan. "Not class conscientious", *The Listener* 93: 2425 (25 September 1975): 416 [letter].

Weekes, Jill. "Mouthpieces for ideas but not characters", *Television Today* 18 September 1975: 15.

"Where was the Army's heroism?", *Radio Times* 208: 2708 (4-10 October 1975): 65 [8 letters, plus a response from Tony Garnett].

Williams, Christopher. "After the classic, the classical and ideology: the differences of realism", *Screen* 35: 3 (1994): 275-292.

Williamson, Audrey. "Drama and documentary – history on the screen", *Tribune* 39: 42 (17 October 1975): 7.

Wilson, David. "Days of Hope", *Sight and Sound* 44: 3 (summer 1975): 160.

The Price of Coal

Banks-Smith, Nancy. "The Price of Coal", *The Guardian* 6 April 1977.

Church, Michael. "Mining a rich seam", *The Times* 30 March 1977.

Cully, Kevin. "Carefully scrubbed for the Jubilee", *Tribune* 41: 14 (8 April 1977): 7.

Dunn, Douglas. "Pitting their wits", *Radio Times* 214: 2785 (26 March-1 April 1977): 4-5.

Hamilton, Ian. "Make It Mine", *New Statesman* 93: 2403 (8 April 1977): 472.

Hastings, Ronald. "Dolphin show with Python overtones", *The Daily Telegraph* 6 April 1977: 15.

Holt, Hazel. "Reality tempered with good humour", *Television Today* 14 April 1977: 13.

Hone, Joseph. "Penholder grip", *The Listener* 97: 2503 (7 April 1977): 450-451.

Lane, Stewart. "Loach-Garnett touch of magic", *Morning Star* 3373/14118 (30 March 1977): 2.

Lane, Stewart. "Reality and the price of coal", *Morning Star* 3379/14124 (6 April 1977): 2.

Murray, James. "Priceless – this new vein of rich mining humour", *The Daily Express* 30 March 1977.

Potter, Dennis. "Cards on the table", *The Sunday Times* 3 April 1977: 35.

Purser, Philip. "Oop for t'sup", *The Sunday Telegraph* 3 April 1977: 16.

───────────. "The Man for all seasons", *The Sunday Telegraph* 10 April 1977: 16.

Raine, Craig. "Vicious & Company", *The Observer* 13 August 1978: 19.

Thomas, James. "Showing the sad, true price of coal", *The Daily Express* 6 April 1977.

Usher, Shaun. "Beg pardon, ma'am, but we <u>were</u> amused", *The Daily Mail* 30 March 1977: 33.

Black Jack

Andrews, Nigel. "A modern period masterpiece", *The Financial Times* 22 February 1980: 15.

───────────. "Hitting the Jackpot", *The Financial Times* 31 August 1979: 11.

Arenander, Britt. "Black Jack", *Chaplin* 167 (22: 2) (1980): 92-93 [in Swedish].

Auty, Chris. "The Movie Fest Marathon", *Time Out* 491 (14-20 September 1979): 19.

Bilbow, Marjorie. "Black Jack", *Screen International* 230 (1-8 March 1980): 16.

Brien, Alan. "Hitch-hiker's guide to cuckoo-land", *The Sunday Times* 24 February 1980: 41.

Buscombe, Edward. "Mannerism, but with its heart in the right place", *Tribune* 44: 9 (29 February 1980): 6-7.

Castell, David. "Loach Party", *The Sunday Telegraph* 24 February 1980.

Christie, Ian. "Hang this for a tale!", *The Daily Express* 23 February 1980.

Coleman, John. "Trial & Terror", *New Statesman* 99: 2554 (29 February 1980): 333-334.

Dawson, Jan. "Home brew", *The Listener* 102: 2627 (6 September 1979): 310-311.

Delmas, Claude. "Un grand Ken Loach pour les enfants", *Jeune Cinéma* 125 (March 1980): 35-37 [in French].

Dignam, Virginia. "Intellectual workers, isolation and tension", *Morning Star* 4267/15012 (22 February 1980): 2.

F.R. "Black Jack", *Positif* 220-221 (July-August 1979): 48 [in French].

French, Philip. "A taste of 'Scum'", *The Observer* 2 September 1979: 14.

───────────. "On the road", *The Observer* 24 February 1980: 14.

Hall, William. "The joys of the chase", *Evening News* 21 February 1980.

Hinxman, Margaret. "Black Jack", *The Daily Mail* 22 February 1980.

Hutchinson, Tom. "Loach: one of a rare breed", *Now* 22 February 1980: 84-85.

I.M. "Black Jack", *Kosmorama* 27: 153 (June 1981): 127 [in Danish].

Lefèvre, Raymond. "Black Jack", *La Revue du Cinéma/Image et Son/Écran* 349 (April 1980): 22-24 [in French].

Leggett, Eric. "A lovely one U must see..", *The Sunday People* 24 February 1980.

McAsh, Iain F. "Total commitment to a non-star system", *Screen International* 230 (1-8 March 1980): 15.

Malcolm, Derek. "Baltimore blows it all on bad taste", *The Guardian* 21 February 1980: 9.

————. "The critic who worked Wenders", *The Guardian* 30 August 1979: 10.

Menges, Chris. "Blowing up 'Black Jack'", *Time Out* 493 (28 September-4 October 1979): 3 [letter].

Millar, Gavin. "Outlaws", *The Listener* 103: 2651 (28 February 1980): 278-279.

M.M. "Black Jack", *Écran* 82 (15 July 1979): 20 [in French].

Prédal, René. "Black Jack", *Jeune Cinéma* 120 (July-August 1979): 15-16 [in French].

Pulleine, Tim. "Black Jack", *Monthly Film Bulletin* 47: 555 (April 1980): 65-66.

Road, Alan. "Black Jack gamble", *The Observer* 3 December 1978: 29-30.

Robinson, David. "An awesome landscape of mistrust", *The Times* 22 February 1980: 9.

Roud, Richard. "America the bootyful", *The Guardian* 26 May 1979: 11.

Ryweck, Charles. "Black Jack", *The Hollywood Reporter* 258: 48 (25 October 1979): 12.

Shorter, Eric. "Men-less girls on the make", *The Daily Telegraph* 22 February 1980: 13.

Shulman, Milton. "Tolly, getting Belle out of a fair mess", *Evening Standard* 21 February 1980.

Simo. "Black Jack", *Variety* 12 September 1979: 20.

S.L.P. "Black Jack", *Cahiers du Cinéma* 311 (May 1980): 49 [in French].

Thirkell, Arthur. "Loser by a neck..", *The Daily Mirror* 22 August 1980.

Vaines, Colin. "Garnett's sunny interval", *Screen International* 167 (2-8 December 1978): 17.

Wilson, David. "Black Jack", *Sight and Sound* 49: 2 (spring 1980): 126-127.

Auditions

Davies, Russell. "Greetings for the silly season", *The Sunday Times* 28 December 1980: 31.

A Question of Leadership

Cook, Stephen. "Film maker accuses ITV of 'nods and winks' censorship", *The Guardian* 12 August 1981: 4.

Fiddick, Peter. "A Question of Leadership", *The Guardian* 14 August 1981: 9.

Gilbert, W Stephen. "Off air", *Broadcast* 1122 (24 August 1981): 11.

"How union ban held up strike film", *Evening News* 3 August 1980.

Jones, Chris. "Ken Loach's view of the steel strike misses reality", *Tribune* 45: 34 (21 August 1981): 6.

Lane, Stewart. "A question of censorship", *Morning Star* 4524/14469 (15 August 1981): 4.

————. "Loach gasps at IBA's 'sharp intakes of breath'", *Broadcast* 1121 (17 August 1981): 5.

Lane, Stewart. "Tory strategy of steel provocation", *Morning Star* 4521/ 14466 (12 August 1981): 2.

"Loach on the steel strike", *Tribune* 45: 35 (28 August 1981): 7 [2 letters].

Pattinson, Terry. "Strike Film in censor storm", *The Daily Mirror* 12 August 1981.

Petley, Julian. "Union Blues", *Stills* 14 (November 1984): 44-47.

Piéchut, Barthélemy. "Muting the voice of Militants", *Free Press* 9 (September/October 1981): 5.

Wyver, John. "A Brace Of Loach", *Time Out* 556 (12-18 December 1980): 75.

The Gamekeeper

Andrews, Nigel. "Edinburgh uphill, London down dale", *The Financial Times* 29 August 1980: 15.

Banks-Smith, Nancy. "The Gamekeeper", *The Guardian* 17 December 1980.

Bonnet, Jean-Claude. "The Gamekeeper", *Cinématographe* 58 (1980): 47 [in French].

Canby, Vincent. "Screen: *The Gamekeeper* Begins British Film Series", *The New York Times* 129 (20 September 1980): II: 5.

Clayton, Sylvia. "Feudal and family life", *The Daily Telegraph* 17 December 1980.

Davies, Russell. "The gods in the plastic shrine", *The Sunday Times* 21 December 1980: 39.

Hood, Stuart. "The Right to Know What?", *New Statesman* 100: 2595 (12 December 1980): 21-22.

Jackson, Martin. "Gunning for a gamekeeper...", *The Daily Mail* 17 December 1980.

LeFanu, Mark. "Sur quelques films anglais contemporains", *Positif* 271 (September 1983): 20-21 [in French].

Lor. "The Gamekeeper", *Variety* 24 September 1980: 18.

Malcolm, Derek. "Thriller that packs punch and passion", *The Guardian* 29 August 1980: 9.

Naughton, John. "Lil' 'ol Dolly Parton", *The Observer* 21 December 1980.

Nurse, Keith. "Gamekeeper in a class clash", *The Daily Telegraph* 18 November 1980.

O.E. "The Gamekeeper", *Positif* 232/233 (July 1980): 76-77 [in French].

Wallace, Melanie. "The Gamekeeper", *Cineaste* 10: 4 (autumn 1980): 30.

Wapshott, Nicholas. "Edinburgh: a celebration of cinematic alternatives", *The Times* 21 August 1980: 9.

—————————. "Renaissance images", *The Times* 7 November 1980.

Wyver, John. "A Brace Of Loach", *Time Out* 556 (12-18 December 1980): 75.

Looks and Smiles

Ackroyd, Peter. "Low drama", *The Spectator* 250: 8060 (1 January 1983): 26-27.

Andrews, Nigel. "Cannes: fewer people, better films", *The Financial Times* 23 May 1981: 12.

—————————. "Cartoon capers", *The Financial Times* 17 December

1982: 13.

Assayas, Oliver. "Le gentil prolétaire", *Cahiers du Cinéma* 328 (October 1981): 60-61 [in French].

Bilbow, Marjorie. "Looks and Smiles", *Screen International* 374 (18-25 December 1982): 35.

Boyd, William. "Dead ends", *New Statesman* 103: 2670 (21 May 1982): 27.

Brien, Alan. "Sellers: the trail that went cold", *The Sunday Times* 19 December 1982: 36.

Brown, Robert. "Looks and Smiles", *Monthly Film Bulletin* 50: 588 (January 1983): 10.

Castell, David. "A brief British summer", *The Sunday Telegraph* 24 May 1981: 16.

Church, Michael. "Dramatic dumps", *The Times* 20 May 1982.

Coleman, John. "Near to the real", *New Statesman* 104: 2700/2701 (17-24 December 1982): 53.

Cuel, François. "Looks and Smiles", *Cinématographe* 70 (September 1981): 31-32 [in French].

Day-Lewis, Sean. "Catholic childhood", *The Daily Telegraph* 20 May 1982: 13.

Dignam, Virginia. "Clouseau brings to life the genius of Sellers", *Morning Star* 4937/14882 (17 December 1982): 2.

French, Philip. "Legacies of Nam", *The Observer* 19 December 1982: 29.

Gibbs, Patrick. "A touch of nostalgia at Cannes Festival", *The Daily Telegraph* 18 May 1981: 10.

——————. "Sellers: happy ending", *The Daily Telegraph* 17 December 1982: 9.

"Grå film om frå arbeidsløshet", *Film og Kino* 4 (1981): 157 [in Norwegian].

Hinxman, Margaret. "Looks And Smiles", *The Daily Mail* 17 December 1982: 22.

Hughes, David. "The tradition of telling the truth", *The Sunday Times* 23 August 1981: 31.

Hutchinson, Tom. "Looks And Smiles", *The Mail on Sunday* 19 December 1982: 3.

Kingsley, Hilary. "Love on the dole and a few smiles", *The Daily Mirror* 20 May 1982: 19.

Kretzmer, Herbert. "The sins of pure repression", *The Daily Mail* 20 May 1982: 23.

Lajeunesse, Jacqueline. "Regards et sourires", *La Revue du Cinéma/Image et Son/Écran* 365 (October 1981): 27-30 [in French; includes biofilmography].

Lane, Stewart. "Beyond boredom and frustration?", *Morning Star* 4757/14702 (19 May 1982): 2.

MacLeod, Sheila. "Adolescent antennae", *Times Educational Supplement* 21 May 1982: 26.

Malcolm, Derek. "The cutting room capers of Clouseau", *The Guardian* 16 December 1982: 11.

——————. "Why Rosie riveted the loud lady in clogs", *The Guardian* 20 August 1981: 9.

Miller, Kit. "A star stays put in the pit", *The Sun* 19 May 1982: 14.

Mosk. "Looks and Smiles", *Variety* 27 May 1981: 17-18.

Nurse, Keith. "Snake in the criminal jungle", *The Daily Telegraph* 21

August 1981: 9.

O.E. "Looks and Smiles", *Positif* 244-245 (July-August 1981): 97-98 [in French].

Petley, Julian. "Looks and Smiles", *Films and Filming* 341 (February 1983): 32-34.

Prédal, René. "Regards et sourires: Chômage ou armée... est-ce bien la seule solution?", *Cinéma (France)* 273 (September 1981): 94-95 [in French].

Preston, John. "Looking outwards", *Time Out* 643/644 (17-30 December 1982): 32.

Purser, Philip. "Push-button responses", *The Daily Telegraph* 23 May 1982: 13.

Ramasse, François. "Regards et sourires", *Positif* 248 (November 1981): 61-63 [in French].

Robinson, David. "Affectionate sense of life's comedy", *The Times* 17 December 1982: 16.

——————————. "British gifts in need of creative guidance", *The Times* 27 August 1981.

——————————. "Exploring the enigma of Vaslav Nijinsky", *The Times* 18 May 1981: 9.

Roud, Richard. "Heaven's Gate creaks", *The Guardian* 21 May 1981: 12.

Smyllie, Patricia. "Dole fear for a star", *The Daily Mirror* 19 May 1982: 17.

Wade, Graham. "Courting with disaster", *The Guardian* 18 May 1982: 11.

Walker, Alexander. "Queue here for quality", *Evening Standard* 21 May 1981.

The Red and the Blue

Banks-Smith, Nancy. "How to get in on the big time", *The Guardian* 3 October 1983: 11.

Barnes, Julian. "The case of the kissing Kinnocks", *The Observer* 9 October 1983: 52.

Davalle, Peter. "Weekend choice", *The Times* 1 October 1983.

Felstein, Roma. "C4 gives Loach prime time slot", *Broadcast* 30 September 1983: 24.

Kretzmer, Herbert. "Two nations beside the seaside", *The Daily Mail* 3 October 1983: 27.

Lane, Stewart. "Focusing on red and blue", *Morning Star* 5179/15124 (1 October 1983): 4.

Last, Richard. "Festival wins for Britain", *The Daily Telegraph* 3 October 1983: 15.

Stoddart, Patrick. "What has happened to the party conference season?", *Broadcast* 21 October 1983: 14-15.

Questions of Leadership

BB. "C4 to show Loach leadership?", *Broadcast* 24 February 1984: 8.

"C4 Loach films in 'censorship' row", *Screen International* 456 (28 July-4 August 1984): 25.

"Central has to abandon the two Loach docs", *Television Today* 2 August 1984: 15.

"Confrontation", *Free Press* 23 (May 1984): 5.

"'Defamatory' Loach films will not be broadcast", *Screen International* 4 August 1984: 17, 21.

Dell, Edmund. "A balanced view of television that leaves room for searching polemic", *The Guardian* 14 November 1983: 21.

Dunkley, Christopher. "The right to air wrong opinions", *The Financial Times* 1 August 1984: 13.

"Four into two won't go – for the time being", *The Guardian* 3 September 1984: 11.

Glencross, David. "Double vision lets you see both sides of the question", *The Guardian* 14 October 1983: 12.

Hewson, David. "'Defamatory' TV films on unions scrapped", *The Times* 1 August 1984: 3.

"Loach among the directors making docs for Four", *Television Today* 9 June 1983: 20.

"Loach films have been buried, claim directors", *Television Today* 26 July 1984: 13.

Petley, Julian. "Union Blues", *Stills* 14 (November 1984): 44-47.

Pilger, John. *Heroes* (London: Jonathan Cape, 1986): 500-503.

Poole, Michael. "Questions of censorship", *The Listener* 110: 2831 (20 October 1983): 30-31.

"Questions of censorial leadership", *The Guardian* 5 November 1983 [letters from W P Rilla and others from the Directors' Guild of Great Britain, and from David Elstein and Frank Chapple].

RF. "Is Loach new C4 'victim'?", *Broadcast* 23 September 1983: 5, 32.

—. "More problems for leadership", *Broadcast* 29 June 1984: 12.

Rusbridger, Alan. "Diary", *The Guardian* 31 August 1983: 15.

"This week in bits", *City Limits* 147 (27 July-2 August 1984): 4.

Thompson, Jan. "Loach 'politically censored'", *Television Weekly* 80 (3 August 1984): 6.

Tremayne, Charles. "A question of balance?", *Free Press* 21 (November-December 1983): 8.

Winner, Michael. "Guild claims Loach docs were held back", *Television Today* 26 July 1984: 15.

Which Side Are You On?

Barker, Dennis. "Channel 4 to screen pit film", *The Guardian* 15 December 1984: 2.

"Coal comfort", *The Sunday Times* 2 September 1984: 47.

Douch, Lucy. "Striking videos", *Morning Star* 6024/15969 (11 July 1986): 7.

Fiddick, Peter. "Media File...", *The Guardian* 10 December 1984: 9.

French, Sean. "Ring of confidence", *The Sunday Times* 13 January 1985: 39.

Hackett, Dennis. "The allure of gossip", *The Times* 10 January 1985: 13.

Hopkins, Tom. "Which side are you on?", *Tribune* 49: 5 (1 February 1985): 10 [letter].

"Ken Loach tells of bid to kill strike film", *Morning Star* 5564/15509 (8 January 1985): 3.

Lane, John Francis. "Loach party", *The Guardian* 12 December 1984: 11.

Myers, Kathy. "A question of censorship?", *City Limits* 166 (7-13 December 1984): 6.

Neyt, Geert. "Which Side Are You On?: Creatieve Stakers", *Film en*

Televisie 344 (January 1986): 34 [in Dutch].

"No Loach say LWT", *Evening Standard* 29 November 1984: 6.

Poole, Michael. "Taking sides", *The Listener* 113: 2891 (10 January 1985): 26.

RF. "Controversial film wins Italian prize", *Broadcast* 14 December 1984: 5.

——. "LWT dumps Loach's miner masterpiece", *Broadcast* 7 December 1984: 12.

Robinson, David. "Empire in decay", *The Times* 2 May 1985: 9.

Tulloch, Marian and John Tulloch. "Television, industrial relations & audiences: representing & reading strikes", *Media Information Australia* 70 (November 1993): 34-42.

Fatherland

Andrews, Nigel. "Down and out on the Adriatic", *The Financial Times (Weekend)* 6 September 1986: xv.

Austin, David. "Worlds gone mad", *The Spectator* 258: 8282 (4 April 1987): 46.

Aziz, Christine. "Soul searching", *City Limits* 286 (26 March-2 April 1987): 14-15.

Banner, Simon. "Drittemann, poor man", *The Guardian* 26 March 1987: 13.

Bartholomew, David. "*Singing the Blues in Red*", *Film Journal* 91 (February-March 1988): 68.

Cart. "Fatherland", *Variety* 17 September 1986: 14.

Counts, Kyle. "'Singing the Blues in Red'", *The Hollywood Reporter* 301: 3 (9 February 1988): 3, 50.

Cunliffe, Simon. "Seek and hide", *New Statesman* 113: 2923 (3 April 1987): 24-25.

Dignam, Virginia. "Deadly bloodsucker in the flower shop", *Morning Star* 6241/16186 (27 March 1987): 8.

——————. "Smalltown shocks", *Morning Star* 6253/16198 (10 April 1987): 8.

F.B. "Lettres volées", *Cinématographe* 114 (December 1985): 66-67 [in French].

French, Philip. "The singing defector", *The Observer* 29 March 1987: 26.

"From East to West in Ken Loach's Fatherland", *Screen International* 532 (25 January-1 February 1986): 16.

Grant, Steve. "No place like home", *Time Out* 866 (25 March-1 April 1987): 24-26.

Henderson, Elaina. "On Location: Fatherland", *Stills* 23 (December 1985/ January 1986): 33.

Hoberman, J. "Emigre Eyes", *Village Voice* 33 (9 February 1988): 65.

Huhtamo, Erkki. "Odysseia valvonnan kourissa", *Filmihullu* 5 (1988): 42 [in Finnish].

Jaehne, Karen. "Singing the Blues in Red", *Cineaste* 17: 1 (1989): 35-37.

Jilks, Elaine. "The song remains the same", *New Socialist* April 1987: 50.

Johnstone, Iain. "Life, death, and own goals in Venice", *The Sunday Times* 7 September 1986: 45.

——————. "Love across the Atlantic", *The Sunday Times (Review)* 29 March 1987: 49.

Lipman, Amanda. "Fatherland", *City Limits* 286 (26 March-2 April 1987): 27.

Malcolm, Derek. "Loach's song for Europe", *The Guardian* 4 September 1986: 11.

——. "Shelf life of sweeties", *The Guardian* 26 March 1987: 13.

Mars-Jones, Adam. "An air of the dog-eared", *The Independent* 26 March 1987: 14.

Martin, Marcel. "Fatherland. Pour...", *La Revue du Cinéma* 427 (May 1987): 33-34 [in French].

Mather, Victoria. "A long-distance love-affair with literature", *The Daily Telegraph* 27 March 1987: 10.

——. "Carry on up the Grand Canal", *The Daily Telegraph* 10 September 1986: 10.

Mayne, Richard. "The discreet charm of the bookseller", *The Sunday Telegraph* 29 March 1987: 17.

Nave, Bernard. "Un film irrécupérable: 'Fatherland' de Ken Loach", *Jeune Cinéma* 178 (January-February 1987): 4-6 [in French].

NR. "Fatherland", *Screen International* 589 (28 February-7 March 1987): 14.

Petley, Julian. "Fatherland", *Monthly Film Bulletin* 54: 638 (March 1987): 75-76.

Pulleine, Tim. "Fatherland", *Films and Filming* 390 (March 1987): 38-39.

Robinson, David. "Gentle charm proves oddly irrestible", *The Times* 27 March 1987: 17.

——. "Shattered dreams", *The Times* 3 September 1986: 15.

Totterdell, Ann. "Ghost of a flirtation through secondhand books", *The Financial Times* 27 March 1987: 23.

"Venise 43^e: Mostra", *Positif* 309 (November 1986): 55 [in French].

Walters, Margaret. "Exploring idealisms", *The Listener* 117: 3005 (2 April 1987): 30-31.

Time To Go

Pallister, David. "BBC highlights Ulster divide", *The Guardian* 8 May 1989: 4.

The View from the Woodpile

James, Jeffrey. "Men only mould broken", *Morning Star* 18296/6948 (10 June 1989): 8.

Hidden Agenda

Adair, Gilbert. "The lying game", *The Sunday Telegraph (Review)* 10 November 1996: 1-2.

Andrews, Nigel. "Dry season down on the Riviera", *The Financial Times (Weekend)* 19 May 1990: xi.

——. "Thrills and spills", *The Financial Times* 10 January 1991.

Bara, Allen. "Belfast Calling", *Village Voice* 35 (27 November 1990): 110.

"Bosses fan the IRA flames of terror", *The Sun* 7 April 1993: 18.

"British entry for Cannes is film defending the IRA", *The Daily Mail* 21 April 1990: 9.

Brooks, Richard. "Time to go filming the great British taboo", *The Observer* 6 May 1990: 55.

Brown, Geoff. "Full-blooded affairs of passion", *The Times* 10 January 1991: 19.

Camy, Gérard. "Hidden Agenda", *Jeune Cinéma* 202 (June-July 1990): 25-28 [in French].

"Cannes row over Loach Irish film", *Morning Star* 18579/7230 (17 May 1990): 8.

Caryn, James. "Seeking Truths in Northern Ireland", *The New York Times* 140 (21 November 1980): C13.

Collins, Martin. "Censorship's hidden agenda", *The Guardian* 24 March 1993: 19 [letter].

Davenport, Hugo. "Hard Left version of the Troubles", *The Daily Telegraph* 10 January 1991: 15.

Dobson, Patricia. "Festival Britain", *Screen International* 754 (28 April-4 March 1990): 8.

"Evasion, censorship and the Troubles", *The Guardian* 25 March 1993: 23 [3 letters].

"Fictional Faction", *The Times* 10 January 1991: 13.

Francis, Ben. "Hidden Agenda", *City Limits* 10 January 1991: 29.

Garel, Sylvain. "Un regard objectif sur la réalité irlandaise", *Cinéma (France)* 468 (June 1990): 14 [in French].

Géniès, Bernard. "IRA, ira pas?", *Le Nouvel Observateur* 10 May 1990: 77.

Glaessner, Verina. "Hidden Agenda", *Monthly Film Bulletin* 58: 684 (January 1991): 18-19.

Grant, Steve. "'Hidden Agenda'", *Time Out* 1063 (2-9 January 1991): 27.

──────. "Troubles shooter", *Time Out* 1063 (2-9 January 1991): 24-26.

"Hidden Agenda", *Le Film Français* 2296/2297 (4-11 May 1990): 34 [in French].

Hill, John. "Hidden Agenda: Politics and the Thriller", *Circa* 57 (May-June 1991): 36-41.

Hirschhorn, Clive. "Twilight truths of a tragic pair", *The Sunday Express* 13 January 1991.

Hutchinson, Tom. "Shooting to thrill", *The Mail on Sunday* 13 January 1991: 36.

Johnston, Sheila. "Cannes Diary: The festival gets serious", *The Independent* 17 May 1990: 15.

──────. "Rushes", *The Independent* 19 April 1990: 17.

Johnstone, Iain. "Matching the nose with a rose", *The Sunday Times (Review)* 13 January 1991: 10.

──────. "Verdicts galore, but the jury is still out", *The Sunday Times* 20 May 1990: E4.

Kauffmann, Stanley. "Stanley Kauffmann on Films: Dealing with Surprises", *The New Republic* 204: 5 (3968) (4 February 1991): 28-29.

Klady, Leonard. "Hidden Agenda", *Screen International* 785 (1-7 December 1990): 22.

Lane, Anthony. "What you might call a feature film", *Independent on Sunday* 13 January 1991: 15.

L.G. "Hidden Agenda", *Cahiers du Cinéma* 447 (September 1991): 74 [in French].

Malcolm, Derek. "Critic's view: Cinema", *The Guardian* 19 April 1990: 28.

Malcolm, Derek. "Depardieu's Cyrano, winner by a nose", *The Guardian* 10 January 1991: 25.

——————. "The plot thickened", *The Guardian* 17 May 1990: 27.

Mansfield, Paul. "The Troubles shooter", *The Guardian* 8 February 1990: 24.

Mars-Jones, Adam. "Married abyss", *The Independent* 11 January 1991: 16.

Martini, Emanuela. "I film in concorso – Hidden Agenda", Cineforum 295 (June 1990): 22 [in Italian].

M.C. "Cannes 90", *Positif* 353/354 (July/August 1990): 88-89 [in French].

Meisel, Myron. "*Hidden Agenda*", *Film Journal* 93 (November/December 1990): 45-46.

Moore, Oscar. "Hot on the press", *The Times* 18 May 1990: 19.

Murphy, Patsy and Johnny Gogan. "In the Name of the Law", *Film Base News* September/October 1990: 13-17.

Murray, Angus Wolfe. "Home truths from Belfast", *The Scotsman* 19 January 1991.

Neyt, Geert. "Hidden Agenda: De flinterdunne democratie", *Film en Televisie* 404 (January 1991): 16-17 [in Dutch].

Norman, Barry. "Barry Norman on...", *Radio Times* 277: 3615 (17-23 April 1993): 34.

Osborne, Robert. "Hidden Agenda", *The Hollywood Reporter* 315: 30 (21 December 1990): 6, 43.

"Outrage over IRA film", *The Sun* 21 April 1990: 9.

Pallister, David. "Smears, skullduggery and Stalker", *The Guardian* 10 January 1991: 25.

Pannifer, Bill. "Agenda Bender", *The Listener* 125: 3197 (3 January 1991): 30-31.

Parente, William. "Shooting to thrill", *The Scotsman* 26 January 1991: vii.

Petley, Julian. "Hidden Agenda", in Nicolet V Elert and Aruna Vasudevan (eds), *International Dictionary of Films and Filmmakers*, volume 1, third edition (Detroit; New York; Toronto; London: St James' Press, 1997): 435-437.

Quart, Leonard. "Hidden Agenda", *Cineaste* 18: 2 (1991): 64.

Robinson, David. "Due respect and star hysteria", *The Times* 18 May 1990: 19.

Ross, Philippe. "Hidden agenda", *La Revue du Cinéma* 474 (September 1991): 37 [in French].

Sawtell, Jeff. "Where truth really *is* stranger than fiction", *Morning Star* 18779/72930 (11 January 1991): 4-5.

Sockett, Richard. "Terrorism concerns", *The Times* 24 March 1993: 17 [letter].

Strat. "Hidden Agenda", *Variety* 23 May 1990: 28.

"Tears and troubles", *The Guardian* 27 March 1993: 26 [3 letters].

Tookey, Christopher. "This proboscis has real panache", *The Sunday Telegraph (Review)* 13 January 1991: xvi.

Usher, Shaun. "Death on the agenda kills thrilling idea", *The Daily Mail* 11 January 1991: 26.

Vidal, John. "Corruption on the agenda", *The Guardian* 17 May 1990: 27.

——————. "Media File", *The Guardian* 28 May 1990: 21.

Walker, Alexander. "Plots and paranoia", *Evening Standard* 17 May 1990: 30.

White, Jerry. "Hidden Agenda and JFK: Conspiracy Thrillers", *Jump Cut* 38

(June 1993): 14-18.

Willmott, Nigel. "Check the mirror", *Tribune* 55: 5 (1 February 1991): 9.

Riff-Raff

Adair, Gilbert. "If you don't buy the politics, we'll shoot the movie", *The Guardian* 27 February 1992: 22.

Alion, Yves Perfide. "Riff-Raff: Métaphore immobilière", *La Revue du Cinéma* 476 (November 1991): 27 [in French].

Amidon, Stephen. "Frontal attack on Hamlet", *The Financial Times* 18 April 1991: 21.

Bear, Liza. "*Riff-Raff*", *Film Journal* 96 (March 1993): 69-70.

Brooke, Chris. "English subtitles spell out the jokes for America's moviegoers", *The Daily Mail* 20 October 1992: 20.

Brown, Geoff. "Belly laughs and bottom lines", *The Times* 27 June 1991: 17.

—————. "Salty talk peppers the rough trade", *The Times* 18 April 1991: 17.

Brown, Georgia. "Men at Work", *Village Voice* 9 February 1993: 56.

Davenport, Hugo. "Laughter on the building site", *The Daily Telegraph* 18 April 1991: 17.

Del. "Riff-Raff", *Variety* 6 May 1991.

Dobson, Patricia. "Riff-Raff", *Screen International* 798 (15-21 March 1991): 11.

Earle, Lawrence. "Rushes", *The Independent* 6 December 1991: 14.

—————. "Rushes", *The Independent* 6 November 1992: 20.

Floyd, Nigel. "Riff-Raff", *Time Out* 1078 (17-24 April 1991): 65.

Francke, Lizzie. "Riff-Raff", *City Limits* 18 April 1991: 24.

French, Philip. "Uneasy idylls", *The Observer* 21 April 1991: 57.

Giavarini, Laurence. "Combat", *Cahiers du Cinéma* 449 (November 1991): 63-64 [in French].

Guard, Candy. "Rough humour", *Sight and Sound* 5: 1 (January 1995): 69.

Jesse, Bill. "A brush with fame", *The Guardian* 18 April 1991: 25.

Johnston, Sheila. "Another brick in the wall", *The Independent* 19 April 1991: 18.

Keller, Keith. "Riff-Raff", *The Hollywood Reporter* 317: 30 (21 May 1991): 11, 69.

Kennedy, Douglas. "Lethal weapon in a theme park", *The Sunday Telegraph (Review)* 21 April 1991: xvi.

Klawans, Stuart. "*Riff-Raff*", *Nation* 256 (15 February 1993): 209-212.

Lane, Anthony. "Where imagination fears to tread", *Independent on Sunday* 23 June 1991.

Lochen, Kalle. "Nyrealistiske drømmer", *Film og Kino* 5 (1991): 10 [in Norwegian].

Loffreda, Pierpaolo. "Riff-Raff", *Cineforum* 310 (December 1991): 72-74 [in Italian].

Malcolm, Derek. "From Mad Max to the mad prince", *The Guardian* 18 April 1991: 25.

Marsolais, Gilles. "riff-raff", *24 Images* 56/57 (autumn 1991): 32 [in French].

Martini, Emanuela. "Quinzaine des Réalisateurs – Riff-Raff", *Cineforum* 305 (June 1991): 31 [in Italian].

Moore, Oscar. "A homage to the hard hat", *Mail on Sunday* 23 June 1991: 39.

Nave, Bernard. "Riff-Raff", *Jeune Cinéma* 212 (January-February 1992): 35-36 [in French].

Neyt, Geert. "Riff-Raff", *Film en Televisie* 415 (December 1991): 27 [in Dutch].

Niel, Philippe. "Des rats ou des hommes? Riff-Raff", *Positif* 370 (December 1991): 46 [in French].

Norman, Neil. "Doctrine in the house", *Evening Standard* 18 April 1991: 35.

Perry, George. "Loach's site for sore eyes", *The Sunday Times* 21 April 1991: Sec. 5, 3.

Ph. N. "Riff-Raff", *Positif* 365-366 (July-August 1991): 91-92 [in French].

Quart, Leonard. "Riff-Raff", *Cineaste* 20: 2 (1993): 54-55.

Robinson, David. "Bawdy eye on a building site", *The Times* 18 April 1991: 17.

Sawtell, Jeff. "Socialist realism is dead. Long live Socialist realism", *Morning Star* 18861/73012 (19 April 1991): 5.

Saynor, James. "Riff-Raff", *Interview* 23: 1 (January 1993): 52.

Sierz, Aleks. "Cutting edge", *Tribune* 55: 16 (19 April 1991): 6.

Taboulay, Camille. "Riff-Raff", *Cahiers du Cinéma* 445 (June 1991): 46 [in French].

Tookey, Christopher. "Where passion failed to prosper", *The Sunday Telegraph (Review)* 23 June 1991: xiii.

Usher, Shaun. "Life's labourers – getting lost", *The Daily Mail* 21 June 1991: 30.

Vicari, Daniele. "Riff-Raff", *Cinema nuovo* 41: 2 (336) (March-April 1992): 56 [in Italian].

Wilson, David. "Riff-Raff", *Sight and Sound* 1: 1 (May 1991): 61.

The Arthur Legend

"Biter bit", *The Daily Telegraph* 22 May 1991: 19.

Gosling, Mick. "The mirror and the miners: the facts", *Free Press* 64 (June 1991): 1, 3.

Milne, Seamus and Paul Brown. "Soviet Union moved cash to avoid rift", *The Guardian* 22 May 1991.

——————————————. "Tangled tale performed by international cast of players", *The Guardian* 22 May 1991.

Whitfield, Martin. "Media 'piranhas' fall out over TV defence of Scargill", *The Independent* 22 May 1991: 4.

Raining Stones

Adagio, Carmelo. "Piovono pietre", *Cinema nuovo* 43: 1 (347) (January-February 1994): 45-46 [in Italian].

Akomfrah, John. "For a richer vision of poverty", *Vertigo (UK)* 1: 3 (spring 1994): 43-44.

Andrew, Geoff. "Raining Stones", *Time Out* 1207 (6-13 October 1993): 66.

Andrews, Nigel. "Simply horribly funny", *The Financial Times* 7 October 1993: 21.

Audé, François. "Raining Stones: La fierté de Bob", *Positif* 392 (October

1993): 16-17 [in French].

Beard, Steve. "Raining Stones", *Empire* 53 (November 1993): 37.

Billson, Anne. "Laughter in a wasteland", *The Sunday Telegraph* 10 October 1993: 8.

Brown, Geoff. "Catholic with the truth", *The Times* 7 October 1993: 33.

Brown, Georgia. "Daily Bread", *Village Voice* 15 March 1994: 48.

C. Tab. "Raining Stones", *Cahiers du Cinéma* 469 (June 1993): 43 [in French].

Canby, Vincent. "What Bob does for a few Bob", *The New York Times* 143 (2 October 1993): 11+ [2pp].

Crespi, Alberto. "Film in concorso – Raining Stones", *Cineforum* 325 (June 1993): 11 [in Italian].

———————. "Piovono pietre", *Cineforum* 33: 328 (October 1993): 52-56 [in Italian].

Curtis, Quentin. "The new de Niro: just a big kid", *Independent on Sunday* 10 October 1993: 27.

Davenport, Hugo. "Loach's estate of the nation", *The Daily Telegraph* 8 October 1993: 18.

Delval, Daniel. "Raining Stones", *Grand Angle* 165 (November 1993): n.p. [in French].

Dobson, Patricia. "Raining Stones", *Screen International* 906 (7-13 May 1993): 38.

———————. "Raining Stones", *Screen International* 907 (14-20 May 1993): 26.

Eaton, Michael. "Not a Piccadilly actor in sight", *Sight and Sound* 3: 12 (December 1993): 32-33.

French, Philip. "No end to the Thatcher's Britain genre", *The Observer* 10 October 1993: 5.

Fuller, Graham. "Raining Stones", *Interview* 24: 3 (March 1994): 34.

Gervais, Marc. "Engelsk realism – mer än en skitig diskbänk", *Chaplin* 36: 250 (February/March 1994): 50-53 [in Swedish].

James, Nick. "Cheeky Monkeys", *Blimp* 25 (autumn 1993): 22-25.

"Julie, kitchen sink star", *The Daily Mail* 28 January 1993: 5.

Khan, Marit. "Money/The Church/Family: for your own personal truth", *Vertigo (UK)* 1: 3 (spring 1994): 39-40.

L.C. "Raining Stones", *Positif* 389-390 (July-August 1993): 53-54 [in French].

Macnab, Geoffrey. "Raining champion", *Time Out* 1314 (25 October-1 November 1995): 163.

Mahon, Mick. "Raining Stones", *Film Ireland* 39 (February/March 1994): 26-27.

Malcolm, Derek. "A rank betrayal", *The Guardian* 22 May 1993: 21.

———————. "Return of the local hero", *The Guardian* 7 October 1993: 6.

Mars-Jones, Adam. "The gospel according to Ken", *The Independent* 8 October 1993: 20.

Marsolais, Gilles. "Il pleut des pierres à Manchester, 'the piss-pot of England'", *24 Images* 68/69 (September/October 1993): 66-67 [in French].

Morley, Sheridan. "Laughter in the rain", *The Sunday Express* 10 October 1993: Sec. 2, 55.

Morsiani, Alberto. "Il bambino e le pietre", *Segnocinema* 13: 62 (July-

August 1993): 62-63 [in Italian].

Mulcahy, Patrick. "Principled laughter", *Tribune* 8 October 1993: 9.

Nash, Elizabeth. "Raining plaudits", *The Independent* 13 April 1993: 25.

Netland, Geir. "Raining Stones", *Film og Kino* 4 (1993): 19 [in Norwegian].

Pilard, Philippe. "A View from Paris", *Vertigo (UK)* 1: 3 (spring 1994): 40-41.

"Raining Stones", *Le Film Français* 2453/2454 (7/14 May 1993): 51, 54 [in French].

Romney, Jonathan. "High gloss, true grit", *New Statesman and Society* 6: 273 (8 October 1993): 30-31.

Sawtell, Jeff. "Loach triumphs over Hollywood", *Morning Star* 195990/73866 (9 October 1993): 7.

Steyn, Mark. "Last exit to Hollywood", *The Spectator* 271: 8623 (16 October 1993): 45-46.

Stratton, David. "Raining Stones", *Variety* 7 June 1993: 39-40.

Tookey, Christopher. "Bright lights in a bleak tale", *The Daily Mail* 8 October 1993: 52-53.

Turner, Jenny. "Raining Stones", *Sight and Sound* 3: 10 (October 1993): 50-51.

Wainwright, Hilary. "Political sightings", *Vertigo (UK)* 1: 3 (spring 1994): 42.

Walker, Alexander. "Alexander Walker", *Evening Standard* 7 October 1993: 32, 41.

Ward, David. "Poverty writ large may spell big-screen success", *The Guardian* 5 October 1993: 4.

Ladybird Ladybird

Adair, Gilbert. "States of mind", *The Sunday Times* 9 October 1994: 4.

Allen, Carol. "A social sledgehammer", *The Times* 26 September 1994: 15.

Andrew, Geoff. "Impact lessons", *Time Out* 1258 (28 September-5 October 1994): 65.

———————. "Ladybird, Ladybird", *Time Out* 1258 (28 September-5 October 1994): 66.

Andrews, Nigel. "Problem mothers", *The Financial Times* 29 September 1994: 17.

Bamigboye, Baz. "Success is a bowl of soggy cereal", *The Daily Mail* 22 February 1994: 7.

Bear, Liza. "*Ladybird Ladybird*", *Film Journal* 97 (December 1994): 30.

Bennett, Ronan. "Still worried about Maggie's children", *The Observer (Review)* 4 September 1994: 2-3.

Billson, Anne. "Throttle to the floor", *The Sunday Telegraph (Review)* 2 October 1994: 7.

Black, Mary and Fred Fever. "The Trouble with Maggie", *The Guardian (Society)* 28 September 1994: 2-3.

Brechin, Marion. "When justice screams in pain", *The Guardian* 28 September 1994: 2-3.

Brown, Geoff. "Shaken and stirred", *The Times* 29 September 1994: 35.

c. ad. "Ladybird Ladybird", *Cinema nuovo* 43: 3 (349) (May-June 1994): 37 [in Italian].

Cadeux, Mike. "Film exposes the need to debate Ladybird's plight", *The Guardian* 15 October 1994: 28 [letter].

Cohen, Nick. "For their own good", *Independent on Sunday* 9 October 1994: 21.

Combs, Richard. "Down and out almost everywhere", *The Guardian* 6 January 1994: 6-7.

Corliss, Richard. "When Love Isn't Enough", *Time* 13 February 1995: 47.

Crespi, Alberto. "Ladybird, Ladybird", *Cineforum* 34: 334 (May 1994): 62-65 [in Italian].

Curtis, Quentin. "A premise that promises too much", *Independent on Sunday* 2 October 1994: 27.

Davenport, Hugo. "Unhappy families", *The Daily Telegraph* 30 September 1994: 24.

Dawtrey, Adam. "'Ladybird' finds U.K. home at UIP", *Variety* 11-17 April 1994: 32.

Dobson, Patricia. "Ladybird, Ladybird", *Screen International* 929 (15-21 October 1993): 28-29.

Elley, Derek. "Ladybird, Ladybird", *Variety* 28 February 1994: 69.

Fitzherbert, Claudia. "Don't shoot the social worker", *The Daily Telegraph* 7 October 1994: 29.

Francke, Lizzie. "Ladybird Ladybird", *Sight and Sound* 4: 10 (October 1994): 46-47.

French, Philip. "Rebellion without a cause", *The Observer (Review)* 2 October 1994: 10.

Guttridge, Peter. "The truth, or something like it", *The Independent* 16 August 1994: 25.

Johnston, Sheila. "The dark side of Mother Courage", *The Independent* 30 September 1994: 25.

Joseph, Bobby. "Cutting like razor blades", *Morning Star* 19976/74154 (1 October 1994): 7.

Kauffmann, Stanley. "Stanley Kauffmann on Films: Flesh and Blood", *The New Republic* 211: 24 (4169) (12 December 1994): 24-26.

Korman, Lenny. "Ladybird, Ladybird", *Screen International* 948 (11-17 March 1994): 17.

"Ladybird Ladybird: The writer", *Sight and Sound* 4: 11 (November 1994): 10-12.

Lyttle, John. "John Lyttle on cinema", *The Independent (Supplement)* 6 October 1994: 9.

Maher, Jackie. "Farewell, my lovelies", *The Guardian* 28 September 1994: 2-3.

Malaguti, Cristiana. "Ladybird Ladybird – Una storia vera", *Segnocinema* 68 (July-August 1994): 34-35 [in Italian].

Malcolm, Derek. "Raining bricks", *The Guardian* 29 September 1994: Sec. 2, 10.

Marriott, John. "Love story with true grit from depths of despair", *The Daily Mail* 30 April 1994: 52.

Moir, Jan. "Rock and role", *The Guardian* 21 September 1994: 10-11.

Molhant, Robert. "Ladybird Ladybird", *Cine & Media* 1 (1994): 8 [in Spanish].

Morley, Sheridan. "Torment of a mother adrift in the system", *The Sunday Express* 2 October 1994: Sec. 2, 54.

Norman, Neil. "A lost Ladybird", *Evening Standard* 3 March 1994: 26.

O.K. "Ladybird: Y a-t-il une 'Loach touch'?", *Positif* 404 (October 1994): 6-7 [in French].

Ostria, Vincent. "Ken Loach, la logique du vivant", *Cahiers du Cinéma* 484 (October 1994): 35-36 [in French].

Palmer, Alasdair. "Care and destruction", *The Spectator* 273: 8674 (8 October 1994): 52-53.

Perry, George. "First impressions", *The Sunday Times* 21 August 1994: 10.

————. "Ladybird, Ladybird", *The Sunday Times* 2 October 1994: Sec. 2, 54.

Quart, Leonard. "Ladybird, Ladybird", *Cineaste* 21: 1-2 (February 1995): 84-85.

Rees, Caroline. "No escape", *Tribune* 58: 39 (30 September 1994): 13.

Rognlien, Jon. "Å være mor – mot alle odds", *Film og Kino* 4 (1994): 10 [in Norwegian].

Sarler, Carol. "Nothing but the truth", *The Sunday Times (Magazine)* 14 August 1994: 43-44, 46, 49.

Smith, Peter. "Filming difficulties", *The Sunday Times* 18 September 1994: 4.

"The 'Ladybird' social worker's own story", *The Guardian* 12 October 1994: 2-3.

"The star from the bar", *Evening Standard* 23 September 1994: 26.

Tonkin, Boyd. "Family misfortunes", *New Statesman and Society* 7: 322 (30 September 1994): 50.

Walker, Alexander. "Verdict on an unfit mother", *Evening Standard* 29 September 1994: 45.

A Contemporary Case for Common Ownership

Blevin, John. "Call for amendments at constitutional conference", *Tribune* 59: 8 (24 February 1995): 3.

Sherman, Jill. "Activists defend Clause 4 on film", *The Times* 21 February 1995: 8.

Wilson, Brian. "Clause for thought", *The Guardian* 3 March 1995: 11.

Wynn Davies, Patricia. "Left-wing director rallies to the clause", *The Independent* 22 February 1995: 11.

Land and Freedom

Alberge, Dalya. "Actors wanted: only revolutionaries need apply", *The Times* 18 September 1995: 17.

————. "Chronicler of war backs battle-scarred cinema", *The Times* 15 August 1995: 6.

Alexander, Bill. "Against Forgetting", *Socialist History* 9 (1996): 93-94.

Andrew, Geoff. "'Land and Freedom'", *Time Out* 1311 (4-11 October 1995): 73.

Andrews, Nigel. "A war between ideologies", *The Financial Times* 5 October 1995: 21a.

Barry, Shane. "Land And Freedom", *Film Ireland* 49 (October/November 1995): 30-31.

Bigas Luna. "Luna eclipsed", *Time Out* 1311 (4-11 October 1995): 26.

Billson, Anne. "Native American princess, fluent in treespeak", *The Sunday Telegraph (Review)* 8 October 1995: 10.

Bojstad, Anneli. "Land and Freedom", *Screen International* 1004 (21-27 April 1995): 17.

"British film wins prize", *The Times* 15 November 1995: 8.

Brown, Geoff. "Animated, but no sign of life", *The Times* 5 October 1995: 35.

——————. "Looking back on celluloid", *The Times* 22 May 1995: 14.

Cable, John. "Fair film", *New Statesman and Society* 8: 378 (10 November 1995): 29 [letter].

Challinor, Raymond. "Growing grey whiskers", *New Statesman and Society* 8: 378 (10 November 1995): 29 [letter].

Christie, Ian. "A film for a Spanish republic", *Sight and Sound* 5: 10 (October 1995): 36-37.

Davenport, Hugo. "A struggle for heart or mind", *The Daily Telegraph* 6 October 1995: 26.

——————. "Outbreak of war on the Croisette", *The Daily Telegraph* 26 May 1995: 19.

Eaude, Michael. "Gracias, Mr Loach", *New Statesman and Society* 8: 372 (29 September 1995): 48-49.

French, Philip. "For whom the bell continues to toll", *The Observer* 1 October 1995: 10.

——————. "War and peace pipes", *The Observer* 8 October 1995: 11.

Gellhorn, Martha. "This is not the war that I knew", *Evening Standard* 5 October 1995: 27.

Gilbert, Jack. "Loach offensive", *New Statesman and Society* 8: 376 (27 October 1995): 35-36 [letter].

Gilbey, Ryan. "Spain 1936 and all that", *Independent on Sunday* 8 October 1995: 13.

Grant, Brigit. "A Land fit for heroes", *The Sunday Express* 8 October 1995: 35.

Herpe, Noël. "Land and Freedom: C'étaient des hommes", *Positif* 416 (October 1995): 71-72 [in French].

Hoberman, J. "Class Action", *Village Voice* 19 March 1996: 65.

Hopewell, John. "Politics get personal in 'Freedom'", *Variety* 24-30 April 1995: 53.

"It's in the Cannes", *Evening Standard* 30 May 1995: 8.

Johnston, Sheila. "Looking back in anger", *The Independent* 5 October 1995: 10.

Kemp, Philip. "Land and Freedom", *Monthly Film Bulletin* 5: 10 (October 1995): 51.

Knibbs, Steve. "UK film misses wider audience", *Evening Standard* 14 November 1995: 53 [letter].

La Polla, Franco. "Film in concorso – Land and Freedom", *Cineforum* 345 (June 1995): 9 [in Italian].

Lamet, Pedro Miguel. "'Tierra y Libertad'. Un pedazo vivo de la guerra civil española", *Cine & Media* 3 (1995): 4-5 [in Spanish].

"land and freedom", *Screen International* 1020 (11-17 August 1995): vii.

Malcolm, Derek. "A spot of serious trouble", *The Guardian* 27 November 1995: 9.

——————. "A winning battle", *The Guardian* 23 May 1995: Sec. 2, 6.

——————. "Homage to Utopia", *The Guardian* 5 October 1995: 8.

Martini, Emanuela. "'Chi scrive la storia controlla il presente'", *Cineforum* 348 (October 1995): 50-52 [in Italian].

Masoni, Tullio. "La triste primavera del '37", *Cineforum* 348 (October 1995): 53-55 [in Italian].

Morgan, Kevin and Paul Preston. "Partisan", *New Times* 30 September 1995: 8-9.

Nathan, Ian. "Land and Freedom", *Empire* 77 (November 1995): 48.

Norman, Neil. "Shooting the pain of Spain", *Evening Standard* 30 June 1994: 28-29.

O'Carroll, Lisa. "Top director's anger at big screen snub", *Evening Standard* 3 November 1995: 7.

Ostria, Vincent. "Grandfather land", *Cahiers du Cinéma* 495 (October 1995): 56-57 [in French].

Petley, Julian. "Land and Freedom", in Nicolet V Elert and Aruna Vasudevan (eds), *International Dictionary of Films and Filmmakers*, volume 1, third edition (Detroit; New York; Toronto; London: St James' Press, 1997): 553-555.

Porton, Richard. "Land and Freedom", *Cineaste* 22: 1 (April 1996): 32-34.

Preston, Paul. "Viva la revolucíon [sic]", *New Statesman and Society* 9: 390 (16 February 1996): 18-21.

Ramsden, Sally. "Comrades up in arms", *Red Pepper* December 1995: 28-29.

Rebichon, Michael. "Land and Freedom", *Studio* 99 (1995): 20 [in French].

Rees, Caroline. "Pain in Spain", *Tribune* 59: 40 (6 October 1995): 9.

Sawtell, Jeff. "A spectre of revisionism", *Morning Star* 20230/74408 (4 August 1995): 6-7.

Screen International 1034 (17-23 November 1995): 10 [letters from Rebecca O'Brien and Steve Knibbs].

Shone, Tom. "Land and Freedom", *The Sunday Times (The Culture)* 8 October 1995: 7.

Steele, Jonathan. "Betrayed from within", *The Guardian* 29 September 1995: Sec. 2, 2-4.

Terrail, Maurice. "Land and Freedom", *Cine & Media* 3 (1995): 6 [in French].

Thomas, Hugh. "Fanning forgotten flames", *The Daily Telegraph* 7 October 1995: 3.

Tookey, Christopher. "Land And Freedom", *The Daily Mail* 6 October 1995: 44.

Wrathall, John. "Land and Freedom", *Premiere (UK)* 3: 9 (October 1995): 21.

The Flickering Flame

Aitkenhead, Decca. "Thirty Years That Shook the World", *Independent on Sunday (Review)* 8 December 1996: 18-20.

Milne, Seumas. "Loach keeps the fires burning", *The Guardian* 19 December 1996: 2.

Odone, Christina. "Manipulative maybe, defensible definitely", *The Daily Telegraph* 19 December 1996: 39.

Sawtell, Jeff. "Which side are they on?", *Morning Star* 20577/74755 (14 December 1996): 8.

Sutcliffe, Thomas. "Review", *The Independent* 19 December 1996: 28.

Truss, Lynne. "Nightmare? More like a dream come true", *The Times* 19 December 1996: 39.

Carla's Song

Alberge, Dalya. "War film based on lawyer's script is tiped for prize", *The Times* 31 August 1996: 6.

Andrews, Nigel. "Love letter to the Bard", *The Financial Times* 31 January 1997: 17.

Brown, Geoff. "Made glorious by this son of New York", *The Times* 30 January 1997: 33.

Charity, Tom. "Carla's Song", *Time Out* 1380 (29 January-5 February 1997): 67.

Crespi, Alberto. "La canzone di Carla", *Cineforum* 357 (September 1996): 68-70 [in Italian].

Curtis, Quentin. "Plenty of action but where is the heart?", *The Daily Telegraph* 31 January 1997: 21.

Dobson, Patricia. "Carla's Song", *Screen International* 1075 (13-19 September 1996): 24.

French, Philip. "Loach misses the bus but Pacino's bard is just the ticket", *The Observer (Review)* 2 February 1997: 11.

Gilbey, Ryan. "Also showing...", *The Independent (Tabloid)* 30 January 1997: 4.

Glaister, Dan. "Travails with my camera", *The Guardian (Review)* 8 November 1996: 2-3, 14.

Hibbin, Sally. "The Plague", *Vertigo (UK)* 1: 6 (autumn 1996): 16.

Hooper, Joseph. "When the Shooting Starts", *Village Voice* 26 March 1996: 25-29.

Hunter, Allan. "Carla's Song", *Screen International* 1050 (22-28 March 1996): 23.

Jackson, Kevin. "It's Shakespeare, Al, but not as we know it", *Independent on Sunday (The Critics)* 2 February 1997: 15.

Jeancolas, Jean-Piere. "Carla's Song: Managua mon amour", *Positif* 429 (November 1996): 41-42 [in French].

"La canción de Carla", *Cine Informe* 678 (October 1996): 48 [in Spanish].

Landesman, Cosmo and Stephen Amidon. "The rest of the week's films", *The Sunday Times* 2 February 1997: Sec. 11, 8.

Laverty, Paul. "Day 28 of shoot", *Vertigo (UK)* 1: 6 (autumn 1996): 15.

——————. "The struggle of memory", *Village Voice* 23 April 1996: 4 [letter].

Malcolm, Derek. "Love's gory", *The Guardian (Review)* 31 January 1997.

Mansfield, Michael. "Sometimes the facts get in the way of the truth", *The Independent* 8 February 1997: 19.

Mulcahy, Patrick. "Latin lament", *Tribune* 61: 5 (31 January 1997): 9.

Quinn, Anthony. "Also showing", *The Mail on Sunday (Review)* 2 February 1997: 40.

Sawtell, Jeff. "Romance and a Latino revolution", *Morning Star* 1 February 1997.

Smith, Paul Julian. "Carla's Song", *Sight and Sound* 7: 2 (February 1997): 38-39.

Tookey, Christopher. "Loach's political song is off-key", *Daily Mail* 31 January 1997: 45.

Walker, Alexander. "Off the buses, into battle", *Evening Standard* 30 January 1997: 27.

Young, Deborah. "Carla's Song", *Variety* 9-15 September 1996: 118.

Index

Notes on contributors

John Hill is Senior Lecturer in media studies at the University of Ulster. He is the author of *Sex, Class and Realism: British Cinema 1956-1963* (1986), co-author of *Cinema and Ireland* (1988) and co-editor of *Border Crossing: Film in Ireland, Britain and Europe* (1994), *Big Picture, Small Screen: The Relations Between Film and Television* (1996) and *The Oxford Guide to Film Studies* (forthcoming). He is currently completing a book on British cinema in the 1980s.

Deborah Knight is Assistant Professor of Philosophy and Queen's National Scholar at Queen's University at Kingston. She is associate editor of both *Philosophy and Literature* and *Film and Philosophy*. She has published in the areas of philosophy of mind and language, film theory and aesthetics, Canadian cinema, and philosophy of literature in journals such as *Stanford French Review, New Literary History, The Journal of Aesthetic Education* and *Metaphilosophy*. Her current research focuses on narrative interpretation.

Stuart Laing is Assistant Director (Academic Affairs) at the University of Brighton. He has published in the fields of cultural studies and media studies, including *Representations of Working-Class Life 1957-64*.

Patrick MacFadden is an Associate Professor in Carleton University's School of Journalism and in the Film Studies Program of Carleton's School for Studies in Art and Culture. His recent research has included Soviet and post-Soviet cinema. In addition, he has been involved in public broadcasting for over 30 years, serving as a writer, host, film reviewer and cultural affairs commentator for the Canadian Broadcasting Corporation, both radio and television, as well as writing for various newspapers and journals including *Take One, Canadian Forum* and *The Nation*.

George McKnight is co-founder and former Chair of the Film Studies Department at Carleton University, and currently an Associate Professor in Carleton's School for Studies in Art and Culture. He has written on various aspects of British cinema, including the representation of class in the 1930s, Len Lye at the GPO, wartime documentary drama, British film genres, and television documentary drama in the 1980s, and has most recently co-authored "The Case of the Disappearing Enigma", appearing in *Philosophy and Literature*.

Julian Petley lectures in media and communication studies at Brunel University. He has published extensively on Loach, not only in Britain, but also in France, Italy and Spain. His most recent publication is *Ill Effects: the Media/Violence Debate* (edited with Martin Barker, 1997). He is a regular contributor to *Index on Censorship*, *British Journalism Review* and *Vertigo*, and is currently editing (with Alan Burton) the first issue of the *Journal of Popular British Cinema*, to be published by Flicks Books.